AFTER THE HAPPILY EVER AFTER

A COLLECTION OF FRACTURED FAIRY TALES

EDITED BY

ANTHONY S. BUONI & ALISHA COSTANZO

AFTER THE HAPPILY EVER AFTER
Transmunande Press, LLC | www.transmundanepress.com
Editor-in-Chief & Co-Publisher: Alisha Chambers
Content Editor & Co-Publisher: Anthony S. Buoni

ISBN-13: 978-0-9984983-0-0
Worldwide Rights
Created in the United States of America

Editors: Anthony S. Buoni & Alisha Costanzo
Cover Design: Dean Samed
Interior Layout: Alisha Chambers

DEDICATION

For my parents, Steve and Mary Buoni: thanks for your infinite wisdom and guidance, filling my life with magic and fairy tales.

-Anthony S. Buoni

For Gram, thank you for being one of biggest supporters, for bragging about me every chance you get, and for that first romance novel you slipped into my hands to read at the hospital.

-Alisha Costanzo

CONTENTS

ACKNOWLEDGMENTS

First, a colossal thank you to all of our wonderful contributors. This beast was the most grueling and wonderful project to work on, and you made the process worth it. Thank you for adapting, growing, compromising, and challenging us. We hope you are as proud of this collection as we are.

Second, a gigantic thank you to Dean Samed for creating this breath-taking cover and teaching us a thing or two about color, composition, and thumbnails.

Finally, a massive thank you to Becky Lynch, our Marketing Liaison, for bringing our authors together and helping us create a community.

IT'S IN HER KISS

Tiffany Michelle Brown

Delilah has developed a fetish of the human-who-was-once-an-amphibian variety. Her predilection has progressed into a full-fledged addiction as three or four times a week, the door to our flat bursts open and a new prime specimen drips pond water onto the Ikea rug in the foyer.

Delilah wears a proud smile and clings to their arms, bright with infatuation, gleaming with accomplishment. After all, her rose-pink lips elicited their transformations. And they are all hers, rescued from the muck and ever-grateful to their savior.

Each specimen is distinctly different, but they all are ambitiously handsome. Last week, Delilah's first catch was Italian. Olive skin, dark, emotional eyes, clothing that only a European can get away with wearing. He was young, so he was probably an exchange student. Her second catch looked like a lumberjack, a man with a full beard, bulging muscles, and enough freckles to create a connect-the-dots coloring book. I half-expected him to produce an axe to cut the lasagna they shared that evening. The third was an older Russian gentleman who moved with innate bravado and had the saddest blue eyes. He didn't speak a lick of English, but Delilah didn't care. She took him to bed anyway, as she does with all of them.

The next morning, she kisses them goodbye. When they've reassumed their froggy countenances, she affixes their legs with a little gold band. It helps her to determine which frogs she's already romanced. Then, out the door and back to the park they go, as if nothing ever happened.

I've lost track of the number of suitors that have come through our door and dampened our rug. Does Delilah know? Does she keep track? Does she delight in her growing number of conquests?

And if she does, is my name at the top of the list? Does she fondly remember me as her first? Or does her lack of lust and passion for me exclude me completely from the ranks?

###

I'd resigned myself to an amphibian lifestyle the morning I met Delilah. I'd been a frog for nearly a year, the result of a tumultuous breakup and a vindictive ex-girlfriend who decided to teach me a lesson. When she threw me into the lake, a note full of expletives, blaming, and mentions of voodoo followed me.

At first, I thought someone would figure it out. My parents ordered a police investigation, but the ensuing search proved fruitless. You don't leave a trace when you recede into a local pond. No cell phone records. No credit card transactions. People say you were completely normal the last time they saw you. And, of course, the woman responsible for the hex isn't going to have a change of heart. Especially when you cheated on her—not one of my finest moments.

As the missing person posters shriveled on lampposts around town and were eventually replaced with the face of some other unlucky guy, I decided I'd make the most of my new life. After all, I'd always enjoyed the outdoors, I'd become an exceptional swimmer, and while I missed a choice cut of sirloin from time to time, I developed a taste for bugs.

While gathering breakfast one morning at the community park, a net dropped over me. I panicked. I jumped; I kicked; I squirmed, but then my little heart raced far too fast, and I grew heavy with exhaustion. I looked up, expecting to see a mean-spirited little boy, the kind that would subject me to light filtered through a magnifying glass.

Through the mesh, a pair of feminine brown eyes gazed down at me. A girlish grin lit up my captor's face. And wouldn't you know it, it was nice to receive a smile for once.

I didn't struggle as Delilah scooped me into her palms and said, "Gotcha."

The internet is a crock of shit. I can find support groups and rehabilitation programs and intervention specialists for some crazy things—people who eat the ashes of their loved ones, Satanic cultists, teenagers who sniff glue to get high—but I can't find anything for sex addicts that use magic to ensnare, manipulate, and then re-enchant their lovers. The lack of resources is maddening.

I've done some medical research, too, trying to discern if Delilah has some kind of health condition that gives her lips transformative powers. Could this be genetic? Some insane recessive gene? But I've found nothing.

I've reached out to local government to express my concern in the recent surplus of frogs in our neighborhood. A state representative emailed me back saying that while he understood my annoyance, the increase in amphibian life in nearby ponds has proved ecologically beneficial. A rare species of fish, recently deemed on the cusp of extinction, now flourishes in ponds and lakes around town.

Since my ex mentioned voodoo in her departure letter, I've been trying to track down dark magic shops in the area, but my searches are spotty and uninformative. Apparently, none of these niche businesses are too concerned with having a web presence. I'm sure they rely on word-of-mouth marketing to keep them in business. "That son of a bitch cheated on you? Well, there's this place you can go to get a potion that'll turn him into a dog. Literally."

My search is frustrating, but I understand how widespread, traditional marketing would pose a safety concern. A plague of frogs would likely descend upon the shop, if only the poor schmucks knew where it was.

The sounds of Delilah and her new pet making love in the next room are enough to make me want to pull off my fingernails, one by one. An overexcited yip here, a bellowing moan there. And always that headboard chipping away at the paint on the walls.

I never hear the sound of lips smacking or muffled calls of pleasure, because Delilah never allows them to kiss her. Not until she's ready for them to leave.

I fold my arms behind my head and stare up at the ceiling. I concentrate on clearing my mind, ignoring the world around me. But then the thumping increases, and out of desperation, I sing a Journey song as loud as I possibly can to drown out their exhalations of passion.

Of course, they continue, and in a moment of madness, I get up from my bed, storm into the next room, and throw open the front door of the flat. I pause at the threshold, anticipation welling up in my chest. Will this time be different?

I move forward, hoping to step into the hallway, but instead my body meets a force field that feels like glass. My cheek slaps against it, making a hollow sound, and I stumble backward into the living room. The impasse shimmers softly in the dim light. Why do horrible, dreadful things always seem to glitter?

I rub my throbbing cheek and slink over to the couch. Just as I settle into the cushions, Delilah climaxes in the next room.

I honestly thought Delilah and I would end up together. She was a different person before she discovered her powers. Curious and strange, but kind and gentle.

I lived in an aquarium the first six months in the flat, along with a couple slugs named Benny and Joon. While I missed roving free, Delilah fed us three times a day, talked to me all the time, and on occasion, let me out to hop around the apartment.

I observed her in a way that no man ever gets to observe a woman—without her knowing, without her planning every word, without her trying to look a certain way. I got to watch the real Delilah. I watched her make pancakes, dancing in the kitchen to David Bowie. I listened as she called her mom every week, just to check in. I saw her in sweatpants and suits and pajamas and little black dresses. I loved it when she turned up music and sang along, completely off key.

I turned away when she brought men back to the apartment because I'm a gentleman. When those men didn't call back or left in a hurry, she'd consult with me. "What is wrong with me? Why can't I seem to keep a guy interested?"

She cried and cried, and her tears pulled me apart.

I'd peer up to her and try to communicate via psychic energy. *There is absolutely nothing wrong with you, Delilah. I think you're wonderful. Those guys are players. You need something,* someone *more.*

After our talks, Delilah would wipe the rejection from her cheeks and blow me a kiss through the glass.

###

I've since learned that the day everything changed for us, Delilah went on a particularly horrible lunch date during which her suitor told her that minor plastic surgery would fix her nose. She came home a flurry of psychotic energy, pacing about, mumbling below her breath, sweating lightly. She howled, sat down on the couch, and her shoulders bobbed. She cried and cried.

I moved to the glass and placed a webbed foot upon it, reaching out to her. I wanted so much to hop out of the tank and comfort her.

A few minutes later, she looked up at the aquarium with red-rimmed eyes. She rose from the couch, blew her nose, and walked over. She unhooked the lid of the aquarium, small muscles twitching in her snow-white arms.

"They say you have to kiss a lot of frogs to find a prince," she said, scooping me up. She raised me to her lips and gave me a soft peck. "There. I kissed a frog. Now send me a prince, universe."

Later that night, a burning sensation swelled in my chest. It became so painful. I was sure I was going to die. My heart raced, and my vision tripled. Glass broke, and I fell. When Delilah ran out to the living room to investigate the noise, she found me in human form, naked, bleeding, and laying amidst what was left of the shattered aquarium.

"Why won't you let me go, Delilah?"

Delilah sits at the kitchen table a few feet away, painting her nails black. She stops and looks at me, concerned. "Is this about last night? I know Duncan and I were a little loud."

"It's about every night, Delilah. There's always some new guy here."

"Oh, don't be dramatic. It isn't *every* night." She blows on her nails. "Besides, I thought we were family."

"Clearly, you're looking for something more."

Delilah gets up from the table and sits beside me on the couch. "Are you jealous?"

Deep down, I am, but I can't tell her that. "I just feel like I'm in the way."

"But you aren't," Delilah says, throwing an arm around my shoulders and caressing the shag of hair at the nape of my neck. "And you mean so much more to me than any of those guys. They're totally disposable. You're…not."

"Why have you never kissed me? After that first time."

"Because I don't want to lose you. You'd turn into a frog again, just like all the others."

You could just as easily turn me back into a human. I don't have the balls to say it out loud.

After giving me a little pat on the knee, Delilah goes back to painting her nails, and I fantasize about the freedom I once took for granted—cool pond water, sunshine on my back, and a world devoid of bullshit romantic entanglements.

###

The night I thought Delilah and I would become a couple, a mere three weeks after my transformation, we sat on the floor in front of the couch, watching a horror film and drinking hot chocolate. As a serial killer skewered his victim with a knife, Delilah huddled into my shoulder, laughing at the fake blood, a smile lighting up her features. I wrapped an arm about her and held her close. A few moments later, I lowered my face to hers and waited for something that would never come.

Delilah squirmed out of my embrace.

"I'm sorry. I just don't…feel that way about you." She crossed her arms, avoiding my gaze, discomfort radiating off her like heat. "You've seen too much…You know too much about me."

I didn't know what to say, so I simply nodded. A tense thirty seconds later, Delilah got up and went to the bathroom. The showerhead sprayed and the door closed. She didn't come out for an hour. And the next day, she brought her first love hostage home.

I'm in the kitchen when Delilah emerges from the bedroom with a man wearing a motorcycle jacket. Per usual, he's got this dreamy look on his face. It's Florence Nightingale Syndrome, and it happens to every one of them. They all love their caretaker until they realize *she* doesn't love *them.*

I used to try to warn them. I'd call out, "Run. Get out of here. She's about to put a spell on you." But before any of them could process my warning and make a break for it, Delilah would pull them into a passionate embrace. Next thing I knew, a frog would be croaking on our carpet.

Delilah grew livid when I tried to save them. She screamed at me, and once, she threw a shoe.

"They deserve to know, Delilah."

"In my experience, men only want one thing, and then they throw you away. Why can't *I* do it for a change?"

"Not every man is like that."

"Are we talking about you now?"

"Yeah."

"I've already made it clear how I feel about you. You're like a…brother to me."

"You kissed me once."

"I was desperate."

"Looks to me like you still are."

Delilah brought home two men that night.

When I stumble across the website, I nearly fall off the couch I'm so excited. The business, The Magic Act, is disguised as a children's magic shop, the kind of place where you can get coins that vanish and never-ending scarves and hats with special compartments for rabbits. But at the bottom of the page, an innocuous link titled "More Magic" takes me to an entirely new site. I have to confirm that I'm over twenty-one before entering.

And then I find droves and droves of magical supplies for adults: love elixirs, pendants with alleged levitation powers, and voodoo dolls. A search box stares at me from top of the page, but I'm at a loss as to what to look for. I type in "escape," and I find amulets that will transport you to other parts of the world and a potion that will turn you into sludge, which can then seep off to freedom. Since I've already been turned into something inhuman, that option makes me a little nervous. And while teleporting to somewhere like Paris or Germany sounds fun, it doesn't feel quite right. I know in my gut that I need to do something about Delilah. Slinking away unseen or simply breaking this hex isn't going to cut it. I have to save the others, too.

I take a look at the links in the left-hand navigation bar of the page, then click on "Spells for Others." I get a long list of product offerings and start to sift through them. No, I most certainly don't want Delilah to fall in love with me. No, I don't want her to die. She's been behaving badly, but I don't think she deserves *that*. No, I don't want to turn her into a toadstool, but we're getting closer.

That's when something labeled "Power Transference Ring" catches my attention. I click on the link, read the product description, and I can't add the item to my basket fast enough.

When I get to the checkout page, I panic a little. I can pay in cash—I've lifted a bill or two from Delilah's purse when she wasn't looking—but I can't leave the apartment. I look through the delivery options, hoping to find a courier service of some sort.

I laugh when I find the company offers delivery via carrier pigeon. I select a timeframe for the bird to arrive and the cash option.

I delete my browser history before closing Delilah's laptop.

The ring arrives while Delilah is "on a walk." A small thump and ruffling feathers bring me to the window. I lift the glass, and a pigeon flies into the apartment. It perches on the couch and lifts one of its orange legs. A small, velvet satchel swings from its talons. I take the satchel, open it, and a ring tumbles into my palm. It's a simple circle of silver. No embellishment, no engraving, nothing to signify it's anything special. Doubt begins to worm its way through my gut. What if this place is a total scam?

"It'll work," the pigeon squawks, and I'm so startled by the noise that I tumble to the carpet. The pigeon edges forward and looks down at me. "You must maintain physical contact with an individual for thirty seconds to fully transfer their powers. The ring must touch their skin the whole time, because it is the ring itself that absorbs the power. Afterward, whosoever wears the ring also wears the power. Got it?" The pigeon cocks its head to the side.

"Got it," I mutter from my position on the floor.

"The Magic Act does not take responsibility for what may or may not happen in correlation with the sale of their products. All purchasers agree to hold harmless The Magic Act and its associates. All sales are final." The bird hops to the carpet. "Do you acknowledge I've recited these restrictions to you and you understand them completely?"

I nod.

"I need a verbal confirmation," the bird squawks.

"Yes, yes," I say.

"That'll be $19.99."

I show the bird a twenty, add a five for a delivery tip, and then roll the bills tightly so it can grasp the money in its talon.

"Thank you very much, and have a magical day." It flutters out the window.

I've never wanted to inflict physical harm on any of Delilah's suitors, but the urge to knock this guy out rests neatly in my ready-to-swing fists as we all eat pho out of Styrofoam cartons.

I have nothing against the guy. He seems nice enough. He's wearing a suit and tie, signifying he's the business type. Maybe he used to work with numbers or algorithms or predictive modeling. Black eyeglasses hang on the bridge of his nose. He's soft spoken and smiles often. He's been polite.

But he's a blockade. With him here, I can't be alone with Delilah. I can't woo her. I can't build the intimacy required to hold her for thirty seconds. The magic ring sits in my pocket like an anvil. I'm hyperaware of its existence, its promise, and my increasing longing to escape.

In this moment, I realize just how much of a captive I've been.

Delilah tosses back wine like we're celebrating something. I sip from my glass and wonder just how sweet it will taste when I've stolen everything from her.

The risk is palpable as I creep into Delilah's bedroom. The window is open and moonlight streams in, bisecting their bodies with light and shadow. My heart thumps in my chest and the adrenaline coursing through my extremities is a warning of danger, but I ignore it. I have to touch her. I have to try to break her hold on me as soon as possible.

The ring rests on the middle finger of my right hand. It feels inconsequential, but I have to believe contact with Delilah with bring it to life.

Delilah's guest snores lightly beside her, his glasses still clinging to his face. She's draped over his body like a blanket, her petite chest rising and falling in a steady rhythm. She looks peaceful for once, the way she did before she started kissing frogs and weaving magic spells with her extraordinary lips.

I tiptoe to the foot of the bed and crouch down on my haunches. One of Delilah's feet protrudes from the bedclothes, white as ice in the moonlight. This is my best shot, so I lie on the floor. If I reach up my full arm length, I can make contact with Delilah's heel.

I lower myself to the carpet and stare up at Delilah's skin for a full five minutes before I'm able to summon the courage to move. With a shaking hand, I reach up, moonlight reflecting off the silver band on my finger. As gently as I can, I lay my open palm against Delilah's foot. She twitches in response, but then settles into stillness.

I count. *One-Mississippi, two-Mississippi, three-Mississippi…*

By *five-Mississippi*, a distinct warmth radiates from the ring, along with a soft blue light. By *ten-Mississippi*, the ring pulls Delilah's power out of her body, and I'm holding my breath. By *twenty-Mississippi*, I'm almost in tears, because dammit, it's working. I know it. By *twenty nine-Mississ*—Delilah pulls her foot away and gasps. I pull my hand to my chest and the ring sizzles with heat and energy.

The bedsprings creak as Delilah sits up. I can imagine her surveying the room, looking for anything out of place, her blond hair swaying with alert movements. She clears her throat, and I squeeze my eyes shut. A moment later, she settles in and pulls the covers up to her chin. Five minutes later, her breathing is deep and steady.

Ultimately, I'm unsure whether the power transfer worked. The ring has changed in color from silver to a seafoam green, and the band is riddled with designs, but is the change due to a partial transfer? Were the "Mississippis" enough to get me to a solid count of thirty, or did I never hit that oh so important number? What now? Do I only need to touch her again for only *one* second, or do I need to start from scratch and count to thirty again?

I'm pondering this over a bagel with cream cheese when Delilah's bedroom door swings open. She emerges in a lilac silk slip. Her hair is tousled, and she wears a lazy, satisfied smile. The guy with the glasses follows her, fully dressed, but his tie is undone and hangs from his neck.

"I had a great night," Delilah says, pulling him close to her on the Ikea rug.

"Me, too."

Generally, I turn away during this part. Delilah's goodbyes are grotesque, because I always know how it ends. But today…

The suit caresses Delilah's hair and then her cheek. "Can I see you again?"

"I'd like that," Delilah lies. She grabs the lapels of his jacket, pulls him in, and their mouths meet. The suit pulls her close, tries to deepen the kiss, but Delilah disengages and steps back, a cruel smile painting her lips.

And then they stare at each other. Nothing happens.

"Can I get your number?" the suit asks.

Delilah looks like she's been slapped, and I nearly choke on my bagel.

"I'm not sure if that's a good idea," Delilah says.

"But…you just said…"

Delilah opens the door to the flat and gestures for the suit to leave.

The suit stands there dumbfounded for a moment, mutters, "Bitch," and steps into the hallway, fumbling with his tie.

Delilah closes the door and locks it. She backs up and sinks into the couch, her eyes wide, her mouth hanging open, tension riding her shoulders. "What…the hell…was that?"

The demonstration is enough to restore my confidence. I slip the ring out of my pocket and onto my finger.

I get up from the kitchen table, scoop up my half-eaten bagel, and join Delilah on the sofa. I worry she'll hear the jackhammer of my heart or notice the sheen of sweat that's suddenly developed on my brow, but she keeps staring at the door as if she can see the suit retreating. The one that got away.

"Here," I say and offer Delilah what's left of the bagel.

She absentmindedly takes the food and raises it to her mouth, her eyes still glued to the door. She takes a bite, smearing her top lip with cream cheese.

"I don't understand," she says. "It didn't work."

I hook an arm around her shoulders, the way I did when we first met, when I thought perhaps Delilah could be the girl for me. She doesn't resist when I pull her close.

"I don't understand it either," I breathe into her hair. "But it'll be okay."

"What if he comes back?"

I can sense fear in her voice. And I suddenly understand. I understand my piece in all of this.

Delilah never wants her suitors to return. That I've always known. She's happy to receive their gratitude, their passion, their lust, but she doesn't want to deal with the intricacies of a relationship. She's okay with the superficiality of it all, because a well-constructed façade is safer than the risk of getting hurt.

I am someone who can never hurt her as much as she's hurt him. Someone who can't leave. Someone who she knows still feels something for her despite her bullshit and greed and restlessness.

And if she can no longer turn frogs into one-night-stand princes, she'll have to try to make it work with me, the person who knows what she's capable of, the greatest tenderness and the greatest cruelty. For her, this is the most terrifying fate of all.

"I could've loved you, you know." I try to keep my voice sweet and measured. "If you'd let me. Why wouldn't you let me?"

And then, I make my move. I pull her to me and bring her lips to mine. She protests at first, but then she sinks into the embrace, weaving her hands through my hair and grasping my shirt in her small fists. I get a sweet, beautiful, ephemeral glimpse at what could've been.

Then I'm holding nothing.

I visit Delilah at the pond once a week. I figure it's the least I can do after all we've been through together. We have a regular spot, a bench at the farthest corner of the park. I arrive at 11 AM on the dot, and by 11:05, she's seated beside me. I tell her about my week—the new job I've landed with a marketing agency, the friends with whom I've reconnected since I've "come back from the dead," the great sushi place I found not a block away from my new apartment. She'll croak in response here and there, and I wonder what she's trying to say, if she's really invested in our conversation or just humoring me. You never know with her.

I conclude each and every visit with a kiss, but I never wear the ring, and as such, Delilah retains her amphibian form, and I return to my normal, human life.

The ring is in a safe in the closet of my new apartment. At first, I thought about destroying it, trying to return it to the magic shop, conveniently tossing it into the sewers. But it didn't seem safe. Or right.

And for some reason, I feel like I need to keep the ring close to me.

It's comforting, knowing it's sitting there behind suits and track jackets and leather belts. Because if my time with Delilah taught me anything, it's that it's good to have a little magic on your side. Just in case.

SLEEVE OF FEATHERS

Claudia Quint

"Stephen, how do you feel about living together with all six of Geileis's brothers?"

The well-intentioned doctor with her degrees framed and hanging on the wall, pulled down her glasses to stare at them, and Stephen leaned forward and fiddled with the cuffs of his shirt as though an animal were caught in his throat, fighting its way to his teeth and pushing out past his lips, recalcitrant, resentful.

"I want it to stop."

The doctor nodded.

Geileis wore the white pleated chiffon shirt today. A diamond necklace Stephen bought her dangled at her throat. Back in those days, Geileis's lips had been locked shut, she would not speak. Now with her tongue unloosed, she might speak of whatever she wished, but neither of them dared. Like veterans returned from war, they skirted around their past, making it impossible to talk with her six brothers always there in the periphery of their every movement, occupying arm chairs and reading books, eating out of the fridge and leaving the milk carton empty on the shelf, traipsing through their bedroom, by god, their bedroom for christ's sake.

It all came crashing down when he found Geileis in bed, nestled between Dylan and Ailill, Oisin cuddling on the left and Ruari at her feet, with Emmet and Cian resorting to floor space when they ran out of room on the bed. Stephen dragged the brothers out one by one, pushing and pulling so they awoke with starts and cries, until she roused, confused and sleepy, to ask him what in the world he was doing.

"Like it's the most normal thing in the world." Stephen contented himself by folding his hands to stop fiddling with the cuffs. "To sleep with your brothers and shut out your husband."

Geileis, mute again, held her chin high. Her silence once struck him as mysterious, lent her an irresistible mystique from the start of their courtship, but now, it maddened him. Why wouldn't she speak her mind? Instead, she retreated into her self-possession, into places he could not follow.

Except for her brothers. All six of them, by god. They seemed to know and sense and feel everything she wanted or thought. If she were thirsty, they appeared beside her with a drink. If she needed the power drill, no sooner had she asked Stephen where he'd last seen it, when Ailill finished the job and hung the ceiling fan for her.

"What does she need a husband for when she's got six men to take care of her?" Stephen sneered, heard the sneer in his voice but couldn't stop it, hated himself for it. In the past, he never would have said such a thing, in such a way before; he had been all forward motion, all chivalry, all magnanimous heart until inside a wretched atherosclerosis slowly took hold, hardening his heart and breeding suspicion where before their life together had been honeymoon hours, blissful romance.

But before, six men did not occupy their marriage and their house.

"Geileis, Stephen has expressed himself regarding your living situation, did you want to talk about your feelings?"

"They're my brothers."

And she said nothing else. As though this statement and this statement alone were the extent of the world, and its very limits, limits which Stephen could not breach. He exploded and threw his hands up into the air before pressing his fingertips to his temples as though to pin the words there before they could race from his brain and through his mouth, finally retreating into the silence that used to be Geileis's alone.

In that silence resided all the things they did not talk about. In that silence lurked all six of her brothers, the years they spent as test subjects in the Cygnus Pharmaceutical Company, Geileis's own step-mother slowly turned them, one by one, into swans. By what alchemical drugs, what modifications, what redirection of cells and mutation wrought such a wicked transformation, Stephen did not know. And his sweet Geileis, working years through her medical degree, graduated with top honors and went straight to the lab where she advanced work on the cure that would reverse it.

He met her in that same lab. Then, he knew her as the rich and pampered daughter of a pharmaceutical magnate, and all around her clung a deep sadness of something lost, her lab tables piled with feathers and the strange presence of six swans, resting in their experiment cages in the room where she worked and slept and would not leave them.

Of course, the truth came out in the end. Quite the scandal. And in the end, none of them had ever recovered from the shock of it, all bound together by seven years of silence and medical torture.

And the silence never ended.

They didn't talk about the brothers and their lost years. And most of all, they didn't talk about Ailill with his one arm, which could not be saved. All that remained was his half-arm, fringed with white swan feathers and where there should be a hand, a wing tip he kept hidden up into a long sleeve. It stubbornly refused to respond to all of Geileis's drug trials, as much as she tried to coax it back to human life. In the end, Ailill refused the skin grafts offered.

Ailill had done it on purpose. To always hold that reminder of the past before them all, insinuating it in every detail of their day-to-day life as though to make sure Geileis never forgot it. *See? See what happened to me? I need you. I need you more than that wretched man you call a husband.*

"They need to go," Stephen said. "And that's final."

The doctor looked at Geileis, and oh, in her silence, she only nodded as though she agreed, but his betrayal must make her loathe him. He was not her knight anymore. Six swans had come along and toppled him from his pedestal.

Stephen did not go home after the doctor's office. He spent the night at his father's house, where for a while, he could gain a measure of comfort without the weight of six gazes all around him, beady-eyed and magnifying his every move. Within him stirred the guilt of abandoning Geileis, but she would have room to think about where their marriage was heading, if anywhere, and a chance to say goodbye to her brothers if that was what she needed.

Things had been so much simpler when she could not speak. He lied to himself and believed he he knew her through and through. The same way one might think their house cat adores them, until one realizes it can never object, raise its voice, say it prefers the salmon flavored tin over the tuna, or that one's socks smell.

And what if Geileis left?

Stephen barely slept through the night, long after he pulled out the mattress from the sofa and tossed and turned. He could not shake from memory the sight of them all nuzzled and hugged close to her in the mattress where he should have been. Yet, she carried on afterward without self-consciousness or self-recrimination, he dared not accuse her of the unthinkable, which would be—No, Geileis was not to blame.

But Ailill…

In the morning, sleepy-eyed and hair sticking up at all ends, Stephen's phone pinged a message. Geileis wanted to meet him at the old tavern where they held the wedding rehearsal.

So this is it. She's going to leave me. There's no other reason to meet in a public place.

He agreed and did not say *I love you, I miss you*, or *I do not know how I should live without you*, but drank the rest of his bitter coffee, thinking of Ailill's mutilated arm and the feathers filling his sleeve, *you can't have her, Ailill.*

He took old clothes from his father's closet, smelling of mothballs but serviceable, even if he had not worn them since high school. Stephen washed, shaved, dressed, and readied himself for battle, taking care to iron the wrinkles out of the old dress shirt before donning it and letting his dad know that he'd likely see him later that night.

The silence that followed, his father's face grew graven, weighty. *You'll get through this son. I'll be here.*

The tavern was an old converted stone mill, sitting at the edge of a slow, trickling stream where the wheel mill turned and diners could see the layout of the sleepy villa across the green fields past the stream. With the sun dipped below, an eerie blue hue cast over the land, and it took Stephen several seconds for his eyes to adjust as he stepped inside the tavern, but when they did, Geileis was not there.

Instead, seated at the bar were all six of her brothers.

Ailill, the oldest and also Geileis's fraternal twin, sat in the center with his left sleeve trailing white swan feathers. Dylan, Oisin, and Emmet thronged him on the right. On the left, Cian and Ruari. In the half-light, they looked like pale versions of each other, not quite exact copies but enough alike to ring a sense of the uncanny: their hair cut the same, the same non-de-script shade of brown, each wearing casual clothes but within the same color wheel, as though they were an unspoken army of six and this, their uniform, their phalanx. They each drank froth capped mugs of beer, and their eyes glittered above their white collars.

"Where's Geileis?"

"She's taken a well-deserved trip for herself until later in the night," Dylan said and gestured him over. "Come now, don't be shy."

"We thought it would do us all well to get to know each other better," Emmet said.

"Indeed, the wedding and the honeymoon came so quick…" Ruari said around the lip of his beer.

Cian finished Ruari's incomplete thought, "…we barely had time to know one another."

Emmet removed himself from Ailill's side. Stephen fussed at his collar and maintained the impression that if he did not take his place next to Ailill, he would be forced upon the seat by the gang of brothers surrounding him.

He approached the bar and took his place, the liquors gleamed on the shelf against the front of the bar mirror. Cian ordered for Stephen. The bartender served him his beer, the same brand as the others. Stephen wanted to refuse, to dash the beer to the ground or throw it in Ailill's face. Ailill's feathers brushed Stephen's bare arm and his hair raised in goose flesh to feel it.

"We need to talk." Stephen prepared his ultimatum: *You leave or I do.*

"Drink first." Ailill's voice wove through the bar noise, so soft it might have been lost in the underside of every dish clatter, but cut through it all the same. Stephen did not desire a full scale argument yet, he had readied himself for a battle with Geileis and without her there, he fell to drinking, heedless, drank and drank until Cian let loose a whoop of amusement and Ruari leaned forward to pound Stephen on the back. Stephen finished the drink and smacked down the glass on the bar counter.

Ailill nodded.

"I know you and Geileis are having a difficult time, and of course, we want only the best for you both, you know that, right?"

Ailill bared his teeth, then the teeth were gone behind a smile. Beer fizzed in Stephen's gullet. He wished he had not sucked it down so quick. What was he doing? Showing off? Expounding on his manliness?

"I think you want Geileis all to yourself."

"She's my sister."

They're my brothers, Geileis had said to the doctor, and now Ailill, in eerie echo.

Stephen snorted. "I'm an only child. Tell me what that's like, having a twin sister."

Ailill's beer mug remained filled. Instead, he took an end of bread from the basket on the bar and tore at the crust, prying a wedge from it. He threw it up into the air, and Dylan snatched it with one hand, setting it on the bar. Patrons filtered out from the dining room where the lights dimmed, thrusting half the room into darkness by degrees.

"We thought that might be part of the problem," Emmet said into Stephen's ear, so close Emmet's sweat and heat radiated from him in a halo. Stephen's skin rippled with unease, he leaned back but this only pressed him into Ailill. The tavern, Stephen believed, was no longer level, it must be on an incline, unbalancing him, so Stephen gripped the bar counter. Another beer appeared in front of him as if by magic.

"Drink," Ailill said, and his voice, honeyed, Dionysian. His eyes, wizened from the folds of his skin where they crinkled like wax paper around the oculus, feathers—*eyelashes*, Stephen corrected himself —fringing the lambent glow of the iris.

Oisin rose from his stool to grip Stephen by the shoulders like an old friend and drew him close to bid him, *drink!* Demonstrating his own eagerness by downing his beer and laughing, raucous, along with Ruari and Dylan and Emmet and Cian, all except Ailill who did not laugh and did not drink but watched Stephen through the bar wall mirror. He sipped at his beer this time, to appease a grinning Oisin, who slapped him on the back.

The bartender wiped down the counter, flicked off the light and plunged the bar into darkness, save the emergency lights by the ceiling, so all things glowed with a strange phosphorescence.

"Where is everyone?"

"We're all accounted for," Ailill said.

"Where are all the diners? Where did the bartender go? Is the bar closed?"

The old mill stood empty, and Stephen no longer cared for this tête-à-tête, no longer cared for working anything out if working his marriage out meant being trapped in this place with Ailill's hostile stare, no matter how good-natured the other brothers might be.

Stephen stood.

"Where are you going?" Oisin asked.

"The place is closed." Stephen's irritation bubbled over, so he gestured, furious, pointing his finger like a stabbing knife at the empty tables, the overturned chairs.

"So it is," Cian said. Dylan laughed. Emmet laughed with him. They ejected from their chairs and clapped each other on the backs, the shoulders. Ruari took off his shirt, unbuttoning it hastily. The others did the same, unbuttoning and walking out the door, one by one until all that remained were Stephen and Ailill, holding their empty beer mugs.

"Won't you come with us, Stephen?" Ailill slid off his stool and pulled off his shirt. He had to work the sleeve over his mutilated arm, and the feathers hissed over the fabric as his shirt fell away.

"You can stop lying," Stephen said.

"Lying?"

"You don't want our marriage to work. For whatever twisted reason you might have. It's fine, I don't care anymore. You and Geileis can have whatever you have together that I obviously can't understand—"

"What are you implying?" Ailill set his shirt on the stool and drank his beer until the foam ran down his mouth, his chin, made a slug trail over his pumping adam's apple. He finished and set the mug down with a satisfied breath.

"You must think I'm an idiot," Stephen said.

"No. Not at all." Ailill's calm was so like his sister's, so like Geileis's. Did Ailill mimic it just to provoke him? Because it worked. "You simply don't understand. And we want you to understand, Stephen. We really, really do. That's why we called you here tonight."

Outside the closed mill, the brothers laughed and called out to one another. They slipped and slid down the muddy river bank and took turns leaping into the water. Their heads bobbed past the window frame and filled the air with their yips and their laughter.

"In some ways," Ailill said with a sigh, "they never really grew up. Not like people do. Come, Stephen, I mean you no harm. Let me show you. It's much better if I show you."

Ailill left. He did not look behind him to see if Stephen followed but, in a moment's time, he was on the other side of the window, standing on the bank with his useless arm curled at his side, the feathers furled from being cooped up in the sleeve all day. His brothers threw water at him from the river, calling names and singing songs. Their drunken chorus reverberated:

Row, row, row your boat,
Gently down the stream,
Merrily, merrily, merrily, merrily,
Life is but a dream.

Stephen made his way out of the empty tavern. Where had the patrons gone? How ghostly the place looked without anyone inside it. He followed the sounds of the brothers from around the building, trailing over the old and ancient mill stones to stand at last by the river bank.

The earth seemed to roll up from under him, threatening to trip him with every step. This slippery reality was not mere intoxication, he noted with dismay, this was a drunk of a different nature. His head, pleasantly floated in the vicinity of the sky near the stars above, and all of him, disconnected and euphoric, still loathed Ailill and wanted to punch him in the mouth.

Or clip his wings. Stephen congratulated himself on his little joke.

"Come with us," Ailill said. Stephen nearly slid down the bank and slipped on mud. Ailill caught him. Stephen, disgusted by the touch of him, reeled back, and Emmet was there to catch him, to steady him and let him find his feet. Stephen need only turn to evade one brother and another stood in his place, ready to receive him with open arms, charming smile, glittering eyes. Dizzy and disoriented, Stephen cried out.

"Let me go."

"You're free, Stephen, we'll not hold you here. You can leave any time."

"You won't let me. You're in my way."

Ruari and Emmet and Cian and Dylan and Oisin all thronged around him like a cage, and Stephen spun, crying out, embarrassed, ashamed, and the sound of his heartbeat grew louder with each passing second until Ailill broke through and set him down on the riverside, where the earth stopped moving, and Ailill's voice close into his ear, Emmet's hand on his shoulder, all of them, so close, my god, would they press him to death on all sides?

There, there, Ailill said, *close your eyes, and all will be well.*

And Stephen did.

The sun loomed ahead, and they burst through rain clouds. His brothers were there, and they were all together, their wingtips brushing and then again, came the gust of wind, sending them faster and floating above the earth.

Up here, they hung suspended in the atmosphere.

Crescent rainbows appeared between storm clouds and shards of lighting, came and went like wisps of cobwebs, there and gone again, and he feared none of it.

Up ahead, Ailill led them. Long sweeps of wing. When he turned, they all turned with him. Ruari and Emmet and Cian and Dylan and Oisin, and now Stephen, but he had but a dim sense of himself as another entity, maybe not even here, maybe not even real.

It didn't matter, because he was flying now.

Down below, the earth itself rendered into a patchwork of verdant green. The black specks were pools and lakes of water, and Ailill knew the way, led them there, so they descended. The air rushed past his face, over his eyes, and the earth loomed up to meet them before they touched down to the horizon itself, falling into the water like leaves finding their places, sending ripples overlapping in every direction.

The distant calls and clucks of his brothers brought him comfort, let him know they were there; they were safe and all accounted for. Their arching necks made bows of white, rows of bone, swimming through the lake and nipping at the water, at bugs and floating bread.

In the evening, when they had eaten and drunk their fill, they nestled in close together with no clocks and no time. Each day folded into the last to become new again in the morning. They slept beak to tail and wing to wing as was their manner, their want, sharing heat and energy and breath. In their bower, they ceased to be separate individuals. The border between where one began and the other ended dissolved, and instead, they were one entity, one white and feathered and creature with no past, and no future.

In the morning, they shook off their odd and fragmented human dreams of a sister who loved them, of a laboratory where they used to be boys, and they took injections by the step-mother whom they did not like and always smelled foul to their noses, a pinch-faced woman who didn't care if they didn't like the needles, and then when the injections had been given, came great and riving pain, a fire on the inside of them and feathers, keratin forming at strange places on their bodies, and that was when their sense of time and sense of self distorted, some ferment in their neurons that rearranged their limbic system, and with it, dictating their cells and hormones how to grow feathers and where to grow them and by what arrangement.

And they were not human anymore.

And their sister—

wife

—wept for them.

But for now, on the waking, none of that really mattered, and the pain of the past was but a distant dream; the universe of their brothers was the only universe that mattered, and only when Cian fell in love did their world disrupt.

Ruari and Ailill pulled Cian back from the swan who kept calling to him, plaintive. She dreamed of little cygnets with Cian, she sent calls to him. Cian, with his big puffed feathers, was gorgeous among all the swans and would provide her with all they might need for love and survival. Cian wanted to go with her, called back to her with all his heart, but Ailill would not let him.

Ailill remembered being human though he longed to forget. And Stephen did not know how he knew this, but only that it had something to do with the barriers dissolved as swans, with their reptilian brains and sense of each other, the way birds move in concert without having to be told, as though by some lizard telepathy, and what he felt through their invisible bond now was Cian's sorrow and his grief to watch his beloved fly away without him, because of Ailill.

Damn Ailill, would let none of them free; he was their jailer and insisted they not mate or mingle, and when Cian asked why, Ailill said when swans mate, they mate for life. If they hoped of ever returning, they must never love, they must hold before them the love of their sister.

So all the brothers kept their hearts and their minds focused on only one thing, Geileis, and Stephen understood, awakening from this dream within a dream—

merrily merrily merrily merrily—

that by force of will, each brother had by accident bonded with their sister as a swan might bond with a mate, imprinting—

life is but a dream—

and in so doing, become twined with her for life, unable to leave, trapped by their own animal instincts into feeling what they did not feel, wanting what they did not want, for to do otherwise would be dissolution and all would be lost, they would reject humanity and remain swans forever.

But necessity was cruel.

In their hearts, they could never be separated now, and they could never want any more love from their sister beyond that which she was willing to give, and so remained, doomed to a half-life, and in that moment, Stephen could never hate them or deprive them of what shred of pitiful love they had managed to attain through their sister, and through her, Stephen as well. For them, Stephen and Geileis's marriage was as close as they would ever have one of their own.

Stephen sputtered awake.

The night flooded back in fractured, jagged images. First, he stood beside the stream with Ailill's feathers brushing his arm and then his arm was Ailill's, and his feathers filled his sleeve. The brothers linked with him, laughing, singing, dancing, then they were in the stream and his shirt came off, floated down the water and was gone, and by then, he did not seem to care. Everything that made Stephen uniquely and individually Stephen was gone like his shirt, gone and floating downstream until all that remained was his twined awareness of Ailill, Dylan, Ruari, Emmet, Cian, and Oisin.

He was them, and they were he. And there followed such a—

life is but a—

dream.

He was a swan, and a lifetime passed as he was a swan, complete with desire and love and sorrow, but as a swan might know desire and love and sorrow, and all the brothers had been beside him, feeling as he felt and knowing what he knew.

Stephen woke in his familiar bed. The mattress cossetted in white. He rose up through the sheets, his head, throbbing and all around him, the figures of the six brothers scattered, some on the floor, and Ailill beside him, face pressed into the pillow, chaste, incorruptible.

Ailill's eyes fluttered and opened wide to take in Stephen, who swore for a split second Ailill's eyes were those of a swan, lambent yellow enclosed with sable.

"Life is but a dream, is it not, Stephen," Ailill said. His arm, serrated with feathers, fluttered in an errant draft.

Stephen lay back down onto the mattress, and soon, all their breathing fell into rhythm, as one creature might breathe. In time, the sound of Geileis erupted at the door, jingling her key into the lock, and she made her way upstairs, breaking the communal silence. With all the brothers crowded beside him, their blood and heartbeats and breath drew a cloud of warmth surrounding them. Geileis climbed into bed with them and nuzzled beneath Stephen's arm. He held her close, kissed her on the forehead.

"How are we?" In her question lingered a different question entirely, asking if they were still married, if they would stay married.

"We're—"

merrily merrily merrily

"—fine." He kissed her on the mouth.

"And my brothers?"

"Can stay. For as long as they wish."

She held him tight, shivered in delight and exaltation and fell to sleep beside him, where all eight of them commenced to dream.

In this dream, they all took flight together.

THAT TIME HE HAD TO MAKE DECISIONS

Amanda Iles

Prince Phillip's life used to be filled with action, adventure, heroism, and focused passion—all things he excelled at. He used to think himself the most fortunate prince. Then he made the mistake of finding the princess he'd spent years looking for, releasing her from a wicked enchantment with a one-sided kiss that felt pretty creepy, so he tried not to think about it, and defeating the most evil witch his world had known, so evil her name literally meant, well…

Anyway, Phillip had made his mistake, and now, he suffered the consequences of his success.

He could only play so many polo matches and hold so many festivals, albeit he could probably dance an infinite number of waltzes. His betrothed, however, disagreed about dancing. She was a fine dancer who complimented his talent, but she preferred to spend her days doing…Phillip was not quite sure what.

Because while he had spent the majority of his life dreaming about and searching for the secret princess, Aurora had spent hers living a life that had nothing to do with him. And even after the whole celebrate-after-the-rescue bit, she still lived her own life—one that pretty much had little to do with him.

At first, he had given her space, figuring she would be drawn to him, like other ladies. But Aurora seemed to be an exception. Oh, they had chemistry, neither of them could deny that, but Aurora did not seem to feel Phillip's presence so charming that she had to be near him all the time. Or most of the time. Or even some of the time. It seemed she really did not feel the need to be near him much at all.

And so, as the months went by and Aurora was no closer to running into his arms or responding to the many texts he sent her daily, Phillip had to admit that his dream of him and Aurora living happily together, dancing every night and doing whatever else happy-in-love couples did may not come true quite like he'd expected.

As their wedding date approached, Phillip had to do something. He was a doer, a slayer of monsters, a fulfiller of dreams, an accomplisher of great deeds. He could no longer sit back, wallowing in his discontentment, which was, after all, quite unseemly behavior for a prince.

He wanted a partner not just in name but also in actuality. Which is why he would selflessly give Aurora the option of ending their relationship, or at least the opportunity to say if she needed more distance.

For a conversation of this importance, Phillip made the bold decision to call Aurora instead of texting her.

His Find My Princess app located her at a bookstore. Perfect. She could be doing nothing pressing there.

Phillip strolled the streets of his capital city. Medieval-turned-modern buildings nestled next to skyscrapers and subway stations. An antiquated inn transformed into a hipster hangout thrived between a Wine-N-Wash Laundromat-bar and a Potions for Swap pawnshop-apothecary. Phillip crossed a busy street, which had designated lanes for buses, cars, bikes, and horses. He adored every part of his kingdom and took pride in his role as its prince.

The walk took care of his nervous energy and provided an excuse should he need to escape the conversation. Perhaps the financial district would encounter a dragon problem.

He could only hope.

As he typed in Aurora's number, he ran into a tiny patch of difficulty. What if she was, in fact, busy? What if she did not want to be called? What if he was forced to—*gasp*—leave a message?

He decided to text first.

Babe

And when she didn't answer immediately, to text again. And again.

Babe?

Hey

What's up?

How are you?

Let's talk.

Can you call me?

A message from her interrupted his next one.

I'm in the middle of something. Can't this wait until tomorrow?

Technically it could…Phillip drew on his superior self-resolve to compose his next message.

Of course, darling.

He received no response. He waited. For hours. Surely, she should have confirmed she received his text. What if she hadn't? Should he text again? Would he seem desperate? What if another text angered her?

The night lasted an infinite number of hours. Even though he turned his phone's volume all the way up, his phone did not *ding* to indicate he'd received a message.

The next day, the royal tech guy confirmed that Phillip's phone was not, in fact, broken. Aurora had simply not felt the need to respond. But a new day meant he could text again. When more hours passed during which Aurora maintained radio silence, Phillip went for a run. He needed to stay in shape in case of a dragon or other mythical creature problem.

When his phone finally rang, interrupting his kick-ass workout playlist, he was so excited he almost dropped the phone when leaning it against his good ear. "Hello? I mean, hey. Hi."

"Yeees?" Aurora asked, drawing out the vowel.

At the sound of her harmonious voice, Phillip regained his composure. "Darling. What's up?"

"You tell me. You're the one who wanted me to call. And who also texted literally forty-six times today."

Damn his inability to tone it down. "Wisdom has it that enthusiasm is a virtue."

"Yeah, but like, over-enthusiasm? That's a problem."

At last, new task: temper his over-enthusiasm. Phillip would work at it day and night. He would be so not over-enthusiastic, he would border on—dare he even think it?—unenthusiastic.

The scrape of fencing swords sounded from her end of the phone. Aurora boasted so many wonderful talents.

"Heellooo?" she said.

Phillip had learned that when she held out her vowels, she grew impatient. To him, though, those long words sounded like a wonderful song.

"Yes, darling, I'm sorry," he said. "I was thinking."

"Oh, honey, I thought we talked about that."

Phillip paused to give a regal wave to some of his subjects lined up at a bus stop, which was so urbanly charming. They bowed to him and all was well.

Someone on Aurora's side of the line grunted and said, "I yield."

"Again," Aurora said, muffled, then clearer: "Phillip. Is there a point to this call?"

"Yes, there is. What are you up to tonight?"

"You're not going to throw another festival, are you?" She sucked in her breath and took a few seconds before speaking again. "Because if so, I can't attend. I have...plans."

"No, no. I thought perhaps you'd like to join me for a camping trip."

Aurora stopped what she was doing, and her side of the call gave off a loud silence. "Seriously?"

"You're constantly reminding me how fairies raised you in the woods. I thought you might like to get away for a night, get back to nature. We could go to the spot where we first met."

"Seriously?" Aurora's voice grew softer. "That's actually really sweet. Let me talk to my boss."

"Your what?"

"The person in charge of my work?"

How could independent, decisive, in-charge Aurora have a job in which someone else told her what to do?

"I'll text you later, okay?" She hung up without waiting for a response.

###

The kingdom's premier outdoor goods store overwhelmed Phillip with so many choices for everything. From the many military campaigns he led, he knew soldiers who would give anything for basic equipment. He doubted they would have a preference for one of the eighteen campfire stovetops that the store carried as long as they had food. Though Phillip had no need for such fancy camping finery—he actually enjoyed sleeping under the stars—he intended to make this trip perfect for his darling Aurora.

Assuming he could make decisions about what to buy.

His phone buzzed, and he smiled when he saw his name for Aurora, *Perfect Princess*, surrounded by every heart emoji he could find plus a kissy face and a sunrise and a rose with thorns.

Her message said:

I'm good for tonight.

Let's do it.

He texted her back a selfie in front of the store's campsite display.

She replied with an eye-roll emoji.

The night would be perfect. He would give her the chance to leave, but her heart would melt at his passion, and they would be happily married and dance together every night. Well, maybe not every night. Phillip could compromise.

Hours later, Phillip wandered around a market, once again confused. This was why he needed beasts to slay and witches to defeat—he knew exactly what to do in those situations as opposed to the more mundane tasks, which troubled him.

He called Aurora, but it went to voicemail. He called again, and his heart jumped when she picked up.

"Hey—"

"Babe," he said.

"Hold on a sec."

Familiar noises came from her end of the phone—Phillip had been in enough fights to recognize the sounds of one—but no one would fight his darling Aurora.

After several minutes, during which Phillip paced the candy aisle, Aurora came back on the phone.

"Hey, sorry about that. What's up?" Her words came out in clusters, as if she were short of breath.

"What are you doing?"

"I had to take care of some people who've been spying on me."

Phillip laughed so hard several of the other customers gave him looks they would never have dared to give him if they knew he was their prince. "Darling, you tell the best jokes."

"Yeah, okay. I'm also in a bowling alley?"

Ah, yes. The crash of balls hitting the ground and pins falling down distinguished themselves. Though not the same noises he'd heard before, he could have missed fighting so much, his brain misinterpreted them.

"So..." Aurora said.

"I need to know if you prefer gourmet chocolate or the more traditional kind on your s'mores."

Aurora sighed a sigh so powerful, it was clearly meant to impart something important.

"I…I don't know what that means," Phillip said.

"You literally defeated evil incarnate. I think you can handle this." Aurora hung up the phone.

Phillip's faithful horse protested being loaded with all the equipment necessary to make a perfect camp for Aurora, but with a bribe of carrots and a promise of apples once they got to the site, Phillip coaxed him to cooperate.

The expansive forest between Phillip and Aurora's kingdoms had always been a peaceful place. Ease enveloped him as he led his horse to the meeting spot—a break in the trees by a lake where years ago he had first seen Aurora before he knew who she was and where a short while later, he officially proposed.

She'd cried when he asked for her hand, not out of happiness but because she knew she should not refuse. They'd been promised to each other before they could speak, and as their parents kept reminding them, the fate of their two kingdoms, their eventual reunification, lay on his and Aurora's shoulders. At least she had been honest with him then. At the time, he'd appreciated it. At present, he wouldn't mind if she would be a little less honest. It was fine, though. As a hardened warrior, Phillip could take blows made by swords or words, even though wounds made by steel were a little easier to bear.

When he arrived, a roaring fire enclosed in a pit of stones greeted him. Two small shelters made of branches, mud, and leaves rested at the edge of the trees. Moss-covered logs served as benches, and a pot filled with savory-smelling food sat steaming on the stone pit.

Phillip's practiced apology for being late was somehow replaced with a stammer and an awkward, "How…when?"

"For the trillionth time," Aurora said, stretching as she stood, "I was—"

"Raised by fairies in the woods. I know." Phillip was both proud of Aurora's resourcefulness and relieved he did not have to try to impress her.

Damn, though. She constantly impressed him. Aurora managed to look both rustic and chic, her shirt matching her boots and her hair tie. The early evening sun turned her hair copper. When she hugged him hello, she smelled like the sweetness of honeysuckle but also a little like acrid gun smoke. Phillip must have craved adventure so much, his senses turned normal scents, like burnt wood from the campfire, into ones he missed.

"You did a marvelous job setting up," he told her.

"How do you sound condescending even when you're being complimentary?"

"I—"

"I was being rhetorical."

As she helped him unload his horse, her hands distracted him. As per usual, she did everything without using the index finger on her right hand, her "finger of betrayal" as she called it. Her finger, she claimed, touched the cursed antique spinning wheel, much against her wishes. Black thread coiled around the entire length of her finger, marring the sight of her otherwise perfect hands.

Phillip was glad to see she wore his family ring and pleased she'd painted his family crest on her accent nail. Her other hand broadcast her family's sigil. Perhaps she accepted their shared future? Phillip was tired of guessing.

Tonight, he would find out how she felt for sure.

Or at least he'd try.

"I thought you'd appreciate my nails." Aurora wiggled her fingers in front of his face.

"How did you have time to do all of this?"

Aurora eyed the many packs they'd unloaded from his horse. "Not shopping for hours? Also, one of my cases grew cold."

"So you work with cases."

"Ye-es."

"Doing what, exactly?"

Aurora's mouth twisted, her perfect pink painted lips looking none the worse. "I don't think I can tell you."

"Can we talk?"

"Must we?"

"Yes." Phillip took her hands to lead her to the fire, where they sat on a log facing each other. "I don't like what I'm about to say, but I have to say it anyway."

"Okay…"

"I'd like to give you the option of leaving…me. Of…of not getting married."

"That was not at all what I expected you to say. Can we hold off on the dramatic gestures for a few minutes while we talk? Phillip, why do you think I would want that?"

"Because you don't seem to like me. Because you always have ten million things you'd rather do instead of spending time with me. You have your own life, which is great for you, but not ideal for me."

Aurora slid her thumb back and forth against the side of his.

Phillip gave her time to think, turning away from her beautiful face to take in the beauty of their surroundings. The lake was quiet at night, a mixture of pink and gray from the setting sun, with faint ripples disturbing its surface. Orange competed against blue for dominance in the sky. Black shadows turned plants around the water into silhouettes. Phillip would have to describe this scene to his biographer. The image of the sun hiding behind trees on the other side of the lake was not metaphorical at all, but also possibly quite metaphorical.

"Phillip," Aurora said. "It's not that I don't like you."

"That's encouraging. Truly, it is."

He stopped her moving thumb, and she met his gaze.

"I love my life. I loved it before I knew that evil witch had cursed me, and I loved it after you…rescued me." She wrinkled her nose, which was quite adorable, but Phillip had enough sense not to tell her so. She squeezed his hands. "The thing is, I was all set to dislike you. I mean, how embarrassing is it needing to be rescued?"

"It's not. You couldn't have prevented the curse from running its course."

"Thanks." Aurora said it in such a way it sounded half-sarcastic, half-not. How wonderfully intriguing she was. "Not to mention you love being the hero."

"I do. But I don't have to rescue you necessarily. The other day, I came across a little bird that had fallen out of its nest, so I put it back. That was as rewarding to me as anything I have done."

"Yeah. You really do need something to do."

"I could dote on you…"

"No. And would that really make you happy? Like, all the time?"

Phillip took a few moments to imagine spending all his time with Aurora. At first, it seemed like a wonderful dream. But then the edges got a bit blurry, and the images started to crack. He'd miss going on adventures. And journeying with his horse. And winning competitions.

"Hello?" Aurora tapped his shoulder.

"I had to think about what it would be like," Phillip said. "Like you, I miss my old life. I want it back, but I also want you in it. Why don't you want me in yours?"

Aurora shrugged. "I was trying to tell you. I didn't like the idea of being rescued and told to marry basically a stranger. Phillip, I'd only met you once before that creepy kiss."

"Let's not talk about that."

"Gosh, what an awful person that woman was. I'm glad you killed her."

"But if I broke the spell, doesn't that mean we have true love? Shouldn't that count for something?"

"Oh, honey." Aurora petted his hair. Playful or romantic? Phillip couldn't tell. "She cursed you, too. My parents weren't the only royalty she was trying to mess up."

"So everything I feel for you… it isn't real?"

"Please refrain from spiraling down into your doldrums for like a minute, okay? Think about everything after you broke the curse. Like, for me, despite my intentions to dislike you, you've managed to impress me with your passion and your earnestness and your genuine desire to excel at whatever you do, whether it's, you know, saving a baby bird or readying yourself to become a king. And you have your…eccentricities…but you're aware of them. Which makes them a little, ugh I hate this word, but charming. Also, not gonna lie, you being super hot helps."

"Are you saying you like me?"

"Yeah, kind of? No, wait. That's not fair. I feel like I'm still getting to know you, but I'm liking the person I'm getting to know. Kind of a lot."

Phillip's heart stilled. His shoulders relaxed. His face felt warm. "I like you too, Aurora."

"Wow. Color me shocked."

"I'm so glad we're finally talking to each other about these things. Aren't you?"

"Yeah. Thrilled. Look, I know this isn't how you imagined things would be between us. You've told me what you've imagined so well, I can picture it myself. But that's not realistic. And it's not what I want."

"Then I'll give you what you want." Phillip's adrenaline kicked in, readying him for the challenge. "You know I'll stop at nothing to make you happy, my darling, my sweet—"

"Less of that is exactly what I want. You're always at an eleven, and I need you to take it down to, like, a six. Even an eight would be okay. Not always, but just sometimes? If you could try to be less…" Aurora took her hands back to grasp the right word but ended up gesturing at him instead. "If you can be less, you know, then I guess I can try to include you more."

Phillip froze, scared any movement might disrupt the moment. "Will you really?"

"Yeah. Just let me figure out how."

Her phone buzzed, making a strange noise against the log they sat on.

"That's weird." The screen on the phone displayed a restricted number. "It's usually you."

She frowned and picked up. Her face changed at the voice on the other end, but Phillip couldn't read her expression. She made a few noncommittal noises before standing. "Give me a sec?"

Aurora paced between the trees, her lithe body imitating the movements of the fairies who raised her.

After a few minutes, she took the phone away from her ear and tapped it against the palm of her hand. She tugged her hair tie out of her hair, and as she walked back to him, pulled her hand through the long strands. "My boss." She sat hard on the log. "Will you hate me if I leave?"

"What? What about our romantic camp night?"

She waved her phone in front of him. "This is kind of really important."

No smile graced the corner of her mouth. Her voice held no touch of her usual sarcasm.

"But…"

Aurora would leave no matter what Phillip said. This was the crucial moment, unrelated to picturesque sunsets or twinkling stars. Using his superior self-control, he reined in his passion and told her what she needed to hear. "I suppose if it's that important, you have to go. You should go."

Aurora smiled, and Phillip was wise enough not to tell her how dazzling she was.

"You just earned yourself, like, a hundred points." She gave him a kiss, way too chaste and quick, before she picked up a small bag. "You still have stuff for s'mores, right? I would eat that instead of the soup I made. It's gross."

She walked away at her usual speed, which was pretty close to a run.

"You'll still think about including me, right?"

Aurora turned back to him. "I could…Or you could try to figure out what I'm up to."

Phillip's heart took a running leap and vaulted over an Olympic-sized hurdle. "Is that an invitation?"

"It's more like a challenge. I just talked to my boss about it. I'll give you a week to follow me and figure out what I do."

"I'll take it." Phillip jumped up. "I'll even give you a head start."

"Babe, I've been like a thousand steps ahead of you this entire time."

Aurora left without saying goodbye.

Which was fine.

They were beyond goodbyes.

Phillip's current vision of the future filled with static, like an old TV that struggled to receive proper channels. He just had to adjust the antenna the right way for a clear picture.

As he settled down to a meal of marshmallows, graham crackers, and chocolate—the type seemed less important than it had hours before—he mentally readied himself to embark on a fantastic adventure.

Phillip held his phone out in front of him, relying on his horse to guide them as they plodded along a park's path. Though Phillip modeled for a hands-off-phones-while-riding campaign, he didn't always follow his own superb advice. Then again, his steed wasn't an average horse. They wouldn't crash.

For the past few days, he'd successfully managed to follow Aurora…to a point.

On the first day, she stopped at her forest apartment. Phillip waited for her, his mother's opera binoculars trained on her door so she couldn't leave without his notice. She came out with her nails unpainted and her fingers unadorned.

He'd texted her: *No ring?*

She'd replied: *Can't wear it to work. You'll see why soon. Also, you're about to lose my trail. xoxo*

Over the next few days, he tracked her until she disappeared. Each time he got close to catching up to her, he grew more determined to find her. Aurora managed to turn her challenge into a game, and Phillip adored her more for it.

As he rode through the park, he pondered. Why could Aurora now share her secrets? Why was her boss now letting her include him? Damn his being a little bit slow.

Perhaps his slowness was why he couldn't interpret Aurora's message. Her latest depicted a flock of ducks. Which made no sense. Nevertheless, Phillip and horse prowled around a pond while he figured out what to do. His horse nickered as a dozen ducks waddled out of the water.

He texted Aurora: *I'm on the duck case.*

She replied: *Weirdo.*

"Keep alert," Phillip said to his horse. Who knew how much one could trust waterfowl? After all, they didn't have separated toes, which freaked him out.

He followed the flock. It must have been quite a sight: a dozen ducks waddling in a line on the side of the road, a dashing prince and his noble steed behind them. He imagined the dramatic music that would accompany this scene in the award-winning movie they would make of his life.

The flock clustered around a storm drain, flapping their wings and stirring up road dust.

One moment, Phillip was looking at a bunch of ducks. The next, they had transformed into twelve beautiful maidens as varied in their appearances as there were people in the world. Though, obviously, none of them as beautiful as Aurora.

Phillip tapped his horse on the head. "Did you see that?"

Two of the women bent down and yanked the cover off the storm drain. They held it aside as the rest descended underground, apparently unworried about dirtying their lavish dresses or stumbling in their fancy shoes.

Aurora ran toward them from the opposite direction. She cut the line to disappear down the drain, pausing to wave at Phillip before descending.

When the last of the duck-women disappeared below ground, Phillip and horse galloped to the drain.

"I will follow them," he announced. He tied his horse to a tree and took a charming selfie, which he sent to his stable boy along with his horse's location for pickup.

"If I get lost in whatever maze awaits me and do not return, tell Aurora I love her. Tell her I died with her on my mind, my last breath her name on my lips."

His horse snorted.

"Fine. Tell her something you think she'll appreciate."

Phillip climbed down the slippery, gross rungs of the ladder. He then ran through a descending tunnel, which opened into a room filled with people playing billiards.

The women walked to a door in the back and disappeared behind it.

Phillip hurried to catch up. A twisting flight of stairs led down to a bowling alley. People shouted, music blared, and balls crashed into pins. Phillip covered his good ear to block the cacophony.

Still the women didn't stop.

Aurora led them to the last lane.

They rushed along the gutter and ducked behind the pins.

Phillip followed. A claustrophobic staircase finally turned into a hallway that went from dingy to elegant in a matter of steps.

A woman near the front held open a wide door for the others. When the last one passed through, she called to Phillip. "Are you coming?"

"You saw me following you?"

"I don't know what I'm more impressed by: your stealth or your intelligence." She pointed to the door, and when Phillip hesitated, she gave him a little push through.

He wove his way around couples dancing traditional dances. Classical music blasted through tall speakers. The dances contrasted the modern décor of the large, finished basement. The other eleven women twirled around the floor, each talking in earnest to her partner.

"Finally." Aurora took hold of his elbow and led him to the side of the room. "I got tired of waiting."

Aurora also wore a gown, which she had not been wearing above ground. The hooks connected with the wrong closures. Her sash slipped out of its knot. Her hair was three-quarters of the way to being a disaster, covered in what looked like ash. She leaned in close, and Phillip leaned back to avoid getting the ash-like substance on his designer jacket.

"This is Headquarters. My boss has wanted me to recruit you for ages, but like I said the other night, I wanted my own life. We already talked more than enough about that, but yeah. This is it. This is what I do. Here's where we report information. Those couples dancing are agents and informants and people who work behind the scenes. Dancing makes it harder to overhear conversations since the couples are constantly moving and tend to stand rather close to each other. Also, if our space is infiltrated, it looks like we're just some weirdos who are into old-fashioned stuff." She spoke so quickly, Phillip's brain needed a few moments.

"What are you saying?"

"I'm an agent, Phillip."

"You're a spy?"

"I mean, it's not exactly like the movies, but sure, close enough. I'm part of the organization that tries to rid the world of evil. You've worked independently in your heroism, which is why my boss wants you, he thinks you'd be a great asset for our cause, but most of us work together. We're more effective that way. We don't all have your single-minded determination."

"You're trying to tell me you're a spy in a secret organization that fights evil?"

"Even you are not usually this slow."

Phillip laughed. The kind of laugh that came from his stomach, that brought tears to his eyes, and made it difficult to breathe. He couldn't see Aurora very well through the tears, but she looked pissed.

"Babe," he said. "Good job. You got me."

"Ummmmm."

"Can it be my turn now? I'll make up some elaborate scheme, and you try to figure out what it is."

"Yeah. This could be a problem." She turned a full circle, searching the room. "Do you want to dance?"

"Always."

The DJ had just put on the second movement of a minuet, not as a delightful a dance as a waltz, but it sufficed. Phillip and Aurora moved slowly in their place on floor, clearly the best dancers in the room.

While all the other couples conversed in earnest, Phillip and Aurora communicated in silence. He gave her his winsome smile. She rolled her eyes. He leaned in for a kiss. She turned her head.

They danced the familiar, automatic steps. Aurora's proximity, her hands on him, and the rhythm of her body against his exhilarated him. The waves of negative energy coming off her, however, dampened the experience. Phillip had done something to make her angry. Whatever she had been trying to do in leading him on a wild duck chase, she had done for him. And she'd ended the elaborate affair with one of his favorite activities: dancing. He had to let her know he appreciated it.

"Aurora."

"What?"

"If you were truly part of a secret organization to defeat evil, I would join you."

"Oh yeah?"

"We would fight together, side-by-side, and go down in history as the best-looking, most talented, bravest couple who ruled their joined kingdoms and fought monsters for the sake of their people."

"Whyyy?" Aurora dragged out the y-sound. "Why do you always have to take it, like, three steps too far?"

Phillip replayed what he just said, counting backwards to find the elusive line between just enough and too far.

"You know I really wasn't joking, though, right?" Aurora tugged at his jacket. "I've been giving you hints this whole time. Please tell me you get that."

"Darling. It's not funny anymore. You have to know when it let it go."

Aurora laughed with no humor, quite an incredible skill. "You're amazing. You know that?"

"Thanks, babe." Phillip closed his eyes, content. Perhaps he did not need to defeat evil all the time. Maybe he would not have to rescue villages or slay monsters. If his life with Aurora could contain these bits of adventures, if he and Aurora could maintain some excitement between them and dance every so often and he could fight a dragon every once in a while, perhaps he needed no more adventures.

He opened his eyes when she shook his shoulders.

"Phillip, I'm not joking. This is your chance to do something, to make a difference, and I'm asking you to do it with me." She seemed serious, but she was so hard to read.

Then again… ash covered her hair. She smelled like gun smoke. Sounds of fighting accompanied their phone calls. The other couples danced with intensity instead of glee. And Aurora kept secrets and liked to disappear.

Ah, yes. She was not, in fact, joking.

"Thank every star in the sky." His heart danced its own frenetic waltz. "I have never wanted anything to be this true in my life. Except you, of course. I wanted you to be real and to wake up and to love me and to want to marry me and—"

"I get it. So that's a yes, then?"

"It's a—" Phillip held back the enthusiasm threatening to burst from within him. "It's a definitely. A definite yes."

"Babe." Aurora shook her head, ash falling around her like dirty stardust. "You are about to have the time of your life."

She pulled him close and relaxed into the dance.

They no longer followed the proper steps, but strangely enough, that didn't bother him.

Even more oddly, he didn't really fear his jacket getting dirty when Aurora leaned her head on his shoulder.

He had more important things to think about—incredible, world-saving, evil-defeating things that made him the most fortunate prince alive.

Which said a lot, considering princes are more fortunate than most.

TEN DAYS AFTER HAPPILY EVER AFTER

Amelia Steiner

I smacked my knight in shining armor on the head with a heavy skillet. He wasn't wearing his armor at the time so he grimaced, but I digress.

On our wedding day, my father, the king, gave us a ton of gold, a full two thousand pounds worth. He also gave us a castle in a neighboring kingdom. The evil gleam in my step-mother's eye and smiles of glee on the ugly faces of my step-sisters quickened my heart. Let them rejoice at my departure. My knight and prince had vanquished all the dragons, rejected my sisters and chosen me to be his bride.

The following day we loaded the horses. We took only the basic necessities as luxury awaited at our castle.

My champion mounted his white steed and I rode a sure-footed mare. He led the string of horses that carried his belongings and the gold. For the journey, he selected two sets of armor, as one was severely dented and probably had but one good battle left in it. He also packed three swords, including a broadsword and a longsword and two jousting lances, one war hammer and a mace. He packed three suits, one for appearing at court, one for lounging, and the other a full suit of mail.

I packed three exquisite gowns plus two for every day. Even though underwear is never mentioned in such tales, you only have to look at the illustrations to know I wear a push-up bra and an enormous number of petticoats. In addition to these, I took five pairs of glass slippers and three tiaras. A single pack-animal sufficed to carry my belongings.

We journeyed through the Hundred-Acre Woods, where there's so much to do, then over a mountain range and into the Dark Forest. As we neared the edge, a group of marauders approached on foot. My defender dispatched the gang in short order.

Heads rolled.

No sooner had he banished the mercenaries when we were assaulted by rampaging boars. He speared one as the rest vanished into the forest. We dismounted to admire our prey.

My prince planted his boot on the belly of the beast. "Dinner."

We'd been traveling on the road for a couple of days and were quite hungry. Normally we only eat at feasts or bite the occasional bewitched apple. We looked around for the pit in which the servants would bury the boar. Not only was there no pit but no servants came running to care for our steeds and offer us mead. We were quite alone.

We decided to press on as we had only the River of Doom to cross before we reached our castle. Lance, as my defender was called for short, tied the boar to his string of horses. We would feast at the castle.

On the other side of the river, lush green meadows rippled in the breeze and in the distance the towers of our castle pierced a cloud of purest white.

"A rainbow would make it perfect."

Lance said, "Where are my minions? I'm sure your father said there would be minions."

"Little yellow-pill men?"

"What? My servants? Where are they? Why are there no cattle or sheep in the fields? No wheat."

"Yes it is quite odd. Perhaps they're napping."

"All of them? And all the livestock?"

My perfect white cloud darkened. I bit my lip. "They must be here."

Lance drew his sword. "Perhaps this land is ruled by dragons. I shall slay each and claim my bequest."

I suggested we return to my father's castle. Crossing the River of Doom did not seem fortuitous.

The thought of battle made my husband giddy.

He held up his sword. "By might and right, I claim this land."

The weight of the gold almost drowned two horses, but through a heroic effort, my knight put each horse on his back and carried it to safety.

Arriving at the castle, we paused at the moat. The drawbridge was up. Lance removed his trumpet. He had been practicing in case there was no one to announce his arrival. His first toots didn't arouse the hare sitting motionless five-feet away, then he gave off a mighty blast, reminiscent of the trumpets of Jericho. The drawbridge remained closed. We journeyed around the moat. An unpleasant one as the moat smelled like a chamber pot that had not been emptied in weeks.

Lancelot reluctantly decided to cross the moat on his trusted steed. He handed me the string of pack horses and encouraged the white stallion to put his front feet into the muck. The animal gathered his haunches and catapulted my knight across the moat. This horse, whose mane had been singed by dragon's breath, turned to follow me to the drawbridge.

Eventually, chains clanked, gears groaned and the drawbridge dropped. Lance, always one for dramatic gestures, removed his hat, bowed low and welcomed me into our kingdom. His horse went first.

"Rubble." My Prince cried.

Cobwebs like hammocks hung from a ceiling with jagged windows to the sky. An owl perched in the corner explained the floor covering.

"Nonsense, just needs a good cleaning." I whistled a tiny trill.

"Why are you doing that?"

"It's a family tradition to whistle while we work." After some time, I managed to clear most of the cobwebs. The place still had layers of dust and my mouth was dry from whistling. No bluebird came to perch on my finger. No dwarfs came to my rescue.

My husband went out to unpack the horses and turn them out into the fields to graze retuning with a grin. "I know what the gold is for, to buy us servants and cattle and sheep."

"My prince, once again you have saved us. Hurry, and please get a good seamstress and some bolts of cloth, this dress is ruined. Who knew cleaning was so messy?"

"Yes, where shall I hurry to?"

"To get servants."

"Where is that?"

We sighed and I said, "I'm so hungry."

"Imagine a steaming bowl of porridge with diced apples."

"Imagining no longer seems to work. I dreamed of sausages, a big one, and still I'm unfulfilled."

Lance said, "Imagine harder."

"Stop, I'm tired of these hunger games. Move on."

"I observed my men foraging when we were on our quests. I shall go forthwith and return with such bounty."

He left.

I had never eaten bounty before but anything would do. I sat in a chair and toppled over. One leg was shorter than the other. I smiled, at last a use for the gold. It took three pieces to level the chair.

When my knight returned I learned bounty was a handful of nuts and berries and green plants with dirt still attached. We ate the fruits while he admired my ingenuity. We leveled three more chairs and a table.

"And what is this for?" I pointed at the weeds.

"Well you wash and cook them."

"Then get me water." I handed him a jug.

"Very well, but I'm supposed to have minions." He turned to leave.

"Wait. Don't get the water from the moat."

He rolled his eyes. A gesture I had never seen before and did not comprehend its meaning. *What was happening?* Before we only had to look into the other's eyes to know we were in love and only happiness awaited us.

He returned with the water. I cleaned the plants while he watched.

"I think you cut off the brown bits."

"Then what?"

"You cook it." He looked around. "But we have no fire. I think it can be eaten in this state."

I said to my protector, "You first."

He divided the greens and ate his half. I waited for the obligatory length of time one usually waited before the poisoned apple took effect. When he didn't collapse, I ate mine.

Almost as soon as we had eaten, my prince said, "I need to talk to you of pillaging."

"Pillaging?"

"Yes, it is how I procure my heirs. I've never done it before because my code of conduct required that I remain pure of heart and body. As we are now wed, I may pillage you. My men quite enjoyed it."

"I've never heard of this."

"I know. My code of conduct would not let me speak of such things."

A slight tinge of alarm. My mother warned me of that which could not be spoken. "What is this pillaging?"

"Well, we are not going to do all of it. I'll not murder the male subjects and set their houses on fire."

"Is that because there are no minions or because we have no fire?"

"Neither, it is because that part does not provide me with an heir."

"What part do we do?"

He smiled and rubbed his hands together. "I tear off your dress and throw you to the ground and mount you. My men found it exhilarating."

"And what did the women do?"

"They ran until they were brought down. Screamed and tried to rip out my soldiers' eyes. I'd rather you didn't do that bit. Shall we have a go?"

I held up my hand to give him pause.

My knight bit his lower lip. "Please, may we chat later? I must stress the urgency."

"A few quick questions. How many times do you intend to pillage?"

He gave me his best Prince Charming smile. "At least once a day for the rest of our lives. It is part of our happily ever after."

He held out his hand to bid me rise.

I ignored it. "I brought with me only five dresses."

"You want to talk to me about your wardrobe? At this moment?"

"I'm afraid I must." *Did my brave knight whimper?* "I have brought with me only five dresses. If you do not wish me to go naked for the rest of my days, you may pillage four times."

His blue eyes widened. "This is terrible. Nothing is mentioned of such travesties."

"Must my clothes be torn off? Couldn't we both undress?"

He withdrew a step and clutched his sword. "Are you trying to disarm me? Have you lost your purity?"

"You may keep your sword."

"Very well. But if it does not give me heirs, we'll have to follow the prescribed methods."

We disrobed. I kept my eyes skyward. A mockingjay perched on the battlement and trilled a song of longing.

My prince led me to the center court yard and threw me down. Stars swirled as my head hit the pavement. Loose rocks ground into my back. While I tried to dislodge the rocks my knight fumbled with other areas of my body.

A cry, "Oooh."

His sword clanged time, *thunk, thunk, thunk,* mimicking his rhythmic thrusts. A louder cry escaped as he collapsed on top of me.

Finally, he gathered himself and looked into my eyes. "My darling, stars exploded, I saw the heavens."

I could truthfully say I too saw stars.

He rose. Pricks of blood dotted his knees. "Perhaps you could make me some cushions for my knees. I think it would be more enjoyable."

I turned so he could see the wounds on my back.

"We could pillage on the grass near the moat. By the way, I slipped the wild boar into the moat. He was starting to stink."

"I suggest we try it in my bedchamber. While sparse, there is some cushioning." As I stood a trickle of blood ran down my inner thigh.

"Did I wound you, my beloved?"

"I'm fine." The blood stopped shortly but the next day a tremendous flow of blood began. I had cramps but otherwise did not feel bad.

"I did hurt you."

"I think this is something else. It feels as if it is coming from deep inside me."

"An heir, already? We are truly blessed."

After four days the bleeding stopped. My knight stayed at my side, looking in all directions for his heir to appear. When things seemed back to normal, my love was eager to once again pillage. "You probably need to practice more."

On the tenth day, after a morning of pillaging, my true love withdrew a scroll from his saddle bags. "Let me share this with you."

"Couldn't you first go in search of bounty and water? I'm hungry, thirsty and dirty."

"Soon, my love, but this will gladden your heart. It is the *Knight's Guide To Happily Ever After Appendix*."

"Where is the Princess's guide?"

He chuckled at my naiveté. "You don't need one. I am your guide and you must follow."

This seemed like the logical place to whack him on the head but he is after all my prince.

He opened his scroll. "Part one is on obtaining heirs. I could have received a bit more instruction in the how to department. All it says is to create many. Part five, section two discusses the uses of heirs."

He looked at me to see if I comprehended and moved to part two. "This deals with defending and maintaining your castle."

"Let me hazard a wild guess. You need minions."

"Alas, yes. You need them for so many things. You get them by paying them gold."

"And yet we have gold and still no minions."

"You're rather testy. This is happily ever after."

I did not hit him.

"As soon as we see a minion, he will be ours. Now part three is on obtaining more gold. For that you turn your minions into an army and invade neighboring kingdoms. They must then tithe to you in gold and other riches. This allows you to get more minions and invade more kingdoms. Part four won't interest you. It is developing the strategy for invading kingdoms. But part five is all about you."

My heart didn't make the slightest flutter. "You said five is about heirs."

"Yes, I'm so pleased you're following. It's rather complex." Still, he remained upright. "You need to produce as many male heirs as possible. For when I conquer a new kingdom, I shall put a son in charge. Isn't it a beautiful plan?"

"That is all it says about me? I'm to provide you with many heirs."

"Yes but it is very important." He glanced away. Worry flickered across his face. "I hope you won't fail me."

"Fail you?"

"Yes, like your mother. She only gave to your father one helpless female heir, you. No wonder this kingdom is in such disrepair. He had no male progeny to protect it. You must do better."

I stood and strode like a warrior advancing to battle.

He rose and gave me a smile meant to disarm a trifling foe. "I know you will do better. You want me to live happily ever after."

I'm afraid I lost momentary control and knighted my beloved with a heavy pan. But knights have the hardest heads of all men in the kingdom. My mother told me that before she left.

"Enough. We are returning to my father's realm today."

"Yes, I've been thinking we need to get our minions."

I donned my pure-as-snow gown for the journey. My husband packed both suits of armor and all his weapons. We crossed the River of Doom and journeyed through the Dark Forest and the Hundred-Acre Woods without incident.

As we neared my father's castle a group of soldiers approached. The leader said, "You must not go closer. The evil queen has imprisoned your father and will kill both of you on sight."

An aura of beautiful light surrounded my prince. "You will follow me and we will slay the guards as I did countless dragons."

The men pledged their allegiance. I was told to move back and keep out of danger. I could hear the clash of swords. At last my prince returned and together we rode through the gates of my father's castle.

The queen stood on a balcony. Her ugly daughters stood beside her, each with a man at her side. Between us and the queen was another full contingent of soldiers.

"You will never succeed in this quest." She threw a poisoned apple at my feet.

I looked into her eyes and did not see evil, but a woman who only wished for happily ever after for her daughters. This was denied as in one stroke of a man's pen her daughters became ugly, she evil, and I beautiful and therefore pure and good. I evaluated these sisters. Each was taller and more formidable than I. Far more capable of challenging the appendix that excited my knight. A male creator wrote our fates, our destinies. Perhaps it could change if parents refused to open books that began *Once upon a time.*

The apple lay at my feet. I bent and picked it up. I wiped it clean on my dress which remained snow white and pure. My prince stood beside me. We both knew my destiny was to take a bite.

The fear in my step-mother's eyes acknowledged her fate. My knight would defeat her, rescue my father and once again come to claim his reward.

I bit the apple, after all, I was quite hungry. I dropped the fruit and offered my hand to Lance. He kissed my fingertips as I swooned.

LITTLE RED HUNTING HOOD

M. T. DeSantis

Seriously, this basket gets heavier every time. I enter grandmother's cottage without knocking. Ten years ago, when I started bringing her food, she told me to just come in. I don't argue with grandma, and it's a good thing, considering what happened with the wolf.

"Grandma." I place the basket on the kitchen table. The cottage hasn't changed much. It's still dark wood and old-style charm. Pans pile atop the woodburning stove in anticipation of a home-cooked meal. I inhale, and aside from the fresh bread I brought, pine and oak season the air. No matter how old I get, this place will always smell like home. "Grandma, it's me, Genni. I'm here."

"Be right out, sweetie." Grandma's voice, as old-style charm as the house, drifts from somewhere in the cottage. She says something in a softer tone.

I halt halfway to getting my red cape off and hung on a hook by the door.

Budding beanstalks, grandma has a visitor. Grandma never has visitors, except for me, Mom, and that guy she met at the Elder Cottage Living group two months ago.

I strain to hear. Whoever's back there is quiet, which means it isn't the Elder Cottages guy, and of course, this is the one time Grandma keeps her voice low.

I hang my cape and go back to the basket.

Two sets of footsteps approach. Grandma enters the kitchen. Her white hair is in its signature bun, and she's wearing her white dress with the red-check pattern.

"Hello, sweetie." Her face wrinkles with a smile and stays wrinkled as she directs a glare over her shoulder. "Oh, for giant's sake, get in here. She doesn't bite."

I freeze. Who does Grandma need to reassure?

The person in the other room sighs. A scrawny guy who's about my age and lucky if he has any muscle steps through the doorway. He's dressed in shades of brown and green. Dark hair frames his stark-white face. He's familiar from his blue eyes to his black boots, but I'm too mesmerized by his narrow arms to give it much thought. They're so small.

"That's more like it." Grandma claps her hands. "Hutson, this is my granddaughter, Genni. Genni, this is Hutson Gunderor, Gunter Gunderor's son."

"Oh." No wonder this kid is familiar. Gunter is the hunter—Gunter the Hunter, wow—who saved Grandma and me ten years ago. Hutson is the spitting image of his dad, except his dad is built, well, like a hunter. I hold out my hand. "Nice to meet you."

Hutson doesn't respond. He's eyeing my hair as if it's going to come alive and flambé him.

I finger the strands. Naturally, my hair is auburn, but since I turned fourteen, I've dyed it with various shades of reds and oranges. The result resembles flames.

Grandma steps on Hutson's foot.

He yelps and shuffles away from the dangerous old lady.

"Nice to meet you, too." His tone suggests he'd rather be burned alive by hair-fire. He takes my hand for the wimpiest shake ever before dropping it and making eye contact with the floor.

What is this guy's problem?

"Very good," Grandma says in her I-have-news voice. Nothing good ever follows the I-have-news voice. "It's about time you two met. The arrangements were made ten years ago, and Gunter asked if I would do the introductions."

What is she talking about?

"You two are betrothed."

The world goes away.

Did another wolf barge in and swallow me whole?

I blink a bunch of times until reality comes back. The words *future* and *husband* flit around in my skull like a fly trying to break free of a jar. I heard wrong. Or maybe Grandma's going nuts in her old age.

"I'm sorry, what?" I say.

Grandma beams. "You two will be wed. Well, not right away, of course, but isn't this exciting for the two of you?"

Hutson's face turns a paler shade of green.

I can't blame him. Betrothed? It's so archaic. Besides that, betrothed to Hutson Twig-Arms? Absolutely not.

"Well?" Grandma lifts her foot to step on something, most likely someone else's foot.

Possibly my foot.

"Great." My voice is flat.

To be fair, Hutson's face is still green.

"Wonderful. Well, if you'll excuse me." He shuffles toward the front door and mumbles something about having to meet his father.

"Of course, dear." Grandma rushes to let him out. "Give your father my best, and tell him we will begin preparations soon."

We will?

Hutson mutters something else before darting out of the cottage and down a path.

"He's a lovely young man." Grandma closes the door.

"You can't be serious." My inner whiny twelve-year-old takes over the second the latch clicks home. "Him?"

Grandma nods, somber. "Yes, sweetie. You didn't think Gunter saved us out of the goodness of his heart, did you? Hunters have to eat, too. He came calling for his payment, and I didn't have it."

A fire to match my hair blossoms in my chest. "So you offered me instead?"

"I did not." Grandma straightens to her full height, a few inches shorter than mine. Even so, she's almost wolf-scary. "I bartered everything I could think of, but nothing was enough. Gunter said he would accept a betrothal of you and Hutson. I had no choice."

"There's always a choice." I fling my hands up. "Like, for example, I could choose not to marry Mr. Stick Figure. He's a hunter's son. He couldn't lift a toothpick, forget an axe."

"Magenta Hood—"

"It's Jenni." Ugh. Why does she have to use my full name? "And I'm not changing my mind. I don't need a man to protect me. I'm capable. Besides, what good will he be around the house? And what if something does happen? What do I offer my father-by-marriage in return for a second rescue? My first born?" I gag on the words.

Oh man, get that image out of my head, now.

Grandma doesn't waver. "I am certain things will work out. Unless you have fifteen gold pieces."

My inner fire snuffs out, and the horrible images vanish like mist. Fifteen gold pieces? No one has fifteen gold pieces, except maybe kings, and those don't hang around the woods too often. "These are the only choices?"

"Yes. If there were any other way, I would do it in a heartbeat." Grandma deflates and crosses to the table, uncovering the basket. "But there is not. Thank you for the bread."

Stillness settles around me as I retrieve my cape and sling it over my shoulders. It's not armor, but wearing it helps. "You're welcome. I'll see you in a few days."

"Genni," Grandma says, attention still on the bread.

I pause with my fingers wrapped around the door latch. If she tells me to have a dress by my next visit, I'm done. "What?"

Grandma's silent for a long time. Her head is bowed, and her shoulders are scrunched up by her ears. The posture doesn't want comfort. "I'm…sorry."

I force myself not to go to her. Hugs will only make this worse. "Me, too."

I wander into the afternoon. Sunlight and shadow play over the forest floor in unpredictable patterns. Birds chirp, way too joyful for what's happened. Overhead, the leaves stretch like the sky turned the color of a dead frog caught between two mossy boulders.

"Goodbye, freedom." I slog down the path toward home, heart heavier than the basket's ever been.

I sink onto a stump beside the path, letting the dead tree take my weight. This is ridiculous. I'm sixteen, and I have to rest during the short trek from the baker's to grandma's? I've never had to stop and catch my breath before.

An image of Hutson bombards me.

Yeah, I'm pretty sure exhaustion has nothing to do with not wanting to get to grandma's. The bogus betrothal and my bleak future have woven into my basket to drag me down.

Okay, enough feeling sorry for myself. I haul myself off the stump, heft the basket, and get back on the path. I'm going to grandma's and facing this if it kills me.

Which it might.

Around the next corner, the cottage comes into view. Happy smoke billows from the chimney. Oh good. At least I'll get lunch out of this visit. I trudge across the clearing, concentrating on food and not the Hutson-issue.

"Grandma." I call as I open the door without knocking. "I'm—"

Grandma hangs, tied, over the stove.

"*Grandma*." I hurl the basket aside and leap across the room, cape billowing. "Grandma, what happened?"

A growl comes from behind me. "Too late, little girl. She's unconscious."

That voice…it chills me all over. I pull my cape tight, but it doesn't help.

The memories engulf me. A gaping jaw. Darkness. Certain death.

Muscles protesting, I turn.

A black wolf stands in the doorway.

It's not the same one.

He died, but, like Hutson, this creature is familiar from its hungry golden eyes to the shock of white hair at its muzzle.

The wolf licks its lips and tilts its head in mock concern. "Oh, what is wrong, little girl? Are you afraid?"

My knees knock together. The icy rasp of its voice brings me back ten years to a day where I faced Grandma's bed and made stupid-kid observations. What big ears you have. What big eyes. Even now, the words spill toward my lips, threatening a repeat performance.

I swallow them like a wolf might a terrified six-year-old girl and stand tall. I'm older. I'm stronger and smarter and tougher. I can get rid of a wolf and save Grandma.

I point to the door. "Get out."

"But I just got here." Human words are so weird in an animal's maw. The wolf kicks the door closed. "Besides, is that the way to treat the son of an old friend?"

My body shakes like a top-heavy beanstalk. So much for my exit or someone walking by and seeing the girl being threatened by a wolf. This *is* how I die. It's just been delayed.

All right, Genni, stop. What about that pep-talk I gave myself—older,smarter, tougher. I fold my arms.

"Let me guess. Your father tried to eat us ten years ago." I don't let the tremble in my limbs reach my voice.

The wolf advances a step. "He did, and what reward, girlyhood, did he earn for doing what he must to survive? An axe in the back."

"He ate my grandma and me." The worst excuse ever in this situation, but it's all I have. Capes and curses, why wasn't I more careful? The first few years after the attack, I checked everywhere to make sure the route was safe. In the absence of a threat, I got lazy, and now, grandma and I are going to be eaten by some revenge-starved wild dog.

"Survival of the strongest," the wolf says.

My head clears a little. "You mean fittest?"

The wolf frowns. "What?"

I get my shakes under control. "It's survival of the fittest, not strongest."

"You..." The wolf snarls. "It matters not. The time for chatter is over. Today, I take the recompense denied my father for so long."

What is it with people's father's demanding payment this week?

The wolf howls, and the door uses the opportunity to open and bodycheck—doorcheck?—the wolf into the wall.

It takes me a second to realize I'm not being gnawed on.

The door is open. There's hope.

"Are you okay?" Hutson rushes inside.

My heart warms. Hutson came to my aid? Maybe he and his arms aren't so bad. He reaches for me and trips over the floor, slamming into the stove.

The world seems to slow. Hutson goes down like a sack of flour, and one of the iron burners pops free. It bounces once, spins, and comes to rest on its side. A stream of fire shoots from below.

"Crap." I grab Grandma and yank her out of the flame's path. The fire burns through the rope.

Grandma and I follow Hutson's lead. I land on my butt, and Grandma flips into a fighting stance.

"*No*." The wolf is up. "I will not lose my victory."

He howls and bounds forward.

"Yes, you will." Grandma yells a bunch of violent-sounding stuff in a foreign language and meets the creature in the middle of the room.

Paws and fists fly almost too fast to see.

Go, Grandma. All that prune juice must be paying off.

Hutson groans from his place on the floor.

I scramble toward him. In all the Grandma-almost-burning-to-death and wolf-kicking, I forgot he was there. "Are you okay?"

He grips his head.

"I think so." His eyes widen. "Look out!"

He shoves me.

I fall back in time to have Grandma's foot miss my head. Instead, she hits Hutson, who crumples again, this time with Grandma on top of him.

The wolf lets out a triumphant howl. "At last, the feast."

My world snaps into clarity. Oh, no way in a kingdom far, far away is another animal making breakfast, lunch, or dinner out of the Hoods. I snatch a broom from the corner and charge the wolf, laying into him with everything I have.

The howl turns to a whimper, which turns to a sobbing sound. I don't let up my assault. I hit and hit and hit until there's nothing but me and my target.

Take that, wolf scum. No one eats my family.

"Genni." A voice reaches through my blur. Grandma's wrinkled hand clamps over mine, forcing me still. "Genni, it's unconscious."

My arms continue the swinging motion on their own for a second before going still. I drop the broom and draw in a long breath.

So that's what blood fury is like.

The world spins.

Tears flood my eyes, and I collapse into Grandma's arms.

She holds me and makes soothing noises until I stop crying.

"Budding beanstalks. You were committed."

I sniff and wipe my eyes. "Me? What about you? Grandma, where'd you learn to fight like that?"

Grandma winks. "You don't think I keep Old Rumple from the Elder Cottages group around for his conversational skills, do you?"

A laugh pops out of me. "I hoped not, but—"

"What's going on here?" A booming voice fills the air.

I straighten and whip around. Hutson's father stands in the doorway of the cottage. His hair is pulled back, and he's holding an axe at the ready. He seems smaller than I remember, but it's probably because I'm an adult now.

"Gunter." Grandma faces our visitor, back straight and hands clasped. "What can we do for you?"

Gunter's blue eyes are hard. "I heard a wolf howl and came to aid."

He gestures with his axe to the wolf's body. "And I find someone's done my job."

"It isn't dead, Father." Oh good, Hutson's conscious. "Just out cold."

Gunter cuts the air with his hand. "I was not speaking to you."

He turns his unforgiving blue eyes on Grandma. "Well?"

Grandma fiddles with the sleeve of her white dress, and I suddenly know why I was promised to Hutson all those years ago. Gunter intimidated my grandmother. I didn't think it was possible, but watching them now, I know it's true.

Hot iron fills me. No one intimidates my grandma into anything.

"Someone did do your job." I point to myself. "If we waited for you, Grandma and I would be wolf chow."

Gunter waves his weapon. "Which is when—"

"You save us?" I snort. "Well, maybe we didn't want to get eaten so you could chop open another wolf. Did that occur to you?"

Some distant part of my mind warns me that yelling at my former savior isn't a good idea, but I don't stop. "While we're talking about it, did it occur to you that fifteen gold pieces is a ridiculous sum to ask in payment and that an arranged marriage is not viable compensation?"

Gunter bares his teeth. "I've never—"

"Been told the truth?"

I'm on a roll.

"Well, it's about time, and here's another dose of reality for you." I point to Hutson. "I saved your son, which means the debt from ten years ago is paid."

Gunter sucks in a breath.

"She has a point," Hutson says, smiling a little.

Gunter's silence is like thunder. Hutson's smile disappears, and he goes back to studying the dust bunnies on the floor.

"Very well." Gunter sticks his nose in the air. "The contract is fulfilled."

He spins on his heel and storms away.

I do a mental fist pump. Oh yeah. Took out a wolf and faced down Gunter Gunderor the Hunter Blunderer all in one day. Who's amazing?

"Wow," Hutson says when his father is gone. "I've never seen anyone stand up to him like that. You're amazing."

My point exactly. I start to tell him I know, but the words get lost. Hutson—inexperienced Hutson—came to help. Granted, his helping mostly consisted of getting knocked out, but who knows what would have happened if he hadn't been here?

I face him. "You were pretty amazing, too."

Hutson turns a greener shade of pale. "Uh, thanks."

The cottage falls into awkward quiet.

"Well," Grandma says after a bit, "I guess we don't have to plan your wedding now."

My world clears as if my head breaks the surface of a lake I've been trapped in for hours. Hutson's not so bad, but I still don't want to get married at sixteen.

"True." Hutson smoothes down a cowlick on the top of his head. "But could we, maybe, uh, you know, be friends instead?"

Friends. It rings like a bell at just the right pitch. Friends are the perfect thing for Hutson and me to be.

"I think we can manage that." I hold out my hand.

Hutson shakes, and the tiniest spark passes between us, warming my cheeks.

Oh man, no way. I'm never falling for this kid.

Though, he's not as useless as I thought.

In fact, those twig-arms of his might be perfect for carrying semi-heavy baskets of bread.

RAINBOW SLIDE

Dana Wright

"How late are your parents going to be out?" Jared said in my ear as his hand groped toward the edge of my shirt. I wiggled away and reached for the TV remote.

"They should be home in about an hour, why?" I shoved the bowl of popcorn from the coffee table at him and moved over on the couch. Flipping channels until it hit a horror movie, I settled back against an overstuffed pillow and tried to tamp my growing irritation. Weeks to arrange this date, and everything was going wrong. *Everything.*

"Jared, can we please just watch the movie?" I growled.

His lips curved upward. "Why? Am I rushing you?"

Yes.

I scooted further down, annoyed at his assumption. *He was supposed to be different.*

"What did you expect? That I'd fling myself at you the moment my kid brother went to sleep?"

Asshat.

A creeper-tastic smile crossed over Jared's face.

What had possessed me to even consider this guy as date material?

He was a football jersey with tentacles and more notches in his belt than I could count. I wasn't about to become one of them. I should have listened to Cindy when he left her stranded without a shoe at the dance last year, but after my long, mono-induced slumber, I wanted some date night action.

Desperate? Maybe.

But *this* wasn't what I had in mind.

"Aurora. I can't sleep. They're outside again." Christopher stumbled into the living room, bleary eyed from sleep, clutching his well-worn bear.

I had no trouble falling asleep at the drop of a hat, but my brother could hear a roach poop on the other side of the house and bolt wide awake.

The Grim Wood was right outside our back door. Without looking, I bet he'd forgotten to put the iron lock on the back gate. Fairy tales were great until they crept into your back yard and ate the family pet. Damned unicorns.

I closed my eyes, my lips pressing together in frustration. He had been listening in on my date.

Again.

I'd told him over and over if I have a guy here, stay in bed. I even saw the pattern from the textured paint on his left cheek where he'd mushed his face into the hallway wall. Last week, I'd caught him snooping on our parents when he'd gotten in trouble at school for flattening a kid who messed with the neighbor girl next door.

Wait till he had a date. I was so going to make him pay.

Better yet, I should take a pic of him in his superhero jammies and Instagram it. See how long it takes for all his buddies to give him a wedgie.

"Kid, your sister said to go to bed." Jared huffed off the couch and loomed over my brother. "Look, there is nothing outside for the hundredth time. See?"

Jared stalked out the back door, stepping into the yard.

"What are you doing? Don't go out there."

Macho boys were all alike. Try to play the hero and see where it gets you.

The original fairy tales weren't fluffy Disney stories. They were filled with death and dismemberment.

And if you were dealing with unicorns…you had better be a virgin.

"It's just a bunch of dumb wild horses. They'll run off in a minute." He turned to the herd, his red and white varsity jacked muted under the security lights. He waved his arms, shouting at the largest one. "Get out. Go on…adios, hairy muchachos."

The unicorn snorted, his horn flashing in the moonlight. His eyes narrowed and his lip curled over too-sharp teeth to be the sweet little lunch-box ponies.

Oh crap.

"Ummm, Jared. You might want to get back inside. Like now."

I edged back from the door.

"Don't worry, Aurora. I got this." With a smug nod, he turned back to the beasts. "Go on. You heard me. Get out."

Jared picked up a brick my mother used to surround her potted plants on the patio. He chucked it brick like a football.

The brick hit the unicorn square in the chest with a dull *thud.*

Nostrils flaring, the beast shook his rainbow-colored mane and lowered his head.

Bad move, buddy.

"Close the door." I pushed Christopher back inside, wishing I could ignore the swirl of color and the flashing hooves. Chris slammed the door shut with a rattle of blinds.

"*Wait.* Let me in."

We peeked through the blinds.

Jared was surrounded.

Chris and I were fine, but left alone too long with Jared and my virgin card would have been punched. Game over.

"You bastards. Get off me."

He never had a chance.

Jared ran, but the unicorns were faster. A medium-sized pink unicorn impaled him in the neck, and a smaller one with blue iridescent hooves dragged him to the ground.

The large one lowered his horn, teeth grit in a determined territorial stance.

"They're really into him."

I nodded. "That's good. Somebody needed to be other than himself."

I couldn't look away.

A few of the smaller unicorns slipped in the growing pool of viscera and dove in for more, their horns covered in gore. Screams and ripping flesh echoed against the glass.

"You think Mom and Dad knew I was having him over?" I glanced out the window once more and flipped the door-blinds closed. "I mean, it's funny they should show up like that."

"Yeah, well. He insisted on going out there." Christopher peered up at me and rubbed at his eyes. Running a hand through his bed-head hair, he grimaced."You really need to be careful about the uber douche lords you keep bringing home."

"Yeah. I know." I eyed the television. "You wanna watch *Zombies vs. Unicorns?* I hear they made a movie from the book. It was on Pay-per-view last night. Kind of looks amazing."

"Okay..."

"You want popcorn?"

Chris whipped around, his attention diverted by the mention of food. "Yeah. Extra butter."

"You got it." I tossed a bag in the microwave. The chocolate covered rainbow sprinkle cupcakes I had made for tonight sat uneaten on the counter, so I took a bite of one.

The rainbow-colored unicorn with the purple mane glanced at me through the kitchen window.

Maybe he wanted some as a side order with horn-dog asshole.

I threw in an extra bag of popcorn and hummed.

The scent of freshly-popped theater-butter-flavor filled the air. Maybe the night wouldn't be a total waste.

Unicorns.

Best bad date solution ever.

NEED TO BE APART

Jody Sollazzo

"Once upon a time in a land far, far away, Westchester, New York…" Cam pauses.

He kisses a line across Emerson's stomach. His lips are moist, biting, and wanting. He rolls her to her side and bites her ample hip, and she squeals.

"…there was a beautiful princess. Everyone saw how beautiful she was except for the bloody beast."

His voice is as thick as the Dublin heat outside of the crisp air-conditioned Hilton. Em almost forgets about the all the hidden trafficking below. How all these people look the same to her. Em almost forgets who she is.

"That's not how it was at all," she says with giggles.

He flips her on her stomach and squeezes her middle like he's holding it together. He kisses across her low back. She moans and longs for the back and forth ride against the crisp sheets. He moves his chest against her raw, molting back. The soft skin of his abs beat against her tailbone. The tickle of it makes her want to break apart with desire.

"I won," he growls.

He bites her ear.

She mewls. She can't help it. The a pinch of teeth spikes a trickle in her brain that pit stops at her vocal cords and roots deep in her body.

"And history is told by the winners."

"Of course you won. Home-turf advantage, but you always win. Because you cheat. Who wouldn't be a slave to that face yapping on about freedom?" she says.

With her back up against him, she can say all the right things that bring out what she wants in him. It's a swift magical spell that gives her the reward of a swifter ass slap. She cries out as her body convulses together in pure pleasure at the pain.

"I am the monster after all," he says.

Then why is Em the one that always sounds like the wounded animal as he finds the pleasure hidden inside of her? He does feast on her like she's a kill. Her cries go silent like a kept princess who can't scream, until she does.

Em splits in half with ecstasy as they come. With him, she can do it over and over without breaking herself. He says she's the only thing that soothes the whole of him. It's amazing what they can do smashing together and breaking apart. They are the two halves.

The light and the dark, with no weakness or pain or toil of the outside.
Their mingled blood has no bounds.

"Your blood test shows you may have some abilities."

The long workday left Emerson in pain. Her knees were inflamed. She had to use her cane to get the pamphlets across the room.

The Philippines brought out all the swelling her Lyme disease had to offer. It did have beautiful scenery. Yet, the view from the splintering Picong, Lanao del Sur Community Center showed little of it. Across the way was a dilapidated fruit-stand. The endless green mountains were too far away in the scorching sky. She forced herself not to think of Ireland and its breezy summer days and humming nights.

This D-positive girl she had to help was poetically named Diwata, which meant fairy.

"My boyfriend already told me about my disease, ate. He's in DFT."

Emerson's heart dropped. This news was nothing but bad. It would make her job near impossible. A fly with mammoth sized wings droned through squeaking, impotent fans.

"Your boyfriend is DFT," Emerson said. "DFT tells you being D-positive is a *disease?*"

"He's going to bring me to America," Diwata said.

The backless top of her own design had the breathable cotton that didn't stick to her and make her itch. Emerson was always prepared. She wasn't good at going off-book, like Cam. She used her TATI checklists:

1) Establish rapport with possible D positive. **Recognize and respect cultural differences.**

2) Obtain informed consent.

4) Do Blood Test

5) Discuss result of test. Go to either A or B

5A: Negative result: use Health Education protocol

5B: Positive result: Congratulate for possible abilities and give info of network for further education and immediately educate on trafficking.

Note: People may be more or less comfortable using terms of folklore. Use language they are comfortable with.

There was no checklist for when a D-positive girl was literally screwed by a guy from DFT. She was sure Diwata wasn't comfortable with calling her DFT boyfriend a dirty fuck-wad.

D.F.T.—Down For Trafficking, Dark Fairy Trade, Drop Fae Torture.

Or whatever DFT really stood for. Maybe the D stood for disease. She fought an urge to go into Sullivan's diatribe: Disease/disability had nothing to do with being D-positive; and no one knew why people with disabilities showed more D-positive abilities.

Emerson's phone tinged with a text.

Cam: *Just got another one done!! How bout U?*

She texted one letter back to Cam: *F*

Diwata texted on her phone, too. Of course, girls from remote villages texted.

Emerson texted the second letter: *U*

All girls would text unless they were trapped in a cult somewhere, or chained in a storage crate—bound. Emerson was here with TATI to make sure none of that happened to girls like Diwata.

Cam texted back: *U want 2 F me?? I could be there in no time.*

Manila was far less than two days away for her coworker and his boundless blood-energy. All the more reason she wasn't going to let some obnoxious Brooklyn-Irish kid win. She *was* Filipino.

Emerson would educate more people than Campbell if it killed her, and if this heat kept up, it might. Diwata was going to be tough. Forget DFT propaganda. Diwata's ignoring-people-for-texting skills rivaled any teenager's.

Emerson decided to be the responsible adult and do some texting of her own. She texted Ms. Sullivan, her field supervisor: *D-positive girl has DFT boyfriend!! How do we save her??*

"Are you texting a boyfriend?" Diwata asked.

The girl stood and stretched and sleeked back dark hair that mirrored Emerson's.

"In New York?" Diwata continued, "What does he do? He doesn't mind the cane because you're pretty? Is he white?"

My boyfriend loves the cane because he has a freak fetish, and he's not an asshole like your so-called boyfriend. He works against *human trafficking, but if you're not on his side, he can be a bit of a tenacious monster.*

"He's mixed-race," Emerson said, "He does his thing. I do mine."

She wasn't here to talk about boyfriends. Emerson steeled herself and remembered the mission of TATI: Teach Against Trafficking Initiative.

Connect any way you can, Ms. Sullivan said once.

Emerson's phone buzzed.

Dylan Sullivan: *You don't SAVE her. Be tolerant of DFTs beliefs!*

Ms. Sullivan was in her PC-the-war-is-over mood today. Sometimes, Emerson wished Ms. Sullivan would get angry again and just admit that DFT was no better than the Wing Rippers and Witch Hunters that turned on others as well as their own. But cold wars were different than all-out-wars. Emerson understood that if you were going to be a career woman you had to stay diplomatic, especially if you were a disabled Bender. Emerson wasn't a disabled Bender, or a Bender with a disability, as Ms. Sullivan would say. Emerson wasn't even what Ms. Sullivan really was, a witch with a disability. Emerson wasn't really fully anything, but Dylan Sullivan was the closest thing she would ever have to a role model.

"So, your boyfriend is a DFT recruiter?" Emerson forced a bright voice.

"No," Diwata said, "He's the boss of them."

Diwata's make-up caked around the edges of her eyes in light brown powered. Her eyelashes clumped in dark slivers. *Connect any way you can.*

"I could help you do your make-up. You would look so good in high fashion, New York brands. Your boyfriend will love it. You gotta go big or go home sometimes."

Yes. Wasn't her body supposed to feel at home here, or half of it? Which half was Filipino? It didn't matter. She had to connect here. She had to beat Campbell. She did almost nothing in halves.

###

Cam's phone answered his stare with a buzz:

Ses Drop+: *Can't U still teach me? These people r just old bruhas.*

Here was a girl who actually wanted Cam's help. Well, a ladyboy. Cam flopped on the bed. They used the term Bruhas in Manila, just like in Brooklyn, with the Spanish influence. Here in the outer islands it was *Mambabarang.* He liked that word even though it was hard to say. He hated the PC term *bender* they used in the 'burbs. He was glad people his age were trying to take back the word witch, as long as they were on the right side.

The sunset over Dapao Lake was a cooling orange ball framed in vines.

These people sucked in more Cheetos and cigarettes than Cam had ever five-finger-discounted from the bodegas in Brooklyn. They also took in more lies.

He texted back: *U can trust the Network. Remember the differences between tapping and binding & the people to stay away from. DFT = Devine Fair Travel, they are anything but & the worst. Remember if anyone offers to take you somewhere—don't go!*

Ses Drop+: *I WANT U 2 take me somewhere!! I could <3 u!!!*

People were addicted to all kinds of fairy tales. Fairy tales led to the same lies. Lies over drops of blood because Drops were all that were left now. Once, Cam was immune to lies. He used to believe all people needed was truth. But after a war, the truth was about what was believed. There was trouble beneath beauty, and he used to think the only way to create change was to be a beast about it.

A knock thudded on the thick bamboo door. Sullivan.

Cam had to shut this text down: *Doll, you can do better than me. I can't take you anywhere. My girlfriend takes me places, and I mess that up.*

Cam opened the door. Sullivan limped in. Their resident Mambabarang. Even in the movement the bosses were mostly witches because most of the Fae blooded were just young Drops, after all.

"You know I'm tougher on Emerson than you because I have to be, right?"

This was her greeting.

"You're tougher on Emerson than me?"

This was news to him. She was always hard on him. Always giving him lectures about power and responsibility. Always telling him to check his privilege, or as his mom would say it: *Get your dick out of your hand and your head out your ass.*

"I'm harder on her because it stops her from going too far." She limped over to the wicker chair and lowered herself down on it.

How she walked looked reckless compared to how she spoke. He was so used to the dichotomy that he normally didn't think about it anymore. Tonight, he was looking at her too closely because part of his brain was waiting for bad news.

"But sometimes, it doesn't work, and when it doesn't work, I need you." She took out a joint and lit it with nothing but the element of electricity around her.

All witches had the ability to work a Fae blood for elemental power. Working a Drop's blood isn't unethical if you do it right. If you do it right, it can only make them stronger, but how many people do something right when the other way was is easier? Sullivan for one.

Cam relaxed. This was just going to be Sullivan telling Cam what he already knew: Emerson was working too hard.

"Uh huh. You know a lecture about over-working is going to go a lot further from you than it is from me. Can I get some of that?"

He reached for the joint. She pulled it away and gave him her round sleepy-eyed glower. It was worth a try. Some nights, she's in a playful mood. He could use a hit. His insides had that twitchy hollow feeling. It had nothing to do with her. Sullivan no longer made him hollow or twitchy. Emerson on the other hand...

"Campbell, focus. I'm hard on her because it stops her most of the time, but when it doesn't, I need you."

Cam went stiff and clenched his teeth.

"What happened?"

"She's been blood-bound in a house," she said.

"She texted you? Not me?"

"That's procedure."

His stomach tightened at her calm. He bounded up and dug through his duffel of useless clothes until he felt the cool steal in his hands, his bladed horseshoe that took nothing short of glamor to get through JFK Airport. Sullivan gave her stern look and stood as quickly as she could. Her round eyes edged.

"Campbell—"

"I don't have time to discuss the finer points of the cold war, Sully. It's Emerson. Beautiful Emerson. Just know I won't fuck it up, but—"

"Cam—" Sullivan said, sterner this time.

"I'm not being possessive of Emerson, or objectifying her, and I'm well aware of the culture here. Of course, that's part of what I'm afraid of. What they could do to her if—if they see her—"

He clenched his fists and shut his eyes for a moment. How could he let her go out there alone? They'd never understand her beauty. They'd destroy it, and he'd destroy them even if DFT wasn't behind it, but they always were.

"She didn't report that she was seen, but even if it has come to that, it's a remote village that has its own belief system and—"

"I know," he says, "The Prime Directive. I swear I won't hulk out or hurt anyone. I'll just get Em."

Cam tensed as some female voices rang out in the hall. They were laughing. It was just the German tourists.

If Emerson was here, she'd make fun of for saying Prime Directive. Sullivan gave him a full smile.

"Bring our girl back in one piece."

She laughed.

It was the equivalent of her professing her love for both him and Emerson. As much as they called themselves field workers, they were all really soldiers-in-arms together.

"She wouldn't like that," Cam said.

But a laugh bubbled up. It swirled around the adrenaline and fear that had nothing to do with this war. Why was his beautiful girl fighting solo?

###

Cam burned across the island to where Sullivan had descryed out Emerson's location in forty-five seconds. He traveled the fifteen miles, grounding himself in earth when he had to.

The ramshackle bungalow was a yellow, wood box with a window that poured out light. Other dwellings lay around with countless island trees. Cam wanted to believe this could go smooth.

Cam breathed thick, hot air through his nose. Night bugs chirped. Something far off howled.

A woman with long gray hair stood near the house but apart from it, as if stalking around an invisible fence. This woman had to be the Mambabarang, the village witch, who put the binding circle around the house.

Her circle couldn't bind Cam's blood. He raced into the house so the witch had no chance of seeing him. He really didn't care about being *culturally respectful.* Emerson was trapped inside. Once in, the pungent odor of salt and rancid vinegar stung him.

"Em."

Emerson's upper-half lay on the kitchen counter. She was on her torso like it was a pot bottom and she was a two-and-a-half-foot-tall houseplant. She wore a lilac backless top, stained with vinegar-water. Two long, pink entrails hung on either side of her. The torso-wide crimson streak along the counter looked as if Emerson slid into place next to the stainless-steel sink. Her normally straight sleek hair hung wet and wild over her face.

"Em?"

She was out. Not good. He didn't see her bottom-half anywhere.

Cam turned to a trembling girl in a bloodied pink T-shirt. The girl's eyes were two shocked black balls with perfect cat-eye eyeliner.

She hugged herself. "Aswang. She's a beast."

Cam sighs. He was tired. This wasn't going to be an easy situation to get out of. He had no idea why Emerson would be so careless.

"What happened, doll? Did you throw vinegar at her? It just knocks her out. Ticks her off."

Emerson had been pissed-off, but why? She was light, too light to move. She was dry and splintery. She was wet and slippery. She was free and high, and mounted and bound. She was torn apart and numb. She was disconnected from…

Emerson had to connect with Diwata. To save her. Right?

No, she didn't care anymore. Emerson literally could do no more. Some people you just can't connect to.

Why did she care so much all the time?

Why did she fight?

She could sleep better with half of her gone.

Acidic juices soured her mind. Emerson's legs had been thrown on the hot roof, but at least, they were dry.

She was reminded of a joke from stats class. A stats professor has his head in an oven and his feet inside an ice-block. He says, *On average, I'm perfectly comfortable.*

Despite her disconnect, on average, Emerson was okay, even if she felt a little…all over the place.

"Ya know, this aswang isn't a bad one. She's a fairy with bad PR."

Was Em dreaming? The kitchen lights buzzed sweet music.

Cam told Diwata that Emerson was good. Cam always told people that Em meant well. He'd say she wasn't really a demon-bitch; once you got to know her, she was actually really nice.

"Did she do your make-up?" Cam asked Diwata.

This was too surreal. Bright painted cards of Manny Pacquiao sat on the counter. Cam and Diwata were blurry, and he asked her about make-up. The only thing that made it real was the heaviness of her severed body.

"I want to kill her," Diwata said. "She's a bad one. She wants to hurt my boyfriend."

Cam did that sexy-angry thing where he pulled his dark hair out of his eyes and jutted out his chin and groaned.

This was a dream. Diwata tried to convince Cam that Emerson was evil, just like every girl who wanted him. But, they'd never come together.

Any minute Cam and Diwata would start making out.

Dream. Dream. Dream.

Why, could this be a sexy memory-reliving-dream in a Dublin hotel rather than a guilt/fail dream in a Filipino bungalow kitchen? Never mind reconnecting with her roots. Em and Cam had been working non-stop for months, and they had little time together. She didn't want to work with him too closely. They could make it a healthy competition that way. Wasn't that how they brought out the best in each other? Why had Em thought that was a good idea?

"Was she walking okay? She bring a cane?"

Cam was always on Em about her cane when she swelled. Maybe this wasn't a dream. She never dreamed about her Lyme. Her dreams wanted her running around and high-school thin.

High school was over. Their beauty-and-the-beast thing was over. Emerson planned on big things before twenty-one.

Being rescued in her motherland was big, right? Cam bounded over to Emerson with his take-charge stance.

"Where's her lower-half?" Cam demands in his sexy-rumbly-voice.

He moved back Emerson's hair. Her whole face cooled with relief. She could see him now even though her stupid eyes wouldn't stay all the way open.

His wings were out, shining with every color that danced in the light. There was a word for that. What was that word? He cupped her chin, and her nether regions stirred, even though they were technically her upper regions now.

"Emmy?"

He stood lean-muscled in a tank top. Those Jared-Leto eyes and almost-triangle jaw that rounded at the end. The wings with a sexy scar. Maybe her big thing really was to be his queen. Cam denied he was the fairy king.

He was half human after all.

But the full-blooded Faes were mostly gone. Whether light or pretty, like him, or dark and ugly, like her, full-bloods were bred-out and dissipated.

Now there was only a drop of Kool-Aid in the ocean. Ninety-nine-point-nine percent of the time anyway. Point-one percent of the time mixed-raced genes and a catalyst-illness made things go sideways.

Or get cut in half.

Cam took out his horseshoe-thingy and used the tip of the steely blade to slice open his forefinger. He put it to Emerson's mouth. This wasn't the taste of him she wanted, that she owed him. But it was so sweet, like the rainbow-light of his wings. Did she taste like the sour, black liquorish of her wings? Ugh.

Ugh.

Emerson sobered up more quickly than Sleepy Beauty, that lazy bitch. Em's head thrummed with the buzzing over-head kitchen bulbs. Her shoulders practically screamed for release.

Emerson was better off sober. The sensation that she'd tried to stay afloat in a rotting ocean for hours was gone. Gone also were the moronic anti-feminist thoughts. What was present was head heaviness. What was present was the complexity that called itself clarity.

Whatever was in Diwata's death-water made Emerson full-blown-out-monster and temporarily basic-bitch-wasted. Emerson did not want to be Campbell's queen. She didn't even want him here. Telling all the girls it was going to be all right.

Campbell had no idea how Emerson had failed this girl, and he could not fucking fix it with his smile or his wings.

"You're an angel," Diwata said. "Don't you know an evil aswang when you see it? They eat babies, you know?"

Cam groaned and pulled his hair back again—annoyed.

His wings disappeared.

Maybe, he finally realized Diwata didn't meet his secret damsel-in-distress turn-on.

Diwata jumped when that weird, old woman pounded on the door. Emerson didn't know what the woman's deal was. Besides bad hair. She just showed up after Diwata doused Emerson, and Diwata wouldn't let the woman in.

"Okay." Cam exhaled with false casualness. "Gotta go. You showed yourself."

What? He thought he was going to swoop in here and say that this was her fault. Emerson forced her eyes all the way open, sporting that creepy doll-button-black that was in every horror movie. She ignored her stupid hormones responding to his hands around her torn-apart torso.

"You showed yourself, *angel*," she stiffened her body but didn't pull away.

"Must make you a demon then. You're going to get yourself killed without me. Don't worry about the cane. I'll carry you."

He had the balls to use that crooked smile as he mansplained.

"Put me down."

She hissed at him. Not a human sound. He always said she sounded like a cockroach. She hadn't even known cockroaches hissed until he showed her on You Tube. She thought it was a city myth.

The old woman yelled and pounded on the door again.

She was clearly a witch here to kill Emerson.

Emerson never learned to speak Tagalog. She didn't have to in order to know that the woman shamed her for it. Like it was Emerson's fault her grandparents wanted her mother to be all-American.

"Stop. You're making it worse. Scaring the hell out of them."

Cam shamed her now, too. He put Emerson back on the counter.

"Em. C'mon. Let's pull you together."

She restrained herself from biting off his pretty face. Even if she pulled herself together and left this all behind, half of her would stay. Stay with Diwata, who was going to become a slave and wanted Emerson dead for trying to stop it. Cam couldn't understand any of that. Emerson barely did.

The woman pounded on the door again.

#

"Do you know the night I've had, Cam?"

Em's pupils dilated her eyes into full-on reflective black pools. They wouldn't stay black, but they always glowed with reflected light.

"No. I don't because you want to do everything without me," he said.

Emerson's blood-stained lips frowned. Her delicate forehead wrinkled. That woman would not stop pounding on the door.

Thank Jesus, the girl went outside to talk to the woman. A shrieking discussion in Tagalog erupted between the two. Em and Cam were about to have one in English.

Em shifted her torso on the Formica. "You have no—"

"*Em.*" Cam's voice tightened and rose. His limbs twitched, and he had to break away from her and pace the little kitchen.

"It's obvious what happened. This girl has a shitty boyfriend, and you just had to say something about it. So, then, shit escalated, and you lost control and showed yourself, and this poor girl freaked out."

Cam refused to let Em speak. He didn't want to do any of this. He wasn't Batman or Constantine. They got to work alone…because their mortal girlfriends died. Cam told himself he wasn't mansplaining. He hated that word. He told himself he had to point out Emerson's obvious over-attachment in this case.

"So she got the Mambabarang to bind you here, and they're probably fighting about the cost of you and who gets to sell your body parts. If I'd been here—"

The unfurling of her wings stopped him.

They awed him every time.

Unlike his own useless wings.

"What did Sullivan say about leaving out your values?" he demanded.

"*I* should leave out my…" Em was furious.

Cam felt removed. Distracted by her wings. Embarrassed about how his own came out before. How they flitted and fluttered. Nothing but flapping microcells made of iridescent light. The single tear made them inoperable.

"…Speaking of shitty boyfriends, this is exactly why I didn't want to work with you here, Cam."

"*I'm* being shitty? This whole trip—"

The witch burst in, yelling.

Here we go.

The girl in the bloody shirt trailed her. Neither seemed to be looking for a fight.

Em's wings beat. They spanned the entire kitchen wall and knocked colorful saint cards off the counter. They were so formidable and solid. Flesh and delicate bone. Made of the golden-sand skin of her body. They had little moles in places. Cam wished he could forget how reckless she was being. He wished they were back in her house in Westchester, and he could be the guy that knew where to take her to in the city on weekends.

The older woman spoke in Tagalog and pointed to the ceiling. He answered her words.

"Don't worry. I'm an angel. I'll take the demon away. Just need all of her."

He might as well make the angel thing work for them. The woman clearly asked the girl for a translation. The girl said a word in Tagalog, and the old woman got something from the top of the crowded family photo fridge. A knock-off Hummel figure of a chubby cherub with wings and a halo blowing a horn.

Emerson pushed her upper body to the edge of the counter. Her talons scraped the yellow Formica.

Out the window, scraps of bloody sherbet tainted the remaining sun. They reflected in her black-well-eyes with the shadow of himself in them

"Angel," the old woman said and smiled at Cam.

"Asshole." Emerson snarled as she pushed off the counter. "Everything is so easy for you."

An entire angry tirade clutched him, but Emerson's upper-half took low flight, a half-foot taller than her *normal* self. She dragged him through the door.

Everything was so easy for him? Which everything was she talking about?

She'd be upset her backless lilac top was stained...because that wasn't easy.

But, Cam being poor-as-shit-was? He didn't have a trust fund. He couldn't just walk away and think about designing clothes-for-wings on Esty.

Em's wings whipped the air. Her two entrail cords flowed like a gown's train.

Maybe Emerson thought the war easy for him when *she* could fight under-the-radar, but every witch wanted him.

Easy E, like Sunday morning. Back when he was nothing but a powerful body to take apart and his mother and Dylan hid him in Emerson's McMansion for protection. She didn't want him there, and he felt like a prisoner. He thought nothing could feel worse, but maybe being released when you wanted someone to hold you close was worse.

Emerson hooked her arms around his shoulders. Despite himself, Cam's body loosened. He leaned back into her chest. She ascended pulling him aloft.

Em could fly.

He couldn't, and not because his wings were only made of light particles or because he sometimes lost control of their visibility. They were rendered useless minutes after he knew he had them. They only thing he mourned was his brother's betrayal. Why would he mourn his wings when never really had them? Why would he need them when he had Emerson?

The sun had set, and the night was cooling. He wanted to just enjoy his brief flight, but his brother's words haunted him.

You may've gotten all the looks, but you're half-mortal, baby brother. You can give me all your mortal-dominant-gene crap, but you'll feel it. You'll feel the time-lag when that demon-girl throws you fast away. The dark-ones aren't like us. They're bound to time.

His brother turned on his full-Fae drama, trying to get Cam away from Emerson when mom was sick, and she almost died. Not mom, Emerson.

Ever since, he worried about his beautiful girl. He wanted to protect her.

Cam couldn't help it. Even now.

No, especially now.

The truth was he was glad for the war. Glad he had to hide in her house, helpless. He more than made up for it.

If anyone was trapped in death and time, it was Cam. He was well aware Emerson pushed him away. He wanted to know why.

Like anyone else, he was scared of what he didn't understand.

Cam dangled from Emerson's hooked arms. The corrugated roof was twenty-feet high and tilted.

She dumped him roughly on it. His ass would bruise.

"*Ow*. What is wrong with you?"

"I don't know. Maybe it has something to do with literally being torn apart while trying to help."

"Well, you go too far and don't accept help yourself. We're up here for your legs, right?"

"No. We're up here to have sex. If only we could find my vagina. This must be so hard for you."

Her voice had that sarcastic stab that wasn't as sexy when directed at him. The stars were brighter as dusk moved away.

"See, this is what I'm talking about."

His forehead ached with knots. She scoffed and majestically pulsated her wings. A white sandal with a delicate, red-pedicured foot lay next to him. He was happy to feel the rest of her legs.

"Right, it's no wonder they think you're a fuckable angel, and they hate me. I totally deserved to have villagers attack me," she said.

He grabbed at her ankles and pulled her legs towards his lap.

He almost told her this wasn't a contest, but then, her ice broke.

"God. Did I really just say *villagers attacked me*?"

He should say something. Answer her.

"Yeah, um…"

No. He was a dumbass. That wasn't the answer she wanted. He was just glad to have her lower-half halfway in his lap. His detachment disappeared like someone had flipped on a switch. His hands felt weak and threatened to shake like they just realized they were really filled with half of Emerson's body. She could give him the rest of it or take it all away.

"I'm a B-movie monster. I'm not even an A," she said.

Her legs tightened around his waist and hugged him. He squeezed the curve of her hips. The old lady and the girl argued in the house. If they did anything else to hurt Emerson, he would Kirk-out. Prime Directive be damned.

"Baby," he said as Emerson's legs squeezed him. If he looked at her, she would get more upset. So he looked where the rest of her body should be. Tropic trees and mountains became dark shapes. "These people just don't know us. I'm sure if they did they'd want to fuck you, and kill me, and I don't know, marry Sullivan."

He was so happy she laughed. Her torso-less hips hugged him. The high rise of her pants covered her torso stump. Her upper-half hovered, and the full moon behind her made her look like a living horror-comic tableau. She was so self-conscious about her torso stump, her two entrails. Cam was fascinated by them.

Whatever miracle of nature that disconnected her also protected her. It sealed off her two halves with blackness when they severed.

Anything romantic when she was severed was out of the question. She had kicked friends out of cars for even joking about it. Her legs clutched him so tight. He shifted himself, curbing his excitement.

He tried for another laugh. "And don't exaggerate. Only two people tried to kill you. Not a village."

"She had some boys get my legs on this roof. I was weak. I was so glad they didn't—didn't try to do anything else. That a disconnected live-one wasn't their thing. Maybe it was the cane. I don't know where they put that."

She laughed bitterly, and the sound of it socked him in the chest. Emerson was so strong. She couldn't ever be vulnerable like that. Not anymore. It wasn't fair.

"It's okay. Nothing else happened."

"I-I don't think you're supposed to be the one making me feel better, and here I was, an idiot, worried about DFT."

"Oh, but you're not a idiot, Cam." Her voice swung-up mirthlessly. "At least not about DFT. That girl down there, Diwata, thinks some creepy DFT Mission Head is her boyfriend. I think he wants to take her for a personal power source."

Her voice broke, and she sobbed. Cam squeezed her waist hard. Em always ended up shedding tears over someone else. She still tried so hard to project her Diva image, but she would never forget this girl's name, Diwata.

"Maybe I'm just a cynical American. Maybe, it is true love. Who am I to say who's a monster and what a healthy relationship is, right?"

"Em. I. Do you want me to find him and—No. You can do that. You don't need me. You don't."

God, his chest hurt. Emerson flew around to her lower-half, hovering above him and her legs. Her pupils shrank back.

Her lovely two entrails dangled.

"No. There's nothing we can do here, and I clearly need you, too. Like it or not, I am the monster, and you're the—"

"You know that's not true. Nothing but lies. I'm no prince, and you're no monster." He wiped sweat from his forehead.

"It's not exact. Ya know, when you take control of a curse to live out a role-reversed fairy tale, you think it's going to be all feminist, or at least fun. But, it just never ends."

Cam shook his head as he looked up at her. His eyes stung with the threat of betraying all of his hurt. Did she just feel stuck with him? Did they lack their fairy tale ending?

"It never ends? Is that why you're with me? You think you're flipping a so-called curse some bitch gave you in high school? She was a twisted Changeling in the body of a boarding school brat."

Emerson scoffs.

"You're being ridiculous. The curse was ended the minute I killed her and took her heart. I'm with you because we're—"

"You don't need me. We aren't fated to be together. You rise above all of it. And me."

He was going to fall apart, but she shimmied her way down to her lower half. Her flowing coral-like entrails coiled into her until everything closed with a sweet smacking.

The sound reminded him of two bodies coming together, not one.

But their bodies were entwined together now. His mouth filled with the sweet night air. He had to shut it. No way did Em not know about one of Cam's body parts lifting from the others now.

"Sorry, I guess I'll always rise for you, like you need that right now."

He tried to shift his hips with her on top of him so he at least wasn't poking her with an erection while she was having a bicultural crisis and maybe deciding to break up with him. She laughed, like a soft bell in his ear.

Relief loosened the knots in his stomach.

"Okay, you win," she said, "I don't need you. I love you. I'm not with you because we're fated to be together. I'm with you because I know we should be together, even when fate tries to tear us apart. But, sometimes, I need to be apart, and if you make an aswang pun, I'll tear up your other wing."

He brushed his lips against hers, tasting his own copper-sweet blood and her salt. She exhaled as a night bird cawed.

"God," he said, "you are so fucking beautiful."

"I'm a bloated demon that's bad at my job."

"Oh, you think you won the bad-at-your-job contest today? Wait 'till I tell ya…"

His voice thinned out in his mouth as with the heat of her tightened around him. This wasn't just the heat of her wings blocking the night breeze that suddenly came, but the heat of her that poured out her cotton pants and into his lap. She tucked her solid wings away and into her body. He kissed her.

"You know, I'm the real creep. I'm sorry I find you so hot like this. Hell, I'm sorry about everything that happened here. The so-called light turning your own people against you."

She giggled. The buzz went down his ear and carried through all of him.

"I like your Asia-phile-ness more than your white guilt, Mick. When full aswangs were being destroyed, your people were off having drunken-orgy fairy-circles. Completely disconnected."

"And we know from our trip last year most still are. But I've been disconnected. I should've realized how coming here would affect you. It's like when we went to Ireland for me. Only not because I'm—"

"—ethereally hot and kickass, and you know that trip was magical."

"I was gonna say white and a guy, but okay."

Cam was going to say something about his nose being a little long-busted, and how she always reminded him he had a four-pack, not a six-pack. How when they were in Ireland, she had to bail him out of jail.

It turned out continuing a brotherly brawl wasn't actually legal there.

As far as kickass, she could probably take him in a fight when aswanged and unbound.

Then Em kissed him open-mouthed and slow.

He forgot about everything else.

Something landed with a hard thwack right beside them.

He shielded her.

"Seriously?"

Huge gray moonlit wings lifted a grinning, wild-gray-haired old woman. She had on a bra with a purple skirt.

An aswang.

She had the teenage girl by the shoulders with an orange gas-lantern that glowed in the black pool of the old aswang's eyes.

Cam's vocal cords twitched in his throat, but he couldn't make a sound.

"My *lola* says to apologize," Diwata said.

Em's cane dangled from her hand. The white of it stood out in the night.

"I wanted you to be bad because you were telling me not to trust my boyfriend." The girl's voice shifted.

The old aswang put her down on the roof, and the girl leaned on Emerson's cane.

"But I know he is bad, like *lola* says. How do you know your boyfriend isn't bad?"

Emerson spoke so quickly her words stepped on Diwata's. She shifted her weight on Cam.

"He saved a lot of people and taught them how to use their own power when he didn't get anything back for it."

Her wings whooshed out of her.

A breeze chilled the now black tropic night.

"Baby, bae…" Cam said as Emerson rose off of his lap.

She looked like a fierce predator, hovering between him and the women. This was one of those times when he didn't know what she'd do.

She flew at the older aswang's well-lined face.

"You can't have his blood. You'll have to kill me first. He's not one of the Fae that hurt you. He's half-human and mine."

The girl gripped the cane tighter.

The aswang spoke in Tagalog, all drawn-out long vowels. The lines on her face remained dark as the lantern lit the rest of her face as she laughed and smiled.

"Baby. She doesn't want me. I think she just wants to talk to you."

"Oh."

The girl sighed and played with the cane, twirling it as she translated.

"She says she's been protecting this place for forty years, but that doesn't mean you can make aswang/angel babies on top of her house."

"Babies? We weren't—We're twenty, I—" A rare Emerson stammer.

The older aswang wagged her finger, like a happy elf with gothic wings.

"Like we can even have babies," Emerson said, "dividing in half during certain times of the month is kind of bad for a fetus."

Cam hadn't thought about that.

"You obviously don't do it when there's a baby inside." The girl scoffed. "My *lola* wants you to come back into the house as a guest. She wants to talk to you about your blouse."

"It's all stained now, but tell her I made it. I have an Esty page."

Eyes back to their upturned hazel jewels, Em beamed.

"So, this turns into a night about your clothing designs." Cam smirked.

"You can go, if you want," she said.

Right. He was going to leave his girlfriend in a village where they were known to hunt her kind as baby-eaters. But, obviously they didn't always. This old aswang seemed like she had a good life. A family pain-in-the-ass-family for sure. She had to have fought battles and won.

So many questions that weren't his to ask.

He was just happy to help keep things together and be along for the flight.

The girl handed the cane over.

He connected with at-risk brats but didn't take their crap, and he certainly wasn't gonna let them jack his girl's stuff.

Cam liked to hold Emerson's cane when she didn't need it.

Just in case she had to come back for it.

Will Tyrone 16/11/16 The Witch Hunter (33 witches + 9 Devils)

TINKERHELL

Michael Seese

The river. I needed to get to the river. The river would carry me away from here, away from them, away from death.

I struggled, staggered. The sweat streaming down my face clouded my eyes, making it difficult to discern the small details of the terrain below my feet. I tripped and fell, far too often. To make matters worse, I grew more and more woozy from the loss of blood. Though I had taken no major blows, the tiny wounds scattered across my body added up.

I crawled. The rough ground—or perhaps traps and barbs *they* had placed—tore into my knees and palms. I had to press on. What choice did I have? I could have given up. I could have rolled over, let them swarm, and said, "Take me, you vile little beasts." That would have been easy. Quick. Merciful.

No. You will not *give up. You will not die here. Damn it, man. Move.*

I willed myself forward and found my holy grail, coming to rest atop not so much a cliff, as a steep, long, treacherous slope. The river, and its salvation, coursed perilously far below. I *had* to find another way there. In my condition, trying to navigate down at this point would have been too dangerous.

But which way to go? In which direction lay the ocean? I'd lost track long ago. I grew more confused, more disoriented. The thick canopy of foliage masked the sun overhead. It would offer me no guidance with regard to east or west.

The sound behind me brought the hairs on the back of my neck to attention. The ominous buzz. I stood. I didn't need to turn around to look. But look I did. There they were. Hundreds of them. Maybe thousands. Eying me. I could wait no longer. I had no other choice.

I turned and leapt. I assumed that after a few seconds I would hit earth and start sliding, rolling, falling, and finally splashing. But I didn't.

Instead, my descent slowed, then ceased completely. I hung, suspended in midair, torn between two forces. One natural, and one wholly unnatural. .

'Twas not the betrayal of gravity that halted my escape They had caught me, and were bringing me back up.

Just before I blacked out, I recalled the words, the warning of the old man at the tavern, the fellow with one eye and tiny little scars all over his face and hands.

"They may only be three inches tall. But they're mean little buggers."

How did I get here? My inauspicious adventure started three days ago, in that very tavern...

Downing a drink, trying to forget my troubles, I overheard the two men sitting next to me engaged in a hushed conversation.

"I don't know about this, James. Sure, you're offering a lot of money. But I've heard bad things about that place."

"They're just rumors."

"What if they're not? Didn't you send Peter out there? And he never came back."

"*You* can handle it. Peter couldn't row a dinghy in a bucket. But you're a solid boatman. And you're the best hunter and tracker in Kensington."

I could lay claim to being neither a solid boatman, nor a mediocre hunter and tracker. But I was broke and really could have used the lucre. I ingratiated myself into their *tête-à-tête*. Being a somewhat rough place, one didn't simply amble up to strangers and say, "Excuse me, and please pardon my ungainly interruption. I couldn't help but overhear." So I broke in boldly, scantly acknowedging them, but rather nonchalantly contemplating my tankard all the while.

"If the man doesn't think he can do it, don't force him to his own doom. They can smell fear. If you have even the slightest doubt, they'll capitalize on it and…" I said, making that thumb-across-the-neck gesture, which implies slitting a throat or, shaving perhaps.

"You sound mighty confident stranger," said the one who had been identified as James.

"Let's just say I've had my share of hunting and tracking exploits." I lied, unless you count hunting down opportunities to scam a few quid, and tracking the whereabouts of the numerous people to whom I owe debts, so as to avoid them.

"I think he's your man," said the other fellow, as he took his drink and excused himself.

James turned to me. "Let me buy you a drink."

"Matthew."

"Matthew, it's a pleasure. I'm James." He nodded to the barmaid. "Wendy, an ale for my friend here."

I thanked the gods of poverty that he offered. I had thought about buying his drink, but doing so would have deprived me of my last shilling.

When the tankard arrived, I took a sip and said, "So, tell me how I can help you."

"Have you ever heard of Neverland?"

Of course I had not.

"Of course I have," I said. Lying quickly had become habit.

"Well, then you know that most of the place is a worthless dump…mountains, plains, mazes, a rock that looks like a skull. But in the center lies the prize: Pixie Hollow."

"Pixie Hollow?"

"Yes, Pixie Hollow."

"More like Pixie Hellhole," intoned a voice from the other side of James. It came from the aforementioned one-eyed and scarred man.

"What?" I said, trying to *not* appear as concerned as I was.

"If you go there, you'll come out calling it 'Pixie Hellhole.' That is, assuming you do come out."

"Pay no attention to him. He's off his rocker." James then lowered his voice. "He thinks there's a ticking crocodile after him."

"It's true. He's real," the stranger said, rabid fear flavoring his voice s. Apparently, losing an eye did not affect his hearing.

"Come," James said, grabbing my arm and leading me to a table and away from the voice of caution, and perhaps even reason, who had not finished his litany of horror tales. "It may be true that the inhabitants of Pixie Hollow can be a little aggressive at times. Perhaps tenacious. Okay, sometimes downright ferocious. But they're basically mosquitoes."

That prompted the stranger to utter the aforementioned comment about "three inches tall."

"So they're *big* mosquitoes. Bring a fly swatter and a butterfly net, and you'll be fine. Look, if it were easy, the pay wouldn't be so good."

"And what exactly is the pay?" I said, struggling to contain my greed-borne curiosity.

"One hundred pounds. Half now, half when you deliver."

"And exactly what do I need to deliver?"

"What else? Pixie dust."

"Pixie dust?"

"Pixie dust."

"Naturally. And how do I get it?"

"You're a tracker," he said. "You find a giggling umbrella, follow it to them, capture one, and she…I mean *it* will lead you there. To the dust."

Of course. Follow the giggling umbrella. And while I'm at it, why don't I find a yellow brick road and follow follow follow follow it as well? Hmmm. That has a nice ring to it. Put it to some music, and you'd have a catchy tune.

"I think I can handle that. So, what exactly does pixie dust do?"

"Look friend, I'm not paying you to play twenty questions with me. I'm paying you to go to the island, get as much pixie dust as you can, and bring it back. If you don't want the job…"

At least, I now knew it was an island.

"No. I'll take it. I can handle mosquitoes."

"You do have a boat, right?"

Of course I didn't.

"Of course I do."

"Great. You're hired." He dropped on the table a small sack, which happily jingled. He took one last sip from his stein, stood, and said, "Meet me back here in one week. You'll get the rest then."

"Count on it."

James turned to leave.

"One more thing," I said. "How do I find it? The island?"

"It's the second to the right and straight on till morning."

Though I was, as already acknowledged, by no means an accomplished seafarer, his directions made no sense.

"I'm not sure I follow you. Exactly what does that mean—second to the right and straight on till morning?"

He just shrugged. "That's all I know. That's all anyone knows."

After he left, I sought out the one-eyed and scarred man whose opinion of Pixie Hollow seemed to run contrary to that of James. Unfortunately, he had disappeared. I slumped down at the bar and ordered another ale.

Where am I going to get a boat? And then providence stepped in once again.

"Sure," said the fellow to my left, to his companion, sitting to his left, "I'll be up in the Highlands for a few days."

"Still hunting that ogre?"

"I know he's out there. I'm going to capture him and bring him back alive. With any luck, I'll get that talking donkey I heard about as well. Since I'll be traveling by horse, I won't need my boat. Feel free to borrow it, if you want to do some fishing while yours is getting repaired."

"Thanks. I may have to do that. Edward says it will be another week before she's seaworthy again. Damned sea monsters. She's moored down at the north docks, right?"

"Yeah."

"What's her name again?"

"*Tinkerbell.*"

"*Tinkerbell?*" He barely contained a guffaw.

"Don't start. My wife picked the name. And since I bought it with the money that she had set aside to remodel the kitchen, she got all whiny about it. So I figured, okay, let her have this one. Trust me, my friend, do yourself a favor and just stay single..."

Quite a propitious turn of events. Within the span of an hour I gained a job, some money, and a boat. (Not to mention a boatload of concerns, questions, and apprehension, but I forced myself to put those aside.) Now, all I needed were some supplies.

The following night, I stole down to the north docks, found *Tinkerbell*, and set sail. I made a conscious and concerted effort to travel light, forgoing foodstuffs. Would not the island have *something* in the way of comestibles? I wanted to ensure that I could *carry* all the supplies I would need:

- A butterfly net.
- A small birdcage.
- Since I wasn't sure what would serve to contain the fairy dust, a jar and a bottle of wine. (The bottle started out full; that would change.)
- Rope.
- My knife.
- A flint, for starting fires.

- And finally, a tin nebuliser, in case I had to spray the little buggers with poison.

The notion of navigating to an unmapped island remained elusive. Despite ruminating over it intently for the better part of the prior day, I didn't have a clue how I would find it. In the end, I trusted in James's assertion that others had made their way there by simply relying on the guidance: it's the second to the right, and straight on till morning.

After rowing for perhaps two hours, I came upon a sign sticking from the waves.

"RIGHT," it read.

I took that to be an indicator that I might be on the right track, if I may mix transportation metaphors.

After several more hours, I encountered another sign.

"RIGHT." So I steered starboard, and redoubled my efforts.

As the sky morphed from black to cobalt, an island arose from the mists.

"That's it. I've done it."

Had I the slightest doubt as to whether or not I'd found the right island, the third sign laid all uncertainty to rest.

"Welcome To Neverland. Enjoy Your Stay."

I rowed into the lagoon, tugged the boat ashore, and stepped out onto the soft, white sand. After so much seafaring, I felt spent and sat down to rest.

My heavy eyelids and weary bones suggested I would be wise to nap, so that I might regenerate my strength and have sufficient reserves for the tasks before me. I had just lain down when a playful giggle touched my sleepish imagination. I envisioned the sweet face of the woman issuing the joyous noise. How nice it would have been to see a—

Wait. A *giggle?* As in a giggling umbrella?

I opened my eyes, pleasantly surprised to see my areverie morph to reality. There, twenty feet out in the surf, stood a radiant beauty. Long, flowing red hair. Bright blue eyes. In lieu of a blouse, she wore a brassiere of two seashells. Purple seashells. She smiled at me and motioned, beckoning with a finger. A playful splash preceded her dash to another rock about five feet further away. Turning toward me, she motioned again, then proceeded to the next rock. This continued ten or so times, until she had reached a point approximately fifty or sixty feet away in the center of the lagoon.

I walked to the edge of the water and jumped to the first rock, large and steady, with a flat top. I skipped to the next, and the next, and the next, and so on, until I arrived at the final plateau.

I sat down, said hello, and asked her name. She only smiled.

Long about this time, I cast a subtle downward glance to drink in the rest of her glory. To my surprise, a long, fish-like tail swayed rhythmically below the blue.

Three days ago, if someone had told me I would soon be sitting on a rock in the middle of a lagoon chatting up a mermaid, I would have quickly and without any sudden movements eased away, as I tend to be wary of the insane. But seeing as how I embarked on an expedition to retrieve pixie dust, which I was to find by following a giggling umbrella. Let me just say that logic would suggest adopting a more forgiving definition of crazy.

She said, "Kiss me."

Such a direct request surprised me, though as a gentleman I always complied with a lady's request. The sun, which had settled into the distant waves, cast a golden glow on the scene.

I leaned in.

Her lovely blue eyes shifted from passion to regret. "I'm so sorry. You should have moved more quickly. Now, it's too late."

She grinned. Her mouth expanded like a bear trap.

She hissed and lunged.

I recoiled, and in doing so plunged into the water, which thankfully came up only to my chest.

Something—somethings—swam around me.

"Stay away, sisters," she said, a feral growl replacing the lilt I'd grown fond of. "He's mine."

I leapt out of the water and onto a different rock—one closer to the shore—in one smooth motion. As I turned to hurl myself back to the next rock, one of the sisters rose out of the water and lunged for my ankle with her razor-sharp-tooth-filled-bear-trap mouth.

I avoided the *SNAP* and jumped. The water around the rocks roiled, and the sisters popped up out of the water like devilish jack-in-the-boxes. *Or would that be "jacks-in-the-box?"*

I made a mad dash toward the safety of the shore, a different mythical minx nipping at my heel with each hop. When I at last reached dry land, I allowed myself a sigh of relief.

Though the other sisters surrendered to the surf-turf barrier, the first girl, the crimson-haired beauty, refused to relent, She crawled from of the water and onto the beach. Even though she had no legs, and therefore could not stand to pursue me, she nonetheless wriggled and writhed, gnashing her teeth. I could have simply come around, grabbed her tail, and heaved her back into the water before making a break for inland safety. But her singular pursuit suggested I take nothing for granted. I fashioned a quick lasso, tossed it around her lower half, pulled tightly, and dragged her away from the beach and into the forest.

She gave up her struggle.

I lit a fire. She roasted up rather nicely. I wish I'd brought some tartar sauce. At least, I had the providence to pack a crisp Riesling.

My hunger sated, I sat back and picked my teeth with one of her pointy little fish bones.

I must admit that she certainly scared the snot out of me, which I would consider infinitely preferable to any other potential effluents. But I survived.

If that's the worst this island can throw at me, I'll be okay.

I napped for several hours before beginning my quest. I wasted the better part of the day escaping the verdant confines of a maze I inadvertently wandered into. My efforts at exit were only confounded by the constant calling out of women's voices, as they looked for their lost boys.

"Tootles."

"Nibs."

"Slightly."

"Curly."

Why didn't these mothers or nurses have their children in prams, where they would be safe?

Exactly how was I to find my way out? Would I find my way out?

Then I heard it: a faint laugh. A laugh that sounded like a baby cooing. A baby *giggling*. I looked back. A dandelion seed approached, then glided past my ear. I cocked my head to listen more carefully.

The sound clearly emanated from the seed.

It does look like an umbrella. This must be it.

The umbrella did not float above the top of the maze, but rather wound its way through the green, twisting hedges. Since it seemed to know where it was going, I followed. In due time, we emerged and the umbrella continued in an easterly direction.

I continued my chase past countless topological challenges, which nearly prompted me to abandon my quest.

Most challenging was the mountain, which—I will admit—took some of the steam out of me. Fortunately, the altitude slowed the seed as well.

After we peaked, my quarry gained speed and raced down the eastern face. The day drew to a close, and darkness overtook me. I feared I might soon lose it. But as the ambient light faded, the little guiding seed illuminated. How convenient.

As it breezed across a meadow, the assorted wildflowers beneath its flight likewise glowed and opened. From them emerged little winged things. The three-inch mosquitoes.

I quickened my pace so as to not lose sight of the seed. But I need not have fretted. Ahead, near a bend of the river, sat a large, shining tree. Indeed, both the seed and the trailing mosquitoes alit on a large specimen of fungus clinging to the bark roughly seven feet above the ground.

More and more tiny tracks of light whizzed across the lea, settling on branches surrounding the flat fungal surface. For mosquitoes, they flew rather upright. If I hadn't known otherwise, I could have imagined them to be humanesque in shape. Truth be told, they resembled little people. With wings.

They buzzed, though its timbre sounded somewhat like tiny little voices.

Despite my curiosity, I dared not wait. I spied a particularly luminescent branch, crept up beneath it, and with one swing of my net captured a number of the little beasts. I transferred them to the cage .

I hurried, even though I could not imagine a reason to fear the little things still flitting around the tree.

Under the cover of the forest, I sat down for a short respite. I must have fallen asleep—the healthy hike up the mountain apparently had been more taxing than I assumed—because when I opened my eyes, the new day had dawned.

I stretched, sat up, and scratched my head. How could I employ these little bugs to find this pixie dust?

Now blessed with plentiful light, I put my face up to the cage to get a better look at my prisoners. Four tiny faces—decidely un-mosquito-like faces—glowered back at me. At that moment, I'd lost all capacity for surprise.

It all made sense: my mission had been to secure pixie dust, which can be found in Pixie Hollow, which is where pixies live. I laughed and shook my head, embarrassed and astounded by the sudden—and now obvious—insight.

Though their voices were tiny and high in register, I could make out a conversation.

"What do we do, Tink?" asked the auburn-haired one with the huge braid at the back of her head.

"Don't worry," said the blonde one in the green, leafy dress. "I've got the tools. It's amazing what you can find washed up on the beach. Are any of your friends around?"

"Wait. Let me see." She closed her tiny eyes. "Yes. Quilliam is close."

"Perfect. Let me know when he's *really* close."

"How can I help?" asked another, this one with long, black hair, and appareled in a blue dress.

"You'll know what to do," said Tink.

"And me?" said the fourth. "A light show, I assume?"

The blonde nodded.

The three turned to the one with auburn hair. She paused a bit as if listening—or smelling—then cried out, "Now."

With that, Tink slipped two flattened, sharpened thimbles onto her wings. She backed up to the side of the cage and flapped furiously, sawing through the minuscule bars. She made short work of my gaol in miniature. In a blink, out they zipped, and I rediscovered a small measure of the surprise I thought I'd lost.

They flitted about me as if they *were* three-inch mosquitoes.

Distracted by the turmoil around me, I failed to react to the porcupine that had stepped onto the path in front of me.

"Quilliam. Fire," squeaked the pony-tailed one.

A volley of barbs sailed off his back, and lodged into my lower legs. Waves of pain coursed upward, gaining strength before launching a unified assault on my spine. I screamed, and fell to the ground.

The dark-haired one flew over to a tree and waved her hands. The leaves synced with her motions. She swept her hands in my direction. The morning dew, still clinging to the leaves, flew off and pelted my face in wave after wave of sharp, speeding droplets. The water stung more smartly than the porcupine quills.

A menacing buzz filled the air. The space around me had grown thick with them.

Before I could run, a flash of light blinded me. The fire in my eyeballs spread quickly thorough out my skull.

"Way to go, Iridessa."

When my brain had cooled enough to permit me to open my eyes, directly in front of my nose hovered a little, flying blond man. He held up a tiny hand and blew dust in my face.

Had he poisoned me?

I rose from the ground and flew.

He must have blundered, as I now had at my disposal a means of speedy, aerial escape. However, the besprinkling was part of his strategy, as I could no better control my flight than, say, an elephant, even one possessed of abnormally large ears. I wished, willed myself to run away. But with my feet well off the ground, I merely spun, back to front. Not only was I getting nowhere while expending considerable energy in the process, but his tactical dusting effectively rendered me a huge, rotating target for their magical weaponry.

More lights flashed.

More water needles stung me.

Rocks and pebbles lifted from the forest floor and assailed me from all sides.

Birds swooped down from the sky and pecked me.

My minor injuries were mounting.

After several minutes of assault, the effects of the dust wore off, and I descended. Once my feet felt earth beneath them, I ran.

I put what I had hoped would be sufficient distance between them and I. The path ahead converged and grew narrower though, unfortunately, not owing to the effects of some optical illusion. The brambles, briars, and branches of the blackberry bushes reached for me, whipping me, slashing me, slicing me.

Rapidly, I lost blood, confidence, and hope. I had to press on. If I could get to the river, I could follow that to the lagoon. To my boat. To escape...

I came around, supine and floating, carried along by a battalion of the little winged abominations. I struggled to move my arms, but found I was fettered by an assortment of cast-off pieces of string: yarn, fishing line, and thread.

Above and behind the crown of my head flitted the blond one, the duster.

"Excuse me," I said. He either did not hear or willfully ignored me.

"Excuse me," I raised my voice. "Might we have a word?"

"Take any word you want. It's yours." His snarky comment elicited giggles from his comrades.

"Where are you taking me?"

He flew around so that we were nose to tiny nose. "You came looking for our dust, didn't you?"

I had nothing to gain by lying. "Yes, I did."

"Foolish human. What were you planning to do with it?"

"Sell it." Again, why lie?

"What for?"

"To be completely honest, I don't know. A gentleman paid me to secure some and bring it back to him. Look, if it's money you want..."

"We don't need your money. We need something else."

"What might that be?"

"We are an open, giving people. But we've always believed it is better to give than to receive."

"I'm not sure I understand."

"Let me put this into terms that your big brain can comprehend," he said, condescendingly, another comment that evoked a flurry of little guffaws from below and around me. "Twenty billion years ago—give or take—there was a cataclysmic event, which we call 'The Big Bang,' a term that your people will glom onto in a hundred years or so. Personally speaking, I'm not very fond of the name.

For what it's worth, it sounded more like a thud. Anyway, after this event, the stars were formed. The earliest stars were much larger than our sun."

He pointed skyward and looked at me quizzically.

"The sun," I said. "Yes, I've heard of it."

"Just checking. Anyway, these first stars were much *much* larger than our sun, and because of this, burned much more quickly than our sun burns right now. After all of their hydrogen had been converted to helium in a process called nuclear fusion."

He looked at me expectantly again.

"Nuclear fusion. Yes, I've heard of that, too." This time, I lied.

"Just checking. Anyway after all of the hydrogen had been converted to helium, then the helium started burning and creating heavier elements, such as calcium, carbon, and iron, blah, blah, blah. However, iron is really strong—you might have experienced that at some point in your life—and as a result cannot be made to fuse and form still heavier elements. So once the star became a big, iron ball, it stopped burning and exploded in a smaller-scale cataclysmic event called a supernova."

The little finger quotations that he used to emphasize common terms, like "iron ball," which he apparently suspected were outside of my vocabulary, had become rather annoying.

"These supernovae explosions served to spew and scatter these heavier elements throughout the universe, and more locally, our galaxy, mixing them with the free-floating atoms of hydrogen and helium, which themselves had begun the process of condensing into a massive disk centered ninety-three-million miles from where we're flying, give or take. These heavier elements spun around the disk, which eventually formed our sun and system of thirteen planets."

"Thirteen planets? You're mistaken," I said, with a high degree of confidence. "There are only eight planets."

"Keep looking. The point is, these raw materials—present at the very birth of the universe—formed the stuff of our sun, our planet, and you. In essence, we all are children of the stars.

"Some of us are just more star-like than others. But you'll do."

"Do? For what?" I could not fathom in what capacity I might serve them.

He laughed. "You wanted to find the source of our pixie dust?"

He held a mirror to my face and said, "You're looking at it. My brothers and sisters. I think it is time we paid a visit to the factory."

COMPANY AT LAST

Brian H. Seitzman

People generally believe that loneliness is a void, a black emptiness of dull sensation and unending yearning. Henrietta Odalin's experience of loneliness was none of this. Her long solitude was blinding white, a sharp blow delivered with enough force to concuss her brain. Her senses were keen, pouncing like a mad cat upon any stimulus to alleviate the sameness of her days, and her yearnings she ameliorated for many contented moments with books.

Etta, as she would have preferred to have been called if anyone ever spoke her name, loved all sorts of books. When she was a lonely little girl, she loved to browse the shelves of libraries and bookstores. The adrenalin generated from a discovery was the only thing that kept her awake through life's monotony.

Always she would hurry back to the protection of her bedroom, though. She hated people staring at her only slightly less than she resented their awkward attempts to avoid looking at her at all.

Etta preferred having no contact with those whom she knew judged her. Thanks to the Internet, she could search for literary treasures online rather than in shops. She relished her privacy now more than she delighted in searching shelves. Seldom were her asymmetrical features made the subject of gawking anymore. She needed never answer tentative questions about her velvety body hair, her peculiar outsized teeth, her glassy green eyes with large pupils and hardly any sclera. Etta knew that her appearance was unsightly, even frightening, and so she hid herself from the eyes of the city.

It had become her habit of late to cover her head and lower face, from flattened nose to receding chin, in the manner of the Arab and North African women seen nowadays on the streets of Worcester. Better to be thought Muslim than a monster, she reasoned, even if a few ignorant people conflated the two. She avoided eye contact and conversation as she went about the infrequent business that forced her from the usual confines of her one-bedroom flat.

Etta's vacant social life disposed her to flights of fancy.

She dreamed of miraculous surgery that could make her face and body normal, even beautiful when her imagination grew daring.

She fantasized about salons, dates with handsome men, and of moving far from dreary Worcester and her tiny apartment on Martin Luther King Boulevard.

Her physical deformities paid her bills; she was considered permanently handicapped by the government thanks to a major curvature of her spine. If not for that twist, as uncomfortable as it occasionally made her, she would have had to go begging for employment and somehow overcome her uncanny features.

Etta contented herself with her reading and her daydreams.

A quiet morning perforated by the pings of raindrops found Etta reading about life in ancient Rome. A buzzer alerted her to a visitor at her building's outer door. She shuffled on uneven legs to the wall-mounted intercom, taking a deep breath before pressing the button to talk. Nobody ever called on her; only mistakes made her buzzer sound. She readied herself to explain the stranger's error.

"Hello. Can I help you?" she asked.

"Good morning, ma'am," came the courteous, measured response, "I'm here to see Henrietta Odalin. I have a delivery."

"Oh. Okay. I'm... ummm... I'm upstairs in 3B..." Etta buzzed the courier in.

A few moments later, three raps rattled her door. Etta hurriedly draped a scarf over her head. The young man standing there extended a black-edged nine-by-twelve envelope and a clipboard.

"Sign on the next blank line, please." He diverted his gaze to the pattern of the scuffed floor tiles rather than Etta, until she returned his clipboard.

The envelope was from the law firm of Vargas and Townhill in Fitchburg. The letter within bore news that a distant relative who shared her last name had passed on. Etta found the decedent's name familiar; she dimly recalled Michael Odalin from childhood. He had been a guest in her parents' home when Etta was five years old. The memory felt warm, as if this relation had been kind to her. Her punishingly loveless childhood, devoid of the slightest parental affection, made the emotional recollection a highlight that lurked in her memory for two decades of cold, bare, metallic life.

The realization ushered in sadness, a regret that she had not spent more time with a man who had long ago treated so humanely a neglected and malformed little girl.

The formal letter explained that there would be a reading of the deceased's will in Fitchburg ten days hence. While not mandatory to attend in order to receive Michael's bequests, it emphasized that Etta's presence was advisable in case questions arose.

Etta was of two minds. She dreaded being in a room with people she did not know. Her family had shunned her long ago. She had not an ounce of love for any of them. On the other hand, the same circumstance made it unlikely that she would ever receive another inheritance. She worried that she should be present to defend her interests, since no one else would do so. Etta argued with herself for the better part of an hour before resolving that she would summon up her courage, cover her face, and attend the gathering.

###

Etta arrived at the law offices of Vargas and Townhill earlier than she had planned thanks to the prowess of a lead-footed cabbie; it was not yet business hours. Had the velvet body hair that hid them not been there, her knuckles would still have been white when she exited the taxi. Etta adjusted her veil and decided to pass the time walking. She so rarely ventured out of her apartment; perhaps she might see something novel today. Still, Etta was sure that judgmental eyes were upon her, that disparaging thoughts were percolating in anonymous observers' minds. She was uncomfortable in the open, trebly so when people were nearby. She checked her watch frequently, impatient for the shelter of four walls and a ceiling.

When she had wasted sufficient time, Etta returned to the building in which the law offices were housed. Upon opening the correct door, she explained her business to the doughty woman seated behind a mottled marble counter. The polite receptionist made eye contact and invited her to have a seat in the waiting area through an uncertain smile.

"Mr. Haviland is running a little late. Can I get you some coffee in the meanwhile?" Etta nodded and found a chair.

There were too many eyeballs here to feel comfortable about removing her veil in order to drink her coffee. She set the cup down and wondered how many of the dozen people scattered about the room were also there for the reading of her uncle's will. Eventually, a pudgy little man with a briefcase rushed by the receptionist's desk. Minutes later, the receptionist informed them loudly, "Everyone here for the reading of the Odalin will, please meet Mr. Haviland in Conference Room B, right this way."

Six of those waiting got to their feet; Etta made sure that she was last in line. Her clumsy gait and the slight thudding of her cane on the carpeted floor were unique among the potential beneficiaries.

The few friends and relations of the late Michael Odalin entered a large room and seated themselves around a long table, instinctively reserving the chair at the head for Mr. Haviland. The plump attorney arrived after they were all seated. He occupied his chair with a faint groan and placed a green folder on the table before him, which he leafed through before looking up.

"Ladies and gentlemen, on behalf of myself and Mr. Odalin, thank you for coming today," Haviland said.

He spoke for a couple of minutes, but Etta let her mind wander. The words were unimportant to her. Her kindly kin was gone, and she didn't know any of the attendees in the room.

Etta was bored by the proceedings.

She paid marginal attention as bequests were revealed to mister such-and-such and missus so-and-so. Enough information diffused her boredom for her to understand that Michael Odalin had been a wealthy man with neither wife nor child. His heirs had been bequeathed cash, land, even the mansion in which Michael had lived. Etta was impatient for her name to be read. Every glance her way in the sterile white light of the conference room made her wish to return to the secure, solitary comfort of her apartment.

Haviland finally read her name from the will in the green folder and informed her of her inheritance.

###

Etta silently bemoaned her rotten luck for the extent of the trip home. Not only had she spent over $100 on transportation to and from Fitchburg, but now she would have to spend some additional sum to have her inheritance hauled from there to Worcester. Michael Odalin had left her a room's worth of furniture. Antique furniture, to be sure, several of which pieces were family heirlooms passed down through generations. She was still fretting over the potential expense of moving her inheritance when the driver dropped her off in front of her building. Etta paid him and slunk to the elevator, shaking her head all the while. The sun was hidden behind the Exchange Building, the sky becoming orange as evening approached.

Etta decided that the way forward was to relax and read about ancient Rome until sleep took her. In the morning, she would make calls to get appraisals from antique dealers regarding the list of furnishings Mr. Haviland had presented her. Then she would see what, if anything, would be worth moving. She reclined on her twin bed and read through the list once more, then switched to learning about problems with Roman plumbing until a deep and dreamless sleep overtook her.

Etta spent her whole morning and much of her afternoon reading Haviland's list to antique dealers over the telephone. All were interested in a few pieces, but none wanted the lot. She connected at last with Krimbret Antiques, LLC. Mr. Krimbret was eager to have all of the pieces save for one chair and an oak chest. More to her relief, Krimbret was willing to travel to Fitchburg, appraise the furniture, and move it on his truck.

Etta was beside herself; she was still in for a windfall of $5000! With that, she could pay to move the remaining chair and chest and have plenty left over with which to pamper herself.

She enthusiastically accepted Krimbret's proposal. The dealer told her he would call tomorrow from Fitchburg with a final bid but would not move a thing until Etta had agreed to it.

Mr. Krimbret was a man of his word. Etta picked her head up when the phone rang minutes past 10:00 AM. Krimbret had arrived at the Odalin manse and gone over the items bequeathed to her. He was ready with his bid.

"I can give you $6,500 for the lot," Krimbret said, "I'm not interested in the Hepplewhite-style chair or the chest, but I'd be happy to bring them back to Worcester for you at no charge, Ms. Odalin."

Etta agreed as reflexively as the jerk of a hammered knee. She decided in that moment that she could use another chair and she could find use for an oak chest. She cast her eyes about her unkempt dwelling and thought of what she might store in the trunk.

"You have a deal," she practically squealed. Her inheritance had turned out better than she'd hoped. The boon would be a much-needed supplement to the monthly pittance paid her by the government.

In fact, Etta whispered to herself as she put down her phone, it was one of her best days ever.

When the delivery driver had come and gone, Etta had her check in her pocket and antique furniture in her cramped living room. She decided that she would move the chest into her even smaller bedroom to use for storing her linens. The gorgeous, finely crafted chair would stay in the living room directly across from her television. The check needed to get inside an ATM; she had never had so much money in her account before.

Joyfully reeling, Etta decided to spend extravagantly on wine of a vintage she had never been able to afford previously. She would toast the memory of Michael Odalin even if she couldn't remember what her benefactor looked like.

Today was meant for celebration.

Etta walked as erect as she could, always looking straight ahead, into a liquor store where she selected a bottle of 1996 Duval-Leroy Cuvée Femme champagne, an investment of $150, as suggested by a helpful, friendly clerk. She left the shop with a brown bag full of extravagance in hand.

She would have danced in the street had her body been capable of it.

A rare smile was riveted to her face, but nobody could see it beneath the floral cotton scarf concealing her mouth.

Arriving home, Etta went eagerly to her refrigerator to chill what she was sure would be a bottle of the best thing she had ever tasted. She settled onto the black upholstered seat of her new chair, resting her feet on the chest that came with it. The elegant woodwork of the chair back pushed hard against her spine and the edges of her shoulder blades. This would never become a favorite chair for comfort, but its beauty as a crafted piece was undeniable.

After her meal, Etta inspected her new possession more closely.

Such elegance.

The feet of the chair were carved into long, thin digits clutching spheres, as were the ends of its arms. The arms and legs were threaded with fine, dark, leafless vines that continued onto the frame supporting the seat. The back was glorious, carved and molded into loops and bends such that there was not a single sharp angle. The delicate patina on the varnish rendered all of the wood a glossy, warm fawn.

Etta was intrigued with the black threads, no thicker than a few hairs, which wound their way throughout the wood. They looked natural, as if they had grown there.

The upper edge of the back swooped upward to a graceful circle carved at the summit into the face of an animal that Etta did not recognize, its eyes shut as if asleep, its mouth broad, its snout shallow. She ran her fingers over the carved visage and wracked her memory.

The beast was familiar, yet she could not name it. She felt the pride of possession and wondered why Krimbret had not wanted to buy such a unique and lovely chair as this. It was the most aesthetically appealing item in Etta's otherwise spartan, utilitarian dwelling.

She treasured it.

Days passed as they always did for Etta: in isolation. There were books; there was the Internet; there was television. Most of all, there was white-hot emptiness for which she did not pity herself. Etta had moved past dejection as a teenager when she had given up the idea of a normal life. She preferred to occupy her mind with knowledge for its own sake. Given her appearance, she was sure it was for the best.

Still, she wished for company. Having someone to talk to, a companion to lift the curse of silence if only such a thing could be bought.

One day more than a week later, after a supermarket outing that left her fatigued, Etta collapsed in exhaustion into the heirloom chair. She read for a few minutes until her chin slumped onto her chest and the book fell from her hands. Etta dreamed wild dreams of dashing exuberantly through caves and chasms. She awoke from her nap an hour later, panting and sweating as though the exertions of her reverie were real.

As Etta gripped the chair's arms to rise from the seat, she noticed bumps in the elegant wood. She was certain these hadn't been present before. When she inspected the places her hands had gripped she found a number of blackened wooden blisters. Casting a broader eye, Etta found such blemishes on every upholstery-free part of the chair. Panic rose, a burning lump in her throat. What could this be? What was wrong with the wood? Was her prized possession rotting away before her eyes?

She searched the web for clues to the cause of the carbuncles, but nothing adequately described the disheartening phenomenon. More disappointing still was that when she turned back from her computer, the lumps were noticeably larger and darker than they had been a mere hour and a half before. Etta scrutinized the wooden tumors and noticed that they were connected to one another by the network of dark threads throughout the wood. The lumps, too, were becoming more prominent by the minute.

Etta retrieved a steak knife from the kitchen and probed one of the now pea-sized bumps on the back of a chair leg. It was as hard as she imagined the wood to be. She tried scraping some of the blemish into a cupped hand. When disjoined from the mass, the sample was like charcoal. She crushed it easily between thumb and index finger into fine black dust. She tried similarly crushing the lump she had scraped; it was as refractory as the wood itself.

Despite the unsightly imperfections, the chair still felt as solid as an artisan's masterful product should.

Etta was at a loss.

Then she thought of Krimbret; surely a man so experienced with antiques could guide her to an answer. She phoned his shop once more.

"I'm having a problem with the chair I inherited. Can you help me?"

"I'd be glad to try. What's the problem?" Krimbret said..

"There are bumps popping up all over the wood. They're turning black, and when I scrape them off, they turn into powder."

"That doesn't sound good," said Krimbret, "Are they wet or dry? Is there a smell?"

Etta squatted next to the chair so that her meager nose practically rested on an arm. She inhaled deeply.

"They're dry, and there is a smell. It's faint, but it reminds me of old paper and rubber."

Etta spoke with Krimbret for some time, but he had no good advice for her. Whatever the wooden bumps were, there was nothing he could tell her about them.

She decided to try an experiment; she would dig one of the lumps completely out of the wood. She looked for the lump she had scraped minutes before but could not pick it out, as if the pimple had healed the wound she had inflicted. She chose a different bump on the back of the same chair leg.

Etta pushed the sharp tip of the steak knife into the rim of the wart, where the black body blended into the surrounding wood. She carved the discoloration's edge in a motion not unlike coring an apple. She dug and pried until the dark blemish fell to the floor. She picked it up; it was dry and rough, and it broke into bits when she squeezed it. It didn't feel like something capable of growth.

Etta was preparing to prize out a second lump when she realized that the hole she had left in the wood was filling with the black mass of a new blister. When she looked closely at the healing wound, there were tiny beads of black liquid around its edge. She smeared the juice on a fingertip and it reeked of spoiled meat and vinegar, nose-wrinklingly unpleasant. She wiped her finger on the waistband of her pants, streaking it with black.

The nodule swelled quickly to overflow the cavity in the pale wood, forming a new verruca.

Not knowing what to do to save the chair and fascinated by events, Etta turned her office chair to face the heirloom. She perched in worried silence. The bumps pushed outward gradually. After an hour, they looked like black fingertips all over the wood. She cautiously touched one rubbery knob.

When she sawed a piece off, however, the fragment became hard, dry, and crumbly. Again, the irregularity she had wounded healed and caught up to its fellows in length.

The black protrusions elongated in perfect slow-motion unison. After a couple of hours, they grew four inches. Then they seemed complete, their length maximized.

Etta gingerly grasped a digit and flexed it about. The cylindrical appendage moved in any direction and bent until its tip touched the wood from which it had sprouted. When she let go, it languidly straightened, like plastic with memory of its shape.

She waited, but the fingers did not meet her expectation by moving.

A jolt of astonishment coursed through Etta's chest; the eyes of the beast that crowned the chair were open. She was sure they had been closed before. Now they were flawless black beads, polished but unreflective.

What explanation could there be?

She bewilderedly traced the visage with a finger. The corners of its wide mouth twitched.

She snapped her hand back from the chair. Her mind fumbled for a reference to such a thing in the multitude of books she had read. The living face of Dickens' Marley manifested in Scrooge's doorknocker in a film adaptation of *A Christmas Carol* she'd seen. A note of amusement was added to the chord of her fear; perhaps three well-intentioned ghosts were on their way.

The frog-mouthed wooden beast whispered. Etta couldn't make out words; it sounded like someone speaking through static on a radio, his utterances small and metallic, distorted and windy.

A will not her own bade her to sit in the chair. Etta had many times worried about the tenacity of her sanity in the face of her sempiternal alienation from the society of the normal, but never before had she felt so certain that she had skidded into madness as she did at this moment. Looking at the seat that surely must have escaped from someone's nightmare, her inclination to sit in the thing made her doubt the reliability of her judgment.

Nevertheless, what had she to lose?

Slowly, carefully, breathlessly, Etta lowered her hindquarters onto the black upholstery of the outré seat, then settled her back into position against the flexible protrusions and hard wood. She rested her arms and noted that the rubbery black fingers on the armrests bent out of the way of her forearm, then looped themselves gently along its length from hand to elbow. The projections in contact with her back, forearms, and legs vibrated subtly.

The chair was trying to soothe her.

Etta's fear abated.

She relished this; the touch of another was as rare as a precious stone in her life.

Calm uncoiled in her mind and tension left her muscles.

When Etta was fully relaxed in this chair, with which she was falling in love, the beast spoke again. Its voice was clearer now, stronger, deeper, and came from close by her lobeless ear.

"Daughter," said the voice of the wooden countenance, "Why lock yourself away? Why are you alone?"

The black fingers caressed her more emphatically now, a massage from a dozen hands. A lump formed in Etta's throat.

"People fear me because I am so ugly. I fear them because of their loathing," she said.

"They are not your people. Men are no more than cattle for your brothers and sisters. You have not yet traveled far enough."

"I don't understand..." Etta trailed off, too much at a loss to formulate a question for the weird wooden face.

"Henrietta Odalin, I am your thrice-great grandfather. My son was Charles Corbett, and I am Horatio Corbett. The child of Charles Corbett was adopted by Sarah Corbett, wife of James Odalin, when your progenitor left the human world. You are not an Odalin; you are a Corbett.

"In you are the reconstituted traits of my consort, Mary Gover. I tell you, Mary Gover was not born for the world of men. She was the legacy of an elder race nearly exterminated in millennia past. A few have survived in secret places. You,

Henrietta, are only in small part human, and in greater part of that race, the Voormis.

"Search yourself, and you will know it true. The Voormi heart of you drew you to this place. A door beneath this building has been sealed for many years, but beyond it is your heritage. You will know peace, solace, and delight with your people, my daughter. Rejoice in the darkness, feast upon your proper food, and dance in abandon before the dreaming god, Tsathoggua. Doubt yourself no more."

Myriad black fingers caressed Etta from head to toe as she mulled over the knowledge imparted by the chair. She was torn. So much was uncertain. People as cattle? Living in darkness and worshiping a deity when she had been atheist for as long as she'd had an opinion on gods at all?

She resisted the new information, incapable of reconciling it with her life of shrieking solitude.

"I... I'm... How is my grandfather a chair?" The absurdity of the question made her smile.

"When I died, murdered by my idiot brother, Mary Gover planted a sacred tree upon my grave. The roots of that tree reached down to my scraps interred in the earth and absorbed all that I am. From that tree, this chair was made by skilled hand and mind. All that has happened since has converged, under my will, to bring us together in this place at this moment. Fear me not. You are my seed and must be preserved. O Henrietta, abolish your doubt, blot out your wavering. We are the servants of the mighty lord Tsathoggua for ever and ever." The words rang true and sweet.

"I believe you."

"Then go to the cellar of this place. Take with you five fingers plucked from this chair that is my body. Grind them to powder and use them to find your way to the home of the Voormi clan secreted below."

Etta dutifully plucked five fingers from the chair and stood. The eyes of the beast were closed once more. She retrieved a plastic sandwich bag from a kitchen drawer and placed the now-stiff black protuberances inside, zipped the bag closed, and pulverized them beneath her velvet fist.

Etta took the elevator to the ground floor. She pushed the button for the basement repeatedly but it failed to light. She would have to find some other entrance.

She exited the elevator and left the lobby through the front door. Etta tossed a pinch of black powder into the air. Despite the absence of wind, the puff of darkness turned sharply to the left, traveling a few feet in a straight line before dissipating. Etta followed, then utilized a bit more of the charcoal dust.

In such manner, she arrived finally at a pair of chained, rusted metal doors. Each bore a massive padlock. Again, she propelled black powder into the air. It flew like an arrow to the door on her left. Etta tugged as hard as she could until the antique lock snapped. She removed the chain. The rusted hinges were stiff and groaned sharply when she pulled the door open.

Beyond the portal was utter darkness. As she waited for her eyes to adjust, Etta breathed in a whiff of heady incense. The inviting odors of fungus and blood beckoned her to a rubbish heap lit only by the sunlight streaming in from the open door behind her. Etta cleared the refuse; her shadow was long and its head melded into the greater darkness of the passageway. This was no natural cavern; its surfaces were brick. Someone had taken great care in building this place.

The darkness swallowed Etta as the door behind squealed closed. With the last rays of sunshine gone, her emerald eyes rapidly adjusted to a darkness that other eyes could not have penetrated unaided. The bag of powder luminesced an icy cyan that barely alleviated the gloom.

She tossed dust into the air at junctions to determine her course.

After some time shuffling through the brick passageways, a glow, as of embers, smeared warm light into the murk. She instinctively froze when she heard voices–not human voices, but canine growls and whines that triggered a sensation of remote familiarity, as if she had heard them so long ago that her memory of them had dwindled almost entirely. The shadows of legs passed between her and the faint illumination from the coals of a fire pit.

"Hello, is someone there?" she called timorously into the darkness. The canine vocalizations grew louder. She recognized them as words though she could assign them no meaning.

Etta held her breath.

Padding footfalls approached. Bipedal shadows drew closer, sniffing audibly. Their proportions were wrong; their legs were too short, their arms too long, and their heights insufficient to be topped with heads so large.

It was too late to run; her uneven legs could never put timely and sufficient distance between herself and whatever these things were.

Her mind raced.

Had the spirit in the chair mislead her?

Would she be torn apart?

Would it be quick?

A calloused, three-fingered hand seized Etta's forearm. The digits were supplied with long, jagged nails. The hand was covered with velvety gray hair, as was the thin arm to which it attached.

Her pulse throbbed in her ears as she fought off the paralysis of terror.

A warm, inviting stink of putrescence enveloped her.

Etta raised her gaze and looked squarely into the emerald green eyes of an anthropoid that bore a resemblance to her. Her apprehension dissolved as the creature pulled her toward the glowing coals; she sensed no malice.

By the light of the pit, Etta could make out a dozen figures. They were the reason she had come. These had to be the Voormis of which Horatio Corbett had told her. They grasped her arm and guided Etta toward the cadre of her gathered fellows.

The little troop regarded Etta with glinting green eyes. They circled her, sniffing cautiously from a few paces' distance. A bold Voormi reached out and pulled at her shirt then vocalized gruffly to its fellows, shaking a hand in Etta's direction. The others responded in kind. Etta understood what they were expressing as one might understand a foreigner's broken language.

She slowly raised her hands to unbutton her shirt. The Voormis were silent as she removed the garment. Etta looked down at her own bare torso and was struck by how well her anatomy, derided and loathed in the city above, matched the physiques of her subterranean kith.

She sucked in a breath of air thick with the rank odor of the Voormis and awaited their response.

The Voormi that had guided her again took Etta's arm and led her closer to the fire pit. The velvet-furred figure squatted, drawing Etta down with her. The rest of the Voormis gathered around, yelping excitedly. The chaperon howled into the darkness and soon another of her race appeared, arms laden with what looked at first to be firewood.

When the creature drew nearer, the timber became human limbs, some wrinkled and brown like smoked meat, some raw and festering. The flesh-bearer extended the gruesome bounty, an offer of hospitality. She took one, a slender brown arm, from her host. The rest of the larder was passed around the circle. They waited, staring expectantly at their guest.

Etta steeled herself. She must do this. She dared not refuse their offer.

Etta bit into the arm. Her teeth, seen as grotesquely misshapen in Worcester, were suited perfectly to the task of tearing chunks of meat from human bone. The flesh was chewy and smoky, the most delicious morsel she had ever tasted.

The Voormis barked and yipped with delight as all commenced feasting.

Etta took another bite.

Its savor was ambrosia.

Henrietta Odalin nee Corbett knew that her solitude had ended forever, for the lifespan of a Voormi is long and never lonely.

WITCH V HANSEL, GRETEL, ET. AL.

Daniel M. Kimmel

MR. CHIEF JUSTICE NIMBLE, writing for the Court.

The facts below, as presented by the appellate court, are not in dispute. Once upon a time, Respondents Hansel and Gretel were travelling through the woods when they came upon a house made of gingerbread belonging to Appellant Witch. They proceeded to—according to their statements at trial—"nibble" upon said house. Evidence introduced at trial indicated that the house was not purely gingerbread but was also made of licorice, gum drops, lollipops, candy canes, and a variety of frostings, including chocolate, vanilla, and butterscotch. There is some indication that more than "nibbling" was involved, but that is not an issue on appeal.

Subsequent to discovering that her house was being digested by Respondents, Witch emerged from her domicile and, upon seeing the Respondents, invited them to enter her abode. Only after their entirely voluntary entry did she attempt to throw both of them into her oven with the admitted intent of baking and eating them. Subsequently, during a struggle, they managed to escape, in the process causing her serious injuries, which have been described as being slow to heal. Respondents filed suit in a court of competent jurisdiction before the statute of limitations tolled, charging Appellent with grievous bodily harm, maintaining an "attractive nuisance" in the form of said gingerbread house, and treble damages for trying to create a video recording of her attempt to hurl them into the oven. This latter claim was made on the grounds that, based on her past activity, it was a fair assumption that she intended to share this video with those who maintain collections of pornographic materials involving baked children. This was brought under section 33 of the Rumpelstiltskin Act, which prohibits recording or distributing materials related to children being subjected to supernatural endangerment. Respondents Hansel and Gretel filed suit as a class action on behalf of all other children, or their surviving families, similarly situated, and said class was certified by the trial court. After a full trial, a verdict was reached on behalf of the respondents. Counterclaims by Witch against Hansel and Gretel for her injuries were dismissed. On appeal, the verdict of the trial court was affirmed, and Witch was ordered to replace her gingerbread house with something constructed out of inedible materials, as well as pay significant damages and court costs. Neither side disputes the facts in the case nor the record now before this Court. Instead, Appellant brings forth an issue of first impression, arguing that the courts below acted in violation of the Constitution by infringing upon her freedom to practice her religion without being subjected to the "political correctness" she claims was imposed by the verdict. Appellant is requesting that said verdict be set aside, and that either a new trial be ordered or, in the alternative, that the case be dismissed. Due to the significance of the issue raised by this appeal, the Court granted *certiorari*, and heard argument limited to the Appellant's claim that the decisions below were, in fact, violating her freedom of religion pursuant to the First Amendment.

Appellant argues that under our decision in Burwell v. Hobby Lobby Stores, Inc.134 S. Ct. 2751 (2014), a corporation is as entitled to religious freedom as an individual, even if it has a negative impact on others who may fall within the purview of said business. In that case, the corporate owners' objection to birth control was deemed to override the requirement under the Affordable Care Act that they assert such objection in order that their employees might obtain birth control through their insurer at no cost to the business. Simply having to acknowledge their objection was deemed to be such an onerous imposition on the religious freedom of the corporation that the Court relieved them of this burden.

In the instant case, Appellant Witch is a Delaware corporation formed in 1993. Under its articles of incorporation, the purposes of the corporation include the promulgation of its religious beliefs, including the baking and eating of "bad children." Such children are defined as, but are not limited to, those who eat, in whole or part, the houses belonging to or maintained by members of said corporation. Under this reading, argues Appellant, punishing Witch for her actions is an act that is impermissible due to its infringement on her right to the "free exercise of religion." Appellant argues that if said verdict is permitted to stand the courts will have embarked upon the slippery slope where placing curses, creating magical potions, or burying the heart of an enemy at the crossroads at midnight might be similarly questioned or prohibited.

Respondents dismiss this argument on the grounds that such "witchery" is tantamount to "Satanism," and that the Constitution was not intended to establish any rights for the Prince of Darkness or his disciples but was only supposed to protect those "good religions" that had been approved by the state. (See "Symposium: Defending America Against the Non-Existent Threat of the Imposiiton of Sharia Law," Paranoid Law Review, 2014.) Numerous precedents were cited to support the argument that witchcraft falls outside the purview of the First Amendment, from the Salem Witch Trials (1692-93) to cases in which evidence of participating in role playing games (RPGs) or listening to "heavy metal" music was deemed, *prima facie*, to be evidence of Satanism, which necessitated both hysteria and a guilty verdict. In oral argument, lawyers for the Respondents went so far as to claim that the religious protection of the First Amendment was, specifically, never intended to protect individuals or corporations professing a belief in witchcraft, and thus, the decision in Hobby Lobby is inapt. Thus, an issue for the Court is whether engaging in witchcraft may be deemed a religious practice protected by the First Amendment's guarantee of religious freedom or was, in fact, never part of the original intent of the Founders.

While the issue is a novel one for the Court, this is not the first time it has arisen in American jurisprudence. The court in West v. Gale 416 Oz 398 (1939) considered a similar claim and found it wanting. Gale was a Kansas runaway who, in the course of a series of misadventures, had dropped a house on the Wicked Witch of the East. She subsequently took possession of a pair of ruby slippers belonging to her victim. West, the decedent's sister and sole heir, claimed that the slippers, by right, belonged to her. At trial, Gale asserted her ownership took precedent by dint of an alleged "good witch" who, she said, had presented the shoes to her. However, no such witch (identified in the record as one "Glinda") appeared at trial. East died intestate and the Probate Court found that, in the absence of a will, West was her sole legitimate heir. The notion that being a "wicked witch" barred West from her inheritance rights under common law was rejected by the court, which ultimately ruled in her favor. Said decision was appealed, but unfortunately, no final determination was made in the case as it was held to be moot due to a.) the dissolution of West and b.) the disappearance of Gale from its jurisdiction.

Nonetheless, we are persuaded by the decision in West that the status of being a witch does not serve to estop a party from asserting his, her, or its rights and, thus, that Appellant does indeed fall into the protected class of corporations professing religious beliefs as established by our decision in Hobby Lobby.

However, once we find that Appellant Witch may assert that her religious freedom is being infringed by the lower courts through sanctioning her beliefs in the baking and eating of miscreant children, it remains to be seen whether such rights are properly raised in the present instance. Respondents argue—not without reason—that being baked and eaten by Appellant would curtail their own rights, as expounded in the Fourteenth Amendment, depriving them "of life, liberty, or property without due process of law." While, of course, Appellant Witch is not a state actor, the freedoms asserted by Respondents are, without question, the mainstay of our legal and social system. So the question before us is one of balancing these two compelling but competing claims: Appellant Witch's insistence that any attempt to curtail or punish her actions would be an infringement of her religious freedoms under the First Amendment versus the desire of the Respondent class not to be baked and eaten.

While there is no precedent that is precisely on point, there are a number of cases that indicate a clear pattern. One such case is Goldilocks v. Papa Bear, Mama Bear, et. al. 516 Goose 749 (1852). In this instance, Goldilocks was in the same position as the Respondents in this case, trespassing on private property while asserting a need that, as was so claimed, overrode any competing rights. In her tort action against the Bear family, Goldilocks asserted numerous injuries, such as from eating porridge that was "too hot" or attempting to sleep in a bed that was "too small." Nonetheless, the court found for the Bears, upholding the ursine precept that "a bear's home is his castle" and that being a "cute child" did preempt the rights of the Bear family to the quiet enjoyment of their abode. Indeed, the defense raised by Goldilocks against charges of criminal trespass and unauthorized digestion are precisely those that are asserted by the Respondent class in the present action.

A similar action arose in the landmark case of Unnamed Giant v. Jack 1028 Grimm 27 (1801), wherein Jack, a young simpleton who sold his cow for magic beans, which his mother subsequently disposed of, insisted that his needy situation required extraordinary measures and that, further, the Unnamed Giant was not harmed by the removal of a gold-laying goose or a singing harp. A summary judgement held that Jack's claims did not serve as a defense against breaking and entering, theft, or illegal cultivation of a beanstalk. Upon appeal the Giant's assertion of *his* right to quiet enjoyment of his domain was affirmed *en banc*.

This leaves us with the question of whether Appellant Witch is properly asserting a religious claim permitting her to invoke the protection of the First Amendment. Respondents argue that, in their view, there is no religious issue here. Appellant is simply making an excuse for wanting to bake and eat children. However, as Respondent conceded at oral argument, there are numerous beliefs that might seem odd to non-believers but are readily accepted by those who are members of that particular faith. Thus, our courts have accepted that shoe size is an acceptable means for determining fitness for marriage [Cinderella v. Step-sisters 556 King. 421 (1845)]; that the owners of houses made of straw or sticks have no defense against huffing and puffing [Pigs v. Wolf 299 Forest 12 (1905)]; and that the rule of *caveat emptor* applies to the purchasers of enchanted fruit [Beauty v. Drusilla 8 Perrault 129 (1805)].

Respondents contend that many of these decisions should not be deemed precedent, particularly when they serve to undermine otherwise successful tales in which a young hero or heroine vanquishes evil. However, a leading legal commentator has noted that while these stories are told and retold in many forms, the courts are bound by a particular set of facts and law and have to pursue matters to their logical end, no matter how absurd it might seem to those wishing it were otherwise. (See "Fractured Fairy Tales: Taking a Fresh Look at Settled Lore," by Jay Ward, 1960, Harvard Judicial Animation Review.)

Therefore, we hold that Appellant's witchly beliefs are not subject to approval or disapproval, but must be accepted as the sincere protestation of faith as has been claimed. That said, any ruling that holds against such beliefs concerning children eating one's home being subject to appropriate high temperature responses is in error. Appellant was correct that these strongly held beliefs are part of her system of religious teachings and practices, and that they were wrongly questioned by the courts below. Consequently, the decision of the appellate court is hereby voided. The case is remanded to district court for retrial or dismissal, as may deemed consistent with our findings today.

THE EYE OF THE BEHOLDER

Sati Benes Chock

Note#1 to the Case File for Unidentified Patient #45:

The girl—heavy with child—and estimated to be no more than twenty years of age was discovered naked in the woods, covered in blood, and sobbing incoherently about a "beast." The only thing in her possession: pages torn from a diary. Since then, she has refused to speak to the hospital staff. There are no buildings other than an abandoned castle in the immediate area, we are thus unable to determine who she is or where she comes from.

-Dr. Gabriel Barbot Villeneuve, Fontainbleu Hospital

March 1

Mon dieu—Father has lost everything.

It happened at sea; the fleet of ships sank during a terrible tempest, and with it, our entire fortune. We are all—father, Ariel, Camille, and I—to move to a farmhouse upon his return. A farmhouse. In the country. I can hardly comprehend the prospect. Surely, our ancestors are turning in their graves.

God help us.

June 15

Merde. The farmhouse is horrid. There are rats everywhere, and strange sounds assault my ears at night. It is terribly hot and every room is filled with the stench of rot. I fear I have bugs in my bed. I think mice nested in last season's gowns; I've already had to throw out half of my things. As usual, Ariel and Camille can't stop bickering. Father says we are to learn to farm, lest we starve.

I think it not such a horrible prospect for Ariel or Camille to lose a few stone.

October 4

Autumn is upon us, and our mood has lightened considerably with the cooler air and splendid foliage. Some village lads have presented themselves at the most opportune of moments—imagine! They wish to labor on our farm for room and board. Now if we can only retain a few girls for domestic tasks, things will improve greatly indeed. But the best news of all is from Father dear, who is traveling once more. Our fortunes have turned, he writes. He asks what we might like from his journeys. I miss my roses, the exquisite varieties our family has bred for centuries, and so I ask him for a sweetly scented rose, for remembrance. My sisters, always standing in front of that stupid mirror, have requested jewels and furs. Do these children learn nothing? Oh, well. At least if the tides change again, we can sell these luxuries for food if we have to. I never want to go without again—I don't care what I have to do.

November 7

Father has done something so, so foolish. He didn't want to tell me, but I coaxed it out of him in the special way that only I can. He purloined a rose from a beastly lord for me and was caught. Now, either he must stay, or I must go as payment for his crime. Of course, I will go. I'd never do otherwise. But I confess that I am horrified at being handed over to a husband sight unseen, even if he does live in a castle.

At least we won't starve.

December 1

I'm at the castle. It is not as bad as I'd feared…oh, dear diary, I lie, 'tis a thousand times worse. The castle itself is quite lovely, with the most amazing windows and large fireplaces. But it's a tad neglected. Chilly, of course, but that's to be expected. As for the cobwebs and dark rooms—nothing a little sunlight and soap and water couldn't cure. I needn't tend to any of that. That's what the servants are for. At least, I believe they must exist, though I've never actually seen one. They lurk in the shadows, delivering meals and retrieving empty dishes. (If only they'd do a bit of dusting or washing while they are at it.) I don't think they like me, though. Their constant low whispering sounds like a hive of bees.

June 15

Diary, I fear my lord 'tis not man at all, but truly a beast; his name is Marand. Sometimes, he has uncontrollable rages, and he destroys the room. He only comes to me after the sun is down, when the shadows are long and the dark rooms hide his ugly countenance. His smell is animal, yet not unpleasant. In fact, mealtimes are surprisingly enjoyable. His wit is sharp, and I enjoy the verbal jousting we engage in nightly. Furthermore, his appetite is quite…hearty. Somehow, despite his temper, I seem to be growing fond of him.

When I sleep, however, I dream that he is not a beast, but a charming prince. We explore secret rooms that dazzle with their opulence, surely they rival that of Versailles—the mirror opposite of the dark chambers we inhabit by day. I can never find these rooms during the daylight hours, and yet, I cannot get the queer thought out of my head that they exist. But back to the prince. He is the most romantic fellow in the world, and in the morning, I awake with flushed cheeks and bed clothing in disarray. Oh, it makes me blush to write these words—and yet! To not write them would allow them to linger in my head, tormenting me.

I almost forgot. The rose garden is the most beautiful I've ever seen, with hundreds, nay, thousands of roses of every shade of red, pink, yellow, and white.

Their scents are all distinct, yet even with so many different varieties, somehow they are not overpowering.

How I miss my family.

July 10

Lord Marand has agreed to let me visit my family. Oh, how wonderful it will be to see dear papa and my beloved sisters. He has given me a magic mirror and ring: the mirror will allow me to see what he is doing at any time, and the ring will allow me to be instantly transported back to him. Oh, I know, diary, this all sounds terribly fanciful, but it works—I've witnessed it.

One more thing. *I knew it.* My poor lord was once a handsome man, but tricked and transformed into his present state by a pair of evil fairies who were jealous of him. He says the only way the spell can be broken is if the fairies are destroyed. I am determined to help him do this just as soon as I return from my trip.

Just as soon as I return. I will not let him down.

August 15

Diary, it is wonderful to be home, but so stressful, too. My family has missed me and begs me to stay longer. I will extend my trip a fortnight, but am terrified for my darling beast—tonight, when I checked the mirror, he appeared to be so pale and unwell. I don't think he is eating. Damn, those useless servants. I'll fire them all immediately upon my return. From here, however, there isn't much I can do. Still, I will check on him in the morning, and if he hasn't improved, I will use the magic ring to return and restore him to health.

Those wicked, wicked fairies must pay.

August 20

Note#2 to the Case File for Belle Beaumont

We have received word of a horrific tragedy from the next village over—a father and two daughters were found brutally murdered. A witness claims to have seen the eldest daughter, Belle, running from the house. While neighbors say that the family appeared normal, they have not remained untouched by hardship—the wife deceased when the three girls were small, a fortune lost. However, a source close to the family insists that Belle had an "unnaturally" close relationship with her father.

After confronting the patient with the possibility of her identity—without disclosing the tragedy that has befallen her family—the patient readily agreed that it was she. When shown a miniature portrait of her father, she burst into tears, kissing the picture and murmuring "*Mon pere, mon bête, mon amour.*"

Two separate witnesses have visited the hospital and confirmed that our unidentified patient is, without question, Belle Beaumont.

It is this physician's concluding opinion that the patient suffers from a number of psychiatric complaints, chiefly, amnesia, delusions, multiple personalities, and quite possibly, schizophrenia. While it is not this physician's duty to determine guilt or innocence, it is also this physician's opinion that Belle Beaumont may be responsible for the murder of her father, Armand, and her two sisters, Ariel and Camille. As such, she is without question a potential danger to others as well as herself and her unborn child, and will thus remain at this hospital until such time as local law authorities can decide her fate. When the child is born, it will be relinquished to the local convent, where the nuns have agreed to care for it.

-Dr. Gabriel Barbot Villeneuve, Fontainbleu Hospital

THE MAN WHO MARRIED BLUEBEARD'S DAUGHTER

Rohit Sawant

From the day she became an addition to our neighborhood, she carried an air of mystery about her. I was on my way home from my afternoon prayer when I ran into a friend. Having returned my *Salaam*, the first thing he enquired, with a wolfish smile, was if I had any intention of visiting my new neighbor.

This was news to me since I hadn't known I had one. The house next to mine was on the market for months but had failed to find a tenant.

He told me about the young lady who'd moved in early this morning. I had woken up late and spent the rest of the day holed up in my studio, which was a corner room facing away from the house in question.

I was unaware of any commotion, absorbed as I was in applying the final touches to a painting I was supposed to deliver yesterday.

But I needn't have worried about missing anything; Hatim, who lived two streets down from my house, filled me in. He was the local crystal ball when it came to women.

She was, he informed me, a singular beauty. Also she had the most peculiar shade of hair.

"Peculiar how?" I asked.

"From what I've heard, she has blue hair."

Shoving him, I let out a snort, sure that I had allowed my foot to be vigorously yanked. But he insisted it was true. On asking how he could be so sure when he himself hadn't seen her, he said, deeply indignant, that he had his sources.

The news about the new tenant I could believe, but I couldn't bring myself to buy the part about blue hair and left the matter at that; I'd find out soon enough.

While I did discern activity in my neighboring house, I didn't see her until a few days later. She hurried across to her door, groceries tucked under her arm, as I left the house. Her whole manner was taut.

But I didn't notice any of that at first.

My gaze was drawn to her hair; God, it *was* blue. Not a startling Cobalt, which is how I'd ridiculously pictured it, but a deeper shade, a Midnight Blue. No wonder I wasn't able to pick it out earlier when I caught the odd glimpse of her through the window.

The corners of her lips tipped shyly up in response to my smile, in relief I suppose that I didn't stare at her; maybe subconsciously expecting it and having a quick eye for colors, I wasn't compelled to.

By the end of that week, we'd graduated to neighborly exchanges. Her name was Subiya. The day I'd learnt it, I had lain awake, repeating it aloud through a grin.

In need of a new palette—the one I owned had begun to splinter and caused all sorts of nuisances, from chaffing the web of my thumb to tiny slivers of wood getting caught in my brush—I'd just stepped out of the house when her door swung open, twisting my yawn into gasp.

There was something quivery about her bearing as she got out: stealing glances, smiling, blinking.

I would've walked away after greeting her, but seeing her linger, I did, too, offering some banal remark about the weather, for which I mentally gave myself a standing ovation.

"I'm making *karak chai*," Subiya said, the announcement sounding more like a question. "You're welcome if you'd like some."

"I would, yes," I said evenly, hoping my exterior didn't betray any of the excitement swelling within.

A while later, I sat across from her, wondering if I wasn't still in bed and all this a dream. She seemed a lot less nervous within her own abode and had a graceful ease about her. I was pleasantly shocked to discover we had a lot in common.

"Would you do me the honor of letting me paint a portrait of you?" I blurted, surprising myself as much as her.

"What?" A childlike puzzlement rounded her features.

She leaned back, leaving me deflated and certain I must've lost any goodwill I'd gained.

The stray lock she tucked behind her ear and absently twisted and tugged at might as well have been my heart. I finally let out the breath I was holding when she answered, sounding far from sure.

"Uh, okay."

Feeling bad at the way I'd put her on the spot, I told her she didn't have to decide right away and that it was okay if she felt otherwise.

A change spread over her features like the untying of a knot as she slowly nodded.

"No, it's...okay," she repeated with a full smile.

I usually work fast. Well, at least when starting out. The dawdling sets in the closer I get to finishing a piece. But I confess, I premeditatedly dawdled even as I prepared my canvas just so I could spend more time with her.

By the time I'd painted in the hooked nose, the swan-neck, the thick eyebrows that were like a bold dash of charcoal with tinges of a dark velvety blue, we'd grown fairly comfortable in each other's company.

Her hair took up the bulk of the work; those lush wavy tresses suggestive of a stormy sea under starlight. Hesitatingly, she asked once if I could paint her hair black.

This was the first time any remark had passed between us about her hair, and the way she said it made my heart crumble. I held her lightly by the shoulders and said, "No."

As my gaze darted from face to canvas after she resumed her position, I was conscious of a change in her demeanor; the smile she cast upon me was different from the one on the canvas, and I knew things had changed.

I asked once about her family. After a pause, she said it was a painful topic, one she preferred not to discuss. I considered promising not to bring it up again; instead, I took her hand in mine, squeezing it. Which as it turned out was the right response; words rarely mean much when it comes to trust.

About a year later, Subiya let the house she lived in and moved in with me as my wedded wife.

She might have been averse to discuss the topic of her family, but about mine, she could hardly keep shut, and my mother and two sisters loved her equally. Sensibility and instant affection for her rendered the odd tinge of her hair invisible to them. And as my youngest sibling Lily put it, it was just hair after all. Local interest in her hair dimmed, and she eventually ceased to be the Three-Legged Pigeon and was merely the three-legged pigeon.

To me, our newly married life seemed filled with daily discoveries and adventures. She, too, must've felt likewise, or at least I hoped, as she filled pages upon pages in her journal every night. I asked her once, playfully, what she wrote about so much.

Meeting my eyes, she flashed a cryptic smile.

To see how socially active she'd grown made me swell with pride. Not waiting till sundown anymore to run errands, dropping by my mother's house, going for outings with my sisters, having a cheery exchange of dialogue with the man next door whenever their paths crossed or he came over with the rent. This latter development left me just a little peevish, though I'd scarcely have admitted it, considering how long it'd taken her to reach that level of ease with me.

When I answered the door one evening, a bright eyed young man greeted me with a big grin and asked if my wife was in.

I was about to make some sort of vague reply asking his business when Subiya's voice called out, "Omar?"

She came over to the door, puzzled but not unpleasantly.

"Your book, Miss." Omar held out the book of poems he carried.

Her frown smoothed over, and she thanked him, saying he didn't really have to. Omar shrugged, saying it was nothing.

"Feel like I've seen him somewhere," I said to her after he left.

"Yes, he works at the library. He—"

"Does he deliver books to everybody's doorstep?" I immediately regretted it when I saw how her face fell.

"I forgot it when I checked out some books this morning," her voice stung. "He was passing by our house to a relative's so..." she said, half-raising the hand with the book.

"Oh, Okay." I nodded. Aware that anything else I added would've sounded strained, an effort to show I wasn't disconcerted.

But I was. The following day, alone, having convinced myself that I was in the mood for poetry, I thumbed through the book, on the lookout for any dog-eared pages with a muffled alertness, until I came to the last page which bore the library stamp, dispelling the brewing speculation that it was a part of his private collection. Feeling sick with myself, I set it back on the shelf.

Still, her casually telling me how she ran into Omar, something that made me think of the early days of our acquaintance when I'd contrive to 'run into her,' or that he helped carry her books or the funny story about his cat, the way she shook with laughter as she related this last bit, I found myself wondering if I'd ever been the cause of such mirth—all this did little to quell the disquiet roiling in my breast.

Finding her hunched over her journal, I'd wonder what she confided in it.

Well, you could always sneak a look, a voice in my head supplied.

I banished the thought immediately.

Not that it would be a hard thing to do; she kept the diary in her unlocked dresser drawer. I had seen her place it there countless times and hadn't given it any mind; until now, that is.

But no! I mustn't even entertain the notion, I mentally said to myself.

Distressed, I turned to Hatim, an unwise choice. He was always suspicious that she wouldn't reveal anything about her past. But I had no other close friends.

He filled my head with ideas I could've done without. "I hear her old man replaced wives by the season. Wouldn't be surprised if the apple didn't fall far from the tree."

I was busy at my easel, working on my current project: an evening landscape, the sun, blood red, dipping behind the corrugated dunes. Poking her head into my studio, Subiya asked me if I wanted anything since she was heading out to the market.

"No, nothing."

"Okay," she chirped and said bye.

For a while, I sat absorbed, drying my brushes. Then rising with a jolt, I made for the dresser.

I gazed at the drawer for a long moment before finally pulling it open. There it sat. Only after emblazoning on my mind the angle at which it lay, did I delicately reach in and pluck the diary out without disturbing anything.

I don't how long I stood there, heart pounding, eyeing the little book clutched in my hands, debating whether I should go ahead and open it. My mind flew back to the moment we'd touched upon her family, the pressure of her hand as she squeezed mine back. A wave of shame washed over me, making me cringe at the grievous betrayal I was on the verge of committing.

I carefully placed it back in the drawer, already feeling better about myself, when I saw my thumb print stamped on the diary's pale green cover. Holding up my hands, as if in accusation, my heart beat a wild rhythm upon seeing my palms lightly smudged in places; and on my right thumb was a smear of red pigment, the blood red of the setting sun.

I almost made a grab for the diary but froze, realizing it'd accomplish nothing except leaving more evidence. I threw a swift glance over my shoulder at the empty room as if expecting her to have magically appeared before aimlessly pacing about, a hand clasped to my mouth.

What did I do?

More importantly, what was I going to do? Even if I cleaned my hands and tried to get the color off I would only smudge it further. Scraping it off was also out of the question.

Exiting the room, the best thing, I decided, was to just leave it be. Maybe she won't notice. And if she does and asks me, I'll tell her I was looking for something and must've accidentally touched it while going through the drawers. I was back in front of my easel going over these things when I jumped at the sound of the door being shut.

She was her usual self at dinner. I thought about asking her if she'd seen such-and-such, that I was combing the dresser for it. I didn't say it though; offering an explanation, especially when none was asked, would only have served to make me look guilty. Still, it was worth a shot. But I couldn't bring myself to tell her. I'll do it sometime, I kept saying to myself with every passing moment until soon we retired to bed.

It was too late now.

If she saw the thumb print, she never brought it up. Not the next day or the day after.

But I never saw her writing in her journal again.

Meeting up with Hatim that weekend, I considered telling him the mess I'd gotten myself into, but being anxious enough already, I thought better of it, suspecting I'd leave twice as anxious, judging from my previous experience, if I broached the subject with him.

That ended up happening anyway.

He had some news about Subiya. About her past, he said.

He told me stories of bluebeards, locked rooms, and slit throats.

I found it all a big load of nonsense. When I demanded where he got it from, he gave an evasive reply about having sources. After a pause, during which neither us spoke, I wrung out a promise from him that he wouldn't go about spreading slanderous stories about my wife. I worded it kindly so as not to tick him off, which would only have resulted in the opposite.

I mulled over what he said later. Even supposing it was true; so what? A good person having murderers for parents or vice versa is not unheard of.

Except for not seeing Subiya huddled with her diary, there hasn't been any perceptible change in her. However, sometimes, I catch a hard glitter in her eyes when she thinks I'm not watching; it softens when they lock with mine. But when I recall that look, it chills me, and just for an instant, I'm convinced that it's all true; and I'm afraid that she *is* her father's daughter.

SMILE-BREAK
Amanda Bergloff

The night is colder than I expected. My hands feel numb, even in my pockets, and I'm shivering uncontrollably. The light from the street makes the window next to his door reflective like a mirror. I look serious with my hood pulled down to keep warm, my eyes barely visible underneath.

He is usually home by nine p.m. on weeknights.

I don't have my key anymore, so I wait outside for him. It feels like I've been waiting here for hours. The cold makes time move so slow.

All I want to do is talk to him without him telling me that I shouldn't be here.

I look at my serious reflection again and remember how much we used to laugh together. Everything was perfect for a time. We were so happy once. We could always make each other smile, even when things weren't so good.

Whenever we got too serious, we'd say to one another, "I think you need a smile-break," and we'd stop whatever we were doing and just smile at each other. Things always seemed to get better then.

I haven't felt like smiling for some time, now.

I don't know what I did wrong. It seemed that he just got tired of me one day, and that was it.

The lights of a car turned down the street, so I step back into the shadows on the side of his house, not wanting him to know I'm here when he pulls into the driveway.

All I want is for him to understand what he did to me.

All I want is for him to know how I feel.

Yes, that's his car. He pulls into the driveway and gets out of the car, looking at his cell phone. I think he's checking the texts I've left for him. The glow from the screen lights up his eyes.

I used to love looking into them. What big eyes he has.

I take a step, and he leans his head in my direction at my slightest movement.

What good ears he has.

Head down, he casually brushes hair out of his eyes with his hand. I notice for the first time what big hands he has.

I step out of the shadows. He smiles at me without thinking…a toothy smile…what big teeth he has.

Then, his smile fades.

The first blow connects fully and drives him to his knees.

The second one severs the artery in his neck.

My reflection smiles under my red hood.

That was just the smile-break I needed.

BENEATH SHALLOW WATERS

Mary Victoria Johnson

"Sir?" The detective says again. "Would you like to sit down?"

Eric blinks, dragging himself back to reality. He shakes his head.

"Your discomfort is understandable, sir. It's always distressing when a loved one dies, especially when you don't know why."

Drowned.

The detective knows this as well as Eric. The question he meant to ask was *how*.

Beside them is the tidal pool, tucked neatly away from the rest of the ocean by a circle of rock. Leaves from a single tree, brown and soggy, float on the surface. The pool is tinged a dark shade of green, totally obscuring the bottom.

"Perhaps I should ask the princess instead, sir?" The detective is anxious now.

"No," Eric manages to find his voice. "No, I'm fine."

Ariel is the last person he wants, for once. She was in town during the accident, so she wouldn't know how his brother, visiting from the country, fell into a shallow tidal pool and drowned when he was an extraordinarily strong swimmer. He hadn't even hit his head; he'd just plain drowned.

Not a whisper of a breeze is blowing, and the surface of the pool looks like glass. Green, mottled glass. The twigs gathered underneath form strange shadows.

Eric closes his eyes in an attempt to steady his nerves. Inhales, tastes the salt in the air. It is the end of autumn, and soon, winter will freeze over pools like this one. Two weeks later, and things may have been very different.

"She's beautiful," Julian said, having just been introduced to Ariel. "You did well, old boy."

Eric smiled, proud. "High praise coming from you, Jules."

"Nonsense." His brother grinned. Then he grew serious. "So, is it true? She was...well, a mermaid?"

Eric doesn't like to think about the time before they were married. When his ship was taken down by a storm and he'd awoken to a song so ethereally beautiful it couldn't have been human. The rest was a blur of enchantment, a mute girl, a sea witch, and events that still feel like a dream months later. When the mute girl came to him after he'd woken up from his trance and told him her story, and he'd loved her even more because of it.

His island kingdom has always been ripe with tales of creatures living in the ocean. Sirens, monsters, horrible things. Ariel and the mermaids are different. Eric knows they are, but he's never been able to view the sea in the same way after their incident with the witch.

"What was the last thing your brother told you before he left?" The detective makes a clear effort to be gentle. "Did he seem out of sorts at all? Nervous? Agitated?"

Eric nearly laughs. "Not at all. 'I'm going down to the shore to see if I can get as lucky as you'. That's what he said."

The shadows form a shape, and despite the absence of wind, ripples flutter over the surface. It's as though right at the bottom of the pool, something is stirring.

"Was he a desperate man?" The detective frowns. He's got an extraordinary amount of flesh on his forehead, forming deep ridges and valleys each time he moves his eyebrows. "Lonely?"

Eric is about to answer 'no', but then out of the corner of his eye, he sees her. She's distorted under the surface, making it impossible to tell where her green cloud of hair ends and the water begins. Black eyes. No nose. White, white skin.

He chokes on the stab of fear, jumping away.

"Sir?" The detective's calm demeanour falters, tone becoming etched with concern "What is it?"

The thing in the water is smiling at him. Her teeth are sharp and thin. They remind Eric of cat claws. Finally, a breeze, whipping in from the north, races across the pool. When the water falls still again, she is gone.

"I don't know," Eric says. Then, after a moment of deliberation, "Get Ariel."

The detective hesitates. "Should…I don't know if I can leave you, sir."

"I said, get Ariel." Eric finds himself raising his voice, a horrible sort of pressure building up within. "Just do it."

Not needing to be told again, the detective gathers his coat around him and runs up the hill toward the castle.

Eric's head pounds. He can't actually remember Ariel in her mermaid form, but he's always been able to picture it. Nothing more than his beloved wife with a tail rather than legs. Nothing sinister. Nothing like whatever reappeared in the tidal pool.

She cocks her head, assessing him. Black, black eyes. An impossibly ugly smile traces a crack across her skin —it's demented, crazed.

He's suddenly aware how alone he is. There's nothing but the empty, rolling sea before him and the barren cliffs behind, and all at once, Eric feels like a lost child without his parents. He considers calling the detective back.

"You took her from us."

Eric flinches. The voice inside his head is painfully uncomfortable, not belonging.

"She is a sister of the sea, and you took her away. How does it feel, human, when we take one of yours?"

"You're lying to me," Eric says, backing away. If only his head could stop spinning, he'd be able to concentrate. Think. "You're not anything like her."

The smile widens. Waves are lapping at the rocks now, gaining momentum with every passing second.

"Eric?"

Ariel rushes down the hill, a few steps ahead of the detective. Her red hair is wild, her face flushed from the cold.

"Darling, I—"

She trails off, gaze meeting with the black one submerged in the tidal pool. Her lips move, whispering a name under her breath, and something inside of him clenches.

The mermaid, pointed teeth still bared in a chilling smile, slowly sinks deeper into the water. Eventually, she's obscured by the murkiness.

"Is that what you were?" Eric asks, hoping he doesn't sound too harsh. He doesn't like new emotion —anger— building up within him.

All the colour drains from Ariel's face at an alarming rate. "You knew that, darling. But I'm human now, aren't I? Isn't that all that matters?"

The detective has dropped his clipboard. Vaguely, Eric is aware of him asking a tirade of questions, but neither he nor Ariel pay him any attention. Their eyes are locked together in a silent struggle to say the words they are unable to find. Eric is surprised by how much guilt he sees in his wife, and wonderers vaguely what she sees in him. Anger? Fear?

"Julian…"

"My sisters are more vengeful than I am." Ariel is pleading, her voice several octaves higher than usual, a single tear tracing a shimmering line down her cheek. "I…I'm so sorry."

What could he say? His illusion of Ariel as a mermaid shatters, and he doesn't like how it makes him feel. The closest emotion he can think of to compare it to is the emptiness surrounding his mother's death, but even that doesn't feel quite adequate. He was young, she'd been painfully distant. This is more internal. The ocean is his second home, and now he's afraid of it. Of the truths it might hold.

Ariel takes his hand in her cold one, desperation tightening her grip. "I'll talk to them. I'll make sure it won't happen again. This doesn't change anything between us. Does it?"

Eric takes a deep breath trying to shake his unease, and forces a smile. "Of course not."

He lets her lead him back up the hill to the castle, away from the tidal pool and the creature within it.

She clarifies a few things with the detective.

He embraces her when she comforts him. He loves her, but she is no longer his little mermaid, and he doesn't want her to be anymore.

"Don't dwell on it. Look at me."

Eric's begun to notice that she uses her innocent appearance rather like a weapon, widening her eyes and shrinking, trying to appear smaller, in order to solicit sympathy. It always used to work, but tonight, it's falling flat. The acting is too obvious.

"Darling, look at me. It's going to be okay."

So he does, and he sees a human.

He also sees the thing beneath the shallow water.

THE THIN BLUE BREADCRUMB TRAIL

Chris Chelser

The flashing lights of police vehicles guided him to the villa's driveway, where erratic blue smudges splashed across the house, garden, and the crowd of curious onlookers at the gate.

Detective Inspector Hans Hauer surveyed the scene, gravel crunching under his boots as he strode up to the house. Several uniforms guarded the cordon around the secured premises; two sergeants took statements from nosey neighbours; the forensic team's van stood parked to the right; and as he passed, one of the Coroner's officers fumbled with a gurney and a body bag.

Say of Smith what you will, but he knew how to kick off a murder investigation.

Hauer identified himself to the nearest bobby and ducked under the cordon. On the steps to the villa's main entrance, a female constable consoled a sobbing elderly lady. Probably the one to have discovered the body. Never a nice experience, whatever the circumstances.

The clumsy white forensics suits already crawled around the inside of the house like ants at a picnic. Not that the owner would mind the intrusion, since the man's blood had spread across a substantial area of the marble patio. Hauer hung back. The dark-red pool reminded him of cheap cranberry syrup, the kind with all the sugar and colorants. He shoved his hands into his pockets and rubbed his thumbs against his forefingers.

A deep breath filled his nose with the iron tang of blood and gunpowder.

Better.

"Ah, there you are, sir. I was just about to give you a ring. Got stuck in traffic?"

Detective Sergeant Ronald Smith bustled over, carrying a smartphone in one hand and a greasy bag in the other. Crumbs dotted his grin.

"Superintendent Cooper's 'brief meetings' are never brief enough." Hauer glared at Smith's chewing face. "What is that muffin doing at our crime scene, Sergeant?"

"Haven't had tea yet, sir. Sorry." He crammed the rest of the glistening pastry into his mouth, chomped a few times and swallowed hard.

Hauer fought a wave of nausea.

"Better you tell me about this enormous man with the equally large beard." He nodded at the body. "Who is he?"

Smith flipped on the screen of his smartphone.

"This gentleman here is, uhm, Gilles de Rais? Well, that's how the maid pronounced it. Apparently a French businessman. Sixty-four years old, but doesn't appear his age because he dyed his hair, obviously."

"How so?"

"You're joking, sir? That beard's black as ink. Even has a weird blueish shine."

"Whatever. Get on with it, sergeant."

Smith had the decency to look chastised. "The bloke's been on the Met's radar for a while now, on suspicion of being involved in a smuggling ring. Hasn't triggered any alarms since he got back from France a couple of months ago. He owns various properties on both sides of the Channel, but this is where he brought his new French bride."

"Oh, wonderful. Bloody foreigners."

"Uhm, aren't you from the Continent yourself, sir?"

Hauer snorted to hide an embarrassed blush. "A lifetime ago, maybe. What I meant is, this has all the hallmarks of becoming an international case. You know how well those go."

He ran a hand over his gaunt face. Focus. He had to focus.

"Let's not get ahead of ourselves. New bride, you said? And he a senior citizen. Not a woman his own age, I bet." He did a quick survey of the nearest rooms. "Where is the grieving widow, anyway?"

"Inspector Hauer? You have a moment?"

He turned to a masked forensics officer in a once-white suit now covered in dark smudges. "This is not good. Not good at all."

He snatched gloves and a pair of shoe covers from a nearby kit and followed the forensics officer down a flight of stairs into the basement. Old-fashioned lightbulbs lit a straight corridor some thirty feet long. Two more no-longer-white suits stood in the only doorway, waiting.

"Please tell me that is the wine cellar," said Hauer as he put on the covers and gloves.

"I'm afraid not, sir." The forensics officer pulled a half-face mask from an equipment bag and handed it to him. "Trust me," she said through her own mask, "you'll want that."

The instant he stepped into the dank room, mask held loosely against his nose and mouth, he understood why.

Aside from a single lamp, the only fixtures in the windowless room were six wooden slabs on shores. Improvised beds, given that on each slab lay a human corpse, all in a considerable state of decomposition. At the back lay mere skeletons, faces frozen in a mocking grin, whereas the bodies closest to the door still resembled a human, if you squinted. The shreds of decaying clothes suggested that at least three of the corpses had been female, although by now only a pathologist could say for sure.

He heard the distinct sound of retching. In the corridor, Smith leaned against the wall and intimately reacquainted himself with his factory-processed muffin.

"God, that smell…" Smith moaned.

Hauer lowered his mask. "Are you referring to your vomit or the bodies?"

"The bodies, the bodies..."

Suppressing a laugh at his sergeant's expense, he still didn't blame Smith. The pine slabs were black with bodily fluids and where the putrescence had dripped between the shores, it had congealed on the cellar floor, forming a noxious crust. Only the most recent body still oozed slime. That stank to the high heavens, but Hauer had smelled worse.

"Next call we receive about a fire with fatalities, remind me to send you out on first response. You haven't smelled death until you've had a nose full of burnt corpse." He glanced around the cellar, shrugging off a memory. "I've seen enough here. Tell the Coroner's men to check first whether any of these lovelies qualify as the last-known mistress of the house. If you need me, I'll be upstairs."

He turned on his heels but stopped at a nasty scratching under this boot. Annoyed, he crouched down to see what was responsible.

In the thick layer of rotting gunk lay a key. A door key, if he was any judge.

"Was this door locked when the room was found?"

"No, sir," one of the white suits said. "The door was shut, but not locked."

"Interesting. This isn't a room to leave open for visitors." He pried the key from the floor and cleared away the slime. The key fit smoothly in the open door's keyhole, so he gave it an experimental turn. With a click, the lock popped.

"If the key to this door was inside, whoever unlocked it didn't care about covering their tracks when they left."

"'Cos they ran away in panic?" said Smith, still a bit green around the gills.

Hauer scoffed: "Do you shut a door when you're in a panic? Of course not. No, this wasn't panic, but they were in a hurry. Interrupted, maybe."

"The neighbours stated that the owner arrived in the middle of the afternoon."

"Then he may well have come home a little too early for his own good." Hauer pulled off the grimy shoe covers and the gloves and dropped them into a mobile hazardous waste container. "Come on, Smith. Let's hear what the Coroner has made of Mr de Rais."

Not much, as it turned out.

"Other than why his hairdresser gave him that ghastly colour job, there is little mystery to the man or his death," the Coroner's officer said as he pushed his glasses further up his nose. "Four bullets to the chest, coming from two distinct angles. My guess is that you are looking for two gunmen, not one, but the boys at ballistics will be able to confirm that."

Hauer leaned over the body. "Tight cluster around the heart. Professional work."

"Those who live by the sword, will die by it. No doubt you will have noticed that Mr de Rais was not entirely defenceless against his attackers." The officer pointed a gloved finger at the semi-automatic pistol resting in the dead man's right hand. "Judging by the gun residue, he fired it. But since there is no other body lying about..."

"We need to go bullet hunting."

"Oh, not for the ones that killed him. No exit wounds, you see. All still lodged inside after tearing his lungs and heart to shreds. The poor man was dead before he hit the ground, I should think."

"What about his wife?"

The Coroner's officer frowned. "Which wife would that be?"

"She isn't here, sir. At least, First Response didn't find anyone else when they swept the house, except for that cellar." Smith shivered. "The elderly maid said that she'd seen her mistress before she–the maid, that is–left to run errands this morning, so I don't think any of those corpses are the wife."

"Then who the devil are they? And where has the wife gone? Did you check the garage?" Hauer said.

"Rich bloke, sir. Multiple cars. Can't be sure if one's missing, but two neighbours stated they'd seen a sedan pull up in the driveway and leave only a few minutes later. They didn't notice any other vehicles." Smith nervously wiped his brow. "Are we treating this as a missing person's case, sir?"

"That depends entirely on the sedan. Did the neighbours recognise it?"

"Uhm, one neighbour thought it was a Vauxhall, but another said it was a black BMW."

"Figures." Hauer snorted. Concurring witness statements were as rare as hen's teeth. "Pull CCTV of the cameras in this street. This house will have its own security cameras, too. Get me a license plate and find that car, and alert Hearthrow, Luton, Stansted, Gatwick, Dover, and anything else with a runway or port that Mrs de Rais is *not* to leave the country. Voluntarily or otherwise."

The license plate number proved less elusive than the car or its occupants. The registration belonged to a black Mercedes E63 AMG. At least the witnesses got the colour right…

More alarming was the Met's file on Rais's dodgier activities. It revealed evidence of several marriages, none of which had lasted very long. Unfortunately, the file contained nothing conclusive on how those relationships had ended, which in turn heaped suspicion on Rais's corpse collection. Smith was tracking the names of known ex-wives, but beyond that, they had nothing but a stack of preliminary findings and photographs to go on.

Hauer's heart sank further when he leafed through the papers that the forensics' assistant had dropped on his desk. The printed photographs meant little unless you knew what you were looking at, but the designation on the report itself made his blood run cold.

"Incendiary device with time delay mechanism."

Shooting Rais had not been enough for these people. They had rigged the gas pipes to blow the house to smithereens after their safe departure. Only a constable's swift kick to the timer and a great deal of luck had prevented a devastating fire that could have killed two dozen police officers. Himself included.

"Smith, any word on—? No, don't answer that just yet."

At the opposite desk, Smith stopped wolfing down a foot-long ham and pastrami baguette. Thick globs of mayonnaise and ketchup dripped from the bread and down the sergeant's fingers, narrowly avoiding the computer keyboard as they fell on a grease-stained wrapper.

"Woo wansusu?" Smith swallowed. "Sorry. You want some, sir? I have plenty of crisps and two chocolate-chip biscuits, if you want."

Hauer stared at the American-style cookies, each one as large as his outstretched hand. Their sickly-sweet, fatty smell drenched the air. "I'll pass, thank you."

"You sure, sir? A man can't live off coffee alone. Look at you, you're skin and bones."

"Food is a prerequisite to keep breathing, Smith, but what appetite I had for such junk food, I was cured of long ago. Now, where are you on those ex-wives?"

"Nowhere, really." Smith licked some sauce from his hand, but froze mid-motion at the sight of Hauer's flaring nostrils. "Uhm, our records show that Bluebeard was married at least seven times, sir, and—"

"Wait. 'Bluebeard'?"

"Uh, yes. That's what they're all calling him. Because of—"

"Yes, yes, I get it. So, seven wives and no trace of any of them."

"Nope. Only lead we have is pretty tenuous. Older surveillance photos show that one of the ladies had a lovely smile but an incomplete set of upper teeth. According to the coroner's first findings, one of the bodies in the cellar has the same anomaly. He says it's genetic and not all that common, so…"

"Seven wives, six bodies, and one widow on the loose. Do the maths." A premature conclusion, perhaps, but in his experience if a piece of evidence looked the part, it played the part.

Hauer stared absently at the office wall while he tried to link the scraps together in search of a bigger picture. What he got instead were gaping holes, starting with motive. Why would two professional hitmen execute a fellow criminal? That sort of thing happened among drug dealers and gangs, as part of turf wars. Of course, Rais had been a suspected smuggler, and smugglers fought vehemently over trafficking routes.

But six bodies in the basement opened up other possibilities. Provided they, too, were murder victims and not some private body farm, Mr Bluebeard's death might well have been revenge. Perhaps one of the wives had been a relative of one of the shooters. A sister, or perhaps a daughter. Speaking of which…

"Was anyone else living in that house, apart from the stiff and his wife? A child from a previous marriage maybe?"

Smith scrolled through his notes. "According to the records, the owner was the only official occupant. Wife hadn't been registered yet, nor the servant. But," he clicked few times, "said servant, Mrs Beaufort, did state that the new wife had brought her sister in from France."

"Do we have a name?"

"Again according to Mrs Beaufort, the wife is called Marguerite, and the sister is called Anna. She didn't remember their maiden name, but the French civil registry should have a record of the marriage. I called the officials there, but it seems they're still in bed at this hour."

Hauer steepled his fingers. "So, not only is the wife missing, but her sister as well."

"Both were seen by Mrs Beaufort and neighbours in the last couple of days, so it's safe to assume that they didn't end up in that cellar."

But Hauer's mind barrelled along another train of thought.

"Rich man takes in a young woman and her sister. The man is killed—two shooters. Expert shots, full frontal, in a firefight. Wife and sister? No, women prefer more subtle weapons. Still, someone killed the husband, set an incendiary bomb to destroy the evidence, while the siblings ran—No, it couldn't be."

"Sir?"

He jumped to his feet, ignoring Smith's questioning gaze in favour of pacing the tiny office. He had to be mistaken. These memories, always at the edge of his awareness, had happened long ago and far away. They belonged to the past, and the past shouldn't influence his professional judgement, whatever the similarities. This was the present, and in the present, he had two fugitive killers and two runaway women, who may be the same persons.

He'd missed a piece of the puzzle. Something he had failed to notice because he hadn't realised it ought to be there. Why did this man die? Either his death was directly connected to his collection of corpses, or it wasn't. If it wasn't, why kill him?

"Of course." Hauer whipped around in mid-stride. "Not missing, but stolen."

Smith blinked, slowly chewing the last bite of his sandwich. "Sir?"

"Think, will you? Your Bluebeard was as rich as Croesus. A man like that has a safe, his wife has jewellery. What valuables were taken from the house?"

Greasy fingers typed faster than should be possible. "Well, we haven't received the list from the insurer yet, but forensics did find a safe in the study, exposed and empty, and a handful of relatively cheap items recovered from the bathroom and the bedroom."

"No gold, gems, pearl strings?"

"None, sir."

Hauer exhaled deeply. As much as the past obscured his focus, on occasion it proved itself a valid advisor. "Smith, I think we've been barking up the wrong tree."

"A robbery? Are you quite mad?" Superintendent Cooper clenched his dark hands into fists. "This man has hidden multiple dead bodies in his house, and you are telling me that it was just a coincidence?"

"As far as the shooting of Rais is concerned, yes. His death might well be merely collateral damage."

"Rais's wife and her sister are missing, Hauer. More collateral damage, I suppose?"

"We have no reason to believe they were kidnapped. If whoever drove that black Merc wanted them for ransom, they wouldn't have shot the one person most likely to pay up. If they killed him by accident, the wife is worthless, and they would have killed her, too. Only they didn't."

"It has been less than twenty-four hours. A ransom demand might still be forthcoming."

"To whom? Their family? Besides, I have never known kidnappers to booby-trap the abduction site, much less place an incendiary bomb."

Cooper's sullen frown approached the quality of a pout. "I take it you suspect the wife."

"I most certainly do, sir. Not of murdering her husband, though. Ballistics confirmed that the bullets in his body match professional weaponry, not a desperate housewife with a peashooter."

"Did you consider she may have fled the violence?"

"We did. Rais drove a Range Rover, his maid told us. We found it parked in the garage, blocking the exit for the other three cars. If the ladies ran in panic after the execution, the only vehicle available was the Mercedes that the neighbours saw."

"So, a straight-up robbery, you say?" Cooper deflated. "Does the evidence even support that theory?"

"They didn't ransack the house, so we missed the theft at first glance. Professional thieves are meticulous, but these culprits knew exactly where to look and what to take. I believe the intended explosion was supposed to erase their tracks, as well as any chance for the insurance company to identify the stolen items. After a fire, insurers consider all household effects lost, so if Rais's jewellery is offered for sale anywhere, it won't raise suspicion. The ultimate fence."

Cooper sank deeper into his chair. "Plausible indeed. And here I was, willing to put money on her killing her murderous husband in self-defence."

"Never bet on self-defence, sir. Especially when it concerns murder in conjunction with theft and arson." The tang of nougat and white chocolate spread through his mouth, trailing after the words. He tried to rid himself of the foul taste, but to no avail. He would need another cup of black coffee to achieve that.

"How about the—" An urgent knock interrupted him, followed by the office door swinging open. "DS Smith, what is the meaning of this?"

"Sorry, sir, but I need the inspector. Aviation Security at Heathrow has found our Merc."

Or what was left of it, anyway.

The Heathrow officers had emailed photos of a mangled, molten wreck on a hotel car park near the airport. Since automotive vehicles in general didn't have the tendency to instantaneously combust, Hauer suspected that the destructive blaze had a little help. Involving a timer, in all likelihood.

"Did the cameras catch them?"

"We're working on obtaining the recordings, sir, but this here might be of interest." Smith grinned as his eyes flitted across the screen. "An AMG turns heads, even at a posh hotel. One of the hotel guests is a real car fanatic, so he parked right beside it for a closer look."

Hauer studied the photo. "The formerly silver Lexus on the right?"

"The same, which is why he came running when it and the Merc went up in flames. Now here is the great thing: in his statement he described two men and two women walking down the same parking lane where he had seen the Mercedes. He remembered because he thought it strange that they all wore sunglasses on an overcast day."

"Eccentricity is not limited to criminals. They could have been anyone."

This reality check didn't curb Smith's enthusiasm. "I checked the photos the responding constable sent, and they show only one other car in that lane, a two-seater. So those four people must have come from the Merc. But I found something else, sir. The car is registered to a shelf company. No activities, just a handful of assets. It is owned by yet another shelf company…"

"Yeeees?"

"...which is in turn is owned by known aliases of–hold on to your hat, sir–the Carlton Brothers." Smith spun his chair in triumph. "Two enterprising criminals who don't shy from putting bullets in someone's chest if it gets them what they want. Bluebeard's murder definitely fits their MO."

Hauer's jaw worked. He'd heard of these two. Greedy opportunists indeed, but hardly organised criminals. One piece didn't fit.

"That bomb in the villa's boiler room couldn't have been fabricated on the fly. They came prepared, which means that they must have been to the house before yesterday." He ran a nail across his chin. "Bring in the maid and show her the mugshots. Let's see if she can tell us more."

"*Ah oui*, I saw them," said the elderly Mrs Beaufort with an accent as thick as marzipan cake. "They attended the wedding. Madame's brothers, you see? Such charming boys, both of them."

"You were at the wedding?" Hauer caught himself before he gaped. "Did Rais invite all his servants?"

"*Non*, *non*, only me. I have worked for him for more than *cinquante*, eh, fifty. Fifty years. He was orphaned. I looked after him. All his life. And now... *maintenant il est... il est...*"

Hauer handed her the tissue box to stem the abundant flow of tears. "Having been a confidante of sorts, ma'am, I'm sure you can shed some light on his many marriages. None of them lasted long, it seems."

Her wrinkles deepened as she scrunched up her face and spat. "*Menteuses*, all of them. Lying, unfaithful girls. Of course he would not stay married to them."

"He divorced them?"

Her expression straightened like a shirt under a hot iron, but she held her tongue.

Hauer held up the evidence bag with the dirty key. "You knew about the cellar, didn't you? You knew what was in there."

"Monsieur Gilles was a good man. Too good for those horrid women. He trusted them. Gave them all keys and said only that room they cannot enter. A simple order, *non*? They tell him they will obey, but they never do. All of them, all of them went in to see what was forbidden."

Ranting on, her broken English descended into rapid French, too fast for Hauer to tell one word from the next. Exasperated, he left the examination room.

In the hallway, he found Smith listening at the door while sipping from a can of coke.

"Sir, are we absolutely certain that Bluebeard's collectibles have nothing to do with the missing wife? It just seems too big a thing not to be connected somehow."

Hauer mentally blocked the ghastly smell of soda. "The Carlton Brothers are no more the wife's brothers than they are upstanding citizens. They infiltrated a rich man's life to rob him blind. Do you really think they gave a damn about a couple of bodies?"

"No," Smith said between sips, "but I'm guessing old Bluebeard did."

A strained sigh betrayed a smidgen of doubt. "Go on."

"Well, Mrs Beaufort said that Bluebeard gave his keys to the wife, right? He leaves, and she can enter all the rooms, even the ones she hasn't seen yet. So she scouts the place for valuables. There's plenty, so the wife and her sister gather it all and call in the Carlton Brothers. They've been pretending to be one big happy family, so should Bluebeard come back early, he will think they're just visiting. While waiting, the wife checks the last room, the forbidden one, thinking there must be more loot in there. But she finds the creepy bodies instead."

"We found the door unlocked. She was interrupted, then?"

"I think so, 'cos what she doesn't know is that her husband had planned it all. He comes back early, she hears him and closes the cellar door but doesn't lock it 'cos she dropped the key in the muck. He asks for his keys back, then finds the forbidden one missing."

"The maid believes he killed his wives for that offence."

"He would've, too, only that's when the Carlton Brothers arrive, and they shoot Bluebeard before he can shoot his wife. Whose maiden name, by the way, turns out to be an alias."

"That's quite a presumption to make."

"Not a presumption, sir. I got an email from Paris saying the name on the marriage certificate is a fake. Anyway, with Bluebeard dead on the floor, the gang has all the time they need to take whatever valuables they want and plant that bomb, which they expect will destroy all the evidence. Next, they get into the Carltons' Merc, drive to the airport, rig the car to burn, and board the first flight out 'cos they think that as far as we know, everyone in the house died in the fire." Smith smirked. "How's that, sir?"

"Not bad, Smith. Not bad at all..." Hauer pinched his forefinger out of habit. "However, if they did slip out of the country, they'll be back."

"For what?"

"Think about it. All passenger luggage is screened. If suitcases full of valuables show up, they would be flagged for closer inspection. And stashing the loot elsewhere to smuggle it out separately takes time and preparation." His forefinger began to hurt. "Chase those CCTV recordings, Smith. I want to know where they went after abandoning the car."

Said hunt turned out to be a wild goose chase in the otherwise surprisingly smooth investigation. The hotel staff had been more than forthcoming with their surveillance footage, but seeing the culprits walk off the hotel's premises was useless without the local traffic cameras picking up their trail.

Like breadcrumbs. Hauer miserably stared out of the office window. Just when you had a solid lead, the birds got to it. Bureaucracy.

"Uhm, sir?" Smith peered out from behind his computer. "I think you'll want to see this."

He sauntered over while Smith tapped the keys that controlled a grainy black and white video on his screen.

"The security cameras give a rough direction of which way our culprits went, but what I found was this."

On screen, coming from the Mercedes, two men and two women strolled across the hotel car park, each with a large suitcase.

"How did they get those bags through customs?"

"They didn't, sir. Keep watching."

The video changed to another camera. The four figures walked to the hotel first, but passed the entrance and crossed to the far side of the car park, out of the camera's range.

"Now, we can't actually see them getting into a vehicle, but the only car to leave in the next three minutes is this one." Smith fast-forwarded to a white van driving up to the car park barrier, and froze the image. "License plate says it belongs to a bakery in Whitechapel. They reported it stolen a few days ago."

"So Heathrow was a decoy. Good job, Sergeant." Hauer purred like a cat playing with a mouse. "Can you enhance the image of the occupants?"

"Maybe I can go one better, sir. Hold on."

Smith plugged another USB-stick into his computer and opened a series of images.

"Nope. Nope," he said every time he closed a window with a photo. "Nope, nope, nope. Ha, there we are."

He turned the screen to give Hauer a proper view. "The hotel's barrier contains a system that scans a car's license plate and snaps a shot of the occupants upon exiting. It's to identify car thieves. Does the trick, I'd say."

Hauer no longer heard his sergeant. He recognised the driver from the mugshots they had shown the maid, but the woman in the passenger's seat...she wore a shawl and sunglasses, but even so, the small office suddenly smelled of caramel, Sachertorte, and whipped cream. On his lips lingered the taste of sticky little fingers stuffing his mouth with colourful gummi bears. All he could eat and more. His stomach rumbled, undecided whether he was hungry or about to be sick.

"Sir? Sir. *Oi*, Inspector."

A sharp yank at his sleeve pulled him from his daze before the words did. "What?"

"I said, the registration number of that van," Smith pointed at his screen, "was just logged by a unit responding to a car fire in Winchmore Hill."

"Well, it would. She loves a good fire."

"Sir? Look, I don't know what you're on about, but they're reporting casualties. The occupants. Don't you think we should—?"

"I think you need to print that photo." Hauer snatched his car keys from his desk. "Bring it. I'll drive."

By the time they arrived, the local fire brigade had already packed up their hoses. They had doused the fire with plenty of foam, but it had been too little, too late. The van's carcass had burnt to a crisp.

When Smith opened his car door, the odours of charcoal, metal, petrol, and sulphur drifted in, along with the distinct smell of burnt flesh. The sergeant sniffed twice and gagged. "You were right, sir. It's at least as bad as that cellar."

Not in the mood for even a sarcastic reply, Hauer only nodded and got out.

A flash of their badges and a quick introduction to their colleagues gave them full access to the scene. A white sheet had been draped over the burnt-out cabin. Hauer lifted one end and held his breath as he peeked underneath. Prepared for the nightmarish memories that the state of the victims would trigger, he pushed the old images back before they overtook him.

"Anything, or anyone, in the back?" he asked the constable in charge.

"No, sir. The firefighters cut the doors open while it was still burning, but the cargo compartment's empty."

"Well, well. Any clue on the gender of the crispy critters in the cabin?"

"Coroner's officers aren't here yet, but the eye witness who called it in spoke of two men, just sitting there. Say, did you expect more victims, Inspector?"

"I did, but then I should have known better." He dropped the sheet. "Tell the Coroner's that their clients are likely to be the Carlton Brothers."

Walking around the carcass, he pressed his hand to the warm, blackened metal. Even as a child, the hot glow after a fire sparked a sense of comfort, of relief. Relief that the acrid stench nipped in the bud, just like it had all those years ago.

Spell broken, he paced towards the constables.

"Paperwork can wait, gentlemen. We're looking for two women and four heavy suitcases."

The uniformed men stared at him in confusion.

"Don't just stand there, go ask around. Two well-to-do women in sunglasses carrying heavy luggage stand out. Someone must have seen them. Smith, you take that photograph and go south with two men. I'll take the other two and head north."

"Sir, do you want a photo to—?"

"No need. I *know* who I'm looking for."

He questioned anyone who might have been around longer than a few minutes, starting with the rubberneckers who had stayed to gawk from behind the police cordon. While he noted their answers, he calculated. The wreck was still warm, but did that mean anything? Not if she used a timer again. Still, neither she nor her companion could have gone far. Gold weighed as much as lead. Alternatively, a suitcase full of paper–bearer bonds, for instance–was barely lighter.

But perhaps *Marguerite* had never planned to go far in the first place: less than half an hour later, his mobile phone rang. Smith. The women had been spotted entering a cottage near the church.

"The sign in the garden says the property was sold recently, so I checked the registers to see who owns it now."

"Let me guess: your Bluebeard."

"Got it in one, sir. There're no curtains or furniture, but I see movement in the living room. One person. Long blond hair, I think."

"Block the exits, but do not initiate a confrontation, you hear?" Hauer panted as he ran in the direction of the church. "Three men are dead because of her. I don't need you to make that four, so call the SCO19 for armed back-up."

Within minutes, he rounded the corner of the churchyard, where Smith patrolled a small gate to a garden.

"Armed unit is on the way, sir," his Sergeant said, but whatever came next faded as Hauer gazed at the house beyond the hedgerow.

A small cottage, half-hidden among yew trees and juniper bushes. A thatched roof and mocha-coloured walls, like the gingerbread houses that old Nanny Katharina used to bake for his sister and him. Even the white facings of the front door louvre reminded him of icing trimmings, and blossoming hollyhocks dotted the brown walls like coloured sugar sprinkles.

Of course Nanny's wards had to finish every last crumb. Every day anew. Biscuits, cotton candy, liquorice, chocolate, lemonade. Until one day his sister had had enough.

His stomach squirmed at the memory and the lingering stench of the burnt corpses clinging to his nostrils didn't help. He pinched his forefinger to stop the queasiness. A tried method, but this time, it failed. He stumbled into a nearby shrubbery for a modicum of dignity while he heaved until nothing remained in his stomach.

From there, he operated on the autopilot of experience. The SCO19 team arrived, guns at the ready, and broke down the gingerbread door. He listened for shots, but heard nothing. Within forty seconds of going in, the team leader declared the scene secured.

Past memories mingled with bouts of obscene clarity as he strode towards the cottage. Stepping across its threshold felt like stepping into another world. The very world he had so wanted to forget when he escaped his past and moved to London.

In the entrance hall, sprawled at the bottom of the stairs, lay a young, dark-haired woman. The angle of her neck explained her vacant eyes as well as the general disinterest in her wellbeing. At the far end of the hall stood the four suitcases. One had been kicked over, priceless jewellery spilling out.

"We've got her, sir. Even if we can't make the rest stick, at least she'll go down for theft," said Smith.

Hauer nodded, but winced when a sudden outburst of sobs assaulted his ears.

Someone wept. Loudly and with the same flair that had brought the law enforcement of his birth town to their knees. He gritted his teeth until it hurt. Much as he wanted to walk away from this nightmare, he couldn't. This had to end. For good.

On the barren floor of the living room, hands cuffed behind her back and surrounded by three policemen with semi-automatic rifles, sat the woman who had crowned herself Marguerite de Rais. The illegitimate queen of a broken empire.

"Why are you doing this to me?" Her blond locks obscuring her eyes as she wailed. "My husband killed those poor women, not I. He even pulled a gun on me and my sister."

She gasped dramatically between sobs.

"My brothers, they saved us. They said to wait for someone to take us home, to France. But then poor Anna fell down the stairs—"

"With some considerable assistance from you, I take it."

His voice, cold and hard, echoed in the unfurnished room. At once, the woman's head snapped up, her red-rimmed eyes infuriated rather than frightened. The fine lines on her tanned skin betrayed that she was of his age–too old to be the dead girl's sister, as she claimed. Yet nothing about her gave away what deranged mind hid behind this act of innocent self-defence.

An old trick of hers, but one he remembered well. And now, she remembered him.

"H-Hans?"

A whiff of lemon drops filled the air.

"Murder and robbery, served with gratuitous arson. I should have known I would find you at the end of this trail." He bared his teeth like a wolf that had found its prey. "Hello, Gretel."

JACK AND JILL

Tom Williams

"Our wooing doth not end like an old play; Jack hath not Jill."
Love's Labours Lost

"See you at the matinee. All bright-eyed and bushy tailed, sweetie. Kiss kiss."

Evan shook his head as the taillights of Larry's Mercedes disappeared into the night. A lift from Larry inevitably meant a sly fondle, but tonight, it had been anything but sly. Evan had to be quite blunt with the old ram, with little effect.

Evan walked down the short path to his door, and began fishing for his key when the unmistakeable footfalls of a child skipping on the pavement broke the silence. He turned and caught sight of the top of a bandaged head bobbing along his fence.

"Wait." It was almost midnight, and this child was out alone. Evan walked back up the path as the youngster arrived at his gate. The boy was no more than nine years old. Close up, under the dull orange light of the sodium street lamps, he could see the bandage was roughly fashioned from brown paper. "What are you doing out at this time of night? Does your Mummy know you're out?"

"I don't have a Mummy. I live with Mrs Dob."

"Does Mrs Dob know you're out at this time?"

"I had to come out, Mister, I'm looking for Jill." The lad's high reedy voice carried a strength that came from desperation.

Evan flinched; it had been more than six months since Jill had disappeared. He stepped back, his knees weak. The boy skipped away down the deserted street.

Evan hurried back to his house, went straight to the kitchen, and poured himself a glass of Malbec from a bottle he started last night. He sat at the table.

The lad couldn't mean Jill Daventry, his Jill. It didn't make any sense. The boy must have been looking for a different Jill.

He poured another glass and rolled a joint.

First, bloody Larry all over me, then, then… It was too absurd. He recited the rhyme under his breath.

Jack and Jill went up the hill
To fetch a pail of water.
Jack fell down and broke his crown,
And Jill came tumbling after.

But that was the first verse. What was the second? He lit the joint and smoked half before he gave up trying to recall the rhyme and went into the sitting room for his tablet. Thank God for Jimmy Wales and Wiki.

Up Jack got, and home did trot,
As fast as he could caper;
To old Dame Dob, who patched his nob
With vinegar and brown paper.

Mrs Dob. He tapped an inch of ash off the joint. That ridiculous paper turban the child had worn. Evan remembered Jack's pinched little face looking up at him, so serious, so sombre it made him smile. Dear Jack, have you lost your Jill, too, you poor thing. He took a deep, lungful of smoke.

Imagine, Jack and I both losing our Jills.

There was a difference though, an important one. Evan knew where his Jill was. Oh, yes, he knew exactly where she was. Hadn't he carried her corpse, twice as heavy in death, across a ploughed field, staggering under her weight as he tottered over the furrows.

He let the smoke out. The splash her body had made as it plunged into the dark waters of the old well, down in Aldermaston near his parents' home, made it all worthwhile. Afterwards he had lain down in the mud, filthy and exhausted but jubilant, free at last of the sanctimonious cow. Fortunately, he had several days to hide his tracks before his masterly performance at the police station. It had been one of his best. He imbued his role of the deserted partner with every ounce of tragedic pathos he could muster.

Still, when the desk sergeant tried to reassure him, "Don't you worry, sir, she'll surface soon," he had almost had an attack of the giggles.

What a stroke of genius to turn his laughter into choked-back tears.

With Jill officially missing, all he had to do was play the abandoned lover until the tabloid squall died away. Thank God she already had a well-deserved reputation as a brilliant but unbalanced writer given to disappearing for months at a time with one or another similarly-unbalanced new lover before returning to her long-suffering partner.

Well, darling, I think you may be disappearing for a bit longer this time.

Evan stubbed out the joint and hit the speed dial on his mobile. *Pizza for dinner, I think.*

A week later, Evan jogged along the towpath. The morning fog lingered under an insipid sun and mixed with the smoke from the narrowboats moored along the canal. Evan had not thought about Jack since that night. Just another of those curious encounters that happened in London with a puzzling regularity, as if the city was so large and complex that even the unlikely became likely.

As he ran under a low stone road bridge, he stopped dead and retraced his strides so that he could peer up at the parapet of the bridge, all stained grey stone against a stained grey sky. What had he seen?

He examined the line of the bridge and retreated a handful more steps. There, just a little taller than the parapet, the top of a child's head.

Back a little further. The eyes and nose of a young boy peeking over the parapet.

"Jack."

"Yes, sir."

"Have you found Jill yet?"

"No, sir."

Evan shrugged. Was it possible that his Jill and Jack's Jill were connected in some way? He smiled weakly at Jack and resumed his jog.

"Please, sir, will you tell her I'm looking for her."

Jack pulled himself up so that his chest rested on the stone edge.

"Sorry, Jack, I don't know where she is." Evan could see Jack's knuckles whitening as he fought to hold himself up on the parapet. Evan shrugged again showing his open palms to Jack, as if to say, there is nothing up my sleeves. A speeding cyclist approached, and Evan leapt off the track. The cyclist flew past and hurtled under the bridge. When Evan looked up, Jack had gone.

The Friday two weeks later, Larry was half-cut during the show and gone on a flesh crawl in Soho. So, no lift home; no big deal. Evan waited until the so-called stars finished signing autographs and posing for selfies before he let himself out through the stage door. Not everyone had gone. A little way from the door, standing beside some bins was Jack.

"You again…I don't suppose you would like my autograph?"

"You know where my Jill is, don't you, sir?" Evan held his face rigid under the child's scrutiny.

The alleyway was deserted. "Don't be ridiculous, I have never met your Jill."

"She told me you got angry, a cold-hard anger."

Evan shivered. That was precisely how the pathologically-literate bitch described him to her mother.

Evan looked down at the diminutive figure. Jack returned his gaze unflinchingly. Was Jack accusing him of being involved with Jill's disappearance?

Evan was no longer finding the little fellow amusing. "Yes, Jack, I know where Jill is. I will take you to her. You wait here. I just need to get some keys." Thank goodness Larry left his keys in the dressing room when he went on a bender.

Jack waited in the alleyway by the stage door while Evan collected Larry's car from a mews around the corner, an ex's place. London was easy to leave at this time of night, Larry's Merc cruised along the M4 smoothly.

"Why do you think that I know where your Jill is?" Evan noted how careful he was to say *your Jill. 'Your Jill'. She's a bloody nursery rhyme character.* Evan glanced quickly at the child besides him. Everything was getting messy because Jack had lost his fictional Jill. Evan could feel anger rising in him like bile.

"She said you had left her in a cold, dark place, and she doesn't know how to get home."

Evan kept his eyes fixed on the deserted lanes of the motorway, pale under a heavy yellow moon. "So, she can talk to you."

"Oh, yes."

"Can she talk to anyone else?"

"No, sir. Only me. I am her Jack."

Evan smiled. *You are such a little egotist, aren't you, Jack?*

They left the M4 at Theale. In the darkness, the narrow twisting roads were strange and unfamiliar, but finally, Evan stopped the car abruptly at a five bar gate. "Time to get out, Jack."

Evan opened the gate, and together, they walked along a track at the edge of the field. The strong moonlight cast the whole scene in a silvery monotone.

Evan took a deep breath, the air felt clean. He could hear Jack wheezing from the effort to keep up.

"Not a country boy then, Jack."

"I don't like hills, sir."

Finally, they arrived at the far corner of the field. There were half a dozen railway sleepers over the top of the well.

"Stay back, Jack. These sleepers are heavy." Evan shifted three aside so that a gap of around eighteen inches opened at the mouth of the well.

"Jill is down there, Jack." Evan stepped back to allow Jack to peer into the aperture. "Can you see her?"

"In there, sir?" Jack leant over, leaning forward on his toes.

Evan pushed him hard. Jack arched over the hole, throwing his arms back wildly, but Evan was too strong, he guided Jack's struggling body through the gap. Jack fell into the darkness, followed by a deep splash. Evan replaced the sleepers and brushed his hands. It had been a lot muddier when he had brought Jill.

Jack and Jill re-united.

He laughed.

This had almost been fun.

THREE LITTLE VISITS

Sita C. Romero

The shaking began again in earnest, even though I blasted the heat in mid-July. I put on my long-sleeve flannel. Satisfied that I had packed the important stuff, I threw the bag over my shoulder and took a last look around. I loved my little apartment on Sixth Street, but I'd never be free of them if I stayed. Running was my only option.

Outside, I ignored the stares and stumbled to my car. Bizarre sights were commonplace at the beach. People watching was as popular as surfing. I didn't care if they stared, they couldn't see inside me. *Just a few stops, and I'm out of this place. For good.*

Momma's house was the first on my list. I pulled off the highway and into the abandoned convenience store parking lot. I flipped out the blade of my pocket knife and yanked my belt from the overnight bag. Peeling back the flannel shirt exposed my hairy, left arm. The heater blew, and in spite of the fever, sweat formed around my hairline. Biting down on the belt, I pointed the sharp blade at my forearm and forced my shaky hand to steady. Pain seared through me, and I screamed into the bitter leather as the tip punctured my skin. I sliced sideways as if cutting a sliver off a block of cheese. Thankfully, it was deep enough, so I wouldn't have to do it again. My skin peeled back, and with it, the microchip. I bandaged my bleeding forearm and wrapped it tightly with the medkit supplies. I opened my door, tossed out the chip, and vomited into the empty lot.

Now, it's only a matter of time.

The trailer park never emptied completely. Compared to other neighborhoods, its occupancy increased in the middle of the day. The working folks of Spring Glen kept odd hours. Luckily, Momma was home.

"I've got to go away for a while, and I just wanted to say goodbye. I knew you'd kill me if I told you over the phone."

"Honey, you're burnin' up. I just don't think now's a good time for you to go. Why don't you stay here, and I'll nurse you back to health. Then you can go." She moved her knitting project off the worn couch and patted the seat.

My flannel was back in place, hiding the hole I had dug. I already felt lighter since the tracker had come out. "You don't understand, Momma. These people. They'll come after me. I made certain—" I swallowed. I didn't want to relive it. Momma didn't need to know. "Promises."

Momma crossed her short arms over her plump middle.

"Promises I don't intend to keep." I broke into a coughing fit. The bile surged up. *Not again.* I made it to the sink, at least, vomiting on Momma's discarded coffee cup from the early morning. Momma stood by me, offering a cool cloth and turning on the water to rinse it down.

"What sort of trouble is this, Jake? Why don't you tell Momma and let me help?"

"You can't help." The sweat turned cold now that the vomiting had stopped, and a wave of heat flushed through my body. "They'll quarantine me, Momma. I'm not going back. This isn't what I signed up for."

"They can make you better, Sonny. They'll fix it."

"No. They won't make me better. They'll treat me like a lab rat. I'm not going. Besides, I'm already much better than I was last night. I'm gonna get better. I know it. I just need some time away. Trust me, Momma. I know what's best."

"Okay, dear. Well, I love you. Let me pack you up a sandwich for your trip."

Momma packed a sandwich and kissed me on both cheeks. She stood stiff. I could tell she was trying to hold it back. But the tears started before I could turn the engine over and wind my way out of the maze of trailers.

At least we got our last goodbye.

Justin lived on a country road off Highway 20 near the lake. He had done better for himself than Momma. He had done better for himself than me, too. I had to stop again to vomit on the way. Still, I didn't want to leave without telling my only brother goodbye. Only two more stops.

Justin had a large home office, and he sat at his big oak desk overlooking the lake. I could see the back of his head through the over-sized window on the second floor when I skidded into the gravel driveway.

I let myself in and shouted up, making my way to his office only to be greeted with a look of concern.

"Jake, what are you doing here, man? Jesus, you look like shit, dude. What the hell is going on?" Justin shut his laptop and came around to my side of his massive desk.

"I think something is fucked up with the transplant. I've been pretty sick."

"Did you call Dr. Strauss?"

"No, man. I don't want any more of that poking and prodding. They promised me the xenotransplant would work. Now, I've got animal parts floating inside me, and you see this? You see how sick I am?" I looked down at my wrinkled flannel shirt. "I'm taking a little vacation."

His posture shifted and he looked me over, disbelief and concern wrinkling his forehead. "Where you headed?"

"I'd rather not say, man. I took out the tracker."

Justin's eyes took over his face. I barked a laugh at the cartoonish-nature of the expression. "Come on. I'll get you a cup of coffee, and we can sort this out."

"No way, man. I'm sure when they realize it's out, you guys will be the first to hear of it. So do me a favor and tell them you haven't seen me, okay?"

"I don't know, Jake. I don't think this is the way to handle it."

"Please? You don't know what it was like living in that lab. Test, after test, after test." Caged, like an animal, in that white room.

"I hear you. Okay, man. I won't say anything. Now you better get the hell out of here. Send me a postcard."

"I'm going to see Jessica before I leave." I swallowed hard.

"Good luck with that." He gave me a knowing look. My sister wasn't the easiest person to deal with.

I hugged my brother one last time.

Jessica lived in the country club. I had to wait at the gate for the guard to call and make sure I had permission for a visit. Sitting in my car behind the barred entrance, I fantasized about breaking through it. I didn't have time for yuppie bullshit. The air blasted cold from the vent. The fever had broken. I didn't need to stop even once to vomit this time. I was getting better. I knew it.

The guard finally hung up the receiver and waved me through. I wound my way back to her massive home and parked in the drive that split her perfectly manicured yard. She stood just inside the doorway, waiting for me. Had Justin called her?

"Jessica, I've had a rough morning. I'm glad to see you." Our relationship was odd. I was glad to see her, but I also never let my guard down.

She hugged me and brought me into her home. Her kids were at school. She was alone in her mini-mansion. Her cleaning lady must've had the day off. "Me, too, Jake. Me, too." She brought me a glass of water and urged me to sit at the kitchen table with her. It was cozier than the usual, formal-living-room gathering. You'd think she could afford some comfortable furniture.

Now that I was at my last stop, I sighed with relief. *Freedom.* I would leave without the fever and vomiting, free from the tracker and on to a place they would never look for me.

Jessica fidgeted with her fingers. She seemed nervous, but she was an anxious person anyway.

Maybe she didn't have her meds or her vodka yet today. Or maybe she's worried one of her neighbors will come knocking and see her white-trash brother sitting at the table.

She fingered her necklace and glanced at the front door.

"I'm leaving for a while, Jess." I awaited her harsh judgements. Momma wasn't all that bright, and Justin was a go-with-the-flow kind of guy. But Jessica, she was the smartest of the bunch.

"It's xenosis, isn't it?" Her voice was too quiet. "You contracted a disease from the transplant, didn't you?"

"I think so. It's the only explanation. But I'm already getting better. So, it's nothing to worry about." I gave her my best reassuring smile.

"Do you know why you're getting better?" Her voice eerily was calm.

"Well, no. But why does that matter? I'm getting better. It's not going to cause any of the problems they warned me about."

"You're getting better because of the porcine antibodies. Your body has the ability to produce them to fight the disease. Ironic. The thing that is causing your disease is also curing it."

"That's good. I'll take pig antibodies if it means it'll fix this." I said. "But if you're telling me this to get me to stay, it won't work. They haven't studied xenosis enough to know what it can do. They'd love it if I brought in a new disease for them to dissect. And, an animal disease transferred to a human? They'll win the lottery with my return. No, thanks. I'll never be free. You wouldn't understand."

She twisted the fat diamond on her finger. "Oh, I understand more than you think. I was just secretive about my procedure. That's why none of the family knew about it."

"Wait. What? You've had a xenotransplant, too?" My voice came out shaky, laced with confusion.

"After I lost all the weight. It was a xenograft, actually. It's the reason I'm not sitting here catching your disease right now. I have the porcine antibodies to protect myself. Wish I could say the same for Mom and Justin."

She never called her Momma anymore.

Horror roiled through my bones. *Contagious*. Why hadn't I considered that I might be contagious? Everything was internal. I thought it could only affect me. "Oh shit. Did you talk to them? Did I get them sick?"

Jessica's gaze darted to the front door. I'm right. She *was* anxious about something.

Looking down into her cup of tea, she was stalling.

She was dragging this out.

I stood and pushed my chair in. "I wish I could stay and chat. I'll check in on Momma and Justin after I get settled." I turned toward the front door.

Jessica grabbed my arm and spun me back around. Her eyes pierced me, blinking, narrowed and fearful. "You've got to go in, Jake. You have no idea what you've done."

"I won't do it. I—" The words died in my throat as a Hummer pulled into the driveway. An unmarked white van followed behind. "Son of a bitch. You called it in."

"It's over Jake. I had no choice. I couldn't let you spread it any further."

"Oh, don't be so dramatic."

"I love you, Jake, and for that, I'm going to tell you the truth."

Men in hazmat suits busted through her front door and seized me. Tears formed in my sister's eyes. She had betrayed me. I never should've come. All I wanted was to get away.

"You have the potential to start an epidemic. I couldn't let you do that."

"You're lying," I spat.

"Let me go." I struggled with the hazmat suits.

"I didn't hurt anyone. I didn't do anything."

They wrestled me out the door as my sister's soft voice reached me, "I forgive you. It's not your fault Momma and Justin are dead."

Serving His Lordship

3-D MONARCH

KT Wagner

Balanced on his tail end, the prince ripples around his dungeon office. He punts swill containers into a corner, sweeps drawings off his desk, and hurls a mug of milkweed tea. It shatters against the stone wall in a not-quite-satisfying explosion of sound and shards.

"Make babies. Prepare to be king. Grow up." He mimics in a sing-song voice and casts around for something else to break. "Never mind what I want, who I want to be."

"Our prince, can we help?"

His upper lip curls at the simpering falsetto of his stick-bug sister-in-law, Lucinda. Wherever she goes, the other sister is right there. Drusilla. His striped skin undulates.

"What is it you need for your wedding this time?" He pivots toward his desk and picks up a sheaf of official-looking papers. Dust billows. "See my purser."

A mound of litter in the corner twitches. His mood lightens. Dropping the papers, he unclasps a grappling hook from his belt and bends into a hunting stance. A scrawny rat snuffles into view, tenses, and sniffs the air. Saliva puddles under the prince's tongue. He closes his mouth and slowly pulls back the arm holding the hook—

"You have to do something about the Cinderellas." Drusilla's nasal twang reverberates through his exo-skeleton.

The rat scurries under the desk. The grapple misses it by a foot. His snack darts out the door.

All eight of his fists clenched, the prince rounds on the sisters. "Get out. Better yet, go catch me a rat, or a squirrel, or something. Don't come back without one, or I'll find other uses for you." He advances on the trembling women.

Antennae waving, Lucinda draws a deep breath and leans toward him. Her sister has no choice but to stand ground with her. Lucinda clicks her mandibles and extends her foreleg in a gesture of peace. "Your father sent us. You have to deal with your mistakes. Our wedding is off now that there are five extra Cinderellas.

None of the bachelor lords are willing to settle for..." Lucinda clears her throat. "...spinster sisters."

The prince tries to sound imperious. "It's not my fault she decided to nap inside the old coach pumpkin during my last experiment. Besides, I'm very upset she pupated without my permission. She's just not interesting now that she changed. It's a husband's prerogative—"

Drusilla expels a hiss of air and her compound eyes bulge more than usual. "*Men.* You know her nature. You should've anticipated—"

"Of course, she gets that self-absorbed streak from her mother's side." Lucinda lowers her voice. "Everyone knows there's a long family history of consorting with maggots—most certainly some of that DNA was responsible for Cinderella's behaviour. And her maternal great-grandmother…rumour is a fairy godmother tarted up the *pedigree*…well, it would at least explain how Cinderella managed to attract an advocate while the rest of us…"

Lucinda and Drusilla sigh in unison.

"Do tell me more." A familiar longing softens the prince's stance. "You know, my mother has fairy godmother in her family tree. I can see myself in some of the old photographs."

Cinderella's step-sisters exchange a look, a tad shy of eye-rolling.

"The extra Cinderellas?" Lucinda prompts. "Bad enough there are all these rotting coach pumpkins around. The king is thinking of limiting your access to technology. Says you're being too careless. We could put in a good word for you, but we have this little problem…"

"I know, I know, the Cinderellas." The prince curls up to ponder. It takes effort to balance on his tail end, and he needs to think. "I suppose I could just marry the rest of them."

The sisters shake their heads in unison. The mud-green side-wings of their shared body rub and emit a high-pitched squeal. Drusilla, her face flushed red, swats at the wings with her forearm but to no effect.

"You zoomed the copier function to one hundred and fifty percent. Our Cinderella is devastated. Have you seen the size of the wings on the new ones?" Lucinda clicks her mandibles. "All that turquoise, silver, and blue. It's blinding. You've disgraced our Cinderella. She's talking separation and maybe even divorce. Her fairy godmother has suggested they move away together."

The Prince straightens. "No, no, I can't lose Fairy Godmother. She's the only one of my kind around here. Can't we just feed the new Cinderellas into the chute of the 3-D printer? Recycle them, so to speak?"

The sisters shudder.

Lucinda hums. "You're such a child. It's time you grew up and got over this Fairy Godmother obsession…started acting like a normal prince."

Drusilla buzzes. "*No.* You can't just recycle the Cinderellas. That would be wicked."

"I could give the extra Cinderellas jobs pollinating the orchards up north or working in the scullery." He stretches. His skin feels tight, but he isn't ready to part with it. His destiny is fairy godmotherhood. The expert editors of *Destiny Quarterly* claim it's too late to tap into gifts once you transform into a true adult. He just needs to unlock his potential to transform others. "Enough. I have work to do. Find them jobs. Figure it out. You're dismissed."

He waves several arms in the direction of the door.

Their huffs of indignation aren't unexpected. Mantis like to bluster and put on airs, especially rare two-headed ones. The king saw fit to name them advisors, and now, his sister-in-laws think entirely too much of themselves.

If he were a monarch, he'd get rid of them, but he has no intention of becoming a monarch, or having children, or doing anything else that doesn't involve tapping into his latent fairy godmother heritage.

The magic he tried to perform with the 3-D printer experiments hasn't worked. Pumpkins turned into pumpkin patches, not coaches. Replicated rats didn't morph into footmen, and they got under foot until he finally ate the lot. He'd never tried one before, and now, he has a constant craving.

He curls and picks his drawings up from the floor. A before-and-after sketch of Cinderella rests on top of the pile. He strokes his chin with four hands. He's expecting too much from technology alone. He'll renovate the mothballed torture chamber. Turn it into a modern surgery and work magic with his own hands. He has five extra Cinderellas to work with.

A thump behind him. He's forgotten the sisters. "I told you to leave."

Plop. Something moist and sticky attaches to his head. None of his arms can reach it. He tries to curl his tail, but it's held down. The noise of the sisters' wings fills the room.

"Time to grow up," Lucinda says. "You're not the only one who can operate the printer."

The prince thrashes. Fine strands of silk waft around his head and down his body. They spin and tighten. He opens his mouth to scream and soft fibers fill the orifice and push down his throat. He gags and struggles. His prison cocoon squeezes and firms. Juices flow from his body, and his flesh starts to dissolve.

The sisters croon. "We replicated your metamorphic gland."

They attach the chrysalid that was the prince to the dungeon wall.

In the dark, it weeps golden tears knowing it will emerge a monarch.

THE SPIDER KISS

David Turnbull

"Come into my parlor," said Herr Tarantel.

Adelaide Muffet hovered in the doorway. Her heart fluttered as Tarantel smiled languorously.

"I won't bite," he said and revealed his pointed little teeth as he flicked lank black hair out of his eyes. When he winked, she sizzled under the heat of her blush.

Tarantel closed in on her with a single stride. His legs seemed impossibly long and spindly. He was so uncomfortably close to her that she could actually feel the moist heat that emanated in pulsing waves from his gangly body.

Adelaide swallowed hard and fought for breath.

"Come." He motioned with elongated fingers. "Step inside."

Adelaide stepped into the parlor, as if stepping into the lair of some predatory beast. There was a musky scent in the air. She took a cautious look around. Other than the untidy preponderance of cobwebs hanging from each corner of the room, there seemed nothing untoward.

"Sit." Herr Tarantel's mouth pressed mugginess against her cheek. Adelaide lowered herself on the sofa, and Tarantel sat beside her.

She bowed her head to avoid looking directly at him. His hip touched hers. The pressure made her pulse quicken. She shuffled coyly to one side. Her underskirts rustled embarrassingly. She clasped her fingers together to stop them from trembling.

"I can help you." From the corner of her eye, she watched as Herr Tarantel appraised her. "The program that I have devised has its roots in the fledgling science of hypnotherapy. My results are unfailingly successful."

A small shiver of excitement trembled at the back of her neck.

"My mother thinks I'll never find myself a man if I while all my time away sitting on my tuffet practicing my needlepoint."

Herr Tarantel edged uncomfortably closer. Their hips touched again. The sharp odor of his pungent perspiration went to straight to her head. Adelaide wedged herself firmly against the armrest.

"How old are you?"

She couldn't help but stammer her reply.

"T-thirty-one."

Herr Tarantel sighed as if he'd just heard the saddest news.

"And still a spinster?"

She blushed once more.

"I'm not comfortable in the company of men. My mother worries."

"Frigidity. More common an affliction than you may think."

Adelaide plucked up the courage to ask what she was thinking.

"You can help then?"

"Oh my dear. I am most positive that I can."

An odd tingling danced along Adelaide's spine.

"Turn your head and look at me."

"I couldn't possibly." But she wanted the exact opposite.

His voice grew insistent.

"You must turn your head and look at me."

Shyness caused her to rest her chin coyly on her chest.

"I don't like to."

Tarantel touched her cheek. She almost leapt out of her skin at the shock of the physical contact. He guided her face in his direction. His fingers went pitter-patter down to her chin, and made her face him, eye to eye. She had to swallow down the gasp that almost escaped from her mouth—as his dark pupils quivered and contracted. Her pulse thrummed a frantic tattoo in her ears.

"Relax," said Herr Tarantel. "I am going to count down slowly from one hundred, and I want you to count down with me. One hundred. Ninety-Nine…Ninety-Eight…Ninety-Seven…"

She absently mouthed the numbers with him. "Ninety-Six…Ninety-Five…"

As she did so, her pattering heartbeat slowed.

"Breath in."

Adelaide breathed in.

"Breath out."

And she did as he bade.

"My voice is soothing to you. You can feel your muscles slacken with each deep breath—in and out—slowly, so very, very slowly. Your eyelids are heavy. Close them whenever you're ready."

Her head flopped back to the sofa's soft headrest. Stark images flashed in front of her. Vast multitudes of fat black spiders dropping down on silvery threads from the clusters of webs in the corners. They scrambled across every inch of her: in her hair, her face, the secret folds of her dress.

Might they be searching for entry through buttonholes and half-open zippers?

Herr Tarantel's voice came from far away, his words jumbled and erratic. His hand rested on her lap. Its weight and prickling heat both intrigued and terrified her. Where might it wander to next if left to its own devices?

Her eyes snapped open.

She jerked upright and lunged to her feet.

"I think I had better leave."

She fled.

"Come back, Miss Muffet." Herr Tarantel called after her. "I didn't mean to frighten you away."

"Did you go?" asked her mother when she arrived back home.

"Yes, I went," she said.

"And?"

"Please don't make me go again."

"Why ever not?"

What could she say?

"I found him unsettling."

"Well, the ladies at the Bridge Club swear by him."

The way her mother's little group of friends carried on, you would think that nothing had changed since the revolution. They still met up to gossip and scandalize in the same shameless way. Sour-faced old bats. But Adelaide could imagine that some of them might gain considerable enjoyment from frequenting Tarantel's fusty little parlor.

"Maybe I'm not so easily taken in as the ladies at your Bridge Club. I feel—drained."

"What does that mean? He wasn't inappropriate with you, was he?"

Was he? Had he been? What would disappoint her more, the fact that he had been, or the fact that he hadn't?

"No. It's just that I found his methods rather intense."

Her mother's finely plucked eyebrow went up in that annoying manner of hers.

"I paid for the entire course, you know."

Adeliade drew a slow breath to calm herself.

"You shouldn't have."

"I have to do something. I can't have you hanging around here for the rest of your days. If your father was still alive."

Adelaide bristled with anger as tears flooded her eyes.

"Father would never have sent me to a man like that."

Her mother's upper lip curled into a pout. "I'm at my wits end. You'll never find a husband carrying on the way you do."

Here we go again.

"Maybe I don't need a husband," she said. "Things have changed since your day. There's been a revolution in case you hadn't noticed."

"A woman still needs a husband."

"Fine. I'll go back. And I'll make damned sure that you well and truly get your money's worth."

"Don't curse. It's so un-lady-like."

Adelaide turned her head slightly so that the unbidden smile that had started to curve on her lips would not be so noticeable. There were things that were far more un-lady-like than cursing, and some them would be highly likely to see you damned.

###

"Would you prefer if I didn't sit down beside you on this occasion?" It was the start of their next session. Herr Tarantel prowled by her side, mirroring her every move.

"I think that would indeed be a good idea if you avoided sitting next to me."

His dark gaze wandered from her face to her breasts to her thighs.

"Sit then."

Adelaide sat on the sofa. She pressed her knees firmly together and folded her arms defensively. Herr Tarantel pulled up a chair so that he was seated directly in front of her. His long legs were sprawled wide so that her own were completely fenced in between them. She couldn't help but notice once more that audacious bulge in his trousers. He pulled the chair in closer. The insides of his thighs almost brushed against her knees. The animal smell of him made her breath shiver inside her throat.

"Relax," he said. "You know what we must do now?"

Her shoulders went taut. Her pulse quickened.

"Count down from one hundred, Miss Muffet," said Herr Tarantel "Are you ready?"

She gave him a small nod.

He counted, slowly exhaling each word.

"One-Hundred…Ninety-Nine…Ninety-Eight…"

Adelaide counted with him. "Ninety-Seven. Ninety-Six. Ninety-Five."

She drifted more rapidly than the first time. Now his willing partner, her resistance relinquished. Her eyelids drooped. It felt as if she was slowly being consumed by the cushioned folds of the sofa.

She closed her eyes and drew a deep breath.

Something traced the contours of her face. The delicate touch of Herr Tarantel's fingers? There came a similar sensation along the raised ridge of her shoulder, then another just above her knee, and another around her midriff.

Panic seized her.

She tried snapping herself out of whatever catatonic condition she'd been lulled into. Deep in a dark, dark well, she could not force her eyes open.

Was this actually happening, or was it an illusion?

The caresses enveloped Adelaide—her legs, her arms, her hips, her thighs, her breasts, her back.

How many hands does he have?

How many arms?

The questions dismayed her.

The possible answer delighted her.

The hands fumbled with buttons and untied bows. He nip-nip-nipped at her neck. Not just nipping—another sensation altogether. What could it be? *Inseminating?* Venomous toxins, passed from his saliva into her blood steam, corrupting and subverting it with a seductive ejaculate?

Defend your honor. Her mother's prudish voice nagging in her head had the opposite effect. It actually made her want to capitulate in an act of stubborn defiance.

Exposed, the myriads of scurrying fingers touched her in embarrassingly intimate places, becoming more forceful and urgent. She let out a long, involuntary moan. Had she the nerve, she would have reached around the back of Herr Tarantel's head and pulled him tighter so that he might spit his delicious poison deeper into her veins.

Her fervor was unexpectedly dampened by Herr Tarantel's voice.

"Wake up Miss Muffett. When I snap my fingers you will awaken."

The loud *clicking* of fingers sent its retort into the very essence of her soul. She felt strangely disappointed at the pinprick of light that grew wider as it illuminated the dark pit of the well.

"Miss Muffet, on the count of ten, you will awake. Refreshed and reborn."

The light around her grew.

"One," he counted. "Two. Three. Four."

Her eyes snapped wide on ten.

She sat on the sofa. Fully dressed. Herr Tarantel sat before her. He showed his sharp little teeth. Perhaps, a pinkish stain about them. She searched his dark eyes for a clue as to what had really happened.

"What did you do to me?"

He smiled.

"I have made you anew. Unburdened the weight around you. The chains of frigidity have fallen away. You are a sensual creature, and you will have appetites."

"I will?"

"You are reborn, my dear."

Adelaide waited with forced patience for her next session with Herr Tarantel. Hours and minutes dragged by. She studied her reflection in the mirror. Her complexion had assumed the tainted gray of the corpse, the white of her eyes inebriated red with the wine of ruptured veins, the flesh on her fingers as black as spider legs.

"How perfectly contrary I've become."

For entertainment, she plucked wings from flies and hung their panicking bodies from the gossamer mesh of a spider web draping the dusty corner of her mother's garret, watching lustfully as the long-legged spider came slowly dancing around his prey. When the mood took, she'd pop the panicky little insect torsos into her mouth. Their sour juices oozing down her throat afforded her an invigorating but fleeting sensation.

More aware of her body's sensual curves and swells, she dared to look at herself naked in the mirror and didn't blush or balk. She soaked and caressed herself for hours on end in perfumed bubble baths in an effort to recreate the intensity of the sensations she'd experienced while under Tarantel's strange induced trance.

The day of her next session was almost upon her when her mother returned one evening from the Bridge Club.

"You're not to go back to that terrible man again." She hung her coat in the hall.

"Why ever not? It was your idea in the first place."

"Well, now, I don't want you to go back. I've heard dreadful things—things that are not for your ears."

"I'm over thirty years old."

"Did he touch you?"

Adelaide turned away so that her mother would not question too closely how bloodshot her eyes had become as she attempted to search them for clues.

"He touched my soul."

In ways you will never comprehend.

"Several of the ladies are petitioning to have him denounced by the People's Assembly. I expect that the Commissariat will issue a warrant for his arrest."

"Then I will see him before he is arrested. You paid for the entire course. We don't have that sort of money to waste."

"We'll manage. Besides, I think I may have found a far more appropriate solution to your little problem."

"You have?" said Adelaide.

"Elspeth Bonnington has a recently-widowed cousin." Her mother beamed.

Adelaide wasn't having it.

For once, I intend to be obstinate.

"No. I won't do it."

"The chances of you getting a proposal at your age are slim to say the least."

"Who says I want a proposal? What law demands that I have to be married anyway?"

"Of course you have to be married. It's the done thing. Since you were a little girl, all I've ever dreamt of is your wedding."

"In case you hadn't noticed, there's been a revolution. Women have been liberated."

"He's only fifty-two. And he has a good job in the Ministry of Statistics."

"Fifty-two?" cried Adelaide. "The Ministry of Statistics?"

Elspeth Bonnington's cousin, bald and bespectacled, was also afflicted with an assortment of ailments: halitosis being the least of his worries. His name was Cedric for heaven's sake. He stood a whole head shorter than Adelaide. His eczema blistered and peeled. Standing next to him made her itch.

His position in the Ministry of Statistics involved the same type of work he had carried out for the King in the Royal Counting House before the revolution, only with a different title and purpose.

"Mathematics holds no particular political allegiance." He boasted, during a short but excruciatingly ponderous courtship. "Income and expenditure. Output and productivity. It all adds up to the same thing. Those in power need statistical data upon which to construct their propaganda. No matter what happens, whether the revolution triumphs or collapses, *I*, for one, will never be out of work."

Her mother cried when they exchanged rings.

The rain drizzled in the wind as they left the chapel made the confetti stick to her waxen face. In a fit of rage, she threw her bouquet over her shoulders with such force that none of the scrambling bridesmaids managed to catch it.

Cedric was a hopeless failure in the honeymoon bed—awkward and clumsy, his hands lacking creativity or imagination. Wet-fish kisses against her lips. The hopelessly miniscule thing between his legs was flaccid and spirit-crushing.

Taking control, she guided him where she wanted. He didn't like her clawing at his back with her sharp fingernails. And he was horrified when she sank her teeth into the stringy anemic vein that pulsed deliciously on his scrawny neck.

"I am the first man you've ever been with?"

"I've never been with another *man*."

A month later, Adelaide snuck out of her marital home and made her way across the city. Cedric worked late, and she intended to be back long before he returned with his annoying, finicky ways. She hurried through the streets as if she was on fire. Her ardour had never once cooled since that last session with Herr Tarantel. With Cedric, she would never fulfill her true potential as a sensual and carnal creature.

She wanted the lustful evolution activated within her by Tarantel's venom to progress unfettered and liberated. She imagined counting down from one hundred as Herr Tarantel's multitude of hands explored every inch of her. She wanted at last to scream out loud with unrestrained ecstasy.

Unfortunately, when she reached her destination, a stark *Entry Prohibited* sign hung on the door, bearing the official red seal of the Commissariat. According to the proclamation, Herr Tarantel had been denounced as a counter revolutionary. No doubt the work of the spiteful gossips at the Bridge Club.

She paced nervously.

What she might do now?

A neighbor opened her window and poked her head out. "He's gone away."

Adelaide found herself infused with a slither of optimism.

Perhaps he had made his escape.

"Do you know where?"

The old lady shrugged her podgy shoulders, making her bosoms jiggle.

"Did he leave a forwarding address?"

"The work camps or the firing squad would be a good guess."

Adelaide swallowed down the lump that rose in her throat.

"F-firing squad?"

The old lady let out a peal of laughter. "What is it with all you young girls, anyway? You must be the fifth or sixth I've seen hovering by his door like bitches in heat."

With that, she slammed her window.

Weeks dragged by.

She whittled away her time reading paragraphs from the copy of *The Validation of the Rights Women in the Post-Revolutionary Era* she insisted Cedric buy her as a wedding present. She became a fervent student of its author, Mary X, dissecting her discourse and the minutia of meanings in a single turn of phrase.

One particular paragraph had her returning again and again:

We are expected to stand in line like pretty maids all in a row, waiting obediently for the first man to come along and pluck us up. Perhaps, dear sisters, it is we who should do the plucking. I say that if we are true to the courage of our convictions then anything is possible.

How might she pluck Cedric out of her hair?

She harvested the strips of sticky flypaper she had hung in the kitchen, devouring flies with a passion. But one bite, and they were gone. She already yearned for something more substantial.

Adelaide's attention turned to the adhesive properties of the cobwebs in the corners and the flypapers that hung in the kitchen. Silvery threads of thought weaved themselves into a plan, as intricate as any web, and, to her mind, just as beautiful in its construction.

Over the next week, she soaked lengths of yarn in pots of warm glue and hung the gooey strands diagonally in a corner of the dark basement. She repeated the process with a second set of strands and a third and a fourth, overlapping and interweaving. She constructed a web as exceptional as any accomplished arachnid.

Over the next few days, she found that fishing wire was far more effective in terms of trapping her quarry. The first mouse squeaked and wriggled when she examined the web. The coating of glue held fast to its brown fur. One of its tiny, tremulous paws tangled and twisted in the wires.

She pierced its tiny, beating heart with one of the sharp darning needles from her mother's wedding dowry.

A spray of warm blood splattered her face.

Moaning, she licked it clean before holding the mouse up to let the blood drip-drip-drip into her waiting mouth and wiped the dregs from her chin.

"Cedric," said Adelaide one night some weeks later, when the blood of mice was no longer sufficient to sate her increasingly voracious appetite. "Do you think you could go down to the basement and see if you could find that darning kit my mother gave me?"

Cedric peered at her over the top of his newspaper, his baldness glinting as it reflected the flicker of the fire in the hearth.

"Darning kit?" He scratched the dry, flaky skin behind his ears.

Adelaide nodded. "Needles and yarn and the like."

Cedric folded the paper onto his lap. "What do you want with that?"

"I need to darn something."

"Can't it wait till morning?"

Adelaide nodded to the hole in his sock where his big toe poked through. "I looked in your drawer. They're all like that. Even the heels are worn through on some of them. We can't have you going in to work looking like a pauper."

Cedric scratched behind his ear again and absently wiped away the white flecks of dry skin that tumbled onto his shoulder.

"Still," he said. "It could wait till morning."

Adelaide looked wistfully across at him, using her mother's trick of blinking rapidly to release a tear. "I feel so guilty. Seeing your poor socks in such a state. It's as if I'm neglecting my duties. If only I could make a start on the repairs."

Biting her lip to stop herself grinning she reached up to brush away the fake teardrop as he rose to his feet in a somewhat flustered manner. "Don't take on so, my dear. I'll go and hunt it out right now."

Adelaide waited by the basement door, listening intently to each crick and crack as Cedric slowly descended the stairs. There came a cry of surprise. Adelaide knew that he had walked straight into her trap.

"Come untangle me."

She slammed the door with triumphal glee and went to bed.

Three days went by before she crept down to check upon her prey. By then, Cedric was as weak and dehydrated as the husk of a dying bluebottle. His arms and legs were splayed out across her trap in awkward angles that betrayed the struggles he had endured.

He groaned, looking at her through gummy half-shut eyes. She carved a series of lesions into her husband. The tangy odor of his warm blood made her shudder.

"Revolutions can be internal as well as external," she quoted directly from the works of Mary X. "I am a changed woman. Changed beyond your ken, poor husband."

The spiders inhabiting the dark and shadowed places wove fine silky strands amongst the sections of her construct—webs within webs within webs. As if stimulated now by Adelaide's fearsome presence the spiders scurried back and forth across Cedric's face and arms. Little pink pimples swelled on his flesh from the venom of their kisses.

"Help me. Get me down from here."

"No." At last, this is what it felt like to be *quite contrary*. Her nostrils flared in anticipation of the feast of the senses that was sure to follow. She stole a taste of his blood from the tips of her fingers.

"Are you trying, in some ridiculous manner, to prove a point?" Cedric's scornful demeaning behavior reminded her of the dismissive way her mother used to talk to her.

"You are not my equal."

Within her web, Cedric recoiled in terror.

In complete control, she became the sum of her parts: libido liberated by the attentions of Herr Tarantel and mind liberated by the prose of Mary X.

"You could so easily become *my* equal, Cedric." She stroked his cheek. "For a single exquisite moment, you could be *my* equal in every way. Did you know that frigidity is a common affliction? It clearly burdens you as severely as your other numerous ailments. But I can cure you."

She urgently kissed and bit his neck.

Adelaide unraveled his hand from the web and held it hard against the intimate place where she yearned to be touched—her fingers pressing his fingers deep into expectant grooves. Her mind raced.

I will take many lovers. I am sure there are high-ranking men within the Commissariat who can easily be seduced into lusting after the erotic kiss of a widow.

"Look into my eyes."

Cedric pursed his lips in a pathetic show defiance.

She laughed in his face.

"Count down with me from one hundred, husband. My voice will soothe you." She leaned in so close that the sensual swell of her lips brushed against the narrow slash of his.

"Ninety-Nine. Ninety-Eight. Ninety-Seven…"

THE PRINCE AND THE FERRET
John Little

I marveled at the long blond strands becoming ashen in my hands. How could something so soft seem to burn so black? Her smile grew hungry, dangerous, and small things from the corner of my eyes watched us, things of fur and feather. They waited, ready and tense, like my own taut muscles.

Her back arched, and a shudder went up her spine, her eyes flashing from blue to a deep violet as the tremors reached the base of her neck. She'd been so soft, so sweet, so bright when I found her, and so warm and joyous when our carriage wheeled away from the castle, but not now, now she was—

"I'm still me, my prince." She peered deep into my eyes, still stirring, twisting, playing with something deep in my chest with her gaze, like I was an ocean and she a storm. "Truly me, more so than ever before."

The next morning, a bright beam of sunlight woke me. My empty bed momentarily confused me, making the memories of the previous day seem a dream.

Had I married?

Had her hair turned black in my hands?

I blinked the sun out of my eyes and pulled the sheets around me, shivering in a draft. I shaded my vision and jumped when I found her sitting at the writing desk across the room. A pen moved without her hand, and she sat in her night gown, left leg crossed over the right, smiling that dangerous smile that I'd not seen until our first night together. Her hair was still cinder black.

"What are you writing?" My tone notably calmer than my palpating heart would have preferred. I'd seen magic before; it flocked to royalty like beggars to a baker's shop. Still, I hadn't been expecting it.

"Something colorful and not entirely untrue." She took a bite of a dark red apple that she'd pulled from a bowl on the desk.

Had those been there before?

"I've felt bitten by a writing bug, a hobby I've never had time for." She dropped the apple to the table, where something black scurried and snatched it up, a mouse?

I narrowed my eyes looking for it, but she obscured my view as she approached, and my gaze drew to hers, those perfectly violet orbs. She reached the bed and crawled towards me, her mouth meeting mine hungrily.

"You've no idea how happy this makes me," she said, laying a hand on my chest and pushing me down.

The pen never stopped writing.

The rest of honeymoon went quickly; we took walks through the woods of the small estate we'd rented to be alone, other than the servants. The proprietors kept several well managed ponds; on these, we launched small boats and lounged comfortably reading stories. Sometimes, she read me bits of her writing, a memoir she told me. I'd agreed that she had a story worth sharing and hung on every word, guilty that I hadn't known the first thing about her history before I'd married her. The ball led me to believe she was a rich, enchanting beauty, though somehow different than what I'd been seen before, which I will admit captivated me.

When I found her at her step-mother's home, I'd apparently seen her more regular attire. The truth of her family's nature slapped me hard. She amazed me with how sweet she'd been, and it made present circumstances more transparent, though I was still missing something.

"After my stepmother and step-sisters ripped my dress to pieces, I'd given up. My chances of going to the ball, at meeting the prince, were dashed. That is, until my godmother appeared…" She stopped reading "What is it, my prince?"

"Your godmother? I haven't heard of any such person."

"Oh, I haven't mentioned her?" That dagger of a smile returned, short and sharp.

"She's whom I have to thank for this." She ran her fingers through her dark hair, and then made a luxurious gesture around her, finishing with my chin in her hand. "And this, too, I imagine."

"So, she was of the magical variety then?" Maintaining my relaxed posture grew painfully awkward with how fast my heart beat.

"Quite and very." Her fingers broke away from me and graced the water, making it bubble and boil.

"A wish then?" I'd heard of such things, reminding me of old mummers stories, and distant family history.

"Indeed, though don't fear, I didn't put any glamour on you or myself. I just wanted my dress, that's all." She leaned back as the sky darkened.

I wasn't sure if I believed her. I didn't feel like I was under any sort of spell, but wasn't that point?

"At least, that's what I'm going to tell the world." She tapped her journal.

Right. A story. My senses became more acute with panic, the sudden sharp and pungent smell of the duck pond. A wind chilled the sweat at my temples, and the wooden paddles of the small boat dug their grain into the skin of my palms, it helped me keep my head. "So, I *am* under a spell?"

"Oh, not really." She said, her eyes dancing like tiny violet fires that ate and laughed at her words. Her dress clung to her curves as she reached forward with an open black nailed hand and laid it on my chest.

My heart skipped a beat, and the world seemed to spin on a different axis for an interminably long moment. When she leaned away again all that remained was a vague stirring that filled in my chest.

"Just a small one. You wouldn't even notice the difference." She made a gesture towards the shore, and I rowed.

The honeymoon over, we returned to the palace, and the valet announced us as we entered the main hall. I could almost hear the cracks of all the spinning heads. Our arrival was met by scores of confused expressions, from servants and relatives alike, and I couldn't blame them. She did look quite different now, but despite the hair and the smile, her frame and face gave her away as the woman I'd married.

My mother approached at once without care for any sort of decorum, which wasn't a surprise.

"You've changed your hair." She sniffed at my wife, her customary long furs wrapped about her, and her expression only a little less than severe. "I wonder at how you did it, wasn't it blond before?"

"Old family recipe," said my wife with a warm-hearted smile. I wasn't aware she could still do that. "A few dyes, some hard scrubbing, a bit of cinder, and everything comes out black."

"I see." My mother deflated a little. Whatever she'd been expecting, my wife's sudden warmth seemed to have disarmed her. A skill that I envied. My mother sniffed again before taking my arm. "Well, how was your trip?"

"Tiring." I said without pause, exhausted. Despite the pleasures of the honeymoon, my nerves had climbed daily as I became increasingly paranoid that I was not myself, and that I'd somehow been tricked into marriage. The worst part was that I hadn't felt tricked, and that I quite honestly held deep love for my wife. Truly, how did one handle the feelings of love with no certainty of their authenticity?

I must have looked as gruesome as I felt, judging by my mother's sour expression.

"I can see that, dear." She ushered us into a small sitting room just off the main hall. "Please sit, you look dreadful. I had a feast prepared for your arrival, but it can wait till later, or tomorrow even, if you're—oh for heaven's sake. Sit down."

I'd thought she was speaking to me for a moment, but I'd already made myself comfortable in a chair with a glass of brandy in hand.

No, she'd been speaking to my wife.

"I know you aren't used to these sort of things, but don't gawk. It's just a sitting room." My mother had apparently slipped past my wife's earlier charm, easily settling back into berating Cinderella. Honestly, she wasn't the queen anymore…but Cinderella *was* staring open-mouthed at the room's painted ceiling—a beautiful beach landscape in all blue and whites.

"It's so…so…"

"Yes dear, I know it's lovely but—"

"Tall. It's so tall." Cinderella made strange grasping motions with her hands as she said it, as if she would bring the ceiling down with a pull. I steadied myself, ready for the crumbling rock and plaster. "It's taller even than the dining room at my father's home."

"I see." My mother gave me a look as severe as I'd ever received. "And this is so fascinating, why?"

I shrugged.

"How do you clean it?" Cinderella examined the top of a large cupboard that sat against the wall, pieces of china and whatnots arrayed across its top.

I blinked and almost spilled my drink when something small and furry ran between two plates painted like gulls. I waited for it to scurry again. My wife's friends didn't take long to move in.

"Why, with a dust broom I would imagine…why? Are you going to clean it?"

I winced.

"No, I won't." My wife's violet eyes flared. Quickly I stood, ready to leap between them. My wife had become a pit viper, or a fire breathing dragon, while my mother, hunched as she was and wrapped in her gray furs, an emaciated field mouse. "I won't be cleaning anything. Not ever again. Not so long as I live."

Something whirled and tightened in my chest.

I really was too tired for this.

"Mother, send for the butler." I said, falling back into my chair, somehow still holding my brandy.

"I beg your pardon?" She huffed crossing her arms. "When did I become a house maid? Send your darling wife, I'm sure she's—"

"Mother. I am tired, and so is my wife." I slammed down my glass on a small side table. "I don't want to embarrass you any further, so would you please see your way out, and in doing so send in the butler."

I dismissed my mother.

One of my wife's familiars danced about the top of the cupboard as I spoke, and my mother made a less-than-graceful exit.

The head butler was a tall, sharp-eyed fellow with chestnut hair and a difficult smile, which wasn't to say he was unfriendly. He simply didn't smile unless he was sure it prudent. It made him hawkish, but he was a good man.

"You called, your grace?" He bowed low.

"Yes, Walter, could you tell me if our belongings are along?"

"They are already taken care of, sire." He spared the quickest of glances towards my wife. I'd known Walter since I was a young boy, his opinion was seldom granted without prying but always proved invaluable. When I had a moment, I'd have his thoughts of Cinderella.

"If sire is feeling unwell, would he prefer I send the guests home?" From anyone else the question would have been presumptive, but Walter knew his business, and mine.

"No, no, let them have their feast and their gossip, that was why they really came, besides it will ruffle mother." I finished my glass. Walter tried to refill it, but I feared my inability to walk after another. "When is it supposed to start?"

"That would be in fifteen minutes, your grace."

"Very well, the queen and I will be retiring, see that no one—"

"I will not." My wife lay her hand on my shoulder. I waited for the twisting in my chest, but it didn't come. "I want to go to this feast. Other than your wonderful mother, I haven't met any of your friends or family."

Only earnest amusement appeared in her eyes. She did seem so gentle now, it almost made me feel...

Something skittered off to the right, and I remembered how she'd been prepared to disembowel my mother. A deep breath helped me collect my frayed nerves. My wife was proving much more trouble than I bargained for. My father had warned me about marriage, but he might have mentioned the part about dark magics and mind control.

"My dear, I am beyond exhausted, but if you wish, I will forestall my collapse so you may mingle." I groaned as I stood, my head heavy from the brandy, my limbs like bars of lead. So much had happened in such a short time, even for an ordinary man. The pageantry of the wedding had taken its own price, and to follow it with the revelation of a witchy wife, well, could anyone expect me not to be tired?

As I stood she suddenly spun herself into my arms and gave me a quick peck on the cheek. "Better?"

"Yes, dear. I feel much better." I lied, trying to assuage her guilt, but then…yes, after a moment, I actually *did* feel better. My lungs seemed to pull in more air, and my muscles didn't feel their own weight anymore. My head cleared like a storm blown over, and I was suddenly refreshed. Astonished, I reveled in the new-found clarity.

I looked at her expectantly for an explanation, to which she merely shrugged before spinning back out of my arms.

"Why hadn't you done that sooner?"

She ignored me and introduced herself to Walter.

I winced as she took one his hands in hers.

"It's my pleasure, your majesty." Walter gritted his teeth, momentarily pained by the break in propriety, but he recovered quickly. "I hope to be of the utmost service to you."

"I'm sure you'll be terrific." She said warmly, her expression seeming earnest. Still, I frowned as the light flickered in the room, had something flown by the window?

"Plenty of time for that later, Walter." I put my arm through Cinderella's. "We've a dinner to attend."

"Quite right, sire." Walter bowed low before running ahead of us. "I'll send someone ahead to inform your mother."

"Right." I took another deep breath and ignored the small creature that darted out the door. "Once more into the breach then."

"It won't be as bad as that." Cinderella pulled closer. "It's *your* family after all, and how *bad* could they be?"

The dinner went well, no one having become quite drunk enough yet to violate the armor of etiquette. The plates were cleared away, and tables emptied as guests filled the ballroom. The same ball room where I first laid eyes on my wife; the same room where my relatives were proving how *bad* they could be, given full glasses of wine and what they thought was fresh blood.

"I'm just saying that it's strange that she change her hair before the honeymoon is through." Cousin Bertrand, a narrow faced weevil if I've ever met one, said across the table. We'd been pals in childhood, more out of kindness than obligation or desire. His wife had an affair with their butler within a month of their marriage, which gave Bertrand the mind to give me whatever warnings he could. I would have cared more, if he hadn't been sleeping with a housemaid.

"I appreciate your concern, but I find her as beautiful as they day I met her. In this, I am willing to grant her whatever peculiarities she's inclined." I faked a drink from my glass. The servants had been fastidious about keeping it filled, but I was determined to keep my wits about me now that I had them again. With Cinderella mingling on her own, I needed to keep a sober eye upon her if I wanted to avoid disaster. "Did I tell you she's a writer? She writes in her journal nigh constantly. It's very impressive."

"Most women are and do." Cousin Silas took a liberal swig of his glass. "I've met few in our circles that don't whittle away their time behind a book and quill. Sure, they may vary in their arts—painting, drawing, singing, music. They indulge in one or all of these, but they are invariably all writers of one kind or another, so unless you find the common to be uncommon, I don't see your point in blathering on about it."

"What a long-winded way of disagreeing." I frowned. Silas was much in the same position as myself, only without a wife; a prince in another kingdom who was waiting for his father to die. If Bertrand was a weevil, Silas was a ferret; with handsome features, a cunning smile, and wavy dark hair, he was sleek, smart, and a great deal more predatory but still a parasite. "And that reminds me, how *is* your father?"

"The picture of health, would that he were framed, so I could add a bit of green or red to his canvas." He took another drink and motioned for one of the servants to refill his glass. In the changing light, his cheeks reddened, and I made a covert motion to the servant not to refill Silas's glass again. He was bad enough when he wasn't searching for the bottom of a bottle. Despite my dislike for him, I couldn't allow the thin veil around his threats to be pulled away, not in public. Silas grinned wolfishly with his last glass of my brandy. On Silas, the expression was less lascivious, and more like a butcher sharpening a knife before a goose. "So, how does it feel to be king?"

"I couldn't say I know, not yet." I expected more from his expression. Maybe he'd drunk enough to be civil or, at least, misjudge his threats. "I've only held the position for a few weeks, and most of that time my mother has been acting in my stead. Though I should think—"

"My apologies, but your drink is so good I'm forgetting my words. What I meant was, how does it feel to be a king…" Another drink, his weasel face curving around his glass. "With a commoner queen."

"She's not a commoner." My words were calm, but my grip tightened on my brandy. "She's from a noble family."

"Though not a royal one?" Silas folded his arms, eyes widening in anticipation. This was the knife he'd been sharpening, my wife the goose. "Quite a drop if you ask me, from royal to noble. They didn't even have a full staff, I hear."

"Silas." My face and neck burned. "You're treading dangerously."

"Am I?" He finished his drink in one long gulp and dropped it unceremoniously onto a passing servant's tray, gesturing for them to refill it. "Don't your family, your friends, have a right to know? Know that your *noble wife*, your *queen*, came from a house with only *one* servant?"

My throat went dry, my anger pumping hot in my veins. "Don't."

"Don't? Don't what, *your grace*? Don't ask why when Cinderella appeared at the ball, that her family didn't have any servants at all. Or even the greater question, why she is called *Cinderella*? What kind of noble woman announces her stains with her very name?" He drank from another glass of brandy, one I'd expressly forbade my servants from offering him. "I dare say, it must feel *very* good to be king, if you can so easily ignore the shame of marrying a chimney sweep."

"You dare." I slammed my glass on a small table, the sound of glass crashing against the metallic tray silencing the room, though I could barely hear it over the torrent of angry blood in my ears. "I don't care how drunk you are. I'll have your—" I stopped, my breath thickening around the sudden whirl of vertigo and deepening pull in my chest.

"Being a servant has its benefits." Cinderella handed the tray and bottle of brandy to a passing footman. My anger collided with the sudden shock of seeing her, liquefying all the rage in my veins into adrenaline. I'd become bottled lightning: patient, latent, ready to burst at the slightest disturbance, my mind racing trying to understand. Had she been standing there the whole time? I hadn't even glanced at her as she filled my cousin's glass.

"They have an uncanny ability of being everywhere without ever being noticed. By their very nature, they are forgotten until they make a mistake. This is only compounded when masters take credit for a servant's work, since it further encourages everyone to ignore the servant's existence." A wild and dangerous undercurrent swept through her. "As *I* am inclined to ignore *your* existence, cousin."

"Your *majesty*." Silas said before belching and blowing liquored breath into Cinderella's face. "I'm only saying what everyone else is too afraid to, and if you think *you're* frightening me, you're greatly mis—"

Silas yowled, nearly jumping out of his skin as he danced about swearing and slapping at his leg.

"God's Bones. Something bit me." He slapped himself if he caught fire, until something small and furry dropped out of his trousers and darted across the room. "Did you see that. A rat. You keep rats in your home, cousin?"

No one seemed to have seen the creature. They had, however, seen Silas's episode. Walter bustled over, weaving expertly between small and large groups, his expression as unreadable as ever. When he reached my side, he bent, waiting my directions.

"Sire?"

"Walter, my cousin has had too much to drink, and I fear he may have indulged in some other form of recreation prior to dinner. Could you see him to his room?"

"Oh no. You're not shooing me away like the common rabble." Silas stumbled, his suit askew and one leg rolled up past his knee. A small bite dribbled blood around his calf. Walter took Silas's arm, acting as though the man leant on him. Silas fought for a moment, but his eyes drooped and his face turned sheet white.

On his way out, Silas vomited in one of the vases.

After the feast was well and done, I grew quite exhausted again and glad to close the door to our rooms behind me. Cinderella stood out on the balcony, talking to someone, but when I approached, she was alone. Though, was that the sound of flapping wings?

"Quite a lively one that Silas. I didn't know you had such weasels in your family."

The night darkened as the sun set.

"Ferret." I said, pulling her close. A sudden torrent of whispering flowed into the back of my mind, each desperate, each wanting me to ask difficult questions, ask about spells, about things that skittered and flew, to ask after my own heart. I ignored them. "Silas is a ferret, not a weasel, he's too full of himself to be a weasel."

"Too fat you mean?" She twirled a finger in her hair, that devilish smile appearing on her face again.

"I wouldn't call him fat, maybe pigheaded."

"I would. I call him a big, fat, greasy ferret." She twined her arms together and stretched, the motion making her dark hair flair out behind her, the wind picking it up in a sudden cold breeze. Her breath came out in a thick cloud as she laughed, drawing circles in the air with her fingers. I marveled at her beauty, the thrill of it, the sudden frost in the wind prickling my skin and tearing my eyes. She looked at me, her eyes shifting from wickedly dark, to loving, brimming a with a radiant warmth despite the chill. "I enjoyed myself tonight."

"Honestly?" I pulled her towards me, her racing heart beating against my chest like a small bird, her excitement goosepimpling visibly across her arms and chest, even in the waning light. I surprised myself by laughing, "I thought that Silas might have ruined it for you."

"Hardly, he might have made the evening." She leaned against me, her hand reaching back through my jacket. "Besides, it was wonderful watching your mother try and explain away what happened. Something about combat fatigue and poorly administered medications? Like Silas ever did anything in the Army."

Her skin warmed mine against the chill, and my heart twisted and melted without pain for the first time, my muscles relaxing instead of tearing. I breathed easily, she was acting like herself again, the nervous woman I'd met the night at the ball, the one just as real and scared as I was, the one I'd fallen for. "Are all the evenings here this wonderful?"

"I should hope so." I hushed a distant dying whisper and leaned down to kiss her soft lips. After a time, we separated, breathing heavily, and watched the last rays of light shift away into the horizon.

###

I woke early the next morning, determined to greet my guests with twice the energy I had shown the previous night. I needed to see what, if any, damage was done by Silas's outburst, though I wasn't going to let that spot ruin the coming day. Still, should he neither repent nor apologize for his actions, he would be removed. I wouldn't tolerate such flagrant mockery of my queen. I said as much to Walter as he helped me dress, he of course proved as taciturn as ever.

"Quite, your grace." He ran a brush over my shoulders.

"Really, Walter? Is that all you ever have to say?" I turned as he adjusted my collar. "I'm beginning to think you've become a bit of a parrot in your old age."

"Quite, sire."

"Damn it man, now you're just being cheeky." I inspected myself in the mirror, a familiar tall, dark haired, modestly muscled man looking back. I'd always admired my father's steely blue eyes, and I was glad to inherit them. "If you're not careful, I might suspect your tight lips an elaborate joke."

"I would never, sire." A razor thin smile flicker across Walter's lips. We both knew what he was about, but that understanding is what made us as close to friends as we could be. He stepped away then so that I could not see his expression, though he would say he did not wish to obstruct my reflection. "I simply do not wish to speak above my station."

"Ah, but you're forgetting, Walter." I gestured to the ornate golden box to my right. He lifted the led with care and placed the crown perfectly. The image in the mirror took me aback, I had yet to see myself wearing it and was surprised at how much I resembled my father with it on. When had I learned to recognize it as a part of his very person? As if it were akin to his stature? Or the color of his hair? It felt heavier than the one I'd worn as a prince, though that could have just been my imagination.

"Sire?" Walter's concern brought me blinking back. My expression grew pale and distant. I clapped my face with both hands to bring some color back to my cheeks, and turned to him.

"I'm fine, Walter." I grasped his shoulder. "And your forgetting that you are the butler to a king now. I'd say that's better than being a reviled second cousin, even if he is a prince."

"Sire will understand if I refrain from comment."

"I would." I gestured for Walter to shut the door, before I motioned him closer, though I knew whispering would do no good against my wife and her familiars, still I spoke quietly for Walter's sake. "So, what do you think of my wife?"

"Her majesty is perfection, your grace." Walter's appropriate response, but I wanted his true thoughts.

"Yes, yes, majestic wonders will never cease in her gentle movements, and her skin would make Aphrodite rip and tear out her eyes, and all those other praises that you're supposed to heap upon her—but tell me, Walter. What do *you* think?" I whispered the question more energeticly than I meant, but hopefully, it would spurn Walter to answer.

"I think she's lovely, sire."

His sharp eyes more friendly than servile, this is what I wanted.

"She seems to be everything your grace had hoped for, and more." He paused, brow furrowed, his set jaw showing he was forming his words carefully. "If her handling of your mother was any inclination of her superior character, then the way she handled Silas was god's proclamation, if you don't mind my saying so, your grace."

He bowed low at this, and I knew I would get no more out of him.

"Good, I'm glad you think so." Walter's agreement eased my mind, so I turned to my day's activities. "Has anyone called on us yet this morning?"

"No, sire." Walter walked to the hallway door.

"I suppose it is still early, if you would call my mother, I have something to—"

An urgent knock made both Walter and I jump, his hand having been mere inches from the handle. We shared a glance, he cracked the door open to speak with the early messenger. To my surprise, my cousin Metsa, Silas's sister, stepped through. She had the same wavy dark hair as her brother, but none of his ferret features; she was rounder in the face like their mother, and frankly, not cut of the same cloth as her older brother. Her most distinguishing feature was her large leaf-green eyes, which always made her look haunted despite how beautiful they were. I choked seeing those eyes that morning, the whites red from crying, the green leaves wilted.

"You've got to come." Metsa pleaded, pulling on my sleeve. "I don't know what's happened to him, but you've got to come."

"Metsa? Has something happened to Silas?"

"Just *come*. I don't know how much time we have…I—oh god." She covered to her mouth and let out a cry before dashing back out of the room.

Something had me expecting blood, but nothing would have prepared me for the fur. I was glad I left Mesta in the hall.

Thick black clumps of greasy animal hair lay strewn about Silas's room, and blood puddled within inches of each clump.

He laid rasping in his bed, his white nightclothes covered in torn holes and sprays of red, thick black fur crowding most of his body, and I shuddered as it slowly crept up his neck, like a living plague that grew thick wiry spires from the flesh.

The squat, mustached family doctor stood to one side of the mangled bed, his white clothes stained with blood, expression grim.

"This is well beyond me, your grace." He waddled towards the small case on the chair behind him, replaced the few bloody instruments, and closed it with a snap. "I'm a doctor, not a wizard, and this is clearly magic, not some sort of disease."

"Isn't lycanthropy a disease?" My mind focused on semantics instead of the crisis at hand, anything to pull it away from what I was seeing.

"If you want to pick nits, your grace. It is a disease, but a magical one. Magic that behaves like a sickness is typically considered a curse." His gaze was hard but tired, softening a little as Silas writhed on the bed, and in a quiet voice, he said, "I'm not entirely sure it's lycanthropy either. I've seen that before working in a small village to the north, and those poor people looked nothing like this."

"How do you mean?" I pulled him farther out of the room. "He's clearly turning into something, isn't he?"

"Yes, but look at him." He didn't as though he had enough of the sight. "Does he look like any dog or wolf you've ever seen? The way his head is changing, and those teeth, he looks more like a weasel than a wolf."

"A weasel…or a ferret." My mind balked at the thought, this was becoming disgustingly familiar.

"Your grace? If there's anything you know—"

"No. Nothing. Thank you. I can see you've done all you can, you may go."

The bloodied doctor left, his clothes and hair a gory mess. I hadn't considered before how much of that blood was his. Seeing that the doctor had done all he could my mind shifted to whom I could summon to help in this situation, and I didn't like my options. The only wizard was a day's ride away, meaning between sending a message and making his way here, it would take two days for him to arrive. I doubted that Silas would last that long. By now, the fur had filled in around his elongating face, and his eyes shifted into soft opals.

Silas let out a fierce growl and bit down on his own arm with new sharpened teeth. He looked, confused, his eyes somewhere between human and animal, then he rent free a chunk of flesh and fur. The wound was deep, burbling up blood. Silas angrily chewed his own flesh before terrible understanding and pain seemed to come over him. He screamed and spat the bloody mess onto the floor, his chest heaving with the anguish.

"For the love of god."

I held his arms down so he couldn't hurt himself anymore.

"Why hasn't he been restrained?"

His razor teeth buried themselves into my right arm. I froze, and to my relief, so did he. I prayed silently as I unclasped his arms. Breaking into a cold sweat, I stepped away when he unseated his fangs from my flesh, blood blossoming through the holes in my sleeve. Nothing about Silas seemed human anymore except for shape of his body, it was proportional to a man, but even that was quickly changing, his arms, legs, and head elongating, becoming distinctly more ferret like.

A hand pulled gently on my shoulder, and I followed without thought, soon finding myself seated across from Cinderella. She wore a dress so deep a violet that it was almost black, her long hair up in a braid. I marveled at her beauty, at her poise, at her warmth. It didn't feel right though, my mind foggy, displaced somehow.

My reddening sleeve dripped a puddle on the floor. A rat hid under a chair, lapping up the blood as it fell.

Cinderella tsked and reached for my arm, I pulled away to keep her from soiling her with my blood, but she grabbed tight.

Fear and confusion swam away, replaced with neat and tidy thoughts, ones with such clear sharp edges that I could have cut myself on them. The problem with these thoughts was that while I was thinking them, I wasn't believing. It gave me a kind of internal double vision, and brought on an entirely new kind of sickness.

I groped with both my hands for something to hold onto, and found that not only had my arm been mended, but my sleeve too. The puddle of blood was gone as well, though the rat wasn't.

"That was a foolish thing you did." Cinderella rubbed the hand of my new arm. "I understand that you were trying to help, but you must think of his nature now. Before he bit at you with words, not caring how much your heart bled for it, wouldn't he now do the same to flesh?"

Impossible to ignore her words, they reverberated in my mind, pushing out other thoughts, but I wouldn't let them, I—

She smiled.

Oh, how she smiled.

My thoughts evaporated.

Her violet eyes danced like flames behind glass, and the room grew dark around me, like it was just the two of us.

"Isn't this fun?"

"You did this then?" The small fragment of thought left in my mind asked. "I knew you must have…when I realized he looked like a ferret I remembered what you said."

"I see, you've managed to put your mind back together, at least a little bit." Her hand twisted and spun near my chest, pulling on something and chocking off my thoughts.

I became blank, seeing and feeling, but only thinking when she let me.

I could just barely see tiny strings from the tips of her fingers.

Where did they go?

"Don't you think Silas is getting what he deserves? What everyone deserves? To see him for what he really is?"

"Coming from you, that's quite a treat." Where did those words come from? I wasn't aware I'd been thinking them, and how they insulted my wife poked at my anger. "As if you care about other people or their desires."

"I didn't say their desires." She sneered as her the hand twisted violently. I could see the strings now; they glistened a faint red, and seemed to be arching from my chest. "I was talking about what they deserved. What you all deserve. Those born with titles and wealth, acting as if they were so much more honorable, so much better than everyone else. Yet, when misfortune falls, they'll even throw their own to the wolves."

I wept at her words.

I wanted to tear off my ears.

She was right. Her own family had treated her so horribly, but somehow, she managed to stay cheerful, warm and caring; throughout all of it, she remained a gentle soul. Somehow, she—

"When did it happen? Was it after we were married? When your father died? When they took your favorite bear away?"

"I've already told you. Though I won't blame you for missing it." She took on the impression of a distressed damsel and cried. "It was when my *wicked* step-mother tore my dress to pieces. And smashed my friends to bits. And then my fairy god mother came."

"I hadn't heard about her killing your friends…so you had a bit of magic before…but the question is, what did you wish for?" My dopplegänger asked. His expression was dark and serious, and with a massive hole in his chest. He sat just to my left, almost out of my sight, and he stayed there no matter how far I looked.

"She stomped on them." Cinderella shook, the flames of her eyes roaring. "My mice and chipmunks. She dug her heels into them, grinding their blood and bones into my torn up dress. My birds tried to help, to stop her, but she broke their necks, and left them crumpled on the floor."

"The wish?" he asked, no trace of my open weeping in his voice.

"I wished for revenge." She said sweetly, uncrossing and crossing her legs. "And for the power to do it, I didn't want anyone, or anything, deciding how or what was to be done."

"What did you do?" He stood, finally stepping into view. The hole in his chest let me see her through it as he moved.

"I killed them." Her features grew wicked.

I remembered it, that deadly dangerous look from our wedding night. I'd forgotten about it, but I could see it now.

"It shows how much the nobles care that no one noticed when a storm of black wings, claws, and broken beaks swarmed the mansion. You know they screamed and screamed, and nobody cared? Weeks now, and still nobody has said a word."

The other me sat down through me—into me, became me, and the strings pulled free from my chest, taking my heart with them. I now bore that hole, and I understood, terribly and truly.

"You're not free, you know." She held the pulsing thing in her hand. "Really, you're worse off than you were before."

"I know."

The room slowly lightened, and I heard the vicious growls and barks of what had once been my cousin. He was shrinking in his clothes, the hole ridden sleeves and blood soaked pants rapidly becoming too large for him. I looked at him dispassionately, seeing him for what he was, an animal in the trappings of a man. He hadn't deserved this, but it suited him.

The first thing I saw when stepping back into the hall was Mesta's tear stained face, her hopeful expression making me want to laugh, still, I could still affect the emotions of a kind king. I put on a mask of warmth, of feeling, and ushered her away from the door, making sure to shut it quickly so that she could not see into the room. I wept with her when I said that there was nothing we could do except hope he'd live until the wizard came. I told her that, no, she should not visit him, and by no means should she open the door just to look. There was no telling what he might do, and we didn't want him to pass his curse onto anyone else.

"I promise, I will let you know if there's any change." I held her hand until a maid came by, and she was helped back to her rooms, where, yes, I would send a message as soon as I knew anything. As soon as she left my sight, I dropped the mask, her distant sobs awoke no feeling in me, like the ring of a bell in a distant room. It had nothing to do with me.

The door open behind me and a large rat ran across my foot. Cinderella wouldn't be far behind.

"You did this to yourself you know," she said.

For the first time, I got a good look at her.

She was beautiful and horrible, like a marble statue covered in black ash and bile. She laughed at my scowl.

"I was content to let you be happy, but stupid. It would have worked out the best for the both of us. I could even send you back to that, but only if you wanted. I can't force you."

"How kind of you." I walked but a few mere steps before a great weight held me in place.

"Don't think you have your freedom." She stepped next to me and whispered into my ear. "You've just traded your heart for your mind."

"At least there's still proof that I had one."

Another rat ran by, this one was longer, with a strange, loping gate. Frowning, something stabbed me in my chest as I reached out towards it.

"Now, now. You don't get to feel."

It rounded a corner to a woman's scream.

Cinderella must have healed his wounds after I left the room, but my mother had stepped on the Silas ferret as it came around the corner, crushing it into an irreparable heap. It breathed its last breaths as my mother fanned herself.

"We really need a way to be rid of these pests." Mother settled herself into a nearby chair.

Cinderella's face grew crimson, such a reenactment must have brought up bad memories.

I reveled in it.

This is how she'd done it; how she'd smiled so many times despite being so dead inside.

After all, you didn't need a heart to feel wicked.

A ROYAL AFFAIR

E. M. Eastick

You will be sorry when they find the body—swollen and putrid, the eyes sucked out by sirens, and the limbs chewed up by sea serpents—washed up on the beach two miles from our perfect castle overlooking the wrecks in the bay. As damp and musty as it is, I thought we would grow old in that place, with little princes and princesses running and laughing and begging to keep the stray elves that sometimes wander into the village from the enchanted forest.

But now, the royal sheets stink of betrayal, and the tapestries loom with secrets. Did you think I did not know? That I had not smelled the dragon blood from a recent conquest or seen the muddy footprints on the stairs? It must be Sir Hendaman. You always did think his jokes were amusing, even when they clearly were not. He is such a weasel. How could you?

A wave flicks up and slaps my face, stinging my eyes in a final appeal: *Are you sure about this, your majesty?* The stones, like goiters down my breeches, clink the reply: *Upon my word, I'm sure.*

The sand oozes through my toes, and I find it difficult to walk. I wish I had kept my slippers on. The water is cold around my chest as my tunic rises like a cloud around my shoulders. The air bubble escapes with a disgusted huff. My throat constricts from the chill, and I wheeze in air mixed with salty spray. The sea rushes into my mouth, my ears, my brain, so quickly that I inhale sharply. The current tugs me off my feet. My lungs scream.

This is it. Farewell my lying, conniving, cheating devil queen. My limbs slacken, loose and free, my whole existence dissolving like mud.

I am vaguely aware of pain, but not in my head or lungs. Something grips around my torso. A kraken? This close to shore? I slap and punch and claw at the vise around my ribs. Be gone, kraken, and let me die with dignity. But what I grab is not the slippery tentacles of a monster. Seaweed? Or hair, perhaps?

It drags me on but not out to sea. It drags me to the shallows, back to life, back to lies. How can I rule with a shattered soul? How can I even bare to exist?

My toes scramble in the doughy sand, and my weight returns. On hands and knees, buckled by the strength of its pull, I tumble up the beach and over shells, which prod and poke like accusing fingers. Shame on my cowardice. Shame on deserting my treacherous kingdom. My lungs spew water and gulp in the smell of rotten eggs.

Through coughs and burning eyes, I see a mountain of hair, black and shaggy, and hear the chuffing breath of a large animal. A dog? Saved by a dog?

My destiny has spoken. I will sentence Sir Hendaman to death and reclaim my bride. Of course, I will. I am King, after all.

"Come, boy."

The voice I know and adore. My queen, my sweet Cindi, has come to save me. With Sir Hendaman out of the way, she will stay loyal and fair, I know she will. She's always been fond of animals, but from where did she get a dog?

As my vision clears, I see my renewed faith evaporating with the seawater vapor rising from the dog's back. The giant, stinking cur smolders and sizzles. The eyes are fire; the teeth scalpels black with blood. The beast seems not to care for his mistress's call as red saliva dribbles through growling lips.

I close my eyes and listen to her call. "Cerberus, come." And yet, the stench grows stronger, and the growl grows louder.

I have judged poorly—an unfavorable trait for a king. It seems the queen has not partnered with Sir Hendaman after all. She has fallen for someone much worse.

DRIZELLA
David J. Gibbs

"Driz? What are you doing up here all by yourself?"

"Well where should I be, downstairs with you and mother? No thanks. You two are exhausting, and besides, I'm tired of all of this pretending crap."

Her sister gasped. "A lady doesn't—"

"Shit in the woods? Of course a lady does, Anastasia. It's not just for bears anymore. What is wrong with you?"

"You are a lost cause. That mouth will get you in trouble. I came up here to see how you were, and you treat me like dirt. There's no need to be mean."

"There's always a need."

Anastasia folded her arms in front of her and rolled her eyes. Driz brushed her hair, in front of the window facing the castle in the distance. Always there, a monolithic reminder of everything she wasn't. All the time she'd spent making herself a proper lady had been a waste. Binding her feet so they were less mannish, as her mother described them, had done nothing save crippling her. And, for what? Even with that archaic practice, her disfigured hoof didn't fit into the precious, glass slipper, losing her one real chance at royalty.

Her anger, bubbling below the surface built to a numbing froth at the reminder of her failed attempt to ensnare a truly good man, as if she were nothing short of a lost cause. No man was the least bit interested in her as a wife, and everyone knew it.

Her mother, however, was still consumed with pairing her with the most eligible bachelors in the county. They scraped the bottom of the barrel for longer than she cared to admit. It was hopeless. Her nose was a bit too big and bulbous while her chest wasn't near big enough, and her less-than-flattering legs were too heavy in the ankles—heredity at its most cruel and unjust.

"I don't understand you. Please come down stairs. Dinner is being served, and mother wants you there. She wants to talk about the upcoming festival and potential suitors."

"Of course she does," Driz said, distracted as her gaze found the castle once again.

"What is that supposed to mean?"

"I'm sure we're having guests. Someone of the male persuasion? Perhaps the duke's son, Marcus? Or no, even better, the countess's nephew, Dylan? That lush drools any time I let him hold my hand. It's disgusting and ridiculously demeaning. Why on earth should I willingly give myself to him? I might as well sleep with Michael, the stable boy."

"Don't joke. The servants might hear you and start rumors."

"I don't care. Are you not listening to me?"

"And I don't think that's what mother meant by inviting them." Anastasia straightened the bow in her hair.

"Oh, of course not. Mother would never whore out her daughters for the highest price. The problem is, Anastasia, that the going rate keeps dropping, and she won't face facts. Besides, she wants to increase her own stock in the community, not ours. And, since she's just a dried up old biddy with nothing to offer, save us, we're the only way she can."

"*Driz*."

"What? It's the truth. You need to wake up, sister."

"That's just cruel. Mother wants what's best for us."

"Notice you didn't say you and me. It's always us, which conveniently includes mother. No man in his right mind wants to be with her, much less bed her, and we are her most precious assets. Wake up."

"Drizella." Her sister's voice squalled even louder this time.

Dramatically throwing a few of the rose petals collected in the potpourri dish, she countered with, "Anastasia."

Her sister turned and stormed out of the room.

Leaving Driz alone with her bitter thoughts, she stopped brushing her hair and gritted her teeth. That bitch Cinderella had it all. Even with sabotaging the ball, the little whelp managed to have a fat fairy godmother bippity boppity booing all over everything to help her out.

It wasn't fair.

Why the hell couldn't she have had a fairy godmother? She'd positioned herself in society. She'd done her fucking time.

"Dammit." She slammed the brush on the table at her side.

The castle loomed in the distance.

She was just passing the time, keeping an eye on the door. Patience was not one of her virtues, and she had to find something to occupy her time. As a proper lady, throwing back a few and smoking a couple of cigars with the boys could keep her more than entertained.

"So, be honest. Why the hell do you come down here sullying yourself with the likes of us?"

"I love the smell, boys." She winked at several men, their eyes wide and voices loud. She was their goddess, and it empowered her like nothing else.

Such a turn on.

She'd left her knickers at home and flashed the men her bare legs often. That kept them off of her and busy trying to start fights with each other. Why had that trick never been taught in etiquette classes? Seemed like an important bit of knowledge.

"She loves the smell." Guster slammed his half-empty mug, spraying foam to those gathered.

"Of course, she does," said another voice from somewhere in the tangled group of men.

The pub door opened. A gasp of smoke escaped from the stuffy confines to the chilly night air. Worn hat shielded the man's eyes. Jakob, the woodcutter—shunned for his role in the Riding Hood debacle. A great deal of money exchanged hands to ensure that girl never made it through the woods. He had been forced to leave and find a new hovel to haunt.

"Boys, I have business to attend to. I'll be back in a bit. Be dolls and make sure I have a full mug when I get back." With a broad twirl of her skirt, she stood, giving the boys a show.

Winding her way through the crowd of people, she sidled up to the man. "Jakob, I was hoping you'd be here tonight."

He grunted.

This was going to be more difficult than she imagined. Jakob was her best option. She wasn't about to give up on him. Besides, she didn't want to go find the back-woods hag living in for a potion. That lady creeped her out worse than the witch in the candy house that didn't answer the door except for little kids. How messed up was that?

"I've been hoping to talk with you." Driz ran her hand up and down the woodcutter's arm, his firm muscles warm beneath her fingers.

"Came here for a drink." He tried shrugging her off, but it only emboldened her.

"So did I." Driz knocked her curled hair from her shoulder in dramatic fashion.

Less than interested, Jakob was intent on the bar. She worked out her next course of action when someone nudged her from behind.

"Then let me buy you one."

Driz faced the man. "Not interested. Back off." Raising his hands, the man moved down the bar.

This wasn't going how she'd hoped. Jakob left, tossing a few coins on the bar on his way out the back door. She couldn't wait any longer. It had to be tonight.

Time to set her plan in motion.

The lantern above the back door flickered, casting the alley in odd light. A familiar scene played out. The ridiculous opium addict stumbled, rubbing his ruined nose across his sleeve as he approached, his pipe in one hand and beans in another. She thought his name was Jack. He'd already cashed in everything he had from the family cow to their furniture. He'd resorted to trying to sell some stupid beans just for another fix.

"Look, Jack. Really not interested in anything you have to offer."

"Listen to me," he said, speech slurred, his nose scabbed and infected.

"Scram." She didn't want to actually touch him to get around him.

"But, I have these magic beans. They're priceless."

"That's because nobody wants them, you idiot."

"Everybody wants these beans. Everybody." He took a long time to blink.

She surveyed the dark alley to ensure they were alone before she drew him into shadows. Jack might be useful after all.

"Jack. Momma might have some use for you yet."

"What?"

She pulled him close, holding her breath, as he panted all over her. Driz avoided his mouth and the rotten stumps of his teeth. His nose glistened with ooze. With practiced precision, she tucked his greasy hair behind his ear.

"God, you smell so good." Jack sniffed her neck.

"You know I'd love to be with you tonight." Her hands rested on his tattered tunic, avoiding the vomit stains.

"Really?"

Fighting back the urge to gag, Driz leaned in close. "Yes, really. I've fought it long enough. I want you inside me, Jack. I want you to take me so badly, but I need a favor first. Can you do me a favor?"

Her fingers traced the line of his jaw, and she gave him a nice view of her cleavage, pulling aside her own tunic.

He stammered and dropped his beans on the ground. "Anything."

He pawed at her and pulled her even closer. Jack's gaze never left her breasts. His atrocious body odor teased her nose with its stench, taunting her stomach.

Somehow, she managed to hold it together.

"Good. Now, listen closely so we can be together."

Something about being in the stable—the hay poking her bare legs, the door open for anyone to glance inside—excited her. Her breath came in fast gulps, her hands touched his chest, hair oily from sweat and lust. Jakob moved inside her as she straddled his prone form. His hands, rough and stained, moved over her porcelain skin, her hair down in long, loose tresses, spilling over her shoulders.

Moaning together, their bodies frenzied, their motions urgent. Trembling, their passion spilled over.

Slick with sweat and desire, Driz fell against Jakob's chest. She wasn't foolish enough not to enjoy herself, but Driz was merely the diversion, taking as long as possible so that Jack had enough time to do as she asked. Driz took a chance enlisting the foolish addict to help her, but she hoped her promise of bedding him would be enough to keep him focused.

Dressing, she noticed Jacob watching her, his face flushed. His muscular chest still moved rapidly, sweat making his hair dark. Giving him an eye full, Driz said, "Thank you for that." Her tone coy. She offered a playful smile, all the while the sinister side of her smoldered away inside. Driz loved the thrill fluttering beneath her heart.

He grunted as he gathered his clothing from the hay. Not much for conversation. He more than made up for it in his lovemaking.

She left the stable, hands still tucking her unruly hair into something less of a mess. While passing the blacksmith shop, someone whispered, "Driz?"

Jack, hiding behind the sacks of cornmeal, held up the crossbow she'd asked him to get.

Perfect.

"I'm proud of you." She hugged him close, his hands clawing at her.

"I did it just like you asked." His hands trembled.

"So you did." She took the weapon. Giddy, she kissed him, holding her breath, but she didn't have much time if her plan was to work. "And, I'll show my appreciation later, I promise. God, I want to take you right now, sweet Jack, but I have to go."

Driz took her hand from his crotch as she turned away.

Sunlight cut across the early morning sky in waves, igniting the clouds with bursts of color. Driz readied herself. Cinderella would pass by her post at any moment. Sliding the bolt along the groove, she notched the crossbow and waited.

Not long now.

Cinderella took morning rides before anyone else in the castle woke.

Gold light spilled through the meadow, painting everything as she waited. The clip-clop of hooves slowed as Cinderella brought her horse to a slow trot. Crouched behind the fallen tree, Driz readied herself and peered down the length of the crossbow at the blonde bitch that stole her life.

Cinderella let the horse graze. Leaning down, she stroked the animal's neck and murmured something softly into its ear. She was so sweet it was sickening.

Breath coming quickly, the moment upon her, she could feel hear heart thundering. It made it hard to hear. Driz couldn't look at her hands because they kept shaking. She steadied herself and took the shot. Heavier than the one she practiced with, the woodcutter's crossbow bucked against her shoulder.

The bolt slammed into Cinderella's chest. She yelped tumbled out of the saddle onto the dusty ground. Driz cocked the bow, loaded another bolt, and closed in on her prey.

She aimed for Cinderella's head.

"Please help me," she said, red tainted spittle dotting her lips as she rolled over. "Drizella? What are you doing?"

"I am helping you get out of my life, bitch."

"Help me," Cinderella said again, her eyes on the crossbow.

"You don't deserve to have it—"

"I was just as surprised as you when the slipper fit—"

"–I do," Driz spat and launched the bolt into Cinderella's skull.

Blood squelched and sprayed across the dirt road. Sure that she was alone, Driz tossed the crossbow near Cinderella's body. Smacking the horse, it ran toward the tree line.

###

She passed the stables and through the gardens to the servant's entrance, her step light, smile wide. To think, she did it on her own, without the help of spells or potions from that crazy back-wood witch..

"Drizella?" Her mother's odd tone made her smile fade.

It was unusual to hear her voice downstairs in the servants' part of the house.

"There's been an accident. Cinderella was murdered."

"That's terrible." She feigned shock.

"Silly girl," her mother said, drawing her finger along the edge of the desk, "I know what you've done. You had a visitor this morning."

"The woodcutter?"

"Jack."

She closed her eyes. Of course, it had to be that idiot.

"He couldn't wait to be with you. He told me about taking the woodcutter's crossbow. You weren't careful enough, leaving your broach and pink bow tangled in the brush."

Had she just taken more time to fix her hair, the ribbon would have stayed, but Driz never wore broaches to the pub because of the clientele. How did it get there?

"I'm not too concerned with this woodcutter fellow. After all the fuss over that tart Riding Hood, he probably deserves to hang for it. I don't want this mess coming to our doorstep. Ladies must avoid such trouble."

Anastasia walked into the room, kissing the top of their mother's head and sitting on the arm of the chair. Driz didn't like this one bit.

"You should be worried, Drizella. Between what Jack knows and the things they've found by Cinderella's body, I'd say things could turn quite dark for you."

"And, what about you mother? I know that father's death was no riding accident."

"What is she talking about?" Anastasia stood, looking at mother.

"How can you not know? She killed Cindy's father, too. You need to catch up. Remember what I told you? It's all about her."

The chair smoldered as their mother's likeness crumbled, sifted like sand through a child's toy. Anastasia shrieked.

"I think it's high time both of you were taught a lesson." Twisted at the waist like a warped tree trunk, the wraith hissed at them, her face a vaporous mask of its former self. The eyes burned with an unnatural blue. The lips covered with lumpy sores. Thick rutted wrinkles cut harsh lines over her face, a ghostly white hue.

The Hag.

"You're the old Hag in the woods pandering potions."

"Far more than that." She pulled a thick, wooden staff from her cloak.

Anastasia stumbled to Driz, their hands reaching for each other. The Hag slammed the staff against the polished marble floor, and it sparked with a green fire that danced to the corners of the room.

"Mother?"

"Not even close." The thing spat and waved the head of the staff in front of them. That's when deep-seeded pain leapt from her midsection, making her scream. Anastasia doubled over beside her, both writhing in pain.

The green fire spread over them, their too large dresses falling to the floor. Driz tried covering herself, but her arms were no longer there. She tumbled. Anastasia writhed as a serpent, twisting and slithering across the floor.

"Yes, return to the garden where you belong. Back to where I found you." The sickening Hag taunted them. "That's it, my darlings."

The open doors and the garden beyond seemed so far away.

The Hag drove the tip of the staff through Anastasia's body.

After a quick twist, she stopped moving.

"Driz, you had such promise." The Hag lowered the staff once again, in a swift and sharp arc.

"Jack. Jack darling are you there?" She called down the winding stairs to the lower level.

"Yes, Lady Tremaine. Please let me out."

"Certainly. I don't know what made Anastasia lock you down here. It's so terrible. I'm distraught. Both the girls locked me upstairs. They fled. I had to use a hairpin to unlock the door."

"Anastasia, too?"

"They were working together."

Jack bowed his head as Lady Tremaine unlocked the cell and released him.

"Are you someone I can count on, Jack?"

She handed him a small cloth sack.

"There's plenty more where that came from. Plenty more. As much as you like."

RUDE AWAKENING

Jonathan Shipley

The second time up the mountainside was even worse than the first. I'd staked all my plans on one time up, one time down, scavenging a bit of profit. Would have worked fine, too, except the Church confiscated my profit. Should have seen that coming. A golden brazier—what self-respecting priest wouldn't want that for his altar? Gold was gold.

So here I was, going up the mountain again. I'd seen an inner cave beyond the entrance where I collected the brazier, but I hadn't paid much attention. My focus had been on the immediate gold. With the mountain occupied, exploring the inner byways wasn't my first choice anyway. The legend of the Lady Under the Mountain sleeping through eternity wasn't exactly scary, but not really comfortable either when it got up close and in your face.

When I reached my destination, I lit my torch to get a look at my prospects. As caves go, not so big, but with enough worked metal to sink a fair-sized galleon. No more gold, unfortunately. Just bronze and copper and brass. Not much profit with all the hauling and crawling.

I took another tour of inspection along the back wall. Bronze swords, tarnished shields, larger-than-life statues, strange bits of armor that I could only guess at. If anyone other than the Prince-Bishop collected antique weaponry, I would have been ecstatic. As it was, the market felt too dangerous. You have to understand that the Prince-Bishop has three full-time Inquisitors on his staff, and showing up with a gold brazier already made me suspect. It takes a lot of profit to risk The Question, as the Inquisition likes to call physical interrogation. More than I could see anywhere in the cave.

A crystal sarcophagus lay on a raised platform in the center of the cave, and I reluctantly stepped over to it. Any last bits of gold would likely be encased inside with the dearly deceased. Made collection into a none-too-pleasant process. At best a moldering corpse, and at worst a corpse that wouldn't stay quite dead. You never knew when you opened a tomb these days.

I wrestled the sarcophagus lid open, alarmed when it lifted on invisible hinges with a soft *whoosh*. A wave of icy winter rolled over me, then faded.

I leaned forward for a peek inside. A statue? Seemed to be a life-sized marble war goddess decked out in full armor. Odd thing to entomb, but better than either of the other alternatives. And it put a whole new spin on the Lady Under the Mountain legend. Except bringing this war goddess to life needed a whole lot more than True Love's Kiss. But all that flitted through mind in a flash because lying there on her breastplate was gold. Just a bit of gold in the form of a ring, but the only thing so far that looked like easy profit. I snatched it up. Good heft to it—worth a half-dozen crowns on any market.

I turned back to the rows of shields, still debating the twenty trips it would take to get them down the mountain.

A clinking, scraping sound behind me.

"Where is it?" The voice soft, barely a whisper.

But it scared the Sign of the Cross out of me. I flattened myself against the wall of the cave, not daring to move, hardly daring to breathe.

"Where is it?" The creak of shifting weight, the clink of metal on metal.

The light of my torch illuminated a mailed hand reaching out to grip the side of the coffin.

Run, you fool, I told myself.

My legs shook and refused to listen.

The top of the winged helm breached the crystal depths, followed by masses of golden hair as the marble figure took on color. Emerald eyes bored into me. "Where is it?"

"W-what?"

The woman underneath the armor sizzled in a tall, blond way. Why are the best ones always weird?

With more creaks, she rose full height and stood on the dais. Her still form made me hope that she had turned back to stone or ice or whatever she'd been before. I didn't have the fortitude for direct confrontations of this sort. Never trust anyone who sleeps in a coffin, my momma told me. Why didn't I listen?

"You're a thief."

My nerves squeezed a laugh out of me. "Just exploring, ma'am. Hamon's the name. Sorry to have disturbed you."

"You have taken the ring from me."

My left fist tightened around the beautifully wrought circlet of gold. My profit margin. But now this. I should have gotten out of there the moment I saw the coffin, but she'd looked like a statue. And more to the point, I hadn't invoked True Love's Kiss as specified in the legend, so none of this ought to be happening.

"Why, I don't know what you mean, ma'am. Lost something, have you?"

"Don't play me for a fool, thief. I can feel the power of the ring in your hand. At least you weren't so stupid as to put it on."

Oh, lord, a magic ring. The last thing I wanted to get involved with. My cousin's brother-in-law played around with a magic ring once. Ended up as a sister-in-law. And a pretty ugly one at that.

"Just a silly mistake," I said with as much of a smile as I could force under the circumstances. "Why don't I just leave it on my way out. I'm going anyway."

"Release it."

She didn't have to ask twice. Already it was tingling against my palm. I opened my hand and the ring leapt the distance between us as though pulled by a lodestone, clunking into her armor with considerable force. She didn't put the ring on, just tucked it away behind her breastplate.

"What is this ridiculous get up?"

"Ma'am?"

"This is not what I remember wearing. Someone's dressed me in armor while I slept."

"Wasn't me, wasn't me." Under different circumstances, the idea might have some merit, but not the thing to say just now. I hoped that she would sink back into her coffin and go back to sleep now that she had her ring back. But she didn't seem to be so inclined. If anything, she looked more alive by the second.

"What is the time period?"

"Late morning, maybe noonish. I'd need a glance at the sun to be sure."

"The *year*, fool."

"The Year of Our Lord 1247. Uh, what year were you expecting?"

"I was hoping for later than the Dark Ages. I'm still a thousand years from home." Her expression turned shuttered and brooding.

I took a tentative step toward the outer tunnel. "Well, best of luck with your wardrobe. I guess I'll be moving along."

"Stay."

I stayed.

"How did you win past the force field?"

"The what field?"

"The flames at the mouth of the cave."

"Uh, what flames would that be, ma'am?"

"No flames?" She lifted a greaved leg over the edge of the coffin and stepped down to floor level. She strode toward the cavern's entrance. "It's true. The force field—that is, the guardian flames have died. And the field generator seems to have disappeared. This complicates matters."

Ominous. She examined the corner where I had picked up the brazier. What did fields had to do with flames? My eyes searched longingly for a back door to the cave, but the rows of helms and shields offered only a solid rock backdrop.

"Who else knows of this place?"

"No one. No one." As soon as I said it, I didn't like the sound of it. It made me seem too much like an inconvenient loose thread. "I mean, everyone."

"Everyone? You make it sound like the local fair."

I'd overshot my mark. "Of course not, ma'am. I don't mean everyone's been trooping through your cave, but everyone knows the legend of the Lady Under the Mountain sleeping until awakened by True Love's Kiss. It's sheer luck that no one's made it this far before."

"More the flames, I think." She paced. "They can't have been out very long."

I followed her movements, trying to estimate my chances of making it to the cave's mouth while her back was turned. I tensed.

"Don't try it. I am not yet through with you. You have awakened me and so must bear that responsibility. It will take some time to recalibrate the chronometric controls…to re-knit the spell that holds me beyond life and death. And the guardian flames must be rekindled somehow—perhaps with primitive combustibles. Where is your home?"

My mouth went dry at the horrible vision of this blond warrior-woman following me back to the village. The neighbors I could handle, but Brother Justinius…I could only imagine our local Inquisitor's reaction.

"You can't be thinking about leaving here. I don't think the world is ready for that. At least, my village isn't. Women nowadays are less…armored, if you know what I mean. Not so much hardware."

Unexpectedly, she laughed a rich, fudgy laugh. "Attention has never bothered me. This could be fun."

And I might be dead by nightfall.

I followed her to the mouth of the cave. Bringing out the ring and cupping it in her palm, she held it before her with intense concentration.

"What are you—"

The ring blazed. A series of sparks flashed and died under my feet. I bolted out of range. If she called up some sort of magic fire, I preferred not to be in the thick of it. But nothing happened beyond a few more sparks.

"It is not to be," she said, tucking the ring away and belting on one of the many swords the cave offered. "It will need a combustion source. Let us go."

My gaze alternated between the steep, unforgiving mountainside and her heavy armor. "I don't suppose you have a winged chariot or something?"

"I've been asleep forever. I welcome the exercise." And my war goddess came down the mountainside hand over hand just like an ordinary mortal. How she did it in all that armor—it made my arms ache watching her.

At the bottom of the cliff, she waited for me to catch my breath, and it struck me all over again that she really intended to come to the village with me. And that would be a disaster. At least the sun already hung low in the afternoon sky, which would put us into the village at dusk and save a lot of questions. Or postpone the inevitable.

We tromped in silence through the woods, but I could no longer contain myself.

"What should I call you?" Lady Under the Mountain felt awkward in conversation. "You do have a name, right? Maybe, Brunhilda or something?"

"Brunhilda?" She gave me a flinty stare. "You people really name your daughters things like 'brown battlemaid?'"

"No, of course not. I just thought…you have to admit—the cave, the armor."

She didn't have to admit anything, apparently. She also didn't offer any other name.

"And have you always lived in that cave?" Though *lived* might not be exactly right for someone who slept in a crystal sarcophagus.

"I'm just traveling through. The cave is supposed to be an out-of-the-way location where I can sleep undisturbed. But apparently not, though that is about to be rectified. Frankly, 1247 doesn't appeal much as an end destination."

Destination? "Where are you trying to get to?"

"Not where—*when*. The downside of chronoshifting backward is a long stasis-sleep back to the present."

"Ah." I had no answer to that. Either she was talking about sleeping off a bad hangover, or I didn't have a clue. Probably the latter.

By the time we reached the outskirts of the village, twilight had settled in right on schedule. Then I made the mistake of trying to cut through the Square.

I expected a deserted plaza at this hour, but I had forgotten about the Feast of Purgation. With the Inquisition, any day could be purgation, but this was the real thing. Kindling was piled in front of the church doors, and Brother Justinius at his most pompous in robes of gold and purple inspected the large stakes where the guests of honor were tied. In a village where everyone knew everyone, no one actually believed they were heretics, but they were old and expendable. Better thee than me—that sort of thing.

She—Brunhilda, for lack of anything better—stopped to study the scene. They had the brazier—my…er, *her* gold brazier—set out as the source fire for the kindling.

"Move on. Move on."

"What is happening here?" she asked.

"Tonight's auto-de-fe," I said. "It never pays to look too conspicuous at such occasions."

"Ritual immolation?"

I confirmed and again tried to herd her back to a side street. She wouldn't move. It got worse.

"Hamon, you unrepentant thief."

I whirled to find Brother Justinius stomping toward us.

"Who is this outlandish woman?"

"A mercenary?" Any excuse in a pinch.

"A mercenary." He gave Brunhilda the twice over. "The Church forbids women to bear arms."

"Which Church is that?" asked Brunhilda.

I groaned. Of all the things she could have said, that took the prize. Not everyone loved the Church—especially around this time of year—but like death and taxes, the Church was a fact of life.

Brother Justinius began seething.

"Just a little joke," I said.

"One does not joke about Holy Mother Church." His face turned redder. "This bears looking into—for the good of both your souls."

Icicles formed on my extremities. He meant an Inquisitional investigation.

"Forget what I said. I have no idea if it was a joke or not. Just met the woman, don't even know her name."

Not exactly chivalrous, but it did shift his attention to Brunhilda. Chivalry only works for the upper classes anyway.

"What do you have to say for yourself, woman?" Brother Justinius puffed up like a pig's bladder, all arrogance and anger. "What is the meaning of your unseemly garb and unseemly words? Have you no shame before your betters?"

She threw back her mane of hair and drew herself up to her full height. It was a lot of drawing. "My *what*? All I see before me is a fool."

"Heretic. Guards, gua—"

The sword leapt from the scabbard into Brunhilda's hand and swept down, its hilt connecting with the brother's head with a hollow *thunk*. He gurgled and slumped to the ground.

I'd seen plenty of people knocked senseless before, but never with these particulars. Inquisitors were traditionally on the other end of that business.

"Are you crazy? Attacking the Inquisition—do you have any idea what they'll do to us? Burn us both, that's what. You have to hide before the guards show up—go back to the woods—or the cave maybe."

"You're babbling. I can deal with these fools." She flourished her sword ominously.

"But *I* can't. There's more than one neck at stake here. I prefer to live out my life without undue pain."

She impaled me with a penetrating stare. "Then I shall finish this quickly," she said finally.

"Not…" I eyed her sword. The aftereffects of a murdered Inquisitor would be ten times more dreadful than a battered one.

"No. No blood this time." She shook her curtain of golden hair and gave another of her rich laughs, the golden ring between her fingers. "Just my field generator and lots of fire."

May my legs be fast and my face forgettable. I prayed, preparing to put some distance between myself and the upcoming fireworks.

Brunhilda's ring flashed like the noonday sun, turning the whole Square into golden flame. And this was the ring I tried to steal? Not one of my smarter moves.

Her voice cut through the golden haze: "Forget True Love's Kiss. This is how to awaken someone in deep stasis."

When my vision cleared, I stood alone in the Square. That is to say, alone with one unconscious Inquisitor. Brunhilda was gone. The sky hadn't fallen in, but golden sparks still filled the air around the stakes. They faded into nothing.

What was wrong with this picture?

From his position on the cobblestones, Brother Justinius gave a little moan. I stooped down beside him, patting his cheek to bring him around. This would be a little tricky.

I started babbling as soon as his eyes flickered. "That strange woman. I can't believe she attacked you, Father. I tried to stop her, but—well, you saw her."

He looked at me with narrowed eyes as I helped him to his feet but didn't actually contradict me. I was counting on a little fuzziness after that tap on the noggin.

"Yes, the woman. Where is the harlot?" He staggered forward a step.

"Gone. I was so concerned about you that I didn't even notice which direction she went."

As his attention elsewhere shifted, I gave in to relief. All things considered, I weathered that rather well. No charges of heresy, no Brunhilda—no more poking around caves for lost treasure, thank you very much. Yes, I weathered that well.

I wanted to silently slip away, but people already were trickling in for the evening's auto-de-fe. By village standards, tonight rated as a big social event, one of the times to see and be seen. And woe unto those that were not seen. So I stayed.

Brother Justinius managed an impressive formal condemnation. Sure, the lighting was poor, but at this point we all should have spotted the problem. But then again, stupidity is popular in my village.

Only when the men-at-arms came forward to torch the kindling around the three stakes did it became painfully obvious—no brazier to light the torches with. Nor was there any kindling. This wasn't a simple matter of who hid the kindling—not that anyone would. It takes a small forest to adequately accommodate guests of honor at an auto-de-fe. Servants had been building the pyres for days. And all of it gone…along with the three heretics of the evening. I was hard pressed not to burst out laughing. Wherever they had ended up, they were better off than here.

Needless to say, it caused quite a stir. So much for this year's Feast of Purgation. I mean, what can you do? No heretics, no Feast. Brother Justinius came off looking like a fool in front of the whole village. A thoroughly wonderful evening in that respect.

Better than wonderful, actually.

I'd managed to lift the good Inquisitor's coin pouch as he lay unconscious on the cobblestones, and I was now two crowns richer. He'd discover the loss, of course, but would no doubt blame it on Brunhilda along with everything else. All things considered, how could he not?

So an all-around good day, yet I wonder.

On one hand, it's a temptation to cast everything in epic terms. Pagan war goddess against the Inquisition, shining warrior against injustice—that sort of thing.

On the other, you can dismiss it all as no-nonsense practicality. She wanted the brazier and kindling for her guardian flames.

Now which of those sounds more like someone who sleeps in a crystal coffin?

I think the answer lies somewhere in a deep, fudgy laugh.

I INSIST
Raven Ashwood

From my bed, where she insists I stay, I watch her through the open doorway of my bedroom. She picks up the plates from breakfast and tosses them in the sink to soak before walking into the bedroom with her dimwitted smile. "Can I get you anything, dear?"

I glare. She smiles. She doesn't understand that my silence is a "no," so I speak. "I'm fine."

She nods eagerly. "Just let me know if there's anything I can do. Okay, sweetie?"

The girl turns before she can see my grimace. Walking to the far end of the bedroom, she makes my eldest brother's bed. The length of the blanket hangs unevenly down the sides, the pillow lays crooked, one of the bottom corners is untucked. The next bed she makes isn't much better. If I made it, the corners would have been crisp, the blankets would have hung even, and the pillow would have been perfectly centered at the top. The rest of her housekeeping skills are equal to that of the bed making: less than adequate. While being only a two-roomed house, it shouldn't be difficult to manage a certain level of perfection. For her, it seems impossible. She also sings while she works. My brothers say she has the voice of an angel. I didn't know angels strained to hit high notes. She loves those high notes.

How do people see her as beautiful? Her dark hair is matted and greasy, her eyes overly large, her nose too thin, her nails dirty and torn. The yellow dress is faded and worn and too short on her, coming up to her ankles, the sleeves halfway up her arms. I'm not sure if she is aware of the few tears she has in the fabric or if she cares about the red and brown stains that speckle her dress. I'm sure it was once beautiful.

After finishing the six other beds, she returns to me. "Need anything before I head into the other room?"

"No."

"All right, then. Just call if you need me," she says with another smile.

I sigh and close my eyes as she leaves. At least her singing is muffled.

"Oh, I almost forgot." I open my eyes when she re-enters. She grabs the edge of my blanket from under my arms and tugs. The look I give her would have made any semi-intelligent creature flee in terror. Not her. She continues to tuck me in bed, pinning my arms beneath the blanket. She pats me on the head as if I'm a small child. "Now, you rest up and get better."

Resting will not make me better. I was born sick and remained frail. While my brothers work mining ore from the mountain, I stay home. Instead, I hobble around the small house and keep it clean. I have the beds neatly made every morning after they leave, picking up their dirty laundry, before I sweep the floor, dust, clean the windows, clean the countertops, and prepare dinner so that when they return, the food is hot and ready on the table. It isn't the easiest thing for me to do, nor the most exciting, but it's still my work. I do it well.

She is dreadful.

I can't watch her anymore, so I close my eyes and try to sleep.

I managed just fine. The house was spotless. There wasn't dust in the deep crack along the mantle or dirt between the floorboards. No spider ever tried to spin a web in dark corners of the ceiling. While there was a small hole in the base of the cupboards, no mouse ever dared to call it home. The meals were delicious, never over- or undercooked. I always made just the right amount, and dinner was placed on the table moments before they arrived. My brothers used to praise me for my work around the house. While sickly, they knew I was capable.

Then she came.

I wake to the sound of a cat dying. Unfortunately, I see not a cat, but instead *her*. I wince as she finishes the final notes of her song. She stands there smiling at me, always smiling. "It's time to get up, sleepyhead."

I feel stiff from laying still for so long. "What time is it?"

"Dinner time."

"Why did you let me sleep all day?"

She laughs. "So that you could get some rest and feel better."

In the weeks that she has been here, I have tried to explain to her that I will not get better. When she proposed the idea that she'll take over my duties so that I can rest up, my brothers eagerly agreed. Outnumbered, I'm forced into bed rest. Regardless of what I say in protest, my words will only be ignored.

I move to get out of bed, and she is right there, one arm around me in an attempt to support me.

"Let go," I said practically growling at her.

"Oh, no. I don't want you to fall."

"I said let me go." I try shaking her off. She grips me harder.

Her perpetual smile is plastered on her face. "But what kind of person would I be if I let you fall?"

I switch tactics: "But how can I get better if you don't let me practice?"

She contemplates this idea. It's almost painful watching her trying to think so hard. She lets me go. "That's a wonderful point."

I force a smile and hobble into the other room with her standing over me. She is my shadow until I reach the dark wooden table that dominates a large portion of the room. She pulls my chair out for me. I sit. The table has been fully set, and the food is portioned out onto our plates. Extra sits in the middle of the table. Tomorrow, she will overcorrect and prepare too little.

I look out the window and wait.

My brothers trudge through the door almost two hours later. They arrive the same time every day. The food has grown cold. I'm sore from sitting on the hard wooden seat. I have not been allowed to touch my meal until my brothers are seated.

But still, I have to wait. My stomach growls again because I was allowed to sleep through lunch.

They each file past the angel. Each of them stand at her chest's height. They are covered in dirt and grime from the mines. Except for our height, I look almost nothing like my brothers. Scars cover their rough skin and calloused hands while mine are soft and gentle. She bends down and gives them each a hug and welcomes them home. After this fifteen minute ordeal, they are seated at the table. We may begin.

The food is cold and absolutely awful. The chicken is burnt. The carrots are limp. The mashed potatoes have raw chunks, and the bread is charcoaled on the outside and barely cooked on the inside. While I barely nibbled on my food to begin with, I stop eating when one of her long black hairs wrapped around a potato chunk.

She chats with my family about their day. They say things that clearly go over her head, but she nods and smiles. The girl knows nothing about the mining business. She can't engage in conversation with them like I used to. Even though I usually stay home, I was able to keep up enough so that any outsider would have thought that I was down there with them.

I wait for them to finish by reminiscing about the peaceful days before she came. They move to the mismatched furniture in the corner of the room. As their fair maiden picks up the table, they play music. A couple of them dance in the middle of the group. I should have gotten up and snuck off to bed or out into the garden.

Her thin hand with the ragged, dirty nails reaches for my plate and then stops. "Honey, you didn't eat much."

"I wasn't hungry."

"Oh, you have to be hungry. You've barely had anything to eat."

I do not point out that this was not my fault.

"I'm fine."

She grabs my fork and scoops up potatoes. "Really, it will be good for you."

"I don't want any."

"It will help you get stronger," she says bringing the fork closer.

"No." I slam my mouth closed. She stabs me in the lip. I yell in pain. The fork clatters to the floor, and she apologizes over and over.

The music stops, and they all look at me. I stumble as quickly as I can to my room. She grabs me.

"Leave me be."

Her hands fall away, and for once, she lets me walk to my bed alone.

It's no surprise I can't sleep. I'm starving. The bread might still be semi-edible. I have to move slow. The slightest sound could wake the girl curled up on a mat in the corner of the room.

I slice a thick enough chunk of bread to satisfy my hunger but small enough that she wouldn't notice.

Maybe I should go for a walk in the woods to help me sleep.

As I walk to the door, my hip catches the corner of the table. I stumble. Before I can stand, she is at my side. She tries to help me. Instead, she pulls me off balance, and I fall again. She yanks at my arms, and I cry out.

I shove her off and stand. She reaches for me once more, and I slap her hand away. "Leave. Me. Alone."

The venom in my voice is enough that she lets me walk into the chilly, night air. I sit on a rock at the edge of our clearing and look out into the woods. Now more than ever, I want her gone. The window shows that she has lit a candle and is pacing. I don't feel bad for making her worry.

I hope that she will go back to bed. But she won't until I've returned. Too tired and sore to wait her out, I head inside.

Crying, she apologizes for hurting me. She doesn't try to help me to bed. She's too busy sitting at the table. She speaks to herself as I walk away: "I'll do better."

I'm sore in the morning, but it does not stop me from wanting to get out of bed. I've woken up sore before, and I'll inevitably wake up sore again. I stretch. My brothers are not in the room.

As soon as I throw off the blankets, one of them says, "He's up."

This stops me for a second. They all stand, including her, around my bed. I'm trapped. No one smiles. Some refuse to look at me. Others line their faces with determination, like they're studying me.

"Honey," her voice gentle, "we need to talk."

She clearly hadn't slept.

"Your brothers and I are concerned about your health and safety."

"Health and safety?" My voice is flat.

She nods. My fall last night worried them because I am sick. "We want you to have complete bed rest."

"Excuse me?" She can't be serious.

"We know you like to do things on your own, but it's only making you worse."

"No—"

"So, you shall remain in bed until further notice. Understood?"

I can't believe my brothers. "You can't agree to this?"

They all nod and murmur. I am more infuriated than I have ever been.

"But don't worry, sweetie, I'll make sure to take good care of you."

My brothers go to work.

She follows them.

They are serious about the bed rest.

I'm force-fed every meal.

I cannot bathe, so she scrubs me with a wet rag.

I use the bed pan.

The few times I attempt to be independent, I'm threatened by her and my brothers.

They will use force if necessary.

I have been in bed for one week.

I can understand why the queen wanted her dead. Laying here, day after day, I want her dead, too. Killing her eats at the back of my mind. Every spoonful, every scrub, every "dear," "honey," and "sweetie" drives me closer to my breaking point.

Sweeping the floor in the other room, she misses a spot.

I know what I must do.

The following day I wait until everyone has fallen asleep before I get up. I creep into the kitchen, pull out a pen, ink, and paper. My letter is short and to the point. I explain how the girl lives in our cottage. I give the old hag directions. I assure her that in a week's time, the maiden will be alone.

Donning a thick cloak and grabbing my walking stick, I step outside. It's a long walk for me, a couple of miles. I do not fear the woods, even at night. I do not jump at the sound of the owls hooting. I do not flinch at the shadows.

Tonight, they are my friends.

Once in town, I drop the letter off to the mail carrier and go home. I do not stop to rest. I must get home before everyone wakes.

A cool breeze shakes the forest leaves, and I press the cloak tighter around me.

I get home with a couple of hours to spare. Shuffling slowly, I make my way back to the bedroom and go to bed. She wakes me for breakfast. I don't protest when she feeds me.

A week passes. I show her that I'm stronger. And I can join them at breakfast. Before the dishes are cleared, I say, "Brothers, and dear maiden, tomorrow, I wish to go with you to the mines."

"But, sweetie," their lady says.

I raise my hand. "Now, I know that I'm frail and cannot do much. But I think it will help me recover if I join you in the mine. Bed rest has given me new energy."

I grin when they approve.

###

The next morning, I follow behind my brothers as we make our way to the mine. I let them go on ahead of me, knowing that I slow them down. I enjoy my alone time, especially since I have gotten so little lately.

Near the mine, I pass a crippled, old woman heading in the opposite direction. A long black cloak that brushes the ground, collecting leaves and sticks as she walks, obscures most of her features; a basket filled with colorful fabric swings on her arm.

The old hag glances at me.

I move along.

I keep up with my brothers on our way home. I'm giddy to return. They assume it's because of my time in the mines. I let them believe it.

The front door is open, and no one sings out of tune. Their sweet angel lays on the floor, still as death. I hide my grin behind a handkerchief and collapse in a chair. Tears spring to my eyes, not for the loss of her, but for the freedom from her.

One of my brothers calls for a knife.

Another says something about her corset being laced too tightly.

As she takes her first breath, I shake in anger.

Her eyes open.

I leave the room.

I'm tired and have a long walk ahead of me tonight.

I climb into bed.

My letter is even shorter.

The girl still lives. They found her in time. Try poison.

I walk with determination. It should not take this much effort to kill her.

I alternate my days between home and the mines. I have no desire to watch my brothers work, even less to watch the girl make a mockery of the housework. I allow enough time to pass so that suspicion won't fall on me when she finally dies.

When morning arrives, I'm less than enthusiastic. But I try to maintain a pleasant attitude. They are all oblivious.

The eight of us gather around and eat breakfast together, hopefully, for the last time. The eggs are runny. The toast is black. The orange juice tastes sour. I will not miss her meals. Regardless, I eat my fill.

My brothers file past, oldest to youngest, giving her a hug goodbye. I'm the last to pass, and I allow her a quick hug, the only one I have never resisted.

On the trail, after my brothers have gone ahead of me, I walk through the brush, letting nature wipe off her hateful hug that lingers on my clothes. She is even horrible at hugging. She grips too tightly.

I pass an old, long-white-haired woman. Dressed in a red cloak, she swings a basket filled with an odd assortment of combs, mirrors, and jewelry. Her appearance differs from the last time.

I don't bow my head, but rather give a very quick, short nod. I want to tell her not to fail again. I remain silent.

I'm impatient in the mines, and my brothers repeatedly ask me what is wrong. I don't tell them that I have a bad feeling that she will fail again. I convince them I'm fine. We return at our normal time.

The front door is closed. Only the birds sing.

I don't give myself enough hope that this heavenly peace will last.

They flock to her. They check her dress. The laces aren't too tight. They shake her, and yet, she does not stir. Perhaps, the queen is not so useless.

They carry her to bed, and we hear a small *thunk*. I shuffle over and pick it up. A decorative comb has fallen from her hair. The golden tips have a red stain. It isn't blood. I'm not sure why the queen expected this to work.

I move to my chair at the dining room table. I sit and I continue to wait.

A few moments later, she stirs.

I toss the comb on the table.

My brothers celebrate.

I rub my face. Someone asks what happened. She only mumbles something unintelligible.

I go to bed.

I'm too frustrated to worry about dinner.

The crescent moon shines bright in the cool, night sky. A few bats fly overhead. The peaceful evening gives me a chance to think. I have been too impatient and too lazy with my plans. I cannot rely on the queen to finish this task.

I must do something.

I'm too weak to overpower her.

I wouldn't be able to stab her hard enough.

Strangling her would be too difficult.

Poison still seems like the best route.

I pace the yard as I try to figure out the best plan. I pause and lean against a tree.

An owl hoots. I look up.

A few days later, my brothers and I get ready to go to the mine. I move slower than normal but still insist that I go. I tell them that I enjoy spending my time with them. As we leave, my brothers order her not to open the door to anyone. I agree.

They hug her for the last time. I follow them outside and into the woods. They outpace me more quickly today. I slow down before I turn back home.

I hobble up along the path and across the yard. Heading to the tree first, I see it.

Shining in the sunlight, the apple seems harmless resting at the base of the tree. I pick it up. The front door is locked. At least she has enough intelligence to listen.

I call for her.

She opens the door. I smirk.

I stumble forward so that she can catch me. Let the last thing she does be something she enjoys more than anything. She ushers me to my chair.

"I knew today would be too much for you." She pities me.

"Yes, I could not take it anymore. I had to come back."

"Well, you will certainly be in bed for the rest of the day."

"That is the best thing."

"Can we move you to the bedroom, or do you need to rest a little?"

"I would like to sit here for a moment."

"Just for a moment."

She started to walk away, presumably to turn down my horribly made bed. I call to her. "Can I give you something?"

She turns in surprise and returns. "Of course."

I hold out the shiny red apple. "For you."

"Thank you. You are an angel. But what is this for?"

"For everything you have done for me and my family."

"May I eat it now?"

"I insist."

She manages three bites before she falls to the ground.

I remain seated and watch as she struggles.

The fair damsel reaches out, her hand wrapping around the bottom of my trousers.

I brush it away.

Her hand drops to the floor.

I wait several minutes.

She does not breathe.

She does not stir.

I pick the apple up. I shut and lock the door behind me. I walk for a while along the trail before I toss the evidence into the woods.

It doesn't take me long to get to the mine.

We walk back to the house at our normal time. While I was slow in the morning, I manage to keep up with them. We arrive. They recognize the silence and rush inside.

Once home, she does not wake.

The moon shines brightly as I drop off my final letter.

She is dead.

Yesterday, they built the coffin.

Today is the funeral.

After carefully preparing her, she is brought out. Instead of burying her in the ground, my brothers rest her in our garden among the flowers. The coffin is made of glass so that they could look upon her beauty.

I'm fine with this.

Being the one that she cared for the most, I'm given the task of planting the first set of flowers around her grave.

I plant it quickly at her head. My brothers follow, their sorrow slowing them down. I wait until they are done before I tell them that I'm heading inside to make dinner. A few of them nod.

As I cook, I smile and look around the room. Yesterday, while they prepared for her funeral, I cleaned. The floor is finally properly swept. The cobwebs that have popped up since she has been here are now gone. There is not a speck of dirt in the house. The beds are made neatly; the corners tucked in tightly and the pillow centered at the head of the bed. The table has been scrubbed. The counters sparkled. I sigh in contentment. The house is back to normal.

I might bake a cake to go with dinner.

Outside in the garden, I can see her clearly in her glass coffin. Her black hair is no longer matted and greasy; instead, it shines. Her ragged fingernails, trimmed and cleaned, are hidden beneath a bouquet of flowers. Her appearance has much improved. Her silence is angelic.

The sunlight reflects off the glass. I smile.

U R NEXT
12/1/16
The King's Jinger

TRADER

Robert Dawson

The ocean holds many kinds of islands. There are the ordinary sort of islands that stay in the same place all the time, solid reliable islands where men and women raise their children and cabbages. Beyond them lie the barren rocks, swallowed and released as the moon draws the tides, where only the selchie folk live, and the shifting sandbars where the cold mermaidens wait to marry drowned sailors.

Then there are hidden islands that appear on no charts. The boats of Land's Men cannot find them except now and again by mischance, and to land there is perilous. The largest islands have been sighted often enough by Land's Men that they have names: Thule, Hy Brasil, and golden Atlantis. But most are nameless to the people of the Land, and on these, the Sea Folk dwell.

Thuriphel lived with his mother on just such an island. Every day, morning or evening as the tide commanded, he would walk down to the dock, hoist the sails of his little boat, whistle up a wind if none blew yet, and sail out across the harbor bar. Out in the open sea, he would cast his net until his arms ached and return on the falling tide.

Some days, Thuriphel would catch nothing, not so much as a sculpin or an old leather seaboot. On those days, he would trudge back through the village, hungry, unhappy and tired. His mother would shake her head and give him a big bowl of plain porridge with a thick slice of brown bread.

"We should get a cow, Mother," said Thuriphel one day. "Then even when I have no luck at sea, we might at least have cream on our porridge and butter on our bread."

"Wishes will not fill the pot, my son," his mother said. "Your fishing earns us so little, and you know no other trade. Now, if you'd apprenticed to your uncle the nightsoil man…"

Thuriphel shuddered. You could tell when Uncle Vath's cart was lurching up the road long before you could see it.

"One day, I'll be a trader like Father. I'll sail to the mainland, earn some silver, and buy a cow there. Valesse's father tells me that is the wisest place to buy cows. Island-born cattle do not thrive, he says, and they give little milk."

And she looked at him with tired eyes and shook her head.

That summer, the fish were scarce, and Thuriphel had come home with an empty boat for three days running. He ate his last crumb of bread, finished his porridge, licked the spoon, and put aside his empty bowl.

"Mother, I am going to sail to the mainland, to a marketplace of Land's Men, and there I will buy a cow."

"We do not need a cow."

"We need the milk, cream, and butter."

"The sea is wide and dangerous."

"Father's boat is seaworthy, Mother."

"You have no money."

"I'll earn some."

"The winds are treacherous, and the reefs are cruel."

"I am as good a sailor as any in the village."

"So was your father." She looked out towards the empty sea.

"I shall come back. It's only a day and a night each way, and a day or two to trade." He kissed her, left the house, and walked down the rocky path to the village, willing himself not to turn back.

Outside one house, his feet lingered. Should he knock? Valesse, cherry-lipped Valesse, would come to the door; and what then? What if she, too, looked up at him and begged him not to go? He bit his lower lip and walked on. He would tell her all about it when he got back.

Every time he passed a field with cattle, he appraised the size of the beasts. Yes, his shallop was large enough to hold one safely. He would tether the cow to the mast, as he had seen farmers do. And soon, they would have butter for their bread.

His mouth watered in expectation.

He swaggered into the village, strode to the house of Ogamain the tavern-keeper, and knocked upon the door.

It opened a few inches, and a weather-beaten face appeared at the crack. "Who's there?" Ogamain said, with breath reeking of starwine and tobacco.

"Thuriphel. I sail for the mainland today. Do you–do you have any cargo for me?"

The grizzled eyebrows raised. "You? I hadn't thought you had the courage. But you are your father's son, and many's the cargo he took past the king's watch-ships. What can you carry?"

"What have you got?"

The door opened further. "I have twenty, maybe two dozen casks of starwine beyond what I need this season. If you still have room in your hold, that is?"

The starwine casks were not large; if he stood them on end and lashed them down, they would fit. "I can take those. What are your terms?"

"One cask for you."

"Father worked for one in four."

"Aye, he did—as a seasoned trader. But I'm risking my cargo with an untried novice."

"I'm as good a sailor as he was."

"That's to be seen, lad. One cask."

Would that buy a cow? It would have to. Thuriphel spat in his hand and extended it. "A bargain then."

Ogamain raised his gnarled hand, spat, and shook. "Step inside."

For an hour, the tavern-keeper talked, listing half-a-dozen customers and the prices that Thuriphel should ask. Thuriphel accepted a glass of starwine, and they drank to success. For two hours, they labored with the barrel-stang, carrying his cargo from the musty darkness of the tavern cellar to the salt air and gull cries of the harbor. The wooden pole galled his shoulder as they took one cask, then another, over the cobbled streets. Finally, the twenty-fourth cask was loaded. Thuriphel stretched his arms and took a lung-filling breath of the sea air.

The breeze sent eager little waves, lapping and laughing against the dock. The afternoon tide was almost high enough.

"Time to set sail," Thuriphel said.

Ogamain began to turn away, then stopped, as if he had thought of something. "Lad?"

"Yes?"

"I won't pay more than one cask for carriage by an untried trader. But if you want a larger profit, I'll show you the way to it."

"How?"

The tavern-keeper reached into his pocket. "I'll trade you these for your cask, lad. They're in high demand among Land's Men. You'll likely be able to sell them for three times what that cask would fetch." He brought out a package wrapped in dry brown leaves and carefully unfolded it to reveal a dozen or so red seeds.

"Windpod seeds? They're never worth as much as a cask of starwine."

"That might be true, lad—in the autumn. They're there to pick off the ground then, aren't they? If you want to go around the village, and see if somebody just happens to have saved some, why, you're free to do so. They'll have had to keep them dry, mind. And wrapped in comfrey leaves and cobwebs in the dark of the moon. And there's some words that need saying over them every month, too. But perhaps you don't want to miss the afternoon tide, Captain." He winked.

"Why would Land's Men pay such a price?"

"Reasons, lad, reasons. For those same reasons, you want to be careful where you show those seeds. If the King's Men catch you running starwine, likely they'll just take a quarter for themselves. They'll ask for half or more, but don't give it to them. Mention my name, lad. But if they catch you with these..." He drew his finger across his throat. "Then you'll want your Trader wits about you."

Was this courage or folly? Thuriphel took the seeds and stepped into the boat. He grasped the main-halyard and hoisted the sail. Slowly, the wind took hold of the sky-blue canvas, and the boat slipped from the land, hopeful gulls screeching around the mast.

For the first part of the voyage, Thuriphel stood at the helm, running before a light breeze and navigating eastward by the setting sun. His sail was full-bellied and silent; even the rush of water on the hull was hardly more than a chuckle. Above, the sky wore a few wisps of cloud, but no stormsign: the fair weather looked set for a few days, and the wind would not change more than a point or so. On the way home with the cow, he would have to tack upwind. He hoped cows did not get seasick, as they said Men did.

Why such a fuss about the windpod seeds? They were pretty, of course. For a few weeks in the autumn, all the children of the Sea Folk picked them from the little bushes, and strung them on necklaces or played tossing games with them—Three Rings, Blind Archer, and Come-To-Me-Come-to-Me. But soon the bright color faded, the seeds split, wrinkled, and grew moldy, and the children threw them away. Old Ogamain was right; it was unusual to see them fresh at this time of year.

Maybe they were intoxicating, like the heady starwine, and hard to give up. After all, selling liquor and tobacco was Ogamain's profession—maybe this was the same but more dangerous? No, surely not. Thuriphel still remembered chewing one as a youngster. The flavor had been so foul that he spat it out immediately and ran to rinse his mouth, but he had taken no harm. But who could say what they might do to Land's Men?

Well, that was the king's problem, and Ogamain's. Today, he, Thuriphel, son of Thastarel, was a trader like his father; he bought what one person wanted to sell, and sold what another wanted to buy. He was not going to force any Land's Man to swallow one. What they did with them was their concern, and all bills were paid when the wind filled the sail.

He looked up. The sun had slipped below the horizon, but no stars shone yet in the dim purple-blue sky. What should he steer by until they appeared? The moon was in its last quarter, not due to rise until a little before dawn. His boat ran before the wind so fast that it left hardly the crust of a breeze for him to take his direction from. Until it grew dark enough to see the stars, the swell would have to guide him: slight, but enough for an experienced helmsman like himself.

He kept his course steady between north-o'-west and west-o'-north. As the sky darkened, his worries returned. If Men wanted windpod seeds so badly, why did nobody sell them when they were in season? When he had overheard his father talking to friends about Trading, it was always starwine that he shipped, with maybe some soft grey wintercloth or dried apples to show the King's Men if they were stopped and searched. Was trading windpod seeds so wrong that Father had refused to do it?

One by one, the stars came out. Thuriphel sat, choosing his position so that the Standing Star was next to the mast. Navigating like this would be simple enough that he could risk some hours of half-sleep. His body rested, and the vexing questions in his head ceased. Only his eyes stayed open, locked to the Standing Star, and his hand worked the tiller incessantly.

Towards daybreak, he came fully awake again. Something in the smell of the water had changed, something in the feel of the waves was different. But what? Somewhere ahead, voices sang faintly in an unknown language.

Mermaidens. They lived on the evasive moving islands near the mainland, treacherous sandbars that might never break the surface, or might extend for miles underwater. Quickly, he shifted his course: north-o'-west, west, south-o'-west. The boat heeled on the broad reach, and the voices were drowned in the crackle of the sail and the rush of water on the hull. If more sandbars lurked ahead, he would never hear the mermaidens' warning.

The safe thing would be to haul on the tiller again, reset the sail, and beat upwind, away from the treacherous sands. With a twitch of the helm, he could leave their danger astern and tack slowly back across the dark ocean to his quiet fisher's life.

Thuriphel-the-Fisher would have tacked homeward and been safe by the fire the next day: but it would be shameful for Thuriphel-the-Trader to turn back with his first cargo undelivered. After a few more minutes sailing across the face of the wind, he let out the sail, bore off, and returned to his original course, hoping that he had gone around the sandbar. Once more, he ran before the wind, ears pricked for any hint of mermaidens' songs in the night.

Soon, the moon rose astern, like a bowl of thick, creamy milk. Its light spilled upon the water behind him, a straight path leading homeward. He ignored it, following instead the invisible way ahead that led to the lands of Land's Men and their markets. When he got there, maybe he could ask a little more than Ogamain's price and earn enough to buy his cow. He could toss those accursed windpod seeds into the harbor and set his mind at ease.

Ahead, something glowed. A fog bank, shining in the moonlight, barred his way, and he could see no end to it in either direction. Thuriphel did not change course: a sailor who could read the swells was as safe in the fog as out of it. Maybe safer—the king's ships would never find him there. And it was a sign that he neared land, with maybe a league left to go. He sailed on into the pale mist and let it enfold him.

By the time he emerged from the fog, day was breaking. On the horizon ahead of him, dark-wooded hills rose. And, to starboard, maybe five minutes away, was a huge ship, ungainly compared with his long slender craft.

Somebody on the big ship called faintly, and the big ship began to trim her sails and put about. Thuriphel laughed. How could anything so awkward catch him?

But, ugly though she might be, the king's ship was capable of surprising speed. She would overhaul him long before he made land. Voices from the deck were already calling for him to lower his sail and surrender in the king's name. A small cannon fired a warning shot, though it was still too far to be aimed accurately.

What had his father said, when young Thuriphel got overconfident? "It's on the last league to shore when you meet the selchies, my son." The selchies themselves were harmless, but where there were selchies to be seen, there would be rocks.

He scanned the water between him and the shore.

There. To starboard, well out from the still-distant land, waves flickered on a rocky reef. Not just one reef, but a glorious line of them, with surf dancing and dashing white against them. The closer he came, the further the line extended. Thuriphel-the-Trader set his course for a narrow gap in the line of tossing crests. His own narrow hull with its shallow draft would slip through with a good fathom on either side, but if the monstrous ship bearing down upon him was as ungainly underwater as above, her helmsman would never risk the narrow passage.

The watchman of the great ship gave a halloo. As her helmsman turned the wheel, Thuriphel pursed his lips and whistled up a gust. It caught the ship in mid-tack, and she heeled dangerously. The cannon fired again, but on the tilting, reeling deck, the gunner had no chance to aim, and Thuriphel skimmed untouched through the gap. From a selchie on one of the rocks came a cheerful hoot.

Thuriphel shouted back without slowing. By the time the king's boat rounded the end of the line of reefs, he wouldbe safely among the maze of islands that fringed the shore.

For two days, Thuriphel followed the coast, ducking into bays and behind islands, finding his customers by the landmarks that Ogamain had told him about. He grew used to the lush greenness, the boxy and ungraceful houses, the stubby boats that looked as if they might as well go sideways as ahead—yes, even the heavy-set forms of the Land's Men themselves.

But those clumsy creatures were shrewd bargainers. Not once had he been able to squeeze an extra silver piece out of a sale. "Twenty-two shillings, lad?" the Man would say. "Nay then—I'll buy when the price comes down again, and drink ale till then. Twenty's my price." When the last cask was sold, though the pouch he kept for Ogamain's takings was heavy, his own was still empty. Could he, would he sell the seeds?

First, he should find out what they really were, and then decide. But how to do it safely? He stood and scratched his head for a while. He walked away from the marketplace to a quiet country road, where he loitered against a tree until he saw a solitary farmer leading a cow.

Thurifel smiled to himself. However horrified the Land's Man might be by what he saw, he could not give pursuit without losing his valuable animal, and there was none around to hear if he raised the hue and cry. Thurifel waited until he drew near.

"Good morrow!" called the farmer. He was young, about the same age as Thuriphel.

"Good morrow, indeed! My friend, perhaps you can help me. I have found these strange seeds. You look like a man of the soil, wise in the ways of plants. Perhaps you can tell me what they are? Or should I search for an apothecary?"

"Why, save us! You've found magic beans, on my soul. My father, may God rest him, told me about them." The young Land's man looked at the bright round seeds with awe.

"Magic? What is their virtue, then?"

"They say that if you plant one, it will grow into a vine so tall that a man may climb to the heavens and seek his fortune. Of course, the King has made a law that none may grow such a vine, lest they grow richer even than him. But it would be a fine risk, I think."

Thuriphel thought of the scrawny windpod bushes, hardly higher than a child, and did not laugh. "You would not eat them, then?" He muttered a charm under his breath and looked across his right thumbnail at the farmer.

"Eat them? Mercy, no. That would be folly." The farmer laughed heartily. And Thurifel knew, from his charm, that the farmer told the truth.

A Trader's duty was to get the best price he could for his cargo. "So, my friend, would you trade them for that cow?" Thurifel asked, trying not to sound over-eager.

The farmer nodded. "Aye—if you're minded to sell," he said, in much the same tone.

Thuriphel spat in his hand and extended it. The bargain was sealed, the exchange made. They wished each other a good day, and each strode away with his prize.

It had been a good voyage, Thuriphel decided. He had a cow, and he had a fine story to tell to Valesse. And, who knew? Perhaps in the rich strange soil of the mainland, a windpod plant would grow taller.

THE PRINCESS QUEST
Shaun Avery

On the day that your quest begins, you look into the distance and see the tower.

Like always, the sight fills your eyes with tears.

Standing beside you, your friend Farmer Thomas lays a hand on your shoulder.

"It just can't be," he says. "You know how the old legend goes. She'll only be with someone who quests for her."

"So why can't that be me?"

But you look at him as you ask the question, and you see the answer on his face. Truth is, you're just not the questing type. You're not big and muscular; you're not handy with a blade. You're just… you.

"You've never left this town. You don't know the things that live out there." Thomas shudders at whatever it is he's thinking. "Dangerous things."

"They can't be *that* bad. Not for a prize so great."

That's right, you think. The princess is a prize. A beautiful one, with hair as golden as the sun, eyes as blue as a summer sky.

You're quite sure you're in love with her.

Which, for some reason, upsets your sweetheart of these last seven years, Rowena.

She weeps when you return home that night and tell her what you're about to do. She calls you awful names in anger, and then in sadness, she begs you to stay. But your mind is made up.

"I can't help it. I'm afraid I love another." You smile and meet her gaze, knowing that your next words will make her understand. "But it's okay. You don't have to be mad. She's a princess."

That's when her eyes narrow, and her mouth curls up into a snarl.

Next thing you know, you're laying outside of the house with a bloody nose and a bruised eye, looking back through the window she just punched you out of.

You never can tell the way some people will react to good news.

###

Frederick the blacksmith seems surprised when you enter his shop. As well, you suppose, he might be.

My word," he says. "What brings *you* here?"

"Hello, Frederick. I need a sword."

"Then you've come to the right place. But may I ask why?"

"I intend to go on a quest," you tell him, "to win a princess's hand."

Though you have to admit, it's probably her *other* body parts that drive you.

"The princess from the tower?"

You nod.

"Then this is a proud day for our town. A proud day, indeed." Then he's walking around the counter and coming over to you. "Yes, a sword you must have. But first let me shake your hand."

You do so.

"And let me buy you a drink for good luck."

This is how you end up in Goodfellow's Tavern. This isn't your expected destination–you'd been planning on beginning your quest straight away–but you enjoy the collective gasp that ensues when you enter with a sword at your hip.

Frederick walks with you towards the bar, where your friend Farmer Thomas waits. Two mugs of ale before him – he must have been expecting you. Seeing that you brought Frederick, he signals Old Man Goodfellow for one more.

You come to stand in front of him.

Thomas seems impressed by the sight of you. "Can I try your sword?"

You're fine with that, but Frederick stops you before you pull the weapon from its scabbard.

"No," he says. "It's bad luck to draw a sword before you really need it."

Slightly alarmed by his comment, you wonder, "do you think I *will* need it?"

"Almost certainly."

"And you'll be needing all the luck you can get," Thomas adds.

"Why? Am I not handsome enough for her majesty?"

"Probably not."

Though this is the friendly, good-natured banter you two have enjoyed for years, today it bothers you. Doesn't he realize that things are different now? That you deserve more respect since you're venturing out on a quest?

The conversation comes to a halt for a moment, as Old Man Goodfellow brings the third mug of ale over. Frederick reaches over to the bar to claim it, whilst you slide in next to Thomas and take your own. Just three men enjoying a drink together. But you have important things to discuss.

"But that's not what I meant," Thomas says. "I meant you'll need luck getting to that tower in one piece."

"How so?"

"Remember what I said earlier? There are *things* out there." He pauses, as if weighing up whether to elaborate or not, whether to tell you more. "Nasty ones."

"Things? Like what?"

"There are the Plagued Lands for a start. You'll have to give those a miss." He takes a drink. "Unless you *want* your face to fall off."

You're pretty sure you don't want that.

"Then there's dragons." Frederick this time, lips still foamy where he just took a sip of his ale. "Great winged beasts with breath of fire and teeth of death."

You snort. "Yes. So they say. But when was the last time anyone actually *saw* a dragon?"

"You could say the same for your princess. She's not been seen in years," Thomas says.

"Yes, but the legend explains that. Only those brave enough to reach the tower can look upon her beauty."

Wiping the foam from his lips, Frederick nods. "That's true."

Your tone is defensive as you look to Thomas and say, "Anything else?"

"Giants, ghosts, gladiators." He takes a big drink as he thinks, almost draining his mug. "Oh, and the Winged Women of the Wicked West."

Frederick's eyes mist over as hears the name. "Now *there's* a legend worth telling."

"I saw someone that met one of the Winged Women once," Thomas says.

The blacksmith shakes his head. "Impossible. No one sees a Winged Woman and lives."

"I never said he was *alive*. I found him–what was left of him–on my farm. Horrible sight, he was." Thomas smiles. "Still, my pigs fed well that day."

You're bewildered by all of this new information.

You look into your mug of ale, as yet untouched.

Thinking that you might need a few more of them before you set off into the unknown.

It's the next afternoon before your drink-induced headache abates enough for you to walk in a straight line, and that's when you say your final farewells and leave the town of your youth.

It's not until you've been walking for half an hour that you realize something:

You're not sure what you're supposed to *do* on a quest.

But you keep on walking, anyway, sure that something will pop up en route to the princess's tower.

You reach the Plagued Lands.

A huge sign warns people not to enter. Still, the smell surely serves the same purpose—an awful reek of death.

It's inconsiderate, making this place so close to the princess's tower. Did they think someone as lovely as her would want her saintly nostrils assaulted by *this* filth every day? If you could only gain access to the area without your skin falling off, you'd take your sword to each and every one of the plague victims for their impudence.

Then you'd show off to the princess.

Who knew *how* grateful she would be for such a selfless act of heroism?

The deviation away from the Plagued Lands takes you over hills and through valleys, the roads beneath your feet opening up to expose a whole new world that you never even dreamed of.

Should you be worried, though?

After all, the vast threats promised by Thomas and Frederick have yet to materialize.

Maybe they were trying to scare you. Because they were jealous of you. Jealous of your courage.

You're resting when this thought occurs to you, lying on the grass in a shade. And you realize you have yet to wield the fine sword that the blacksmith made for you.

You want to feel the power in your hands.

But you remember his warning.

Won't this bring bad luck?

"Don't be stupid," you say to yourself. "Who needs luck?"

And then you unleash it.

Hold the weapon aloft.

You imagine running in through a few of the disease-ridden denizens of the Plagued Lands, slaughtering the foul souls whose stench of decay must so perturb the lovely princess. You fantasize about bringing her their hides. Then the princess showing you hers…

The image makes you more eager than ever to see her.

So you sheath your sword and walk once more.

And soon you come upon the town.

You're worried, at first, that you've just walked in a huge circle, that Thomas is about to appear at any moment and laugh at you.

And if he does…

Your eyes narrow.

Your hand tenses on the hilt of your sword.

On further inspection, though, this is not your town at all. It's just one similar to yours. And, luckily, that similarity includes a tavern.

You walk into it, eager to taste ale once more.

But you're a little disappointed by the reaction when you enter.

No one turns to look at you and gasp. Instead, the people inside carry on drinking, as if you're not on an important quest.

But never mind.

They'll know soon.

The whole *world* will know, when your name joins that of the princess in the legends they tell.

This makes you smile as you take a seat at the bar.

The bartender looks disturbingly like Old Man Goodfellow, and he says, "What can I get you, son?"

"Well, I don't know. What would you recommend for someone on a very special quest?"

"How about this?" He pours.

Not quite, it must be said, the response you were hoping for.

To add insult to injury, when you've paid for your ale, he doesn't do what he should do, doesn't enquire as to the nature of your quest and then sit enraptured before you as tell him your tale. No, he just moves down the bar and serves somebody else.

You're shocked by this, and you start thinking up ways you can embellish this story when you tell it to princess later. You take a swig of your drink, picturing the look on her wonderful face as you do so – then gag. Whatever it is he's given you, it's a lot stronger than what you're used to at Goodfellow's tavern.

Nice, though.

You could get a taste for the stronger stuff. Now that you're an adventuring man.

You're about halfway through the mug when the man plonks himself down on the empty chair next to you.

"Did I hear you say that you're on a quest?"

"Yes, I am. What of it?"

"Looking for anything interesting?"

"Just trying to win the heart of a good woman."

"Never had a heart myself," he says. "What do they taste like?"

You drink a little more, trying to work out if the stranger is joking with you or not.

But there's no smile on his face.

"Not a literal heart. A…" you falter then, not quite sure how to put it. The best you can do, and it is feeble even to your ears, is, "a heart of love."

"Sounds like an odd sort of quest."

He could be right. So far it hasn't seemed like much of a quest at all. Just a rather long and tiring walk.

"You should go and talk to Henry. He knows all about quests and stuff. You might have even heard of him."

"I see." You drain the drink then place your mug back on the bar. "And where might I find this Henry?"

"Big house on the end of town. You can't miss it."

"Thanks." You stand, placing a few coins down on the table. "Have a drink on me."

"Lovely." He signals to the bartender for service. "Good luck with the quest."

You walk through town in merriment, excited at the thought of talking to another quester.

What sort of man will this Henry be? One happily retired from the world of adventuring, or a sad old man bitterly missing the thrills of long ago?

Neither, as it happens.

When he opens the door to his house, which is indeed big, you greet him with the words, "Hail Henry, fellow adventurer. I am on a quest to meet the beautiful princess who resides in the tower on the edge of the horizon." Or at least, you try to. In actuality, he cuts you off at "am," and bids you follow him inside the house.

You do so.

"So good of you to come and see me." Henry leads you into a huge front room. "I don't get many visitors these days."

"But how can that be?" you say, amazed that an adventurer such as he – and such as yourself, of course – is not idolized and worshipped by this town and others. "Don't they want to hear the tales you have to tell?"

"People tend not to like the way I tell them." He sits, gaze straying to a door at the end of this room.

Sitting down across from Henry, you take the chance to examine him further.

He looks familiar.

But how can that be, when you have never left your town?

Perhaps he once passed through. On the way to some far off land.

He looks back to you, saying, "Do I understand that you quest, too?"

"I do, sir."

"People only quest for one of three reasons." Henry's gaze flits away to that door again for a second. "They are love, gold, and destiny."

He looks back to you. "Which is yours?"

"Love, sir. I'm in love with the princess from the tower."

And that is the truth, is it not? You may have thought your true love once lay with Rowena, but ever since Thomas told you the story of the wonderful princess, you have realized that this is not the case. Only the princess can fill the gap in your heart. The princess and her love. And touch.

"I know of love," Henry says. "Perhaps you've heard of me. Though in the legend, they say that I'm a prince."

And then it hits you.

Where you've seen him before.

In storybooks read to you by your dearly departed parents.

"You're the prince who was left with the beautiful woman's shoe. And then had to try and track her down."

"Half right. I was never a prince, though." He winks at you, stands, and beckons you to follow him. "They just added that bit to make the whole thing sound more magical."

You remember the nights when your parents told you those stories. The whole thing coming alive in your imagination, the love blooming in your heart. You always loved those tales. And the story of the shoe – the story about this man here before you, this Henry – was always one of your favorites.

"It worked." You walk after him. "Was she truly as beautiful as they say?"

"She was all right, I suppose. Truth was, it was her stepsister I was after."

"Which one? There were three."

"All of them." He grins back at you. "Ugly girls are always dirtier, you see."

Then you're standing at the door he has been glancing towards.

"But some things are better than girls." Henry pushes open the door. "Even dirty girls."

He steps through the door into a room softly lit with candles. A room with a serene feel to it. Akin to a place of worship, like the church your parents used to take you to as a child.

"You know how to impress this princess of yours?" He glances back at you as you follow him into the room. "Slay a dragon for her. They always like that."

"Is that what's in here? Dragon skin?"

"No." Henry gives a crazy little laugh. "That would be weird."

He walks to the other end of the room.

There's an altar in the corner, strengthening your feeling that there's a reverential aura to this area. The candles that light the room are stood there on the table. But they're not alone. No, there's a shoe on there. A woman's high-heeled shoe. Just like in the legend they used to tell about the man.

He lifts up the shoe and rubs it against his face. Moaning slightly as he does so, rapture in his eyes.

"You didn't go searching for her?" you ask him. "To see whose foot it would fit?"

"No," Henry replies, and he starts to lick the shoe. "Me and this little baby get along just fine."

Well, you think, heading away from the town later in the night, *that's legends for you. They're never quite the same in real life.*

Still, he's given you some clues about what to do next, at least. All you have to do is find a dragon. And then slay it.

Simple.

Not the sort of thing that small-town life has prepared you for. But you need to move beyond your humble roots if you're to win your princess's heart. And then probably lie about them.

So you search for a dragon.

You remember, from stories you were read as a child, that they live in caves. So that's where your search begins.

In the first cave, you find nothing.

In the second, you find rats.

They're nasty little things, but a bunch of rat's heads won't impress the princess. That said, you've not eaten in a while, so they still have their uses.

You head back on your way, well-fed.

Burping a little.

But you manage to keep them down.

The next cave has a skeleton in it, and you think your luck is in. Perhaps a dragon pulled its victim in here and consumed its skin, leaving only bones behind. Maybe this is its lair, and it will return soon, to find you and your sword waiting.

But after three days and nights, you realize that this cave probably *isn't* a dragon's domain. That the guy just crawled in here and died for some other reason.

"Useless." You kick the skeleton.

Then you head back out.

It's probably fair to say that you're feeling a little demoralized by this point. The nourishment you received from the rats has gone, and you're dehydrated, too, the ale from the tavern just a happy memory. That's probably why it happens.

You black out and stumble from a cliff-top.

Naturally, your first thoughts are of her. Of the lips you'll never get to kiss. The hips you'll never get to touch. The –

Then all is blackness.

When you wake, you're in a cave again.

Wrapped tightly in a blanket.

A fire crackling next to you, warming your body.

A big, green face looking down at you.

"Hello. I'm Leonard the Dragon."

You groggily pull yourself into a sitting position. "What happened?"

"You were falling from a cliff. Lucky I happened to be flying past at the time."

You grin. You'll have to let Frederick know his theory about drawing your sword before use is totally untrue.

"So you saved my life?"

"Of course. Why wouldn't I?"

"Well, I sort of thought you guys ate people like me."

"Dear me, no." He gives you a thorough looking over. "Though *you* look like you could do with some food, if you don't mind me saying."

He's not wrong. They may have temporarily filled a whole, but those rats you ate weren't exactly high in nutritional value. In fact, you probably used up twice the energy catching them as you did eating them.

"I have bread and apples and meat Feel free to take some," Leonard says.

"Thanks," you say, and head over to his little food pile.

"I notice you carry a sword. Are you a warrior?"

"Not quite." You're standing with your back to him as you eat. "Not yet."

"Oh?"

"I'm on a quest. To reach the tower where the princess lives."

"Oh yes. *That* tower."

You pause, a loaf of bread moist and half-eaten in your mouth. "What do you mean?"

"That tower is high indeed. How do you intend to gain entry?"

That's a good question, and not one you've really thought through in any way. So you're a little uncertain as you reply, "I'll just knock on the door. When I tell her all the things I've done, she'll let me in."

"I see. What things have you done?"

It's on the tip of your tongue to say, "Killed a dragon." Thankfully, some sense of self-preservation kicks in, allowing you to stop yourself. Still, it pleases you to see how easy you find it to boast of your exploits.

"Oh, just travelled far and wide," you say.

"Commendable. But that's not quite what I meant."

You eye your sword, lying on the floor of the cave.

"No? What did you mean?"

"There is no door. It was bricked over some time ago."

Of course, it was. As a further test. Only the strongest and cleverest would be able to get to her.

"There *is* a window. At the very top of the tower. Maybe you could be like that other fellow they talk about, the man who climbed the woman's hair to reach her."

You've heard this story, too. You're not too eager to stake your life on it, however, after hearing Henry's less than romantic re-telling of another old fantasy.

"Or, I could fly you to the top of the tower."

You look back at him.

Then down at your sword.

"I really wouldn't mind," he adds.

You think it over.

You realize that, on one hand, this could be the answer to all of your problems. He could fly you up and into the tower, and that would be the quest over and done with. But what have you really got to tell her about so far? How are you going to impress her when you haven't really *done* anything?

But then you remember your last conversation with your friend Farmer Thomas.

"Have you ever heard of the Winged Women of the Wicked West?" you ask, taking a sidestep towards your sword.

"Why, yes. But you should stay away from those. They're dangerous. Not to be trusted."

"Funny you should say that."

And you grab your sword and plunge it deep into the heart of the dragon that saved your life.

When it's done – when he's stopped twitching – you try to decide which piece of him you should cut off to present to the princess.

The head would make a pretty good gift.

But how are you going to carry it?

You decide to trim a little bit off his tail, and you stick it in your pocket for safe keeping. Thinking maybe you can come back later, with your love in tow, and show off your handiwork.

By the time you're done with the dragon's corpse, you're pretty dirty, your clothes covered in green blood. So you find a nearby lake and dive into it fully-clothed, and then strip to let your garments dry out in the sun.

You take the chance to look at your naked body.

You've lost weight since you started walking; your physique is in better condition than it has been in years. This is only right. Your old self was good enough for the likes of Rowena, but not for the lovely princess.

That said, it is your mind you'll need soon. You'll have to convince one of the Winged Women of the Wicked West to fly you to the tower, so you can drop in through the window that the late Leonard the Dragon mentioned. But how will you do that?

You decide that you'll know when the time comes.

Then you settle down to sleep.

Knowing that your quest is almost complete.

There might not be a warning sign posted near it, but the Wicked West looks just as dark and unwelcoming as the Plagued Lands.

Just beyond the Wicked West, shimmering on the horizon, the tower that holds your love looms ever closer. You just need to find an airborne guide to get you there.

So you walk onward.

It's a while before you see one of the Winged Women up close and personal; they're mostly just specks in the sky. Until you've been walking for about ten minutes, and one of them drops down and stands before you.

That's when your breath catches in your throat.

She's absolutely *gorgeous*.

Her hair is dark, her torso magnificently toned. The wings that spring out of her shoulders are vast and wonderful, and the silver harness that covers her chest leaves just enough to the imagination to make you want to see more. Even her voice is seductive as she says, "What business have you in our land, stranger?"

You should probably reply here.

But it's hard to find the words.

The creature is stunning, so stunning that you're only just now remembering to breathe around her. And you think back to your time spent in the town, the time before you were a mighty adventurer. How you could have ever thought that someone as plain and ordinary as Rowena was the person you wanted to spend the rest of your life with?

"Well?" the Winged Woman demands. "You'd better answer me – some of my sisters won't ask so politely."

That's a scary thought. Scary enough to make you explain, "I wish to hire someone with wings."

"What for?"

"To, uh…to fly me somewhere?" you offer tentatively.

She glares at you. "Is that supposed to be funny, little man?"

"No." You worry that she'll either fly off and leave you or dive in and eat you. "I'm serious. I really wish to hire you."

"Hire me? With what?"

"I have money." You go to hand her some coins.

She knocks your hand away. "Money is useless here. What we want, my kind takes."

But you're aware that her voice has changed.

Softened slightly.

Her eyes seeming to slide over you, lingering on certain parts.

It's been a while since anyone but Rowena looked at you that way, and it's nice. But you have to remain focused. The princess is the woman for you. The *only* woman.

But…

If this is the only way…

The Winged Woman comes a little closer, saying, "aren't you curious to be with one of my kind?"

You weren't. Not until now. Your old friend Thomas could not claim the same. Back at the bar, you hadn't really known what the Winged Women would look like. He had to explain it, descriptions growing increasingly graphic and crude the more he drank.

"Don't you want to know if all our parts match up?" she asks, within reaching distance.

The princess, you think.

Then her hands are upon you.

You're doing this all for the princess. Aren't you?

"*I'm* curious," the Winged Woman says.

Her face is inches from yours. Eyes looming large before you.

"But be warned," she says. "Women are the dominant ones in our species."

"Dominant?" you say. "What does that mean?"

She shows you.

"Oh, it's so free up here," you say, soaring high above the ground in the Winged Woman's hands. "It must be great to spend every day like this."

"It has its moments."

You're sore and tender, and you've got scratches in places it'll be hard to justify to the princess, but that's okay. See, you're on your way. The tower coming into sight, the quest almost complete. Part of a dragon's tail in your pocket and some fine stories to tell the princess.

"Big place," the Winged Woman says, looking at the tower. "You going to live there?"

"That's the plan."

"Well, if it doesn't work out, come track me down."

"Thanks. But I'm sure everything will be just fine."

With a slight shrug, she drops you down on the window ledge and soars back into the sky and away.

You take a chance to look back down at the ground before you enter.

You've made it.

You're here.

"My love," you say, and you climb through the open window and into the tower. "I have arrived."

And this is it.

The moment you've been waiting for.

"I brought you a little something," you say, and pull the dragon's tail from your pocket.

Then you gag.

It smells bad.

But no matter. Any minute, the princess will rush out and cover your face with kisses. She will press against you with the body you've dreamt of for so long.

Any minute now.

"Princess?"

What if she's not here? Now that the Winged Woman has gone. Since the door is bricked up, how would you get out?

Worse…

What if someone else got here first?

Your hand falls to your sword.

That's what if someone else got here first.

You move away from the windows.

It's so dark and gloomy in here…the shadows seem to swallow you.

You sniff again.

The smell's familiar.

It's death.

Like back in the Plagued Lands.

But it's not coming from the dragon's tail.

She steps out of the shadows.

Comes towards you.

A crown dulled with age on her head.

What *remains* of her head.

"Princess?"

She rushes you.

You don't have time to draw your sword, but even if you did, you could never hurt her. Not the princess. The princess who was locked up here not because she was waiting for a hero to rescue her, but because she had the plague. The princess who legend had turned into something quite far from the truth.

But you can't help how you feel.

And you still manage to croak out the words "I love you" before she eats your face.

NO MAGIC NEEDED
Kayla Bashe

Elle can tell when people had an image of her in their mind, when they talk to that image instead of her.

Her father had an image: the dutiful daughter, head bowed over her needlework, listening to him read with parted lips and endless loyalty. This image was happy to mend an endless stream of jackets and sit by his bed for hours.

The real Elle sat still at his deathbed, counting the seconds between each breath. He'd always been so foolishly sentimental about their run-down old estate—about the apple trees in the garden and the bodies buried underneath. She counted ten seconds after his gasps ceased before injecting panic into her voice and calling for the doctor. She never mended another jacket again.

Her stepmother and stepsisters had an image: the meek, scullery girl humming to bluebirds, grateful for every scrap of food, happy to manage the finances and the meals and the cleaning besides. This image wept and harbored no thoughts of vengeance.

The real Elle bargained at the market, wrangling last week's bread for half the cost. Enough sugar and her city-bred relatives would never be able to tell the difference. She saved every penny in a hollow knot of her mother's graveside tree. *They* thought she was wishing. Talking to ghosts. When conversation drifted towards her from an open window, her shoulders shook with laughter that she knew looked like tears.

Two months before the ball, she bought three yards of blue silk, hidden in the back of the donkey cart under the new curtains. She rented the carriage the night before.

The night of the ball, Elle tied her corset so tightly she could barely breathe. The prince didn't want to hear her speak. Her head was as light as her feet when she whirled across the ballroom floor, but her smile was brighter than her diamond earrings.

The Prince had an image of her as well, of course. Royal blood has no bearing on one's intelligence. He thought her beautiful and pliable and pink-cheeked. So grateful to be rescued from her horrid, horrid relatives, hiding against his shoulder when he sentenced them to death. This image thought only of the palace aviary and giving pennies to the poor. This image did not cry and cross her legs on her wedding night; she was grateful to be buried beneath the ceaselessly thrusting bulk of a prince.

Now, the entire continent has an image of Elle, one transported through ballads and broadsheets, portraits in pen. This image is a young widow, her husband tragically gone from this world after only one month of wedded bliss. She speaks with eloquent sorrow of the man who lifted her above torture and restored her family's estate, of how it was love the moment their eyes met mid-waltz.

Now that her husband is dead, the neighboring kings will war. They think she needs wishes to keep her hope alive. They think she needs magic to succeed.

Clad in the mantle of fairy-blessed innocence, Elle will steal their thrones. She will destroy their sovereignty and crush their crowns like glass beneath her small, slippered feet.

11/2/16
The King's Dragon People

AFTER THE GIANT

Josh Burnell

It's been six months since the giant fell from the sky, on a brisk, autumn morning in the Enchanted Valley. Men worked the fields, drawing sweet, plentiful vegetables from the valley's wondrous soil, children chased chickens that were so large and friendly they rarely had the heart to eat them, and women made pies in small, provincial homes, gossiping about the odd boy that lived at the foot of the Enchanted Cliffs. His only family was his grandmother, and his only friend, a cow.

But everything changed when a series of thunderous claps echoed through the land. Rhythmic, like chopping wood. The women drew from their homes, and the men raised their eyes to scan the pillowy white clouds that filled the heavens. Then suddenly, a great crack tore the sky apart, and everyone dove for cover. Later, a young boy named John would say that, for a split second, the sun went out. His friends would heartily agree, though in truth, they'd covered their eyes, too frightened to look out from the bushes in which they hid to see it for themselves.

And all would remember where they were when they felt the shockwave as the monstrous body of a giant smashed down upon the town. The head crushed the town square, burying the fountain beneath its monstrous crown. The torso fell across several blocks of shops, demolishing the entirety of downtown, slaughtering the jovial afternoon crowd. Only Mrs. Kensington's bakery was spared, missed by inches as it slipped between the giant's cavernous belt loop.

The monster's right arm came down at an angle, sweeping a thousand feet of farmland from the earth and casting it a mile across the valley, while its left slammed down on the church, burying Father Branworth in the rubble of the holy structure he built with his own two hands.

Its buttocks obliterated the textile mill and crushed the mill's four dozen workers, including Mrs. Fitzpatrick, who for years had told friends she'd never survive to see her thirty-second birthday, a promise she kept by a week.

Last to fall were the legs, one unimaginably massive trunk collapsing the buildings that lined the dock, smashing the Armory and the Fish Market, while the other leg drove through Thomas Wilkins's cow farm, crushing half his herd and sending the others stampeding toward the hills at such a flurry that they knocked down the fence and didn't stop running until they'd either drowned themselves in the river or marooned themselves halfway up the Enchanted Cliffs that surrounded the valley.

All in all, the giant's body killed half the population of the village, more than two-hundred souls. After the shockwave, only two buildings remained miraculously intact: the aforementioned Kensington's Bakery, though most townspeople found the pastries bland and the bread too hard, and an outhouse east of the town square where the valley's breezes carried its stench toward the trees.

And when the dust cleared, it would have proven a testament to the human spirit that the people of the Enchanted Valley should pick themselves up and rebuild, but the dust never cleared. The cloud, knocked free by the giant's unimaginable weight slamming into the valley's soft soil, filled the sky with ancient minerals. And while the cliffs had once been the cause of the valley's perfect weather and moderate temperatures, now they served only to trap the dust cloud and blot out the sun.

Within days, the crops died and the townspeople coughed up dark globs of phlegm and sneezed ropes of black snot. Dr. Mallory, the community's only surviving physician, called their condition the Dust Cold, and their skin turned gray and pallid.

The sick were given token prescriptions of bedrest and clear liquids, but they soon found that they couldn't sleep in the tepid air and the cloud had tainted the water. Once the pride of the townspeople, their water was a glittering, refreshing liquid that was often bottled and sold to travelers at a premium, but it was now consumed as little as possible. One sip turned the tongue and two sips caused diarrhea. Few ever attempted three unless they were truly desperate.

And so, with the crops dead, the cattle slaughtered, and the water ruined, the people of the Enchanted Valley turned to the only resource they had left: the monstrous body of the giant. First, they stripped its massive clothing, sewing the stiff canvas pants into tents to replace their homes and cutting the tunic into squares they used as blankets.

The skin they dried and cured. Some attempted to make clothing out of it, but it was too tough. Others tried to eat it, but they found the consistency similar to two-inch thick leather. Finally, the McCords, a family of sheep herders whose flock had fled with the cows, sliced the giant's skin into strips and sold it as rope. They made a good business until Thomas Wilkins, the cowhand, cut the veins from the giant's wrists and found that they were much stronger for tying off the townspeople's wares.

The giant's left arm was butchered, the meat of the bicep cut into massive, yard-long steaks. Families took them to their tents and ate the meat bland, until Patricia Bennett, the town chemist, devised a way to harvest salt from the giant's melon-sized sweat glands. It satisfied the townspeople for a while, but the technique was time consuming and expensive, and soon, only the wealthiest of residents could afford the luxury.

The blood was bottled and served, and while it satiated their thirst, it turned their lips and teeth black. Sadie Devlin, formerly a cook at the Tavern lost beneath the giant's monstrous left shoulder, was the first to realize that the blood of the arteries deep in the giant's arm tasted sweeter and had a more pleasing mouth feel than the blood of the veins, which were more easily accessible at the surface of the giant's two-story tall wrists.

Soon, Sadie and a group of other connoisseurs were bottling blood from all over the body. The plasma from the feet they found to be bitter, but rich, while the liquid from the head was thick and sweet and made the drinker feel warm. The vein blood was less pleasing but easier to come by, while the artery blood was soon in high demand by the wealthy.

And so, the people of the Enchanted Valley did their best to survive the terrible plight that had, literally, befallen them, and though their day-to-day lives often involved horrors unimaginable just a few months before, Sadie's resource brought a joy to their lives.

That's when the problems started.

Despite his brief ten years, John could feel the tension growing in the valley. His father, once a farmer, now a calf monger, was a strong man with a neck lined with ropes of muscle. Before the giant fell, his father would come home at night, lift John into his giant arms and rustle his hair with hands brown with dirt. Now, his father returned from a long day of cutting and curing strips of flesh from the giant's left calf, and fell into a chair at the table, his hands black with dried blood.

Their house had been shaken to its foundation by the shockwave, so they lived in the shadow of the giant's left foot, on a small rise called Foothill, in a tent barely large enough to contain John and his parents. It consisted of a small cook-fire, a wooden table they'd rescued from their old house, and two mattresses made of scraps from the giant's socks, stuffed with the giant's thick, wiry leg hair.

One night, John came in from playing to find his father falling asleep at the dinner table and ran to him, flush with excitement.

"Papa," he shouted, "at school today, Stephen Willoughby told us they opened the giant's stomach and found a person living inside. A little girl in a pink dress that smiled and sang songs about the sky."

But his father only sighed.

"They opened the stomach weeks ago, but weren't no little girl in there. Just more Stench."

The Stench, as the townspeople had come to call it, emanated from the giant's stomach and chest cavity a few months after they'd cut it open. It hovered around the Enchanted Valley like a fog, smelling of stale sweat and rotten meat. The townspeople were annoyed but undaunted, and after a few days, they managed with the assistance of perfumed cloths they wore over their mouths and noses, and this worked until a team of excavators unearthed the giant's massive heart.

The search for the heart had been a long one, as for weeks, men had delved deeper and deeper into the monster's body cavity, the chest alone more than fifty-yards high, to find the organ. They took to the task out of curiosity, anger, and as the brave Chester Copperpot said "Because it's there," but the men all returned in failure, and Chest Copperpot never returned at all.

Soon, the organ took on mythic proportions, symbolic of the giant's power that, in an instant, had changed the lives of everyone John had ever known, and as communities sprung up around the body, a tacit truce evolved over ownership of the heart. Everyone knew it would be located eventually, but when it did, they silently agreed to leave it be.

And so the day came that a team of men did find the heart. Word of the discovery moved quickly through the valley such that dozens of townspeople were in attendance to see the organ's reveal, but, as if to reinforce the community's brittle truce, it did not arrive with victory, but instead, brought with it a monstrous cloud of Stench.

All in attendance got sick including John's young twin sisters Ellen and Avery. They'd skipped to the chest cavity to see the great unveiling, but they came home stumbling. Vomiting and fainting led to coughing up blood and boils on their soft skin.

More than three dozen people died within a week, including Ellen and Avery, and the heart was thenceforth left alone.

"I need you to do something for me," said John's father, as he finished a bowl of calf stew, a dark slop John's mother prepared from calf meat and foot blood and seasoned with ankle cartilage and shaved toe nails.

"Don't," John's mother interrupted, from where she was darning socks at the table.

"He needs to learn." John's father gestured for John to come closer. "I need you to find Connor Macintosh. He left three days ago for the Head, and we think he's still there. I need you to find him and give him a message. Can you do that?"

"Of course," John said, eager to be treated like a grown-up.

Connor Macintosh was one of his father's oldest friends. Before the giant fell, he was a blacksmith that made all of the town's farming tools with steel; now, he carved blades and shovels out of the giant's massive ankle bones.

"What do you need me to tell him?"

John's father slipped him a small bit of paper, folded over on itself and sealed with a stamp of the giant's earwax. "Give him this note. Tell him it's from the Foot Men." That's what John's father and his friends called themselves, the Foot Men, the strong, hard working men that worked at the far end of the giant's body, harvesting the tough flesh from the feet and legs.

John's father hushed his voice. "And don't show that letter to anyone, not even yourself. It's a secret. You know what a secret is, right?"

And John nodded because he'd known what a secret was since the day Ellen and Avery died. His mother had called him into the tent and asked him to sit beside the small mattress the girls shared, while she ran out to fill a pitcher with water at the twins' behest.

Once their mother was gone, the sisters coughed and weakly confided in John that they had a gift for him, a small pebble, one of two they had found while digging through the refuse knocked free from the giant's toes. The pebbles were warm and green and seemed to glow even in the dark. His sisters wanted him to have one and make sure they were buried with the other - for luck, they said - but John had to promise not to tell their parents, as their father grew increasingly wary of anything that came from the giant.

So, John took the pebble, stuffed it low in his pocket and kissed his sisters as they slipped away.

And so, the next morning John packed a satchel with calf jerky, marrow cakes, and a skin filled with bitter foot blood. His mother also gave him four pennies for the journey, not enough to rent a cart or purchase a meal, but all she had. As the crow flies, the trek from Foothill to the Head would take a few hours, but now, with myriad tent cities and wreckage to wade through, he expected the walk to take him a full day, so he packed a bedroll as well.

He left early, when the air was cool and the scent of the giant's body hung low and quiet to the ground. Foothill was a small encampment, but still one of the largest on the Giant's Road, the dirt path that started at Foothill and wound all the way to the Head, and as John left the town, he waved proudly to his friends, children with black mouths that grinned and waved back.

The first encampment John passed beyond Foothill were the Calf Mines where the Foot Men worked. Scaffolding ascended the giant's leg, reaching fifty-feet into the sky. With it, John's father and his neighbors climbed the giant's massive limb and cut out the meat that was their livelihood.

At the base of the scaffolding was Calf City, where the meat would be processed, weighed, and cured. It was run by Governor Wallace, as were all of the processing cities that dotted the giant's body. Calf City, Waistburg, Bicep Town. Governor Wallace ran them all and kept the majority of the profits. John's father, on the other hand, made a penny for every ten pounds of meat he could bring down, and all the free steaks he could carry.

Because steaks were plentiful in the Enchanted Valley. It was blood that was in demand.

Beyond Calf City, John passed a myriad of travelers' villages, tiny encampments where people seemed to stop for the night and never leave. In the shadow of the giant's kneecap, he purchased a skewer of Candied Marrow from a street vendor, an old man with a pink hat made from the soft tissue of the giant's foreskin.

"You alone?" the old man asked. His speech was slurred and his breath smelled of vinegar and ammonia. John had heard that the vagabonds that wandered the Giant's Road were known to ferment the monster's urine, turning it into a kind of sweet wine.

The old man narrowed his eyes at John. "Sometimes, I think the folks that got crushed were the lucky ones."

John had seen his uncle's body after it was crushed by the giant's heel, so he couldn't fathom what the statement meant, and twisted his brow in confusion.

"What?"

"Think about it," the old man said, pointing to the giant's massive knee cap, where a team of excavators had cut a cave to harvest the giant's soft cartilage. Then he laughed so loud and aggressively that John moved on, confused, and so distracted that he couldn't enjoy the Candied Marrow and cast it into the shrubs that grew around the giant's towering thigh.

###

When the sun peaked and the temperature rose, John donned a scrap of canvas cut from the giant's undergarments and tied it around his mouth and nose. His mother had touched it with rose water, the only possession she rescued from their old home. Its scent reminded him of her smile, when his mother's teeth were still white, and her hair fell in brown ringlets around her face. In the memory, she grins at him in his old room, with his twin sisters and a father that still knew how to laugh.

The canvas did its job to distract from the Stench as John walked on past Thighville and Waistburg, but soon, it became unbearable. He kept walking, breathing through his mouth and putting the cloth away as the tall tents of Organ Town took shape in the distance.

When the people of the Enchanted Valley first harvested the giant's body, they avoided the torso as long as possible, knowing that the organs would be the messiest to deal with, the hardest to manage. So, when the time came, it fell to the most impoverished of the Valley's people, the most desperate, to do the deed. And when they cut into the cavity, slicing into the side of the giant's chest, carving a path between its monolithic ribs, thousands of gallons of blood and other fluids spilled out.

Excavating the torso was filthy work, and the people that did it became accustomed to that filth, the blood that was too plentiful to wash off and the organs that were too viscous to avoid. They lived blood-stained lives that could end at any moment, cut short by a collapsing rib or a pocket of Stench.

Organ Town became home to people that liked to live quick and loud. Brothels sprung up everywhere, make-shift taverns and gambling dens.

John's father once said that there was no law there, only survival.

John held his satchel close as he entered the village, listening to his feet squelch in the bloody Giant's Road, as filthy men and women moved past him and disappeared into tents that were covered in black handprints.

"Aye," came a call and John turned to see a woman standing outside a massive tent made of four of the giant's ribs, sunk low in the ground, tied at the top with lengths of vein, and strung with skin cut from the giant's side. A faint image was centered on the tent like a crest. It was a massive tattoo - a skull and crossbones - like the one his father had gotten when he was a boy and his mother used to smile at when she knew he wasn't looking.

"You coming from Foothill?" The woman said, stepping away from the tent. She wore a long peasant skirt and a tight corset from which her breasts, which John only in recent weeks found interesting, threatened to spill out.

"I am." He stood tall and deepened his voice, trying to sound older.

"I thought so. You're too soft to be from Organ Town and too polite to be from the Head."

"I'm John."

"Maris is me."

John smiled. Maybe Organ Town wasn't so bad after all.

Suddenly, shouting surrounded them, as men and women rushed past. John and Maris followed them to a gathering behind the tent, where a man stood over an empty barrel.

"They took it. They took it all" he shouted. The man had dark skin and a thick, black beard.

Maris leaned down to whisper to John.

"That's Valdor. He be the leader in these parts. Someone must have stolen the Rations."

Rations, as the villagers had come to call them, were the remaining dry goods—oats, grains, beans, and wheat - that had been salvaged from the town after the giant fell and before the dust cloud contaminated the crops. As meat was so plentiful, Rations became worth more than money and were often used in its place. In Foothill, most of the Rations were stored in a small tent at the center of town, but three days ago, Brandon Willoughby, Stephen's father, had found the tent empty. The Foot Men were certain that someone from Organ Town had taken them and had met in the woods every night since to discuss how they should handle it.

"It's them," Valdor hissed, he face red.

"Who?" asked one of a dozen onlookers.

"Those people at the Head. The damned royals. They already have everything, but they still want more, so they take from the likes of us."

"You're talkin' crazy," shouted Maris. The group turned their filthy faces toward her. "Them's at the Head have plenty of Rations. Why would they want ours?"

"They don't want our Rations. They's only taking them to distract us." Valdor leaned his thick forearms on the empty barrel, training his eyes on the group. "They's coming for the heart."

"They can't," shrieked someone.

"It's ours," said another.

"You're damn right, it's ours," answered Valdor. "We's the ones that live in the shadow of the chest. We's the ones that brave the Stench every day."

"We can't let them take it," shouted the crowd, their jeers and cries reaching a din that turned their faces red and drove their fists to the sky.

But Valdor only smiled. "We can't, and we won't."

John trembled, his eyes darting at the faces around him, so overwhelmed by their fury that he didn't notice when Maris seized his arm and dragged him back to the Giant's Road.

"You need to go. It's not safe here for a boy from the Foot. Hurry home, stay inside, and tell your mother you love her."

"But I'm not going home," said John, planting his feet. "I'm going to The Head."

Maris's mouth twisted in concern. "What are you going there for?"

"My father needs me to take a message to his friend, Connor Macintosh."

"The Blade Man?" Maris turned away. "Whichever way you going, you best be going quick. Organ Town ain't no place safe for children. Pretty soon, ain't no place on the Giant's Road gonna be safe for anyone."

John walked and didn't stop. Outside of Organ Town, where the Giant's Road returned to the dry, dusty state he was accustomed to, John met a small child that sold him a square of bread for a penny, but when he bit into it, he realized it was just a slice of one of the giant's fibrous scabs, rolled in dandruff. Still, he ate it, because he'd already finished the marrow cakes and because, to a boy from Foothill, even scab was a treat.

He kept walking and as the sun disappeared from the sky, the Enchanted Valley took on a sickly hue of yellow. He passed a small encampment called Nipple Square that his mother told him to avoid at all costs and, further on, saw the women of the Finger Lakes washing their laundry in a small waterfall created by the giant's massive left hand crashing into the river. Beyond that, he found the Elbow Bridge. It cost two cents to cross, the last of his money, but it saved him having to trek through the damp, dark Armpit Cave.

Finally, he rounded the shoulder and saw, for the first time, the giant's massive head. It stood one-hundred-and-fifty feet tall, and as the sun disappeared behind the monster's nose, it drew a monolithic silhouette of skin, bone and cartilage on the orange sky. He passed beneath an arch, made from one mammoth golden tooth, and continued down the Giant's Road. High torches lit the way, fueled by fat from the giant's chin, guiding John past the large flowing tents of the Enchanted Valley's richest inhabitants. They were made from the soft flesh of the giant's lips, strung with hair dyed blue with the pigment of the giant's eyes and decorated with paintings drawn in every shade of blood.

The people of the Head feasted on the soft, luxurious flesh of the cheeks and slept beneath blankets sewn from the giant's feather-light eyelashes. Unlike the Foot Men and the Organ People, their mouths were not black as they drank the giant's refreshing, clear saliva, and when they celebrated, they did so with the most expensive bloods from the brain and the arteries closest to the heart.

He followed the Giant's Road to where it ended at the monster's colossal ear, and there, a staircase had been erected to the Governor's Mansion. Originally, Governor Wallace made his home in a stone castle at the top of the town square, but it had been crushed by the giant's head, so the governor had his new mansion built in the same spot, positioning it on the giant's long, flat forehead, a stunning, bleached white structure made of the giant's teeth and strung with the feathery flesh of the eyelids.

The Head's residents were amassed at the foot of the staircase, dressed in silks and lace, cut from the giant's collar. John slipped through the crowd to find the governor standing at the front of the group, a squat man with a thick mustache and a head that consumed his neck. He held a scepter carved from the giant's tooth, crowned with an enormous, polished gallstone.

"Just this morning, I received word that another of our members had their Rations stolen by the men of the Foot, and still the Organ people dig further into the cavity, releasing more and more of the Stench into our precious air.

"This cannot stand. We can no longer sit idly by and watch Foothill foster criminals and Organ Town destroy our homes. The question we must ask is no longer whether or not we will fight, the question is whether or not we strike first."

Grumbles ran through the crowd. John inspected their faces, witnessing mumbles of assent and moans of concern, but mostly, what he saw was fear.

"And so," the governor said, "I've decided the time has come. We must take up arms this instant and prepare to defend what is ours. We must show them that we are superior, that we are strong and mighty. And that power rules from the Head."

The governor raised his scepter high. "Tomorrow, we take the heart."

The crowd cast off their uncertainty and erupted in shouts of excitement so furious that it shook John to his core. Their faces lit with anger, and their fists waving weapons in the air. The servants, standing at the edges of the group, worried for their safety and the safety of their friends and family back home.

Terror shot through John and he dove back into the crowd. He had to get home, he had to warn Maris and Valdor and his father at Foothill. He'd forgotten his task, what he'd come all this way to do. He had to tell them that the Head was coming.

He bumped into the townspeople, drawing shouts of anger and confusion, but he kept going, emerging from the gathering and sprinting down the Giant's Road, getting halfway to the arch when-

A firm hand grasped him, dragging him away. He fought, screaming and clawing, until he was tossed into the dark of a small tent and looked up into the furious red face of his attacker, the man he'd come to find, the Blade Man, Connor Macintosh.

"John," said Connor, "what are you doing here?"

John sat on a small stool, hovering over a cup of Tear Drop Tea amidst the Blade Man's wares. The scent of flowers and the sting of salt wafted up from the drink, but John found himself too overwhelmed to enjoy it.

"They're going to war."

"Yes." Connor's broad shoulders sagged low. "Yes, they are."

"The people of Organ Town are, too. They know the Head is coming, they know they want the heart, and they're prepared to fight for it."

"I know that, too, John."

Connor's sad eyes drooped at the corners to meet a thick gray beard. He had no mustache, as was the custom of the Foot Men, and his neck rippled when he was thinking, just as John's father's did.

"The Foot Men have heard rumors for some time that there would be a battle for the heart. Your father sent me here to sniff it out, because, as the Blade Man, I can go places others can't and hear things when people think no one is listening. I saw Valdor in Organ Town and heard his woes, and met the Governor at the Head, and listened to his anger, and it became clear that the rumors were true. I'd hoped that battle wouldn't come. Unfortunately, it's coming sooner than I imagined."

"Then let them destroy each other," John said, savagely. "Let the Head and Organ Town battle over the heart until nothing remains. Afterward, my father and the other Foot Men will bring the valley back together."

"Open the note, John."

John pulled the note from his pocket, the small slip of paper his father had sent him all this way to deliver in a conversation that seemed so long ago. He broke the seal made from the giant's ear wax and revealed its brief message: AT DAWN WE TAKE THE HEART.

John's heart sank. "How did you know?"

"The Foot Men have been talking about an attack for weeks, but I'd successfully held them off. And when I left, your father agreed not to do anything until I got back, but when I saw you, I knew he'd changed his mind."

"But they can't. They're outnumbered. They won't survive."

"Deep down, your father knows that. All the Foot Men do."

"Then why? Why fight if they're just going to lose?"

"Because the people of the Enchanted Valley are tired, John. Tired of squabbling over scraps, tired of drinking bitter blood and eating bland steaks, tired of living in the shadow of the lives they used to have, lives they're certain were better. Sooner or later, that exhaustion turns to bitterness, and that bitterness turns inward, and people go in search of someone to blame. The head blames the feet, the feet blame the guts, and the guts blame the head. They might solve it if they could work together, but if they can only find fault in each other, they'll only succeed in tearing themselves apart."

"But it isn't their fault." John's face burned and tears stung his eyes like the Stench. "It's the giant's fault."

"But that's the problem, John. You can't punish an act of God, so you punish yourself."

John opened his mouth to protest. He didn't know how to stop it, but Connor must. He was older, wiser, but when John looked at his face, all he saw was sadness and surrender, and he lost something he didn't know he could: hope.

He sprung up and threw months of anger and confusion into his feet, bursting from the tent. He ran away from the Giant's Road, away from the Head, beating his feet across the dirt where grass no longer grew, running beneath the dust cloud that hid the moon, into the darkness until the shouts and cheers of the people of the Head fell into the distance, until he reached the barren, lifeless trees at the edge of the Enchanted Valley, and he ran until he came to the foot of the Enchanted Cliffs.

Then he climbed. His hands gripped the shale walls and his feet dug into the dusty rock, lifting him higher and higher.

He climbed until he could see the Giant's Road winding into the distance, and he climbed until he could count the torches of the Head, the cook fires of the Finger Lakes, and the bonfires of Organ Town. He climbed until he could make out the giant's entire monstrous shape, extending the length of the Enchanted Valley, and the towns and villages that made up life on the Giant's Road. And still he climbed until he found himself inside the dust cloud, his eyes watering in the haze. It filled his mouth, heavy and metallic on his tongue, and still he climbed.

Finally, he blinked the dust from his eyes and raised them to the sky where the moon hung high and full and impossibly bright. He found a perch on the edge of the cliff, a rocky outcrop, and sat, taking in the heavens, so pure and black and filled with enumerable twinkling stars. It seemed like a lifetime since he'd seen those stars, and with them came a rush of memories: his father chopping wood, his mother growing vegetables, his sisters chasing the chickens in the yard of their old house.

He looked down, straining through the dust cloud to trace the lights of the towns that lined the Giant's Road, then to the edge of the Enchanted Valley, and that's when he saw it. Thick and brown and hundreds of feet long, like a rope that had fallen across the valley floor, a rope the width of a tree.

Except it wasn't a tree, it was a beanstalk.

Flush with excitement, John descended the Enchanted Cliffs, moving toward it. The end had landed a few miles from the giant's right arm, but John wasn't interested in the end, he was interested in the root.

So, he followed the mighty trunk, now dry and brittle, as the moon dropped lower in the sky. His feet hurt and his hands were bloody, but as the first rays of sun peeked out from the edges of the valley, touching the dust cloud with a sick, mustardy glow, he saw where the beanstalk had been chopped down. It ended in splinters, still attached to a massive stump, so large it tipped up one corner of a tiny house. Beside it, a fence encapsulated a small pasture, and a small patch of newly turned soil was marked with a crooked, wooden cross that read: GRANNY.

Inside the cottage, John heard whispering and shuffling, someone having a hushed but feverish conversation with themselves. He knocked hard on the wooden door, but the conversation continued unabated, even as he knocked again.

Finally, he pressed on the door and watched it swing wide with the sound of tearing wood and fall hard onto the planks of the floor. It revealed a small room, open to the elements, with a crumbling fire-place still filled with smolders. The only light were the thin rays of virgin sun that slipped through the cracks in the walls, illuminating the dust in the air.

"Did you come from the sky?" begged a scratchy voice and John turned to regard a sickly man of about twenty with sunken eyes and a scraggly beard. His clothes hung in tatters as did the skin on his face, and he was sitting on a pile of pebbles.

"What?"

The man crawled across the floor to John, sending the pebbles skittering in all directions.

"Did you come from the sky?"

John's mouth went dry and he pressed his feet into the floor to keep from running. "No."

"Good," said the man, returning to the pile of pebbles, sifting through them, inspecting each one, frowning, then tossing it aside.

John followed him into the room, knelt down and picked one up, rolling it around in his fingers, feeling the smooth yet soft coating that enveloped it, and realized it wasn't a pebble at all.

"You stole the Rations," he said.

"The beans. I stole the beans," the man said, continuing to inspect each one and then tossing it aside. "Have to find the magic, have to stop the giant."

And all at once, it came to John: a magic bean that grew a mighty beanstalk, a beanstalk that reached to the sky, a beanstalk that was chopped down, that collapsed in the Enchanted Valley, and brought a giant with it.

"It was you." John seized the man by his paper-thin shoulders and slammed him against the wall. Then his hand found the blade, the blade from the Blade Man, and pressed it to the wild man's throat. "You brought the giant. You destroyed the town. You ruined *everything*."

"I didn't do it," sputtered the man. "But I can stop it."

"What?"

"I can fix it."

John stepped back, his hand still gripping the blade made of bone.

"How?"

The wild man dropped to his haunches and crawled back to his pile of beans.

"There are more. Other magic ones. I have to find them. To stop the giant."

"Other magic beans?" John reached deep into his pocket. "Like this one?"

He produced the pebble, the final gift from his dying sisters. It glowed, soft and green, in his hand. When the wild man saw it, his eyes grew large and his mouth dropped open.

"*Yes*."

"This is it?" John asked.

"Yes," the wild man shouted, his fingers twitching.

"This will stop the giant?"

"Yes."

The wild man dove forward and snatched the bean away, then crawled across the room and paused in a ray of sunlight, holding it on his open palm, studying it with awe and wonder in his tired eyes.

Then he dropped the bean on the ground and crushed it with his foot.

"What are you doing?" John said, feeling his stomach drop, his hope pulverized with the bean. "You said you would save us."

"I did."

"But you *crushed* it. You crushed the bean, and now my father is going to war and Organ Town will be destroyed, and everyone will die. You said you would save us from the giant in the valley."

"Not the giant in the valley," said the man, his eyes trembling with fright. "The other one. The live one that's still in the sky."

John left the man, who returned to his pile of beans, as the sun took shape on the edge of the dust cloud.

And within minutes, the sound of swords made of bone striking knives made of teeth rang out through the Enchanted Valley, followed by shouts of victory and cries of anguish. Smoke rose in the distance, first from one fire, then two, then more than John could count.

He couldn't stay at the house, where the wild man was too crazed to fathom the damage he'd done, and he couldn't return to Foothill, where his father was engaged in a fight he couldn't win, and he had no desire to see Maris in Organ Town or Connor Macintosh at the Head.

He couldn't see them because he wanted to blame them, to hold them accountable for everything he'd lost, but it wasn't their fault; it was the giant's, the giant that fell from the sky. He hated the monster, he wanted to punish it, but Connor was right, you can't punish an act of God. Unless, of course, you know where there's another God still alive.

So, John walked to the forest, where the bodies were buried, specifically, those of his young twin sisters, Ellen and Avery.

For there, John knew, was another magic bean.

BLUE WEDDING

Dimitra Nikolaidou

First, he feels her, like a sea breeze or the rain in the air. Then, he swings the double-doors open, and there she is, back turned, her long blue hair dripping water on the marble floor.

Her name pulses in his throat, but still he dares not utter it aloud.

"That was quick," she says without gracing him with a backwards glance. "But then again, you have always been good at stalking."

"Stalking?" It takes him a moment to blurt out the next words. "I was not stalking you. This is my castle, remember?"

She turns her head, and her sea-cave eyes pierce his words and kill them in his throat.

"Oh, I do—all too well." The menace in her voice makes his heart jump at his throat—only a fool is not afraid of the dark waters, and he ceased being a complete fool the day she left him, to go back to the sea. He swallows hard and lifts his white-gloved hands to show he means no harm.

"I am sorry," he says. "I apologize for my tone. I just did not expect to ever see you again, my lady, not even on a day like this."

"A wise assumption. I never meant to return."

Yet here she is, seven years after her escape. "What changed?"

"I could hardly miss my own daughter's wedding."

So she found out about that. He is not surprised, really; not even a desert prince, raised on wine and smoke, would have escaped the water's eyes—and his own castle blooms under the heavy Eastern rains, overlooking a vast, dark sea.

And he thought himself so clever the day he stole her shawl twenty years ago, forcing her to be his wife. What other lord had gotten himself a true fey for a consort, a queen of the wild beholden only to his will? Who else sailed his bed on the waters of the world every night, had children born with ocean eyes, and could pray to the seas and have his prayer answered on the spot?

Well, no-one else, that's who. The rest of his cousins brought earthly wives to the king's banquets; no matter their beauty or their dowry, they never outshone his own bride. Every time they arrived at a feast, the other lords' envy dripped from their skin, like Melusine's tears dripped the day she came out of the sea to find her shawl missing and him standing over her, clutching it tight in his hand.

Thankfully, the village witch warned him of her wiles; she would pretend she had a heart and speak of a mother waiting for her beneath the waves. None of it was true, of course—her kind had no familial bonds, loved no other but themselves.

What does she want here today, the day of his daughter's wedding? She dressed in a flowing gown of blue and silver, a diadem of fallen stars atop her head as if she expects to be seated by his side at the feast.

"My daughter, yes, of course. I take it you want to be present at the wedding?"

"Isn't that the protocol for the mother of the bride?"

She smiles now, a novel sight. "Not when she is considered dead and gone by all, her children included," he says with as much care as he can muster.

"Ah, that. Well, I would hate to scare the guests. I will make sure to remain unseen, so don't you worry."

His cannot stop his disbelief from furrowing his brow; she softens and her voice turns warm. "Worry not. Would I ever spoil her wedding?"

Would she? He does not assume to know.

"I am not aware of what you would and would not do, my lady," he says, and takes a few careful steps towards her. Now that the shock of seeing her again after all these years subsides, the familiarity born of a long marriage settles on his shoulders like a well-worn mantle. "I was a fool to think I knew you. I won't make the same mistake again."

"You were a fool to steal my shawl and make me your wife by force." The voice remains soft for now, and he relaxes even more as he comes to stand by her side.

"I know that now. I was a besotted idiot, and you did well to leave me behind."

Oh, he was lucky she simply left him instead of flaying him once she got her shawl back; he was not a fool to think that she came to love him in the meantime, so the only explanation he could think of was that she did not want to leave her human children all alone in the world.

The children; those she does seem to love, in her own elemental way. And how they turned out, despite their parents' cruel history. No wonder the whole kingdom is here today, to join in their joy.

Shoulder to shoulder with her, he looks down at the wedding preparations. His daughter gave him no trouble over his choice of husband. She is clever, and they both know she will bend anyone she marries to her own will. The only thing she asked for, once he announced her the match, was a nautical theme for the wedding: she wanted barges, a sea shell made of flowers and sweets that looked like foam and just a hint of salt mixed with the spun sugar. Oh, she knows her strengths, this daughter of his, knows how to turn her fey heritage to her advantage. She would get her happiness, or the world would crawl.

"You are smiling," Melusine says.

"It is a happy day, made happier by your presence." Despite the compliment he pays her, he keeps his voice neutral; he is as a man on the prow of a ship, safe only as long as he keeps his distance from the wide sea.

"How come there is no second wife to share the day with you? You must have had your fair share of offers."

"I am afraid my lady will not appreciate the answer."

"Oh?"

He holds his tongue, deliberating. The truth will make her mad, but he was never in the habit of lying to her, and now, she watches him, her inhuman eyes intent upon the truth.

"If I tell you, will you tell me something I want to know myself?"

"I might."

"I will take it." He would never have, before, when he had her shawl and there was no way for her to refuse him anything, but all this was in the past. "The truth is, I could never marry anyone else after having been married to you. I swam in the moonlit sea, and after that, everyone else was a glass of mud served to me cold."

He feels her disgust ripple her surface and closes his eyes, hurt to see how she angers at his expression of desire. Nothing new here of course, but having the shawl used to make it matter less, made it kind of fun.

Now, the intensity of her repulsion cuts him like a thousand sharpened corals.

"Is it my turn?" he asks.

"It is."

"How did you find the shawl? I had hidden it too well, and you would need my blood to open the chest."

Surprise makes her take her gaze of the window, and she turns to him, eyebrows arched in disbelief, lips parted. Another rare occurrence. "Of all the things in the world, this is what you want to learn from me?"

"It is." It drives him mad to this day. Every time he wakes up, he regrets his choice of a hiding place all over again, thinks of what he could have done differently to keep it hidden, keep her his. Wonders who could have betrayed him—the guards? The village witch? Some lover she took back then?

Better to know and be done.

"I promise. You will learn before the day ends," she says and turns again to the feast outside the window, her brief interest evaporating. He wants to punch the indifference out of her face, but self-preservation prevails. At least, she cannot lie; he will know what robbed him of his happiness before the sun sets over the lake.

"Thank you," he says. "Shall we descend? The guests await."

"You may go. I will find my way and a hiding place, too."

Of course—they are not a couple anymore. How easy it is to forget, standing beside her.

"I am sorry," is all he can say.

"It doesn't make a difference, my lord." Her voice is once more a river of venom.

He wasn't lying to her, when he said this was a happy day; standing by his beautiful daughter in their pearl and flower laden barge, his heart so full of joy he forgets to breathe. Not even the king's own wedding had been as perfectly painted as today—and it had not even cost him a chipped silver coin, for men competed to marry Melusine's daughter to the point of renouncing their right to a dowry and offering to pay for the wedding day themselves.

Not that it matters. He would have given up whatever his daughter asked of him and more, just to see her smile as she does now. She does resemble Melusine, but he is painted on her features, too. Her face is the last place on earth where the two of them remained united.

He looks back to the shore for his former wife, but she has kept to her word and is nowhere to be seen. If he knew her at all, she would only show up at the end of the day to deliver the answer she had promised and be gone.

No matter. Wise men do not regret what they cannot fix.

He stares straight ahead, at the groom's golden barge moving towards them, flower petals spilling from the sides, banners flowing in the breeze. It is more magnificent than their own vessel of course, given that the boy's father had more land and was so much closer to the king, but this only means his daughter is leaving him for an even better life, and she would do so in a splendid manner. A bridge would soon unite the two barges, ornamented with silver nets and sea creatures made of gems, and she would walk it to find her groom on the other side.

Life, taking its course.

Perhaps, he should look for a bride for himself, now that his passion has ebbed, and finally leave the past behind.

His daughter beams at him, and he smiles back, as gracefully as his overflowing heart allows.

"Are you happy?" he whispers to her. His hand barely touches her long blue veil.

"I am, father. This is the day I have been dreaming of for years."

He laughs and lets go of her veil. Her husband doesn't stand a chance against her, and he can tell she knows it; her stance is poised, but he senses the naked blade underneath. The barge approaches, the bridge extends trembling under the weight of its jewels. He whispers for her to move, and she lets go of his arm and steps on the white and silver filament, gliding towards the rest of her life.

And in the middle of the bridge, she stops.

Come on, my love, do not make a fool of me. Be brave.

His daughter turns to him, pushes her veil back from her eyes, and spits in the water.

The music halts on a screech. The boys in the groom's barge stop tossing petals aboard. The bride's eyes are two lakes of scorn.

"You want to know who found and returned her shawl, father?"

His blood bursts ice-cold.

"Never crossed your mind, did it? Not even when you knew that it took your own blood to open the lock, the blood that flows inside me?"

He wants to scream and hurt her; anger hammers his head now, but at the bottom of his heart, all he can find is an abyss of regret.

"Good riddance, father. I hope you die in pain and alone."

And for the second time in his life, the waters open and swallow what is more dear to him than life. Only instead of Melusine diving in, she now bursts out of the water, clad in the depths and crowned with dead stars, engulfing her radiant daughter. Embraced in blue, they descend together in the depths, no glance spared for the stunned court, the abandoned groom, or his own dissolving self.

The bridge stands alone, drenched in water, silver nets torn away. Unraveled, the pearl sea-creatures fall away into the depths.

He wants to dive after them, to drown regret at the bottom of her lake, but the waters will never have him. Muted in the empty barge, he is left to drift back to dry land.

TAMING THE BEAST
Kevin Hopson

The creature had been tracking him. Ruben was sure of it.

He smelled smoke from the nearby chimney as he lay face down in a dusting of snow, the moisture penetrating his shirt. Leaves crumpled beneath him as he shifted his weight, the late November breeze taking hold of the damp fabric and making Ruben shiver.

Too much noise. I have to keep still.

Ruben buried himself under the red cloak. Though tight, the shroud was long enough to conceal his entire body, including the snug hood over his head. Ruben's left hand stung. The blood dripping from it provided a clear trail for the beast. He winced at the pain.

Early morning sunlight trickled through the trees, blinding him. He tilted his head, allowing a large oak tree to block the hindering rays. Ruben spotted the girl twenty yards ahead. Hidden behind a pile of chopped wood, she peeked through a small opening. He offered a reassuring nod, his right hand gripping the hatchet tighter.

A mockingbird overhead ceased its singing, cut off by a snort. Then a louder one. Ruben put his face to the forest floor and played dead. The snow tickled his nostrils.

His heart thumped, the pounding threatening to tear itself from his throat. The beating inside his ears so loud that Ruben feared the beast would hear it. He slowed his breathing.

Crunching leaves alerted Ruben to the beast's location. Ten yards out, the creature maneuvered off to his left. A drawn-out growl came next. Ruben didn't dare look. Not yet. Based on the silence, he assumed the beast was stationary, possibly even within striking distance now. Ruben, about to roll over on his back, hesitated when it spoke.

"Fool," it said with a deep, throaty voice. "I know the girl is close. I can smell her."

Ruben sprung to his feet. The giant wolf, twice his size, sprinted toward the wood pile. Ruben ran after it, hatchet in hand. He couldn't match its speed and feared the worst. He could throw the axe, but what if he missed or the girl stood up?

Ruben ran as swiftly as he could. The wolf's powerful body increased the gap between them.

It soared over the wood pile.

A horrifying roar.

A deathly scream.

Ruben willed his legs faster, almost too scared to look.

The wolf lay on its side, a blade sticking from its chest.

The girl trembled, but he couldn't tell if from anxiety or fear or both. Ruben lifted the hatchet to deliver a final blow. The wolf's chest rose and fell, slowing until the yellow glow of its eyes faded.

"It's dead, Father. How did you know?"

Ruben lowered his hatchet.

"That it would come for me."

"I didn't. I hoped it would work. You did the right thing. It would have killed you."

"I know."

"It was just an animal." He wrapped his arm around her. "You're nothing like it. Thanks to your grandma, you're so much more."

"Yes. I am," she said, her irises glowing yellow."

SWEET REVENGE
Charlotte Bond

"I don't know, Gretel. I mean, we've only got Old Wainwright's word about what he saw, and he's not right in the head," Hansel said. He kept his voice low since they weren't standing far from where his wife crouched in the stream, washing his shirt.

Gretel put her hands on her hips and gave her brother a stern look. "He's old. Not stupid. And what about the smell he described?"

Hansel winced and Gretel pushed her advantage. "What other creature smells of both decay and gingerbread?"

Hansel's gaze drifted past her, into the dark woods at the edge of their village.

"Sweet gingerbread, a smell to make your mouth water." He shook himself, shoulders hunched as he resigned himself to her plan. "Fine. We'll go and look. Will that make you happy?"

"Yes. For now."

Hansel huffed in exasperation then walked off. Gretel went in the opposite direction. Inside, relief at having enlisted his help was mixed with trepidation about going into the forest again.

She returned home to find her father busy in the fields behind their house and her stepmother lying in bed, indulging in one of her regular afternoon naps. There was no one to see Gretel as she collected her bag and changed into sturdier shoes.

She met Hansel at the edge of the forest. He had his axe over his shoulder.

"Like old times," he said, as they set off through the trees. She gave a snort of laughter.

"Except this time we're going of our own free will."

"True. And we've no need of stones or breadcrumbs to find our way back again." Gretel and her brother shared a smile. Three years ago, it had taken them several days of wandering to return to their home after escaping the witch's cottage. But upon hearing their tale, the villagers set out in search of it. When they found it, they'd painted red marks on the trees to keep people from stumbling across the cursed place in the future. To find it now, all Hansel and Gretel had to do was go past all the markers that warned them to turn back.

They walked in silence. Gretel's head filled with the stories about the horror that had haunted the village for the past few moons — tales of a creature skulking on the outskirts, too large for a wild dog, too hunched for a bear. It hissed and scuttled and recoiled from the light, meaning that no one had done more than glimpsed it, except Wainwright. Recalling these stories now made her feet heavy, as if her body was rebelling from returning to that foul place.

Hansel, in contrast, whistled and walked with a light, almost skipping step. Family has gone to his head, and Gretel envied him somewhat.

But below the mild bitterness and jealousy, a warm glow of joy kindled over how her big brother was making his way in the world. All she needed to do now was find her own way.

Drawing nearer to their destination, the trees clustered around them, forcing Gretel to walk close behind Hansel or risk being hit in the face by the branches he pushed aside. The birds in the trees fell silent while the scuttling creatures in the undergrowth grew louder, as if a whole host of rats were teeming around them.

Hansel swallowed nervously. "Gretel, maybe we should-"

"Too late. We're here."

The witch's house had fallen into ruin. Large sections of the gingerbread had rotted away to reveal the wooden structure underneath. Gretel shuddered, thinking about the nights she had spent curled up against those walls inside the hut. Hunger had gnawed at her stomach while the tempting smell of gingerbread filled the air, infuriatingly unreachable on the other side of the wall.

The chocolate that coated the roof tiles had melted in the sun, blackening patches of grass where it dripped down. The sugar-panes of the windows were still intact but covered in an army of ants.

"The oven's round the back, isn't it?" Hansel's voice rasped. He licked his lips, his eyes darting nervously this way and that.

"You mean you don't remember?" Gretel asked.

Hansel looked at the house uneasily. "Every strut and every layer. Come on."

He led her to the rear of the decrepit cottage where a large clay oven stood. Memories stalled her in place: the heat of the fire, the weight of the door as she struggled to close it in time, the sickly smell of roasting flesh. When they left, the door had been closed and bolted. Now it hung open.

"An animal could have opened it," Hansel suggested. His tone indicated just how unlikely he thought this might be.

"An animal?"

"Yes. Maybe. Or it could have just swung open on its own. It has been three years, Gretel. Things break." He stepped forward with caution to the open door. He crouched down and peered inside. Gretel came up to stand behind him.

"Empty." He closed the oven door, lifting the latch just as Gretel did that fateful morning. The moment he pulled his hand away, the door swung open again.

"The latch is broken. That's why it's open."

"And the bolt?"

He shrugged. "Not there. Must have fallen off. It doesn't mean anything. It doesn't mean she escaped. Take a closer look yourself if you don't believe me."

Gretel clenched her fists, impatience with Hansel simmering inside her. She knew that seeing for herself was the only way to be sure. She did a circuit of the oven and knelt down by the door. She looked inside, wary in case something looked back at her, but the inside was too gloomy to make out whether a skeleton rested on the floor. The only way to know for sure was to crawl inside and check, and nothing would convince her to do that. The bolt lay in the grass next to the over door, as if it had fallen off like Hansel said.

Walking away from the clay monstrosity, she couldn't help glancing over her shoulder, certain that the burned witch would be closing on her. Any normal human would not have survived three years in an oven, but who knew what powers a witch might have, or how they might survive what would kill anyone else?

"Feel better?" Hansel gave her a sympathetic smile.

Gretel wrapped her arms around herself.

"No. Not in the least. But we should get home. It'll be getting dark soon. Even if you don't believe it's the witch stalking the village, I don't think you would want to be out after nightfall, would you?"

Hansel shuddered. "On that point, little sister, we absolutely agree."

That night, Gretel lay awake. An unwed girl in her parents' house, she retired to bed early. Living with her step-mother, although always challenging, had become more so when Hansel left. Her step-mother seemed to see Gretel's continued residence here as a calculated insult to her.

I bet she's working on a way to leave me in the forest again.

Her father would never stand for it a third time.

Probably.

Their house was a small affair, with a main living area taking up two thirds of the space. The sleeping quarters took up a section at the back, the rest stored crockery, pans, and farming tools. A doorway with a curtain separated the living area from the sleeping quarters.

A shadow fell over the curtain.

She shut her eyes, feigning sleep.

The curtain swished aside and soft footsteps crossed the floor. A rustle of skirts and a pained grunt meant that her step-mother knelt down by Gretel's bed.

Gretel fought hard against the urge to open her eyes—sure that her step-mother watched at her.

She nearly cried out when her pillow shifted as her step-mother slid her hand underneath it. Gretel's eyelids must have fluttered because her step-mother spoke in a calm, soothing voice, completely unlike her normal one. "Hush, Gretel dear. It's just me. Go back to sleep."

Gretel forced herself to relax, and a few moments later, her step-mother retreated. She counted to one hundred and opened her eyes. The sleeping quarters were empty.

Her gaze fixed on the door, Gretel felt beneath her pillow. Her fingers touched something hairy, and she pulled her hand back.

She sat up to uncover the object underneath her pillow. Her step-mother had put there a crude dolly made of woven hair. It had a loop for a head and tufts of hair sticking out for arms and legs.

Gretel shuddered.

What on earth is it? Why's she put it under my pillow? Gretel guessed she wouldn't like the answers.

She picked up the dreadful object, holding it between thumb and forefinger at arm's length, as if it were a particularly corpulent spider she wanted rid of. She placed it under her step-mother's pillow instead.

Gretel settled back into bed and once again failed to find sleep when her parents retired for the night. Gretel made sure to curl up right on the edge of her pillow to dissuade her step-mother from checking on the charm.

Gretel lay in the darkness and waited for the other two people to fall asleep.

A thirst burned in her throat. Only when her father and step-mother's breathing became slow and measured did she risk climbing from her bed.

They kept a covered pail of water by the door, which was refilled each morning. Gretel went to it now, a wooden cup in her hand. There was only a small amount left in the pail, but half was enough to quench her thirst. She drank slowly, not wanting to return to the room where she'd lain awake for the last few hours.

Her gaze drifted around the room then settled on the last glowing embers of the fire. She couldn't stop her mind from going over the stories again. Old Wainwright, the wagon-maker, had been a respected member of the community until his wife died two summers ago. After that, he spent more time at the local tavern than he did at home. His deterioration into village drunk had been quick and absolute, but Gretel remembered the kind, conscientious man who had often given her a slice of bread to chew on as she sat and watched him hammering and planing. He might be querulous now, but the fear she'd seen in his eyes as he'd spoken about what he'd seen a few weeks ago, led her to trust his word.

"'Twas terrible, low to the ground, crawling or limping like an injured beast. It were all hunched over and black. It smelt both awful and so, so sweet, like if you smeared honey on a dying dog." Most of the villagers had scoffed at that, but Gretel had not: she remembered that awful smell of roasted human flesh, so terrible and yet so tantalising to an empty belly. "And I shouted at it, and it looked at me with red eyes that wept bloody tears and...and..." He had been drowned out by shouts and jests then, but Gretel had heard enough to rouse her suspicions.

The laughter had died and the rumours had grown when they'd found the third dead dog in two weeks; each one had been torn to pieces, the heart gone and the ribcage showing teeth marks.

Outside the cottage, in the dark night, a dog howled. The noise brought Gretel back to the moment. She held her breath. The howl came again but was cut off by a sharp yelp.

Just a master, throwing a boot at his dog. But she conjured up a cowering dog, shrinking away from a hunched, limping creature.

I have to see. I have to know.

She stood up, her legs complaining after sitting on the floor for so long. She crept to the window and peered through the shutters. The cottage had fields behind it, the village square in front of it, and the woods beyond that. The moonlight shone brightly on the square. It illuminated a slumped shape hauling itself along with its twisted hands.

The breath caught in her throat. The world constricted to a tiny peephole. The figure was clearly human; it reached out and dragged itself along with two arms while two legs scuffed the ground ineffectually behind it. It lifted its head, a misshapen nose sniffing the air. The burned, blistered face was that of the witch.

Gretel ducked down, her hand clasped across her mouth to hold in a scream. Her gaze flicked to the sleeping quarters; should she wake her father?

No, I'm being foolish. This is just some strange vision, a waking nightmare brought on by thinking bad thoughts in the dead of night.

She forced herself to stand again, to muster the strength to look through the peephole. She imagined the open and empty moonlit square. But when she put her eye to the hole, the witch was inching her way over the wide, empty space. The monstrosity was closer than before and undoubtedly headed for Gretel's cottage.

Gretel pulled back from the window and rushed to the door. The heavy wooden plank that her father used to bar the door on windy nights had lain idle, propped by the door, for most of the summer, but now, she seized it. She staggered over, lined up the plank then let it fall into its brackets. It landed with a dull thud. She expected the noise to wake her family, but nothing in the hut stirred.

A scratching at the door sent Gretel backwards. That hunched figure crouched on the other side, her wickedly sharp talons raking at the wood. The insistent noise transfixed Gretel. Her stomach cramped, the water she'd drunk like an icy block.

Suddenly, the scratching ceased, and that was so much worse.

Gretel's heart stuttered at the rasp of the witch dragging herself across the ground outside.

Has she given up? Is she leaving?

Then a new, terrifying thought occurred to her. Gretel dashed towards the window. She reached up to the top hook, slipping it into its loop a split second before the shutters shivered with a blow from outside.

Gretel stumbled back. The shutters trembled again, and the bottom bowed inwards.

Mastering her terror, Gretel rushed forward to slip the bottom hook into its loop and secure the window.

The slats blotted out the shining moonlight. Through a gap in the shutters, a blood-red eye glowed at her. The pupil was a tiny black dot in crimson orb. A bloody tear leaked onto what remained of the lashes before trickling down the blackened cheek. A wave of cloying decay mixed with sweetness swept around Gretel, and she gagged. The witch hissed at her, and the eye vanished.

Gretel stood still, holding her breath. All she could hear was the thrumming of her blood in her ears. Then the scratching at the door began again in earnest.

Her heart hammering, Gretel backed away to the farthest part of the room. She sank to the floor, her knees pulled up to her chin. She stayed there all night, keeping a silent vigil.

The witch would scratch at the door before trying the window again.

Several times, the witch shuffled around the outside of the cottage, looking for another way in.

A short while before dawn, the scratching stopped altogether.

Gretel waited a little longer before crawling to peek out of the window. A hunched shape clawed its way back into the forest, and Gretel let out a long, quivery breath. She staggered back to bed, exhausted. Her initial fear had gradually evolved during her vigil into a mindless panic then a kind of detached thoughtfulness. As dawn brightened the sky outside, Gretel closed her eyes and found sleep at last.

"Gretel? Gretel?" Her father's gentle voice roused her to a dozy wakefulness. She opened bleary eyes to find full daylight. Her father's face turned from concern to relief. "Thank God, girl. We thought you might have had the sleeping sickness. It's nigh on lunchtime."

Gretel sat up, confused and alarmed. "Sorry, father. I didn't sleep at all last night."

"You certainly made up for it this morning."

"Is that slut up yet?" her step-mother called from the main part of the hut.

Her father's jaw tightened with displeasure. But his voice was pleasant. "Yes, my love. She's awake. No cause to worry."

Her step-mother muttered in response; her father rolled his eyes—all the defiance he was capable of.

He left, and Gretel got up. Her step-mother banged plates and cutlery around on the table as Gretel dressed. When Gretel walked through the curtain, her step-mother was waiting, her gaze cold and suspicious.

"Decided you're too good to get up for your morning chores, girl?"

"Sorry, step-mother." Gretel retrieved the slab of butter from the shelf and took it to the table. Then she got the bread she'd baked yesterday and brought that over, too. All the while, her step-mother's spiteful gaze crawled across her skin.

No doubt looking to see whether I'm suffering any ill effects from her charm.

"Your father said you didn't sleep well," her step-mother said as Gretel sat down at the table. She didn't meet Gretel's gaze.

"No," Gretel said evenly. Then, with unaccustomed sweetness, she asked, "How did you sleep?"

Her step-mother's gaze flicked to the curtain, filled with uncertainty. Gretel kept her expression carefully blank. "Fine. Like normal people."

"Why didn't you sleep, lass?" Gretel's father asked with concern.

"I thought I heard something scratching at the door," Gretel said. Her step-mother glanced again at the curtain, a worried frown creasing her brow. "I got up, and put the bar across the door and latched the windows. Just in case."

Her step-mother gave an imperious sniff. "Just coincidence, husband. I told you, it was a dog, or something worrying at the wood."

"Or something." Her father's brows drew together.

Gretel felt her heart jolt with apprehension. "What is it? What's happened?"

Her father shifted in his seat. "Oh, nothing. I just found some marks on the door this morning."

Gretel stood to investigate.

"Really, Gretel, it's fine. Nothing to worry about," her father said hastily.

Gretel opened the door. The bottom third was rough and splintered with several claw marks clearly visible, picked out by a dark substance within them. Hand trembling slightly, Gretel touched it. It was sticky. She held it to her nose then tentatively placed her finger on her tongue. She'd only tasted treacle once, but it was unmistakable. The tingle of it now brought back so many unwelcome memories.

She turned to find her step-mother gone. Gretel's gaze drifted to the curtain just as it was thrown back. Her step-mother stood there, her lips pressed into a thin, white line; two spots of colour bloomed on her cheeks, and her eyes blazed.

"What's wrong, my love?" Gretel's father half-rose from his seat with concern.

Gretel met her step-mother's glare with a calm smile. Her step-mother stormed back to the table.

"Nothing's wrong. Just eat your bread and meat, then let's all be on about our day. There are many jobs left unfinished from this morning."

Gretel sat at the table once more.

So, step-mother, you found that horrid little doll under your own pillow, did you? And just what do you think of that? What was it supposed to do — make me awaken with a fever, close to death? Or did you put it there to draw the witch to me? Did she crawl across the village square, drawn by your little charm? Aren't you lucky, then, that I barred the door? Otherwise, it would have been you she dragged from bed.

The rest of the meal passed in an uncomfortable silence.

When she had eaten every last crumb of her meagre meal, Gretel asked, "What job would you like me to do first?"

"Muck out the goat, then I have a very long list for you."

As the day drew to a close, there wasn't a part of Gretel that didn't ache with weariness. Beneath that physical pain, burned a bitter grievance. Her step-mother might have done *some* of her chores this morning, but apparently not. Even the hearth hadn't been swept. And Gretel's day had been made even longer by her trip into the woods while her step-mother took her customary nap. She'd chopped and hauled wood, laying it carefully to set the trap she'd envisaged last night when she'd kept watch. When she'd returned to the cottage, her step-mother scolded her for taking so long to sell the hen's eggs but hadn't guessed where she'd been or what she'd done.

With a whole day's chores to fit into a few hours, Gretel didn't stop all afternoon. The sun sank in the sky. Eventually, she only had the washing to take in, and she was done. As Gretel dumped the basket of clean clothes inside the door, her step-mother looked up from her darning. "Don't forget the water bucket, Gretel."

Gretel stared at the bucket in astonishment. "It hasn't been refilled yet?"

Her stepmother's mouth twisted into a sneer. "I can't exactly do it with my bad hip, can I? And your father has been out in the fields all day, digging up food so that we might eat tonight, and your-"

"All right. I'll do it." Gretel snatched up the bucket, trying to hold her temper in check.

Her step-mother's mouth quirked at the corners, holding back a smug smile. If Gretel's father had been here, he might have suggested that he could do it in her place. Or even insisted that his wife do it; after all, her bad hip hadn't stopped her going to the well before when such a trip offered her the opportunity to gossip with her friends. But Gretel knew none of her own words would sway her step-mother.

She dumped the few pegs she'd been holding into the basket, picked up the empty pail, and set off towards the forest. The well was above an underground spring in a clearing not far from the village; in fact, Gretel's house could be seen from the well. Yet even during this short walk into the forest, Gretel's skin began to prickle with unease.

Whatever had terrorised the villages these past few weeks had only come at night, no reason to be fearful during the day. Yet terror raced through her limbs the further she walked from the village.

The hairs on the back of Gretel's neck stood up. She turned round and examined the way she'd come. Children played with a hoop in the village square. The blacksmith paused in his work to watch them with a smile. A normal, contented scene, yet Gretel felt utterly removed from its familiarity and safety. The trees pressed close around her, their branches snagging in her hair as if they meant to haul her up and away from the path.

Gretel quickened her step. Her toes snagged a tree root, and she went flying with a cry. The pail flew out of her grasp as she tumbled to the ground. She sat up, wiping her hands on her skirts and rubbing at her bruised shins. Horror sickened her. The pail was on its side, its base facing her. The little dolly made of twisted hair had been pinned to the underside.

Gretel leaned over and unfastened it. The hair left a greasy stain on her fingers. She had the overwhelming urge to throw it as far away as she could, but a sixth sense made her pause. Maybe this could be used to her advantage. She tucked the little dolly into the pocket of her apron.

The grass to her left rustled. Gretel stood up quickly and searched for the source of the noise. A crouched, black shape emerged from a patch of long grass. Two red eyes peered malevolently out of a burned face. Then the witch scuttled forward on all fours, straight towards her.

Gretel turned and ran. She ducked below branches and leaped over roots. Behind her came a terrible rustling as the witch scampered in pursuit, moving faster than any half-burned creature had a right to.

The witch wasn't gaining, but she wasn't falling behind either.

Just a little further, almost there.

Gretel's heart pounded; her breaths were short, ragged gasps.

She glimpsed the grey expanse of the cliff up ahead and put on a burst of speed. The path was now nothing more than a game trail, uneven and narrow, but that all worked to her advantage. She reached the clearing and was careful to leap over the patch of grass between the two white stones she'd placed as markers. She slammed into the cliff and turned to face her pursuer.

The witch gave an inhuman squeal of glee to see her prey cornered. She sped up, heading straight between the two white rocks.

For a sickening moment, Gretel thought her trap had failed and that she really would be torn to pieces. But then, the witch was yanked upwards, a startled scream escaping her cracked lips. She bent double, clawing at the rope on her ankle that held her suspended upside down. She thrashed wildly, panicked gurgles coming from her throat.

Gretel steadied her breathing before she walked towards the sprung trap.

The witch increased her manic attempts at freedom. She hissed at Gretel, her taloned, bony fingers stretching out towards the girl.

Gretel stopped just out of her reach.

This close, she could see what a charred mess the creature was.

The old woman who had imprisoned her and Hansel had been old and mostly blind but still healthy and strong. This creature was wizened, its limbs little more than bone and burnt sinew.

Pity for the creature tugged at Gretel's heart until she looked into its blood-red eyes; they shone with a mad hunger.

"If you were a sick dog in the village, we'd slit your throat and call it a mercy. I shut you in an oven, and yet you still clawed your way out. Just what-"

A scream made Gretel spin round. There were only two narrow paths that lead to this cliff face, and Gretel had set a trap across both of them. The witch was caught in one, her step-mother now caught in the other.

As Gretel approached, her step-mother groaned in pain.

"My ankle. Oh, my hip." Her eyes, dazed with pain and shock, focused on Gretel. Her lips drew back in a snarl. "Gretel. You wicked child. What have you done?"

Lying on the grass was the bread knife. Gretel picked it up. "I think the question, step-mother, is what were you planning to do?"

Her step-mother's eyes roved wildly. "I was planning to slice the witch open and save you, you ungrateful child."

"Were you indeed? Then why not come up behind the witch, rather than sneaking up behind me, along a different path altogether?"

Her step-mother's lips opened and closed, but no words came out.

Gretel sighed and turned away.

"Wicked child. Don't walk away from me. Cut me down."

"Oh, I will." She climbed into a patch of undergrowth, squeezing through tree trunks to where the counterweights for her two traps had been concealed. Using the breadknife, she sawed through her step-mother's rope and felt some satisfaction at the indignant squawk as the woman fell to the ground.

Then she cut through the witch's rope. The charred bundle of flesh and rags fell to the ground where it writhed like an overturned turtle.

Wide-eyed, her step-mother said, "What have you done, you stupid child?"

Gretel smiled. "Why, stepmother, I'm leaving you in the forest just as you left us. Only I will be kinder than you were. I will leave you with a little something extra. Here."

Gretel tossed the little black-haired dolly so that it landed at her step-mother's feet. The witch's head snapped in that direction, her bloody eyes drawn towards that dark charm above all else. She reached out her spindly arms and dragged herself across the clearing.

"Gretel. Gretel." Her step-mother scrambled backwards, her bad hip making it impossible for her to stand. "Gretel, come back. Child, I'm sorry. Come back and help me."

Gretel walked out of the clearing. Unmindful of the shouts behind her, she bent down and picked up a handful of white pebbles.

As her step-mother crawled frantically away into the undergrowth, the witch hauling herself after, Gretel walked back towards the village.

She dropped the little white stones as she went, marking the path out of the forest, just as her brother had done all those years ago.

A little way along, she dropped the breadknife as well.

After all, it seemed only fair.

The Bramble Witch
11/6/16

ASHES

M. Regan

His memories of the previous night are hazy at best.

The consequence of drink and revelry is that he can picture nothing of the ball clearly. His guests' swirling gowns blur one atop the other, phantasmagoric; champagne bubbles distort the features of his partners, making it all the more difficult to differentiate one candidate from the next from the next when asked about his preferences the following day.

He nurses water from a crystal glass. The residual pounding of feet reverberates inside of his skull; the waltz-beat of his hangover grinds his molars. Liquid sloshes within his cup in much the same way that his thoughts slosh between his ears.

A ray of gilded sunrise catches off his glass. In a flash, he recalls moonlight glinting off a shoe.

That one, then, the prince mumbles, the command coming from beneath his splayed arm. It hurts to move his mouth. Everything hurts. But he endures the discomfort, as a quest to find that slipper's owner will distract his advisors long enough to allow him some much-needed sleep.

Whoever fits that slipper will make as good a bride as any.

His advisors return with a girl who reminds the prince of the sunrise catching off of glass.

She radiates brightness. Fragility, too, in how she sits. She is pale and gold and delicate when she bows her head to him, pledging loyalty and love. Those who had been there upon her discovery relay in detail how she had fainted dead away, and needed to be carried to the carriage. She waits before him now with naught for luggage but the slipper his men had returned, and a wire cage draped in cloth.

The cage squeaks. She blushes.

"You will forgive me," the girl says, eyes demurely downcast, "for not curtsying as I ought. I am afraid that if I stand, I'll simply swoon once more."

A charming notion, he decides. *She* is charming. Suitable for a Prince Charming, surely. Finding equal pleasure in her curls and the ivory pale of her bosom, the prince graciously grants the requested forgiveness. He grants, as well, her plea for a room with a fireplace. Then he joins his intended upon the bench, hoping to more fully enjoy the perfume of her.

Notes of mugwort, yarrow, and rosemary waft through the air. A headiness like that of burning leaves. The fragrances meld, smothering a spicier scent. Something about it is familiar. Implacable.

The prince does not waste too much effort on remembering the aroma's name. Remembering this lady's name is far more imperative. Unfortunately, it is also far more difficult. The party has left hundreds of ghosts dancing around in his head; beyond the haunting tingle of certainty that they have met before—which, of course, they *have*—the prince is unable to recall *anything* about this girl. What they may have spoken of at his gala, or what she might have worn. Beyond that shoe of hers, all is a mystery.

In retrospect, the prince regrets the vices he had allowed himself.

But the past is the past, as they say, and their concern is the future. What happened then is not as important as what will happen next. Soon they will be married, his reign allowed to begin; they will have plenty of opportunities to reacquaint themselves after that.

For the time being, he is happy just to sit beside her on embroidered cushions, delighting in the warmth that radiates from her body.

It reminds him of fire.

Their wedding party is magical, as is befitting of royalty.

Their wedding night is less so.

"You would deny your husband?" He scowls, senses addled by wines and the pungent stench of herbs. The sweetness clinging to his bride curdles his nose hairs. Her choice in cologne is becoming intolerable, as is her propensity for dramatics.

"I would not deny my lord anything." The lady is polite, earnest. Still, her claim is difficult to believe when paired with a wheeled chair barricading the door. "But sir, the day has been long. A long night atop it would do neither of us good."

"What about the day was long?" Try though he may to contain it, the prince can feel himself sneer. Exasperation curdles his lips, then creeps into his voice. "The ceremony? You sat through it. The dinner? You sat. You did not dance a single step, so busy were you with *sitting*. We met at a ball, did we not? And yet, you could not find the strength nor energy to favor your prince with a single waltz."

"I am afraid I am still recovering from shock, my lord," the newly-crowned princess says. Her tone is firm, but there is an apology in her eyes. They shine, pale blue, around the frame of the jamb. "My prince's patience will be rewarded, I swear. Just a day or two more, I am told. My husband can endure that long, can he not?"

He can. Of course he *can*. He just does not *want* to.

"I must tend to the fire, my lord. Good evening."

It seems, though, that he will *have* to, given how she locks the door.

The princess had been gifted an extravagant fireplace, just like she had wanted.

He is not particularly interested in her reasons for asking this. To hear the kingdom tell it, his bride had been a slave before his proposal. This is unlikely. Still, with how romantic the rumor is, the prince is unsurprised his palace's servants have taken such nonsense to heart. Perhaps this is why they insist that their new lady feels more at home sleeping before the hearth. He hears the maids call the habit endearing. They only wish she would be careful when dozing; more than once, they have found her quarters reeking of burnt hair.

Beneath the chandeliers of the dining room, the prince finds himself considering his bride's curls. They are perfect and silken.

They are unsinged.

For no reason in particular, he wonders what happened to her wire cage.

When she finally deigns to lift her skirts, the prince wishes desperately she hadn't.

"What the hell—?"

A gag burbles up his throat, scorching the lining of his gullet. The hand thrown over his mouth is the only thing that keeps him from spewing bile across the floor. Acid eats away at his exclamation with the same voraciousness it does his esophagus, his palm. He reels back, retching. "What the *hell* is this…?"

The girl before him blinks, glancing downward with nigh-revolting innocence.

"Why, they are my feet, my lord," she says, dangling the putrid meat over the edge of her bed. Blackened skin crackles around pus-crusted threads; she wiggles the shriveled blisters of her toes. "I worked hard to earn them, too."

"*Earn* them?"

"Well, they weren't always mine." The princess' explanation is as sweet as her smile. Gelatinous excretions ooze in greasy slugs down her shins. "But I wished and I wished that they were. I wished so very hard, in fact, that I summoned a fairy godmother to me. She granted that wish, as you can tell, but I had to do all sorts of things to prove I was worthy of my coveted prize."

Something suppurates in the space between her stitches, the secretion clouded with sickness. Fluids follow a path forged by dissolving flesh; the sinews of her tissues erode into strings. Sallow dew pearls upon the bone of a swollen ankle, the oppressive heat of the fireplace worsening its stink.

She shifts. A rancid droplet nearly falls atop the prince's knee. It misses, hissing instead on the marble floor. He wants nothing more than to cringe away from that ichorous puddle, to scramble to the door and run screaming through the castle halls, but he finds himself unable.

The hearth is hot. So hot. *So hot.* It pushes down on the prince's shoulders, penetrating the withered husks of his lungs. It entombs him. It amalgamates the horror and disgust that are festering in his bowels, stealing all vestiges of his strength.

He cannot stand. He cannot move. He cannot breathe.

The princess' gaze flits towards the fireplace, the first hint of anxiety in the flutter of her lashes.

Or perhaps what he sees is insanity.

"You should kiss me, my lord," she says. There is a warning in the whisper, wrapped up like her cobbled legs around his hips. Strips of rot peel free of the heels that chafe against his back. An empty cage glimmers in the corner, its bars illumed by the finger of fire that is creeping over the grate.

"My fairy godmother says *you should kiss me.*"

Ashes pop in the heart of the hearth.

"You should do it *now.*"

He does not want to know whose ashes.

"You should do it *quickly.*"

He does not want to know…

"My *lord….!*"

He does not want to know.

"*Please*, before she—!"

The coppery sizzle of her spittle leaves burns atop his tongue.

Somewhere in the darkness, the midnight bells toll.

The princess sings a pretty tune as she wheels herself over the grounds, pausing only to cleave a rat from the mouth of a barn cat.

Upon further consideration, she takes up the cat, as well.

"My fairy godmother will love these." The lady coos to her attending prince, cradling the poor, paralyzed animals. "Don't you think, my lord?"

She gifts him a beam as bright as sunrise catching off of broken glass. It is splintered and beautiful.

Her prince, ever the gentleman, offers a smile of his own.

"I do." He places a hand upon her crown.

The other is upon the head of his dagger.

RAVEN, ROSE, AND APPLE PIE
Jaap Boekestein

I do not love Machtaine. I am married to her, but love only flows one way between us. I am supposed to love her, as the maiden who was saved from the dragon by the fierce warrior, but I simply can't.

She is boorish; she is brutish; she didn't kill the dragon because of *me*. No, I was just a convenient road to fame, to wealth and lands. A petite demure princess, in mortal danger, the damsel in distress. Save her and marry her, and you get half of her father's kingdom. That was the deal. So Machtaine did. Fearless warrior from a long line of warriors with plenty of warrior relatives. Was my father afraid to refuse the marriage, or was he happy with all the sword hands?

I do not know.

Father commands; I obey.

Like I have to obey Machtaine now.

I do not love her; she stinks of horses and dogs. Stable hands are more cultured than my husbandwife. I shudder when she touches me. I almost gag when she kisses me. She is so *filthy*.

I want children, boys and girls. It will never happen. Even if Machtaine would allow me to sleep with a man, the fruit of that union would be born out of wedlock. Bastards, every one of them. I cannot burden my children with such a curse.

No children.

How I hate her.

The wind pulls at my hair; my braids are all undone. I can see such a distance from the highest tower of the castle: yellow fields and darks woods, silver rivers and hazy gray mountains with white peaks. It is beautiful. Will this be the last thing I see before I throw myself from the window? What will I think during the fall? Will I feel regret, or fear, or freedom? Will it… will it *hurt*? God in Heaven, forgive me.

His song saves me. The sound of the lute reaches even the highest tower. His voice…

Beautiful.

A minstrel is at the gate, asking to be let in with a demonstration of his skills. He is young; he is handsome, wearing bright colors.

I step back from the edge.

I have been saved.

Charlemange is his name, and he is all I ever dreamed of. His speech is refined; his manners are impeccable; his songs and stories are wonderful. He is handsome, of course, with his hair flaxen like mine, and his beautiful eyes, dark smoldering coals. I dream of how our children would look, but I hardly dare to look his way.

Oh, if only...

In the woman's chamber, of course in company of all my ladies in waiting, I listen to his tales of faraway lands and noble deeds. He has come here to hear my story, he tells us. How the princess was stolen by the dragon, and how the beast killed champion after champion.

I blush, and pretend it is the summer heat.

Charlemange sings a song about a sweet little bird, bathing in a sparkling spring. The words are innocent, unless you know how to listen. When he looks into my eyes, he knows I know.

Come bathe in me,
sweet love.
Let your singing,
flow my waters.

Oh yes.

Spread your wings,
beautiful songbird.
Pearls of water,
on your feathers

If only…

The filthy bitch. She took him. She bedded him. She practically dragged him to the bedroom and mounted him like...

Like...

I hate her.

She had her pleasure with him, paid him, and discarded him. Charlemange, the sweet voiced man-whore. The pox to your tongue and to your manhood.

I cry and cry. My ladies blame my malady on the weather, an upset stomach or whatever, but they all know. They all know I wanted Charlemange, even if I could not get him. I *wanted* him, but I would never have dared to… to… I am married. I cannot. I only had my little guilty dreams, nothing more. A minor sin, is it not?

Machtaine the she-beast, my husbandwife, did not hesitate. I do not know if she was aware of my feelings; I do not know if she even cares, but the vows of marriage did not stop her. I hate her.

I hate her.

I want to die, but I am a coward. His voice did not save me on that tower. I would never have jumped. I have not been back.

Instead, I chose the coward's way to die: I will starve myself to death.

The food they bring me, I hardly touch. The wine they pour me, I only sip. My only activity is staring out of the small window, waiting for the Angel of Death to come.

Machtaine visits me, once. She brings me the still bleeding heart of a stag. "It will give you strength. You need it, little one."

She waits for my response. That smelly hulk of a woman, the husband I never wanted. Soon, I will be free from her,

My ladies in waiting have deserted me. Is it my temper, or do they feel the end is near and do not want to be contaminated with the touch of Death?

I do not care.

I do not need them: scared little mice, bleating lambs, grunting piglets; that is what they are.

Death, please come quickly. I beg you.

The crowing of the raven wakes me. The big, black bird sits in the window. Is this then the Angel of Death, disguised as a bird?

I study the raven with feverish, doubting eyes.

Why would Death bring me a red rose?

For this raven carries a rose in its beak, red.

I reach out. Maybe it is not Death, but it certainly is a sign. *Roman de la Rose*, how many times have I not listened to that poem?

The black bird hops just out of reach of my gasping hand. How thin are my fingers; how little flesh remains; how long and crooked are my nails. They look like claws or thorns.

"Come here, *Messieurs Sable*, what do you have for me?" My voice croaks, these are my first words in days.

The beady eyes peer at me. I advance a little, ever so carefully.

The raven flies out of the window, and I almost cry out: "Wait. Wait."

Instead, I lean out of the window, trying to catch the black feathered messenger.

In vain of course. I hang out of the window, the fresh autumn air kisses my hollow face with a thousand pin pricks. The wind's caress makes my eyes water: precious tears run down my cheeks and chin.

The raven with the rose sits in the tree closest to the window. It nods its head, as if beckoning me to follow him.

I nod back.

Am I insane?

Perhaps.

Probably.

Hunger and fever, despair and hate. My soul is tainted. My mind is gone. I see things that cannot be. I talk to birds. I have heard of saints experiencing such things, but I know I am not a saint. I am a wicked, empty, spoiled girl.

Yes, I know I am. Do not think I am stupid.

I get up. My gown is now too big for me; the fabric is so heavy. It does not matter; the weight does not slow me as I fly down the winding stairs. Round and round I go, running after rosie, and I don't fall down.

The raven waits for me in the garden, still with the red rose in its beak, still in the tree.

I approach, and he flies away, though only a small distance this time, just to the tiny courtyard door. I understand.

On and on we go, unnoticed, unseen, and unheard. How? Do not ask me. From the garden to the wall, down to the main courtyard, out of the gate, the muddy road from the castle, and the far smaller but just as muddy path down in the dark wood.

My guide flies and waits, and I stagger and follow.

The woods are supposed to be dangerous. Wolves, the ladies in waiting whisper, those beasts will kill and devour travelers. And robbers, of course, even worse than wolves. Those beasts will rob and rape and kill travelers. They won't gnaw your bones, though, unless the winter is extremely cruel.

The raven guides and protects me, or maybe the woods are not that dangerous after all. More likely, Machtaine has killed most of those monsters. All that blood and fighting and death is something she enjoys.

I reach a clearing.

A hovel crouches close to the ground, as if it does not want to be discovered. The lovely smell of freshly baked gingerbread fills the air.

The raven alights on a small outdoor table. The rose rests in a simple earthenware vase.

Panting, I wait. I understand this is not natural, but what does it matter? I am already doomed. Have I caught the eye of demon or a warlock? What kind of monster has lured me here? *Big eyes, big ears, big mouth.*

I shiver.

Here, deep in the dark woods, there is no one to save me.

I don't want to be saved.

I want to be damned.

Take me, use me, kill me. I am already dead.

"Hello, sweet little thing," an old woman's voice crackles. "I see you followed Phaedrus all the way here."

Her name is Lucia, and she is a witch. Or at least, she does not deny it when I ask her.

"Why did you sent a raven with a rose to me?"

"Phaedrus, dearie. He is a little bit vain and likes to hear his own name."

"Why did you send Phaedrus with a rose to me?"

I sip the tea Lucia has brewed for me. It is heavy and spicy. I taste acorns and sage, pine needles and dried mushrooms.

"I am going to teach you how to bake a pie, dearie," Lucia says.

"A pie?" A baffling task.

Lucia nods. "An apple pie. Serve me this dark winter, and I will teach you how to bake an apple pie."

"Why should I want to learn that?" Anger creeps into my voice.

With an old crooked finger, Lucia tickles Phaedrus under his beak. The bird seems to like it. "There is a beast in these woods, my dear, running rampant. It hunts and kills and disturbs the ancient balance. That has to stop. So you are going to bake her a pie."

Her. Hatred curlded my innards.

"This is the same beast I dread?"

Lucia feeds the raven a crumb of bread.

"And this special pie, this apple pie, will release me from the beast?"

Again only silence for an answer.

Speak now or forever hold your peace.

The old woman holds her peace.

My mind gallops like a wild stallion. "Why can you not bake the pie yourself?"

"I am only a poor old woman, dearie. I cannot feed the beast."

I can.

I can, but I hesitate. I was ready to die, ready to meet my fate, to be torn by demon claws or raped by what- or whomever lured me into the dark wood. But now I have an alternative.

I *could* kill.

Rid the earth of Machtaine for good. Of course, I still would be damned, but I could enjoy a few years of happiness in this earthly vale of tears.

No. Yes.

It is wrong, but I will do it.

I will pay for my atrocity, I promise myself. The moment Machtaine is dead, I will throw myself from the highest tower of the castle, straight to Hell to burn forever for my sins. This time I will not hesitate.

Or maybe I will eat myself a piece of the cursed pie, who knows. I will take my own life after I end hers, the manner is not important.

"I will help you," I say. "I will serve you this whole winter, and I will learn how to bake that special apple pie. And then, I will feed the beast."

"Good, dearie. I will enjoy your company," says the witch.

I gesture in the direction of where I suspect the castle lies: "Won't I be missed?"

Lucia grins and nods. "You have a sharp mind, child. That is good. Don't worry, Phaedrus will take your place."

"Phaedrus, how…?"

Lucia snaps with her fingers, and the raven flies up. It shrieks and flaps, and threads of light and smoke swirl around him, engulf him. One, two, three heartbeats later, the smoke clears, and a young woman stands in the clearing.

It is me, or at least I think it is. Am I really that thin? Are my eyes really that big? Do I really look that sickly?

Apparently, I do.

The woman opens her mouth, and a raven's shriek comes out.

"Hm, that won't do," Lucia says. She smiles. "I know the solution. Your ladies will find you in your room, in a deep slumber. Whatever they do, they cannot wake you. Phaedrus will sleep all winter, and you will serve me all winter. When the spring comes, you will take Phaedrus' place and wake up."

"After which I bake the beast a pie. A special apple pie."

Lucia-the-witch nods. "So will it be."

I serve all winter and learn a lot. Most things I do not want to learn, at first. How to clean, scrub, and dust. How to feed the two pigs Lucia keeps, and how to make porridge. And do not forget washing clothes in ice cold water or spinning rough wool into threads. I work, and I grow—cooking is another one of my lessons, as is butchering and baking—and I learn. In the evenings, when I am tired to the bone and the few embers in the hearth and a single oil lamp hardly chase the darkness away, Lucia tells stories and sing songs.

At first, I am too tired to listen, too weak, but I grow stronger, and I start to take notice.

"There once was an old man whose thieving son was to be hanged," Lucia starts one night.

"Three hedgehogs were lost in the woods," Lucia starts another evening.

"*Sweet red, sweet thread,*" the old witch sings, "*Bring me bread, take me to bed. Sweet red, sweet thread.*"

Are they all nonsense, those stories and songs? No, they are not. They are lessons; they are wisdom. I do not always get their meaning right away, but Lucia is patient. She tests me, makes me see.

I am her apprentice; I realize one day. I am becoming a witch.

The princess who in secret became a witch, who will one day be a queen.

I shiver.

Two powers combined could create something evil.

My breath is a white cloud.

I stop feeding the pigs for a moment.

Is this what I want?

Yes, of course.

Of course.

I yearn to be back in the warm castle, with hot baths and fine food. I want to be a princess; I want to have a good husband, handsome and wise, a good dancer and lover, kind and strong and well mannered.

I want that. Yes.

Somehow, I am angry when I go back inside.

Stories and songs and a knowledge of herbs and all that grows and lives in the woods.

"This is Dancing Lily, a tiny plant that grows between the roots of elms. Dried, it helps against morning sickness."

"This is Bear Claw. It will repel flies and mosquitos."

The magic is in the words we sing and the gestures we make when we prepare Dancing Lily and Bear Claw and the hundred and one other things. At least, I think it is magic. It has to be, has it not?

Winter is cold and long and dark, but one day, spring is there.

"It is time," Lucia tells me. "Time for you to go back and wake up. Time for you to bake an apple pie."

Back home. Back to my clothes, to fine food and perfumes. To all those things I have left behind.

Back to Machtaine, whom I will have to poison.

Taking a life…

I hesitate. "Am I truly ready?"

"You are, dearie." Lucia puts a hand on my shoulder. It is an old woman's hand, but she is not frail. Far from it.

"But what if…?"

"You will be fine." Lucia gives me a pat, already guiding me. "Come now, get wood, lots of it, I am going to prepare a bath."

The bath is a huge iron cauldron; the water is so hot that steam rises from it. I lower myself into the cauldron, all the way, from my little toes to the last of my golden hairs. Lucia-the-witch adds herbs and sings, stirring the water with a huge wooden spoon. "*Little duck, little duck, come swim with me. Duck, duck, you little duck, come swim with me.*"

When I finally get out, I am all soft and clean.

I am reborn.

"And now, it is time for you to leave."

Tears consume me when I walk down the muddy path. Golden hair, green dress, red cloak, winter white skin. If a woodsman would see me, he would think me a faerie, but I meet no one. Saplings sprout everywhere in the woods, looking for light and warmth. I cannot give any because my heart is heavy and full of sadness and doubts.

Sadness because I have to leave dear Lucia. I liked the old woman; I loved her like a mother.

The doubts—they are not about me returning to the castle. No, I belong there. My uncertainty is about baking that fateful pie. I do not love Machtaine, but do I want to kill her?

No.

But can I live with her?

No.

Still doubting, I reach the castle. Just like the last time, when I followed Phaedrus the raven, nobody notices me. Through the gate, the courtyard, the stairs, and I am back in my old room. A body that looks like mine lays on the bed. White skin, golden hair, eyes closed. I look well fed. I touch the other me, lips on lips, ever so slightly.

It is the kiss of life.

The other me rises. Her arms become wings, her robe—exactly the same kind of robe Lucia has given me—turns into black feathers. The face is the last to change.

Phaedrus sits on the bed and looks at me with his black animal eyes. He nods.

I nod back. I know what is expected from me.

Such revels to celebrate my magical recovery. Musicians, nimble jugglers, fire breathers, a roasted pig above glowing coals, gaiety, and laughter. Machtaine sits at my side, touches my hand time after time, as if she cannot believe I am real and that I am back.

"She slept at your feet, every night," tells my oldest lady in waiting.

"She prayed for you, every night," says another.

"She fed you and sponged you with rose water," says a third. "Every night."

Did she? I look at Machtaine… My husbandwife had changed. Gone is the boisterous warrior; she is only a shadow of the woman she used to be. Her face is hollow, her hair long and unkempt, her skin dirty and black.

She loves me, I realize.

I have to poison her, I know.

Two nights and two days pass.

On the third night, after the twelfth hour, I wake up in the kitchen; I am kneading dough. Phaedrus sits in the window, watching me. Three unnaturally red apples—sorcery, in springtime apples should be old and shriveled—wait for me on the kitchen counter.

Appalled, I step back. "I know it was the deal, but I do not want to kill her. I cannot. I refuse."

Phaedrus flies up, shrieking, his wing touches me.

The change is painful. Like giving birth, I imagine.

Before my eyes, Phaedrus turns back into me. And I? A robe of black feathers, wings instead of arm, talons instead of feet, a beak instead of a mouth. I have turned into a raven, into Phaedrus.

"No. No." I cry, like the shriek of a carrion-bird.

I want to attack her, the false me. She makes a simple gesture, and I freeze on the spot. I am silent and helpless; I am a raven. I have to watch the false me baking a pie.

No. No. I fight, or at least, I try to but all in vain.

The apple pie is finished. The false me takes it out of the oven and puts it on a plate. It is hot and smells delicious. The evil me make a gesture, and without a sound, I fly after her.

We go to my chambers, where Machtaine sleeps. The poor woman looks terrible. Her winter-long wake and the shock of my return have exhausted her. Is this the woman who killed a dragon to save me? It hardly seems possible.

Machtaine wakes, says something. The false me smiles and feeds her a slice of the apple pie. I am paralyzed, unable to move, to speak, in numb terror.

My husbandwife chokes; she falls back on the bed, her body convulsing.

I shout, a cry escapes from my throat, half raven, half human.

The false me does not wait. She takes a few quick steps and jumps. Before she touches the ground, Phaedrus is a raven again and flies away.

I… I am back in my own body one more. I hurry towards the bed. The cursed apple pie is on the floor.

She is dying, my husbandwife, the woman who loved me.

A winter's worth of witch's wisdom fills my head. Why had Lucia taught me all those things? I can save Machtaine. Maybe.

I take her in my arms. I sing. I evoke ancient spirits. My tears wet her face, but I keep singing. I will save Machtaine, although it means my own death. I cannot let her die.

Machtaine is poisoned. Machtaine is dying.

I am not.

I touch her face. I kiss her lips. she breathes the air from my lungs.

First, I do not think the magic will work, that all is in vain.

But I see the change.

Machtaine's black hair turns paler, her skin becomes smoother, her face changes utterly.

A hundred hasty heartbeats, and I am looking at my own face, or to be correct, the face that once belonged to me. I wear Machtaine's face and body. By all accounts, I am Machtaine. I am the one who is poisoned; I am the one who will die.

The poison shows no mercy. Darkness embraces me as a greedy lover; the very last moment before I close my eyes, I see the woman with my face open hers.

I am Machtaine. I am strong. I killed a dragon and won the hand of a beautiful princess. I eat the steel bleeding hearts of stags. Poison? Ha! Poison cannot kill me.

I wake up.

She sits at my bed, the beautiful blond girl I have always loved. She smiles.

A raven sits in the window; it seems to smirk before it flies off.

"I love you," says the delicate blond girl.

"I love you," I say, and I take her in my arms.

MORGIANNA AND THE COFFEE-HATING GOVERNOR

David W. Landrum

Trouble began when the new governor took the rulership of our city and the small kingdom that surrounded it. To his credit, he did not achieve his position as ruler through murder, intrigue, and machination. The city council elected him. and he seemed competent. His dislike of coffee, though, got a laugh at his inauguration. The drink came to our city from Yemeni port of Mocha and was all the rage.

Since the episode with the forty thieves brought wealth and prominence to me and my dear wife, Morgianna, I served on the council and got to hear the governor's inaugural speech. *Is he joking?* I chuckled audibly. *Couldn't he see that shops sold it everywhere, and people consumed the beverage in large quantities?*

We took it as a funny quip about the governor's preferences, which were quite different from those of the people in our city.

He ruled with compassion and skill, and we on the Council of Elders thought we had made a good choice. But like many men and women who are highly capable, he had one serious flaw that blemished all he did. Rafiq—this was his name—had let the more extreme imams whisper in his ear so that his religion took on a narrow, dogmatic, and ascetic coloring.

After a year of being quiet, he enforced his views.

Our city is diverse and liberal in outlook. Religion is a private matter. The rules of our Islamic faith were generally kept, but plenty of room lay afoot for those who practiced other faiths. Christians made up about a fifth of the population. The Muslims were mostly Sunni, but a number of Shi'a and some Sufi lived in within our walls. Thousands of Jews lived and worked in our city, the Druze made up a sizeable community, and Europeans, mostly merchants who were our connection with markets in those northern countries, constituted a large enough population that they maintained three churches that corresponded to their various divisions.

The governor, we found out, also did not like diversity of religion.

He appointed men who were severe and conservative to ministerial positions, often bringing in outsiders rather than choosing from our population. He also dismissed Jews and Christians who had served in various capacities in the city and provincial officers.

Now, if you read certain commentators, they insist unbelievers should not hold positions in the government and military, but we had opened doors in those areas to Jews, Christians, and Druze who did their jobs with efficiency and skill.

Rafiq sent them packing and appointed fundamentalists in their places.

"There's going to be trouble," Morgianna said.

"He's just a bit fanatical."

"Wait and see. It will get worse."

And it did.

He harassed non-Muslims, making them wear identifying marks: ribbons and a certain type of sash for women, wristbands and red belts for men. When the citizens protested this decree, he gave them a long, chiding sermon about following the law and said he meant no harm to nonbelievers. In fact, he wanted to protect them.

"What if they wander into areas off-limits to unbelievers? If this should happen, we can identify them and prevent them from intruding into sacred precincts."

We puzzled over this because we could not think of any areas that *were* off-limits to non-Muslims. Even non-Muslims can enter a mosque if they follow proper protocol. And the distinctive marks only seemed to make our neighbors who held to different faith more visible for the thugs he hired to harass them.

My wife, who is a Christian and had to wear a red sash, came home one day with a swollen eye.

The servants put cool cloths on it.

I knelt by her bed and asked what happened.

"One of those thugs who call themselves the 'religious police' struck me."

Rage filled me so much I trembled. Morgianna touched me on the cheek. "Don't make trouble."

"Why did he hit you?"

"Because they identified me as an unbeliever—and because I was talking with Zarah and Shora."

"Since when is talking with friends a crime?"

"They said a Christian should not be running her mouth—that was the phrase they used—with Muslim women. They told Zorah she was immodestly dressed. They harassed Shora, saying she was a spy for the Persians."

Shora was one of the several hundred Persians living in our city. I had never known of anyone impugning their loyalty.

"Then they asked her if she were Sunni or a Shi'a. She didn't know what they were talking about. They pushed and shoved her. I went to her aid, and one of them hit me and knocked me down. They laughed and spat on me. Then they shoved Shora to the ground and went their way."

Conjuring calm, I paced the house. Morgianna joined me, likely afraid I would do something rash. Her right eye bore a blue-black circle that had it swollen shut.

That a man could strike a woman filled me with disgust and loathing.

Eventually, Morgianna felt well enough to go to the nursery and care for the children. I walked to a local tea shop and found a group of my friends. I heard more of what the governor was doing to disturb the peace of our city.

"He's placed a tax on us, Ali Baba," Yaakov, a Jewish friend of mine from childhood, said. "A lot of my people are leaving the city in fear of persecution."

"Doesn't he read the scriptures? We are to treat the People of the Book—Jews and Christians—with honor."

"He sees only want he wants to see." Namir, another long-time friend, kept his voice low.

We sipped our tea and tried to get on other topics, but talk inevitably drifted to the governor. Jalal, a Christian, said he threatened to close all the liquor stores in town. They were run by Christians, since Muslims are not supposed to drink alcohol—though I can attest that a lot of us break that rule. Jalal might have trouble finding wine to serve at his daughter's wedding feast next month. Tama needed a permit to build a storefront inside the city walls, but the office that issued such permits had been staffed entirely by Jews. The governor had dismissed them and the new-hired thugs and cronies did not know how to do their jobs.

Qasim told us the governor had banned coffee.

I went home miserable. Two men—accompanied by armed guards—met me in the entry hall. They conducted me into my own living room, where a portly, richly dressed man had made himself at home, sitting in my favorite chair and smoking my hookah. He blew out a cloud of smoke and regarded me for a moment. "I am Hamza, agent of the governor. You are Ali Baba, a wealthy, law-abiding citizen, who has served on the city council. We note, however, that you are married to an unbeliever."

"I am married to a Christian woman who is a believer in her particular faith."

"An unbeliever. You cannot serve on the council unless your wife is willing to convert."

She would not do this. I would never want her to. The look in my accuser's eye, however, told me I was marked out. The matter would not end here. After he and his guards left, I went in to Morgana's bed chamber.

Wet from a bath, she lay cooling on the bed, her resplendent body uncovered—her strong frame made trim by years of work as a slave girl, her beautiful round breasts, strong, flat stomach sloping to the nest of black hair where her thighs came together, and her long, delicate legs. The swelling in her eye had gone down. The contrast of her lovely nakedness and the bruises on her cheek suggested the former peace and harmony of our city and the violence of the new rulership.

I fought down a surge of anger, sat on the side of her bed, and stroked the hair around her intimate parts.

"Are you feeling better, Morgianna?"

"Better. And I've been thinking."

That was what I had hoped for. Morgianna had outwitted the forty thieves. A governor who would be so stupid as to try to ban coffee and liquor would be no match for her.

My stroking had its effect. I undressed, and she climbed on top and lowered herself on to me. I lay back and enjoyed the pleasure of her embrace.

When we both had gotten our joy, we wrapped in blankets and walked into the entrance hall, which had an open ceiling. Deep rivers of stars glistened. The moon shone its half-face amid them. A few night clouds glowed in its silver light.

"We need Shatara." Shatara was a prostitute, a slave to Issam. A childhood friend of my wife, she had suffered the ill-will of fate when her owners sold her into this sad trade after her sixteenth birthday. After wealth came to us, we tried to buy her out of slavery, but her owner would not hear of it. She made him too much money; and if she gained her freedom, many powerful men in the city would be angry with him because they frequently wanted Shatara and none else.

"How will Shatara help us?" I asked.

"We'll get them together and see if she can lure him into a trap I plan to set."

"He's a fanatic—a religious fanatic. He's not going to hire a prostitute."

"I think he will. Shatara tells me that many of the men to whom she is sold are highly religious. Every coin has two sides. We are shocked when we hear of supposedly saintly men or women exposed as fornicators. Those who repress their natural desires make the darkness inside of them grow so that eventually they fall into the very vices they ardently denounce."

"I would like to believe we could trip him up that easily."

"I didn't say it would be easy. But I think we can."

Two days later, Shatara came to our home. Issam gave her freedom of the city. She had two children, and he threatened extreme cruelty to them if she ever used her freedom to flee from his service. She came with a brace of guards since her beauty made her a target for abduction and two young attendants. I sent the soldiers and her attendants to separate rooms and instructed the servants to give them refreshment. Morgianna and I received Shatara in the main hall.

Shatara's Ethiopian and Persian decent gave her a lovely face with large eyes, a wide mouth, and a thin, straight nose. Her graceful body radiated a lustrous dark brown. Tonight, she wore a blue outfit that managed to be modest and seductive at the same time.

We reclined and ate. She and Morgianna talked non-stop about their childhood days. Both had grown up slaves, but their owner had been benevolent—as benevolent, it should be said, as a slave owner could be. When he died, his children inherited the girls and sold them off, Morgianna to my father, Shatara to Issam.

"It is time to discuss the purpose of which we invited you here, Shatara," Morgianna said. "Let's go up on the roof."

We climbed the spiral staircase. A waxing gibbous moon shone bright in the star-glutted sky. While the main hall was secure, our roof, once the door leading the stairway was closed, offered absolute secrecy. Still, we stood close, a circle of three. Words can carry. One must be cautious even in the most secretive of places.

With her form illumined by moonlight, Shatara resembled a goddess from ancient legend.

Morgianna revealed her plan.

"I don't believe the governor would want a woman. He has three wives—and if I can be blunt, I'm sure there are plenty of women in the palace who are at his disposal."

"I don't think he would consort with any of the women there. It would be known. As for his wives, they will not fulfill the desire he has to transgress."

"Why are you so sure he wishes to transgress?"

"When we make a thing the center of our life, we must push other things from the center to the edges of our affection. However virtuous he appears, he wants what he denounces more than anything else."

Rafiq had of late railed against "fornication, whoredom, and houses of ill repute." He had not tried to close the town's many brothels, but I expected him to set down such a decree any day.

In the morning, I learned he had taken the first step by ordering that prostitutes must wear a bright yellow sash around their waist anytime they went out in public.

The governor had the habit of stalking about the city in disguise to make certain people obeyed his edicts. He seemed especially obsessed with his ban on coffee and frequently sniffed out coffee bars. His obsession led him to make sale the beverage a capital crime.

But the city's thirst for coffee led many bold entrepreneurs to set up clandestine booths in sides streets and hidden parks, resulting in a thriving trade in banned commodity. They had scouts who would warn them if one of governor's thugs, or the governor himself, came their way, and they would gather their wares, fold up their stands, and flee.

By design, two mornings after our meeting, and on one of Shatara's days off, she and Morgianna emerged from an alley, took out cups of coffee they had purchased earlier and sipped. Rafiq came around the corner, spotted them, and whistled to a squad of soldiers.

He gloated as they secured the woman. "Violating my decrees. You are drinking the blood of Satan himself. But I'm not surprised to see an unbeliever and a prostitute engaging in such behavior. You will both hang in the city square to serve as an example to all."

Shatara and Morgianna fell on their knees and pleaded, as my wife told me later.

"Mercy, my Lord," Morgianna wept. "In the name of the Almighty, be merciful."

"Do not leave my children orphans," Shatara sobbed. "In the name of the Compassionate One, spare our lives."

He enjoyed their abjection and made a pompous show of denying their pleas.

The Grand Vizier hurried up and whispered something to him. He maintained the bland, parsimonious look he used when exercising his office, but his eyes showed distress. City officials later told me that he could not put the women to death.

"It is not against the law to drink coffee, only to sell it," he explained to the governor, spreading his hands and making a show to appear mild and judicious.

He had to be careful. One of the women was Morgianna, wife of Ali Baba; the other was a woman favored by innumerable influential men in the city, and the governor did not want to make more enemies.

We had consulted with a lawyer to make certain my wife and her friend were in no real danger of being arrested. Morgianna, ever the trickster, knew what the Grand Vizier had told Rafiq but still acted stricken with terror.

"Mighty Rafiq, merciful and benevolent ruler and Server of the Most High, spare us, and I will tell you how you can become the richest king in all Islam." This, Morgianna said, formed the weakest link in his chain of her plan. Would he take the bait? Would he trust a woman to tell him how to become powerful and prominent? Was he ambitious enough to think he might enforce his morality on all the world of Islam from India to Spain? The governor pondered as long as a minute.

Finally, to Morgianna's relief, he agreed to hear them.

"If this is a lie or a ruse, pain such as you never imagine possible awaits you—and your wayward friend."

He took them back to his palace led them to a sealed room, and turned to them.

"Let's get to the point. I don't have time to waste. How will you enable me to be the richest king in Islam?"

"Have you ever wondered, Governor Rafiq, at the sudden wealth of my husband, Ali Baba?"

"I have not lived here long enough to have seen his fortunes change—but the story of his sudden rise to wealth has been told to me."

"I can show you the hiding place of that wealth and the magic by which one gains entrance to the horded gold that makes him a rich man."

At this point, he might have had her tortured to find the secret of my wealth. But two things interdicted that course of action: one, he would be afraid to antagonize the council after the grumbling his harsh rule had engendered, and to show cruelty to a council member's wife and a woman well-loved in the city might cause a revolt; and two, he wanted Shatara and could have her in a magically-isolated location.

He said that he would meet Morgianna and Shatara just outside the city, alone.

"No treachery, or you will die lamentable deaths. You understand what I will do to you both?"

They nodded, trying to look fearful but secretly rejoicing that he had taken the bait.

"If you don't want to be an exercise for my torturers on how much pain they can inflict and for how long, be true to your word."

A shrewd and cautious man, Rafiq would not normally have put himself in potential danger by going out alone and without an escort to protect him from assassination or abduction; and the political mood being what it was, he would never, under normal circumstances, have left his palace unescorted and possibly have ridden into a trap. He also did not take hostages or arrange to have the families of Shatara and my wife killed in retaliation if anything happened to him, probably because he feared raising too many questions by taking precautionary measures that would suggest some secretive action on his part.

Riches paved the road to power, and he wanted power. I imagine a man like Rafiq wanted to be the sultan, and as Morgianna had said, his lust had temporarily taken the place of his religious convictions. It had occupied the center of his soul, pushing religion to its margins.

They rode, their journey illumined by moonlight. The trip to the Cave of the Forty Thieves took about an hour. When they arrived, Rafiq took Shatara's hand.

"I'm going over here to see the full moon on the face of the small lake."

She smiled. "So am I."

As Rafiq led Shatara away from the cave, Morgianna said, "Open sesame."

Close to the water, he seized and kissed Shatara, his hands undoing the back of her dress so her pretty breasts—dark brown with black nipples—tumbled out. He squeezed, kissed, and licked.

"I thought he was going to eat them," Shatara said.

He began removing her garment.

"Not here, my Master. In the Cave of the Forty Thieves, there is a sleeping chamber where I keep a bed with perfumed sheets and many pillows. Let me spread my thighs for you in that beautiful bower of softness where we will not be seen by the prying eyes of shepherds or travelers."

His animal lust took over, but he agreed with her.

She fastened her garment.

Holding hands, the two of them followed Morgianna into the cave.

Rafiq marveled at the piles of gold and silver bars, the coffers of coins and casques of jewels, and the rich things—clothing, furniture, gold vessels, finely wrought weapons—piled from floor to ceiling.

But he had not entered the cave to gaze upon wealth.

He asked Shatara to lead him to her bed.

Morgianna had told her friend they might drug the governor or knock him out.

Shatara shook her head. "We might fail if we try to do those things. Let me have him, my sister."

"But I need to close the door so no one stumbles on to us. He must not hear it."

"He won't hear it, I guarantee. And don't feel bad for me. I do this sort of thing for living. It's all in a day's work."

After a few moments, the bed creaked, and Shatara shouted, moaned, and squealed.

Morgianna said the magic words. The rock doors came together and darkness descended. She lit a torch that cast flickering orange light on the gold, silver, and jewels all about her.

After a while, the noise of their coupling ceased. Shatara shuffled to the main part of the cave wrapped in a sheet.

As Shatara bathed in the lake, far enough off that she could not hear, Morgianna said the magic and closed the door. Shatara and put on the extra garments Morgianna had brought in her saddle bags.

The two of them rode off into the night of stars and moon.

"Of course, we won't leave him there to die," my wife told Shatara after they had ridden back and we were drinking wine in our secure room. "I would never put a soul to a fate that cruel. I left water, food, and lit a candle for him so he could see his supplies—and a chamber pot. I left enough food for a week."

"He may not need that much food," I said.

Morgianna and Shatara gave me puzzled looks.

"There's talk of a *coup*. The governor's absence will embolden those plotting to overthrow him."

This happened only a day later.

A group of disgruntled soldiers and armed citizens, and no doubt, quite a few coffee drinkers stormed the palace only to be told the governor was missing. He had left no word of his location. After a day and night of fruitless searching, the council announced a new governor—one, they said, who would be much more equitable.

Once the new governor had secured his place and driven out the criminals and blaggards Rafiq had hired as enforcers of his tyranny, Morgianna and I went to free the former governor.

Rattled but generally in good health, he ranted about God being on his side and how he would raise an army and come back to take the city by force.

"You have no support in the city—and I think you may have some difficulty raising an army. My advice would be to accept your fate and go make a new life somewhere else."

We gave him gold—enough to comfortably establish himself somewhere else—and took him to a small town on the Euphrates where he could catch a boat. He thanked God profusely—Morgianna and I not at all.

Back home, we negotiated for the release of Shatara and her children. I told Issam it might be a good idea for him to sell her to us, and he had enough savvy to agree because things were so up in the air politically. I was willing to give up a good portion of the wealth in the cave for Shatara's ransom, but Issam settled for a small payment so as not to antagonize me.

Morgianna and I provided a home and money for Shatara at once and her children. Today, she is married to a man who is fully aware of her past and who loves her with all his heart—and, I might add, is the envy of everyone in our city for having married such a beautiful woman. He is an excellent father to her children.

No word ever came of Rafiq. Some say he settled in Yemen. Some said he had sailed to India.

And I compliment Morrigan, who had entailed much personal risk to get rid of Rafiq and to free her belovéd friend.

"Always the trickster. There is no way anyone could get the best of you."

"You get the best of me," she said.

And I did—more treasure than was hidden in the cave.

BROTHER SWANWING

R. C. Mulhare

While his brothers felt relief to have returned to human form, the youngest son of Lír wished at times that his sister Fiona had more nimble fingers with her needle and more material at hand. Thus, he too would have resumed his human form in full, but instead, he returned to the family's holdings in Antrim with a swan's wing in place of his left arm, a reminder of the sleeve that Fiona had not the wherewithal to sew onto an enchanted shirt in order to transform him back into his true form.

Once back among his people, he soon discovered that he could not bear people's gazes upon his left side. Even if he wore his cloak draped over the limb, common and noble alike, turn their gazes toward it, even when they sought to avoid looking upon it; he could hear their whispers among themselves when they thought he did not hear them:

"That is he, that is Declan, the youngest son of Lír, that's the young man with the swan's wing for an arm."

"That's the one who was turned into a swan, along with his five brothers." For stating aloud what all could see already pricked him to the core of his heart.

"If only his sister had been quicker with a needle, he would have two sound arms."

"Shut your mouth. At the least, he has the form of a man again."

When the chatter grew too loud, he would look them in the eye, letting them know he had heard every word.

He could still sit a horse and swing a blade, but could no longer draw a bow nor hold an offhand weapon nor a shield, though sweeping his wing out from beneath his cloak could and did confound an opponent while they sparred, yet the weapons master warned him that he could not fall back upon this trick too often.

His sister and her maids took the time to refit his shirts and tunics to accommodate the change in his form: pushing a wing through a sleeve, thus bending the longer feathers when the fabric confined and crushed them, hurt more than he anticipated, and this called more attention to his condition that he cared.

He approached Lír, telling him of his troubles, of his shortened circumstances, now that he could fight and hunt with but one arm.

"If you would allow, I would take the cowl at the monastery of Kildare," he said, kneeling at his father's feet in the solarium of their manor.

Lír lowered his shaggy brows and shook his head. "No son of mine, not even my youngest, is running away to hide among those lamb-men and women," he said.

"And where else could the youngest son of a chieftain go, when his kinsmen and kinswomen look at him as if he were a two-headed calf?" Declan met his father's gaze, showing no fear.

"Suffer their gazes. What can they do to you?"

Declan wagged his head. "It is more than mere looks. People talk when they think that I cannot hear, and you have, without a doubt, heard that the nearer chieftains' daughters hardly give me a second glance except to stare at the wing where my arm should be, before they whisper and laugh among themselves."

Lír chaffed, turning away, clearly giving these concerns no further thought. "If you cannot bear the scoffing of women, perhaps you are better off dwelling among the lamb-men and their pallid god."

His father had not given his word to his son to let him take the cowl, and yet had not in so many words forbidden his son from taking this course, and so he departed, head bowed, wing folded at his side.

One of his grandmother Mechtild's handmaidens found him in the passageway, and seeing his drooping wing and bowed head, gently took him by the arm and guided him toward her mistress's weaving room.

Mechtild lifted her gray-haired head from her loom with its web of colored threads, her gray eyes grave as she read his face and form. "What troubles you, youngest son of my daughter?"

He told her of his desire to retire to Kildare and take the cowl and of his father's blunt mockery of his desire. Mechtild listened in a gentle silence. When he had spoken himself dry, she put a hand upon his arm. "Do not let the growls of the old bear trouble you. If you wish to take the cowl, set forth to Kildare and go with my love and your sister's love. If anyone shall take you without scrutiny, that would be the brothers and sisters of Brigid." It came to him as little surprise and yet as a relief that she would give him such a blessing. She filled the place of mother to him at the passing of his birth-mother, and she had not approved of Lír's second wife. Perhaps, she had foreseen the trouble she would cost him and his children, with the faery tricks she had played, in a bid to displace her husband's sons.

And so that night, when the rest of the castle slept, Declan took a small satchel of clothes and dried meat with a small bag of coin that his grandmother packed and hid in his clothes chest and set forth on foot, for to saddle a horse would have alerted the stable grooms and roused their suspicions.

For days, he walked, passing fields and forests, sleeping in copses and avoiding villages as best he could, the better to avoid the gazes and questions of the villagers, and so they would not know where he had passed, and thus spread word of where he had gone, which could trail back to Lír. At length, his supply of food at hand ran out and he grew too hungry to avoid venturing into a town that he might find warmth and food on the hearth of an inn. Though his coin bought him food and drink as readily as the next man's coin, it could not buy him a moment's peace from the stares and whispers of the other patrons when they glimpsed what hid beneath his cloak. One old toper deep in his cups, on spying the wing where the youth would have had an arm, bolted from his seat and out into the night, swearing by the powers that he would never take a drop of the water of life—at least till the host at the next inn offered him a drink with which to steady himself. That night the youth slept in the stable without the ostler needing to bid him go out into the night.

Footsore, in need of washing and with his wing drooping beneath his cloak, Declan arrived at the gates of Kildare, where the porter took one look upon him and thinking in his simplicity—for the porter possessed a simple, kindly soul—that an angel had descended to approach the gate, forgetting to hide one wing from the eyes of man, opened the gate and brought Declan into the guest house. The youth told the brother porter that he would fain see Father Abbot and Mother Abbess.

"I shall see that you speak to them today, once you have rested," Brother Porter replied, while seeking out the best of the fresh bread and the smoothest apples in the guest-house pantry, and a pitcher of the cleanest water. "It must be long and tiring journey from heaven."

Declan opened his mouth to chasten Brother Porter, but closed it, too tired to correct him.

After Declan had rested and put on fresh clothes, Brother Porter brought the youth to the study which Father Abbot and Mother Abbess shared. Both looked at him surprise, for Brother Porter may have exaggerated in describing the new guest, but he could see neither fear nor scrutiny in their gazes.

"And what brings you to Kildare?" Mother Abbess asked, relieving the awkward pause.

"I hope to take the cowl and company with the brothers who dwell here," Declan replied. "There is no place left in the world for a man with only one stout arm."

The Mother Abbess and the Father Abbot looked to each other, conferring together in low voices, the Father Abbot taking a second glance at the cloak draped over the young man's left side.

The Father Abbot replied steepled his hands together. "We have heard tell of you and your plight, for at times, we host travelers unable to find lodgings, and they bring with them stories of things they have seen or heard,"

"Yet, that said, you must know that this is not a place where one may hide from the world," the Mother Abbess added. "The cowl is not meant to serve as a mask."

"Then whatever place is there for a man to dwell? I cannot fight well with but one hand." Declan's heart sank in his chest.

The Father Abbot lifted a gentle hand, calling for calm. "We did not say you could not stay with us. For we shelter many cast out by the world, on account of the weakness of their bodies; we only said that you may not take the cowl. By the rules of our order, a man must have two strong arms in order to serve the All Mighty to his level best."

"Fair enough." One must honor the rules of one's host and the ways of a place that has welcomed one as a guest, the better to respect their hospitality, even when those rules confound one's mind.

He soon settled among the folk who dwelled within the walls of the Abbey, who likewise could neither take the veil or the cowl or who lacked a calling to it: the crippled, the disturbed of mind, the blind, the deaf, the mute, those lacking limbs, and those too simple to care well for themselves and needed gentle hands to assist.

And yet he thought himself an outcast among them, for he still met with stares and whispers from the other guests, at least till the monks and nuns chided them for treating him so, and until he worked in the fields, paired with Finnian, a man with one arm, the right one lost when a stone had crushed it whilst he worked as a quarryman. Together, they sowed the fields, one holding the sack, the other casting the seed. He had to push himself in order to keep up with the other man, but he embraced the challenge, the better to earn his keep, which earned Finnian's teasing fondness.

"We have but one pair of arms between us, but we get as much done as two men," Finnian said with a cheer that Declan found hard to resist.

The summer passed, full of work and growing accustomed to working with but one hand. He discovered that he could use his wing to shade his head on the hottest days, and with the size of it, he could shade companion while they rested, or use it to offer Finnian and himself shelter from a rain shower.

Harvest time drew near, and the brothers, the sisters, and the stronger of the guests set to gathering the corn and barley. Declan and Finnian had the task of threshing the grain. One day, whilst they worked the threshing floor, flails beating the golden grain at their feet, they heard horses' hooves approaching, three riders with their hoods raised despite the sunlit day. They reined in at the edge of the threshing floor, only then did they lower their hoods. Declan, gazing out from under the shadow of his wing, which he had raised to better shade his eyes and see the approaching riders, recognized his three middle brothers.

"What brings you here?" Declan called to them.

Finnian lowered his flail close to his side, as if he would use it as a weapon in case it came to that. "You know these men?"

"Yes, my brothers, or three of them, the ones closest to me," Declan said.

"We came to give you warning, Declan," his third eldest brother, Conor, called back.

"Lír has found where you have taken refuge, and he rides here with his army," his fourth eldest brother, Fiacre, added. "He will not let you hide like a rabbit among what he calls the 'lamb-men'."

"We came to warn you and to help you to flee," his fifth eldest brother, Aidan, said. And he looked to the fourth horse they had brought with them, tethered behind Conor's horse.

Declan shook his head.

"Nay, I will not leave this place. I have made a home and a life here, and I will not abandon it so easily." His words came to his lips so readily that they surprised him, and they brought a warm smile to Finnian's ruddy face.

"Would you bring a battle to these peaceable men and women?" Conor said.

Declan stood his ground. "Nay, but I will not return to the household of a man who mocked my frailties and would not allow me to leave on my own terms."

"As you wish, but we warn you, we have but a day's start on our father and his men," Fiacre said.

"Then let us speak to Father Abbot and Mother Abbess. There are monks and nuns in our company who were warriors before they took the cowl or the veil. If it came to that, they could muster them to defend the Abbey."

And so, they spoke at length with Father Abbot and Mother Abbess in their study. Mother Abbess wanted to call upon the lord whose lands bordered those of Kildare from the west, but Father Abbot stood with Declan's inspiration, rather than risk pulling a neutral man into the quarrel.

"And with what would we arm our brethren?" Mother Abbess asked, her brow furrowed beneath her wimple.

"The harvesters are using scythes and sickles and flails, which offer some match against men on horseback," Father Abbot replied.

Mother Abbess spread her hands in frustration. "Would we stoop to this for but one man?"

"My brothers and I would lead whatever muster you might collect from among your people," Conor said. "He is our brother and we must defend him. We have an advantage that would favor you."

"And what would that advantage be?" Father Abbot asked.

"We know how our father would think, how he would command his men. He might well stay his hand before launching an attack, or he might attack in order to flush out our brother."

"You speak of me as if I were a bird that he has hunted," Declan said.

"And what would change your father's mind so suddenly between two possible courses?"

Fiacre shifted, uneasy. "It would depend on which way his mood ran that day."

Aidan winced, for they all had, at one moment or another, experienced the brunt of their father's darker moods. "And of late, he has been very wroth."

"If that has been so, perhaps I should meet him at the gate and make my intent be known to him there."

Mother Abbess tilted her head, curious and with a motherly concern. "And what is your intent?"

"That I will not be taken from Kildare, nor will I let him assault this goodly place," Declan said.

On the next day, the sun stood halfway to its zenith when Lír and his warriors arrived at the gates to Kildare. But he found Declam already standing without the gates, his cloak cast aside to uncover his wing folded against his side.

"Have you ceased to run, Declan? Have you seen for yourself how weak these lamb-men are?" Lír asked, still mounted upon his charger.

"No, I have not seen weakness in them, but I have seen how kind they are. My brothers would lead those among their company who were once warriors against your men, but I would not have them risk their lives for my sake."

"And so you would surrender?" Lír asked.

"I would not give you that satisfaction, either." Declan fled, heading for the millpond near an edge of the abbey lands. Lír gave chase, but Declan knew the abbey lands well, and on foot, he could slip through hedgerows and run through thickets and stands of trees that Lír could not ride through with ease.

As Declan reached the edge of the millpond, his companion Finnian burst from a thicket of rushes and tried to grab Declan by his wing. Declan whipped it free and nearly struck his friend with it.

Declan shook him off. "What are you doing, Finnian?"

"I cannot let you run away like this."

Declan turned one shoulder to his friend. "And I cannot go back with that man, nor can I let him attack this place."

"And what then would we do? Cast yourself into the pond?" Finnian said, reaching for Declan's arm. "I cannot let you. You are as a brother to me. Between us there is but one pair of arms. Would you tear that apart?"

Lír and his closest warriors rode up, his three middle sons and some of the abbey folk, monks, nuns and guests alike trailing the heels of their horses. Declan turned, distracted at their voices, when the soft ground beneath his foot crumbled, plunging him into the millpond. Finnian tried to grab at Declan's arm. Instead of stopping the fall, he only fell with Declan, the both of them sinking into the water, beneath the surface and into a deep drop-off in the bottom of the pond…

At that moment, a pair of swans flew up from the pond, circling over it, over the mill and over the heads of the crowd on the bank before they flew away toward the south. What the folk who witnessed this event saw in the moment, the telling would depend upon the teller. Lír would say that that his son dragged his companion into the millpond after him.

Father Abbot and Mother Abbess would say that one or the other fell into the pond and struggled to help each other out, but the weight of the water drenched their clothes and pulled them to their death.

Lír ordered the monks to dredge the millpond, and Father Abbot had them comply, but they found no trace of either man, and so Lír and his men rode back to his holdings.

Later, Father Abbot and Mother Abbess wrote the pair into the annals of the abbey, honoring them in their passing with the orders that they could not easily grant to them in life.

The tale grew in the telling, though the harder souls among the listeners would say they drowned, throwing away their lives or losing them in an accident and their fall had merely frightened swans already among the rushes.

The brighter souls might say that St. Brigid had seen fit to work a miracle and had transformed them while they struggled beneath the waters and thus they arose anew, transformed into swans.

Some even claim that each swan had slightly ruffled feathers upon one wing, as if that wing might have had another, much different form, alike to the arm of a man.

BLOOD—NOT ROSE

Megan Fuentes

I am awed by my masterpiece. Tinted blue by moonlight, its true colors are red and white. The two colors together make me ache.

Someone gasps. My blade jumps out of my hand and clatters to the ground. Jamir standing behind me without his walking stick surprises me, but the absence of castle guards is a greater shock after the commotion I'd made.

"I do not regret what I have done."

He sighs. Whether in acceptance or disappointment or resignation, I cannot tell.

"They were a force of destruction for this country—you know that as well as I do. They were sabotaging all that your father had worked so hard to achieve."

"I know." He sighs again, hobbling closer to me. Our marriage had been a forced one—the king's dying wish was to see his lame, younger son married, and I had been an ideal candidate, being without ties except to my sister. Still, we got along fine. What does he think of me now, standing here, in his brother's bedchamber, obviously guilty? Even after five years, I still cannot read his face.

"No, you don't understand. It's not just that he was poison to the kingdom. It was her, too." I am powerless to stop all that I've wanted to reveal from spilling out of my mouth. I find myself rushing through the words. "I was the one who killed Mother when I came out of the womb, not her. She was the firstborn, the most loved because she looked so much like Mother, while Father could barely look at me. Her subjects so revered her because of her story: escaping the huntsman, fleeing into the woods, living as a doting housemaid for those dwarfs until she was offered that damned apple, and then kissed by a prince—the prince *I* brought to her after she was found half-dead in the kitchen. And I was the one who convinced the huntsman to give Stepmother pig hearts in place of ours, and worked in that tiny cottage day and night while she was their pretty little songbird. I am the reason she was here in the first place, and I'm treated like Stepmother used to treat us."

Jamir stands in front of me, using the bedpost for balance. He makes no move to comfort or confront me. Tears flood my eyes as if a dam has burst. My words are barely distinguishable from one another, but I have to continue.

"I saw the gold—the *taxes* the new king had demanded, and in a time of famine. And she just *watched* the kingdom fall. Even when the dwarfs were gathered up and made to work like slaves in the mines, she went along with it. Everything was all right so long as she was loved and taken care of and could turn a blind eye. I couldn't bear it another second. I'd rather swing from a noose than see another day under their rule."

Exhausted after my declaration, I collapse at first onto the bed, but recoil and fall to the floor when my hand finds my sister's still-warm blood. Animalistic sobs rack my body. Even now, I am not crying because I am repentant. I am crying because I have finally said aloud what has been haunting me for half a decade. Undoubtedly, I will be imprisoned and probably put to death within a fortnight. That does not matter to me. Jamir is wiser than his brother ever was or ever would be, and I have no doubt he'll find a second bride—this time, one of his own choosing. The kingdom will have a proper ruler, and *that* is what matters.

"The sheets are a red mess," is the first thing the new king says.

A few more minutes go by while I compose myself. Eventually, I can stand, and he repeats himself.

"Yes," I say cautiously. "They are. Red. Like my name."

"No. *Not* like your name, Rose Red. Not a color for flowers—the color of blood. And it does *not* belong on the king and queen's bedsheets."

I tremble once more, disturbed by his tone. Meek and gentle Prince Jamir never sounded so cross before. So commanding and dominant. And yet he is enigmatic as ever. "What...What, then, do you propose we do?"

He considers this, rubbing the back of his neck. He looks at me, then the corpses. His gaze settles above the headboard, far past the wall.

"We have them dyed."

BEAUTY AND HER PRINCE

Clara Lawryniuk

Belle's hands quivered as she prepared for her marriage bed: removing pins from her long, black hair so that thick waves of it cascaded down her back, cleaning her face of cosmetics and removing jewelry. Tonight promised to be the culmination of Belle's joy. She could not recall a more ecstatic moment. Tonight, Belle and her prince would consummate not simply their marriage but their love.

A love that overcame great odds and adversity, Belle smiled at her reflection.

Four maids attended her before the wedding, primping and coiffing and setting each detail of her appearance until it was perfect. The same retinue offered to undress her as well, but Belle insisted on doing this task herself. She wanted to use this time alone to collect her thoughts and reflect on the eventful day. Though nearly three months had passed since she came to live in the castle, first as a prisoner and now as its mistress, the staff still grew accustomed to Belle's particular needs. Most peculiar to them was her desire, from time to time, to do things herself.

Some of Belle's stubborn independence stemmed from growing up the daughter of a rich merchant who tragically lost his fortune, forcing them to relocate to the countryside to live more modestly. Now, she was married to a wealthy prince. Poverty and luxury and the spaces in between were no strangers to her. If her rises and falls in fortune had taught her anything, it was to always expect change and to rely most on her own strength and resourcefulness.

Belle took a deep breath to soothe the butterflies in her stomach and brushed out her hair. Over the course of the ceremony, every guest in attendance and even the priest himself had told Belle she was beautiful, but no compliments mattered more to her than those of her beloved prince. When the prince regarded Belle in all her wedding regalia for the first time, the smile that warmed his face made her knees tremble. The man her prince had transformed into, after she lifted his tragic curse, was like the mythological Adonis incarnate. Thick blonde hair that fell to his shoulders, a distinguished face with a strong jaw, pouty lips, and piercing eyes the color of a stormy sea. Her prince had the power to render her speechless with a smile or breathless with a look.

Standing in front of the altar, his hands clasping hers, the sunlight beamed through the stained-glass windows, and a rising wave of exultation started in Belle's chest and brought tears to her eyes. Her body could hardly contain such joy. Upon seeing the couple together, guests gasped and remarked that they were as lovely as angels; no prettier groom and bride had they ever seen.

When Belle finished undoing all the finery of her wedding day, dressed in nothing more than a snow-white silk nightgown, a worry overcame her. Would her prince still find her desirable, naked and undecorated, now that he was just as lovely, if not more lovely, than her? She did what she could to dismiss the thought. Before his transformation, she had never felt insecure about her appearance or worthiness. If she could come to love a beast, surely her prince could want her without pretense.

Belle scurried down the candlelit corridor from her own private chambers and timidly entered her prince's empty bedroom, prepared by the servants for their comfort; a crackling blaze roared in the fireplace, a decanter of wine and crystal chalices were laid out on the table along with a bowl of overripe pears, and the enormous bed had fresh cotton sheets. Elaborate arrangements of roses decorated the mantle and end tables. They were her prince's favorite.

If Belle had asked her father for some trinket as a gift instead of a rose, would she be here now? Likely not.

Belle was all the more grateful for her good fortune, that fate had brought them together.

Belle poured herself a little wine, hoping it would soothe her nerves and give her boldness. Though her body flushed with desire, her inexperience made her shy. Fear of the unknown tempered the desire she felt, but she told herself she must be brave. She would do what she could to put her apprehension aside in the name of their marriage and happiness.

"Is that my darling princess?" Her prince's voice startled her out of her contemplation. His smoldering tone made it clear he was pleased.

Belle faced him, stammering, "I—I'm not—" She blushed and quivered under his scrutiny. His robe left much of his chest exposed, the light of the fire danced across his gorgeous face, and Belle once again fell speechless.

"Seeing as I am a prince and you are now my wife, that would make you a princess." His gaze poured over her hungrily as he closed the gap between them. "My princess."

He took Belle's face into his strong and supple hands, hands that had never toiled, hands that had long been lonely, and he kissed her deeply.

The prince stroked Belle's hair and cheek.

"My angel, you saved me. I don't know what I did to deserve you, but I need you. You are the best thing that has ever happened to me, and now you are mine at last."

He undid the ribbons on her bodice with lust in his eyes.

Her body tensed, and his fingers halted.

"What's the matter?" Was that displeasure she heard, or had she only imagined it?

Belle didn't know what explanation to give. Her nerves and mind were betraying her.

"Nothing's the matter. I just…" She decided honesty would be best.

Her voice barely rose above a whisper. "I'm frightened. This is all so new."

Her prince had insisted they be married mere days after Belle had lifted his curse, saying he could bear to wait no longer.

"I'm sorry," was all she could think to say.

Her prince frowned and shook his head.

"Belle, I'm asking you to trust me." His brows furrowed in a doleful expression. "Don't you trust me?"

It pained Belle to see him this way. The last thing she wanted to do was disappoint her beloved prince with her foolish, girlish fears, especially on a night as monumental as this.

"Of course I trust you. I love you." Belle feigned confidence. She buried whatever reluctance and lingering fear deep down where it could be forgotten. She kissed him once more, as passionately as she could, then removed her nightgown, letting it slip to the floor until she was naked before her prince.

Their first fight seemed tame enough. It came nipping on the heels of marital bliss. But what it set in motion, like ripples, or an avalanche launched by a few careless footsteps, burdened Belle with guilt and regret.

Looking back on that period—after their wedding, but before her thoughtless mistake—Belle marked it in her mind as the ideal she ever-after sought to recapture. Much like the innocence of youth, nothing was ever going to be as pure and secure again. Trust was not something earned, but something given from the first that could be diminished over time if one was thoughtless.

And Belle had been thoughtless.

Usually their meals were filled with light-hearted banter, playful innuendo, and the sort of questions or stories a couple shares as they continue to get to know one another. But as time passed, they had less and less to talk about. Belle did what she could to be entertaining despite the strain.

On that night, her prince paid more attention to the fire burning in the hearth than her attempts at conversation.

"Is something the matter?"

"I'm fine," he said unconvincingly.

Belle decided not to pry and thought a story might lift her prince's spirits. She often told him stories from the books she'd read.

"Have I told you the story of Orpheus, my love?"

Her prince shook his head, his eyebrows raised in curiosity.

She did her best to tell the tale of the legendary poet and musician Orpheus, who could make even the Gods cry with his music, and how he tried and failed to save his beloved wife Eurydice from the underworld.

By the end of the story and a glass of wine, her prince's mood was cheerful and engaged. He smiled with rapt attention as she reached the climax, where, despite the warnings, Orpheus looks back to check on Eurydice only to lose her forever.

Her prince went to pour himself more wine and found none left. He scowled and shouted toward the kitchen, a bellowing growl that startled Belle.

"*Curse* you all."

A servant appeared, one of the thin, young men who cooked in the kitchens, worry written all over his face.

"Yes, master. You called?"

"Why am I out of wine? And why in God's name have we been waiting so long for the main course?"

"Beg your pardon, master. Please forgive the delay and this, uh—oversight." He gestured to the empty decanter.

"I could care less about your apologies, you fool. Quit wasting time making excuses and rectify the situation, or I am bound to get more wroth with each passing minute."

Her prince could be temperamental, but Belle was shocked to witness him be needlessly cruel.

The young man rushed off without another word.

Her prince grimaced at her with rapacious eyes. He wanted her to say something, but what? He gripped her forearm, squeezing it firmly.

"Are you just going to sit there gaping at me like that?"

Belle closed her mouth and tried to swallow the lump forming in her throat.

"Why didn't you speak up?" His grip tightened.

"I didn't know you wanted me to. And honestly, I think you were too harsh with him. He said it was a mistake-" He squeezed her arm so hard his knuckles turned white, silencing her.

The servant returned, carrying two full decanters of wine. How much did the young man overhear? He left in a haste.

Alone again.

"Why are you trying to embarrass me? I won't have you undermine me in front of my staff. You're supposed to be on my side." Her prince let go of her and slumped back into his chair. Belle ignored the finger-shaped, red marks on her arm.

The anxious storm brewing in Belle's mind cared only for reconciliation.

"You're right. I apologize. I should have been more supportive." Belle tried to construct a reasonable justification, hoping if he saw things her way his anger would dissipate. "It's just that I don't like being too hard on the staff. I want them to think well of me. We see them every day, and they do such a good job of taking care of us. I try to show a little gratitude for that. Besides, some of them I even count as friends."

Belle didn't have anyone to talk to besides her prince, and at times, she grew quite lonely. She was fond of one young woman in particular, a chambermaid by the name of Mary. The two were close in age, and what started as idle conversation while Mary tidied Belle's chambers led to a bond forged over a mutual love of fairy tales, folklore, and poetry. Mary was charming and sweet, with a quick wit, and made Belle laugh so readily it was easy for her to forget they were mistress and maid rather than two rambunctious farm girls. Spending time with Mary gave Belle great joy and comfort, while making her homesick as well.

"Being friends with servants is beneath you," her prince said.

"Well, I don't see a problem with it. Some of them are quite pleasant company, and it can be so lonely here."

"How could you be lonely? You have me."

Belle held her tongue. She sensed a trap waiting for her if she responded.

When she did not take the bait her prince sneered petulantly. "We were having such a lovely time and you had to ruin it."

The blame hit her like ice water.

They finished the rest of their meal in the sounds of cutlery scrapping against plates, the clinking of glass as he poured himself more wine, and breaths heavy with disapproval.

Belle wanted to undo the damage she'd done. But she could not grasp coherent thoughts through her anxiety. It stood her every hair on end. She ate nothing and clenched her fists in her lap.

She desperately hoped her prince would break the unbearable silence, whether to reassure her or scold her; by then, she did not care.

Yet to Belle's dismay, after her prince's fifth glass of wine, he took his leave without so much as wishing her goodnight.

In the wake of their fight, Belle did not see her prince for three whole days, the longest they had been apart since their wedding. Each night, she waited and hoped that he would summon her for a meal or to his bedroom, but no one came for her, and she was left to her own agonizing thoughts.

She replayed their conversation in her head many times, until she was intimately aware of her every misstep. By the end of the second day, like some caged animal gone mad, she tore up the bouquets of roses that decorated her chambers and threw them into the fireplace. The satisfaction from watching the flowers ignite and turn to ash was fleeting.

On the third day, she refused to eat as penance. Mary tried to visit Belle, but she turned her away each time. Belle did not want to make the situation any worse than it already was.

Belle took this time to plan her apology and to generally commit herself to becoming a better wife. The prospect of hard work did not concern her. She would use the same discipline that had helped her learn multiple languages, or to translate great works of ancient Greek poetry into French, or to turn herself from a city debutant into a useful farm girl. If she could learn how to navigate and appease her own father, who had a notorious temper, then surely she could manage it with her prince.

On the fourth day, Belle was visited by her prince.

It came as a surprise, as he rarely came to see her in her own chambers. He was all the more splendid looking because of how much she had missed him. His smile sent a wave of relief over her. The thorny pain in her chest dissolved for the first time since their fight.

"My darling, I've missed you." He took hold of her shoulders and kissed her. "Come take a walk with me, the weather is lovely."

Belle was too shocked to respond. He spoke to her as if he had never been upset. Had their fight and the torturous days after been nothing more than some terrible dream?

"Get dressed and meet me down in the parlor as soon as you can."

Belle grabbed his arm, stopping his leave, and hugged him, squeezing as tightly as she could.

"Thank you. I love you."

Belle took a few breaths to calm herself and a few more steps. A few breaths. A few steps.

This ritual helped clear her mind and instill composure, at least on the outside. The important thing was to appear calm; even if beneath the surface, she panicked, like deep water churning around a drowning body while the lake's surface remained smooth.

The ritual also bought her time, time she needed to prepare.

Belle braced for the encounter, rehearsing what she would say, forming predictions of what her prince's responses might be, and plotting the most peaceful paths of conversation.

She reminded herself explicitly, lest she forget, the topics she mustn't tread on.

Interspersed with her thoughts was a warning she repeated to herself again and again, like a prayer: *You won't ruin anything tonight.*

The moment her prince sat at the head of the dining table, she tried to assess his mood. Discerning correctly whether he was pleased to see her or if his mood was foul, whether he was morose or angry or deep in his cups on any given night was a necessary skill. It allowed Belle to anticipate her prince's needs.

She was his wife, after all, so it fell to her to keep him happy.

The entire household depended on her.

'Just do what you can to make the master happy." The head of staff, Mrs. Jardine, told Belle after her prince had forgiven their first fight. 'Master treats everyone more kindly when he's happy. Things have gotten so much better for us since you arrived, mistress."

And she could not hesitate or stall, because if her prince had any sense that she was making calculations about him, he may think something was amiss, or worse, suspect deceit.

Her prince valued trust and honesty between them above all else, so he sought to root out secrets whenever he could. The endeavor needed to be swift, discreet, and accurate as it meant the difference between a pleasant night and her ruining everything.

She did all of these unspoken, intricate rituals, because she loved him and wanted him to be happy. He had suffered so much, and she had the potential to give him contentment, even bliss. What sort of cruel and selfish woman would she be if she didn't give it all she had? Belle had the strength to make him happy, which made her happy, more or less. It pleased her to please him.

The darkest parts of winter came and went, and Belle and her prince could hardly make it through a day without some spat. The tension between them was only made worse by being cooped up inside, with relentless snows and little sunlight. Boredom had a way of souring her prince.

Did he look for reasons to be offended?

More and more bored and restless, because he could no longer go out for riding or hunting, he drank to pass the time. He criticized his staff, berated them at any opportunity, and threw fits when his whims were not satisfied. He asked for elaborate meals and was incensed when told they lacked a particular ingredient. He made his manservant, Old Thomas, play endless games of chess with him and was bitter when he lost. He teased and flirted with the maids and became indignant if they showed even the slightest sign of fear.

"Why are you afraid, girl? I'm no longer a beast. Can't you tell the difference, or are you stupid?"

Her prince would oscillate between indifferently ignoring Belle for days and demanding her attention. When he did take Belle to bed, he was rough and fast with her. No longer did he take his time to speak to her sweetly, caress her body, kiss her gently, or compliment her. She could never find it in herself to deny him, though, hopeful that sex would soothe him and improve his mood, while also worried about the repercussions of refusing him.

Sweet to her only in those post-coital moments, he buried his face in her hair and whispered desperate pleas in her ear. "I love you, my wife, my darling, my angel. You are the only thing that keeps the pain at bay."

In those moments, Belle wept softly with relief, her tension alleviated as she cradled him in her arms, once again able to glimpse the sweet man she loved so dearly.

When he asked, she told him they were tears of joy, and he believed her. Stranger still, part of her believed it, too.

"Please, you can't say anything," Belle pleaded.

Horror and disgust swept across Mary's face. "My lady, what has he done to you?"

Belle dismissed the bruises on her wrist and arm as mild. Her pride hurt far worse.

The previous night, they had fought. About what, Belle could not clearly recall, the circumstances and details all a messy blur.

She had apologized, cried, and pleaded, but her prince refused to believe her.

"If you were truly sorry, then you would stop making the same careless mistakes. Yet here we are again. It's like you want to hurt me, Belle." His words haunted her.

Wearing a long-sleeve dress worked to hide the bruises, but Mary had somehow caught a glimpse of her purple wrist.

The predicament tied knots in Belle's stomach.

"It's my fault. I asked him to do it. I was being hysterical, and I thought if he saw how sorry I was, well, then he would finally believe me." She held up her wrist. "This would prove it."

What seemed like a perfectly logical decision at the time surely sounded ludicrous to an outsider who didn't understand what was at stake.

Mary took Belle's hand in hers, trying to examine the bruises.

"And why in God's name are your words not sufficient? People apologize with words, my lady. This is beastly."

Belle pulled away.

"Don't say such a thing. He might hear you, or someone might tell him. You know how sensitive he is about what people call him."

If only she could find a way to help Mary understand the complicated situation she faced.

"He's not a beast, truly he isn't. He's not a bad man and if you knew him like I do, you would see that. It's true he's not perfect, no one is, God knows I have countless flaws of my own, but these demons he carries are not his fault. He was cursed and alone for so long. It had an effect on him. His body might be restored, but his mind and soul are still healing. And I want to be there for him. Help him. If my love could save him once, it could save him again."

Mary frowned, but her voice was soft and compassionate.

"That is all very noble of you, my lady. But you don't need to be a martyr. And maybe it's true your love can save the prince, but I don't think that excuses his hurting you. You don't deserve that."

"But I do," Belle said. "You see, the whole predicament is my fault. If I was just honest with him and not such a coward, he would believe what I say. But words aren't enough any longer. I have to prove to him, beyond a doubt, my repentance, my love."

Mary looked at Belle, mouth agape with concern and dread.

"What would you have me do?" Bitterness seeped into her voice. "Leave him? Abandon him when he needs me?"

Her prince had been distraught, broken, when she left to see her father for the very last time. He had almost lost the will to live. She couldn't bear to put him through that again.

She could be strong for both of them.

Mary sat there silently, tightlipped, her eyes downcast.

"And where would I go? My father is dead, my sisters despise me." Saying it aloud brought the full weight of her circumstances down on her.

"I'm so sorry, my lady," Mary said, somehow affectionate and melancholy at the same time.

Belle avoided Mary for a few days. The whole conversation had left her uneasy. Furthermore, she feared that somehow the prince would find out.

One morning when Belle missed Mary and wanted to put the awkwardness behind them, the chambermaid was nowhere to be found.

When Belle went to the kitchens to ask after her, the servants' faces blanched as they stole knowing looks at one another.

A pang of dread clenched Belle's stomach.

Only when she raised her voice and demanded someone tell her what was going on did one of the older cooks finally speak up.

"Mary's been dismissed, mistress."

No matter how much she fumed at them, they refused to explain any further.

It grew harder for Belle to wake and rise from bed each morning. Deep down in the core of her body seeds of dread germinated, but she insisted to everyone, including herself, that her malaise was just some passing illness, rooted in her weak body rather than her bruised heart.

From time to time, the dissonance between what she told herself and how she felt was so grave she wondered if she was losing her mind.

Ever determined, Belle grasped at how to get back to the happiness she once had, the joy of the halcyon days leading up to and after their wedding.

If only she weren't so flawed and selfish. If only she weren't so difficult. She should be grateful for everything her prince had done for her.

What he asked for in return was so simple.

Yet again and again, though she desired to please him, she failed. Whatever the solution to this predicament, she would find it.

Her journal, which once would have had bits and pieces of poems, or notes on deciphering Greek, were now filled with ideas on how to be a better wife and diatribes on her own shortcomings.

When she was young, her father told her she was clever.

"You are as brilliant as you are beautiful," he had praised her.

But neither her father nor anyone else knew the truth about her, as her dear prince saw it. He knew her for what she truly was and loved her still, as she was convinced no one else would. Her prince forgave her many flaws and saw potential in her. She wanted to be the woman and the wife that he wanted her to be—she just needed to get out of her own way and stop sabotaging herself.

Then came a day when they had a visitor, the first in a long time. He was a worldly traveler passing through, who needed a place to lodge and was lucky enough to arrive on a day when the prince felt generous.

The traveler joined them for dinner that night, and Belle warmed to him instantly. She relished the stories he had from his travels through Bavaria, Russia, and even the Ottoman Empire. He was young and handsome in a rugged, weathered sort of way, but Belle hardly cared. She simply enjoyed learning about the big wide world that she had once dreamed of exploring herself.

Her prince seemed to enjoy their guest as well, so Belle did not anticipate the ambush that wait for her in his bedroom that night. She found him standing with his arms crossed, posture rigid.

"I don't like the way you were looking at him," he said the moment the she closed the door.

"I don't know what you mean. I wasn't looking at him in any sort of way."

"Don't play dumb with me. I saw how you fawned over him. It was embarrassing."

A familiar sort of panic unsettled Belle.

"You have it all wrong. I was just enjoying his stories."

"Oh is that all?" He closed the gap between them and towered over her. "You love his stories of far off places and grand adventures? Are you really so eager to leave? Hate it here so much, do you? No one is keeping you here. You are no longer my prisoner."

Disorienting her with his accusations, he pushed on before she had any chance to get her bearings.

"Do you think you'll go away with him and be happy? Do you think he'd want a girl who's been with a beast?"

"Don't call yourself that."

"You're stupid to think he'd want you. Well maybe for a night. You are beautiful after all. But he'd abandon you on the road as soon as he'd finished fucking you."

"I never said I wanted any of that."

He spun a fantasy that she was powerless to stop, like slipping off the edge of a cliff into nothingness, like the foundation under her feet crumbling.

Belle desperately needed to find a handhold before she was cast out and abandoned.

"I don't want anyone else," she said. Her speech grew frantic. "I want you. You've been so kind to me. I'm grateful for everything you've done. I love you. You're not a beast, you're my beloved prince—"

He slapped her across the face.

"You know what I am. Do not lie to my face." His voice boiled with rage.

Belle bent over limp, trying to keep from falling. She cradled her face in her hands, pain emanating from her mouth and nose. This was not the first time he had used force to silence her or stamp out her hysterics.

But this was different.

Belle had clung to the belief that her prince was not capable of striking her.

She saw a thimbleful of blood in her palms.

Her prince's face went pale; his features frozen. Belle could read his thoughts. He had meant to do it quickly, mildly, a way to regain his control over her and the situation, but he had been too reckless and forceful. His whole demeanor changed, his jaw and shoulders stiff with shame.

Her prince scooped her up into his arms, whisking her away in a hurry. With her head against his chest, she could hear his rapid heartbeat, his breath flighty and on the verge of tears. He took her into his bathing room and gently laid her in the empty tub.

Indeed, tears welled in his eyes. Anguish contorted his face as he examined her.

"I'm sorry. I didn't mean to—" He fought for composure, his hands gripping his legs for support, claw-like fingers digging into his thighs.

In a daze, her face ached, growing more painful as sensation returned to it, piercing through the initial numbness. Dizzy. Disorganized. How bad was it truly? She wanted to say that she knew it had been an accident, but the words did not come out.

"Belle, I'm going to leave you for a moment to fetch some hot water. I'll be back soon, I promise. Everything is going to be all right." His voice shook, and he forced confidence. "I'll take care of you. I'll fix this."

With that, he was gone.

A sort of dim but persistent fear of death entered her. She gathered her wits as best as she could and stood up, despite the lightheadedness. When she could not find any linens on hand, she used her skirt to clean her face and staunch the blood. To her relief, the trickle of blood lessened.

Was her nose broken?

Her thoughts grew distant, muffled.

All she had left was her sense of self-preservation. She concentrated on tending to her face to keep from fainting.

Her prince's voice barked at someone in the corridor outside his chambers.

"I said I can handle it myself. You won't be needed. Now go fetch some more hot water, but don't bring it inside. Leave it here for me." He entered and locked the door behind him.

Rushing back into the tub was pointless. Let her prince find her sitting on the floor in her undergarments, ripping her blood-stained dress and tending to her face.

She searched his face and found relief.

"Oh, thank God." He had a large bucket of steaming water in each hand, which he set on the floor before hurrying to her side. He hugged her tightly.

"Thank heavens you're all right. I'm so sorry, Belle." He cried, his whole body trembling as he held her close.

Still in shock, she wrapped her arms around her prince and stroked his head.

"I'm a monster. A beast." He sobbed. "Look what I've done to you."

Belle did what she could to console her prince. She forgot her own injury until the metallic taste of blood left her nauseated.

The weeks following were like the glorious dawn breaking after a night filled with haunted dreams. All of her struggling and fighting and stubborn loyalty was finally rewarded.

Her prince was sobered by the experience, his love and devotion to her apparently rekindled.

"I promise to spend every day of the rest of my life working to become a man who deserves you." He told her one morning as they woke.

She longed to believe him.

Her prince did all that was in his power to make amends, endlessly apologizing, doting on her, lavishing her with gifts, keeping his drink in moderation, and generally treating Belle like his most precious possession.

He had arrangements of roses placed in her chambers every few days, and as soon as one started to wilt, it was replaced.

He bought her dozens of books, ordering the manager of his estate to track down whatever rare and unique books could be found in the neighboring towns.

His kindness and generosity exceeded even what it had been when they were newlyweds.

He no longer raised his voice to Belle and doted on her affectionately, kissing her and holding her hand whenever she was near. He sent her notes adorned with sweet words, inviting her to join him for meals or in his bed at night. Belle had never seen him so gentle.

At first, she was wary, and though she smiled when his gaze met her own, and though she was genuinely grateful for his tenderness, she still watched him closely. After weeks of such treatment, after the bruises had faded and the swelling in her nose healed, had the beastly remnants of her prince finally been tamed and laid to rest?

After weeks of unwavering kindness, Belle dared to hope.

A couple months into this kindness, Belle's monthly blood failed to arrive.

Belle told no one and hoped that it was simply late, as it had been before in times of sickness or stress. She did not allow herself to entertain the possibility, banishing the thoughts when confronted with them, as if thinking had the power to make it true. Deep down, she did have a preference, which her denial and reluctance revealed.

Belle braved the days.

At night though, her body betrayed the truth as she cried herself to sleep. Belle dreamed of a little girl with black hair and freckles like her own, but each time the little girl came close enough to hold, her freckled skin was black and blue.

Belle would wake with a jolt, alone in the dark and inconsolable.

She cried because she did not know how long she could hide her pregnancy from her prince. She cried because she did not know what he would do to her when he found out. She cried because she knew sooner or later they were going to reach a breaking point, and she was terrified of the day she would learn what it was to be broken.

The Knave of Swords
11/20/16

AS YOU HAVE LEFT ME

Raven Ashwood

Unmoving, the girl lie beneath the glass top casket. The gold base glistened in the sunlight. Her once-white skin now had a grayish hue, the once-shiny black hair now dull, the ruby-red lips now pale. Her hands were folded delicately across her stomach, a withering bouquet of wildflowers in her frozen hands. The beauty she had in life had begun to vanish. This worried the prince, who had stumbled across her coffin in the forest. He had brought her back to his castle and set her out in the garden, surrounded by red and white rosebushes.

For three days and nights, he sat by her coffin, barely eating and sleeping. Occasionally, he lifted the glass top and stroked the girl's hair, caressed her face and arms, kissed her softly.

He paced, knowing her beauty would soon be gone. When the sun rose on the fourth morning, he called for a servant. A young woman came running. "Yes, sire?"

"Fetch me the old witch from the village," the prince said.

"Sire?"

Her hesitation made him bellow, "*Now.*"

As he waited, the prince paced alongside the coffin. When the sun peaked, he placed a hand on the glass top. "Soon, my dear. Just a little longer."

The young woman finally returned from the village. An old hag followed slowly behind, stooping over a cane cut from a thick, knobby branch. A black-hooded cloak covered her matted gray hair and grimy clothes. Under the hood, a long scar cut across her cheek, through her eyebrow, and into her hairline.

She hobbled toward the impatient prince but did not bow. "And what may I do for his majesty?"

"Her beauty fades with each passing day." He caressed the coffin as though he caressed her face.

"Beauty tends to do that, Highness. What would you like me to do?"

"I want you to bring her back."

The witch narrowed her eyes at his request. "Is that all?"

The prince longed for the withering beauty within. "When she wakes, I want her to stay forever young. I do not want to watch her become an ugly, wrinkled old woman."

"So it shall be done." The witch's smile revealed yellow, crooked teeth.

She rested her bony hands on the glass, waving the prince out of the way. Muttering under her breath in an ancient language, the woman chanted, running her hands across the smooth surface. Head back, she shouted her final words toward the heavens.

"All that's left is for you to kiss her." The old witch turned away, resting her hand on the servant's shoulder. "Help me back to the village, girl."

The prince impatiently pried off the glass lid. It fell atop the rosebushes, smashing the petals. Ignoring the stench rolling off her body, he kissed the decaying beauty.

After a pause, her eyes fluttered open.

The prince smiled. "Hello, my love."

The girl could not move, her body stiff.

She was terrified, her senses dulled.

The prince lifted her from her coffin and carried her into the castle, calling for a feast to be prepared. He ordered servants to get her ready.

The heated bathwater loosened her muscles, and her hearing returned, although distant and muffled at first. Her vision cleared enough so that she could see shapes shifting through a fog of gray.

The distant sensation of servant hands scrubbed her flesh.

The girl could not resist. Her body was too tense for her to move away, to tell them to leave her alone. So she could only sit there, trapped, as they dressed her in a heavy, bright red gown. She struggled under the layers of fabric. She could not have undone the little pearl buttons up her back even if she had the strength. Skilled hands twisted her hair into intricate braids. They brushed a light layer of makeup to her face to restore the gray skin to its original complexion, applied red paint to her lips, and sprayed half a bottle of floral perfume on her.

By the time the servants helped her out of the room, down a set of stairs, and into the dining hall, most of her hearing had returned. She could hear the gentle music being played in the next room. She could see again as well, though colors dulled to a gray tint. A sickly, sweet smell filled her nose, mingling with the perfume and the aroma of bread and smoked meats.

When she entered the room, the prince rose from his chair and came toward her. In the center of the high ceiling hung a large chandelier with a handful of candles missing. The faded and discolored tapestries matched the worn out rug beneath the table.

He wrapped his arms around her and kissed her forehead. He laughed as he led her to the table. "The smell hasn't faded yet, but give it time, my dear. Until then, let us celebrate."

The girl did not eat as those around her devoured the feast set in her honor. She didn't desire food, her reality not entirely sinking in yet.

Each woman around the table wore a large dress, many blue or red. Each man wore a stiff-looking formal coat with more buttons than necessary. As the guests ate, they chatted, food and wine dribbling down their chins. Halfway through the meal, the prince called a servant to fill her plate and insisted she eat. The mounds of food on the table consisted of various smoked meats, fresh greens, a platter of apples and pears, and a few plates of burnt bread.

She could not taste any of it.

Up close, the prince was neither handsome nor charming, as she had heard. His hair was greasy and flakey, his teeth crooked and yellow, skin marred by deep, pitted scars. The clothes he wore were dingy; a button was missing on his coat. There was a small tear near his breast pocket. While they ate, a mustard smear appeared on his chin. He wiped grease from his mouth with his sleeve, leaving a stain.

After the feast, the prince led her up to the stairs to a room with a high ceiling, several tapestries depicting various battles, and through the window was a breathtaking view of the forest and the distant mountains beyond. A large four-post bed was centered against one of the walls; a fireplace directly across from it.

A bedroom fit for a princess.

The prince led her into the room and leaned down to kiss her. He stopped and wrinkled his nose, frowning. "In the morning, I'll have the servants draw you another bath. Afterwards, we shall plan the wedding." He gave her a quick kiss on the forehead. "Goodnight, my love. Get some sleep."

He left her standing in the middle of the room. When the door closed, any hope she had left her, but did as she was told. After several hours, she climbed out of bed.

Not tired, yet not awake either—merely conscious.

The next morning, the servants found her standing at the window. They prepared the bath and attempted without success to rid her of her smell. She went through the same routine as the night before: clothes, hair, perfume, and make-up before she was taken to the prince. Greeting her in the same fashion as he had before, he carried her off to plan their wedding.

Servants brought out fabric and cake samples. Later, they paraded around ribbons and flowers. All the while, the girl sat there. While she could move, it was painful. She let the prince and the servants tend to her as they saw fit. Asking without answers, the prince inevitably chose the most appealing, most delicious, and most wonderfully smelling of the options. She longed only for peace—for that eternal sleep he stole her from.

In the morning, the servants made the water hotter and scrubbed her harder. They caked on the makeup and added more perfume. Day by day, the prince commented on her beauty less and less until one morning when she entered, he neither came to her nor said anything besides, "Sit down."

The servants removed the final cake samples, bouquet examples, and table setting options from the room for the day. The prince did not stand as he normally did and offer his hand to her. Instead, he watched the servant girls, all young ladies about her age, walk out of the room. His attention most fixed on the young woman who had fetched the old witch. When they were all out of the room, he said, "The wedding will be held off until we can do something about your smell. Remain in your room until then."

He stood to walk away and spoke in her direction without looking at her. "Even if your odor is dealt with, you will not leave until your appearance can be fixed as well. It's hard to believe you ever had an ounce of beauty in you."

With that, he walked out the door.

She did not move for a long time before she did as she was told. She waited in her room. For what, she did not know. The servants came in multiple times a day to bring a tray of bread, cheese, apples, chicken, and wine. She barely picked at the food, which still had no taste to her. They scrubbed her now twice a day, but the smell only got worse. The servants applied her makeup and perfumes more heavily.

The girl passed her time sitting in a chair by the window. Neither moving nor speaking, she could only think of her former life and her new one. The servants finally gave up on scrubbing her after a week of her being confined to her room. They gave up on the makeup as well. Her once beautiful white skin was now discolored with shades of yellow and dark brown. Her shiny black hair had dulled. Slowly, her already thin figure shrank. Her eyes sank farther into her skull.

The girl finally stopped eating, hoping it would lead her to her end. Two weeks passed, and she remained in the chair; there was no need to move. She sat there looking toward the mountains, toward her former home in the woods.

She had no longer feared what would become of her and waited for the end. She had been peaceful in death. Then the prince stripped her of her eternal bliss without her consent. With each passing sunrise, the hope that she never saw him again, that he would disappear, grew stronger.

During her weeks of isolation, only one had stomach enough to brave the room. The servant who had fetched the witch snuck in every few nights and followed the same routine. She crept forward, slowly stepping into view as to not startle her.

Even with her lady's faded senses, the servant never did.

After a moment of silence, the young woman would ask the same question, "Are you still alive, my lady?"

"I am as I have been left," she said.

Another pause before her second question, "Is there anything I can get you, my lady?"

It was too great an effort to shake her head or say no.

Her silence was the simplest answer.

"Maybe something to drink? I could make a fire, or get you a blanket."

She remained for a few hours. Every so often, she repeated her offers, but she never did ask her lady how she was. There was no need. Her suffering was as clear to the young woman as if it screamed at her.

With every day that passed, her skin grew darker and more withered. When she was first awoken and brought down to the dining hall, there was a tiny bit of light in her eyes, a minute suggestion of life in her. Each time the young woman visited her, that hint of light faded in her sunken eyes.

After four weeks had passed, the doors of her room opened. The food was removed, but not replaced. Instead, a few servants and the prince entered, cloths tied around their faces.

"Is she dead?" the prince asked a servant. The stench was worse than ever before. She had become much thinner and her skin had bad large patches of orange and brown.

"I am as you left me," the girl said.

"How is it possible that you have grown more repulsive than before?" The prince scrunched his face in disgust. "Bring the hag in."

The servants parted and allowed for the old witch to hobble in. Her cane made a loud *clack, clack, clack* against the stone floor with every other step she took.

She did not cover her nose and seemed unfazed by the stench of decomposing flesh.

"Yes, Your Majesty?" the witch asked when she came to stand before the prince.

He gestured to his once fair maiden. "That is the outcome of your treacherous curse."

The witch merely cocked her head at the prince. Her voice conveyed her sarcasm. "Treacherous curse? I did not curse her to the ways of nature."

"I ordered you to make her forever young." The prince roared at her.

The witch smiled her toothy, yellow grin. "And so shall she remain. Never shall she grow old. Not a single wrinkle shall mark her face, nor should a single hair turn silver. She will not age a single day past the day you had me curse her."

The prince fumed. "I wanted beauty, and instead, you gave me a rotting corpse."

"Beauty and perfection are not permanent, nor shall they ever be."

"You are a witch."

"So I am."

"You could have kept her beautiful."

"I could not." The witch spat like she warded off evil. "What is dead can never truly come back to life. I did the best I could."

"The best you could?" The prince laughed sarcastically. "Look at her. You could have done better."

"Better? I could have, no, should have done nothing. That would have been better. She will still rot; there is no use in arguing otherwise."

The servants were still.

Only the girl had moved at all. The bones in her neck creaked as she turned her head to watch the dispute.

The prince's face turned red. "So be it. You shall *burn* at sundown for disobeying my direct order."

The prince left the room. The servants rushed to follow, not out of fear or loyalty but rather to escape the stench.

The girl turned to the window again as the witch got dragged out of the room.

That night, the light of the fire danced across the palace lawn just out of view of her window. It didn't bother her not to have seen it. While the witch was at fault for her current state, the girl had no desire to see another person suffer because of a command from the prince.

The following morning, her doors flew open again. The prince returned with several servants and demanded that she stand. Two servants, one was the young woman who visited her regularly, came to the girl's side to assist her. No longer did admiration fill his eyes nor love fill the prince's voice. "You are stinking up the castle."

Desire bloomed in his eyes as he caressed the young servant-woman's cheek. "How is it possible you were once as lovely, if not more, than this beauty right here?"

The girl felt the servant flinch and tighten her hand around the girl's arm, but the servant did not retreat from his touch.

The prince dropped his touch. "I am sending you to the dungeon."

She did not argue. She did not resist. There was no point. It took too much effort, effort she didn't care to exert. She allowed herself to be supported and guided by the servants to the dungeon where she was to remain until she rotted away to nothing. They left her standing in the middle of her cell. The servant girl was the one who locked the door. She gave the princess one last sad look before turning to leave.

It did not bother the former beauty any as she walked to the wooden bench bolted to the wall.

She sat down and stared at nothing.

She could only mark the passing of days by the light fading in and out from a window high above her.

It pained her less to watch the unchanging walls than to watch the outside world. The dark, cool, and musty walls seemed fitting to her. Her small cell bore no sign of life; nothing beautiful. There was no color in the room.

Three days passed before the servant girl could return to her lady. "My lady, are you still alive?"

Her voice was weaker than before. "I am as I was left."

Instead of asking what she could get her, she crossed the cell and knelt down. "My lady, I have brought you something."

The girl looked down at the bowl in the young woman's hands. It looked like someone had poorly mashed an apple. "I mashed this apple for you, my lady, and let it soak all day in a strong poison. I offer it to you in hopes that it will end your suffering."

The girl opened her mouth.

The servant girl returned the next night. She whispered in the dark. "My lady, are you alive?"

The princess said, "I am as you have left me."

She exhaled her defeat. "Is there anything I can get you, my lady?"

The girl studied the young woman before her. A bruise had formed across her cheek. "Come closer."

Her command surprised the young woman, but she did as she was told. A small cut revealed itself on her cheek.

"What happened?"

The young woman touched her injuries. "I made the mistake of rejecting one of the prince's advances."

"I see."

"Is there anything else I can do for you before I go, my lady?"

"Yes, there is something."

The young woman nodded, a smile quickly spreading across her face. "What may I do for you, my lady?"

"I have an idea."

Two nights later, the young woman returned as she had been asked and unlocked the cell. Helping her to the door, the young woman offered to carry her. They followed the path the princess had taken from her first prison to her second.

They stopped outside a large door.

"I've done as you have instructed, my lady."

The girl smiled. "Good."

She entered a room similar to her former except much grander. The girl walked toward the four-post bed, determination propelling her forward.

A fire roared in the fireplace.

She crawled onto the bed toward the sleeping figure.

Her movements took effort, but it was effort she was willing to give.

She touched his cheek. "Wake, my prince."

The prince's eyes flew open, and he let out a startled cry. A hand covered his nose. "How did you get in here?"

"Are you not happy to see me, my prince?" the girl asked.

"Get out," he ordered, pointing to the door with his free hand.

"I promise to leave and never return, on one condition."

"Why should I?"

"I will just return otherwise," she said.

"What is it?"

She gestured toward the table next to the bed where two glasses and a bottle of wine had been placed. "It's the wine you chose for the wedding. Share one glass with me and allow me to make a toast. Then I will leave you alone."

He snatched the bottle from the table and poured two small glasses. "Get this over with and then leave."

"A toast," she said as she raised her glass toward him, "to life and beauty."

He watched her drink her glass. When she finished, she looked at his and said, "I'm not leaving until that glass is empty, my prince."

The prince sniffed the dark contents of glass before he drank it. "Now get out."

She nodded and climbed out of the bed.

"What are you waiting for? *Leave.*"

She stood by the door, unmoving. The crackling fireplace mixed with the sound of his breath.

"I'm waiting."

"For *what?*"

It took effort, but the girl smiled a twisted smile.

The prince opened his mouth to say something but choked instead.

He tried again. Still nothing.

His fingers clawed at the collar of his nightshirt, already loose, as if that would resolve his problem. It didn't. He gasped. He reached out to the girl, fear filling his eyes. His fingers almost brushed the front of her dress.

She stepped back, watching and waiting.

Eventually, he dropped limp.

She arranged his arms. The prince tried to resist. She turned his head to face her, forcing him to see only her. He attempted at calling for help, but nothing but a tiny squeak came out.

She draped herself over the prince's frozen body, curled to his side and nestled into him, resting her head against his shoulder.

After the last bit of firelight faded, the former beauty spoke to her prince in a low voice. "We are as we will remain."

BEWARE THE FAIRY'S PRICE

Lillian Csernica

Alisia filled her pitcher from the clearest part of the fountain. The old beggar woman drank, then smiled.

"Sweet, well-spoken child, I grant you a gift. Whenever you speak, flowers and jewels shall fall from your lips."

Indeed they did, prompting Alisia's greedy step-mother to send Kerry, her step-sister, back to the fountain. A grand noblewoman waited there, alone and in need of a drink. Kerry scorned her, too busy searching for the old beggar woman.

"Evil hearts breed evil words," the noblewoman said. "To you I give all things scaled and slimy."

And so Alisia married the prince, and Kerry had to flee the village, the snakes and toads her only friends.

"Lord Uthbrey is waiting." Queen Sylvia sat on her throne, gowned in scarlet and ermine, glittering with diamonds. She arched one thin brow at Alisia. "I trust you'll be obliging?"

Alisia bowed her head, gaining a moment's freedom from all the endless smiling. Her long blonde hair had been woven into complicated braids around her tiara, giving her a headache. Her emerald satin gown was so heavy with embroidery and pearls it made her back hurt. Standing beside Alisia in his wine-red doublet and trunk hose, his wavy dark hair perfect, Jeremy still looked the ideal heroic prince.

Lord Uthbrey, stout and gray and debonair, stood at the far end of the throne room with his attendants. Queen Sylvia rewarded Lord Uthbrey's attentive look with an encouraging smile. At his word, two of the pages in his brought forward a small, round table. On it sat a tall object covered with a silken veil. Lord Uthbrey approached the throne and bowed.

"His Most Royal Majesty, Wallace the Fourth, presents his compliments on the occasion of Their Highnesses' third wedding anniversary."

Lord Uthbrey lifted the silk away, revealing a slender alabaster statue. The hair and gown were bright with gilding and tiny jewels. It was Alisia herself, captured in the essence of the fairy's curse.

"Speak, Alisia." Queen Sylvia smiled, her eyes cold. "Is it not a marvelous likeness?"

A wave of dizziness swept over Alisia. She should have been a mother by now, a normal woman with normal healthy babies. She glanced at Jeremy, that lying coward. He married Alisia at the queen's command. On their wedding night he'd had her bound and gagged, taking her virginity with all the care he might show some drunken prostitute. In his eyes she was a freak, a pretty monster who spat out gems and flowers on demand. Monsters. A wild impulse gripped Alisia, making it easier to force her lips upward in a sweet smile.

"His Majesty is most kind."

As the words passed her lips, three sapphires, a white rose, and an orchid fell. No amount of good manners and diplomatic training could prevent the gasps and astonished looks from the members of Lord Uthbrey's retinue.

"Indeed, my lord, I am overcome. You must be my companion at dinner." Alisia turned and made a deep curtsy at the throne to hide the defiance burning in her heart. "If Her Royal Majesty will allow me the pleasure."

"By all means."

Ignoring the smug satisfaction in the queen's voice, Alisia took Lord Uthbrey's offered arm, her empty heart brimming with fresh purpose.

While darkness still covered the land, Alisia dressed quickly and pulled a morning robe on over her traveling gown. Tucking her feet into fleece slippers, she arranged herself in her cushioned chair and tried to look calm. The sun lightened the eastern sky when the door opened to admit Alisia's maid Mina and a younger girl of perhaps twelve. Both girls bobbed curtsies.

"This is Lora, Your Highness."

"Good morning, Lora. Do you remember me from the village?"

Lora's brown eyes widened as she watched the flowers and gems tumble into Alisia's lap. "Yes'm. You'd pick the apples up high where us little ones couldn't reach."

"Do you remember my sister Kerry?"

Lora turned white and shied back against Mina's skirt.

"Oh, Your Highness, please." Mina crossed the last two fingers on her right hand in the sign against evil. "Don't go asking about her!"

"Do you know where Kerry lives?"

Lora shook her head hard.

"Your Highness, *please—*" Mina began.

"I only want to help Kerry. No one will ever know Lora told me where she is."

Mina whispered to Lora, who kept shaking her head. Alisia sorted out the clutter in her lap, letting the flowers fall into the basket beside her chair. At last Lora answered Mina's coaxing with an indistinct mumble broken by sobs and sniffles.

"She's out in the swamp, Your Highness. A day's ride south from the village."

Alisia shut her eyes against the unspeakable possibilities.

"Thank you, Lora." She scooped up a handful of gems. "You may have one, if you like."

Lora crept forward, eyes wide. She chose a smooth round bead of milky jade. Both girls curtsied and Mina hurried Lora out.

Alisia kicked off her slippers, laid aside her robe, and stamped into her riding boots. Her bag was packed and ready. She swung her heavy cloak around her shoulders and fastened the brooch. With luck, any servants who glimpsed her would think she was just another Malrovian guest out for an early ride. Ahead of her, the door opened.

"Aren't we busy this morning?" Queen Sylvia stood in the doorway, barring any escape. She was no less imposing in her fur-lined satin robe. Even at this hour, diamonds sparkled from her wrists and throat. "I'm told you had a visitor."

"Just a girl from my village, Your Majesty. I was feeling homesick."

Queen Sylvia regarded her with a flat, hard stare. "I can hear the truth from you, or I can get it out of the child herself."

Alisia's heart sank. "I want to find my stepsister. To help her."

"You are now a member of the Royal Family. You should be devoting your whole attention to the negotiations with Lord Uthbrey."

Alisia kept her eyes down. Family? They treated her like a special type of servant.

"Speaking of that." Queen Sylvia tapped a collapsed fan in her hand like a threat. "After tonight's feast, you will sing, wandering from table to table, scattering your jewels and flowers among our guests. It should make for quite a charming spectacle."

Alisia kept perfectly still, denying Queen Sylvia any hint of the anger and desperation churning within her.

"You have failed utterly in your primary duty as consort." the queen said, warming to her usual theme. "In three years' time, you haven't shown so much as a single sign of bearing sons."

Alisia's cheeks burned, part shame, part anger. The emptiness inside her had become a constant ache. Still, it was better this way. Far better that Alisia bore no children who would become more pawns in Queen Sylvia's endless schemes for land, wealth, and power.

"If not for this gift of yours. I'd have insisted Jeremy set you aside for a more fruitful wife. Since you cannot give him heirs, the very least you can do is be of this much use."

Nagging, accusing, condemning. Just like Alisia's stepmother. Alisia raised her head and met the queen's glare.

"So I'm of no use?" She walked over to the balcony doors and flung them wide open. "Look at your royal gardens, blooming with thousands of my flowers. Look at your soldiers, armed and armored thanks to the jewels I provide."

"You speak well enough when it suits you. Ungrateful words, at that."

"I never asked to be brought here. I never asked to be Your Majesty's trained monkey, spitting out trinkets for everyone you want to impress."

"*Silence*." The queen took a deep breath, smoothed one hand over her hair. "From now on, you will not leave these rooms unless and until I send for you."

With that, the queen stormed out.

Moments later, Mina peeked around the edge of the doorway. "Shall I fetch your breakfast, Your Highness?"

Sudden stone cold hatred filled Alisia. Queen Sylvia could have allowed her to use at least a portion of her gems to improve the lives of the common people. Better medicine, education, investments in their businesses…Alisia could have been doing so much good. Three years in this pretty prison had taught her one sure lesson. The queen's ultimatums yielded to her greed and vanity.

"You can fetch me Lord Uthbrey. Tell him I'd be delighted to go riding with him this very morning, but I'm afraid he'll have to ask Her Royal Majesty first."

Alisia tied her horse's reins to a low-hanging tree branch. Here the honest trees gave way to twisted oaks and blighted willows. An unhealthy stink tainted the air, the smell of swamp gas and rot. She leaned against the saddle, stiff and sore and longing for sleep. Once Lord Uthbrey and his attendants had ridden deep in the forest, Alisia let her horse follow its nose, browsing among the weeds and grasses. No one expected her to run off, so it had been easy enough to escape. Two days of hard riding brought her to this foul place.

Alisia peered through the tangled branches and murky light. A hovel sat wedged between two willows, its warped roof sagging under the weight of moss and fallen leaves. Smoke leaked from the crooked chimney. Fear and fatigue made Alisia doubt the wisdom of what she was about to do. She could still go back. The queen would be furious, but that would be far outweighed by her relief over the safe return of her personal treasure chest. Alisia's fists clenched. She marched up to the hovel's door and knocked on the splintered wood.

"Kerry? It's me, Alisia."

A large crack split open the upper left corner of the door. Alisia reached up to stuff two garnets, a pearl, and a tulip through it. They hit the floor with a muffled clatter.

Inside the hovel, a chair scraped back.

The door creaked inward an inch, revealing a bloodshot blue eye.

"It is you."

Kerry threw the door wide open. The sudden gust of fetid air made Alisia's empty stomach lurch. The three years hung on Kerry like thirty. Her face was lined and haggard, her black hair filthy. She wore stained and greasy rags. Her feet were bare, callused and muddied. Toads and snakes scrambled around her ankles in a mad rush for freedom. Alisia clapped one hand over her mouth, fighting down the urge to scream and run.

"Why are you here?" Kerry's mouth twisted with suspicion. She prodded the gems and flowers with a dirty toe. "Don't tell me they threw you out, not when you can still do that. Don't tell me you're here to make it all better. After all this time, you're finally feeling guilty?"

Kerry grabbed Alisia's arm in a bruising grip and dragged her inside the hovel. The walls were covered with snakeskins. Beneath Alisia's feet crunched long, slender skeletons. One area of the floor had been swept down to the hard-packed dirt. Snake skulls outlined a circle, their fangs pointing inward. Inside the circle lay patterns soaked into the dirt with—blood. It had to be blood, taken from little animals who were now nothing more than a pile of rank pelts flung into one corner.

Alisia yanked her arm free and spun around.

Kerry's forearm blocked the doorway. Her sudden smile frightened Alisia even more.

"You want to help me, little sister? Good. You aren't leaving here until you do."

"What do you mean?"

"I'm going to work another Summoning. Only this time, you'll be the one calling that fairy bitch. After all, she likes *you*."

Alisia flung herself under Kerry's arm, tumbling across the muck. She leaped up and ran, making straight for her horse. Behind her, Kerry squawked a string of nonsense. Alisia's knees collapsed beneath her, sending her sprawling face down in the mud. Kerry's heavy steps squished closer.

"Little Miss Princess, with her flowers and diamonds and pearls!" Kerry grabbed Alisia by the hair and jerked her head up. "Why do you give a damn if I live or die?"

Snakes slithered through the mud inches from Alisia's face. More small but heavy bodies crawled across her back.

"Answer me!" Kerry caught a fat black snake behind its head, thrusting it at Alisia so its fangs stuck out.

Alisia's eyelids slammed shut. She shrieked until her throat was raw.

"Answer me or I'll make you eat it."

"I just want a normal life." Tears gushed down Alisia's cheeks.

"I want someone to love *me*, not these." She slapped at the muddy gems. "Don't you want that, Kerry? Don't you want a husband and babies and a decent, normal life?"

Kerry flung the black snake away and hauled Alisia to her feet. "I'll tell you what I want, little sister. I want everything you have. I want the palace, the prince, the pretty clothes and good food. I want it all."

"You can have it."

"Not like this, I can't." Kerry grabbed Alisia by the shoulders and shook her. "It should have been me. I was supposed to marry a prince. Mama said so. Instead she had to marry that penny-pinching mumblecrust who fathered you."

Lizards and snakes spilled down between them. Forked tongues prodded Alisia. Cold claws scraped at her skin. She screamed, trying to twist out of Kerry's brutal grip.

"Say yes, Alisia. Say you'll do it."

"*No*."

Kerry hissed and spat. Alisia's scream died, crushed out of her by the coils of some enormous unseen snake.

"You know the fairy will come to you. Say yes."

"Won't be—a *witch*."

The phantom snake squeezed inward. Alisia feared her bones would break.

"I can let it eat you. It will swallow you slowly, bit by bit. Plenty of time for you to go mad while it drowns you in bile."

"Stop it."

The coils crushed. Something covered Alisia's head like a damp, mucky hood.

"Last chance, little sister. Will you do it?"

Burning acid seared Alisia's scalp, stung her eyes, blinding her with agony.

"*Yes.*"

The coils vanished. Alisia collapsed in the mud, sobbing.

Midnight found Alisia just outside the ring of snake skulls. The wavering flames of a dozen candles called evil shadows from every corner burned with a stink that brought unwelcome thoughts about the exact source of their tallow. Inside the ring sat two rough wooden dishes. One held entrails and the other blood.

Kerry stood on the far side of the circle. "Remember, no matter what you see, stay out of the circle."

Alisia nodded. A cold, rusty horseshoe hung round her neck on a strip of tattered cloth. The iron should protect her. If not, its weight made it a useful weapon.

Kerry chanted in a low, husky voice. The candle flames streamed upward, then settled back again. A wet, rotten stench rose from the floor. Two small creatures popped up inside the circle. The first was pink and hairless as a baby mouse, its one yellow eye glaring out of its forehead. It plunged its snout into the bowl of blood. The other had greasy black fur split by a gaping mouth full of jagged teeth. It fell on the entrails, chomping and slurping. Alisia bit her tongue against the scream fighting to burst out of her. Kerry knelt and cooed at the little horrors. They chittered and huffed at her. She looked up at Alisia.

"Tell them. Now."

"I—I want to talk to the fairy who put the spells on us. Bring her here, right now. Tell her Princess Alisia needs her."

The two creatures whuffled at each other and disappeared.

"Will they do it?" Alisia asked.

"They'd better. Or it will be them in the bowls next time."

Kerry crouched at the edge of the circle, watching the center with eyes full of mad, desperate hope. A burst of rainbow brilliance made Alisia cry out and clap her hands to her eyes.

"I warned you, you wretched little hag." That voice. Cool, haughty, infinitely superior. "I told you never to lure me here with that name again."

Alisia lowered her hands. The fairy stood there, her silky white hair bound into a coronet braid, wearing pale lavender gown embroidered with wildflowers and a silver circlet set with the milky gleam of moonstones. At her feet lay what was left of the two little monsters.

"You? Here?" The fairy's amethyst eyes narrowed, and her lip curled in disgust. "So, the hateful sister and the virtuous sister are reunited? How things do change."

"Please," Alisia said. "Take back your gifts."

"Why should I? You earned them." The fairy sneered at Kerry. "You most of all."

Kerry's hatred simmered in her eyes. Her mouth opened.

"Silence." The fairy snatched up the hairy monster and jammed it into Kerry's mouth.

Kerry fell over backward, gagging. The fairy stepped out of the circle and smiled, thin and cold. "Did you really think your petty little blood magic would bind one of us? I am the Countess Benaille. I should kill you for your presumption."

"Leave her alone." Alisia stepped forward, anger giving her courage. "What she is you made her. Just break the spells and we'll never call on you again."

"Why should I? You both lead the lives you deserve. You in a palace, her in a sty."

"I do not deserve the life you've given me. You've made me a trained monkey, a *freak*, a glorified court jester."

Countess Benaille frowned. "Once I sought to reward virtue and punish vanity. I see before me a wasted effort. That one is no better than she ever was. But you." She bent to pick up a single white rose lying on the dirt. Breathing in its scent, she shook her head. "So ungrateful you dare insult me. Spoiled, selfish, haughty. Everything I once knew you were not."

Alisia met that disdainful look with every ounce of strength she'd built up facing Queen Sylvia. "You said you wanted to reward virtue and punish vanity. Is that true? Or are you just one more lord's daughter who likes to torture helpless animals?"

Countess Benaille flung the rosebud into flowers piled at Alisia's feet. The flowers withered, shrank, crumbled to dust. "Prove me wrong, Princess. Prove virtue still dwells in your heart. Give your gift to your sister, and take hers in exchange."

Those horrible scaly monsters crawling out of her own mouth? Alisia made herself think of Kerry before her courage failed her completely. Kerry would take her place in the palace. Kerry would have all the lovely things she'd ever dreamed of. Kerry would very likely sass Queen Sylvia into some kind of fit. Alisia would make a new home for herself, with hard work and patience. She was no stranger to either.

"I will." She watched the rose and tourmaline fall. "Tell me what to do."

"A simple matter. Like so many enchantments, it must be sealed with a kiss."

Alisia hardened her heart against the terror of it. She walked around the circle to where Kerry still lay. Kerry's eyes held that wild, frantic hope. Alisia knelt beside her and smoothed Kerry's filthy hair back from her brow.

"Tell Father I love him. He'd best forget about me."

Alisia stood in the throne room a few steps behind Kerry. A long afternoon spent scrubbing away the layers of grime had taken years off her. She wore a new dress of dark brown wool. Her braided hair now gleamed with red highlights.

Queen Sylvia sat on her throne, frowning in deep distrust. Jeremy lounged beside her on a cushioned chair, fondling the ears of his favorite hunting dog.

"You claim the fairy took Alisia away to the place where she'd already hidden you," the queen said, "then told you it was time the gifts were traded."

"That's right, Your Majesty." Kerry nodded. "She said something about magic and the laws of balance."

Queen Sylvia watched the rain of gems and flowers patter down around Kerry's feet. "Since when do fairies care about rules and laws and such?"

"I wouldn't know, Your Majesty. All I know is, here I am." Kerry caught a few gems in her fist and rattled them like dice, making the assembled courtiers wince.

Queen Sylvia studied Alisia with an intensity meant to strip her bare. "Have you nothing to add?"

Alisia shook her head.

"You do realize what this would mean? Your marriage annulled, your rooms given over to your step-sister, your life as Royal Consort at an end?"

Alisia nodded.

"Will you not say a single word? You put on quite a display the last time you stood before me."

Kerry took a step forward. "You really don't want her to speak, Your Majesty. Not unless you want to watch what happens when a hooded swamp rattler bites someone."

All the courtiers backed away. Some already glanced down in distaste, wearing that look Alisia had seen all too often on Jeremy's face. As if reading her thoughts, Queen Sylvia turned to Jeremy.

"Have you anything to say? After all, Alisia is your wife."

Jeremy gave both Alisia and Kerry the briefest glance, then shrugged. "Hardly makes much of a difference."

"So he's like that, is he?" Kerry muttered under her breath.

Alisia smiled. If revenge had been her main purpose, she couldn't have done better than wishing Kerry on Jeremy and the queen.

Queen Sylvia clapped her hands. Two of the guards stepped forward. She fixed Alisia with a brilliant smile. "Throw the ungrateful little wretch in the dungeon."

"Why bother?" Kerry asked. "You have me. You don't need her anymore."

"My dear, ignorant peasant girl, she has lived under this roof for three years as the wife of Prince Jeremy, who will one day be king. No other man will ever touch her."

Kerry scowled. She thrust both hands at the guards and snarled. The guards dropped to their knees, clutching their heads.

"Stop it." Alisia's hands flew to her mouth. A muddy lizard and a bright red snake struck the flagstones at her feet. They struggled together, fighting free to slither back between Alisia's ankles. The scrape of claws on her skin made her scream, bringing forth even more scaly monsters. The room whirled around her. Triumphant laughter rang in her ears. Queen Sylvia or Countess Benaille? It hardly made much of a difference.

Alisia woke to find herself lying on a wooden bench inside a cold, damp closet made of stone. Ruddy light came from the one torch that burned in the corridor, showing her the bars across the little window in the door. She sat up, tried to stand. The stiffness in her joints told her hours must have passed. How long would she have to wait? The queen did so enjoy executions.

Outside, footsteps and voices came toward the cell. The ring of keys jingled in the lock. The door swung open, revealing Queen Sylvia.

"I want a private word with her. Private, you understand?"

"But—Your Majesty, the snakes—"

"Our dear little princess wouldn't hurt me."

The guard hurried away. The queen turned a cold look on Alisia.

"At a loss for words, my dear?"

The queen's features blurred. Her midnight blue gown rippled away into lavender trimmed with glittering dewdrops. Countess Benaille now stood in the doorway.

"Have you come to gloat?" Alisia asked.

"Did you really believe the queen would just let you go back to your village, carding wool and whelping some farmer's brats?" Countess Benaille shook her head. "You're a fool. But you are an honorable one. I'll give you that."

Flattery from a fairy was even more dangerous than scorn. Alisia turned away. Countess Benaille stepped inside the cell.

"I could get you out of here, you know. If we came to a satisfactory arrangement."

Alisia was so tired of living according to everyone else's whims. She sighed, sinking down on the wooden bench. All she wanted was to go home, wherever that might be.

"Come back to my court with me," Countess Benaille said. "Attend me as my lady-in-waiting. Perhaps you'll catch the eye of a fairy lord." The Countess sat down beside Alisia and laid an arm around her shoulders. "Your babies are waiting for you."

Alisia's head jerked up. "Babies?"

"It's neither my fault nor yours," Countess Benaille said. "The truth is dear Jeremy spends more than just his time away from you. Spends so much that he's no use to any woman hoping for a child."

So it *wasn't* Alisia's fault. Relief gave way to rage. Alisia sprang through the open doorway. Invisible hands closed on her arms and spun her around, pinning her against the wall opposite the cell. The cell door slammed shut. The big iron key turned in the lock. Countess Benaille screeched, pounding her fists against the door. She screamed again, this time in pain, and shrank back, whimpering.

Kerry popped into sight beside Alisia, holding a black cord strung with snake bones, feathers, and what looked like tiny eyes. She stepped foward and laughed.

"You forgot about the iron, didn't you? It blinded you just long enough."

"You will suffer for this." Countess Benaille's voice was icy. "I promise you that."

"Maybe, but you'll get yours first." Kerry held out the necklace to Alisia. "Put this on. Wear it as far as the borders of the kingdom, then burn it."

Alisia pointed upstairs, then spread her hands in a wondering gesture.

"I'll tell the old bat I thought the fairy might come to rescue you," Kerry said. "You'd already escaped, but I got here in time to trap the fairy in the cell."

Kerry dug into the bag hanging off her shoulder and pulled out a large pouch. Alisia recognized the weight of it, heavy with gems. Kerry pushed it into Alisia's hands.

"Now get going."

"Alisia," Countess Benaille said. "Free me. Leave me here, and there will be no escape from those who will avenge me."

"Go on. I'll take care of her." Kerry grinned. "Iron shackles. Iron knives and pincers and mulling rods. I can't wait."

"*Alisia.*" Raw panic colored Countess Benaille's voice. "I gave you three years of royalty. Now I've given it to your step-sister as well. Let me *out.*"

Alisia hesitated. She clenched her eyes shut and braced herself. "Break the spell on me." Scaly rustlings slid down her skirt. She swallowed, tried to breathe normally. "And swear all of you will leave Kerry alone. Then I'll let you out."

"No." Kerry scowled. "She's mine. You can't let her go."

Alisia stepped up to the cell door. In Countess Benaille's eyes blazed the same look Kerry had worn, that same mad, desperate hope for freedom and peace. Satisfied, Alisia gripped the iron key.

"Swear first," she said. "Then break the spell."

"Very well." Countess Benaille mocked in singsong. "From this moment on, I swear on my life to abandon Kerry to her own stupidity and see to it my people meddle with her no further."

"And?"

"Let me out. The iron interferes."

Alisia opened the door. Back stiff, eyes narrowed to slits, Countess Benaille walked out of the cell one dignified step at a time. She covered Alisia's mouth with one hand and snapped her fingers.

"There."

"Thank you." To Alisia's intense relief, nothing but breath left her lips.

"Your troubles are far from over. This is all the help you'll have from me." Countess Benaille vanished in another flash of rainbow light.

The guard rounded the corner. "Here now, what's all this noise? Where's Her Majesty?"

Kerry pushed Alisia behind her. "Just let her go."

"Her Majesty will have my head."

"Tell *me* what you need," Kerry said. "You'll have it, I promise you."

The guard watched the gems and flowers fall. Once more Alisia watched desperate hope kindle in the eyes of another person.

"It's my little girl." The guard spoke in a rush, glancing back over his shoulder. "Her leg's not right. Can't walk, can't run and play—"

"The Royal Physician will see her tomorrow. Now, keep anyone else away."

The guard made a hasty bow and darted back the way he'd come.

"Remember." Kerry held out the revolting necklace to Alisia. "Wear this as far as the borders of the kingdom, then burn it."

Alisia nodded. She was oddly reluctant to leave Kerry. The ordeal had brought them closer together, far closer than they had ever been. "With Father away, you're all the family I have."

"You're wasting time."

Alisia's heart sank. "I—I suppose I was foolish to hope you might feel any closeness to me. You have what you've always wanted. A sister was never part of that."

She worked up the nerve to slip the horrid necklace down around her neck and begin the long walk toward her new life.

"Alisia." Kerry held out a blue glass marble half the size of a hen's egg.

"Take this. It will help you find your father."

"But—but why? I thought you hated both of us."

"You came back for me. You wanted the fairy to break the spell on me as well." Kerry's eyes gleamed with welling tears and forced herself to meet Alisia's gaze. "You didn't have to do that."

Alisia clasped her sister in a fervent hug.

BEWARE THE MOUSE

James Pratt

The sun set, the moon rose, and the Mouse came out to play. She wasn't a real mouse, of course, but dressed in dark gray tights, leotard, and snug cowl complete with a pair of ovals affixed to play the role of mouse ears, she certainly looked the part. And it was no mere artifice. Like her namesake, she was swift, silent, and most active at night.

Slinking along the ledges and parapets of the royal castle, the Mouse kept vigil from the shadows. Her patience was rewarded by the sight of a pair of dark figures scaling the wall beneath one of the guest bedrooms. On that particular night, the bedroom was occupied by a young sultan from a desert kingdom in the hoary East. A recent string of burglaries had struck a handful of noble households and in light of the sultan's extravagant arrival even a dunce could have deduced who the next target would be. While the Mouse normally spent her nights opposing the machinations of unscrupulous nobles, tonight she would defend a foreign king.

Climbing onto the bedroom's terrace, the figures slipped in through the open window and emerged a few minutes later, trophy in hand. The pair were quiet as cats, but silence was the Mouse's element. Even real cats wouldn't have heard her coming up behind them till the three stood only a few strides apart. The presence of not one but two burglars was unexpected but not beyond her capabilities. The Mouse was nothing if not formidable.

"I've been looking for you," the Mouse said.

Clouds parted, bathing the terrace in silvery moonlight bright enough to grant a clear view of the burglars. The Mouse had expected a man, but the figure was clearly female. She, too, wore a mask and tights, but her outfit was much darker, perhaps deep blue or even black. Affixed to her snug cowl were small triangles reminiscent of the ears of cats.

"Edda?" a familiar voice said.

The Mouse's eyes widened, not at the speaking of her true name but at the voice which spoke it. It was a voice she hadn't heard in years and would have been perfectly content never hearing again. "Gudrun?"

The burglar chuckled. "Well, well. Adelgiese, say hello to our sister."

The other burglar looked from Gudrun to the Mouse and back. "But if that's Edda, who's the Mouse?"

"Edda is the Mouse, numbskull. I'd say it's a surprise to see you here, but this is your home, what with you being *queen*. It's nice, very spacious."

"I like the curtains," Adelgiese said.

To Edda, the Mouse was no mere disguise. It felt much more real to her than the life of royal privilege she led during the day. Her life up till the moment she first donned the costume sewn with her own two hands were a distant memory. But faced with two flesh-and-blood ghosts conjured from those half-forgotten memories, it was Edda, the old Edda, who spoke. "You…you two are cat burglars?"

Gudrun's smile wilted into a regretful frown. "After our sister made good and abandoned us, we had to make a living somehow."

Memories of words spoken at their final parting swept Edda away and left The Mouse in her place. "I was never your sister."

Adelgiese's confusion was much more sincere than Gudrun's show of regret. "But you lived with us. We gave you a place to stay and food to eat."

The Mouse's upper lip rose into a near-snarl. "No, my father gave you and your wretched mother a place to stay and food to eat. After he died, you repaid his kindness by treating me like a servant."

Gudrun's tone was innocent but her raised eyebrow an accusation. "Were you too proud to earn your keep?"

It was not the endless hours of sewing, scrubbing, and cooking that clenched the Mouse's hands into fists but the memory of a younger Gudrun claiming Edda's room and possessions for her own. "Earn my keep? In my own father's house?"

Gudrun raised her hands. "Keep your voice down. You wouldn't want to be caught out here anymore than us."

Adelgiese inched a step closer. "Are you really the Mouse?"

"I am," the Mouse replied, still watching Gudrun.

"But you're the queen. You're royalty. The Mouse is an outlaw-hero of the common folk."

"It wasn't so long ago that I was one of the common folk," the Mouse reminded her.

Gudrun snickered. "And yet here you protecting a man ten times as rich as your own dear husband."

"You're trying to rob a foreign king. Wars have started over far less. I'm protecting the kingdom's interests, not the sultan's."

Brow furrowed, Adelgiese stared at the Mouse as she struggled to reconcile two very different prospects. "You married a prince and became a queen. You got your happily ever after. Why wasn't that enough? Why did you become the Mouse?"

It was a fair question and one that Edda had asked herself many times in the weeks leading up to the Mouse's creation. Watching Gudrun out of the corner of her eye, she turned to Adelgiese. "You're right. I went from sweeping cinders to living in a castle. I got my happily ever after. And I was happy for a while. But the more time I spent among the royals, the more I came to realize just how disinclined they were to acknowledge the plight of the commoner. I pleaded with my husband to consider certain reforms. He's not heartless but even he insisted the system was beyond reproach."

"A reasonable position considering how well it's served his bloodline," Gudrun said.

The Mouse's gaze flickered to Adelgiese and, seeing she was keeping her distance, went back to Gudrun. "Yes, above his reproach but not mine. I had to oppose the royals' schemes without incriminating myself. Recalling the outlaw-heroes from the tales of my youth, I conceived a plan. First, I needed anonymity in the form of a masked identity. My inspiration came from memories of rescuing mice from your step-mother's cat Mephistopheles. To ease my loneliness, I sometimes kept them as pets. I would become as a mouse, quiet and unassuming yet ever-present. Using skills I developed during my years of servitude, I designed and sewed a costume. Thus, the Mouse was born."

Gudrun mimed wiping away tears. "Such a tragic story. My heart breaks. You received a fairy tale's worth of good fortune, and it still wasn't enough. The greatness I could have achieved with the opportunities handed to you."

Smiling, the Mouse pointed at their outfits. "Is this not the greatness your mother groomed you for? Skulking about in masks and tights?"

Gudrun's pretty features became an ugly sneer. "You should talk. And mother is a realist. When one door closes, she doesn't wait for another to open."

Adelgeise nodded. "She waits for someone else to open it for her. That's just good manners, her being a lady."

"Shut up, Adelgiese," Gudrun and the Mouse said together.

"Sorry," Adelgiese said, voice dropping to a murmur.

The Mouse frowned. "So you're saying your mother sent you here? Does that mean that wicked old thing is still creeping about?"

Gudrun face darkened for a moment then relaxed into a faint smile. 'Wicked old thing' was in fact a fair assessment. "Creeping and plotting. Simple burglary kept a roof over our heads. What we've taken from your guest, the sultan, will give us much more."

"And what's that?"

"His precious lamp."

"That battered old lamp he calls his good luck charm? You don't really think it's valuable, do you?"

Gudrun shook her head. "It's what's in the lamp."

The Mouse couldn't help but smile. Her old step-mother had been a cold-blooded pragmatist in all ways save one, a firm belief in superstition. "You mean that story about a djinn? A wispy tail instead of legs and skin blue as the winter sky? You can't be serious."

Gudrun's sneer returned. "You of all people shouldn't scoff magic. We know what happened the night of the royal ball. Oh, what a pretty dress you wore."

"Very pretty," Adelgiese said.

It never occurred to Edda that her step-sisters knew the unnatural nature of her good fortune. "How do you know?"

Gudrun exchanged glances with Adelgiese then looked back at Edda. "Certain…talents run in our family. Mother's great-aunt used such talents to become a queen till she was undone by her own step-daughter with the help of some nasty little dwarfs."

"It sounds like your family has a problem with step-daughters," the Mouse said.

Keen on the subject of princesses since her youth, a grin spread across Adelgiese's face as she spoke. "Great-Auntie's step-daughter was a true princess. The stories say her skin was fair as the driven—"

Gudrun shot Adelgiece a warning glance. "Hush. Not just step-daughters. We have a sister who was a bit like you were in the old days, a dreamer who lived in her own head. She stayed behind with our penniless fool of a father when mother took us away for a better life. Now, she lives in a crumbling castle, the prisoner of an unnatural beast or so the rumors claim."

"We're not supposed to talk about her," Adelgiese said.

Chuckling, Gudrun crossed her arms. "It's all right. Edda is family. Speaking of family, they even say one of our ancestors is a fairy. Not a wish-granter like yours but a magnificently wicked one who put an entire kingdom to sleep and hid it behind a hedge of thorns. Mother couldn't do something like that, but her talents are real enough."

The Mouse rolled her eyes. While her old step-mother had expressed a firm belief in spells and such, she'd never demonstrated any actual knowledge of the craft. "And why weren't these talents put into play before?"

Gudrun's perpetual smirk wavered and her voice became deadly serious. "Because unless you're a fairy, magic always comes with a price."

Adelgiese shivered. "It's true. I…I don't like to be alone with mother anymore. She scares me."

Gudrun glanced at Adelgiese then back to the Mouse. "Believe it or not, we don't begrudge you your good fortune. We just want a little fortune of our own."

The Mouse might have asked them about the modest fortune amassed by Edda's father and squandered by their own mother, but night was fleeting and a plan was beginning to form. "Over the years, it's occurred to me that you two were as much a victim of your mother as me. Well, not exactly like me. I was treated like a slave whereas the both of you were merely tools to achieve your mother's goals. I don't begrudge you the opportunity to better yourselves. But not like this."

Gudrun squared her shoulders. "So, it's a fight then?"

The Mouse smiled inwardly as the details of an idea she'd been ruminating over for months fell into place. "No, it's an offer."

"What kind of offer?" Gudrun asked. Set to listen but ready to run, she always assumed the worst.

"Join me. You have the right skills and I'm tired of being one person doing the job of three."

"Will we get to wear costumes?" Adelgiese asked. Despite her love of princesses, she'd found masks and tights much more to her liking than corsets, petticoats, and frilly things.

"Of course." The Mouse turned to Gudrun who glared back. "How about you? Are you ready to step out of your mother's shadow and find your own path?"

"By walking yours?"

"Every step can be the beginning of a new journey, even if that first one falls on someone else's path. What do you say?"

"I say your philosophizing is atrocious."

Gudrun and the Mouse stood motionless, staring at each other while Adelgiese shuffled her feet. At one point, Adelgiese raised a hand like a student asking permission to speak but dropped it immediately when the other two gave her a withering look.

Finally, Gudrun sighed. "Fine. I'll step on your path, but I'm not promising how long I'll stay on it."

"Fair enough," the Mouse said.

Adelgiese clapped her hands. "The sisters reunited."

"Quiet," Gudrun and the Mouse said together.

"Sorry."

HAUNT US NO MORE

Jenn Tubrett

The mud on the path seemed irritating but not necessarily problematic. However, when Gretel's heel sunk in, she slipped and landed hard on her left hip. She let out a cry.

She was all right, not injured, just tired.

And sad. She was so sad.

Gretel searched for a place to rest. She hadn't planned on taking a break, even though she was only one day into a two-day trek. The wonderful thing about never being able to sleep well was that, when necessary, she could get by on very little.

The sun was out, but the dull light meant she couldn't see the pebbles Hansel left for her, so it was as good a time to rest as any.

She abandoned the main path, found a mossy patch, and sat leaning against a tree. Eyes closed, she reminded herself that, even though this self-assigned mission was the most difficult of her life, she only had to do two things.

First, she had to find her brother.

Second, she had to kill him.

Three days earlier...

1

Gretel turned over, kicked her legs out of the blankets, and flipped her pillow to feel the cool side on her face. She lay still, willed sleep, then turned back, and tucked her legs in. The texture of the ceiling beams was waved and wrinkled, like beach sand after the tide rolled out.

With a sigh, she gazed at her sleeping husband, envying his ability to do it with such ease.

Giving up, she rose and crossed the room to the rocking chair near the window. She glanced at the book on her bedside table, but decided against turning on a lamp. She didn't want to wake Rainer. He had a long day tomorrow; he and her father were turning the soil on the east field, the biggest on their farm. She crossed her arms onto the window sill and rested her head. The cool draft from the window and familiar sight of the moonlight on the vast field between her cottage and the large farm house soothed her.

They purchased the farm fifteen years before, which cost less than half the value of the pearls and precious stones she and her brother had brought back with them from their harrowing adventure in the woods. Some would call it thieving, or—more aptly—grave robbing, to fill her apron and Hansel's pockets with the valuable belongings of the old witch who had held them captive.

Gretel called it payment.

She had slaved a month for that hag, working until the blisters on her hands cracked, bled, and blistered again. She came as close to starving to death as she had to going mad. She must have been half-mad to have done what she did.

I saved us.

Her head grew heavy on her folded arms.

As she dozed, the air suddenly smelled sweet—like cane, chocolate, and icing.

"Crawl in." The old witch's voice clawed like high wind through a splintered board. "See if the oven is hot enough."

Gretel jumped, rocking the chair back like she was falling. She closed her hands around the chair arms and took a breath.

You're in your home. You're not a child anymore.

Gretel's anxiety wasn't always this bad. Usually, she didn't think much about it. But today was the first day of November—the day their father abandoned them in the woods for the second time. The first time they had found their way home by following the shiny pebbles her brother left to mark their route. They did not have as much luck with the breadcrumbs.

They were gone an entire month.

Every year, that month proved difficult for the both of them.

A lamp was lit in the main house, but the distance made it impossible to tell in which window. It must be Hansel's room. She stretched the tensing muscles in her back and retrieved a robe from her closet.

"Gretel?" Rainer said as she bent to put on her shoes. "Where are you going?"

"To see my brother." Her whisper matched his sleepy tone.

Rainer propped himself up onto his elbow, his muscular arm bulged pressed against itself. "At this hour?"

"He's awake."

"I'll go with you."

"No, please," she said, perhaps too quickly. Hansel did not dislike Rainer, at least no more than he disliked anyone else, but she doubted he would be pleased to see him just now. "Get some rest. You'll need your energy tomorrow."

He nodded, his disheveled, sand-colored hair falling in his face as he rose from the bed.

"Darling, really. I'll only be gone—"

"I know." He gave her hand a gentle squeeze as he passed by, and his large hand swallowed hers. At the window, he struck a match, lit the lamp, then smiled at her. "To help you find your way back."

She returned his smile and slid her arms around his waist, resting her head against his chest. It struck her how lucky she was to have found someone like Rainer. Most men would find it somewhere between amusing and irritating to have a wife afraid of losing her way on her own land. Rainer just wanted to help.

A large man, standing head and shoulders over her, he was strong, patient, and fiercely protective. She had married him, not because she loved him, although that came later, but because he made her feel safe.

For Gretel, every other quality a man could possess came second to that.

The walk across their land had a sobering effect on her. This was silly. She would see Hansel tomorrow, and who's to say that he even wants to see her tonight?

Things were different when they were in the same house. Perhaps, she would offend him by walking this distance in the dark and cold merely because of a lit lamp. However, by the time she decided to turn back, his shadow flickered the light as he paced.

This was the right thing to do.

The front door creaked as she slipped through it. To her left, her father's axe from his woodcutting days was mounted to the wall. She kissed her fingers and tapped the handle.

"I never understood why you do that." Her step-mother said.

Gretel tensed and panic swelled deep in her chest for the second it took her to place the voice. "For luck."

Hedda was in the parlor off the entrance. Two blue wing back chairs were placed comfortably along the back wall. Hedda sat in the chair on the right, jabbing away at her needlepoint.

"I apologize for the intrusion." Reluctantly, Gretel moved into the room but only past the entrance. "Thought you would be asleep."

Over the years, Gretel's relationship with Hedda mended. When she and Hansel first returned, her father had told them his wife died to spare himself the shame of telling his children that he had abandoned them for a woman who deserted him in the same month. Hedda returned a year later, and Hansel always insisted that she came back because she had gotten word of their good fortune. Hedda swore she only heard about the purchase of the farm when she made inquiries after finding the cottage empty. She had wept, apologized, and begged forgiveness. For reasons Gretel did not understand, her father loved this woman, and when he asked their permission for her return, Gretel convinced Hansel that it was the right thing to do.

For years, they simply tolerated her. A cold tolerance, but Hedda did not push for more.

Gretel eventually warmed to her, but only after the birth of her siblings.

Arilda and Audrik came into their lives eleven years ago tomorrow. They were twins, like herself and Hansel. Not feeling some affection for a person was impossible when you had the love of two sweet children to bond you. However, Gretel supposed this phenomenon was strictly between women, it certainly did not have that effect on Hansel.

"What brings you here?" Hedda asked.

"I've come to see my brother."

Hedda's lips formed a hard line. "We have to speak about him."

Gretel's head dropped, and suddenly, she was exhausted. Whenever Hedda wanted to speak about Hansel, the conversation was always the same. "We're not doing this."

"There are places for people like—"

"I will not see my brother locked up. Do you have any idea what that would do to him?"

Hedda set her needlepoint down on the end table between the chairs and slid forward in her seat. "He's not well."

"This time of the year is hard on the both of us."

"*Every* time of the year is hard on Hansel."

"He has his bad days, but he'll recover, he always recovers."

"This is different, ever since you moved out, he's different. Gretel, I'm scared. I'm scared for my children. I'm—"

"Stop it. My brother has never hurt a living thing in his life. Unless that changes, I don't care if he's difficult to be around, I will not allow him to be sent away."

Hedda deflated back into her seat. "Bless your faith in him. I don't know how you do it."

"I do it gladly," Gretel said, as she left to find her brother.

For a long time, Hansel was Gretel's one comfort. He remained strong while she barely held on to her sanity. Until she met Rainer, her brother was the only person who could make her feel any amount of safety. As Gretel recovered, Hansel deteriorated, as if her good health gave him permission to fall apart. He had been there for her; now, she had to be there for him.

The hallway was wide at the top of the stairs. Hansel's room was at one end of the hall to the left, Arilda and Audrik's room was around a curve on other end to the right. The room her father shared with Hedda was between the two, directly across from the staircase. Her room was once beside Hansel's, but six months after she moved out, he tore down the wall between them. She knocked, and his heavy footfalls grew louder as he approached.

"Hedda, for the last Goddamned time—" The door opened a sliver, the growl of his lips softened, and his brow relaxed. "Gretel? What are you doing here?"

"Couldn't sleep," she said, quietly, not wanting to risk waking the children. "Saw your light."

"I'm glad." He ushered her in, scanning the hallways as if she might have been followed.

Hansel's dark slacks were dusty, his white shirt discolored around the collar and under his arms, and it hung from his slim body. His dark hair was overdue for a cut, standing up on the left; he often ran his fingers through his hair when agitated, and by the look of him, she was surprised he hadn't tugged it out completely. His eyes were sewn with red lines.

Paper crumbled under her feet.

Hansel took down the wallpaper and marked the walls in etchings that detailed every inch of the forest that surrounded their home. Their farm land was near the old cottage. The same woods they were lost in as children. During their adolescence, they spent hours in those woods, learning the land. Hansel—at first with Gretel's help and later alone—walked every bit of the forest and carved all of it into his bedroom walls, but his obsession with the woods wasn't about preservation.

He was trying to find the candy house, to prove to everyone that it was real.

As a child, Gretel had been outraged that her father and her step-mother didn't believe their story. As she matured, she understood why. The story was just so farfetched. Between the witch, the chocolate walls, and the swan that flew them over the river, yes, it sounded like the imaginings of children who had suffered a great deal. They may have exaggerated some of it in their minds, but a woman had held them captive, planned to cook and eat them, and Gretel shoved that woman into an oven to save their lives.

Such a story was too fantastic for a rational adult to accept.

"I think I figured out why we couldn't find it." Hansel walked back to the wall with a carving knife, his feet crunched over the curled and torn wallpaper on the floor. He ran out of space on his own walls and moved on to her old walls. "We were on the right track, but here, just past the river, there's a path—"

"Hansel, that path led to a dead end at the foot of a mountain."

The lamp light flickered, splashing his shadow in lunatic forms behind him.

"It was charmed. We grew too old to see the path. Magic, Gretel, if we had only opened our minds to it, we may have walked right through. We still can." His hand snagged hers. "I'm going tomorrow. Come with me."

Her heart thudded at the prospect of going back into those woods, but she kept her breath steady. "The twins. It's their birthday tomorrow. Pa and Hedda have a supper planned, we're all—"

"The next day then."

She released him and walked into her old room, considering her next words carefully. His request was no small feat. They would have to trek for two days through the forest to get to a path that she knew would be just as impassable as it had been six years before. What would Hansel do when they got there and his *magic* refused to reveal the path he was so certain of? What would she do if he had a complete break down so far in the forest?

"What if," her words were thin as she mustered the breath to speak these words, "there was no magic?"

He set his knife down on the window sill.

"What if we remembered it wrong?"

"Don't." He yanked his hair. "Don't you dare. It was real, Gretel. It happened."

"I'm not saying it didn't." She kept her tone level and soothing. "I'm only saying that there are certain parts we could have…embellished in our minds."

"So, the swan?" He went right to the most fantastical part.

She lifted her eyebrows, an expression that she hoped looked gentle and not as anxious as she felt. "The swan boats at the park."

As he drew away from her, his dark eyes shrunk to slits and his lips tensed, forming lines so deep that Gretel could see what he would look like in ten years.

She followed him. "Anyone could have left one of those by the river. Perhaps we only imagined that we were flying when we were actually paddling."

"There was a witch—"

"Maybe she wasn't."

"She held us captive."

"Yes, but did you ever see her perform any magic? I didn't. Maybe she was just a cruel and deeply disturbed old woman."

"She lived in a house made of *candy*."

"Was it though?" Dangerous territory, but she came too far to turn back.

"We ate it." He threw his arms out, as if her words were meant to crucify him.

"We ate pieces of candy that we pulled off the front." She reached for him but he avoided her. "She could have baked parts of it and the rest could have just been paint and carvings. We were there a month. It never rotted or melted—"

"Because it was *magic*."

"Hansel." She was ashamed at the volume of her voice but could no longer hide her frustration. "It might not have been. You must see that."

"No." His voice boomed. He grabbed hold of her arms, yanking her to him with such force that her head snapped back. His fingers pinched her biceps like he might tear the muscles away from the bone. "It was magic. She was a witch."

As he shook her, the face of a monster resembling her brother popped in and out of her field of vision. Her stomach turned as the room shifted and jerked. She lost all sense of her position; everything was moving out of place around her. "All right. She was. She was witch, Hansel, just stop."

He released her to the floor. Breathing heavily, she looked up at him. From this vantage point, he looked larger than he had ever seemed to her, and she wished she were an inch tall so she could scurry away unnoticed. He held his hands before him as though they'd offended him, done evil without his consent.

"I'm sorry. I didn't. I never meant to. Damn it." He slammed his fist into the wall.

Her knees shook as she got to her feet and the air was heavy, pushing her back down. She reached for him, cursing the tremor that moved through her hand; it would upset him to see her like this.

His knuckles were busted and bleeding. He tried to retreat to the other side of the room. "Get out of here."

"I won't." She placed her hand on his shoulder, clutching firmly so he wouldn't feel how she shook.

His lips folded and his tears streamed; he pulled her to him and cried into the top of her head. "I'm so sorry."

"It's all right. It was an accident. I'm fine." She really was; he hadn't actually hurt her, just scared her. She should have known better than to push him when he was in such a state. "Let me help you with your hand, please."

He nodded and sat on his bed. Gretel took a folded towel from the top of his desk and a glass of water from his bedside table and sat beside him.

After moment in silence as she wiped the blood off of his knuckles. "Hearing you talk like that. It frightens me."

"Why?" She used her fingernails to pluck out a few splinters.

"Because if you believe that, then I might be mad. If I'm mad, they'll send me away."

"I would never let that happen."

"It was real, Gretel. She was a witch."

"You're right." She wrapped the towel around his injury.

Hansel needed to sleep. She knew that the second she saw him. She nudged him, so that he lifted his legs onto the bed and rested his head in her lap, and began to sing a song he used to sooth her during years of nightmares and restless nights.

When the wind cuts through, it's hard to stand
And home is a distant shore
I am here with you, holding your hand
These ghosts will haunt us no more
No more, no more, these ghosts will haunt us no more

2

At the twins' birthday dinner, the table was decked out with all of their best accoutrements. The tablecloth was a thick, red velvet, and they set the polished brass candlesticks, even though the sun was still up and lighting the candles would not be necessary. They set the silver and crystal wine glasses, with wine for the adults and apple cider for the children.

Hedda sat at the head of the table. This was not tradition, but no one ever stopped her, certainly not Gretel's father. Dinner had been served, but Hansel's seat, on the end, was still empty. When Hansel entered, Gretel smiled at him, but the rest fell silent. Rainer stiffened beside her. He saw the bruises on her arms but swore to her, reluctantly, that he would not do or say anything about it.

"Who put this here?" Hansel gestured to the plate of meat and vegetables.

"I did," Gretel said.

Hansel couldn't stand to be served food. It was something he would only allow Gretel to do, and she knew to never put very much on his plate.

They both had their quirks.

Gretel feared getting lost.

Sometimes, when she did housework, she would find herself gripped in panic and would have to stop to remind herself that no one forced her to do it.

Hansel shoveled his scant meal down and stood to make his exit.

"Well, it was certainly kind of you to make an appearance for your brother and sister," Hedda said. She had given up on insistence that Hansel show an interest in his younger siblings years ago, but couldn't help getting a jab in every now and then.

"Oh, was that not to your liking? All right." Hansel returned to his seat. "How about I tell you a story about when your sister and I were your age?"

A cruel smile shot into Hansel's features.

"Hansel," their father said, gaze dropped into his soup, "I don't think—"

"You see, back then we lived in a modest cottage. Does anyone remember what Pa did?"

"Pa was a woodcutter," Audrik said, proud to know this small piece of their family history.

"Very good."

Perhaps because their father was such a timid man, Audrik had always looked up to Hansel and collected his small bits of half-interested approvals eagerly, as if they were rare coins.

Hansel's face, although still masked in feigned good humor, grew dramatically grim. "But times were tough for the ole woodcutter. There had been a drought and a fire. The family was at risk of starving. But his lovely wife, your mother, had the perfect solution."

Hedda rose, her thin body threw a shadow over the table. "That's enough. Arilda, Audrik, you are excused."

"No. They will sit. They will eat. And they *will* hear this story." Hansel's level determination frightened Gretel, her breath stuck in her body, freezing her below the neck as her embarrassment heated her face.

"Please, mother. I want to hear," Audrik said, giving Hedda his most round, innocent gaze.

Hedda sank against the table and placed her head in her hand, pressing her eyes shut.

Their father examined his soup with a twirl of his spoon.

"Hansel, please," Gretel said, barely louder than a breeze. A part of her wanted to shake him. Tell him that he was mad to think any good could come of this. But another part of her, the larger and more powerful side of her mind, was frozen.

"Your mother decided the best way to preserve herself and her husband was to take the children deep into the forest," he paused and looked from one child to the other, making sure he had their full attention, "and leave them there."

Hedda's weeping muffled against her hand, interrupting the silence. Audrik's eyes widened as he looked to his mother to confirm or deny this part of the tale, and Arilda looked to Gretel for the same.

Gretel wished that she was blamelessly asleep in her chair. Under the table, Rainer's hand rested on her knee and gave it a gentle squeeze to remind her that he was there and ready to act however she saw fit. She clasped his fingers.

"Would you like to know what they found in the forest?" Hansel, clearly pleased with himself, leaned casually into his high backed chair.

"Yes," Audrik said quietly, although his uncertainty was clear in his unmoving brown eyes.

"A witch."

"A witch?" Arilda's voice grew small and shook.

"Yes, an ugly, evil, old witch. She invited them in with the pretense of kindness and the promise of a hot meal and comfortable bed. How long did that last, Gretel?"

Gretel attempted to shake her head at him but only managed to jerk her chin.

"About ten hours. Ten hours before she locked me in a cage so small that I couldn't stand and left me there for a goddamn month. Force feeding me every day to make me fat enough for a hearty stew. Gretel didn't fare out much better. The witch locked her to a chain long enough to move freely about the house, forcing her to do all the cleaning, oh, and the cooking, even though she let her nearly starve to death. Apparently, one fat child was enough. Who knows, maybe emaciated children were a different kind of delicacy. She beat Gretel, too." His voice quivered. "Not every day, but most days."

Gretel felt the smack of the floor as she landed, after the hag yanked the chain clasped to her ankle, and the lashes of the broom handle landing on her legs, ribs, and forearms as she cowered, trying to protect her head and face. She heard herself screaming apologies for whatever it was she had done wrong that day. Rainer squeezed so tightly that her hand would have hurt if it weren't such a comfort.

Arilda burst into sudden and loud sobs. This broke Gretel from her paralysis. She let go of her husband's hand and pulled the girl into her arms.

"Shhhh, it's all right."

"But I'm scared of witches." The girl wailed, huddling in her older sister's embrace. "You said they weren't real."

"They're not sweetheart. There was no witch."

Hansel swiped his plate off the table, and it shattered on the floor.

Gretel held Arilda tighter as she flinched at the noise. "She was just a mean old lady."

"Stop." Hansel stood, sending his chair toppling over.

"She was probably driven mad, living so far out in the forest by herself."

"You promise?" Arilda asked into her shoulder.

"Yes, I promise." Gretel brushed a piece of blond hair out of the little girl's face to reveal her gaze.

"I swear." Hansel moved around the table toward them, his pointed finger leading him like an arrow shot from a rigid bow line. "If you don't stop this right now, I'll—"

Rainer slammed his fist into the tabletop, rattling the plates and knocking over one of the brass candlesticks. "You'll what? What will you do?"

Gretel nudged Arilda to her mother. Hedda gathered her child up; however, their father remained remarkably interested in his soup.

"Stop." Gretel tried to step between them, afraid that this could come to blows.

Rainer held out his arm to stop her. "Answer the question, Hansel."

"Nothing. I would never hurt her."

"Never? So you had nothing to do with the bruises on her arms?"

"Is this true?" Hedda's voice revealed a quiet betrayal.

Gretel pulled at the sleeves on her arms to keep them hidden. "It was nothing."

"It was *not* nothing. You need to stop treating this as if it's nothing." Rainer's tone made her flinch. He'd never raised his voice to her before.

"I need a word with my sister," Hansel said.

Rainer released a low, humorless chuckle. "If you think I am going to allow that right now, you truly have gone mad."

Hansel reached around her husband, holding his hand out to Gretel.

Rainer knocked him away.

Hansel charged forward.

Rainer nudged Hansel on his chest. The simple move took very little effort on his part, but it sent Hansel stumbling into the wall.

"Stop," Gretel said, taking hold of Rainer's arm.

He spun, and for a moment, she thought he would yell at her again. But, after one look at the thick tears resting in the lower arcs of her eyes, he exhaled and pulled her to him in a quick embrace. "Let's just go home."

She hesitated, Hansel was glaring at the back of Rainer's head, his own eyes filled with tears, his cheeks redder than the tablecloth. Gretel did not want to leave him like this.

But she knew how this ended if she tried to go to him.

She took her husband's hand and led him toward Hedda and Arilda, taking the long way around the table so they wouldn't have to walk by Hansel and risk another outburst.

Hansel rushed in behind Rainer.

"Gretel, wait," he said, and made another attempt to get to her.

"Enough." Rainer held out his arm and glanced over his shoulder. His voice so sharp that Gretel winced. "My wife and I are leaving."

Gretel could not leave without giving her brother some assurance that they were all right.

Hansel grabbed the brass candlestick from the table, and she had only enough time to scream, "no," before he brought it down on Rainer's head. Rainer stumbled into her and she fell to a seated position.

Hedda cried out, and both children sobbed.

She shoved them to their father. "Take them out of here."

"Rainer." Gretel shook her husband. A line of blood ran down his face and the guilt she felt in seeing it crunched in her chest.

"Here." Hedda was beside her, having scooped some ice from the wine basin and wrapped it in a napkin.

Gretel held the ice over the injury and glared at her brother.

He dropped the candlestick as if it had grown hot and burned him.

When Rainer groaned, and opened his eyes, relief flooded Gretel so strongly that she feared she would faint. He winced in pain, and his gaze shot to Hansel. In a lurch, he tried to get up.

Gretel threw an arm around his chest. "Please."

He relaxed and rested his hand over her arm. "We're leaving."

"Yes." She nudged his forehead with hers. "Thank you."

Hansel bent to assist her as she helped Rainer up.

"Do not touch him." She spoke these words loudly, appalled that he would dare put his hands on Rainer after what he had done.

Hansel drew back as if she had spat a live flame at him, then turned and stomped out of the room. They remained frozen as his footsteps blared up the stairs and his bedroom door slammed shut.

Hedda helped them as far as the door before Rainer stopped her. "I'm all right, Gretel can get me home."

Hedda bit her bottom lip and looked at Gretel.

"What is it?"

"I was hoping to speak with you."

Gretel pressed her face into Rainer's shoulder. "Hedda, please, not tonight."

"This can't go on. I have children to think about."

"All right, we'll talk about it." This wasn't a lie. They would talk about it, but there was no way Gretel would agree. "Just not tonight."

"Tomorrow afternoon?" Hedda said, locking her in.

"Fine."

Satisfied, Hedda turned and walked back into the dining room.

As they were leaving, Gretel glanced up the stairs and caught a glimpse of Hansel's lanky and slouched shadow as he slunk back into his room.

3

"I'm going with you," Rainer said as Gretel rose late in the morning. She'd been up most of the night, too frightened to let him go to sleep, afraid that he was more injured than they realized. "I know you're not going to see Hedda, she's probably not even back from her morning errands yet."

"Please." She couldn't stand for Rainer to see her comfort her brother after what Hansel had done, and as disgusted as she was by his actions, she knew that was exactly what she would do.

"I don't care."

"I care." She stood by her rocking chair, putting on her shoes, just as he had found her the night before.

"I can't let you be alone with him. I won't."

Having Rainer protect her from Hansel was the as humiliating as having him protect her from herself, and perhaps that was exactly what he was doing. She looked out the window, ready with another argument to keep him here, but something was wrong with the main house.

What exactly was so unsettling?

No smoke came from the chimney.

The morning was cold, even if the fire had gone out during the night, by this hour, someone would have restarted it.

Gretel ran, ignoring Rainer as he called after her. The cold air on her bare arms and the sting in her lungs didn't slow her.

Inside the house, out of habit, she kissed her fingers and reached for their father's axe. If she had ever needed good luck in her life, it was now.

The axe wasn't there.

"Oh, no."

She ran to her brother's room. Empty but for the shredded wallpaper on the floor.

Rainer stood in her parents' doorway with a hand over his mouth and nose.

"Don't," he said as she approached.

She looked anyways.

Blood splattered the back wall and pooled around the bed.

Her father's hand hung over the side. She recognized it by his ring and not by the pulpy red mess of the man attached to it.

She uttered a cry and clutched the wall as she moved out of the room and around the curve of the hallway. A voice in her head told her eyes that they were mistaken, she didn't actually see what she just saw, couldn't have.

A crumpled bloody mass was heaped in the hall.

Hedda lay face down, a large gash separated her shoulder from her collar bone. She stood for that hit, and her blood splashed in a wave on the wall. Her head was flattened to the floor with bits of brain, teeth, and bone stuck in the pool of drying blood.

Gretel imagined her brother with the axe, bringing it down on their father first. Mentally, their father was the weakest of the household, but physically, he was the only one who would have been capable of stopping him, so he had to be taken out before anyone realized what was happening. Then Hedda, scared, as she screamed and ran. She could have gone down the stairs and out the door, but she passed the staircase and ran toward her children's room.

The children.

She ran to their room, Rainer protested, but she couldn't process his words. She had to see that they were okay, and she believed they would be. In spite of what she had seen, she couldn't think that her brother would hurt them.

Audrik lay on the bed, his arm detached at the elbow from where he had lifted it as he tried, and failed, to stop the axe from cutting through his face. His death, unlike Hedda and her father's, had been one swift swing of the axe.

"Dear God." Rainer whispered behind her.

A trail of bloody footprints led around the room and toward the closet. Gretel prayed that Arilda's attempt to hide had been successful, even though the path was proof that it hadn't been.

The blood and the two small feet made Gretel faint.

4

Gretel saw exactly what she had expected, a nearly regrown path, choked with limp and dying weeds, at the foot of a mountain. She lifted her chin, ready to scream and collapse, but if she did that now, she wasn't getting back up.

Rainer didn't know she was here. She swore she would be fine at home if he went out with the search party.

Gretel had to find Hansel first.

The group was not a search party; they were an angry mob with pitchforks and torches and all.

They called him Kinslayer.

Baby killer.

Rainer promised that they would bring him in, lock him up somewhere safe where he could get help and hurt no one else. Sure, he was a large man, but trying to stop that mob, he was more likely to be strung up beside her brother than convince them of anything.

Her brother would have no redemption.

This was her fault.

Hansel was her fault.

All the times she comforted him and forgave him, all the times she refused to listen when Hedda insisted that he needed to be sent away, had brought them to this. Yes, it would have destroyed him. But her younger siblings, completely blameless in the mess that had made him what he had become, would still be alive.

This was her fault. She had to be the one to make it right.

Gretel palmed the hunting knife.

She wouldn't scare him and hurt him as the mob would.

This was the one kindness she had left to give.

The pebbles Hansel had left sparkled a faint trail for her when the moon came out on the first night of her search. The pebbles stopped at the base of the mountain.

Magic, Gretel.

If we had opened our minds to it, we may have walked right through.

Could he have been right? Why would he lead her all this way with no indication of where he had gone from here?

It's magic.

She let what she knew fade away and opened herself up to what else could be there.

Before her was a clear path, decorated with flowers that should have died in this cold fall. The moonlight lit a row of shining pebbles.

She ran, afraid that it would disappear again if she tarried.

Around the first bend, the cottage appeared as it had been when they were children, with the chocolate walls and candy cane door frame. It was grotesquely cheerful, the bright icing lined the windows like eyes, pretending to be friendly. Her mind screamed at her to run and her body tensed as if it would listen, but she forced herself through the door because she was so certain that her brother was inside. "Hansel?"

He cowered in the back of the main room, cheeks drenched in tears. "Gretel?"

He rose to embrace her. She fought the urge to recoil as she spotted the dried blood on his clothing and let him pull her into an embrace.

"Oh, Gretel, you found me."

She rubbed his back with one hand. "Of course I did."

There, right along the vein, one good cut on the neck, and he would bleed out before he knew what she had done.

"I had to get out of there."

"I know, Hansel, I know."

"I had the strangest dream, that I took Pa's axe. That I...that I...I wanted to go to you, but oh god, where did all this blood come from?"

She cried with him, not because she had to kill him, but because she couldn't.

No matter what kind of monster he had become, he was still her twin, the sunset to her sunrise, the ocean to her shore. One could not exist without the other, and she could not exist without him.

This place reminded her of the boy he had been, the boy who had reached his arm out of the cage to hold her hand and swore to protect her. The boy that had run to her when she awoke screaming. The boy that she watched deteriorate and did nothing to stop it. If she used the knife on him, she would have to use it on herself.

"It's all right. It was only a dream."

"But the blood."

"We can't go back."

If the only other option was death for them both, why shouldn't they stay here in this magical place, where no one could find them, and he could hurt no one else?

Gretel sat on the floor, and Hansel curled up beside her with his head in her lap. She stroked his hair and sang.

When the wind cuts through, it's hard to stand
And home is a distant shore
I am here with you, holding your hand
These ghosts will haunt us no more
No more, no more, these ghosts will haunt us no more.

TIPPING THE CUP

J. Rossi

from: <unknown> reply-to:undefined
to: clruthenford@gmail.com
date: Tue, Jan 26, 2016 at 3:23pm
PM subject: Hey Cafe Cutie

Now that I have your attention.

We met at the coffee shop today. I got your email and refused to give you my number. I was not playing hard to get. I was saving your life.

Please keep reading. You don't have to believe all of this yet, but you need to know it.

You need to know.

You know this story. It's been told and told again—a bedtime story, fabled to be written after one fateful day on the Isis to entertain three small girls. This story was bought out, sold out, and made into cartoons and movies. You've heard it. You know it. You were entertained.

You clapped your hands, sang the songs, and went to bed at night. Not one doubt or fear in sight.

But you have no idea how far down the rabbit hole you really went.

The bleeding won't stttooop, so I don't have a lot of time. You would think in someone's last moments they would try to reach out or get help. No, I'm sitting at a computer, typing my life story with enough duct tape wrapped around my middle to hold together a faulty Cadillac converter and bumper on a cross-country trip. I have a twenty-two loaded with sage and sandalwood-filled bullets inches from my left hand. Best part is, it's blessed and will kill anything. Even me. Because what I'm about to become is what I've been hunting for a long time. I'm dying, and as nature intended it is my place to go naturally or with a little assistance…To tell the truth, I've lived far too long. I've seen too much. Anyone I wanted to help, I've buried or killed myself.

I have to keep going before I lose too much blood.

Look outside your window.

What do you see? Do you see buildings, cars, random people? Do you see crime, destitution, poverty?

Do you see your reflection in the dark? Eyes so old that they are tired staring back out of the fourth...fifth body they inhabited in a couple of centuries or so.

Fuck. I sound nuts. Amuse me, will you? Keep reading.

I'm too cryptic. I'm pretty jaded actually. I haven't had a normal human conversation in so long.

I'm sorry.

I'm going to open your eyes. My days of keeping things in check is over. I saw you today, and I knew you were the one. You're the next. No, I was not flirting for your email...okay, maybe a little. But you need to know. You need to know who you are.

I can hear the whispering in my bedroom like it was yesterday.

I was a child no more than 7. It came from everywhere. I was chosen young. The transition our kind go through sporadically is highly atypical, so my parents had no way to expect it. We are not quite like other people ,my dear. With time, you will unfortunately know this. It always starts with the voices; they called me. Beaconed. Lulled. Anyhow, the voices can be intoxicating. If you hear them in adolescence, you are left to believe you have lost your mind. You have not. It simply means they have found you. Here's what's most important, if you don't listen to me, please listen to this.

They will come to you as the object of your greatest desire.

For a 7-year-old child, it was something I had begged my parents for, well for what seemed forever. My sisters had cats, grinning evil little things. They got into everything, and I took the blame. I despised cats. I don't so much now. The ornery little bastards hold so much knowledge.

Anyhow, one summer day I saw it sitting in the field seemingly staring at me. It was everything I ever imagined and I wanted to name it but that hardly matters now.

A beautiful white rabbit, mine for the taking.

I chased it; it ran. Into the woods I went. Did I live near the woods? I don't recall. Actually I wouldn't recall the next three or so years of my life. I do remember I was in the most splendid blue and white dress. It was the day of my mother's birthday and we were to have a tea party. She had dressed us all so well. Lorina in red, Mary in white, and I in blue.

I need a minute. More tape. So much blood. I thought of recording this, video you know...but you can't trust reflections...you need it on paper… or typed. It's safer.

Where was I? Oh yes, I ran. The woods. The whispering. The music.

The rabbit.

It jumped into a hole, and I stopped. I never jumped. I was never the dim witted, silly and curious child I am portrayed in fiction. That's what everyone wanted me to think. I needed to be told it was all a dream. I needed it to get past my childhood. But as many things as you will find out about this...I did not jump.

I stopped. I turned.

Darkness seeped from the hole and I ran. I knew that place was bad news. I sensed a great evil. It was malice and hatred and it was hungry. Before I knew it I was running back home, back to my sisters, mother, father and ornery frustratingly messy cats. I wanted to be home. I never felt the need to escape so badly in my life.

I could almost hear my mother call my name.

I could taste her biscuits and scones.

I could feel her hands holding me tight before putting me to bed.

The last thing I could recall were her eyes. Magnificent blue eyes. Like an ocean, or a sky.

I could see the house. I was almost home.

This darkness caught me by the hair and pulled me back so violently my neck and back cracked as I hit the ground. The pain shot up all around me all at once but I was frozen on the cold earth. I wanted to move but I couldn't. The darkness wrapped around my wrist so gently and tugged.

Then it tugged again, and again until I moved back.

Then I was sliding, slowly backwards. It was taking me back.

And it was singing in the most beautiful voice.

They're in the music.

I saw my feet twitching as it pulled me by one arm slowly back through leaves and mud and twigs. I remember the cold. It was freezing but my spine and hair was on fire.

My tears soaked my cheeks and blurred my vision. My little house faded in the distance. I couldn't turn my head to see it. I could feel it.

No one saw me. No one was there to help. I was going to that hole and then, God knows where.

Nowhere.

Everywhere.

I wonder where I went.

Wonder what land.

There.

Everything ground against my legs tearing the sensitive flesh away bit by bit. My jaw wide open. Not one sound came from me. I couldn't scream. I could only watch the sky as I was pulled inch by inch towards that hole.

I knew when I was close. The whispering was loud. Like an applause.

She's here. She's here. Pull her in.

These holes are everywhere. They open in sequences, there is a pattern. They...just keep reading.

I'm falling.

I was dragged down and I fell what felt like forever. It was.

The tearing. All my skin. Or was it?

Scream for us little one.

The next thing I remember I was in a boat.

My father was there screaming at a man named Charles who was holding my head. I was tied. I was gagged. I was thrashing and in the most pain I had ever felt. I was alive. But how? I don't know if it was night or day but we were rowing.

It was the fourth of July 1862.

We were on our way to Oxford University, to The Conclave. This world is full of shit secret societies.You will learn that very quickly so tread lightly. Some are here to rule it, others suppress it and there are the eclectic few that are solely to save its inhabitants. My father and this Charles were part of the latter.

I was a mess. There were passages we used to enter that I still can't find and I've had my hands on the archives before. Anyhow, I was brought in. John was there on internship. That poor bastard had to document everything. He took pictures. Thank heaven for him because If I hadn't seen the pictures I would have believed the lies my father wove to cover it all up.

I was put in a room and they tore it out of me.

Pulling, tearing.

It took days...weeks.

Short time. Long time. What was time.

Late. Too late?

Oils, chanting, cutting. There might have been a chicken or two. It was a mess.

Blood. So much blood. They got the darkness out of me.

But not all of it.

I was kept under lock and key for years. I was brainwashed into thinking it was not real. The worse disservice anyone could do to you now is tell you it is not real.

It is real.

We are real.

They are real.

I spent my youth chasing it, continent to continent. They found me before I found them.

It's very fucking real.

Hell is coming.

Creatures of old are coming as demons and things that you cannot wrap around your imagination should you attempt to conjure up your greatest fears. They will want you my dear because you are of us. You were born to fight. Fiiuigj. Fight it. Fight it and keep your humanity while saving everyone else's. The Conclave was disbanded in 1910 for lack of membership. Everyone was turned or dead. This is so important, if anyone approaches you stating they are with them just run.

No one is your friend. No. No one wants to "just help you." Trust me, the sooner our kind is gone the easier the overtaking will be.

I can't put everything in here. This email is already too long.g..g

Read it all. Over and over and over.oocj. Read it...know it.

I'm ruuning oout tiiime. It's nearly morning and I need to die before the sun comes up or our next conversation will end with me tearing out your throat with my bare teeth.

You will taste of them I know it. Not of us.

No.

I'm losing it.

Stop thinking this is a joke.

This is not a YA book and no I am not going to sparkle, sprout hair or anything romanticized and downplayed in that half assed smut they call fiction. Im sorry.

Fiction is fixtion. They do so well with fiction here. I love to read. Beautiful tales.

All made to make you look the other way. Well LOOOOOK. LOOk.k k.

This my dear is not. Fiction. Notyt fake.

I'm…I've seen too much. I will be of them. Of them. Taste….how they taste..knas

The beginning, the things that were here before they were not, this place was covered with them. They lingered, fed, fucked and fought their way to practical extinction. There was an order to things but it was all flesh for flesh, bone for bone. They were locked away into their own pocket of reality mostly by their own elders. We were nothing but meat suits and play things. We would not have survived had they stayed. The time of man came but it is coming to an end.

The time of man is ending. ENDEDDFjkbnkj…..

They are late for a very important date. Recall that line?

Pay attention.

Your veins… in them.

You are of us.

I wish I could give you more. Time. Imew gfe ….

Attached you will find several PDF's. I've gathered everything I know, and all my maps and diagrams in these files. The story, the full story you have it. Save them, copy them, send them to yourself. Save yourself. Have it printed. Have it made. Tell nth the world.WOE…..WORLD…lknlknsei

I know this seems insane. I asdfjasnf I know. l

you'll know what to do when theeey cofwf come for you.

Theyyyy will come h...soon.

Live with dignity. Die with resolve.

You're great-great-great...you get it,

Aunt Anne...not Alice. Anne. My name was ANNE.

PSSssssSSss

Don't die alone. ....['pmk

and leave now.

RRRRRRRRRRRRRRRRRRRRRRRRRRRRRRRRRRRRRRRRRRRRUuuuuu uuuuuuuibknlnnnnnnnnnnnnn

12/8/16
Dancing With The Cat

WHETHER THEY PIPE US FREE

Daniel Hale

Paul the exterminator was called out minutes before turning in for the day, in the chillier half of one of the soggiest winters on record, to one of the worst ghettos in the city: a potholed, crumbling estate that looked like it belonged in Baghdad (the exterminator did not know where Baghdad was, but had decided it was probably a cesspool of villainy that was responsible for most of his country's problems), only to find that the address was another decrepit apartment block among many, completely pitch dark.

Paul approached the lobby's door. He had a number of faults, born mainly from his stubborn refusal to consider anything that wasn't shared or imparted by one of the guys at Malloy's Thirsty Business or the Reverend Dr. Cletus on the Shining Beacon News Network. He was, however, an experienced exterminator and was familiar with the sounds of vermin about their business.

Paul heard a cacophony of tittering activity. He pressed face to the glass doors, cupped his hands around his eyes.

Seconds later, after sprinting to his van with impressive speed for a man of his waistline, Paul the exterminator removed a small, leather-boundbook of handwritten phone numbers from his glovebox. He traced his fingers down the accompanying descriptions: VIRUS, RAPID. CORPSE, RIPENED. HUMAN, GLOWING…when he found what he needed, he tapped the word EMBASSY and dialed.

The call went to Gregor, which he hated. Remore or Fielden, the heads of the Pied, would have been better suited for it. The two of them had surpassed flutes long ago, could now do the job by whistling, or even humming. Instead, it was his problem.

He'd only just completed his induction, been in his posting no more than three months with fuck all to do. To think he'd been starting to resent the monotony of it; the Pied had assets and investors that went back centuries, enabling its members to pursue their individual interests in their considerable downtime. Gregor played with the idea of performing again, as well. And now, a call.

Gregor's free time came with caveats, of course. Each of the Pied was required to walk once a month in the designated fiefdoms adjacent to their territories. Another incursion might occur, as well, but of course, nobody thought of *that.*

Now his peace was shattered. The incursion was here in his jurisdiction. He had a duty, as the resident piper of the hamlet (as the Pied insisted on naming the territories), to see the Accords were met.

He got his equipment together, taking his time about it. His palms and brow sweated, his hands shook, his heart pounded, but he could not bring himself to hurry up and meet the second incursion in the history of the order.

Gregor put on the suit that, in theory, would mark him out as an ambassador to the people of the nation, and put his civilian uniform on top of it.

He assembled his flute, a weathered, brass affair that must have had half a dozen owners before it knew Gregor's lips. All the while, he failed to ignore the dread shooting bile up his throat.

He'd live the life of a musician, which held more filthy mattresses and cold rooms than popular opinion believed. He tried learning more in-demand instruments, but the flute was the only one he was comfortable with. Between working two jobs (waiter and cashier, as menial as it got), he took up the occasional gig with experimental bands or played for tips in a wine bar.

That was where a portly dilettante in a ludicrous purple suit with pink cravat approached him. Gregor was fairly certain that Remore was not as smart as he liked to act. The man affected an air of mystery that came off fairly well until you got to know him. But he had charm, and Gregor eagerly accepted the offer of a drink after the show.

"You really had them enthralled." Remore reached across the glass-topped table, laid his hand on Gregor's arm. "Excellent work as ever."

The suggestion of a certain subtext made Gregor aware that he had no head for wine. "Have we met?"

"I've watched you from afar. The tone is familiar and carries quite a ways, and then it's just a matter of looking for the crowd." He gestured to the surrounding tables. "Pity you had the wrong audience, else you could get them to follow you anywhere. This bunch can recognize it, but you'd have to get them a little more relaxed before they'd be prepared to follow."

"I don't understand."

Remore beckoned a waiter. "Shut the music off, please," he said as he pressed a roll of bills into the waiter's hand.

To Gregor, he asked: "Do you know how you truly captivate an audience? It isn't with a popular tune, or a familiar one. There is a register that strikes in the mind by surpassing the ear, and it can only be reached by a small subset of minstrels. You've got a sliver of it in you, and with a bit of work we can help it to blossom."

Gregor set down his glass down, prepared to make his excuses and escape. He could recognize a pitch when he heard one, though he couldn't decide if the man was a charlatan or a nut job. Before he could, Remore rose to his feet and cleared his throat.

"If I could just have your attention for a moment." The conversation shut off as immediate as a radio.

Customers turned in their chairs.

"We've a small bit of entertainment yet to go, if you would all just indulge me." He tapped Gregor on the shoulder. "After you, my boy."

Gregor stood, suddenly awash with thousands of itchy pinpricks as the gazes of the patrons settled on him. His stage fright, never quite dampened down, subsumed his wine-boiled buzz. Not knowing what else to do, he raised his flute and blew a note.

Remore, a second later, hummed a note. As one, the customers twitched their heads, as if they'd all been caught thinking the same lightning-bolt image. Gregor experimentally blew three more.

Remore's hum matched him now, and for the duration of those three notes, a serene stillness held the audience.

Remore nodded expectantly at the stunned Gregor, who nodded back, raised the flute again and played.

Snippets of his musical repertoire, Gregor jumped from one tune to the next. Remore matched his every challenge, keeping up with his lead before, somewhere, overtaking it. Gregor lost track of his songs to a distant, unceasing note.

The sound didn't surpass human hearing. But he could not name the note. This existed between the registers, an all-encompassing melody that might have been there all along, albeit at a much lower key. Brought into the audible, it flooded everything else out the mind before swirling down through your veins and nerves, filling your body like fog in a bottle.

When they finished—Gregor had no idea how he knew when to stop blowing—Remore sat down. The crowd shook themselves, looked to each other with a little apprehension, but the moment passed from their memories as suddenly as it arrived, and they returned to their wine and their easy talk.

"And that's the least of what we can do," Remore said to Gregor, who was still standing and clutching his flute in trembling hands. "We can get their attention, but this lot won't listen to anything new for long. They've forgotten the high speech, can only fathom a fragment of it. With the right ear, though…the right mind, ah. Then what music we can make. Please sit down, my boy."

And Gregor sat, and he had listened, because cynical as he was, ill-used as he thought himself to be, he could not turn away from the promise of the outré. This was the hope that had been with him since he was a boy in grade school, when a nervously-cheerful woman in a cowboy hat had taken a guitar and commanded a room of first graders into clapping their hands and singing along, a feat that, to young Gregor, was nothing short of magical.

Then he'd seen the most of what he could do and what it would be used for.

His cellphone buzzed, either Remore or Fielden calling from their offices in Karni Mata, in India. They would have received the alert when the exterminator called him.

He left it shaking on the bed. Distasteful as he found this business, he would see that it was done with a bit of solemnity, without them fussing at him.

The exterminator was leaning against his van (Rodent Rapture Services) in a badly lit part of the city. Perhaps the hardest part of Gregor's training was braving the urban sprawl, particularly those parts of it ranked of the unseemly. Even now he could never quite visit these places without feeling ill at ease.

The Pied walked where the Nations were, played where they could hear them; the roofs of listing towers, the garbage heaps, the docks and the sewers and the ruins-to-be. Gregor had walked them all in his time and had subsequently acquired and conquered phobias of heights and confining spaces and disease. His social phobia, meanwhile, was stronger than ever.

The exterminator was a squat, bullheaded fellow with a small bush of a beard plastered on his fleshy chin. Gregor tried to look imperious and knowing as he adjusted his cap, flute hanging lamely from his right hand.

"First day on the job, they told me that if I ever saw a rat doing something weird to call that number." He hitched a thumb over his shoulder to the unlit apartment building. "I dunno what you people think is weird, but it's as fucked up in there as I can imagine."

"What did you see?"

"Shouldn't you know that?" He glanced at Gregor's flute, piggy brow scrunched as he tried to decide how seriously he should be taking this. "So what're you gonna do now?"

You're a follower of ancient wisdom. This guy is a working stiff with bad facial hair. Act accordingly.

"Whatever is happening in there is worse than you know," Gregor said, adopting a wisp of mysticism into his accent. "The consequences of its spreading are incalculable. You will hold the burden of that if we cannot stop this."

He hefted his flute, a little more sure of himself.

He quoted a bit from the speech new members were given at Karni Mata. "Forces and allegiances coagulate from the minds of beasts. Let them run, and they shall slay. Wield the word, and we may hold them in our sway."

It didn't sound quite as good coming from him as he'd hoped.

"You're a fucking loony. I knew it." He returned to his van and slid into the driver's seat. "Have fun in there while you can, weirdo. I'm gonna do what I should have done in the first place and call the police."

"No. Please." Gregor played, but he was so frazzled by how badly he'd messed things up that he could not carry a simple tune.

In any case, the exterminator was no longer willing to listen, a mix of disgust and pity on his face.

"Okay, buddy. I've had enough of this." He rose from his seat, hand reaching to his side.

Gregor scurried off to the tenement, wishing he'd had his own phone. Remore would be furious enough that Gregor hadn't called. If the police got involved and came here to find him cavorting in a building full of corpses? That would be that.

Do the job and get away.

Gregor strode through the doors and into the darkened lobby.

And stopped.

The floor was not a writhing mass of gray and brown bodies. Disgusting, but anyway, there weren't enough rats. It was difficult to judge in the darkness, but there was movement going on; organized movement. Columns and congregations of rodents scurried to and fro along the filthy linoleum. It was the purposeful activity of a hive of living creatures, all engaged on errands unknowable, all at home on their turf.

Now, there could be no doubt. The Nation had staked a claim for the first time in centuries.

Gregor felt a lump of ice crawl down his throat and into his gut; he had not been aware that he'd hoped for a false alarm.

He put his doubt aside. No time to dither; the police weren't likely to hurry about a call from a slum like this, but no good could come of them facing off against the rats. None of the Pied knew how the Nation would fare against a human agency. Best to defuse it before it went that far.

Gregor willed the tremor out of his fingers, unzipped the nondescript exterminator's jumpsuit.

His uniform was an outrageously colored nightgown of mauves and magentas and fuchsia and other, less easily recognized shades that interspersed and orbited them. A random clash of colors as far as Gregor was concerned, but supposedly, it marked him out to the Nations as an official representative of the Pied.

Gregor raised the flute once more. His lips took shape to form the notes before he played.

"There are anthropologists who will tell you that man devised music before he ever invented language. That he needed rhythm and repetition before he could assign it meaning."

That was the lecture Fielden gave Gregor and his fellow adherents, along a twisted and rancid stretch of the Ganges. Kryora, the dreadlocked, waspish girl, gazed about the weathered buildings and the lapping, muddy water with a studied solemnity. Alricks, a sour, pudgy type, saw only the lumps of nondescript garbage, and his bottom lip curled out in moping suspicion.

Gregor watched the turtles: two tottering, shelled forms crawling slowly along the shoreline. It was hard to tell if either was aware of its surroundings, but it made Gregor sad that these poor animals wallowed in waste not even their own. Would he get in trouble for picking them up and taking them home?

Fielden tapped a sandaled foot meaningfully in the squelchy sand and raised his eyebrows at Gregor. He was a humorless man with a scarecrow's physique, his thin nose like a sliver of triangle of carrot nailed to the rind of his face. The fact that his pomposity put Remore's to shame did not help him any. Gregor pictured him leading the rats by playing his nose like a kazoo.

Fielden resumed his lecture. "In this, they are likely not incorrect. Of course they overlook the fact that music is *superior* to language. It is language expanded, encompassing mental and emotional subtexts that no human tongue can quite manage. Meanwhile, as we set ourselves above the beasts of the field and the fowls of the air, they share a rapport that transcends their every word and deed. Consider the mournful wailing of cetaceans in the wintry brine, the fleet-winged raptors cresting the wind with a cry that announces that they are living, rushing death. This is the orchestra of communication, a worldwide network that our stunted species is excluded from.

"Thus, I believe that music was not the ancient precursor to language. Rather, language is a mistake, an error that superseded its mother in our collective psyche, rewiring our minds to exclude the orchestra of life that surrounds us. Now, the appointed visionaries of our species can only marvel at the flutter of a butterfly's wing, or the navigational dances of bees, with no hope of deciphering the myriad melodies in the twitch of a whisker or flutter of a fin. Even we of the Pied can only achieve an approximation of the song, which to the creatures of the Nations must seem like a primitive's pidgin flattery."

That was as may be, and at the time, the whole thing still seemed like an impossibly elaborate fiction. But then, Fielden caught sight of the two turtles struggling in the muck and removed a small piccolo from his pocket.

To the students, he said: "I don't expect any of you to manage without one of these on hand. In all likelihood, you shall never be called upon to use them except to maintain our presence in the Nations' various territories. One day, however, the Accords may be challenged. We might even face war with a bestial Nation. So you must be prepared.

Fielden played a shrill, listing number that paused the turtles, and they stared at him a bit (a feat that might have been impressive if performed by something nominally more aware than a turtle). Then, the two turned and made their careful way to Alricks, who was standing near a cloth-covered lump in the surf.

"The turtles of the Ganges were bred to feed on the corpses of those who come here to die. Hundreds were released into the river, but the project was fraught with oversight problems and corruption, and their numbers soon dwindled." Fielden nodded to the lump by Alricks' feet, as if to ask for clarification of this irreverent fact.

Alricks leapt aside with a yelp of disgust. Now, Gregor could see the suggestion of shoulders beneath the rags, and the deflated, leathery mask that clung to the skull like shrunken saran wrap.

The turtles crawled for the corpse.

That was the day that made Gregor mistrustful of the whole business. For all that Fielden and Remore talked about the Hamelin Accords and primal communion, they never hesitated to show off before their inferiors, casting their spell over the urban-adapted wildlife that had shadowed humanity since the dawn of civilization. They made foxes dance on tiptoe and rats stack into tumbling towers. They sent pigeons smacking into windows and dogs leaping off bridges. They hummed casual cruelties, whistled conditioning commands with all the petty surety of spoiled heirs.

Those first few nights of training, Gregor, Alricks, and Kryora would sit together in their room in Karni Mata, more for comfort than companionship, listening to the scurrying of the rats that were allowed to roam the temple. Their flutes were always confiscated upon turning in. Sometimes, Kryora would whistle, trying to call the rats, but they never came.

It was dangerous power, too easy to abuse. You didn't even need musical talent, really; just a tone that struck a chord in the minds of animals. Gregor never grew used to it, and began to dread those occasions when he was called upon to play. All those times on the roofs and in the heaps, along trap streets and down tenement hallways, calling for the silent majority of cities…

This was different. Those times he had been an intruder, an anomaly into the lives of vermin. Now, he was an ambassador crossing the border into a country of unknown capabilities and intentions.

And he was alone.

Gregor's eyes adjusted quickly. The rats stopped where they were, turning to follow the source of the noise. He was playing an old favorite, a soothing, roundabout tune he'd devised as a child. He tried to let it come naturally, to not think about the rising sound of countless tiny paws rushing down the stairs, or what might happen to him if he stopped playing.

None of the Pied knew how the first incursion happened, nor why it had been the rats. It was an inexplicable bit of Hitchcockian karma, an uprising of humanity's most loathsome neighbor, in an age when people were only just beginning to lose themselves in the senseless wash of reason. To the people of Hamelin, it must have seemed like a new catalog of plagues were being visited upon them.

Clearly, the Piper had been some lucky, nameless nomad who retained a rare affinity for the rodents. More likely, the entire story was a parable, a neat shrugging off of an undertaking less easily arrived at.

Remore and Fielden only recited the bare bones of it, offered nothing in the way of artifacts to verify it. The music, they believed, was enough.

Gregor waited as more rats filled the lobby, crowding the floor to the corners. He pictured a thousand bolt holes, bored into shoddy sheetrock, streaming with retreating furry bodies as they vacated their new homes. The previous residents were probably past caring.

He couldn't think of this as communication. The things were just staring at him.

Better get on with it.

Still playing, Gregor took a step into the sea of fur.

A circle opened amongst the rats.

Gregor kept his breathing steady, and the tune even, as he took another step.

Through the lobby to a door beyond, a few seconds of agonizing silence to get it open, picking up the tune again to lead the rats through, and out through the back.

Gregor could feel the gaze of the skittering mass, hear their paws on the grass and their nonsense chittering. He badly wanted to run, but thought of this swarm suddenly cut loose and chasing after him was too much to bear.

Police lights whooped down the road. Gregor led the rats in a circuit beyond the tenement, down an embankment and an open field of gravel that overlooked a stretch of freeway.

Damn the costume.

What would the early-evening traffic make of him, a transient jester, conducting rats across the way? He could not imagine, but the rats had to be dealt with. Of the many commandments of the Accords that had been drummed into him, Fielden had harped on about disposal the most. This was the only way.

Gregor stood at the tree line, the restless rats squatting behind him. His song had grown increasingly ragged, his breathing difficult. He tried to focus.

Saturday-evening traffic was a furious current of light. Gregor reached out from his mind, shaped the intention in the music.

Away.

The rats streamed past the musician, who kept his flute aloft and live in the maddened rush. Tires screeched and scraped along a sudden field of bone and blood. Racing metal swerved and met in a scintillating crash, raining jewels of shattered glass on bloodied tarmac.

Gregor was already away before the collision settled. He'd remembered something just as the rats stood dumb in the oncoming glare of a noxious-breathed monster. The other part of the Accords, the one that he'd never thought too deeply about. The balance.

It shouldn't have been him. It would have been fine if it was anyone else. Even Alricks and Kryora could have done it, but not him. He'd never thought it'd have to be him.

And it would have to be done, and it would have to be done here. If Remore and Fielden had indeed been truthful, then there was no avoiding it.

But it couldn't be *him*.

He had to call them. They would be furious with him, of course, for not reporting in. Probably doubly so for leaving the job undone. But what could they do to him?

Gregor arrived at his apartment following a hazy sequence of stutter-start processions. His cellphone was still on the bed, its screen glowing patiently. Either they were waiting, or had given up, and were coming for him.

Seventeen missed calls from Remore, the last from five minutes ago.

No messages, no texts.

Gregor hit the number.

No answer. He caught himself listening for the approach of footsteps in the hallway outside, followed by frantic, slamming knocks on the door. He redialed.

They couldn't ignore him, surely? This was the single most important event in the history of their order, and he'd excluded them from it. They'd be frothing with desperation, palpitating to know that it had been met to its completion. Gregor could convince them, he was sure of it.

The ringing had stopped. The call was answered.

"Remore? Are you there?"

Gregor heard…he listened closely. Quiet static, whispering from a distance down the wire. The scratching expanded in his ear, divided and split into a rustling mass, interspersed with a thousand squeaking voices.

Gregor sat there a while, listening to the noise. He pictured the scuttling, restless shadows in the corners of Karni Mata, always alive with movement. He remembered the gleam of black, inscrutable eyes above twitching noses and quiet, ceaseless squeaking.

He remembered the dumb attention of the people in the wine bar, and the words of Remore.

They've forgotten.

Maybe the rats remembered and had guessed he wouldn't go through with it. Maybe they saw their chance and didn't care. The Nation would come to claim its damages in person.

But Gregor had to try. Resetting the balance would be the only way to fix it.

Hamelin was the town that lost its children. The Piper honored his debt.

Gregor opened his window, looked out onto the city, and prayed to be forgotten.

Then he lifted his pipe and played.

TROLL BRIDGE

Robert Kibble

I've waited a long time for a boy to walk past alone. Adults usually stop them: "It'll collapse" or "It's fenced off." I hate that. When I was young, children ignored fences. Of course, when I was young, the fences weren't here. People walked along this stretch of the riverbank, enjoying the little ornamental bridge. They only blocked it off a few years back, and since then, I've gone hungry. I've had plenty of time to think, to plan, and to change.

I need carefully-crafted mystery now, so he'll climb over that fence.

A breeze to refresh him on this hot summer's evening.

His curly blond hair reacts to the wind, and he turns.

He'll think the river blows strange breezes.

Two ducks swim below me, a tasty snack if I was hungry enough. I've been that hungry before. The goose I scavenged two weeks ago—that'll keep me going. No one misses geese…swans, though. They've got those metal bits round their legs, which I have to bury.

The boy wanders over to the fence. He'll see the crack running up the side of my bridge, or the missing bricks in the top-right corner. Maybe the bent railing. He won't see the joyous proportions of the arch that make it perfect for me to hide, except when rowers go past. If they're concentrating, I stay hanging as they pass. Sometimes, a bored rower looks, and I pull myself up into the bridge.

I haven't spoken in a long time. My voice will sound odd, even to me.

I whisper. He should be able to hear. "Hello."

He steps a little closer, trying to find me.

"Hello?" His voice is high, nervous. I like him. We'll enjoy talking.

"Come closer."

"Who's there?" He takes another step. "Where are you?"

"I'm under the bridge. Step over the fence and let me have a proper look at you."

"Who are you?" He puts a hand on the fence. That's a good sign.

"I'm a troll. If you come closer, I'll let you see me. Who are you?"

"William," he says, an uncertain tremor in his words. "I don't think it's a good idea."

I pop my head out on the river-side of the bridge. I see him with my own eyes, for a second, his wide green eyes stare into my own, a moment of connection. He's wearing a school uniform, smart black blazer and trousers, wearing through at the knees. My size will reassure him. I am a little troll, at least I am now. Obviously, I can change size when I need to, but he won't need to know that. At least, not until we've got to know each other better.

Curious now, he puts his other hand on the fencepost and a foot on the lower beam.

After years of waiting, finally someone's coming. It's so good. I hope my smile is warm.

I wait until he's on my side of the fence.

Such a lovely boy. He doesn't realise how important he is to me. *Come closer...*

"Where are you?" he asks all sweet, but he doesn't know what I'm like.

I pop my head out again, and he steps back. He doesn't appreciate my teeth or my skin. He doesn't know I was considered a good-looking troll, an age ago. That once upon a time I had a wife and children. And friends. I haven't seen another troll in so long. I haven't spoken to anyone in so long. I haven't eaten in so long. I mustn't think like that.

"Hello, William." I come out completely, up on the side of the bridge. I need him to walk across it. "Come closer."

I sit down, cross-legged, and he looks me up-and-down. Well, looks at me, anyway—I don't take much upping and downing.

"What are you doing here?" William shuffles from foot to foot. His hands find their way into his pockets.

"I live here." I've been stuck here, in fact, for a long time. That's why I need him.

"How come I've not seen you before?"

I could ask him the same question. There's something in his eyes I can't place. I need him closer. "I only let the most special people see me. Are you alone?"

I shouldn't have asked that. Not so bluntly. He comes closer.

He sits down, opposite me. Almost on the bridge. Nearly, but not there yet. I need another step.

"Yes. My parents live over there, that house with the statue by the water. They're having a drink in the pub. They've got a little boat that comes and picks you up, you know?"

I smile at that. Such a gloriously boyish thing to be excited about.

"Come here," I say, holding out a hand.

He shuffles forward. He's on the bridge. Now.

"William, there's something special you can do for me."

I've waited long enough. Finally, I can find peace. All I have to do is let one victim go, and I won't be tied here any longer.

"You are quite safe." He keeps staring at me, right into my eyes. I expected a reaction, either fear or relief. His stare is unnerving. "In fact, you've set me free, just by talking to me here. I'll be forever in your debt."

William stands up. He's growing. I stand and try to grow, too, but it isn't working. He leans forward and puts his hands on the ground. Bumps form on his forehead. He's growing horns.

"That's such a shame, poor troll. I believe you meant it, too, but you should've known better than to invite a Billy onto your bridge."

NIGHTINGALE

Matthew Brockmeyer

June 30, 1972

The Historical Society of Humboldt County, California

The following is an interview with Daniel Timbourne, the last-known living witness and survivor of the notorious 1910 fire that burned down a section of the Eureka red-light district from First Street to Second Street.

Q: Can you tell us a bit about yourself?

A: Sure. My name is Daniel Timbourne, and I'm seventy-six years old. Born in 1896. I'm a retired carpenter and lifelong bachelor. No kids, no grandchildren. I never knew my mother. She died in childbirth, having me. I was raised by my sister, who wasn't but five years older than me. My father worked for the Bendixsen Shipyard till they closed in 1901, then he became what I guess you would call a hobo. A drunkard. Never saw him much. I suppose he never got over my mother dying, and every time he looked at me, he saw what gone done and killed her and drank that thought away. So, me and my sister, Katie, was on the streets a lot back then. Looking for what work we could find. Sometimes looking for a handout, panhandling and whatnot.

Q: Can you tell us a little about Old Town Eureka at the time of the 1910 fire?

A: Well, it wasn't called Old Town then, as it was a new town at the time. They called it the Water Front, and A Street to D Street was The Tenderloin. The entire area was "wide-open," a polite sort of way of calling it a red-light district. The sporting houses were accepted, so long as the girls stayed inside, and Police Chief Frank Cloney saw to it that they did.

Wild there back then. Horses and the first cars competed head-to-head in the streets, plus they put in the electric street car system in 1907, so accidents were pretty common. Ragtime music filled the air, pouring out of the sixty-five saloons and thirty-two brothels. The Alpine Brothel on Second Street, which is now Eureka Books, Aunt Sue's Sporting House, the High Lead, the Logger-Club-Rest, and the Star. Madame Ruby Smith ran a cat house in the Oberon building, and the Iron Gate right there behind the old Episcopal Church on Fourth and E. But the biggest and most notorious of them all was Madame Sheri's Palace, which sat perched on the edge of the bay, right where Waterfront Drive meets I Street.

Q: And you worked for Madame Sheri at the Palace?

A: Yes. Yes, I did. My sister and I both. I swept the floors, cleaned up spilled drinks, helped with the dishwashing. Was what you would call a go-for. You know, go-for this, go-for that. My sister, she started out same as me, but eventually ended up doing what she had to do.

Q: What was it like working for Madame Sheri?

A: Actually, back then everyone just called Madame Sheri, the Empress. She ruled that lower end of town. Called it her garden. I can still remember the first time we stepped into that mansion, the biggest Victorian on the lower end of town. Built Queen Anne style. It had over-hanging eves and big polygonal towers poking up into the sky, and those rounded shingles that look like fish scales. Painted pink, with purple trim, and the black water of the Humboldt Bay sparkled behind it. They called it the Palace because a palace is what it was.

Q: And how was it that you came to work for the Empress?

A: Well, a few years before the fire, Katie and I were looking for our daddy, who'd gone off drinking. We hadn't seen him in days. At that time children weren't supposed to visit First and Second Street, but we were hungry.

We wandered the alleys of the Water Front and the Empress spied us. She was a big woman. Huge. Wide as a pallet of bricks and probably as heavy, too. She stood there on the redwood-plank sidewalk in front of her mansion, dressed in the Victorian fashion that was still popular: a long-sleeved gown with a prim, high collar, tight corset and layers and layers of crinoline. Women would dress like that to show that they were too wealthy to work and could afford maids to do their housework and help them dress. The Empress' gowns were always all black, which wasn't uncommon back then, though some folks wondered if she was in some type of mourning. But she had a peculiar cameo necklace she wore that always seemed a little strange to me and gave me the creeps. Embossed upon it was the Virgin Mary with her hands clasped in prayer. A relatively common image. Yet crimson tears ran down her cheeks.

When the Empress seen us there in that back alley of rotting trash and shadows, she shouted in her thick, French accent, "Children. Children. What are you doing out there? You know young ones aren't to be traipsing around here in the lower end of town. You are up to no good, are you not?"

I didn't know exactly what traipsing meant, but wading through garbage hoping to find our father didn't seem to fit this definition. Nonetheless, I didn't say a thing. But my sister was a pretty little thing with long, blonde hair and arresting blue eyes, and she was spunky, full of fire.

"No, ma'am," she said back, hands jauntily placed on her hips, not seeming to be embarrassed of her torn skirt and dirty sweater. "We're looking for our daddy."

A street car rattled by noisily, and somewhere a horse neighed and stomped its feet.

"And who is your father, little one?"

"My daddy's name is Frank Timbourne."

"Oh, you are the Timbourne children. I see. You look hungry. Are you hungry? Come on in, I'll give you breakfast, and then I have some work for you. You do want to work, don't you?"

My God how we were hungry. And—oh—how we wanted work. Anything steady that could put just a few crumbs in our bellies on a regular basis.

So we stepped out of that back alley, the air thick with the dank, fishy scent of the bay, and up to that redwood-slab sidewalk with that pink mansion looming up over us like an owl might loom over a mouse.

"Welcome, welcome, *mon cherries*." Madame Sheri opened the door wide and beckoned us in. "*S'il vous plaît, s'il vous plait*, do enter."

And we went on in.

The first floor was an opulent saloon. A big redwood bar gleamed with mirrors and racks of liquor bottles, a piano in the corner. Dark-purple, cloth wallpaper and ornate moldings and trim. The backrooms were for gaming and had roulette wheels and blackjack tables. A grand staircase led to the upstairs where the girls lived and worked.

There were no customers, for it was Sunday and the Empress never did business on Sunday. The front doors to that big Victorian mansion clanged shut when church bells rang through those dusty streets.

Katie had always been a tough girl. Some might even call her bold, though she was rock-candy sweet, and she just strolled on in. But I was nervous. Hell, I was downright scared. I mean, people said all kinds of things about the Empress. Her very name invoked legend.

Madame Sheri had come to Eureka from San Francisco. But before that she had run some houses in New Orleans. She was from Louisiana, Baton Rouge to be specific. And rumors just abounded about her. How she was involved in voodoo cults. How her family were once famed slave dealers, now shamed and impoverished after the war of the states. They claimed she was an opium dealer as well as a Madame and had left San Francisco because of a war she was in with some particularly nasty Chinese gangs over the opium trade. Now this rumor did have a certain amount of legitimacy, for Chinese were not allowed in Eureka at the time. That ordinance was passed in 1885, and they didn't rescind it till 1959. So Eureka would have been a good place to hide if you were looking to escape them Chinese gangs.

A few girls lounged about in their skimpy dresses, sipping tea and giggling amongst each other. Amanda, a pale-skinned and freckled redhead, who I had a real clamoring going on for, but I was only twelve years old. Lauren, a raven-haired beauty with long black lashes, would sometimes give me a wink that set my face ablaze. And the Empress's inner circle, which were her African servants.

None of them spoke any English. Only French, or some creole Frenchy stuff. Exactly how she had come across them was a source of heated debate. Some said she imported them from Haiti where she had gone to learn about voodoo and black magic. Others said that back in Louisiana slavery was still going on in them backwoods plantations, and they were slaves she had inherited. Now, you got to remember that this was only some fifty years since the end of the Civil War, and lots of old timers still remembered slavery. Lots of Southern folks came to Eureka for a new start after the war. Outlaws and Confederates and such. Hell, you still see Confederate battle flag stickers on the bumpers of pick-ups today.

Q: Can you tell me more about these African servants? This inner circle?

A: Sure. They were all there that first day and I met each one of them all formal like.

Abelard. Behind his back everyone called him the Zombie. He stood at a height of six foot eight, made even taller by the gleaming-black, beaver-skin top hat he wore. He was quite an imposing figure and had the uncanny habit of standing as still as a statue, his white-rimmed eyes staring blankly out from his dark, stony face. He spoke little and folks were generally afraid of him. They said the most awful things about him. Saying he wasn't even human. *A servant of the devil and a demon from hell is what he is*, they would whisper. But when Katie and me stepped into the Palace, and the Empress introduced us, he smiled big and his eyes twinkled with friendliness, putting both of us at ease. He took off his hat and bowed so low I thought his head would hit the floor. Then he looked me right in the eye, still holding that sweet grin, and said, "A votre service."

I didn't understand and just sat there feeling foolish. The Empress laughed that deep, hearty laugh and said, "Relax, *cher garcon.* He just said he's at your service."

Quiet as a mouse, I didn't know what to say to this big, hulking African man before me. But my sister went and curtsied like a princess, saying, "*Merci, monsieur.*" Where she got that French from I'll never know, 'cause we hadn't caught a lick of schooling. Musta picked it up somewhere.

Well, like I said, folks were afraid of him: the way he'd stand behind the Empress with that scary, emotionless gaze. But often he'd give me a wink or a smile. Sometimes, he'd come up to me around midnight, when I'd be so tired and worn out, not knowing if I could change the wet, sticky sheets or mop up mud no more, and he would give me that kind smile and say, "*Monsieur, viens par ici.*" I'd follow him to the kitchen, and there would be a slice of apple cobbler and a steaming cup of joe. Just the jolt of sugar and caffeine to get a young buck through the night and into the dawn. So he was always nice enough to me, and I grew to even love the big guy.

Then Josette. She never seemed to take to me. Always watching in the distance. People claimed she cast spells that seemed to befall anyone who crossed paths with the Empress. Sometimes, after an argument or tiff with the Empress, people might get sick, or suffer some odd misfortune, like their livestock falling over dead, or one of their children going missing. She was dark as midnight, with puckered lips and eyes that were beautiful but always seemed suspicious. Deeply suspicious. And angry.

And the Nightingale. I'm sure you heard of him—a midget, I guess you'd call him a dwarf 'cause of them big hands. He was the piano player. A mute. A master musician. Amazing. Wore a round bowler, and a fresh, clean, linen shirt with a gleaming-black bowtie. Of course people said all kinds of contradictory things about him, too. Said the devil took his tongue. That he was a demon, and the Empress and Josette had cut it out in a voodoo ritual to bind him to servitude. That the Chinese gangs cut it out for snitching on their opium rings.

He spoke through the piano. He could make that beast sing.

In the early dawn, when the sun poked its head up over the horizon and them orange rays filled the room, the Empress would say, "Nightingale, play me *Petite Tonkinoise*," and he would dance his fingers over those ivory keys. The Empress, laying there on her silk couch, would cry. As the tears slipped down her big, round cheeks, the girls would come and sit beside her, wrapping their arms around her. Abelard would take off his top hat and stare sheepishly at his feet, and Josette would sway in the doorway, her gaze not so suspicious for a moment, like we were a family. A bunch of misfits, losers, and orphans, sure, but we were bound to each other like a family might be. We sure as shit didn't have no one else, and that's for certain. And those were happy days, all of us together with the song of the Nightingale filling the air with sweet melodies.

It wasn't long before my sister became a soiled dove and joined the Empress' stable. I wasn't ashamed for her. Many a good girl did what they had to do to feed themselves.

As tradition dictated, the Empress brought my sister down to Daly Brothers Big Store and bought her some of the finest and most fashionable clothes. Then she put her in a phaeton, which was an open carriage of sorts drawn by two horses, and paraded her through the streets of the Tenderloin for the benefit of perspective clients. Katie later told me that at one point she looked down to see our father laying drunk in the gutter by the edge of a slough.

They made eye contact.

That was the last time she ever saw him.

Neither of us ever heard a word from him again.

But you know, we were happy. Katie made plenty of money. Price back then for a date was a dollar fifty, but Katie could charge two.

Everything took a bad turn when the Empress got that pianola, or player piano as they're sometimes called. She had that thing shipped all the way from Germany. Back then everything came in by boat.

The day the pianola arrived started off sunny. Abelard and I, along with a few other laborers, sat at the wharf, waiting for H. H. Buhne's tug boat to tow the ship to shore; the sky was clear and blue.

Abelard was stoic and silent as ever, his dark face stony below that tall top hat, but he seemed agitated. Often he would sneak a little smile at me, or place one of his big hands gently and reassuringly on my shoulder, if only for a moment. That day, he did neither.

It took ten big men to lift the crate carrying the player piano onto the carriage. The axels groaning under the burden, the horses strained, the sky grew dark and rain peppered the gravel streets. By the time we had gotten that big crate into the parlor and carefully pried the boards apart, a full blown storm blew in off the bay.

The pianola was a thing of wonder—a Welt-Mignon behemoth made of gleaming black wood embossed with lines of gilded gold. Ornate panes of glass revealed the gears and pneumatics within it. The Empress bought rolls and rolls of music for it to play.

Nightingale hated it.

Refused to even look at it.

The Empress would insert a roll of paper into it and turn it on, the notes would come ringing out, and she would demand that Nightingale play along with it. But he would not. He would sit at his piano, staring down at the ivory keys with his hands hanging at his sides.

"Oh, you sentimental little fool," the Empress would say in her thick French accent, and carry on to the girls about the wonders of modern technology and how it was a new world.

Eventually, Nightingale stopped playing all together and wouldn't come down from his room. Some said he fled in the night and was gone, angered that the Empress had replaced him with a machine.

Of course she procured a roll of music containing *Petite Tonkinoise*, and she would put it into the player piano and lay on her silk couch, teary eyed as it played. But it wasn't the same. That machine had no heart. No feeling. And the girls would seldom come and wrap themselves around her. Josette wouldn't sway in the doorway, and Abelard would not take off his tall hat. Things felt different, and a melancholy seemed to fall over the Palace.

But that wasn't the only thing that changed with the delivery of the pianola. By securing a shipment from Europe, the Empress also made inroads with the shipping industry and secured routes for other merchandise. Opiates to be precise. Opium wasn't even illegal in those days. Not until the Harrison Narcotics Act of 1914. Hell, you could stroll on down to the Pacific Pharmacy on F Street and buy it. But that was watered down laudanum. And if you tried to buy in bulk, anything more than a small amount that took away a headache, you were looked down on and soon whispered about. The Empress procured large shipments of a refined product whose purity and potency was legendary. I never saw them, but I heard they came in brick sized bundles, wrapped in crimson paper, with that image of the Virgin weeping blood embossed upon them.

I understood the girls wanting to smoke a little of the stuff. Katie's strain showed in her eyes and how she walked: as if she was ripped apart inside.

But they weren't smoking raw opium. The Empress knew smoking it was relatively ineffectual and had a chemist purify the opium into black tar heroin and instructed them in how to inject it with a syringe.

Some of the girls nodded out and couldn't stop their scratching, digging their nails into their skin till they bled. The ones that ceased to function as ladies of the evening would disappear.

It scared me.

I told Katie one night when I found her scouring the cupboards, looking for chocolate.

"You've got to slow down with that stuff. You're not looking so good, and I'm worried."

"You don't understand. I need it." Her watery eyes begged me not to judge her. "This isn't the Empress' only house, you know. There's another one, on the other side of the wharf. A small, dark place, where she entertains business men and senators. The elite. And they do things. Have rituals. And they hurt girls. Hurt them bad."

And like that, my tough Katie burst into inconsolable tears.

Then that Italian pimp Dmitry. He had this girl named Florence. Baby faced and cute, who ended up leaving him for the Empress.

One day, Dmitry burst into the Palace, angry as hell. "I know what you are up to. Turning these girls into addicts so they spend all their money on your dope. You're nothing but a slave driver."

Abelard hauled him out the back door and into the alley and dumped him in the trash. "And this is your cracker, huh? Got you a big'ole, black cracker to take care of your white slaves. This ain't the end of this. Hear me, you voodoo bitch? This ain't the end of it.

Two days later, the police found Dmitry swinging by his neck from a rafter in his little, back-alley house. The coroner ruled it a suicide. Though how had he managed to sever his own penis and scrotum and shove them so far down his throat before hanging himself?

Seems the Empress had all the right people in her pocket and on her payroll. She was a smart lady. And practical.

I don't know if it was Dmitry's big mouth or just all that heroin flowing up the coast that led them Chinese to Madame Sheri.

Near dawn on a Sunday morning, the place was relatively empty, a few loggers and fishermen up with the girls in their rooms and a couple of local drunks at the bar.

I swept up the mud from the loggers, a never-ending job. The pianola played a ragtime song, and a few of the girls nodded out on the sofa. The Empress sipped tea and whispered with Josette when the door flew open.

Six Chinese burst into the parlor, dressed in their changshan, head-hugging prince hats, and braided pony tails.

They beelined for the Empress, dao swords raised over their heads.

Abelard crossed his arms and retrieved two small pistols, one grasped in each hand. He fired, filling the room with the acrid smell of gunpowder.

Three of the men fell.

Josette pulled a straight razor from a garter on her leg and sliced a man's throat open.

Abelard charged another one, grappling with him and falling to the floor.

The last of the Tong stepped up to the Empress, howling and ready to strike.

It happened so fast.

The Empress raised her arms to defend herself from the blow when the most bizarre thing happened.

Nightingale returned.

He saved the Empress.

No longer the little African man in the bowler hat and bowtie playing the piano.

He was naked.

He had leathery, black wings, like a bat might have.

His eyes as yellow as a daffodil.

And his mouth. It was horrible.

He came flying into that room and grabbed that last Chinaman by his pony tail, pulled his head back, and ripped a fountain of blood from the man's throat.

The Empress wept hysterically.

"Oh, my Nightingale, I knew you'd be back. I just knew it."

And that demon Nightingale, fell upon her bosoms and pressed its ugly head against her shoulder. It tucked its wings in against itself, and cooed as she stroked it.

The drunks gawked. A few lumberjacks stood frozen on the steps. The Empress pulled herself up, little Nightingale still wrapped in her big arms, and pushed a logger aside, disappearing up those big, grand steps.

I ran out the door, something inside just compelling me to get away, and stumbled down to the water. I stood staring at that black bay for a spell, my mind a beehive, when the distance grew orange.

I hightailed it back to see the Palace engulfed in an inferno.

Half that block burned down as the sun rose over the bay and the fog rolled in against the crackling blaze.

My sister did not make it out.

Not many of the girls did, high as they were.

No one ever saw the Empress again.

Rumors abounded that she survived the fire and set up shop in some other town: Crescent City, Portland, Seattle.

The authorities ruled out arson, even though some fellow down at the saloons was bragging about having torched the place.

I left. Went down to the coast of Mendocino where I learned to be a carpenter, working in Fort Bragg.

They pulled many a body from that place. And though the corpses were charred to a point past recognition, there weren't no midget's corpse in those smoldering remains.

Perhaps that's another reason I left that strange town behind. The idea of that demon alive there was too much of a burden for me to bear.

THE HEALING POWER OF SEVENS

Randy D. Rubin

The seventh skull, beetle-eaten, boiled, and bleached white as snow is at last in my trembling grasp. It has been seven-hundred-seventy-seven years since I was first bewitched, since I was poisoned and left for dead. I have searched for these skulls for what seems an eternity. I took the first two easily enough, putting enough of a sleeping potion in their jugs to put an elephant down, and as they slept, my blade sliced their heads off like carrot tops.

The third one I split with his own pick axe.

His head came off in a few well-placed whacks.

They kept me a prisoner here in this sty.

They allowed me to cook and to clean for them.

On the fourth, I used his blade-sharpened shovel to pry off his skull.

Chopping through bone made it curl-tipped and blunt.

The fifth and the sixth were at work in their mine. They swung their heavy tools at the walls of rock, chipping away indiscriminate cavernous miles of my life.

I grew older, I grew bored, and I soon tired of them.

They did not grow. They were short of mind and body, short-sighted, short-tempered little men, and they chipped away at me with their short but heavy tools, wanting to rock my walls.

All the while, I'm waiting and wanting and wishing for my prince to come and spirit me away before it was too late. The dumb one and the doctor, yin and yang, fire and ice, gone from their heads filled with knowledge and the bliss of ignorance. It took seven days for the beetles to clean the dumb one's skull and only seven hours to devour the sum of the doctor's knowledge.

I have the last one's skull, and I've made a fitting resting place for it among the skull trees of his brethren. He sits on his own pedestal, my favorite of all the seven dwarves, for he was too shy to take me when his brothers had their turns. He was Bashful. I believe that was their term of endearment.

I think the more adequate term is gay.

He never touched me, so he was taken last.

I have bleached his bashful brain bone a clean, bright Snow White.

Like these seven little bastards used to call me.

THE DRAGON

R. Judas Brown

Lavender knew no one would come for her. Bad things happened to the daughters of poor, dairy farmers every day. The best she hoped for in life was a good marriage arrangement to a solid provider. Her dad only just found that arrangement with the town miller, a man her dad's age. His apprentice looked like more fun, but the miller was well off.

Then she had been taken.

Fire from the sky.

A slam from behind, knocking her flat before the ground fell away impossibly fast.

Trees and rivers rushed by as she hung from yellow, bony talons until the darkness crept mercifully into her vision to steal her terror away.

She awoke on a bed of sharp sticks in a cave reeking of sulfur. Confused, she stood slowly, trying to find some semblance of sanity in the dark. A glowing sliver of daylight burned around the covered mouth of the cave.

Her feet froze before she had taken a full step as what she thought was a boulder in the dark shifted.

A long tail whipped as a pointed snout swung to regard her. It filled the cave entrance, a giant, scaly mass—a creature renowned for merciless violence and calculated malevolence. Lavender jerked back, tripping on the hem of her skirt in panic. Hands and arms scraped along jagged edges as she fell into the pile of sticks. When she came face to face with a skull, the truth shuddered through her.

The terror started with a shake, starting small at first, which grew until the pile of bones rattled. She flung herself back. Far-off, someone screamed. Full-throated, it echoed through the rock, rebounding until the sound assaulted her from all sides.

Lavender wanted it to stop. She needed the gibbering, shrieking wretch to shut up and quit hurting her ears. Lavender needed quiet so she could think.

Her throat hurt.

She forced her mouth closed, and the scream trailed into a whimper. The dragon snorted, like an amused human, and in the short flare of light, she saw them. They perched in a pile of scorched gravel and melted slag. Oblong and leathery, the brief gout of flame backlit them, and through the membranous shell, each contained a curled shape, already the size of a mastiff.

Old tales left no doubt what baby dragons ate.

A terrible, sleepless night passed. The gurgling rhythm of the giant reptile's snoring was joined sporadically by the arrhythmic tapping from the nest. Toward dawn, the sound sharpened. Bursts of activity grew more frequent and insistent. The dim early-morning revealed spider-webbed cracks across the chitinous surfaces. She told herself that she imagined the shifting of the shells. If true, it wouldn't be for long. As the day brightened, hope faded.

Outside, a shout. It repeated, and on the third try, it was joined by what sounded like a skillet hitting a breadboard. The dragon snorted awake. Slitted-eyes cracked open, and the beast rose to fill the chamber. Stomping heavily, it emerged with a deafening roar.

Lavender was left with the eggs, one of which rocked against its siblings.

Defiant roars joined with painful grunts. The booming rush of fire blew through the cave entrance with the parching heat of an oven as a horse screamed.

Pieces flaked and fell.

A short talon, the size of an index finger, broke through. It disappeared, and a puff of flame shot out of a leathery snout. Jaws snapped as it worked at the opening. With a resounding crack, it gave way, and the beast's head was free. Yellow eyes filled with a hungry malevolence.

Lavender didn't have the strength left to cry.

It pushed against the shell, and a single wing came free to beat against the outside of the egg before sharp steel slammed through its collarbone, piercing deep into the body and through its heart.

Lavender slumped against the wall, pulse pounding as she struggled to catch her breath.

The man was tall, larger than the miller's apprentice, and covered from head to toe in metal. He moved from egg to egg, slamming his sword deep into each, working it back and forth. Gore and ichor pooled on the floor by the time he finished.

Hand under the edge of his helm, he worked at some unseen strap and lifted it from his head.

Ringlets of dark hair escaped from his sweat-dampened cap to and brushed away from steel gray eyes. Short stubble did nothing to lessen the strength of his chin, nor the fullness of his lips. He surveyed the cave before his gaze locked on her, still slouched, panting against the wall.

"Well, pleasant greetings to you."

He smiled, and Lavender found it much harder to catch her breath.

"Where is the dragon's treasure?"

"I-I saw no treasure."

Lavender rose to her feet. His gaze traveled over her body, pausing, then eventually returning to her breasts. She clutched her arms around herself, suddenly aware of the way her fear-sweat made her clothes cling to her body.

"I don't see any place to hide gold, but that doesn't mean there's nothing of value. What might be your name?"

He stepped forward. Without thought, Lavender tried to step back, but the cave wall had her firmly trapped.

"La-Lavender."

"Lavender…Your Highness," he corrected as he stepped close, lifting a hand to hold her chin. The silence stretched out, and Lavender balled one hand into a fist to keep it from shaking.

"Lavender, Your Highness."

"Good. I do deserve something for my trouble, don't you think?"

His other hand reached behind her to find the small of her back. His grip almost as hard as the wall as it pulled her closer.

"I—"

His mouth pressed roughly onto hers. Blind panic set in. She opened her mouth to protest, and his tongue, meaty and wet, pushed in. Lavender struggled, but he held her tight. She couldn't breathe, and the cave closed in around her. Just as pricks of light popped at the edge of her vision, he relented, stepping back.

"I think this is your first time, hmm?"

The cave walls spun around her, and she clung to the frayed edges of consciousness. For a moment, she was glad for his steadying arm at her waist. Had she fallen, she would have passed out, and she did not want to be around him in that state. As she desperately searched for an escape, his perfect mouth formed the warmest smile.

"I'm sorry, fairest. Please, let us leave this bloody work."

Lavender let herself be led from the cave. Her legs wavered like river reeds as she walked. At the entrance, she slipped on loose rocks, and a hand supported her in a far too familiar place, and was gone. She squinted in the late morning's brightness.

The earth was scorched in wide swathes around the gashed and bloody beast. Small fires still burned in scattered clumps, one of which looked like a horse next to a man's charred corpse.

A gasp slipped from her lips, drawing his attention.

"Poor Bernard. He was a good squire that knew his place."

He guided her around the flames and over a small hillock. She almost balked as he entered a copse of trees, but his arm still held and supported her. In the middle of the trees, a large warhorse stamped nervously around the edge of a small lake. As he lowered her to a fallen stump, her legs gave out and a wild tremble shook her body.

Lavender looked wildly up at him, waiting for him to lunge, to feel his hands imprisoning her as his weight held her down. Instead, he backed away, hands raised in an easing gesture.

"I want to apologize for…what I did. The blood was hot after the battle. You must understand. I couldn't help myself."

He squatted. His gaze didn't leave her, but he seemed more in control.

Her sweat cooled as her heart slowed.

"My name is Prince Justin. I am afraid I have been at court too long, grown too used to people knowing my name and playing childish games of power. You must understand."

Lavender's brain tried, desperately, to piece together reality. Dragons and a prince, like she was in a festival mummer's play.

"I beg you to forgive me and erase the stain on my honor."

"Of course. You did save me, Your Highness. "

"Excellent," he said as he stood and went to the horse. He calmed the beast, shushing it as he worked to control the bridle and avoid the odd gnashing bite. The stomping eased, and the flaring nostrils gentled. For her part, Lavender followed suit by getting control over her own, racing, emotions. When he returned carrying a saddle bag, she choked down the remains of her anxiety.

"I am sorry about your squire. He was brave."

"Yes. He did as told, for the most part. His distraction worked as planned though I had hoped to see him live, or, at the least, find some coin to pay his family."

"It is good of you to think of them."

"Isn't it? Well, I am afraid my horse will be too skittish to ride us out of here today. We will spend the night. Tomorrow, we will begin the journey back to my father's castle."

"But. I- Your Highness, I would very much like to return home. My poor dad must think me dead."

"No. With Bernard dead, you are my only witness. I can take a piece of the beast to show its death, but will need your witness to prove my hand slayed it. And saved you, of course."

"But I was in the cave. I saw nothing but the eggs."

"I will tell you about it. How else would the poets and bards know my struggle? Later. Right now, I need to clean up. Make a fire."

He tossed a small pouch at her feet that flipped open to let a small striker and stone tumble free, a bit of frayed rope tangled around them. Without waiting for an answer—he was a prince—he sat heavily and worked at the straps of his knee cops. Lavender choked down a protest; it seemed petty, and he had saved her. Her legs felt mostly solid as she stood, so she left him there, pulling at his armor.

Gathering wood took longer than it should. Once out of immediate sight of the pond, a real fear remained. Away from the prince's sword, every rustled bush and odd chitter made her jump. When the breeze shifted to bring a wisp of sulfur to her nose, she shook again and stumbled back to camp as fast as she could, all the way promising herself she wasn't running. No matter how fast her feet moved, she wasn't running.

She burst into the clearing, gulping air. She turned, looking for the prince. Except for the horse quietly foraging, it was empty. For one panicked moment, she thought he had abandoned both his skittish beasts in the name of quieter travel. Then her breath caught in her throat.

He stood at the lake's edge, naked except for his small clothes and the afternoon sun filtering through the leaves. His back was broad and muscular. His armor-matted hair was now a rich chestnut wave that reached between his shoulder blades. Effortlessly, almost with grace, he stepped out of the small clothes and into the clear water. He was as firm down through his calves. Her pulse echoed in another part of her, turning her away.

As fire burned in her face, she swore a chuckle carried up from the water.

A small fire crackled by the time he walked up behind her. Her ankle throbbed from her dash through the woods and an unseen root. Lavender focused on the pain, grasping at her anger. He had ordered her like she was his servant, but she couldn't keep thoughts about his state of dress from her mind.

At least, it's twilight lest a blush give me away. Though, I won't see as much.

He stepped past her, now wearing trousers, though his broad chest remained bare. Hard as she tried, her gaze kept drifting back to its thick lines.

"Your pardon, my lady. A prince must travel clean—image, you see—and I fear Bernard's poor horse carried my fresh tunics."

Lavender nodded agreement, schooling her face to hide what her father called "doe eyes".

"I see."

"So you do. The food will be light tonight. Tomorrow, we will sleep at an inn. The next night you will be my royal guest. The better to spread word of my victory?"

"As you please."

Justin handed her a parcel from the saddlebag along with a short, sharp knife. Undoing the rough linen, she found a hard cheese, a loaf of bread, and a few dates. She thought briefly of arguing, but she understood where a dairy farmer's daughter stood in the presence of a prince. She cut the bread and cheese, offering him the larger sections. They ate in silence for several minutes as the sun faded.

The first pinpricks of stars peeked down from the indigo sky.

Justin hummed. As the tune gained direction, she swayed and words emerged from the melody.

Lavender had heard better voices. This song was far different from the lively tunes played during harvest festivals, the music reserved instead of energetic. Instead of a lusty washerwoman or foolish man tricked by elves, his songs told of kings and knights, the pageantry of life at court, and princesses of golden hair trapped in towers or courted by honorable lovers.

Lavender drifted to sleep under the stars, new music filling her dreams.

The miles passed slowly. Lavender sat atop the prince's horse; he walked alongside, hand on the bridle. Nervous when he first lifted her onto the massive beast, his hands on her waist and the reassurance in his voice eased her fears.

While the horse lazed his way down the road and the sun crossed the sky, Justin regaled her with stories of court. He told her tales of his embassy to far off lands, of travels across the great seas, and his training as a knight. Finally, after a brief stop at midday by a cool stream, she asked the question that had bothered her dreams and worried at the edge of their conversation the whole day.

"The songs you were singing last night, are they real? I mean, is that what life is like away from the farm?"

"I think that it's what some people think life is like, what they want it to be like. Had you never heard them before? Some are quite old but have been favorites at court since my grandfather's reign."

"Truly, no."

"What are your songs, common songs, like?"

"We sing about the harvest and the Goddess. The things that matter in the village, they must seem very small to you."

"A wide world, and you are content the stay blindly at home? Yours must be an innocent existence."

Her cheeks flamed at the not so innocent thoughts she had as she watched him down by the water. There was an awkward pause as she chased taut, muscled thighs from her mind.

"You don't think they're real, the songs, Your Highness?"

"When we get to my father's castle, I will be a prince. Here, alone, I am Justin."

He looked up at Lavender, brow smudged with road dirt, and her cheeks burned at his attention. When he chuckled, she couldn't help but duck her head away.

"My tutor, Charles, would say it is foolishness."

"And you…Justin?"

"I think I would say that foolishness has its place."

The conversation lapsed. As the road wended on, Lavender hummed his songs, and his eyes twinkled at her.

As the light outside faded, the inn's taproom took on a glow from the candles and the small fireplace dominating the eastern wall. The majority of the tables had started empty, but as word of the royal guest spread, more and more onlookers trickled in. Farmers from the surrounding countryside and townsfolk who never made it farther than the next village would file in, look around the room as if searching, before finding a table where they could cast surreptitious glances at their table.

Lavender couldn't decide if Justin was so used to the gawking that he showed no notice, or if he possibly had eyes only for her.

From the time they had entered the village, he had barely taken his attention away. When he had, as he ordered the food and rooms, it had returned quickly, and with an intensity she could feel. Even when other women, with far looser bodices and more they weren't hiding, approached, they simply didn't exist. Her cheeks warmed, not at what they offered, but that she rendered such dangerous women harmless.

She struggled to keep her thoughts at the table, not between bedsheets.

The two of them seemed to move through different worlds, yet here they were. Together.

"This has been refreshing," Justin said, mirroring Lavender's thoughts and causing a flash of heat to run up her neck.

"You honor me, Your Highness."

"I am used to the women who populate my father's court. Every word, every action is done for gain. You don't think that way, do you?"

"I don't know what could make someone so jaded that they could not just enjoy your royal company."

"No guile. No hidden motive," he said, pursing his lips into a distracting bow.

Had she upset him? His gaze was far away, leaving her alone to fidget with the remains of her food and formulate an apology.

Justin cleared his throat. "Do you know many legends about dragons?"

"Fairy stories aren't something I had much time for, even as a child. I have heard some about wizards and knights fighting to save their lovers. Glorious castles…" The girlish lilt her voice reached embarassed her.

"Yes. It didn't turn out to be just a tale, did it? I have the claws to prove that when we get to the palace. And what of the rest of the stories? Every man who has a woman of marriageable age, and some who aren't, bargain with my father for a chance to wed into the royal family. Those with fame want my coffers. Families with wealth want my power. Men with power want my throne behind their machinations as a sign of legitimacy. You would want none of that?"

Lavender's heart dropped from her chest, and the warmth that had spread up her neck became fire in her cheeks. She fought for breath against a bodice that seemed suddenly far too tight, pulling at it under the table in a vain attempt to loosen its ties. The question hung in the air between them.

When she was finally able to answer, her voice came out surprisingly steady.

"I could not imagine wanting anything more from a husband than for him to be who he is."

"The stories do speak of maidens beyond reproach."

The prince looked through her, weighing and appraising. Lavender steeled herself to hold up under his gaze.

I'm not as tiny as I feel. I am as much a woman as any stuffed strumpet.

With a curt nod, he gestured over one of the spurned wenches. He waved the plates away, and she flounced off, arms full.

Justin rose and circled the table. Lavender made to rise, but his hand directed, unmistakably, that she remain seated. Proud tears threatened, then her mouth dropped open as he, His Royal Highness Prince Justin, dropped to one knee in front of her. Silence crashed over the taproom. Lavender trembled, her body threatening to go loose, as all eyes centered on their table. He couldn't—

"Lavender, will you be wed to me and sit by my side as Princess Consort?"

How could—she would have to ask her father. He would have to ask her father. They had just met. This was—

Storm clouds gathered in the ridges of his brow. She was ruining the fairy tale. Her fairy tale. She tried to make the words sound like a line from her favorite mummer's play.

"My noble prince, 'twould be a great honor to be your lady wife, whatever your station."

Prince Justin smiled as the taproom erupted in a cheer.

Trumpets fanfared into the clear summer sky as pennants snapped in the wind whipping through the castle's stone crenellations. Lavender rocked in the war horse's saddle where she sat sideways across her rescuer's lap.

No, her betrothed's.

She could settle into that word in a very physical way. She shimmied her shoulder deeper into the crook of Prince Justin's arm, imagining the strapping chest underneath the plate and chain that still smelled of soot from the great wyrm's breath.

She told herself she could do this.

It was her happy ending.

As they passed through the streets of cheering onlookers, ever closer to the high walls of the castle, reality set in. As Lavender wrung her clammy hands and shrank deeper into Justin's chest, she felt like nothing so much as a little girl playing dress-up.

To his credit, the Chamberlin barely hesitated when Justin introduced her as his betrothed. Lavender still noticed.

They followed him down a long passageway lined with more glass than any farmhouse. The garden beyond burst with flowers and flitting birds of every hue. If not for Justin's hand guiding her along by the arm, she would have fallen behind in her awe. Instead, by the time they stopped, her breath came in gulps and her arm throbbed under the loose sleeve of her chemise.

The chamberlain slipped between two large doors that shushed closed behind him. Beside her, Justin shifted aimlessly. His unease contagious, she found her other hand repeatedly balling in the side of her skirt before smoothing it back flat.

After a couple of minutes of eternity, the rush of twin doors thrown open jerked through her body.

"His Royal Highness Justin and the...Lavender."

An audience chamber stretched before her in shining tile and opulent gold, large enough to fit her dad's house next to itself and space to walk between the two.

Justin strode forward, leaving her no choice but to move with him, even though all she desperately wanted to do was hide. Along the edges of the room, groups of courtiers milled. They turned to watch. If she looked behind her, would she find the crowd filled in behind them like a pack of wolves cornering prey?

Then, they stood in front of the throne, and terror chased mere anxiety away.

Justin swooped down into a deep, graceful bow. Belatedly, Lavender tried a curtsy, struggling to remember the coquettish courtesy she had seen the tavern wenches use toward Justin. Halfway down, she teetered before catching her balance. Somewhere behind her came a snicker, and her eyes burned as she bit down on her lip to stop a tremble.

"We hear that congratulations are in order, my son."

"Your Majesty, Father, I have slain the dragon for your honor. Its dew claw and those of its young, are yours for the glory of your throne."

Justin held out a bag that crusted at the bottom with dried blood. A murmur ran through the crowd.

"You must be weary from the battle and journey. Where is Bernard?"

"Bernard charged forward. Bravely done, but foolish. Lord Estaran will know his son died with honor."

"Again you return without your squire, but not alone this time it seems?"

"Yes, this fair maid was taken by the foul beast." Justin pitched his voice to carry through the hall. "All know that a dragon quenches its bloody appetite with only the noblest and most virtuous virgin flesh."

"So she is noble then. We have been misinformed?"

"Father, natural order has proclaimed her so. The very natural order that proclaims the rights and nobility of those who sit upon our thrones, our liege lords. It is what tradition and nature demand. As such, to codify nature's will, Lavender is to be my bride and take her place at my side as princess consort."

"I see. Let us speak of this in my chambers a moment. But first—"

The king descended the stairs of his dais. Lavender kept her gaze downcast and her muscles taut to still them when he stopped directly in front of her. Old hands, hard and sharp as daggers, took hers and raised them to cracked lips.

"My dear Lavender, before I retire with my son to council, allow us to extend our warmest welcome to the family."

His eyes were jagged glaciers.

Whatever passed between father and son behind closed doors, the announcement was made in the king's court and heralded through the land. That much she easily gathered by the endless procession of tailors and seamstresses that paraded through her chambers in the next few days. Her life became exactly as she had pretended with her husk dolls. At first.

Her days filled with the softest silks, and the jewels tied around her slender neck rivaled the stars. On the third day, a boisterous little man with a funny mustache taught her dances, yelling in a guttural language when she placed her feet wrong. A spinster followed, mouth puckered and dry, who taught her how to eat, frowning disdain at her choice of forks. Each day seemed to bring another torment twisted from her girlish dreams. Finally, after a particularly horrid dance lesson that left her feet sore and near tears, Justin came to her.

"Your Highness. I-I am happy to see you. I tried asking about you, but only the guards will respond to me. They said they couldn't leave, and weren't allowed to let me look for you myself. "

"Court is a dangerous place for the unwary. You must try to understand. There are those who would use you, hurt you to get to me. Once you are mine, this will be worth it."

Lavender bit her lip, struggling to control the frustration tumbling through her.

"I am afraid my responsibilities are going to pull me away until our wedding night. Is there anything I can do to ease your time until we can be together?"

She drew a deep breath, before the words fell out in a rush.

"I would ask two boons of you, my betrothed. If my father could escort me down the aisle, giving my hand to Your Highness, my day would be all the sweeter. Also, when we arrived at court, we passed a garden the likes of which I have never before seen. It would ease the wait for our day. Might I visit, with proper escort, of course?"

The prince's smile made Lavender's insides loose and warm despite it all. He crossed the room to her and took her hands in his. As he lifted them to his lips, a warm pressure rushed through her hips and up her spine.

"I will send for your—our father. As for the garden, I cannot bear to see you unhappy. Lavender is my most cherished flower, and flowers need the sun. Give me some of your patience while I arrange it. You will be in full bloom on our wedding day."

A thrill jumped through her, and she managed a nod of agreement.

Five days passed. The dance instructor refused to give up, the spinster never smiled, and the seamstresses came for ever more measurements.

They were five lonely days. In the time between visits, when she tired of pacing the room, she napped. When she could sleep no more, she flipped through the gilt-paged holy book on the vanity, trying to make sense of the lines and loops stretching across the pages. Finally, she just stared at the wall and cried.

The sharp rap at the door choked her sobs.

Lavender dabbed at her eyes with a kerchief. There would be no helping the splotches. Unsure, she eased the door to her chambers open. Outside, a steel-eyed guard stood, fist poised to knock again.

"His Highness invites you to join him in the Royal Garden."

"I would be happy to. Allow me a moment to compose myself."

Lavender turned back to her room, intent on her wash basin as she shut the door, when a hob-nailed boot stopped its momentum.

"His Highness is not accustomed to waiting."

After being kept to her chambers against her will for so long, frustration boiled, but the glint in the guardsman's eyes had a brittle edge. She might be his liege lord's promised, but he obviously saw her as no more than a cushion-kept prisoner. Despite wanting to look presentable when Justin saw her, it seemed best not to test him.

He led her through the castle halls. As they passed servants and courtiers, distinguishable from each other by the cut and make of their clothes, their eyes followed. Half-hidden behind feigned disinterest or mock bows lay stinging scrutiny. She ducked her head to hide her puffy eyes and school her step to show what the spinster had called a "lady's carriage." By the time she entered the garden, her skin throbbed with shame.

The larks trilled.

Their songs filled the courtyard, echoing from the stone walls. Hummingbirds darted flower to flower. The deepest violets pushed against walking paths that led to roses larger than her hands. Morning-glories crept up walls where honey bees bumbled between blossoms, then slipped up into the sky, carrying their treasure back to the hive. The world erupted in a breathtaking spray of colors.

Lavender closed her eyes and tilted her head back. For the first time in what felt like months, the sun warmed her face. A whisper of a breeze stirred through the garden, carrying the scent of each flower to her. A wren whistled a merry tune, which joined the larks' to blend a seamless harmony. Arms raised, she floated on her every sense, lost to time.

As long as she had this refuge, she could endure whatever struggle the capital could offer her.

"My brightest flower among all these plain things? They will wilt of shame lest you are careful."

Reality fell, and the courtyard spun.

Justin grabbed her before she fell. Closing her eyes, she forced the fantasy away, allowing herself to steady before trying one of the curtsies she had practiced so much.

"Your Highness startled me. I lost myself in your wonderful garden. "

"It was and affectation of the late queen. It reminded her of her family's winter residence when she was a child. Somewhere is the bench she would retreat to when my father was unbearable."

"She had fine taste. I am sorry I will not have a chance to meet her."

"Yes. I suppose I feel the same about your family."

"My mother died when I was young."

"Your father, though, I would have liked to meet."

Lavender's stomach dropped.

"My knight said the home was burnt to a shell. None had seen him since your disappearance, so it is best to be realistic. Here, now. I've got you. Don't dwell. Look at this garden. It is yours."

Lavender clung to consciousness. The sounds became a riotous assault. Feelers cracked mortar from stone. The butterflies snatched from the air in hungry beaks. Beneath the cloying floral smells hid the rot of the unkempt plants devouring what had once been the queen's refuge.

His brow darkened as he called to her escort.

"My lady is weary. See her back to her chambers. Dearest, I am afraid I will not see you until our wedding. Know that you will not leave my thoughts."

With that, she was handed to the cold grip of her guard. He hustled her through the halls, half-shoving her ahead of him. She stumbled, but his pace never wavered. She might have cried out in pain, but she was beyond feeling.

The same looks, some from the same people they passed earlier, mocked her in the halls. Through corridors, around corners, and past the nondescript wood door to her chambers was a foggy memory. The room she so recently wanted to escape now wrapped her in security.

At least, it still had a sense of routine.

Time disjointed.

She was in bed, then in the middle of a dance lesson. The master screamed at her, but there was no name left to be called. Not until the morning of her wedding did she find a spark of hope.

In its lace, pearls, and hoops, the beautiful dress brought her back.

Her maids bathed her. The seamstress dressed her, sewing final alterations as bells tolled throughout the capital. Her ladies-in-waiting arrived, each a daughter of some important personage, were introduced, and she didn't mind when they retired to the opposite side of the room to war amongst themselves for primacy.

When the knock at her door finally came, she answered with purpose.

The late queen's brother, who had been chosen to stand in her father's stead, proffered a hand. To his credit, she barely noticed the sneer that curled his lip at her touch. He bowed formally. She curtsied. The numbness deep inside her was joined by the spark of a growing fire. She was marrying a prince, in his castle. With Justin's love and authority behind her, the trials would soon be over. Maybe she could set things right.

As they entered the hall, a murmur ran through the crowd, admiration rather than mockery. The royal wedding had demanded the best, and they crafted as a work of art. This was a princess's wedding.

She lifted her chin to the courtesans as high as they had lifted their noses to her. In a recess to the left of the royal dais, bows drew across taut strings, and the crowd quieted. When they stopped before the prince and his groomsmen, she curtsied once more to her escort. To her surprise, he bowed deeply in return.

"Thank you for letting me escort you, princess. It was an honor to stand for you."

"You have our welcome." She tried out the feel of power on her tongue.

There, in front of the king, witnessed by a crowd of strangers, they said the words tradition demanded. For a moment, despite the pain, she realized her dreams.

Lavender sat at the head table next to her new husband. By courtesy, she was Her Highness Lavender, Princess Consort. Examining the castle's feast hall, she hoped she did not look nearly so out of place as she felt. She picked the wrong utensil from the treasure of silvered metal laid in front of her. Snickers. They appraised her like a faire merchant inspected a calf.

Mimicking the face of her spinster tutor, she glared them to silence.

The titters faded.

Justin talked to any who would listen. The feast would continue until sundown when the scraps were carted out to the beggars. Until then the plates, truncheons, and especially the glasses were kept full. No matter how set their owners seemed on emptying them.

As the afternoon wore on, more and more ale replaced the food. The water disappeared in favor of wine.

Jesters japed, nobles drank—a royal wedding.

Well-wishers approached.

There was a lot of toasting.

As the wine flowed, Justin's songs became slurred and bawdy. When the reception escalated to shouting, a florid duke took offense. As the men wrestled, jostling tables, the king stood up. A hush fell over the crowd, and a pair of guards jumped to hold the prince.

"It is time for Prince Justin and his new wife to retire to their bedchamber."

A cheer went up from the hall as Lavender's ladies-in-waiting appeared at her side. A nervous twist jerked through her stomach. She had thought about this since that first night. The physical reality of him.

Tears threatened her. This was it.

Her ladies escorted her through the crowd. The people jeered openly. Strange, rough hands reached between her maids to grab at her. She stumbled as one hand found a lacing at the back of her bodice, jerking the knot free before one of her escorts could slap it away. A looseness spread across her shoulders. If it slipped, her corset and chemise would cover her modesty.

Behind her, they cheered for the a conquering hero as his knights guided him away from the head table. A catcall carried above the raucous. After the long wait, she needed to be his, to feel his strength around her-- inside her.

A large bed draped with opulent blankets and furs dominated the prince's chambers. With only the flame from the fireplace to light the room, the edges and corners lay hidden in flickering shadow. Before she could protest, her ladies finished the job of unlacing her. They slipped off the bodice and corset, sending pinpricks along her skin as circulation returned.

She stood barefoot, nothing covering her but the gauzy chemise. The ladies filed from the room. The last turned back, clasping Lavender's hands with the first bit of true compassion she'd seen in the capital.

"I know this is your first time. The prince can be…energetic. Relax."

Her final lady-in-waiting spun and hurried from the room, leaving her alone and confused.

Rough laughter proceeded them.

The prince and his escorts jostled in. Lavender had nowhere to go. They stopped abruptly, openly leering.

She crossed her arms to cover herself.

Justin held his arms out, and his men undid his jerkin. The meaning of their murmured words as he undressed to his small clothes were plain.

She shrank into the shadow, hoping the darkness would conceal what her shift didn't.

Offering a few coarse words of final encouragement, and some not subtle glances in her direction, they left the room.

Justin slid an iron bolt home behind them.

They were alone.

"Don't be shy. I've waited for this."

"Oh, I have, too."

She stepped into the light, willing her arms to her side.

"I have wanted nothing but to be held by your arms, my prince."

He met her at the foot of the bed, chest and arms thick and smooth under her hands as she sought their protection. He leaned in close, and she tilted her head toward the hollow of his shoulder. Lavender sought a moment of peace in the sheltering strength of his presence.

His mouth pressed hard onto hers.

She pulled away from the pain, pushing at his chest.

He followed her, tongue probing into her mouth. Pushing against him, she arched her back, seeking space, but his arms, well used to sword and shield, were granite. Panicked, she beat against him without effect. Her feet slipped out from under her in the struggle, and he pushed her away, flinging her hard onto the bed.

Her breath came in ragged gasps as he stood over her. Fierce protection morphed dark and menacing. She darted a glance toward the door, but he grabbed her knee, fingers digging painfully into the joint.

Roughly, he pulled her toward the edge of the bed.

"Oh, no. I've been forced to wait far too long," he growled.

She kicked his thigh.

The back of his hand cracked across her cheek and set the room spinning.

He let go of her, but she was too stunned to move.

He shed his small clothes, his cock hard and red in the dim light.

Lavender clawed at the bed, pulling to scramble away, but the blankets slipped. He yanked her back.

She screamed.

Again his hand lashed out, and her body went limp around her.

"You are too good to pass up. A woman of marriageable age that legend said was beyond reproach, even if most of the court know you are some country simpleton. Better yet, you were cheap, without even a father to auction your flower. You will just cost me a few good fucks until you get me a son. You get the better end of the bargain because you get me."

Her chemise ripped away.

Her stunned body denied her a final defensive struggle as he thrust into her.

The world went numb.

Lavender shared his bed chamber several times a month when the midwives claimed she was ripe. She gave in to avoid punishment.

After months with no sign of a son, the punishments came whether she fought or not.

The vengeful ember that had carried her through the nuptials faded.

She became a different class of servant.

Lavender learned to smile and wave. She learned to accept the beatings as better than the alternative. She listened to loose words from servants and chambermaids and learned of the barmaid who had been given to knights when she cried too much. A kitchen waif fell off a parapet after leaving the prince's chamber too early in the evening.

The tales were numerous, and the people recounting them did so with a savage gleam in their eye.

The pain echoed through her.

Lavender retreated into drink.

Whether through duty or sympathy, her servants more than willingly kept her ewer full.

Fire lanced up the side of her face, cheek to temple.

The swelling would not flower into an ugly bruise.

She had plenty of experience with the difference.

She eased her legs over the side of the bed. The rugs that covered the floor saved her from the cold stone but did nothing for the aching in her hips.

Lavender added a bit of wood to the fire. She let go of her robe, allowing it to slip to the floor.

Like my dignity.

Sequestered away from any chance visitor wandering into her room, she let herself cry.

A knock at the chamber door came earlier in the day than usual. Her fingers curled into her palm, nails stabbing to drive the tears away, before it eased open. The usual maid was followed by a young man, no older than a page. His face went crimson when he saw her in just her chemise, and a spiteful part of her was glad for someone else's discomfort as he ducked his head.

"Your Highness." He bowed, eyes still downcast, offering a polite hand she ignored.

The maid proffered a small woven blanket, a present from some baroness currying favor, and wrapped it around Lavender to save him any more embarrassment.

"Who might you be?"

"I am—I am Count Farfallo's eldest, Jeffrey. My father bids me deliver a gift to His Royal Highness."

Count Farfallo was master of a few rocks and a goat herd far from the capital. The young man shifted, and his face maintained a bright red. The maid excused herself. Leaving her alone with a man this young wasn't proper, but everyone knew she wasn't a proper princess.

"Why then are you in my chambers, young master?"

"I, ah, heard that the prince—that is, your Lord Husband, had spent the night here and would be returning the next several nights."

The time was right.

"That is true."

"Then, please accept this, Princess Lavender the Pure, as a token of my father's loyalty." He presented a rectangular box.

Lavender struggled not to snort at the heralds of the kingdom's stylized name for her.

She accepted the box: polished to a bright sheen, the top stone-inlay held the royal crest.

Justin would no doubt accept it publicly, mock it privately, and have it locked in a room, out of sight, to gather dust.

She slipped open the latch and raised the lid. A sharp breath slipped between her lips at the sight of the forbidden treasure.

Whatever the box lacked in grace, it held the most beautiful dagger Lavender had seen. She shut the lid, focusing on keeping her hand still.

"So I am, young master. It is beautiful. Know that I accept this gift with many thanks in His Highness's name. I will ensure that he receives it and knows of your father's generosity."

The boy beamed at her, bowed again and left.

Her door had no bolt, only a simple latch anyone could open from either side, but she made sure the door was shut firmly after peaking into the hallway.

Jailers made sure none of their prisoners, even a slight girl, had weapons.

With trembling hands, she removed the shining poniard, its crosspiece a pair of stylized dragon's claws and slid it into the folds of a blanket underneath one of her pillows.

She had waited before for a monster to kill her.

Unable to escape, fear consumed her.

Death is better than some lives. This time, I will slay my own dragon.

Imitating People Screaming
12/3/16

FIFTEEN HUNDRED NIGHTS LATER
Helen Dring

My king and I have never been much for sleeping, but the time he creeps in to my chamber grows later–or earlier–each day. I do not ask where his other hours are spent. I do not need to; I have seen them, teenagers with honeyed mouths and liquid hips who entice him. These are small betrayals, and when I think of him with them, the mother in me thinks only of the fact that, but for me, those girls would be dead by morning. Better to be a mistress for a lifetime than a bride for a night.

The sun rises when his weight sinks in to my mattress beside me. He was always formidable, even in his youth, but age and riches have made him seem gargantuan in my bed, so much that I am relieved that my marital duties fall to others.

Apart from one.

His eyes are wide, and in them, I see my sons and grandsons. My daughter's deep, caramel eyes and her wide nose. Our lives, lived and still living, and I remember the first night I slept in this chamber.

A gamble, that night. A roll of dice I had no way of knowing would fall in my favour.

I have won, I think.

"My queen." My husband leans to his side, his hand stroking my cheek. "Please, tell me one of your celebrated tales."

The tale in store for him will delight. "Of course, Sire. But first, a drink?"

He nods.

I climb out and walk to the silver tray placed on my dresser, the silver pot filled with thick and bitter coffee.

Fuel for the tale-teller.

Besides it sits a tiny glass vial. The doses in the vial reduce every day, and the royal physician has warned me he will not be able to procure more for several months. I try to make it last.

Yesterday, I used only three drops in my coffee.

Today, it must be two.

It will still not last long enough.

My kingdom has lasted–flourished–because I can spin a world with words. I am a mother, and now a grandmother, and all those little lives that build themselves up beneath the palace walls have grown because of me. He would have had my father wring my neck just hours after wedding me if it were not for my stories, for my mind.

And now, I am losing them.

Losing it.

"Scheherazade. Quickly, my queen."

I stir the coffee and lay the tray on our bed, grasping my cup quickly.

He drinks his coffee in three gulps as I sip mine. He is impatient, like a young man waiting to take his lover. I still, after all these years, enjoy making him wait.

"To Sinbad, then." I say.

"I have heard all of Sinbad's voyages." Shahryar whines, and his petulance betrays the boy that still lives inside the man.

I stroke his hair softly "Yes, but have you heard of what happened when he returned home? For Sinbad lived many years after his voyages finished, but not without adventure."

"Go on."

My tongue works wonders on my king. The light comes up as I talk, and by the time the day is in full swing, Shahryar sleeps in my chamber.

It is where his nights always end, where his days begin.

Fifteen thousand nights he has spent listening to me spin him stories.

I must have less than a hundred left.

We do not talk about it. He knows, although he says nothing.

A force works inside of me, a creature that threatens to eat me from the inside.

My memory fades each day, my stories become tattered and frayed.

My king is still an oil painting–fresh and vibrant and the colour of spices at market.

It will hurt to leave him.

I did not expect to love him. I came to tame him, to keep him from the cycle of maiden-killing that plagued us.

But the heart cannot resist forever my only husband.

But I will leave a family, a kingdom, a place that has known peace for many thousands of days.

I hope my loss will not restore his love of violence, that my stories will seep into his veins and keep him kind.

He can be a good king, if he remembers how.

THE PROBLEM WITH HAIR

Juliet Boyd

Rapunzel walked past the ladies of the court. As usual, their eyes were greener than the forest. The forest that surrounded the palace. The palace that surrounded the courtyard, where she was forced to spend her days being observed by those very ladies. Oh yes, the men were allowed out with their horses, their swords and their armour, but the women? They were left to play games of jealousy and spite. She remembered, with no small amount of despair, what her dear husband said when she and the twins came to live there.

"Please grow your hair back to the wondrous length it was when I climbed up to see you in the tower. It was so beautiful and fine, and to see it grace your delicate features again would make me the happiest man alive."

Her initial reserve had not been purely because the idea of walking around with it trailing behind her through the endless corridors of her new home filled her with dread. Her voice wobbled as she put her concern into words.

"You don't think I'm beautiful without it?"

The look of horror on his face told her all she needed to know. How could she refuse to do something so simple for the man she loved more than any other?

An impulsive choice. Her husband was hardly there with all the quests and political negotiating. When he did come back for a brief stay, he never mentioned her hair. He probably didn't think he needed to anymore.

That was the job of everyone else.

"See that Rapunzel. Thinks she's a cut above the rest of us, because she needs five maids to help her wash that hair."

"I heard that whole families of spiders live in there."

"Did you know, they had to make the crown bigger to fit over her head, because there's so much of the stuff piled up on it? I mean, look at how she's got it done up today. All knots and swirls. So pretentious."

It had to stop.

She dabbed at her eyes with a lily-white handkerchief, let out a loud sob, and hurriedly ascended a narrow staircase up to the parapet. She stopped at a spot that was equidistant from the two guards along the south-facing walkway—guards she hoped wouldn't pay too much attention to her for the next minute. She leaned over the outer edge, hair first, climbed onto the wall, gritted her teeth, and jumped.

The screams from the women in the courtyard, who without doubt had been paying particular attention to her antics, echoed against the stone that enclosed them.

"She jumped. She jumped."

"She must be dead."

"The princess. She's dead."

If she wasn't mistaken, she heard a hint of glee in the tone.

Her husband put a finger to his lips as he hauled her in through the window. She had known he would be strong enough to hold on to her locks, but rushing through the air, unable to break her own fall if anything went wrong, still gave her a fright.

He helped her remove the hay padding beneath her dress and untie the intricate pattern of knots her hair had been bound into around her body to avoid decapitation as a result of the jolt.

He took her in his arms and hugged her tight. "How long do you think we should let them suffer?"

"Oh, at least an hour." If suffer was the right word.

He might no longer comment on her hair, but the way he touched it with such reverence, every time he returned to the palace, made her heart flutter like an angel's wings.

And he was always full of good ideas for sorting out of difficult political situations, even if they were just the ones created by the women of the court.

SNOW WHITE AND THE TALL POPPY

Somer Canon

Snow White drifted into the dining room in a way that only a woman of her breeding and beauty could manage. The king glanced at her coolly.

"My queen," he said, returning his attentions to his soft-boiled egg.

The high-born queen stuck her tongue out at her king when he wasn't looking and took her seat.

"Are your eggs satisfactory, my king?" She asked dutifully, examining her gleaming nails. She felt an urge to throw her plate at him when he didn't answer, but her violent longings halted when the current prince, her son, walked into the room.

"Good morning, Father," the boy said, observing formalities. His father wouldn't acknowledge him. He came to his mother's side and kissed her cheek.

"Mother," he said in his sweet pre-pubescent voice.

"Good morning, my darling," the Queen Snow White said, adoration warming her voice.

The prince sat in the seat next to her and ate the large breakfast placed before him, the comfort between he and his mother making the chasm between them and the king more noticeable.

Snow White smiled as she watched her son eat and her fingers traced the large diamond at her throat, a wedding present from the dwarves. They were dear to her because of the aid they offered when she was on the run from the witch Grimhilde.

She missed the dwarves terribly and regretted that they never got to meet her beloved son. After she had married, her father's kingdom had been absorbed by her husband's family. Her new father-in-law soon got word of the group of dwarves who mined stupendously beautiful jewels, and in short order, her friends were enslaved and forced to mine for and craft jewelry for her husband's royal family. Snow White herself refused to wear the pieces that were made by the blood, sweat, and lost independence of her friends. Alas, she had been alone in her boycott, and worked to death within five years, the dwarves were crushed by the greed of the people that she had to call family.

She held little malice towards her husband over that horrible affair, and instead, saved her ire for her father-in-law. She visited the graves of the dwarves on the day that greedy man drew his last breath and laid fresh forest flowers on them by way of hoping for peace for their kind and hearty spirits.

No, the hard feelings that the Queen Snow White had for her royal husband were more present. His disinterest in his wife and son, his constant absence from their lives, and the constant stream of mistresses in and out of his chambers caused a slow resentment in the queen. Their first-sight love burned out fast.

The queen snapped out of her brooding when her son wiped his mouth with his fine-cloth napkin and kissed her on the cheek again, declaring that he had equestrian lessons. She smiled fondly at him as he left. His dark hair resembled both parents, but the way it curled under at his pale neck reminded the queen of her own father, someone she had lost early in life. Her son reminded her often of her father, but she would have loved him regardless. He was her masterpiece. When he was gone, she quietly left the dining room without eating.

Late that afternoon, the queen was in her grand bed, panting and sweating. Ferdinand, her son's equestrian instructor was on top of her, kissing her milky breasts and teasing her, withholding himself, making her squirm beneath him.

"Ferdinand." She pleaded, buried her hands in his dark coarse hair, and pulled him up so that she could stoke her flames in his deep kisses. As he kissed her, her aching need for him became too much. She wrapped her legs around his narrow hips and pushed him into her, his girth opening her and easing the pain of such intense desire.

"Oh yes," she cried out. "Fuck me, Ferdinand."

Ferdinand chuckled as he moved, and she knew that it was because her talk during lovemaking shocked him. She clawed his back, and as his movements increased, her hips bucked in time with him.

"Yes. Yes. Harder, Ferdinand. *Faster.*"

As she climaxed, she bit down on her lover's shoulder, making him spasm inside of her.

After, they held each other under the brocade sheets of the elegant bed, each lost in their own reverie.

"I love you," Ferdinand said.

The queen smiled. His dark skin gleamed with sweat, and he was still flushed from his amorous exertions. He was rakish and handsome, and she felt herself grinning whenever he entered the room. His looks aside, she had come to find his affections endearing. He was not ashamed to tell her that he loved her. He said it often.

"If only we didn't have to hide."

"Indeed." The queen fantasized about having Ferdinand several times a day, every day. How nice would it be to enjoy the meals outside of her chambers with good company and be with a man who acknowledged her son.

"I'd do anything for you. I'd do anything to make you happy." Ferdinand leaned in to speak against her throat.

"I know." The queen patted his cheek with a pale hand.

"Do you think the king would ever take equestrian instruction?"

"Not at his age," Snow White ran her hands over her soft bedsheets still swimming in her post-lovemaking euphoria.

"It would be advantageous if I could be alone with the king and away from the castle." Ferdinand propped himself up on an elbow and met the queen's gaze intensity.

The queen regarded the man who had been her lover for the past year. For the first time, distrust snaked into her estimation of him.

"I will not continue sharing. I deserve to have you to myself." Ferdinand pulled her close.

The queen squirmed from his embrace and rose from the bed.

"I must go about my duties now, Ferdinand." She draped her ethereal form in a silk dressing gown and scrutinized the man in her bed with an impatient look.

"My queen." Ferdinand bowed in an exaggerated way and dressed and left her chambers, slamming the door behind him.

Later, Snow White, troubled queen, walked the halls of her castle alone. She preferred solitude after an afternoon with Ferdinand, as her ladies-in-waiting tended to have loose tongues. She didn't care that they knew. No. They couldn't know about the downstairs room and her inheritance.

She descended a long and twisted flight of steps, down into the bowels of the castle and to Grimhilde's old, spell-crafting room. The large heavy door was locked, but she used her gnarled, tarnished key and lit a few candles once inside.

She took a drink from an obsidian bottle, the liquid inside ensuring that her precious son remained an only child. As the liquid warmed her from the inside, she opened the doors to the large armoire at the end of the room.

Hanging inside was the magic mirror so-prized by the witch Grimhilde.

Snow White protected the mirror, giving a decoy over to her husband to be destroyed. She grew to understand the value of the mirror and believed that its potential outweighed its past misuse.

Mirror, mirror, I call to thee.
Questions need answers, now come to me.

Grimhilde recited the incantation to awaken the mirror, and upon repeating this, Snow White became the new steward of the spirit within the looking glass.

The reflection of her own face twisted and swelled until the spirit in the mirror stared back at her.

"I am here," the mirror said in its metallic baritone.

"Mirror, Ferdinand's affections trouble me. He does not want to share me, and he's suggested a way to dispatch the king in order to have me to himself."

The mirror smirked. "Your feelings for both Ferdinand and the king are complicated."

"Yes." Tension pulled her shoulders high.

"There is love in you for both, I see. But you are not sure who would be better."

"Yes." How could she decide?

"The king's indifference to you is bred by familiarity. He is used to novelty and indulgence. It has little to do with you and more to do with the king being unable to shed his spoiled childish tendencies. But know, queen, that this indifference may someday befall Ferdinand as well. Familiarity, to many, is the antidote to love."

"And what of Ferdinand's feelings for me?" Snow White wrung her hands, and her head ached in anticipation.

"Ferdinand is hardworking, but he is ambitious. He craves you as a prize. Ambition, such as Ferdinand's, is never sated. It merely shifts. If Ferdinand were able to dispatch the king, this would not be satisfied for long. He will want more, and his attention will land on the one person who holds more of your heart than he could ever hope to."

The queen held her pounding heart hostage beneath her breast. She hoped that what the mirror said next was not what she was expecting.

"Your son will fall the same as his father at the hands of your lover if he is allowed to win you."

Fear stuck her in the heart.

Snow White slammed the armoire closed and dashed from the room, running as fast as she could, hoping that the king would be easy to find.

Ferdinand could not have her son.

She burst through another heavy door, startling the king and his advisors as they poured over official documents. She stood before them, panting and not bothering to smooth her wild hair or right her wrinkled gown.

"My king." She collapsed into hysterical sobs on the floor.

"The queen and I shall speak in private." The king said, waving his advisors from the room. He crossed the large expanse and knelt before her, raising her chin with a finger. His brow creased in concern. "What is the matter?"

"I have something to confess."

Three days later, the black-clad Queen Snow White sat on her throne overlooking the execution platform behind the castle. The king stood to her left, his hand on her shoulder. Ferdinand stood below, eyes locked on her, rage flashing through his features, his hands tied and the hooded executioner beside him.

"For the crimes of making inappropriate and violent advances toward her majesty, the queen and for threatening the life of your sovereign king, Ferdinand, you will now die." The king's decree rang clear, and the assembled crowd bristled.

The executioner jerked Ferdinand to his knees. Snow White, as befitting a woman of her superb royal stock, looked on stoically as the head of Ferdinand was laid on a chopping block. The man who, as the king believed, had forced himself on her and threatened his life when rebuffed, accepted his fate quietly.

Snow White had watched many executions but was surprised at her inner calm as she watched her former lover in his final moments. Once the mirror implied that her precious son might be in danger at the hands of that man, her choice had been made. He had to be stopped. The queen placed her hand over the one on her shoulder, thankful to the man who was unknowingly saving their son.

The queen didn't react as the axe slammed down several times, crunching through bone and pulverizing skin. She looked down her nose as the head finally fell to the wooden floor with a wet thud. The king nodded his approval when the executioner lifted the dripping trophy to them.

That night, the queen sat with her son in a reading room, regaling him with tales of her youth and the dwarves, as she often did. Her precious progeny was so entranced with her story that he didn't see his father enter the room. When the king's presence was finally noted, he smiled and nodded before taking a seat in the chair next to his wife and lighting his pipe.

The queen nodded amiably at her husband and continued with her tale, inhaling the sweet scent of his pipe tobacco. Warm memories of him tickled her mind. She chanced a peek at him and saw that he watched her with interest. She felt a blush rise in her cheeks, as that was a look familiar to her since Ferdinand had, until recently, given her the same scrutiny. She told her story, tentatively happy and at complete ease with in her husband and son.

BEANS TALK

Edward Cooke

All because of some stupid fairy story, Jack Spriggins wound up in no end of trouble.

Jack liked stories. He heard a great many of them in the Blinkered Nag, where he spent the bulk of his time. Some considered Jack clever for outwitting the giant, but time passed with no sign of a sequel. Real geniuses left lasting and practicable traces, like the intellectual colossus who invented beer.

The richest man for miles around, Jack bought a great many beers for himself and his permanent or passing friends. As a happy result, he got to hear a great many stories, the vast majority pat and predictable: he could foresee the ending having heard only the first few words. As a less happy result, Old Ned the innkeeper kept sneaking his prices up, until it got to the stage where nobody could afford to drink at the Nag unless Jack propped up the bar.

The life of a barfly suited Jack rather well. Besides beer and stories, Jack liked women. Though they all seemed keen at first, what with him being the richest man for miles around, it proved terribly difficult to hold their attention once they got him to admit that he still lived with his mother.

Jack had never seen this particular fellow before, the one who told him the story that got him into trouble. He hoped never to see him again, especially since women liked a good story, too. Ermintrude and Gretchen had left the Nag at the same time as the storyteller, who was supposed to spend the night in the Nag's draughty garret. Jack knew this because he had paid Old Ned's exorbitant overnight rates as a favour to Ermintrude.

He hadn't imagined the fellow would pose any sort of threat. A loud voice was by far the storyteller's greatest and perhaps his only asset. Jack didn't like to shout: yelling so hard for his mother to bring him the axe caused lasting damage to his throat, and this phobia left him a man of few words.

Not so the storyteller. When he stood on one of the Nag's ramshackle tables to tell his tale, however preposterous, everybody stopped to listen. The Nag offered its punters no other entertainment besides darts—worse than no entertainment at all.

"Once upon a time," he said, and the Nag held its breath.

"Once upon a time, there was a very rich man—"

"And his grandmother was a wolf," one wag said.

Everybody else told him to shut the heck up.

They wanted to enjoy the story, and even if it did turn out to be one they had all heard many times, they had never before heard this loud fellow tell it and might never hear him again.

"The rich man believed in a god called God, and one day he got up and stood before an assembly of people who all believed in God, too, and he told them a story."

Some heckler said, "Oh, no. Not metafiction. It gives me a headache. And it's so last century."

"'I used to have only one dollar to my name,' he told them—a dollar, you see, was to them what a gold piece is to us—'and I gave it to God because a fiery evangelist told me to. I believe God loves a generous giver, and that's why He made me the rich man I am today: because I gave him everything I had.'

"Now a sweet-little-old lady, sitting next to him in the very same pew, leaned over just as he sat himself down. She said—"

"'Goodness,'" somebody said, "'what big teeth I have.'"

Jack nodded to Old Ned. Old Ned stirred himself from counting his takings long enough to remove the heckler.

Ermintrude drew her chair a little closer to the storyteller's table. Gretchen remarked to anyone who would listen what a low-cut blouse Ermintrude wore that evening. Old Ned refilled everybody's tankard on Jack's tab.

Once order was restored, the storyteller said, "The little old lady said, 'I dare you to do it again.'"

The storyteller fell silent. The Nag grew perplexed. The patrons hoped for a story about a gingerbread house or some other luxury they could never afford. They hoped the storyteller would cast the usual aspersions on the grass widows inhabiting such desirable properties. Little old ladies were always rich, a sure sign of trafficking with Satan.

Finally, Hendrik the Village Idiot said, "What does it mean?"

"It's a story. It doesn't mean anything," the storyteller said.

"All stories mean something," Hendrik said. "So tell us what this one means."

"If it means anything, it means we should be wary of flukes, one-offs, the luck of the draw. Inductive reasoning is a great scourge and leads to all sorts of unwarranted superstition. We can't say we know what the world is really like until we have investigated it thoroughly and systematically, not merely anecdotally."

"I still don't get it," Hendrik said.

The storyteller sighed. "Any fool can succeed once, but it takes a real man to succeed twice."

Nobody said anything, because the storyteller was a stranger, but every eye in the Nag made its way by a variety of roundabout routes to the far end of the bar where Jack stood.

Gretchen yawned and stretched and said she'd better get home. The storyteller offered to accompany her. Ermintrude said that Gretchen had drunk too much as usual, and it would take both Ermintrude and the storyteller to carry her home, especially when wearing those preposterous heels.

Everybody else had business elsewhere and faded away until Jack was left with Old Ned, Hendrik, and Tom the Village Drunk.

"That was a stupid story," Hendrik said. His frown deepened until his forehead resembled gnarled ancient wood. "No, wait. I get it. The old lady was really a witch, who only pretended to believe in God so she could sell her wards and hexes at His assemblies. And the rich man was an allegory for deficient labour relations and the need for checks and balances on a burgeoning bourgeoisie."

"You're a lovely man. You know what? I'd die for you, if I had to," Tom said.

"Time, gentlemen," Old Ned said.

Jack paid up and went home, but he couldn't help thinking about the story and its implications. He turned it over and over in his mind. He couldn't sleep.

What if he had just been lucky?

He always supposed his own adventure demonstrated order in the universe, but what if randomness and chaos had thrown him a bone, all the better to disillusion him?

The following morning, a course of action came to him as clearly as some divine whisper.

He couldn't do it until after he ate breakfast. If he didn't eat breakfast, his mother would be convinced he must be running a temperature and make him visit the apothecary. His mother had great faith in the apothecary, who used to be a consummate professional. These days, Tom's hands shook so badly he could hardly hold his own pestle.

After breakfast, his mother made him sit down and browse through an entire brochure of woodcuts depicting modish kitchens.

"Do you think our oven is big enough for a small child to hide in? Because I don't."

Jack agreed that they ought to get a new oven as a matter of urgency. He would have agreed to anything, just to get himself out of the house and on the way to market.

He hoped against hope that he might meet a stranger on the way, but the only person he encountered was Ermintrude, coming out of Gretchen's house. She offered to go with him to market. She wanted to pay a visit to the haberdasher and get some new buttons for her blouse, all the old ones having fallen off during the night. But Jack insisted on going well in front of her, in case the sight of Ermintrude holding her blouse half-shut frightened off the sort of stranger who purveyed magical beans.

He reached the market and hesitated, depressed that all you could do with money was buy either consumables or trinkets. When Ermintrude arrived, he bought her some new buttons, a diamond necklace, and a couple of cows she liked the look of. Minutes later she was bored with all her new purchases. A pumpkin-shaped carriage caught her eye, but Jack was out of cash—he had spent all the gold pieces his mother had made the previous day. He hadn't even enough left to pay Old Ned for that evening's session at the Nag.

Ermintrude set off for home in sky-high dudgeon. Jack steeled himself to follow her, thinking how much he would prefer to face a grumpy giant. He shambled past the florist's stall at a snail's pace. At the back of the display, neglected and crammed into an insignificant pot full of weeds, badged up simply as 'Houseplant—Sure To Brighten Your Dream Cottage', was what looked like a stripling beanstalk.

It took Jack a matter of moments to retrieve one of Ermintrude's errant cows and exchange it for the pot and its contents. This close to closing time, the florist seemed disinclined to haggle.

Ever the gentleman, Jack walked Ermintrude home. She complained the whole way that one cow was no use without the other, not when they had come as a matched pair. Such a pity the world didn't understand the value of stories: if only the storyteller had had any spare cash, and if he hadn't had to stay behind at the inn cosseting his muse and nursing his hangover, Ermintrude was quite certain he would have bought her a whole herd of cows, and the carriage, and the title deeds to the castle on a cloud she hadn't even bothered to mention because Jack was so notoriously tight-fisted. Everybody in the village said so.

Jack bore her lament as stoically as he bore the beanstalk in its cumbersome clay pot.

They returned to Jack's mother's house. Ermintrude complained how pathetic her diamond necklace was and how much she would have preferred a castle on a cloud and a flock of unicorns to go with it. Jack's mother said that she knew just how Ermintrude felt, and the two women sat down and ogled the kitchen brochure from beginning to bitter end. Then she caught sight of Ermintrude's new cow through the window and was quite certain it belonged to her, or had done before her lackwit son had handed it over in a most unfair exchange. A bitter argument broke out, the women agreed on nothing except that it was all Jack's fault.

Ermintrude left under a cloud, taking her cow with her. As soon as she had gone, Jack's mother stopped berating him about the cow and started berating him about squandering on loose women all the gold pieces she had worked her fingers to the bone to mint from those bloody useless golden eggs.

Jack suffered this soliloquy in silence. He wanted nothing but to sit by himself in one corner and wait for the beanstalk to grow tall enough to convey him into the clouds once again.

He fell asleep and dreamed that he was at an assembly dedicated to the worship of a god called God, and a fellow rich man got up to speak to everyone present, except it turned out he spoke directly to Jack.

"What do you hope to achieve by going up there again? You know what'll happen, even if you do come back alive. It won't be enough for the little people down here. You know why? Because nothing is ever enough for them. In fact, if you gave them the moon, they'd say there was a piece missing."

"How about you? I thought you believed in a god called God. What has he got to say about all of this?" Jack asked.

"They say God lives up in the clouds. When you were up there, did you happen to see him?"

"I most certainly did not."

"Are you quite certain?"

"I am. Absolutely."

The rich man shook his head forlornly. "Our holy book tells us plenty about God, but there's one thing it forgot to record."

"What's that?"

"Just how big God was."

STEP-MOTHER

Deanna Smith

My name is Cindy Charming. I'm not, just so you know. Husband is, but that's his gig, and if it makes me squeal and giggle and blush when he's pouring it on, that ain't nobody's business but our own. I sure as hell didn't spawn these three hooligans without some learned interjection from him.

We tied the knot ten years ago. A fabulous fairy tale wedding, of course. A little creepy when the in-laws asked how much torture I'd like to lay on my step-mother and step-sisters, but you've really got to hand it to them, they went all out to make sure I felt welcome to the fam.

Thing was, it just didn't matter to me enough to care if my step-mother and sisters were stuffed into hot iron boxes or forced to wear razor blade shoes or whatever weird-ass thing Queen Mom had up her sleeve. All I could think right then was Cripes Almighty, I am not going to piss this woman off if this is the kind of entertainment she offers for a wedding.

I mean, isn't torturing your evil step-family more of a birthday thing?

I walked away from my old life ten years ago. Not long enough a time to get over a childhood of abuse, Queen Mom says, and I know she's off in her S-and-M fantasy, but she's not me. After catching my three little hell spawn trying to drag the moat monster into the castle, I've got to wonder. Sure, they're cute, and sure, I laughed my ass off once I'd smacked their little bottoms and sent them to their rooms, but I wonder.

If the moat monster had eaten someone, it wouldn't have been nearly so funny or cute. Or if it ate one of them. Granted, the moat monster is about as ferocious as a bean bag, but…I'm a princess now. I'm loaded. When I take the kids down to the kitchen to learn how to cook, if they ruin the bread or break a crock of milk, no problem. If they wreck their clothes playing in the mud, or if they embarrass me by asking why Mommy was sitting on Daddy's lap naked, we just deal with it.

Making sure that the kids are well cared for no matter what, even if the husbeast and I cack it, is a big priority for me. They will not end up as scullery maids or dogs' bodies if I have anything to say about it, and as it turns out, I do. Even wrote it in that my dingbat fairy godmother needs to do a little bit more towards their welfare than provide fancy party wear if the kids are in an abusive situation.

I mean, come on, Fairy Godmother. Seriously. A party dress and shoes? You know what would have been better? Anything. Call the freaking cops. Sure, the party dress and shoes helped to snag me the hottest prince anywhere—yeah, so I'm biased, sue me—but I'm positive I could have caught his eye and everything else without an enchanted ensemble. Also could have cut out the creepy grand duke fondling girl's feet, too.

I walked away from the abuse ten years ago. Long enough time for me to really think all this over, to have my own family, and to look back with clear eyes. I made peace with my step-sisters long ago. They were victims just as much as I was. I mean, look at them. The ugly fairy had a full on beat down on the poor girls, then turned them over to a woman that couldn't tolerate imperfection. That's some cruel shit, and I spent most of my youth laying in ashes.

They're okay, now. Dru's got a little wifey of her own; she came out about the time I was helping them learn how to make what they had work and fell for the gal I hired to teach them dancing and charm and all that. Dru went into engineering, though, and they adopted a few kids. Prissy's become the lioness of society, and between you, me, and the adoption agency, those kids Dru and her wife adopt are Prissy's. I tease her and tell her I'm going to make her marry this guy or that, and she just laughs and says that all the single men in society will revolt if I do. I'm pretty sure she's right.

And then, there's Step-Mother.

I remember when Papa first brought her home. She was so elegant. Refined. Perfect. She wasn't beautiful, but she was handsome. Prissy and Dru were miserable as they stood beside her. They had to be as self-contained and perfect as their mother, and they were crushed at losing their father.

We weren't allowed to be friends. We weren't allowed to play together. We couldn't even sit down and share with each other how much we hurt from losing our respective parents. They had their rooms, and I had mine. They had their governess. I had mine. We barely even saw each other.

Step-Mother wasn't a thing like Mama. Maybe that's what attracted Papa. Or maybe it was that they each had just lost their beloved.

She hasn't changed much if at all in ten years. Though she's certainly not sitting pretty in Papa's country manse, wearing the finest widow's weeds and black blacker than black with a little purple, she may as well be. She's as pristine in prison grays as she ever was.

The jailers make her work. She does laundry; she bakes, she scrubs, she sweeps—everything she ever forced me to do. Then she sits and reads. I watched her through the bars on the door for a while. Finally, I had the guard open the door.

She nodded politely but kept reading, a finger held up. When she finished the paragraph, she set the book down and regarded me like I was a total stranger. Or her best friend. It was hard to say. She was the undisputed mistress of the resting bitch face.

"Why?"

I had all kinds of questions. I'd fantasized this conversation for years. Before I even left home, I wanted to know why more than anything. Why? Why do you hate me so much, why did you treat me like you did, why did you even marry my father in the first place…but it all boiled down to why.

She had nothing to say to me.

I wanted to pace, but I wasn't going to be the one that lost it here. I wasn't going to break. I'm not a confused teenager with a lot of vermin for friends anymore. I am a grown woman, I will be queen, I have a wonderful husband and three varmints loosely disguised as children, and possibly another one baking because I'm late, and there was that whole thing with Mommy sitting naked on Daddy's lap.

Prissy and I really need to sit down with the palace physician and discuss birth control. Dru's a freaking saint, I swear, all of our spawn are happily evil.

While I waited for her to crack, Queen Mom's words whispered in my ear. Visions of iron maidens, thumb screws, racks, whips, and chains paraded across my mind. I can make her answer you, dearling. You shouldn't have to wonder why you, and your step-sisters were so ill-served.

The Queen Mom is seriously the more evil between she and Step-Mother. Instead of being a raging bitch, Queen Mom uses her evil for purposes of good, if that makes a lick of sense. Let's just say that no one lies to her more than once.

Yet, as I was dwelling upon all of those tortures that Queen Mom twittered and burbled about—I kid you not, she has a happy song about them, and it's disturbingly catchy—Step-Mother abruptly shuddered and looked away. All I can figure is my face gave away the guilty pleasure I take in envisioning Queen Mom's suggestions.

"Your father was a weak man." She barked out the words, cold and harsh as ever. She always did talk like that, now that I think about it. I'm not as special as I thought.

"However, I was not in the position to turn him away. My first husband had been killed in an accident, and my parents arranged that I should marry your father before I had even completed the proper mourning period."

I stopped myself from asking why again.

"One would think that a decent man would refuse such a situation, but he was completely absorbed into the notion that a girl must have a mother. That overcame all else." Her voice was flat and hard. It startled me. I never thought of that.

Papa had been obsessed. I needed a mother. I must have a mother. Instead of mourning Mama, he put everything into replacing her. Every reminder of Mama was gone before he even brought Step-Mother home. And probably all memory of Step-Mother's first husband was erased just as completely.

I needed my mother, sure. She hadn't been dead six months before Papa married Step-Mother. I didn't meet her until he brought her home. You'd think he'd have wanted me to at least meet her before committing to her. See if we got along, little things like that.

I wasn't blossoming into womanhood and sloshing hormones all over the house. I had a perfectly good governess, after all. What I really wanted, what I really needed, was time with Papa to heal our loss. I never got that. I got a Step-Mother.

She never mothered me. Ever. At best, when Papa was alive, she would treat me like the daughter of an associate, polite and reserved, which was about how she treated her own daughters, honestly, but you would think it would upset Papa. It didn't seem to bother him at all.

"It was nearly intolerable. For the first time in my life, control over my own life was nearly in my grasp, only to find I was too young to be a widow and forced to marry yet another man I had little in common with and less affection for. I was not a wife. I was a step-mother."

Ouch.

"Then, when your father died, I discovered that nothing had been willed to me. Once you were of age and married, everything became yours. Or rather, your husband's. I was nothing to him. My daughters, who certainly needed a father, were less than nothing."

I was glad that I was leaning against the wall because that rug yanked out from under me pretty hard. I couldn't dispute that. I remember trying to share Papa with Dru and Prissy, but he would say things like he shouldn't sully their memory of their own father. Which, now that I think about it...

That was a pretty damn strange thing for a man so intent on having a mother for his daughter to say.

"I no more wanted them than you. Yet I was honor and duty bound to deal with all of you."

You know, I suddenly understand why Queen Mom is so cheerfully vicious. She had to change the way women were treated in this kingdom from scratch. She had to claw, bite, and fight through unfair laws and stratified social morals, and did it all with a merry song on her lips.

"I taught them to be the worst wives I possibly could." Step-Mother sniffed and looked down her nose at me. "So perhaps they would be fortunate enough to be cast aside and left to live their own lives. I sent you to the scullery, so you wouldn't find that husband who would take your inheritance and throw me out. And if he did simply take your inheritance and throw you out, you'd be able to find a job."

"Things have changed, Step-Mother."

"Your father's will didn't."

Wow. I didn't expect this, but I probably should have. I never did anything that would make Step-Mother hate me, and I wrestled with that night after night. We were never so poor that I was a burden on her. I wasn't a bad kid. I didn't resent her. I scarcely had anything to do with her before Papa died. I wasn't even constantly reminding everyone of my Mama.

Step-Mother didn't hate me. She hated the situation, and had no way out. I couldn't even imagine marrying someone I didn't know, let alone like, and not only had she done that, but had two daughters from it.

My beloved Papa. He really was weak. He wouldn't face Mama's death. He wouldn't face raising me. He married a woman rather than heal, and then refused to take any real responsibility for her or her daughters.

Everything could have been so different. But, as the husbeast says, we must live in the now and think of the future because the children will go feral and possibly devour us if we don't keep a step ahead of them. I can't really remember why we thought having more than one would be such a good idea.

"What is it that you want?" I asked.

"Certainly not to be magically redeemed by your forgiving and understanding heart," she said with a facetious hook of a sneer to her lips, "I may not have ever had control of my own life, but I do have my pride. Just go."

"Don't flatter yourself. I don't forgive you. I don't trust you. I don't like you. You may have gotten a short stick, but you chose to let it make you bitter. You chose to let it break you."

"You were not there, you have no idea of the pressures upon me." She still tried to play the regal widow, but I'd see that act before from her. It still didn't fly.

"Oh, really? Because I didn't learn about the unfairness of things while being forced to work as your scullery maid? Get off of it, old woman. You were as weak as my father. You snapped like a twig."

The cell was silent.

I finally smiled again.

"We can't change the past. We can only change the future, and only if you want to change it. What do you want?"

SHE OF SILKEN SCARVES

Alisha Costanzo

"Are you ready?" My mentor adorned her reaper's hood, disguised as a craggily, old woman.

"Yes, Madame."

She produced the poisoned apple, laced with a drug that would make me sleep like the dead; only my brain would record everything. One bite, and I will be at the whim of whoever finds me.

Cupping the gleaming red fruit in both hands, I took a breath to soften my nerves, and Madame Grimm pinned a charm to the bodice of my dress, a forget-me-not serum. If they discovered me, I'd inject myself to erase all knowledge of my mission and my agency. A fail safe I hoped I wouldn't need.

I bit the apple, the sweet juices mixing with the bitter taste of the sleeping drug.

My body grew heavy.

I slipped the antidote capsule behind my lower lip so that when Prince Charming kissed me, it would bust open.

Madame Grimm caught me, laying me half on the grass and half on the path to my secret lair, where the DWARVES will find me and contact the kingdom.

Dirt worked its way under my fingernails as I dug. The sweet spice of basil mixed with the fresh manure. Not a job for a princess, or an agent, but it assured the eldest prince—my husband—wouldn't bother me. Weeds resisted as I tugged them from the soil, tossing them into the pile on my right.

The scent of waterlilies bloomed in the breeze. My new sister, Lindsay, thunked her empty wicker basket beside me and fell with the grace unbeknownst to a common slave. I have to admit that I preferred my cover story much more than hers—even with those seven little sneaks taking peeks at me in my knickers.

I can't blame them. Assignment makes one antsy after all.

"Morning." Her voice sang like a mockingbird's.

"It's past noon."

Her shears gleamed like her hair in the sun. "So it is."

The pink in her cheeks and red at the nape of her neck meant her Prince Charming had kept her late. A perk of the job—or a duty in her case. The younger brother had a few unbecoming fetishes.

She dropped a fabric sack between us before she freed a lily with her shears. The pale petals brightened her mouth as she breathed in its sweetness. I pulled a few thorny leaves and tendrils before I reached for the sack.

On top was a smaller bundle, wrapped in a scrap of terrycloth, which I palmed as I scattered a new row of groundcover seeds. I wiped the dirt on my apron and slipped the cloth into a pocket.

"How is your father?" Lindsay snipped free a few more blooms.

My father is long dead, but the man who stood for him at my royal wedding sends parcels to me without suspicion. "He sent word of being in the tropics on a new HOPE mission. He'll return in two weeks."

An impossible feat, but Lindsay nodded as she gathered her bouquet of lilies, knotting them in twine before leaving me to my weeds. I dug and pulled and scattered for more than an hour before I returned to my rooms to wash.

Doctor Mansfield's assistant waited in the sitting room as a servant poured him tea. His fat fingers pinched a cucumber sandwich as he smiled up the older woman, ever the charmer. His small size didn't get in his way.

"Good afternoon, Geoffrey." I sat across from him as tea steamed up my cup, and Merdine pushed the plate of biscuits toward me. She knew my weakness. "Thank you. I can top off our tea. You've been wonderful."

I supposed I could be a charmer, too, when need be. It was now my namesake after all. She bowed and retreated, sealing us in with the click of the door.

"How's the doctor?"

"Tied up with a new experiment." Geoffrey scratched his over-sized bald head with those squat fingers like the air in the castle made him itch. "I prefer your perfumes to his rotting vegetables."

"No luck with the peas?" One lump of sugar plops and fizzes in my tea, a dash of milk swirls in the dark like stormy sea clouds. I've become far too spoiled.

Geoffrey's cough reminded me of why I was here. The Charmings, rulers of the Western Kingdom, have been poisoning the Southern Kingdoms, testing their inoculations on the weak, the old, and the pregnant—giving way to birth defects and other cancerous side effects. The most prominent created a new race, the little people with shrunken heads and underdeveloped frontal lobes, that were easily subjugated to the mines and fields.

The Zika Virus, the kingdom explained it away, was a product of an unkempt and uncivilized society. That and unruly mosquitos.

"No, he's more focused on beans for this trial."

Reverse-engineering the GMO soybeans was a hat trick all on its own, but we needed a way to link them to the vaccines. That was the DWARVES's job.

Mine was to supply them with the uncontaminated source, although the genetic breakdown from their botanists would be better.

My guest pinched the bridge of his bulbous nose, and I pushed the plate of biscuits toward him, dropping the terrycloth-wrapped beans between it and his cup and saucer. "A pinch of sugar might help that headache."

He nodded, his gleaming dome bounced reflected light into my eyes.

I bowed my head, and when our gazes met over the towering tea pot, the package was gone.

"Well, Princess Abigail, I must be going. Thank you for the refreshments and the chance to exchange pleasantries."

We stood together, although he disappeared behind the edge of the table, and bowed to each other.

"If you see my father, tell him I greatly miss his stories, especially the one with the green dragon," I said, searching Geoffrey for the parcel and finding no bump or bulge to give away its hiding place.

"May the white rose grow in the shadow of its red sister." With a curt nod, the little man left me to my tea.

Lindsay didn't show for our usual garden meeting. At breakfast, her pallor allowed her lack of usual conversation and her early departure to go unheeded. Our need for documentation to disrupt the next round of vaccines grew more and more dire.

I collected a fresh bouquet of red roses to deliver to my sister before tea. Guards stood outside her parlor and stopped me from knocking.

"Well, this is highly untoward. Is this how you treat your future queen?" Dirt clung to my nailbeds as I plucked at the rose petals. Throwing my weight around in such a way ruffled feathers, which I didn't want. "Why do you keep me from my sister?"

The guard grew two inches taller, blinked, and refused to meet my gaze. I suppose intimidation was the way of a ruler. But still…

"By her own request, Your Highness, Snow White."

"I will have her personal refusal." My knuckles tapped in triplicate, so that she would know I stood opposite the door. "And Abigail will do just fine, thank you."

His nod didn't distract from the sweat beading along his forehead. Madame Grimm had been right, surviving poison did provide me with a mysterious and dangerous air.

The over-sized wooden door cracked, and one bruised eye shown in the space.

"Lindsay, what—"

Her delicate nails pinched my shoulder as she yanked me inside. I rubbed away the fleeting pain as the door slammed closed behind me. Lindsay braced it with a strip of iron. Her petticoats stained with metal grease. The same smeared her white skin, camouflaging the litter of bruises blooming along her chest and the backs of her arms.

The roses in my hand found their way to the side table with no vase or water basin. Water spilt across the floor, glass and ceramic shattered in an arc toward the bathing room. Blood dotting the stone and carpet between. The room matched in its disarray, but I couldn't catalogue the discrepancies.

I yanked a handkerchief from my bodice and dabbed the streaky tears on my sister's cheeks, soothing her as she battled with her breath. With her leaned into me, we both sank to the floor, and I brushed the cinder dust from her hair.

"I've done something wrong. Something unforgiveable. I couldn't stop myself. I *couldn't*." Her fingers left smudges on my wrists, ash and oil.

"Hush. Hush. It can't be that bad."

"All the knights and horsemen could not save me from this. Not even Grimm."

Heart and breath in sync, light flared around my vision. How on earth could it be *that* bad. Unless...

"Show me." I stood, dragging her up on her bare toes.

She grew more steady as anxiety poked itself between my ribs, and I followed her into her bedchambers.

The room was destroyed, the layers of bedding skewed off the frame, down feathers dusting the far end of the room. Her wedding portrait tore in half, pierced by the high-back chair at their writing desk. The wooden frame splintered at the sides.

More glass and oil—sickly sweet but metallic—pooled in front of the fireplace, coals glowing faintly under the gray-white powder. More décor scattered broken or in disarray, but I found nothing unforgivable in this room. Items could be replaced or recommissioned. The maids could clean it.

I couldn't quite place the nagging terror she'd warned me of, but alarm clanged deeply in my gut.

"Well? Where is your unforgivable crime?" The words no soon as left my lips as Lindsay pulled back a layer of blankets to reveal a hand, an arm, and a foot, the rest buried under the upturned bedding.

A noose tightened around my heart.

"He wouldn't stop. He wouldn't—he kept striking me, swinging that belt along my back." She hiccupped and covered her trembling mouth. "The buckle...he had it around my neck. I—I swear he was going to kill me."

"Maybe we can say it was an accident." I pushed the rest of the bedding against the wall to uncover the body. Prince Phillip lay naked minus the belt wrapped around his hand and torn pants, revealing the long arc of his thigh and the source of the blood ruining the carpet.

Feathers stuck to his lips, bent and dyed red. Nose crooked and swollen. Blue eyes turned white with death. Chest snaked with molten bruises. If the state of her rooms weren't enough to signify the nature of their fight, the condition of his body was. She truly did fight for her life.

But I didn't need the details, no one would listen to them anyways.

"Nicked his artery?"

Lindsay nodded, gaining her composure by the inch.

"Second time I surprised him in one day." Her gaze caught the red feathers, and her fingers traced the purple ring around her throat. I imagined him holding her down amongst the destroyed down comforters, feathers flying around them from her struggle. "The first was a well-laid kidney punch that opened me up to break his nose."

"I hope you have a few more tricks up your sleeve. Dress in something dark, outer-ware. You'll run."

"Run where? To the ruins of nowhere, to the slums of shrunken heads?"

"To somewhere that is not here. It doesn't matter. Right now, you must dress." I pushed her toward her bathing suite as I rustled up a set of garments and supplies.

A hood hid the gold of her hair and the bruise of her eye; the cape concealed the circle around her throat and glass adorned her feet. I carried her bag to the door, a small parcel she could climb with packed with the necessities.

She uncovered a thin rectangular box and slipped it into the pocket of my skirts, underneath my silk scarves. "I found it two nights ago. Couldn't break into it. Get it to Madame Grimm."

"Don't even think about it." I pinned her broach to her coat and patted her shoulders. "Ready?"

One sharp nod.

I took up a rose and dropped a bit of DEW as Lindsay lifted the bar from the door.

In the hall, I smiled and swung the rose, detonating the Debilitating Evaporated Whimsy in the guard's face, singing a sweet bird song. He repeated it in a brusque baritone.

Lindsay slipped past, down the hall for the escape hatch to the underground. I ran after her, down the stairs in the opposite direction. The guard repeated the notes I'd fed him, and they echoed down to me twice more before the effect cleared up.

I slowed when I reached the more public halls. Rose stem spun between my thumb and forefinger. Steps even and matched by breath. I walked to the library with purpose.

The package turned out to be a mirror, a comm with an impossible encryption code. Every password, every reiteration of the step-mother's motto, and no success. I had a few pieces of tech in my tea room, hidden in my trinkets.

A heavy gaze weighed on my shoulders, touching the curls falling across my neck. I closed the case and hid it in the folds of a book before I stretched. Untucked corners, my scarves loosened around my waist.

Not many come to the depths of the bookcases.

On my feet, I met the strike of a sly henchman, whipping a silk end to slap him. The other end came loose, and I wrapped him around the center, spinning him across a table and into a set of arm chairs.

A broad man, too broad to be a high-level spy. The slender ones maintained their stealth. Many of us had tricks and tools, too.

The henchman grew twice his size.

A troll.

Damn.

Silk wrapped in my fists, I dove onto the table for leverage and hurled myself around his neck. Shoes hammering the thing's chest, I barely missed the knob of flesh hanging there. A toe. I twisted the scarves tight and rode him into a short stack of books. A slap sent a shock through the silk, frying the troll and flailing his limbs.

We tumbled the wrong way, and I rolled out from beneath him, trapping my scarves under his body weight.

The door on the north corner opened and closed with a snap.

I hustled around the stacks, tucking and pinning my dress back in order, and met my husband in the open floor of this wing.

"My love, you're flush. What on Earth have you been reading?" His smile blinded me, dazzled me. So many times, I've wondered if he had it enchanted. A smile like that couldn't be natural.

"How will I keep it a secret if I tell you?" I let my breath exaggerate to draw his eye. It worked.

Two fingers to his chest, I tip-toed him back into a chair, following across his lap.

"Did you know that others rarely come this way?" I leaned in to nibble on his ear, drawing a smaller scarf from my bodice to run across his skin.

His hands found the openings to my dress with practice. We fit together so well, and he liked my sneaky wild side and the scarves. Henry wasn't ever anything but princely, even as we grasped each other and he came for me.

Satiated, he was easy to distract and send off to his duties, learning to be king.

And I cleaned up the troll.

Luckily, the package was safe, and I tied it back into the folds of my dress.

But I couldn't get it out of the palace fast enough.

The reflection didn't change when I returned to my rooms. The fairy dust, the hair drive, the pearl comb, the mirror just deepened my frown with each turn.

A staccato series of taps rattled my back window. A mountain blue bird cooed at the glass as I opened the window. He lifted his leg and offered me a NOTE. I offered him a few seeds in payment.

Placing an opulent stone on the windowsill, I sang a few notes, and the bird grasped it with one foot.

Back to his flapping wings, I pressed the button along the side of the small, black nodule. A wisp of blue and white poured from my fingertips, forming a wide grin.

"Agent White, Mission Shrunken Head is awash. Operation Vaccination has commenced in the southern quadrant of the Eastern Kingdoms. Twenty-thousand pregnant women have been forcefully injected with the TDaP. Over a hundred deaths reported from resistance, excluding the unborn. Take Agent Cinder and resume Operation Beanstalk before the Reseed. Your mission, should you choose to accept it, will be to destroy supply of modified seeds and seedlings by any means possible. This message will self-destruct in three, two, one."

I tossed the nodule into the fireplace as it sparked and lit the top wooden log in silver flame. Fingers numb from the charge, I shook them and cussed under my breath. Operation Beanstalk wouldn't be easy without Lindsay, and Grimm didn't know about the comm or my partner's escape.

Tucking the mirror away in a shadow box, I slipped into a dress more comfortable for lunch and my visit to my own garden afterwards.

Everything was normal. Perfectly normal.

I spent the next seventy-two hours dividing my days between entertaining my duties as future-queen-in-mourning and trying to locate the seedling nursery, but I met blank walls with missing doors or publicly guarded entrances to the laboratories, where I was not permitted.

My nights balanced distracting my husband with much-needed pleasure and sitting, pacing, and swearing at the mirror comm with no success as the kingdom mourned their fallen prince.

None seemed to know of his hidden monster, or if they did, his beauty and charming words fooled most. I powdered my face its signature pale, rubied my lips, and coiled my long dark hair for the proceedings, rituals, and banquets.

And a hunt went out to rescue Lindsay.

Or persecute her as the only suspect.

With my husband asleep, I sat at my table in my rooms, reviewing every inch of the castle in my mind until the clomping of horses, clinking of armor, and urgent calls of soldiers broke through the dull humming of the castle's white noise.

I rushed to the balcony, fear squeezing my ribs harder than a corset as the cold air turned the sweat down my back to frost.

Four soldiers on horseback rode into through the south entrance from the farmlands and the nobles. Riding straight in the saddle of solider number two was my partner. The only indication was the blonde tendrils escaping her lowered hood.

Please have taken your forget-me-not, every scrap of hope inside of me screamed for the possibility it would prove her innocence.

My feet flew over stone and carpets and steps.

Servants and guests emerged from cracked doors as I descended to the back of the castle, where only family was allowed—and sometimes, not even then—to find three men guarding a collapsed princess in one of the cells. Her sobs slight but constant.

"You've found her," I said, announcing myself before they might discover me.

"You're not permitted to be here." The guard closest to me grew in girth to block my view of Lindsay.

"What type of folly is this? I am the future queen of this fair kingdom. Who are you?" A dangerous sense of commanding touched my voice.

He relinquished me one small bow. "I am the faithful servant of our *present* queen, and she gives the order that no one speak to the widowed princess until she has."

Repositioning myself, I wiped the sweat down my skirts as I peered around his elbows. "I just want to see her. I need not speak."

This didn't seem to counter his orders as he shifted his step so that the full view of my sister showed her puffy redness and wet cheeks. Feigning weak knees, I fell closer to her, our arms grasping each other's out of instinct.

She sniffled loudly as she searched my face. The panic in her eyes further fed my hopes. The forget-me-not cleared all memory of her crimes.

"I—I don't know where I am," Lindsay said.

I wiped the stray hair from her face and nodded, keeping my word and my silence. Pulling her head to my shoulder, I held onto her until the queen arrived.

The mother of all looks did nothing but frighten my poor sister more thoroughly.

My hope shriveled to dust.

###

With my partner jailed and no progress with the comm, I spent more time outside the castle walls than I should have. My excuses were moderate—mourning, hurt, anger, and my propensity for nature and dirt. I even brought a basket to aid in my disguise.

If I could not get into the castle's labs, I would find a lead in the farmlands and gardens.

And I did.

The crops were uniform and abundant in the farms, rows of corn and soy grew three times larger than any I remembered from my childhood.

Yet the plants growing in the noble gardens were smaller, less bright, and more irregular—more natural. This must be where the queen gathered her food. How they separated their targets from their friends.

My better judgement squashed by a fierce hatred and need for revenge, I set fire to the edge of a far garden and watched as it jumped through the hay they used to fertilize the ground and protect their root vegetables. In minutes, it spread to the other rows, and I fled to a home I had not visited in some years to meet a friend.

I had to hurry as a trail would appear soon.

The modest three-room cabin brushed with cobwebs and crusty dishes changed little from the months I spent cultivating my undercover story. The same green-hatted gnome bowed to let me through to the rooms below. The buzz of electric lighting exaggerated the stark contrast of metal and wood.

At the bottom of the narrow steps, a long hallway led to a series of laboratories before widening into a vast open area. Geoffrey greeted me at the mouth of the room, hands clasped over his stomach.

"We weren't expecting to see you here so soon, but we did hear of your conundrum. Doctor Mansfield is testing a new mod that might interest you. Follow me. And do not deviate. As I'm sure you remember, the other DWARVES grow quite absorbed in their experiments to the peril of those passersby."

I surely did. We had to postpone one of my excursions to lure my husband away from his castle because an explosion singed my eyebrows off. The smell of burnt hair still made me itch.

The doctor's current project—one of many as I've been assured—sprawled across an acre of horizontal tresses and a quarter of the vast open space. Green beanstalks twisted and curled around hanging lights and ceiling fans, into the slates of vents and under doorframes.

"Yes. *Yes.* This is the right one. I've done it. *I've done it.*" Doctor Mansfield clapped his chubby hands, hopping and spinning in place. His round spectacles magnified his eyes as he blinked at us. "My friends, I've done it. Come. Come look."

He rushed forward, fighting his way through the blankets of tendrils, vines, and stalks to lift one precious plant with the same bulbous beans I saw in the commoners' crops.

"You reverse-engineered the GMO soybeans." Optimism flanked me. "How long until you will know what substance X is?"

"Six weeks." Bifocals perched on his bulging forehead, he scrutinized the pod and the leaves around it, poking his way inside to prod at the bean.

Crops will be harvested by then. At least three more waves of vaccination will be forced on people in that time. And who knows what other secrets they planned to unleash on the populace.

I had a purpose here. "Dr. Mansfield, I need a way to destroy these crops and their seedlings before they're harvested. I'm sure they'll speed up whatever plans they have with the prince dead."

"Ah, yes. My condolences. Your partner was a good agent."

"She was." The queen did not believe her, blinded in part by the death of her favorite, spoiled son and in part by the truth in the evidence. Lindsay had killed him in self-defense. "What is this new mod you were working on?"

"New mod. New mod. Aha—*new mod.* Yes. This way. Come. Come." He set down his pet project and tottered out of the vines with a practiced ease. At a secondary work station, other plants mingled with metal and chemicals. He climbed onto an elongated work bench and started mixing ingredients: purple rose, red moss, a bubbling blue chemical, and a few miniature-components and swirled them together. Violet steam billowed from his beaker before he turned it out into his hand. A blob about the size of a gold coin giggled in his hand.

"I call it FOG."

It exploded upon his tossing it to the ground. The metal components jingled against the tile and a fog rolled out across the room.

"Hey, some warning next time."

"Where'd it go? Where'd it go? Cinnamon Bun."

Achew. "Well, goodbye soup."

"Come on. That's the third time this week."

"At least this one smells like roses."

"Make a caffeinated one of these next time. I'm really drooping here."

"This batch is explosive with similar components to the DEW drop, but this one will have these mini-micro-nano-mechanical spores that will spread across miles with each devise."

Geoffrey coughed and waved the smoke free of his face before straightening his suit.

Doctor Mansfield started the process anew, this time with a few smidgeons more of this and that. "Add Oleander and few personal concoctions—patents pending—two death caps and a pinch of sugar."

The liquid bubbled high as he dropped in the last ingredient from a vile in his chest coat pocket. The steam shrank back and blobs plopped in the triangular beaker bottom like they were manifested out of thin air.

Settled on the chrome table, Doctor Mansfield bent to examine his creation. "That-a-girl. Such a smart little thing. See, I taught the nanites to group in a certain number, and they've formed their own, separate devices as I specified. Such perfect contraptions."

Crazy, indeed. But this dwarf was certainly not stupid.

"You brilliant man with your big brain."

The doctor's smile bunched his cheeks like a ruddy child, and he waved his hand at me, murmuring endearments as he finished his work.

He packed them in the fashion of some special fertilizers I'd bought from the Southern Kingdom's capitol, and they fit nicely in with what I brought in my basket to dig truffles and plant roots that I wanted to transplant.

I kissed his bald head and winked at Geoffrey before I zig-zagged out of the lab.

In the cabin, a different smoke laced he room—one of burnt grass and vegetation.

Outside, gray tinted the sky, but the fire had died.

I took the trail back the way I'd come.

Royal guardsmen blocked the road a half of a mile down.

"Stop where you are." A meaty, metal hand held aloft as if to stop me in my tracks. Randall, a knight who worked closely with my husband, pulled his helmet and smiled as I drew closer despite his command. The opposite of Henry, Randall was dark and rough and battle scarred, but he wore it well and always with jest. "Snow White, why ever do you skip around the forest? Do you not know there are creatures out here to gobble you up?"

"Call me that once more, and I'll have you in the stocks again." I pulled a daisy from my basket and tucked it between the metal of his armor. "Now, show me to my husband, as you are here, he must be close by."

With a good-natured-but-mocking flair, he gestured for me to follow him, hand offered to maintain my balance and grace as we descended into the woods and back to the crops that I'd set aflame.

Henry stood amongst a few noble men, hand to his chin and furrow in his brow. He nodded, attention on the seething smoke of the extinguished fire.

"Sire, the princess to see you."

My husband blinked a couple of times, shaking himself away from his thoughts. He looked at me before he saw me, his arms dropping from his chest as he stepped forward to greet me.

"Abby, what are you doing here?" His arms came around my shoulder. Sweet smoke clung to his clothes as if even the grim reality of what I'd done could not penetrate his perfection.

"I was out, visiting my old friends. It's been so long since I've seen them all, and I needed a different…" My hand flittered around my head. "…space."

His large hand brushed the loose strands of hair dusting my neck, and he pulled me closer. "I know."

After an appropriate time, I turned to the devastated crops. More than half burnt and the other half threatened by the ash. Solemnity consumed many of the bystanders, whom appeared to lack diversity.

"Randall, take Rosenbergs and their servants to gather supplies from the fruit cellar. And escort the princess, there's no need for her to make her way alone." Henry pulled my hand to his mouth. "I will stay to gather more evidence."

And the implied royal duty lay with me to ensure these people were taken care of.

"Of course. You must do your duty and do it well." Squeezing his hand, I surveyed the scene once more as Randall gathered our group. "Are there signs of foul play?"

The stern line of my husband's brow locked on ignition point. "An accelerant. We've gathered samples and should know its contents soon."

As hard as I tried without seeming suspicious, I did not successfully procure the evidence samples Randall carried with him, but the fruit cellar prickled the skin between my shoulders. The space was larger than the walls portrayed.

With the proper excuses made, I stopped at Lindsay's cell. She sat in a fresh gown but not one of the lavish reds or purples, rather a dingy, simple brown that kept her clean and modest. The bags under her blue eyes spoke of her lack of sleep and appetite.

"You should eat. There's no point in torturing yourself now."

"I can't seem to..." Her voice and half-hearted gestures proved her fatigue. Tears wet the corners of her eyes and tops of her cheeks with an ever-present glistening. "They say I did horrible things to my husband. And his mother does unspeakable things to me. I have no answers for her. I don't even know who I am."

I set my basket down and settled myself on a small stool beside the bars of her cell. "You were a young girl who slept beside the fire with soot and cinders in her hair because your evil step-mother made you a slave. But after years of servitude, an invitation to the ball fell in your lap. With your ingenuity and a little bit of magic—or luck—you made a dress and dazzled a sweet prince.

"You knew better than to dawdle and fled at the end of the night. When the charming prince sought you out so desperately, you gave way to the fairy tale and came to live in this castle with us. And you were happy for a little while."

Lindsay shifted closer, leaning herself against the bars like the story held some type of familiarity for her. "Until?"

"Until the novelty of it all wore off, and you were stuck with a man who would never be king, who resented his lack of power and the laws that made it thus. He took it out on you."

"So I did kill him?"

"You survived."

For a few more days in a cold, damp cell with the red queen breathing fire down upon her. I took her hand and gave it a squeeze. "You will die. Even though it's not your fault, there is no way out of this."

She choked on a sob.

"It's better that you know. Don't waste your energy wondering what if. Okay?"

Her silent nod drew her away from me and into a world of thoughts I could not dive into, so I gathered myself and my things and made my way to my rooms.

The next day, Lindsay confessed, requesting a speedy execution. She got her wish. An overcast morning carried with it the chill from the mountains, and I huddled under an old traveling cloak at the fringe of the crowd as my partner—my sister—stepped up the wooden steps of the scaffold to the gallows.

Her blonde hair whipped around her as though giving a final plea for freedom.

The queen sat on an elevated bench amongst the crowd, my husband standing beside her. He petitioned to save me from the horrors of justice. They both glittered in the clouds' reflection.

I stepped further toward the forest as the hangman settled the noose around Lindsay's throat.

The gems of her blue ball gown twinkled like the night she'd crashed our New Year's party, challenged Phillip's pride, and sealed her entrance into the kingdom.

The rope tightened and the man read the charges against her.

"Do you have any last words?"

"May the white rose grow in the shadow of its red sister."

A needling pain panged deep in my heart. How could she remember those words? Had someone gotten to her after I did? Flipped a switch inside her brain that I didn't have access to?

I couldn't watch my sister fall, so I ran before they dropped the world from beneath her feet.

This was the perfect cover to implement the FOG, although my calculations said I couldn't destroy half of the GMO crops with the set amount Doctor Mansfield had given me, so I made the remaining choice.

I targeted my own food supply. If the elite has to eat the commoners' crops, surely, they would not release the last chemical needed to produce substance X.

No, not with the results I'd seen from their handiwork thanks to the fire I'd set. Henry invited me to more meetings as I'd been a witness to the crime—in a sense.

Their plan had several moving parts, which I'd already known. Operation Vaccination was meant for the severely impoverished, for those groups of humans who were valued as less than by the queen and the other eleven elite families. The casualties were small-scale compared to the culling they had planned.

Henry made it a point that I eat the food offered me in the palace and nowhere else.

The DWARVES discovered the inert agent in the GMOs by accident more than a decade ago, but the crops were few and far between, grown for alternative resources rather than human consumption. But they'd taken over the market within the last two years.

Recent healthcare regulations caused riots in many of the smaller western kingdoms, and the results of the TDaP experiments in the Eastern Kingdom proved to activate something inside of the recipients who relied on the government supplied food. Their nervous systems, hearts, and brains were affected—killing one-in-two-hundred.

But what Henry didn't tell me, what I overheard of whispered conversations was that a third ingredient—something airborne—would spread disease and death further, targeting the specific groups they wanted to eliminate.

And they wanted eighty-five percent of us gone.

Them.

It didn't matter who.

They weren't allowed to play god this way.

I dropped the FOG at the furthest most corner of the noble's territories I could reach on foot, and I used the ensuing fog to cover my tracks around the castle.

The path Randall took me a few days before led me home through an underground tunnel and up through the fruit cellar. Candles lit the room instead of the electrical lights, which we often did for ceremony.

Why the fruit cellar?

Again, that feeling of the space being larger than it seemed. An air current stirred the flames. A draft came from the east corner of the room and a crack revealed itself.

I knew it.

But if the candles were lit, that meant someone hid there now. I shouldn't get caught here.

I braved the mist instead.

Wiping myself off inside the southern foyer, I exclaimed about the fog in the most princess-like way I could before hurrying to my rooms, where Henry met me with a sad smile, a plate of bonbons, and a bottle of wine.

We drew a bath together with rose fragrance, and he held onto me as though he feared I'd fade away.

It took two days until the crops showed signs of damage and a full week before the smallest specs of rot. A pattern emerged from the store room. Once a week, the candles were lit in the evening as they were last night.

My plan commenced tonight.

Geoffrey and the other DWARVES rigged carts to hold as much as they could of the radical supplies the kingdom held in their secret underground level. We'd utilize the tunnels I found when I'd taken my preliminary walkthrough to ransack their provisions.

I examined the non-perishables and was surprised at the variety of survival gear they had, like the castle would fall to ruin and they would have no choice but to survive in the wilderness. Honestly, that prospect wasn't ideal, but I'd been there.

It wasn't so bad.

A bin of obscure items made my hand twitch for the mirror comm I'd routinely hidden on my person since Lindsay's execution. I bet I could find the means to access it with enough time.

Which I didn't have.

The DWARVES clanged against the far tunnel door. Twenty of them filed in with five giant carts and set to work.

I rummaged through the bins of trinkets and wires, pulling the comm free to check pieces against it.

Something in the fourth bin reacted, springing loose a tiny needle that pricked my thumb. My blood brought up a screen with a blinking line, asking for the passcode. I ran through my list, every possible combination of family history I could recall from the Northern Kingdom.

"Damn it. Open says me." Exasperation stained the collar of my dress with sweat.

An icon jangled, ringing like an old-time phone.

Seriously?

A screen opened to somewhere else, video played of the person on the other side of the comm, hidden in shadow, but the ceiling there…the red and gold looked all too familiar.

"Does that say Phillip?" Henry's voice sprayed out of the speaker before his beautiful face fell into focus. "Abby?"

"Oh god. Henry?" The DWARVES clanged behind me. I made a show of surprise and fear, fumbling my thumb to shut the comm down.

Shit.

"Agents, it's time to move. We've been had. Go. Go. Go."

We were out the door in under a minute, racing through the tunnels, but the sounds of pursuit followed.

Breaking from the group, I engaged a foursome of armed knights, pulling the bladed-scarves from my waist. The spray of their blood hidden on the deep red of my battle dress as I dodged their swords and sliced open their throats.

I fled as their bodies dropped to the dirt, away from the planned escape route. A set of footfalls remained steady behind me, the scrape and cadence one all too familiar. Stuffing the scarves away, I dropped a bit of DEW on my finger and slid to the wall past a corner.

Jogging feet stamped closer, closer, closer, and I spun out to meet him.

"Abigail?"

I pulled my husband into a kiss, savoring the taste of him.

Detonation.

Four simple notes.

He sang them back to me as I ran.

And ran.

And ran…right into Randall.

Behind him stood the red queen.

"Hand over your scarves, Snow White." My mother-in-law's youthful jowl lined with pride and vengeance. "Let's not have another Cinderella fiasco."

Heart struggling to keep beat, I fought to breathe as I unraveled my weapons slowly, placing them in Randall's waiting grasp.

He yanked me forward, anticipating my attack. The forget-me-not hidden in the crease of my fingers.

But the knight miscalculated, and the needle sank into the queen's side, right between the boning of her corset.

Bewilderment rounded her smoky eyes before a group of guards came to haul me off.

I don't know what was worse. The boredom or the bare wooden slats under my corseted back.

I awaited no trial. The new king had no need to pull his wife through such proceedings, especially with a queen mother incapable of running their kingdom.

Besides, all of the parading and fanfare wouldn't have sparked a glint of guilt in me. The private accusation in his eyes was enough, compounded by the niceties he ensured me in the dungeon—bonbons and a sweet wine to remind me that he'd loved me for real.

He never asked me why, only if it were true.

I told him the truth without saying a word, crushing the last traces of faith in me he had.

After three days of guilt and boredom, six knights escorted me from my cell and walked me through the castle, out to the courtyard, and up the steps of a scaffold. I stood above a trap door as the rope fell against my shoulders.

The hangman read my charges as the sea of people cheered.

Above them, in his royal throne, sat my husband. His glassy gaze started the tremble in my fingers. Tremors overtook my shoulders and knees for a flash before I willed them under control. I would stand proud until they dropped the world from beneath my feet.

Beside the king stood his new right-hand man, Randall.

Sharp, dark eyes twinkled with respect rather than condemnation, and his mouth moved.

May the white rose grow in the shadow of its red sister.

The noose tightened around my neck as a team of planes rustled the leaves behind me. Breaching my view, they trailed a puffy white chemical-laced smoke across the sky.

THE BIG BAD WEARS RED

Ryan Chu

The Wolf sits there in his hot neon pink suit. It's not just normal hot neon pink—the kind that you see splashed on street signs at your local red light district—it's spelled out in all CAPS and screams bold. It's a neon pink that shouts louder than all the loud drunks in here and says, "Look how quirky. Look how fancy. Look how goddamn friggin' cute I am." The Wolf sticks his black wet nose into his martini glass and moves the olive around with it.

"Woof." He snorts up the olive and shoots it at my chest. I think it gives me a bruise.

He laughs, thinking it's the funniest gesture in the entire history of man. I just smirk, hope he sees the sarcasm, and sip my beer that's gone lukewarm. The Wolf picks up his martini glass with both his paws and drinks what's left.

"Bartender." He knocks the glass down. Right when it shatters, the bartender is there gently placing him another one. He shoves a five down the man's shirt as the man bows with the elegance of a ballerina.

"Thank you, Mr. Wolf."

"No, thank you, bartender." He gulps and shatters the next one. "Another, bartender, please."

I can't remember the first time I met the Wolf. I'd like to say I came across him when I broke bad for a few years, working for a shady real estate company. I would work with a few animals—Wolf being one of them—and we'd tear down little piglet's houses to make way for the shiny and cute gentrification. But I think we met earlier. It was probably Mr. Richardson's class, Advanced Stylistic Prose, room 31B. Wolf was the loud one in that class—chiming in whenever absolutely least necessary, telling poor, meek Richardson of "Bukowski, Shakespeare, Wordsworth—they were all hacks," or how "prose like that is just tepid water. Where are the waves? The tides that become Tsunamis and drown us in the ocean, which is life," and all the while he loves the sound of his voice as his tongue touches each syllable. He'd give a good howl intermittently throughout class. Somehow through all of that, he said, "We are friends."

"Now, where was I?" He sips his wine and smiles as if the wine gave him a smart-business-plan idea.

"Oh, yes. I like you. I like you a lot, man. I consider you my best friend. 'You're not like all the other boys.'" He does his tired impersonation of my ex.

He laughs.

He always laughs at his own jokes. "But for real. You're the cream of the crop in terms of friendships. Sheep was a douche. Snake was a douche, so was Bear, Rock, and Holly, but you are a class act. A great man, but you're too negative."

"How?"

"Like saying this place is 'hell.'"

"So? Just cause I don't like this one bar. I like a lot of things, Wolfy. I said your suit looked nice today. I like that ice cream shop we go to after brunch on Sundays. I like my parents, bagels, donuts, your parents, and milkshakes. I'd say I'm a pretty positive guy actually."

"You might like a lot of those things, but there's a lot of anger in you."

"What—"

"Well, when we first came into this bar, your steps seemed heavier. There was a big weight on you, making you stomp all over this bar. Being one fuck of a Gloomy Gus, looking at all the bartenders with your I'm-Gonna-Kill-You look. Then just talking about how you hate that guy, this girl, that old man, that midget at this bar. Yeah, you do seem like a pessimist. You seem like a huge fucking pessimist." He was panting really hard, looking like he was gonna tear me down with a gust of his breath.

"Guess, I got a little pissy, too."

I took another sip of my beer and looked into the Wolf's deep black eyes. They were soulless but entrancing. He smirked. I looked away before I thought I'd be sucked into that abyss.

"Remember when we fought in the war?" He pushed away his empty martini glass and picked up another one to his left—couldn't remember when he ordered that one.

"War?"

"Yes, the war. The Great Big One."

"The Great Big One?"

"No—sorry my mistake. The Great Big Fat Pizza Pie one."

"Sorry, I don't remember fighting in a war. All I know is that I'm a hunter."

"Damn it, man. The *war*." He downed that martini and picked up another one from under the table. "The war. The nitty gritty war—the one in the jungles. We slept in the trees at night, and in the day, we dredged through enemy territory, trying not to step onto landmines—but god knows at least someone stepped on one each day. Remember Giraffe, Alligator, and his cousin Crocodile—all gone cause Giraffe drank some of that indigenous booze one night and was too drunk in the morning to even care to be careful. The shitty rations we ate, which were just frozen peas, ham bits, and corn meal mashed together. The dirt, the humidity—"

—the sulfur, smoke, gunpowder plastered all over my face as I mowed down three pigs. The blood, the yells of pain. The diarrhea I got when I ate those berries that the wolf said "Never, ever eat under no circumstances." The times I called my mom to come and "take me away from this foreign land. I want to live with you and play videogames all day." My friends are dead, lying in front of me—legs blown off, asking me to end them. The patch of the giraffe's skin laying at my feet, the countless times that bloody patch-worked image snuck its way into me. It was a buffet. I always thought of picking them up from the floor, putting their bits into my knapsack, thinking I'd make a stew of beef, ham, chicken, pork, and something kosher. The time when we infiltrated that straw hut, shooting random piggies, me taking a bullet in my thigh and having Wolf hoist me over his shoulders and carry me ten miles back to the base. "I got you, bud," he said countless times as the humidity made my wound even more uncomfortable. We got home, got decorated, got plaques that said we were heroes—the president even took us for a meal at Hometown Buffet, which was quite good, but I wish I didn't fill up so much on carbs and went for the steak instead.

"Yeah, I remember." I could taste those mashed potatoes and those fried fishes stale from the overheated aluminum.

The sulfur filled my lungs, and I coughed.

"Hell of a life we lived." He turns his attention to the jukebox, the bartenders, some people who look vaguely familiar, the speakers, and his seventh or tenth cocktail glass that just randomly appeared, too. He smiles at all. Tells everyone with his eyes that we are all going to be fine tonight and that nothing ever ever bad happens when the Big Bad is over here.

Everyone nods meekly. Even the jukebox shift a bit by its small peg legs, trying to back itself.

A nice place, the Wolf would think. A nice place, indeed.

I wonder about all the things he did before me, all the people he met, who they met, maybe there were a thousand people like me and I was nothing special.

Wolf mutters. He gets up with the best idea in the world, he goes over to a blonde, college-aged girl sitting at the bar. He leans beside her, sipping his martini, opening his narrow mouth—probably talking about politics, gender/race/class distinctions, feminism, Marxism, whatever these college people were into.

She laughs.

She spills her beer on the floor, while laughing at how funny he is and how smart and intelligent he is, and how he knows how to talk, and yes, oh yes, how witty he is. He motions for the bartender and gets her another drink.

I think I hate the Wolf.

Yes, I do. He's a dick.

I hate the way he talks, the way he laughs, the way that he talks to girls. He's an idiot, a fake. One of those people who just likes to hear himself talk. He starts slow, letting each syllable hang off his tongue, and when he notices he has a person's "undying attention and intrigue," he starts spouting out jargon and phrases "sprinkled with *intellectualisms*."

And people like him for it—love him, actually.

I finish my beer and drink one sitting on my left.

I finish that and drink another and another. Numerous beers. Great beers. Healthy beers. Beers that make you want to make love to everyone in the room and forget about them right as you climax.

Sounds like my ex-wife.

Haha Haha Haha, that's a joke.

Where's the laughter in here? No one has a sense of humor. They're are all too stupid to know what humor is. They are all dead inside and filled with cow menure. There's nothing less funny than a cow. If I had to say it, cows were probably the worst comedians. Don't know a fucking punchline and just stare out into the distance as they get milked by some inbred hillbilly fuck.

I finish the-who-cares-which-beer, and there are no more beers to pick up.

The Wolf chats up the girl, moving his paws slowly towards hers on the counter. She giggles and blushes as he gently grabs her hand. This all seems too easy—it's an act, a sham, a movie scene being shot in front of me, and I'm too drunk, too dumb to see any fucking cameras.

Director, say cut and end this scene, get the bodyguard to take me away in the stretch limo so we could find some prostitutes to lay me.

He laughs, but it's more of a howl. He's scratching the newly laminated bar, but no one who works there cares. They laugh, too, and attempt his howl, but stutter into grunts and coughs. One of the bartenders sends a neon orange drink his way. It's a Persimmon Punch, a Tangerine Twister, the Lone Gunman—some name he came up with on a drunken night, and when he uttered those words, the bartender on duty put some things together and slid it to him.

Only the best service for the Wolf. Anything for the Wolf. On the house for the Wolf. The Wolf. The Wolf. We all love the Wolf and would love to fuck him if he would have us.

The Wolf now has his arms around the blonde girl, who looks younger and younger as the Wolf nuzzles his polished cue-tipped nose against her peachy cheek. The move is clean, smooth, but it makes me sick, feel stupid for some reason. I need another—

"Beer, sir?" A waiter dressed in a clean-cut unoffending outfit stands calmly by my side. How long has he been there? Did my rage exhume my thoughts into wispy fumes? Did he see the distress signal and come by to quell it with alcohol?

"Thanks."

He sets it down.

I reach for my wallet.

He shakes his head. "It's on the house."

"Well, let me pay for my other drinks."

"Nope, that's taken care of."

"Well, I bet no one is saying I can't tip and—"

"Taken care of too." He leaves and half the beer is already down my throat. A frothy, coffee mixture. This one.

As the waiter leaves, the Wolf holds up his glass and winks at me from a distance. The blonde girl is nestled firmly in his embrace, using his fibery arms as a pillow cushion.

It all makes sense.

The pint glass breaks between my fingers. There's blood on my hands. The unoffending waiter is by my side again. He has a dustpan and a little broom, brushing all the bits into it. He puts them down and snaps. Another unoffending waiter appears next to me and swabs my hand with alcohol using a cotton ball. They are both invading my personal bubble, yet they don't feel like they are. They make me feel warm, comfortable. Maybe it's their beautiful faces without a trace of acne, blackheads, nor scarring. I don't even know what race or gender they are actually. I want to kiss them and make love to them. Put these naughty guys into bed, cover them like a warm summer breeze into them. When they clean, I'm in no rush, no state of panic. There's no last bus to catch home. No test to take in five minutes. No last minute bride in the chapel who won't marry you if you don't exactly come when—

"How long have you been working here?" I smile. I smile for the first time tonight. I smile for the first time in a long while. I think.

"Just started today." He's about finished with the sweeping. His broom brushes gently over the laminate to scan for those covert shards.

"Nice. I don't recall wait service here before."

"That started today also." He's intent on finding every little bit, looking closer at the table.

"What made management change?"

"The owners changed today." He's finished with the cleanup, so is the other unoffending person. "Just two hours ago. Anything else, sir?"

"No, I'm fine."

He bows to me and disappears behind the bar.

So this is it. Huh?

I walk over to the bar. The wolf is licking the side of her face, getting her soppy and sticky.

"Hey, Wolf…" I might have said that a little more ominous than intended, but I don't care. I'm going to kill him tonight. Break his jaw, shove mackerel down his throat, until he can't speak anymore, until all he can do is gurgle back bits of food onto the girl, and she'll probably be disgusted by him and not want to talk to him anymore. He's the one—the cause of all my misery. He's the demon, engineering my downfall. He's an ugly fuck. Just one shot, a kill, a stab, and he's gone.

"Hey. Hey, man! What up? Did you meet Shannon?" He playfully shoves the girl, and she giggles. She slams into me and spills some pink drink on me.

"Whoops." There's a whole bottle of perfume spilling from her lips.

"No, it's a 'whoopsie', Shannon." The Wolf chimes, now clenching a cigar between his fat white teeth.

"Oh, right." She laughs a tiny *hehe* from her lips. "Whoopsie, Mr…Mr. Man."

"Mr. Man. Mr. Man. Shannon, my dear, you crack me up." He swivels his claw. A bartender comes, places three shot glasses on the table and pours tequila. The wolf grabs one and holds it in the air. "To Shannon. A comedian, philanthropist, entrepreneur, pedophilia, manure, and lover of the fine arts."

"Cheers," says everyone in the bar. They all grin at us, as if they all saw us come out the door at once, with our hair frizzled and ties askew, and me, Wolf, and Shannon all have the same exact grins on our faces.

That's it. No war. No Richardson. No shady gentrification company.

I remember the Wolf.

I remember the first time we met.

It's a lovely spring day in the woods. I just killed three fat rabbits, and I was delighted to bring them back to my grandma's house because she always liked the taste of rabbits. Plus, my little sister would be coming to visit, so I was extra happy and extra glad that we had three fat rabbits to eat to be extra satisfied.

I could imagine the scene as I got closer to Grandma's cabin. Grandma would be sitting at the head of the table, while my sister and I would sit across from each other, and three steaming rabbits with shiny red apples in each of their mouths at the center. In the background, a fireplace—even though we didn't have one—and a butler bringing out a giant turkey on a silver platter—we definitely didn't have that either. It was going to be postcard perfect.

Then there was a yell. Sounded like my Grandma's. Another one, this time it sounded more youthful.

Oh no. My sister.

So I ran, sprinted, took out my rifle, cocked it, kicked down the door, and threw up all over the mat. The Wolf on top of my grandmother, riding her wearing my sister's red cape. He stopped, turned around, and smirked.

"Well, looks like we got another contestant." He howled. "Join in. We could use some brawn."

"No." Grandma sounded as if she was knocking on Death's door, but her slap on Wolf's butt disproved that theory. "That's my grandson, Wolfy. There is too much family involved—"

"Family?" I stared at the ceiling to avoid looking at her saggy breasts. The bathroom door opened, and out came my sister, her long blonde hair covering her nipples and a plastic leaf shielding her vagina. She crossed her arms and pouted.

"What's going on? I thought we were doing the Adam and Eve roleplay."

"We are." Wolfy got off my grandma and sat upright on the bed. "She's Eve, I'm Adam and you are God here to spite us!"

"*No*. I'm Eve, Grandma is the deceitful snake, you are God, Wolf, and you said my brother gets to be Adam."

"What?" I gasped.

"C'mon just one more drink, man." The Wolf pats me on the back, and I'm ripped out of my memory.

I lunge for a bar knife by the lemons and limes and point it at the Wolf's neck.

"A little thirsty are we?" The Wolf smirks, the same one as always. His arm is wrapped around Shannon, who is laughing, oblivious to the fact that I have a knife an inch from the Wolf's throat. He snaps his finger. "Oh, bartender. Can my friend over here have one of those delicious IPA's you have?"

"Anything for you, Wolf." A pint of beer slides right to me without spilling a drop.

"This guy." Wolf wraps his arm around me, drink in another hand. "I've known you for a long time, man. I have to say, I have never had a friend like you. You're my best friend."

He steps on the stool and raises a glass in the air. "To Friendship."

"To Friendship," responds the bar patrons. They all take a sip. Even I take a sip. Unfortunately, even when I want to kill him, he's still able to convince me to have a drink. I finish that one, and I have another.

A portly man comes up to me, makes a dirty joke, we laugh, and he buys me a shot.

The Wolf thinks the portly man's joke is funny, so he buys him a drink and me a drink also. Shannon then announces that the portly man is funny, so all drinks are on the house for the rest of the night. I ask the bartender for some whiskey. He gives me two. I drink two, then ask him for, "some more whiskey, please sir."

So he gives me five.

I'm trying to puke into a toilet, but I miss and hit the floor. I fall back, lying next to the bowl. My hands are red, a deep cut on each palm. There's a bloody bar knife next to me. It's time like these when I wonder if inanimate objects have feelings and were pretty pissed that I got blood over them.

I also wonder if I'm in the men's bathroom.

The stall door creaks open, and there's the Wolf. He's as clean as when he first came into the bar, no cuts or stabs. His hot neon pink suit is untouched. He has an umbrella drink—tropical.

He laughs.

"Well, didn't you just get a little crazy." He twirls the umbrella around its way through the grenadine, the ice, and takes a sip right through it. "Getting all stabby. Getting all weird, and kinda gross."

There's the pass of liquor through my breath. My mouth is dry, and it's hard to keep focus.

"I must kill you, Wolf." A statement this time. No anger or sadness passes through. It's declarative. It's right. It's some mundane deed that must be done, like pulling a weed. "You must die today. Please, just die."

I hold the knife, the tip pointing at his chest. I imagine plunging it through the fabric. The blade probably sticking itself just halfway as I manage the blade through the bone, sinews, and muscles.

He won't fight it. He'll accept it. He's gracious that way.

"You're right. I will die today." He sips his drink and looks down meditatively at it, swirling it around, then downing it one gulp. "So will you. So will Shannon and her bartenders and those fine-ass stools I told her to buy when she got this bar."

"Why?" I lower the knife. He kneels down to set his glass gently on the floor and whips out a cigarette. I toss him my lighter, and he nods at me.

"Our sins are catching up with us. I know because I can just feel it. The Pigs, Mr. Richardson, your hot sister, and your even hotter grandma will all want to kill us. They are conspiring together, I tell ya. You and I are the real targets. Shannon, the bartenders, and those fine-ass stools are unfortunate collateral damage. And I know what you're thinking. Let's just run the fuck out of here. Let's get away to Hawaii, drink some tequila sunrises as the sun rises, and be done with it. Except, we will never be done with it. They'll keep hunting us down, killing other innocent people along the way, and every day, we'll be wondering when they are going to get us."

He drops his cigarette, stomps it.

"Well," I say. "What do we do now?"

"We live. Live to the brink. Live until the bombs drop and possibly after that, too…"

"Live? Sounds like a new concept to me."

"Try it."

"Yeah."

"We got all the time in the world if you believe in it hard enough." A wink, nice touch. "Let's waste it all."

Then I'm on all fours, crawling towards those hot neon pink pants. So hot. So neon. I leap the last few inches and pull them down. There it is. His big hairy cock. The size of my arm. It's hard, rock-fucking hard. I love it. I reach for it like I'm a ten-year-old grabbing the biggest fucking lollipop in the candy store. I grab his perfect butt and get his cock in my mouth.

"Oh ho." He howls. "This is living right here. Living to the max."

I go slowly. Back and forth so I can feel the veins, the foreskin, the cusp and all.

I can hear a plane flying somewhere.

Back and forth. Back and forth, and maybe lick him some, too.

"You sure are taking your time."

A Fairy Ship, A Hooded Girl
and Grandma's White
Underwear
Will Tanzer 11/27/16

ALICE ON THE ANALYST'S COUCH

Linda G. Hill

Alice's psychiatrist, the esteemed Dr. Dinah Fell, promised her the nightmares would stop. And to the doctor's credit, she seemed to know what she was talking about; six months after the incident when seven-year-old Alice fell asleep under the tree, they had. That was, however, fourteen years ago.

Fresh out of college, Alice found a job quickly—to the dismay of many of her peers who had exceeded her in marks, but not in popularity—in the accounting industry for which she had studied. She hadn't wanted to admit, even to her sister with whom she shared an apartment, that she suspected the leering man in human resources hired her based on the length of her legs and the cut of her blouse rather than her qualifications. He reminded her of someone with far too many teeth for the size of his mouth.

But regardless, she left her car at home and took the bus to work, knowing that parking spaces downtown were prime real estate. She walked the two blocks from the bus stop—about all she could stand in stilettos—and approached the receptionist at the paneled desk that fronted the office of Queen and Jack Inc. The middle-aged woman with a red bouffant hairstyle studied Alice from top to bottom. Her tight-lipped moue indicated her disapproval of the young woman's tight sweater and short skirt, but she conceded that there was, indeed, a Mr. Topper waiting to see her in his office. The secretary stood and told Alice to follow.

"I'm Rose. You'll come to see me only when you leave for the day, so I'll know to take messages. You will not come to me for copies, faxes, telephone books, coffee, or favors of any sort." She stopped at a door at the end of the long hall and placed her hand on the knob.

"Good luck." She opened the door, and walked back in the direction from whence they had come.

The dark room glowed faint from the sunlight between the thin slats of the closed shades and a candle upon the massive desk to the left. Alice squinted at the outline of a man sitting behind it.

"Come in," the man said in an amused voice. "The light will come on when the door closes behind you, unfortunately."

Alice did as she was told, and sure enough a light came on: a spotlight shining directly on her and blinding her every bit as much as the dark had.

"Come in. Get out of the spotlight so you can see me."

Alice did. A skeletal being in a top hat sipped tea from a china cup and grinned at her as though she were the punchline of a joke.

"You're the new girl, I presume?"

"Yes." Alice straightened her skirt and stood at her full height.

"I'm Jack Topper, the owner of the company. You may call me Mr. Topper. Mr. White will be in to show you to your desk..."

The door opened, and a man shot through, crossed to the desk, tossed an envelope on it, yelled, "I'm late!" and left just as abruptly.

"Apparently, Mr. White has other things on the go at the moment. I'll show you around myself."

They left Mr. Topper's office with the boss in the lead. Down the corridor, they turned right into a large room with rows upon rows of cubicles. At each desk they passed sat a person diligently working. The click of computer keys filled the room.

They arrived at a cubicle, empty but for a metal office desk with a stack of papers, a computer, and a deck of cards.

Mr. Topper lifted the cards and slipped them into his pocket.

"You'll be here. Your instructions are on the computer. If you need anything, press this button," he indicated to a red button under the edge of the desk, "and Mr. Cherry from HR will come to help you."

"Thank you," Alice said.

She sat down to work.

No matter how confused she was, she didn't press the button—she had no desire to see the leering man from human resources again.

Back home that night, Alice found her sister cooking up a pot of spaghetti, which was odd since her older sibling didn't usually cook. In fact, she was a clutz in the kitchen at the best of times.

"I thought it was your birthday," she said. Poised with a wooden ladle over a large aluminum pot, she wore an old fashioned red-and-white-checkered apron that Alice didn't recognize.

"It's not until next week," Alice said.

"Ah well. We'll celebrate your unbirthday then."

Alice made a mental note to look up her psychiatrist.

It took Alice three weeks to get an appointment at with Dr. March. Dr. Fell, it turned out, had not only retired, she had died. In the meantime, Alice kept herself happy at work. Apart from the occasional sighting of Mr. Topper, always with a cup of tea in hand, even when he was outside having a smoke; and Mr. White, who was always late for something or another, the job was satisfying.

What surprised Alice the most was the relationship she formed with the previously leering but now not-so-bad Mr. Cherry. Or Garfield, as his parents unfortunately called him. Upon getting to know him, she decided that though he had too many teeth, the fact could not be counted against him. He was quite a helpful fellow.

Even if he did keep showing up in the most unexpected places and frightening her out of her wits.

For instance, the grocery store fruit and vegetable aisle, when he offered to squeeze her melons. In return, he had asked her for a favor as well. Apparently, she was the only one who could properly check to see if his banana was ripe. When she questioned the wisdom of his only buying one, he told her it was all he needed.

By the time her appointment with Dr. March arrived, Alice didn't need him anymore.

Sure, aspects of her new job, nay, her life of late, reminded her eerily of her dream, but things were leveling out. Her size hadn't changed—she hadn't grown tall or small—and no inanimate objects or animals talked to her. In the end, she wished that she had skipped the appointment.

For what Dr. March told her was this:

Dreams can recur. It doesn't matter if it's been days or years or decades, they come back. And when the nightmare was as involved as Alice's had been, they are more likely to not only come back but can feel like they last for weeks. Her Friday-night appointment left Alice the entire weekend to stew over this.

Was she asleep and dreaming?

It didn't seem that way when she woke up in the morning, but anything was possible.

When she stopped at the grocery store for crackers on Saturday afternoon, her new friend Garfield was there.

Mr. Cherry smiled with his usual toothy grin. "Good thing I ran into you. Mr. Topper wanted to see you in his office on Friday, but you'd already left. I told him that I sometimes celery you in the vegetable aisle, so he asked me to tell you he expects you in his office first thing Monday morning."

Alice was so intrigued, and a little bit frightened, over what Mr. Topper could possibly want to see her about that she completely forgot to ask what Garfield meant by "celery." It didn't matter, however. She figured it out in a dream that night.

"Stalk," the dream told her. "Celery stalk."

When Alice arrived at work the next morning, things were different, and not in a good way. Rose wasn't at her desk, where she always was. In fact, no one was.

The place seemed deserted.

Knowing that she was supposed to see Mr. Topper first thing anyway, she knocked on his door. Applause came from within.

She opened the door slowly—entering a room uninvited was a risky prospect in Alice's experience, particularly when she didn't know if she was awake or dreaming. The lights were off as was customary in Mr. Topper's office, but by the dim glow of the sun through the slats, she observed the entire staff standing in a crowd around the desk. So many people were there, it was impossible to tell what was going on. In her curiosity, she forgot that when the door closed behind her she would be spotlit.

They all turned to look at her, standing at the door with her hands curled at her chin. She stepped out of the spotlight, and the crowd parted: there at, or rather on, the desk, Mr. Topper lay face down with his trousers around his knees. Rose knelt beside him with wooden paddle in her hand, poised to spank him on the bum. Her red hair arced dramatically to almost the height of the ceiling.

As her gaze fell on Alice, her eyes widened and so, finally, did her customary moue.

"Off with her head."

Alice, reclining on Dr. Fell's couch, recounted her dream. The good doctor was taken aback when she was told she was in it and that she had both retired and died.

But Alice had gone on with her story uninterrupted, and now that she had reached its conclusion, she awaited Dr. Fell's comments.

When none were forthcoming, she looked up to see a mummified version of the woman who had, seemingly only an hour ago invited her in.

GARFIELD NOIR
Nathan Smith

to be read with a lit cigarette

I hate Mondays
I say to Odie as we sit on the Brooklyn Bay
Lookin' over the waves passing by.
John died four days ago.
Stepped outside to a hail of bullets
from angry lasagne vendors,
upset at unpaid debts.
John, for all his flaws, was an affable guy
and as I watched him die
I tried to stop the bleeding
John died about 3 p.m. on the 20th of April.
A date famous as Hitler's Birthday and for the landing of Apollo 16.
It was also a Monday.

HAIR

Gregory L. Norris

Sometimes, all it takes is a glance out a window to see the world in a vibrant new light. A van sits parked in your pebbled driveway, and a handsome prince dressed in shorts and a matching brown polo shirt delivers the package you've eagerly awaited. You think the carton in his powerful arms, carefully packed full of expensive hair extensions, is the final puzzle piece that will make your day perfect. Then you realize it's only hair, and maybe what you really needed to feel complete was his smile, his chivalrous offer to carry the package to the upper level of your tower by the beach—lovely Sugar Beach, with its dunes of fragrant salt marsh roses. A true prince in every way, even the name stitched onto his shirt says so: *Joe Prince.*

Yet another glorious summer day greeted Maritzia. The cobalt color of the August sky, visible above her comfortable antique brass bed with the porcelain finials, the music of the waves, and the hint of marsh roses infusing the salty ocean air instantly inspired her.

Salt marsh roses grew wildly along the sand dunes of Sugar Beach. According to local legend, the original plants were swept off the deck of an Orient cargo ship steaming toward Boston by a violent Atlantic gale. They'd drifted ashore with the tide, taken root, and prospered in Cormorant Point, much like Ritzi herself.

She woke refreshed, with a clear vision of her new collection, which would be unveiled during New York Fashion Week in less than a month's time. The salt marsh roses growing around the base of the Lighthouse where she lived had inspired her coloration. The window boxes and whiskey barrels spilling over with royal purple petunias and fresh herbs along the gallery outside her studio in the old lantern room had also translated into her palette. Dusty pink, amethyst, and rich green textured fabrics covered the dress forms in the little studio, whose tall windows faced the water.

Two years ago, Ritzi had drifted ashore to Cormorant Point, just like the roses, with less than a hundred dollars in her purse. Orphaned at a young age, she'd sewn her own clothes from the time she was a teenager—a talent she had since turned into a wonderfully successful career after working as the personal assistant to the town's most famous celebrity, interior designer Dame Claudia Gothel. Several of Claudia's wealthy clients, well-connected fashionistas, had fallen in love with Ritzi's wardrobe. An original design here, a ball gown there, and the rest had happened in short order.

Her favorite coffee cup in hand, Ritzi glided along the gallery balcony, drinking in the daylight and daydreams between sips of the robust breakfast blend, light on sugar and cream. The Lighthouse had called to her from the moment Ritzi came ashore. The wooden structure, three stories tall and rising up from her herbs, flowers, and the beach roses, had belonged to one of her best clients, who was happy to let it go for market value and the occasional one-of-a-kind couture gown.

For the first time in her twenty-five years, life wasn't merely good. It bordered on heavenly. Apart from the finishing touches, her new collection was complete. The hair extensions for the models had arrived, as had the shoes she'd had custom-designed for the line. She lived in the Lighthouse, which realtors and developers—even her former boss, Claudia—had coveted owning before Ms. Cope, her society client, recognized Ritzi's vision enough to sell it to her. And then, there was her princely deliveryman…

Ritzi was gently caressing a cascade of velvety purple petunias, lost in her thoughts, when she heard his voice.

"Hullo up there." His deep tenor drew her out of her daydreams.

Ritzi glanced down to see a beach god peering up at her. He had dark spiky hair and carried a surfboard, wore sunglasses and dog tags, camouflage pants cut into shorts, and flip-flops. She recognized him instantly, even without his delivery uniform. A man that handsome was hard to forget.

"Hello down there," she said, fighting the urge to smile but failing.

"How's the coffee this morning?"

"Delightful. The waves?"

"Don't know yet. Why don't you come down and find out with me?"

Ritzi thought about the elegant two-piece suit she'd designed for the new collection. Oh, the temptation. "Can't. I work from home, and it's almost time to punch the clock. The boss is a beast. Duty calls."

"Yeah, I know all about duty." He tapped his dog tags.

"I bet you do."

His smile, aimed up at her and revealing perfect white teeth surrounded by a day's growth of dark scruff, widened. "So, your name's Maritzia? I remember it from the package."

"Ritzi," she said.

"That's different. I like it. Prince. Joe Prince."

"I remember that from your shirt."

"Great to meet you, Ritzi."

"And it's always nice to meet a real-life prince."

The handsome young man shrugged. "I try my best. So when does that beast of a boss let you out? This prince would love to take you out to dinner tonight, wherever you want."

"She's a real taskmaster, my boss, but I say the chances are good she'll let me out of my chains around dinner time. And I hear the food at the Blueberry Café is exquisite."

"I like blueberries," the prince said.

"Me, too, Joe."

"Then that'll be me knocking on your front door at six o'clock."

Ritzi tapped the manicured nails of two fingers against her coffee cup. "Make it five-thirty…if you'd like to join me for a delightful cup of coffee before dinner."

Joe nodded, saluted, and resumed course, marching backward through the sand on his way to Sugar Beach, his eyes tracking her until he was out of sight. Could the day be any better? She had her career, her new collection, her lovely home, *and* she had met her prince.

But right after Joe vanished behind the flower-draped dunes, a phantom chill tumbled down Ritzi's spine, the unmistakable sensation of being watched from somewhere nearby at its source. Turning, she faced the house of her nearest neighbor, and Dame Claudia Gothel stood on her patio, arms folded, a wicked scowl on her face, visible even from the distance.

For the rest of the day, Ritzi attempted to focus on the demands of her career. She had a collection to finalize, three gowns for local clients, and sketches for next season's line calling to her. Her little studio in the lantern room with its tall, ocean-facing windows was a wonderland of high-end textiles, color-coordinated and stored on shelves or in bolts beside the cutting table, buttons, beads, jewels, and shoe racks, all of it guarded over by a small militia of dress forms.

Still, thoughts of the handsome soldier-turned-surfer-and-delivery-driver chased her, no matter where she turned. She already knew about Joe Prince's heroics overseas. All of Cormorant Point's visitors did, too, thanks to the banners written on white sheets stretched across overpasses along Route 7 and yellow ribbons tied around local oak tree trunks. He was the seaside town's favorite son, safely returned home from the war.

"Joe Prince." She sighed, returning one of the lush hair extensions she'd been admiring to its container and tipping a glance at the clock.

Ritzi escaped the confines of the studio for the warmth of the sunny afternoon spilling across the gallery. She picked up the watering can and gave each of the herbs growing in the garden of planters a healthy drink. The basil and Rapunzel lamb's lettuce, radishes, and escarole made wonderful salads, which she had existed on for light lunches and dinners all summer. *Dinner*, she thought. The time for her dinner date with Joe Prince inched steadily closer. Fresh warmth ignited within her at the notion, teasing her nipples into hard points. She settled a hand on her thigh, within inches of her most-sensitive flesh, and shuddered. Thoughts of him had aroused her.

And then Ritzi heard a single deep, hollow knock at her front door.

She lowered the watering can and hurried down the staircase that wound along the inside of the Lighthouse's outer wall. Had Joe, her new potential prince, quit the waves early for that offer of a cup of coffee? Beaming, Ritzi opened the front door. But her smile soon fell flat, for standing on the other side was her neighbor and former employer, the famous Claudia Gothel.

"Ritzi," the other woman said, a frigid smirk at one sharp corner of her mouth.

"Hello, Claudia," Ritzi said.

"Expecting somebody else?"

"No."

"No special deliveries from our local hero?"

Claudia was flawlessly dressed in a pale yellow top and white slacks, heels, and plenty of rubies the color of fresh blood around her neck and on her long, slender fingers. She would have seemed a vision of beauty in the glorious afternoon sun, except that as Ritzi was about to comment on her allusion to Joe Prince, the lone cloud in an otherwise unblemished sky suddenly passed in front of the sun, and a dark shadow engulfed her. This made the powerful negative energy Claudia radiated visible and undeniable.

"Are you going to invite me in, dear or must I stand out here, waiting for it to rain?"

Ritzi blinked herself out of the spell she'd fallen under. "Of course. Please, come in."

Lips pursed tightly, Claudia strutted into the Lighthouse. Her eyes roamed the lower level's sitting area, drinking in the details and perhaps judging Ritzi's choices in color and style. "You have coffee?"

"I was just about to put on a fresh pot."

"Good. You should remember the way I like mine—you poured enough cups for me when you were my assistant."

The venom infusing Claudia's words was so perfectly metered out, so couched in pretty disguises, someone who didn't know her as well might have missed the delicate digs. But not Ritzi. Claudia's reaction to her resignation hadn't been graceful, and for a solid week following her move into the Lighthouse, Ritzi had heard the shattering of glass coming from her closest neighbor's home; likely, she'd assumed, expensive trinkets and treasures Claudia purchased at the local high-end shops on the boardwalk to sell to her clients, pitched in a fit at the nearest wall.

Claudia ascended the staircase to the second story, which contained Ritzi's sunny kitchen, washroom, and bedroom, the latter housed in what had been the Lighthouse's Watch Room until the early 1920s. Again, Ritzi sensed her unexpected visitor was absorbing all that she could about her surroundings, perhaps judging her choices through the eyes of an interior designer known nationally for her unique point of view. But Claudia also walked in a way that suggested she owned the place or was entitled to it.

"You've done a remarkable job with the Lighthouse," she said.

"Thank you, that's a huge compliment coming from you, Claudia."

Ritzi busied herself by making a fresh pot of coffee. She chose the hazelnut blend, Claudia's favorite.

"You know, dear, I petitioned the Cope family for many years to sell me the Lighthouse. And then dear Jessica Cope—my good chum from childhood, school, and Cormorant Point society—turned around and gave it to you. An outsider, an urchin."

Ritzi switched on the machine and revolved to see Claudia had begun rearranging the vase full of wildflowers she'd picked from the dunes only that morning. "She didn't *give* me the Lighthouse. Jessica felt my vision was perfect for the property," she calmly explained. "You know, Claudia…"

Claudia winced. "Please, dear, don't go on. The way you say my name. So heavy and inelegant, galumphing, with the emphasis on *clod*. It really insults me."

Ritzi drew in a deep breath. "Neither my purchasing the Lighthouse from Jessica Cope nor the way I say your name are personal attacks against you."

"Against me?" Claudia tittered a laugh, the sound as harsh and humorless as the smile it emerged from. She turned away from the flowers, which now looked limp and dying after being handled, and faced the shell-ringed mirror on the wall. There, Claudia teased a stray lock of hair. The rest of their exchange passed through reflection.

"My dear, from the moment you arrived to our fair little town in your sad rags and cheap shoes, you've been a parasite, feasting off my good graces. You've poached my clients, stolen this house out from underneath me, and rewarded me by leaving my employ without sufficient notice."

"Excuse me, *Ms. Gothel.* But that is just not true."

She could have reminded Claudia about what a beastly witch she had been to work for, how many times Ritzi had resolved design issues for her, only to have Claudia take full credit for the fixes, and how Ritzi's clients had approached her, enthralled by her ability to create stunning one-of-a-kind clothes. But, Ritzi knew, when a woman weaves the threads of her talent into a successful business, there is never any shortage of detractors who will believe she walked over the backs of others to get there.

"And now, I see you throwing yourself at our local hero, the delivery man. *My* delivery man." Claudia 's cold reflection frowned in the mirror. "Be warned, dear Ritzi, for now you have crossed my last line."

Ritzi folded her arms and took a bold step closer. "What?"

"Joe Prince. He's off limits to you. Stay away from him…or else."

Ritzi gasped, "Are you insane?"

Not until Claudia's smile returned in the mirror did Ritzi's inner voice answer the question for her. Yes, Claudia was.

"Joe Prince is mine. You've stolen enough from me. If you try to take Joe as well, I'll make you pay very, very dearly."

And then, before returning to the staircase and leaving the Lighthouse, Claudia spun around and snapped the talons of a hand covered in blood-red rubies in Ritzi's direction, Svengali-fashion, as though placing a curse upon her.

Ritzi opened the door, her earlier excitement at dining with Joe dampened by a creeping sense of unease. Claudia was unhinged and, Ritzi already suspected thanks to that weeklong thunderstorm of breaking glass following her resignation, capable of violence.

But Claudia hadn't returned. Standing on the other side of the door wearing a striped button-down dress shirt, the top two buttons undone to show plenty of chest hair, blue jeans, and sandals was Ritzi's handsome prince. He'd arrived with a beautiful bouquet of daisies wrapped in colorful paper.

"Hi," he said, extending the flowers toward her. "I hope you don't mind."

Ritzi's worries about Claudia Gothel evaporated. "Mind? They're lovely."

"Then it's a perfect match, Ritzi. I really want to do this right." He tucked his hands into his pockets and shuffled his big feet. "I gotta be honest—you're the hottest girl I've ever seen, and I've been on most of the continents, you know. I want this date to be so amazing that you'll want another. And another after that. And…"

Joe *was* a prince. He opened doors for her—his truck's as well as at the restaurant—and pulled out her chair when they were seated. There was rarely a dearth of conversation over delicious salads and succulent seafood, but she appreciated those rare moments because they gave her occasion to study his handsomeness on the other side of the centerpiece candle. His eyes, vibrant emeralds, had seen terrible things in the war overseas, if the worry lines around them were an indication. He loved to surf waves and ride a skateboard. His dad had fought in Desert Storm. He'd learned how to treat a lady properly thanks to his mom. He liked his new job because it kept him grounded to his past and present life in Cormorant Point. They were both happiest, they learned, living near the ocean on the scant few miles of New Hampshire coastline.

Joe was a real man, despite his boyish smile, yet still wonderfully, miraculously boyish considering the man he'd become during the war.

Dinner at the Blueberry Café exceeded Ritzi's expectations on all counts. Following leafy salads with summer tomatoes and a light balsamic dressing, grilled scallops over wild mushroom risotto, and a blueberry cobbler—which only seemed fitting considering the name of the café—they strolled along the quaint boardwalk, lost in the joy of one another's company. It wasn't until Ritzi caught sight of the Lighthouse in the distance, the glow from her studio in the former lantern room a bright beacon above Sugar Beach, that she remembered her encounter with Claudia.

"Can I ask you something?"

"Anything," he said good-naturedly, a mischievous snarl on one side of his unshaved mouth showing a hint of white teeth. "Well, almost anything. Don't want to scare you off on our first date."

They sat on one of many wrought iron benches facing the pier, he in a jaunty man's pose, she in a pensive huddle, with arms wrapped around her chest.

"What's wrong, Ritzi?"

"Do you know Claudia Gothel?"

"Everybody knows Dame Claudia," Joe said.

"Have you and she, ever, you know…"

"Ever what?"

"Dated?"

Joe snorted a laugh. "I deliver packages to her house and office all the time, but that's it. I don't drink my coffee with just anybody, you know."

Ritzi drew in a deep breath and expelled it on a humorless chuckle.. "She likes your coffee beans, that's for sure. And she thinks I'm invading her territory by offering you a cup."

Joe faced her directly. Ritzi fell into the hypnotic pull of his vibrant emerald gaze, his eyes glowing visibly in the lights from the boardwalk. "That territory is all mine, not Claudia's, and I invite whomever I want into it. I want you here, Maritzia."

He leaned closer, took her hand, and kissed its back.

"She's one mean black widow. Dame Claudia Gothel's not my type."

Relaxing, she cupped his cheek. "And what is your type?"

"Guess," he challenged, and then crushed his lips against hers.

They went on dates every night for a week and sometimes met up during the workday. Once, Joe arrived at her front door in his shorts, shades, and flip-flops, his surfboard by his side.

"Want me to teach you how to ride goofy-footed?"

She had other opportunities and projects to consider, and the fact she'd never been good on a balance beam, let alone a wave. But sometimes, the best thing a person can do is throw caution to the wind, clock out for the day, and spend a sunny summer afternoon at the beach, enjoying the company of a handsome prince.

The salt marsh roses were at the peak of their bloom, the sky was bright and cloudless, the color of comfortable denim, and though she fell off Joe's surfboard more than she rode standing atop it, Ritzi couldn't remember a time when she'd ever had so much fun.

"So this is my new line." She proudly extended a hand in invitation for her prince to enter the lantern room.

The flowers Joe had given Ritzi the night of their first date prospered in her favorite green sea-glass vase atop the cutting table, surrounded by her sketchbooks.

He told her he didn't know much about fashion. That was because, for as long as he could remember, he'd strutted down Life's Runway dressed in desert fatigues and dog tags. But then he surprised her by asking, "Is there a seat for me in the tent at your big fashion show?"

Ritzi coyly traced a finger down the elegant bias cut of the dress draped on the nearest form, the raspberry cut, cutting in on her dance around the dress form, giving her a graceful spin across the lantern room floor. "I want to be there. I love that you're so passionate about your art. You turned your creativity into something real and beautiful. You're a dreamer who made her dreams come true."

Ritzi beamed from his compliment, knowing that sometimes dreamers dream big and their fondest dreams do get rewarded. But she was also forced to remember that sometimes the fulfillment of a hardworking dreamer's aspirations can polarize the jealous into behaving badly.

Ritzi faced this bitter truth as Joe playfully led her through another spin around the studio and out onto the balcony. For when she twirled to a stop, she faced her nearest neighbor's house. Claudia sat beneath a large yellow beach parasol, her eyes hidden by dark sunglasses, binoculars clenched in the talons of one hand, and the look on her face, frigid in the sun, was terrifying to behold.

The storm rolled in during the night, a violent gale likely rivaling the tempest that had spilled flowers from a distant land into the Atlantic, ultimately transforming the face of the New England shoreline forever. A cold and steady downpour fell, and the crash of the waves against Sugar Beach would have deafened had Ritzi not closed up her little tower against the ravages of the weather.

The phone rang while the coffee brewed. It was Joe.

"No surfing today. It's monstrous out there."

Ritzi poured. The rich aroma inspired a kind of internal warmth, as though her insides were smiling. "I agree. A good day to stay inside and cuddle."

"I'll be right over."

That notion warmed her more.. "I'm going to try to put in a full day's work, Joe. Dinner tonight?"

"Pick you up at six?"

"Look forward to it." She blew him a kiss over the line; Joe captured it and promised to send back the real thing when he made it to the Lighthouse's front door.

A ribbon of cold air whistled up the staircase, carrying with it the ghostly moan of the wind. Ritzi shivered—a rarity during that warm, vibrant summer on Sugar Beach. She'd been so absorbed in her work and the invisible specter of worries creeping around the glass walls of the lantern room that she hadn't noticed the lateness of the hour until the gust traveling through the Lighthouse embraced her and stirred the hairs of the long, lush extensions laid out across the cutting table.

The extensions were designed to give the models massive hair volume; glorious ponytails reaching almost to the floor, mirroring the drape and sweep of the clothes. She'd ordered a dozen in all, and though expensive, they were an integral part of the styling. The plan for them after Fashion Week was donation to charity for women going through chemo.

Even before the ghostly breeze whisked up the staircase and into the lantern room, Ritzi had paced the floor, questioning certain choices, including the hair extensions, which had seemed so clear and brilliant until that afternoon. Something dark was in the air; a malaise conjured forth into existence by the storm. Rain splashed against the windows, and a heavy fog shrouded over the Lighthouse and surrounding beach.

The front door clattered as it struck against the wall. Had the wind blown it open? Or perhaps, she wondered, hurrying down the staircase, could Joe have arrived earlier than expected? But the feeling in the air worsened and the gooseflesh that broke suddenly across her arms spoke to another, darker explanation.

Sometimes, it is best when a woman trusts her worry.

Ritzi's front door stood fully open, letting in the rain and wind. The shadows of an early, false dusk swirled beyond the frame, a brooding twilight ushered in by the gale's gloom. Ritzi might have believed the storm's fury had forced the door, if not for her own nagging intuition and the line of wet footprints leading into the seating area.

"Close the door, dear," Claudia said.

Ritzi gasped, both stunned and outraged by the other woman's bold intrusion into her home. Then she saw that Claudia was holding a pistol in one ruby-covered claw, and cold fear smothered every other emotion.

"I said, *close it.*"

Heart galloping, Ritzi did as ordered. The storm pushed against the door in outrage, screaming as its access to the house was denied. A deceptive, throbbing calm settled over the tower's lowest level. Claudia rose and aimed the gun directly at Ritzi's face.

"Claudia, please put that away." Ritzi said, to no avail.

"You know, looking at you, I feel the same way as when I see an antique globe in one of those upscale junk shops out on Atlantic Avenue. I sometimes go out there in search of a bargain for a particular client. See a globe. Give it a spin. Watch borders that have since been redrawn a hundred times blur and fade. Countries that have lost their names. Worlds that no longer exist. That's what you've done to me, dear Maritzia. You've destroyed my world."

"Claudia, I haven't."

Claudia's crazed eyes snapped fully open, like shades drawn too tightly. "You stole the prince of Cormorant Point, after I warned you to stay away from him."

Shaking with rage, Claudia fired the pistol.

Luckily for Ritzi, the quiver in the other woman's hand botched her accuracy. The wall beside Ritzi's head exploded in a shower of splinters. Claudia retrained her aim as Ritzi ran in the only direction she could, higher and higher up the staircase, until she reached the lantern room and there was nowhere else to run.

She locked the studio's door behind her and circled the small room twice. With the telltale clomp of Claudia's heels pursuing her up the staircase, the only clear way out of the Lighthouse now was down, over the gallery's railing. But dropping to the beach three stories below would likely be a jump to her death, and even if Ritzi did survive the fall, what would stop Claudia from finishing the job once she attempted to hobble away?

Claudia pounded on the door. "I'm not happy with you. Open up at once, or this will only get worse."

Ritzi reached for the telephone. Either the storm or the madwoman on the other side of the door had killed the line, and her cell was nowhere in sight—the kitchen, she remembered, left beside her favorite coffee cup following that last phone call with Joe.

"Maritzia," Claudia sing-songed. "You're testing my patience."

Ritzi's eyes darted around the studio in search of a weapon, anything she could use to vanquish her attacker. But what good were pinking shears against a pistol, or fabric up against a .45? Then she focused on the hair extensions, so long and lovely and vital to the success of her new collection for Fashion Week.

Sometimes, Ritzi thought, random convergences might not be so random after all. She needed a ladder, and fate had provided her with a rope. There might still be a magnificent showing at the tents, even without the hair extensions. But there would be no new collection by Ritzi if Ritzi herself didn't survive to unveil it.

As if to cement the point, a gunshot tore through the door, slamming into one of the dress forms and knocking it onto its back. Ritzi gathered up the extensions and, moving as quickly as she could, she knotted one with another, creating perhaps the most expensive rope in modern history. Wasting no time and with Claudia hammering on the studio's door, Ritzi hurried onto the gallery.

Instantly, the angry gale tried to sweep her off the balcony, accomplishing the madwoman's villainous scheme for her. Digging in and keeping focused, Ritzi wound one end of the rope around the railing, tied it twice, and then climbed over the edge.

From the corner of her eye, she caught the glare of headlights from Joe's truck as he pulled into the pebbled driveway. Fresh hope surged through her.

"Joe." she cried out.

He stepped out of his truck and into the rain, glancing around in search of her. "Ritzi, where are you?"

"Up here, on the gallery." Clothes soaked through, her hair plastered to her face, she added, "It's Claudia. She's in the Lighthouse. She has a gun, and she's trying to kill me!."

As if on cue, another bullet tore through the lantern room. One of the big glass windowpanes shattered.

The prince leapt into action. Joe hurried across the wet sand, stumbled, recovered, and was soon waiting directly beneath the balcony. "I'm here, Ritzi. I won't let her hurt you."

"I made this—" Ritzi held up the coil of rope.

"Good, now Ritzi—*Ritzi*—let down your hair."

She cast the rope over the edge of the tower's precipice.

The hair extensions didn't reach all the way to the sand, but slowly, resolutely, Ritzi climbed down. Because sometimes, you just have to believe that everything will work out for the best in the end, and that a prince will be there to catch you, should you fall.

THE SECRET LIFE OF BLANCA SNOWE

Saryn Chorney

In hindsight, Blanca Snowe remembered her wedding day clearly and fondly, yet with a flurry of mixed emotions. A porcelain beauty with hair so black that it looked more like midnight blue when the sun reflected against it, to all in attendance she glowed as a perfect bridal vision. Handsome, doting and kind, Prince Chandler proved himself charming in every possible way. Besides, he saved her life the day they met.

When it came to cinematic-meet-cute scenarios, theirs was top notch. Everyone told Blanca she was lucky—and she agreed. Not only was she marrying a true prince, but she also had seven best men, in lieu of bridesmaids, who would do anything for her.

For better or worse, Blanca was too young and inexperienced at the time to fully understand the future implications of all this male attention. She had no idea how much she would come to crave variety and adventure beyond the trappings of her fairy-tale marriage.

The tragic events of Blanca's childhood were at least partially to blame for her present condition. Blanca's mother died in childbirth, and her wealthy father, the lord of Fairest Landing, raised his beloved only-daughter by himself. Although he lavished Blanca with love and affection, he missed having a wife. When Blanca turned thirteen, he remarried. Unfortunately, his new wife, Hilde, was a manipulative and vain woman with a suspicious agenda. Mostly, she busied herself spending her new husband's fortune on beauty products. Hilde ignored Blanca; she passed the majority of her time in the toilette, mixing ointments and talking to herself in the mirror. Perhaps that wasn't so odd, though, as Blanca spent the majority of her day talking to the birds, bunnies, squirrels, and stray cats in the courtyard of their estate.

Although the Fairest Landing police officially declared it an accident, Lord Snowe died suddenly from an allergic reaction to one of his wife's homemade tonics, which he mistook for mouthwash. Hilde made a big show of appearing devastated, but after a month of official mourning, she debuted a new youthful look and entertained suitors. To her disdain, most of them took a shine to Blanca, who was sixteen by then. In juxtaposition to her innocent beauty, the girl also had an alluring countenance that intrigued men. This infuriated Hilde, who gave a handsome sum to a handsome hitman named Hunter to make Blanca *disappear*. Mid-kidnap-and-chop-up plan, Hunter found himself pitying his pretty prey. Instead of offing her, he dropped her off at a so-called safe house where seven merry men lived.

Blanca crashed with the merry men for two years, and the house was the party pad of its kingdom. She gained quite the voyeuristic education from Doc, Twink, Bear, Jock, Art, Top, and Bottom. Despite their hedonistic lifestyle, the merry men were caring foster fathers. Doc, the eldest merry man and de-facto leader of the household, was particularly protective of Blanca and more acutely aware of her age and naïveté than his housemates. On the night of Twink's birthday party, he cautioned Blanca to stay in her room as hijinks were bound to ensue after midnight.

"Come on, Doc. I'm eighteen, not eight. Besides, Top and Bottom explained the birds and the bees to me."

"Don't try to grow up too soon, lovely girl," said Doc. "One day you will be old like me and look back on your life with longing for the innocence and simplicity of your youth."

Blanca pouted and reluctantly agreed to stay in her room that night.

She laid in bed, envisioning the revelry in her mind's eye while listening to the music and loud (and dirty) conversations going on throughout the house.

Someone knocked.

Hoping Doc changed his mind, Blanca hopped out of bed and swung open the door.

But a gorgeous drag queen in a red wig, heavy makeup, and a long sleeve emerald-sequined gown stood there. Blanca did not recognize this character.

"Oops. Honey, I'm so sorry. I thought this was the powder room." Blanca couldn't quite place her familiar voice.

"Don't worry, I can't sleep anyway," said Blanca.

"Oh, are you experiencing somnambular troubles? I have the perfect antidote." The drag queen fished a lime-green lollipop out of her clutch.

"Suck on this, and you'll be out like a light in two minutes. I promise it tastes so much better than Nyquil."

Blanca opened up the plastic wrapping and took a lick. "Mmm, sour apple?"

"That's right. Sweet dreams, pretty girl." The drag queen abruptly slammed the door shut.

Exhausted, she stumbled back to bed, her head hitting the pillow and the half-sucked sucker falling onto the floor.

Alas, while the merry men were busy with their various peccadillos, the not-so-mysterious drag queen's bewitched lollipop poisoned Blanca. She didn't wake up the next morning, and when the clock struck noon, Doc discovered her missing from brunch with the crew. She was in a coma. Twink blamed himself, and in an especially dramatic display of emotion, he fainted and fell down the stairs. He broke his neck and died on the spot.

As for Blanca, the doctors said she could only be cured by a magic kiss from the right prince. As fate would have it, Chandler matched as her kiss donor.

Like all the men before him, Chandler was smitten with Blanca, asleep or awake. And as the custom follows, Blanca was swept off her feet and married to the man who saved her life. But sometimes, happily ever after has an expiration date, and for Blanca, the seven-year itch set in. Chandler was a good husband, and she loved him, but what does an eighteen-year-old know about marriage? She was twenty-five, a grown woman now, and the time she spent living with her seven merry friends and the circumstances of her near-death experience had changed her, both physically and mentally. The poison wreaked havoc on her reproductive system, and the doctors said she'd likely never be able to have children. Chandler loved her all the same, but Blanca fell into a depression upon hearing this news, and eventually, she rebelled against her innocent-and-pure-as-snow nature along with it.

Prince Chandler was a diplomat and traveled to faraway lands a lot for work. He was focused on his own business and, to a degree, neglected his wife and her emotional state. Blanca was left alone for weeks to her own devices, so she snuck off to other kingdoms where nobody knew her.

She met the first of her secret suitors at a nightclub in Hamelin. His nickname was Pipes, and he was the singer in a band. Like many of his female fans, Pipes' voice and his rock star swagger bewitched her. In private, she loved how he sang to her after they made love and strummed up little impromptu ditties about her while they were in bed. He was sweet but could often be petulant and cocky. Plus, Blanca's marital arrangement tormented him.

This eventually unraveled their ill-fated romance.

In a cockney Hamelinish accent, he chided her. "Come on tour with me, love. Your marriage is rubbish."

Every time, Blanca shook her head. She'd stroke his beard and massage his back, neck, and chest, cooing at him to "just enjoy their time together." The musician entranced her on stage and in bed, but she understood the realities of romancing a rock star. He would always privately entertain fans and groupies, too. The moment she was officially *his* would also be the moment she'd lose Pipes forever.

During this first affair, whenever Chandler called from his long-distance travels, guilt consumed Blanca. But once they were reunited, he'd call her "Snow Bunny" and sweep her into his arms. They'd make love and Blanca would remember all the things that made her feel cozy and content in their relationship. She eventually cut all contact with Pipes, who wrote an entire album, "The Blanca Album," about her.

Ultimately, the experience with Pipes made her appreciate Chandler even more. And that lasted for a few months, until he went away on business again, and she met Wolfgang.

Wolfgang was a traveling salesman. He worked for a luxury furrier and dressed to the nines. Their dalliance was short but kinky: Wolfie liked wearing women's undergarments. She gifted him a red negligee with a little hoodie attached, and they spent a week role-playing in bed. Blanca had a lot of fun with Wolfie, but the relationship didn't run too deep. On their last night together, he opened up his suitcase and pulled out two costumes.

"For you," he smiled brightly, holding up a woodsman's denim overalls. They smelled of dirt and pine trees.

"Ummm, for me?" Blanca asked.

"Yes, and these are mine," he said and held up a long flannel nightgown and large pair of floral granny panties. He winked. "Are you game?"

She wasn't.

When he left town, Blanca bid him farewell, fine with the fact that she'd never see the wolf man again.

Next came Hansel. He was a gorgeous male model whom Blanca met when Fashion Week came to the kingdom. Contrary to popular belief, Hansel did not work out a lot or eat healthfully. In fact, he was addicted to sugar in the way that others in the industry fell victim to cocaine or heroin. At first, Blanca enjoyed letting him eat whipped cream from her belly button and snort Pixy Stix off her chest. However, his creepy and lesser attractive twin sister and manager, Gretel, became jealous of the time they spent together.

On Valentine's Day, he invited Blanca to his fancy hotel room and melted dark chocolate all over her milky white skin. As he lapped it off her, Gretel stormed into the room and pelted them both with strawberries and various other pieces of cut fruit.

"She gets chocolate, and I get an Edible Arrangement? After everything I've done for you? Are you implying I need to diet?"

Clearly their affair had gotten messy. Blanca slipped out of bed and hopped in the shower, leaving the dysfunctional siblings to bicker it out. She breathed a deep sigh of relief when the duo left Fairest Landing at the end of the week.

"Good luck in Milan." She hugged Hansel goodbye while Gretel scowled in the taxi. "Think of me while you eat Stracciatella gelato."

This cycle of on-again, off-again men continued for years: Jack B., Pete Pan, Mowgli, Robin H., and all three Musketeers. Blanca had a steady stream of discreet lovers, and Chandler was none the wiser. Every time he returned home, he'd reap the benefits of his wife's increased libido. Their union stayed intact despite her tendency to stray.

Aside from sexual satisfaction and the passion of the moment, none of her affairs ultimately made Blanca any happier.

One night, the sad princess made a wish upon a certain star.

"Are you there Twink? It's me, Blanca. I know I haven't been a model wife, and I won't even make excuses about my childhood and my stepmom and the coma, blah blah blah. I just want to say that I know I haven't been honest or loyal or especially true for many years. But if there was one miracle that I know I don't deserve—but I'm still just going to throw it out there—I would wish for a child. I want to love and care for someone more than I do for myself."

Up in heaven, Twink nudged the Blue Fairy, granter of stargazers' wishes, and asked her to consider Blanca's request. Blue acquiesced. She descended from the heavens and told Blanca, "Prove yourself brave, truthful, and unselfish, and some day, you will be a mother."

As the years went on, Blanca grew older and wiser. Her double life had run its course; she was no longer compelled to run around behind her husband's back. In fact, the two split up amicably after Chandler matched as a kiss donor for yet another sleeping princess named Beauti. Blanca wasn't mad; in many ways, she was excited to live her own life without some pestering sense of guilt or being taken for granted by her absentee prince. Beauti was young and simple, and she worshipped Chandler in a way that Blanca never could. She approved of her ex-husband's new relationship. They were a better match.

Blanca joined a "Princess Problems" support group and dedicated her free time to volunteering at an animal shelter, as well as taking care of the now-elderly Doc, Art, Bear, and the surviving members of the merry-boys club. Blanca was no longer so young herself, and well past childbearing age—had it even been a possibility in the first place.

She hadn't slept with Chandler, or anyone else for that matter, in almost a decade.

In fact, she became quite the old cat lady, adopting a number of orphaned felines.

Gaining weight and experiencing morning sickness shocked her. Sure enough, the Blue Fairy had finally granted her wish.

Weirdly, Blanca's symptoms also included coughing up hairballs and a light scratching sensation inside her belly. In a miracle of Immaculate Conception (or Cat-ception, as the case may be), Blanca gave birth to a kitten. He was a striped-orange-tabby cat with black feet.

"I shall call him Boots." Blanca held her pussy-son close to her breast.

The old princess loved the magical feline with all her being, and he was raised as a real boy who spoke and wore clothes. After his mother's passing, Boots would go on to become a famous, swashbuckling hero in his own right.

But that's a story for another day.

WOLVES IN SHEEP'S CLOTHING
Jenner Michaud

B.B. Wolf rode his Harley down the winding road, his wild, unprotected mane tussled by the wind. He was big, and he was bad, and no one would get away with kidnapping the man who gave him a career.

Wolf slowed as he turned onto an unmarked mud path. Careful not to splash his shiny hog, he drove on the edge of the dirt road where it dried and cracked into a brown mosaic. Rows of dead confiners camouflaged the kidnappers' shack. Wolf turned off the engine. A flute, loud and off key, rose from the structure. He grinned. Fifer was home.

After stashing his bike, Wolf fought his way through the muck in his spiked, leather boots. Twenty feet from the shack, he called to the homeowner over the cacophony of the tortured instrument. "Fifer. Come out of that eyesore of a pigsty."

A straw hat appeared in the uncovered window, and a cheeky pink face came into view. "Private property. Go away."

"Where's Mr. D.?" Wolf asked.

"The renegotiation of our contracts doesn't concern you."

"You signed the contracts, stand by them. You'd be nothing without Mr. D."

"I can't blame a one-trick pony for not understanding ambition."

"I can't blame pigs for not being gentlemen."

Fifer sighed. "It doesn't concern you, but I rewrote our contracts. Walter needs to sign them, and you need to stay out of the way."

"I can't believe you have the nerve to use his first name."

"We're done here, Wolf. Buzz off."

"Just release Mr. D., or you and your fat brothers are going down." Wolf rammed into the downtrodden home, shaking it free.

"You Big Bad Wolf," Fifer said from inside. "Stop it, or I'll make you regret it."

"There's nothing you can threaten me with."

"Red's a lovely girl. It'd be a shame if anything came between you."

"Leave Red out of this, you cross-eyed swine." Wolf huffed, and he puffed as he levelled the dwelling with his bare paws. Fifer and his crew were gone, and all that remained of the shack was a jumble of broken boards.

"I'll get all of you pigs." Wolf roared and returned to his bike.

B.B. Wolf rode his Harley down the winding road, his mane covered by a dented helmet. He was big, and he was bad, and he had the bruises to prove it.

The trailer park's cobblestone driveway shook the few teeth left in his jaw. Wolf parked and cut the engine before dismounting. The squealers inside made more noise than a band of coyotes.

When he couldn't find a doorbell, Wolf tapped on the door.

"Hello boys," he said, disguising his voice by adopting a high-pitched sing-song. "I have some cakes for you."

Someone wearing a blue sailor jacket with a big black tie cut his way through the white smoke. The window next to the door cracked open, and tendrils of burning skunk drifted out. "Howdy, Wolf. What's up?"

Wolf pressed his snout against the screen and coughed. "Come out here, Fiddler. You and your brothers have messed with the wrong Wolf. What have you done with Red and Mr. D.?"

The door flew open, and Wolf readied to battle. But instead of one of the kidnappers, the woman who owned his heart stood in the doorway.

"Go away, B.B." Ice laced her words.

Wolf's mind raced to understand her reaction. Why did she look so angry that he had come to rescue her? "What's wrong, Red? Have they hurt you?"

She pulled the crimson hood over her long, brunette hair. "You lost the right to ask me anything when you went out with that maid. I don't know what you saw in that tramp. Her stupid shoe got more social media coverage than she did."

"But nothing happened with Cindy. I just—"

"You and your lies. Leave me alone." She slammed the door.

"Her pumpkin broke down, and I gave her a ride. That's all," Wolf said though the window screen. "Please, Red. You've got to believe me."

Smoke whirled around Red's hood. "You're only begging me now because that shoeless girl is back with Charming. I'm not stupid. I know his posse beat you because you seduced his girlfriend. That's all the proof I need."

"You're my one and only, Red. I've never lied to you. I mean, not since we—"

"Go away before I shoot you myself, you lying bastard." The smoke swallowed Red, and Fifer's plump face replaced hers at the window.

"You heard the lady. Scram."

"Why you thieving swine. Hiding in there with your stinky brother. Leave the girl alone, and release Mr. D."

"Don't worry your little brain about things you can't understand. Go knit, or something."

"You can't hold people against their will."

Fifer snorted a laugh. "Trust me, Red is here of her own accord. Oh, the stories she's heard about you. My, my. You've been a Big Bad Wolf." Fifer shook his head in mock disapproval.

"Why, you—"

"You'd better leave before she finds the shotgun. She's so heartbroken, she can't see straight. But I'll be a true gentleman and help her take aim."

Wolf threw a punch at Fifer's snout, but the pig had been faster and moved out of the way before he connected. Wolf howled in pain as his paw broke through the screen and its jagged edges tore through his skin.

The giggling resumed, and Fifer peered out. "What a loser you are, Wolf. Just retire already. No one needs you. You're dated and irrelevant. Passé. Expir—"

A gunshot rang out, and Wolf ran to his motorbike. "You haven't seen the last of me, you pigs."

In his rush to leave, Wolf pulled hard enough on the bike to tip it over, pinning himself underneath it in the process. The humiliation was enough to muffle the new howl of pain wanting to explode out of him.

Fifer walked out of the trailer and smirked. "Better put that helmet back on before Red sees your receding hairline."

Wolf huffed, and he puffed as he righted the bike. "I'll see you again, Fifer."

He drove off, hoping he would make it back home despite the thick black smoke pouring out of the clunking engine.

B.B. Wolf rode in a taxi, the grey peppering his mane showed at the roots. Locked in the back seat, Wolf said: "You're going the wrong way. Go back."

The cabbie snarled. "Shut up. You shorted me on the fare, so you no longer have a say on where I drive you."

A moment after the car screeched to a stop, the door opened on Wolf's left, and the cabbie dragged him out by the collar.

"This is how far your rolled up coins have gotten you." The cabbie dumped Wolf to the side of the road. "Walk the rest of the way, you half-breed mutt."

The taxi's wheels spun on the road's shoulder, splattering Wolf with pebbles and dirt. He dusted himself off and walked towards his destination.

More than an hour later, he reached the tall gate and leaned on it, huffing and puffing with exhaustion. After climbing the wall and fighting through the barbed wire topping it, he dropped to the other side, his clothes tattered and clumps of fur torn out.

The sound of barking dogs greeted him at the front door, but there was no sign of actual guards. Wolf stood on the welcome mat, wiping his dusty boots on it.

"No need to wipe your stupid footwear. You're not coming inside."

Wolf found a camera next to an intercom. "Too cheap to have real dogs, eh? Open the door, Practical. I need to speak with Mr. D."

"He's not here. Try the castle."

Liar. Wolf rang the doorbell. "And tell Red I need to talk to her, too."

"The girl ain't here either so bugger off. Tell you what, I'll open the gate. That way you'll still have some fur left by the time you get to the road."

The gate whirred open at the end of the driveway, and the recorded barking resumed through the speakers.

"Is that the best you can do?"

A thin spray squirted out of the speaker, covering Wolf in a malodorous mist.

"Arrgh, pigsty stink." He moved out of sight of the camera and spat.

"I gave you fair warning. Leave before we take it up a notch."

"Little pig, little pig, please let me in."

"Not by the hair of my chinny chin chin." Laugher burst out of the speakers, Fifer and Fiddler's laughter joining their brother's.

Three for one. Wolf licked his snout. He grimaced and spat, the taste of pigsty flaring anew in his mouth.

"That's enough. Release Mr. D., or I will tear your house down."

"I'd like to see you try," Fifer said. "You should enlist reinforcements stronger and scarier than you."

"Yeah, like a poodle," one of the brothers said.

Wolf nuzzled the camera. "I am going to tear this house down even if I have to huff and puff."

"Hard to do with emphysema, Old Man," Practical said.

"Tra la la la la la," the brothers chanted.

"We'll see what you have to say when I pig out on bacon tonight." Wolf licked his snout before spitting again. He searched the yard for something flammable, but it offered no leaves or branches, not even dead grass.

Fifer appeared on the second-floor balcony and flipped Wolf a cloven hoof, breaking into laughter. "Get a life."

Wolf howled as he ran to ram the front door. A water balloon smashed him in the face, stopping him in his tracks.

"Very mature." He shook the water off, annoyed it hadn't washed off any of the mist's stink. "What's next? Uncurling your tails?"

He shuffled aside, avoiding a falling, flaming bag. He retrieved it, careful not to light himself aflame in the process. *Thanks for the fire, pigs. I'll burn your house down.* "Drop it," a voice ordered behind him. "Turn around, nice and slow."

Wolf dropped the still-lit bag and raised his paws, spinning around. A cop pointed a pistol at his chest and another approached with a bucket. The second cop threw water on the flames, splashing Wolf in the process.

"Hey. Watch it."

The bucket-cop drew his gun. "Don't give us trouble."

"I've got him covered, Mickey. Get him to the car."

"Why are you arresting me?" Wolf pointed to the brothers gathered on the balcony. "Arrest them."

The first officer motioned at the band of brothers. "Could you join us down here? We'll need statements."

Fifer waved. "Of course, Donald. We'll be right down."

Wolf pleaded his innocence without success as Mickey dragged him away. They passed the gate and the cop deposited him in the backseat of the waiting car. The car took off before the cop could climb in.

"What's going on?" Wolf asked the two men in the front seat. Both wore dark suits rather than police uniforms.

"Setting things right," the passenger said in an accented English. "Ms. Hood is pretty shaken up. I think those pigs spun her a very tall tale."

Wolf could not place the familiar men. "Red knows the truth?"

"We've helped her understand your situation with Mr. Charming was a misunderstanding. It's clear that your story and his don't belong together. And as for the three little pigs, I think they revealed their true colors, and she'd parted ways with them before we spoke with her."

"I can't thank you enough for clearing things up with Red, sirs."

"Please, call me Wilhelm," the passenger said. "This is my brother, Jacob."

Wilhelm and Jacob. Brothers. Did he know them? Did it matter? "What about Mr. D.? Is he safe?"

"Those pigs are more talk than action." Jacob's accent matched his brother's. "Their motives are financial in nature, and your current employer will be fine. I must admit we've been keeping an eye on you for some time, and we hope you will soon leave his employ."

"Leave Mr. D.? Why, I could never—"

Wilhelm faced Wolf. "My brother and I would like to offer you an opportunity to redirect your, shall we say, limited career aspirations. Leave this fairy tale world and take a chance to…expand your repertoire."

Wolf smiled as he imagined the pigs out of his life, then turned serious as he thought of Mr. D. "I'd love to move on, but I owe Mr. D. He plucked me out of obscurity, gave me a great career. And I signed a lifelong contract."

"We will take care of any legal issues with your current employer. All we need is for your approval to proceed."

Wolf swallowed. "Are you also making an offer to the pigs?"

Wilhelm shook his head. "There's more than pigs out there, Mr. Wolf. Perhaps you would consider something a little more…grim?"

"Grimmer, you say? Interesting."

"We believe your performance could exceed your predecessor's. He had some issues with our vision."

"What issues?"

Wilhelm waived his hand in dismissal. "Let's not worry about him. He's not around anymore."

"He quit on you, did he?"

"One could say that. Regardless, Jacob and I think you've not yet reached your potential."

"Yes." Jacob locked gazes with Wolf in the rear-view mirror. "We have grand plans for you, Mr. Wolf."

"As well as for Ms. Hood. She's on her way to her grandmother's house and looks forward to your reunion."

Red wants to see me. Mr. D. is safe. The pigs can eat my dust. Everything is right again.

"I can't thank you enough for what you've done. When can I start?"

"*Wunderbar.*" Wilhelm pulled out his phone. "I'll call the goats and set it up."

PEA SOUP

Claire Davon

"Peas again?"

Giselle's upper lip curled at the congealed green pulp.

Prince Marius frowned from the opposite side of the table.

"My darling, what is wrong with the peas?"

Tapping her plate to cover her displeasure, Giselle pushed her fork through the paste, the color the only indication that they were once a vegetable.

Peas, always peas. Cooked. Raw. Boiled. In soup. At least, she didn't have to pretend to feel the pea under a mattress again.

"Why must it always be peas?" She met her prince's gaze. He was a handsome man, and now that his silly requirement for a princess had been met, a loyal husband.

Puzzlement formed lines between his eyes.

"We always have peas. The king likes peas. It's his favorite vegetable. We sell many to the royal court. You know that, my dear."

She did know that. All too well.

Others would call her lucky, but Giselle manufactured her own providence. She always had.

She remembered that night—as did many others judging from the times it was mentioned in court. Whenever she went out, whoever she encountered, they invoked the story of the princess and the pea.

Nothing about her arrival had been random. Timing her entrance so that the castle could not turn her away in the torrential downpour, Giselle counted on his mother being there and insisting that Giselle sleep on a bed of twenty mattresses and twenty feather-beds. Giselle readily acceded to the demand when presented with it.

She knew the condition, of course. The prince and his hands stopped in her tavern on their way back from another holding. The horsemen got rip-roaring drunk and howled with laughter at the prince's test. If a woman were a real princess, she could feel a pea under twenty mattresses and feather-beds. As if a woman that thin-skinned would make a good wife for the prince's rural lands. The hands agreed he needed a woman of sturdier stock. Princesses from all over, unknowing of the prince's foolish matrimonial condition, slumbered on the comfortable bed, only to be ejected the following morning.

Since then, Giselle plotted and waited. When she gained entry to the castle, Giselle forced herself to stay awake. She found the pea buried deep in the bottom of the first mattress, one that couldn't be felt in a thick set of britches, never mind under over three dozen of the best cushions in the county.

Royalty had odd requirements for marriage, but it got her what she wanted. The next morning, after making an elaborate show of a restless, horrible night, Giselle emerged to a sea of expectant faces. The prince produced the single pea and declared her his bride.

After six months of marriage, Giselle understood why a pea was the tool used to determine her worthiness. Peas were their cash crop, the mainstay by which this holding made its money. Cultivating it kept this small castle and the surrounding acreage going.

She gave her husband a bright smile and turned to the mush again.

Peas. Ugh.

A farming holding such as this one never lacked for chores. Tilling. Weeding. Caring for livestock. The crops needed constant tending and cultivating. Peas of all colors grew in thick rows, dominating the other crops.

When her chance came to snag a prince, Hecelin created Giselle, a name more suited to royalty. Inventing a kingdom not easily reached was a necessary part of the tale. Marius lacked the resources to check on rulers in Africa, although she would have thought her light skin and chestnut hair may have told him that she did not hail from that savage continent. Perhaps in time, after she spit out an heir, she would reveal the truth. Until then, she remained a princess from a distant land.

"My prince," she said the next day, trailing her hand across his shoulder and lowering her lashes at him. "Must peas always be the winter crop? What if we tried planting other things?"

She would kill for an apple orchard.

Marius looked at her as if she'd spoken with a forked tongue.

"Are you mad, woman? We rotate our crops around the fields, but one must always be peas. Peas are what the king wants, and peas are what he shall get."

Unattractive when stubborn, his face settled into a sour expression, lines forming on his brow and cheeks.

She caressed the back of her husband's neck. Recognizing the futility of continued argument, Giselle stroked him one last time and stepped away from the throne. To her delight, the polished silver metal of the doorframe reflected how the prince's gaze lingered on her backside.

In some areas, they were well suited indeed.

She checked the stores and ensured they had enough supplies. No longer worried about her next meal, Giselle felt it prudent to check. The remembrance of her empty belly still clung to her like a shroud.

Close to the storeroom, one of the stable hands stopped her, holding his hat in his hand. There was something knowing in his avid gaze that made her heart pound.

"Princess, a word."

Giselle's eyes narrowed at his too casual tone. As mistress of this household, he should have begged her leave before approaching her. The serving woman in her responded to his command. Giselle straightened her spine and forced herself to meet his gaze with the haughty look she had seen on the queen. Her princess title and station should have deterred such familiarity.

The earthy-stink of horses clung to him. Patches of dirt covered his face and clothes. Giselle wrinkled her nose to mask her familiarity with the odors. A princess should be disgusted.

"What is it, stable man?" She stepped into the storeroom and bade the man follow.

A crafty look crossed the man's weathered face, and he made no effort to hide his masculine appraisal.

"Aye, you're a clever one, but not as cunning as old Lyman. Ye didn't think I'd recognize the barmaid that served us in that village, did you? Didn't think any of us would know you all fancied up. It took me a while, but I remembered you. No princess, just another servant like me."

Giselle schooled her face to remain impassive, making no outward show that she acknowledged his words. Images danced in her mind as she turned over the possibilities. If his overprotective mother found out about her deception, Giselle could be put aside or worse.

"That is audacious." She should have accounted for this, yet she hadn't.

"P'rhaps we will go back to the bar, and then we'll see, ain't that right?"

Little chance of the bar patrons spotting the wench that served them tankards of ale.

"You wicked man. I will have no part of this."

"Don't try and fool me. I've been watching you. I ain't asking for much, but I know my silence is worth sumthin'."

Giselle squirmed. The barmaid once called Hecelin wanted to run.

Heaps of clay containing lime carbonate for the crops, and pea harvesters piled out in the hallway. She considered the small curved hand tools.

"We'll work out something fair, at least for me."

She had evaded a baron's roving hands when he thought to molest a barmaid. She had survived her parents' death and the plague at the age of ten, leaving her with only a handful of chickens. She survived the road with its bandits and ruffians, and kept her honor. She survived working as a drudge for a knight. She survived being a barmaid, hauling heavy tankards, and wiping beer off her clothes night after night. She could survive this.

The rustle of footfall behind her alerted her to the man in the doorway.

"What is this?" Her prince's cool tone belied the stiff set of his jaw. Awareness flashed in his eyes, telling her he understood more than she had imagined.

"Sire." Lyman almost shredded his hat.

Marius missed nothing of the dirt and stench that clung to the stable hand.

Giselle controlled a shiver at his abrupt shift in demeanor. This was not a man who dealt in peas. This was a ruler.

"Serf Lyman, I believe."

The other man nodded, his tongue flicking out to wet his lips.

"Do you presume that you should accost her over items more properly discussed among men?"

Lyman's fingers shook—the hat took more damage between his hands. "My prince, she is not…"

Marius waved his hand. Lyman stopped talking. She would have to learn that trick.

"She is my princess. She is my wife. That is all that matters. I should dismiss you with no money and no recommendation."

Lyman paled.

"I should, but I give you to the princess." His gaze turned to Giselle. Putting a finger to his lips, he didn't speak for long moments. Giselle shifted from foot to foot as his silence stretched into seconds and then minutes. "Perhaps a promotion would be in order."

Her husband gained new respect in her eyes. Rather than turn the man out, Marius intended to make him grateful. Former maid Hecelin didn't like the idea of keeping Lyman close after his threats, but royalty did things differently. They had required a woman to find a pea under twenty mattresses and twenty feather-beds to be wed, after all.

"Do you have a sweetheart, Lyman?"

"Aye, I do, prince. We do not yet have enough—"

"I shall see it done. It is the princess you are grateful to, horseman. Do not fail her, or the consequences will be grave."

Lyman bowed and retreated. Giselle watched him go, turning the idea of mercy over in her head. In her previous holdings, the man's fate lay at the end of a noose for daring to speak to his superiors. Perhaps this way would work out better. Time would tell.

"Did you think I did not know?" Marius asked, stroking her cheek with a feather-light caress. "Insisting on a princess who could feel a pea under even one mattress was a stupid test. Mother's friends in town were aflutter with the idea until Mother decreed it. She always inspected the beds, and I despaired of finding a wife, until a clever barmaid came to my rescue. Why do you think my hands revealed my secret to any woman who would listen? You did not disappoint. What is your name?"

Giselle coughed, her hand covering her mouth for a moment. "Once upon a time, there was a maiden named Hecelin who knew she could do better."

He continued his caress, his thumb brushing over her lips until they parted under his touch. Giselle shivered, turning her face into the stroking, like a cat. "Perhaps, I will call you that name on occasion. I would not want it forgotten."

Giselle warmed, her body reacting to his touch. A quick glance at the tightening of his trousers told her he was also affected by their closeness. There would never be a better time to bring up their cash crop.

"Marius, about the peas."

"I have entertained discussion of new crops with the farmers. Peas sustain us. But I am not such a fool as to think the king will always want them. I must not do this in haste for fear the king will take it as an insult. Do not rush me."

He had more strength than she had credited him for.

"My prince." She slid her arms around him, linking her hands at the small of his back. His strong, warm body beckoned, its changing contours hard against hers. Marius undulated, making a small noise when she pressed her body against his.

"I am not yet with child." She spoke in a soft tone, pressing kisses against his neck between words.

Marius groaned. "I do not take your meaning."

Hecelin lifted her face to his. "If I am not with child, do you not think we should change that? I know a pile of mattresses in a corner of the tower that needs some attention."

He brushed a kiss over her lips. "Aye, princess. Lead the way."

In time, she might even learn to love pea soup.

BEAUTY AND THE BEAST: THE BEAST WITHIN

Lorraine Sharma Nelson

"Why?" Adam said, arms rigid at his sides.

Belle shifted her gaze away from him, concentrating instead on the long-stemmed roses strewn across the enormous banquet table. "What do you mean?" She picked up a lustrous purple rose and inhaled deeply.

"Belle, look at me."

Sighing, she turned to her husband.

"What's happening to us?" he said.

Belle's heart twisted at the raw emotion in his voice. She wanted to cross the short distance between them and take him in her arms. To whisper that everything was perfect; that they were perfect.

But she couldn't.

"I don't know what you mean," she said.

"Yes, you do." He took a step toward her, gazing from his great height, and she marveled again at how his broad shoulders gave the impression that they could carry any burden.

"You're moving away from me, my love. Please, Belle." His voice dropped to a hoarse whisper. "Please, tell me what I've done wrong. What has caused this…distance between us."

He stroked her cheek with a calloused finger. A prince with hands as rough as the farmers that worked the land. Whoever heard of such a thing? He was not afraid of hard work, her Adam.

And she had loved him for it.

Once upon a time.

Belle shook her head. "It's…it's not you, my prince. It's me. I…I miss my Beast." She focused on the shiny gold buttons and elaborate brocading on the vest he wore.

There. She'd said it. Finally.

Tears pricked her eyes, but she refused to cry.

A heavy silence filled the sunlit morning room. She gripped the back of a chair to keep her knees from buckling.

"Belle, I *am* the Beast," Adam said, his voice clipped. "I'm still the same. Inside. Where it counts. Do you not see that? How can you not? What–?"

Belle held out a hand to stop him. How could she explain what she couldn't understand? She had to try, for both their sakes.

"Sit down, Adam." She gestured toward the gold-plated loveseat by one of the bay windows. She seated herself carefully, smoothing out the skirt of her gown, which rippled and shimmered around her like a lavender waterfall. Adam remained standing, his stance rigid, his face like carved marble. Belle's heart ached to see him so tortured. She patted the seat beside her.

"Come."

He approached as if afraid of what he would hear. Oh, Goddess, she was cruel to torment this man who would do anything for her. He should be enough. Would be for so many women—like her sisters. *So, what's wrong with me?*

When he was seated, careful not to touch any part of her, Belle tried to put into words what had taken her the last month to realize: that this man seated beside her—beautiful, well-bred, the picture of grace and elegance—was a stranger to her.

"Adam, please try to understand what I'm about to say to you." She swallowed before plunging ahead. "When we first met…when you were still the Beast, I was terrified. I'd never been so scared in my entire life. I…I really thought you were going to devour me."

Adam shifted in his seat, and Belle quickly placed a hand on his arm. "No. I'm not saying this to make you feel any guilt. Please, just listen."

She thought he was going to say something. Instead, he gave a curt nod.

Belle gently squeezed his arm. "Once I got over my fear, or rather, when I realized you weren't going to eat me, I saw sides of you that challenged me in every direction, every day. You were arrogant, childish, quick to anger, slow to reason, and very, very accustomed to getting your own way. In your world, your word was law, and the Goddess help any man or woman who dared contradict you."

Belle stopped when Adam's expression filled with complete disbelief. Dismayed, she pulled her hand away. "Adam? What—?"

"And that's what you miss?" His voice dropped to a deep rumble that vibrated up her spine. "That childish, immature, ranting, raving, beast-like creature?"

Belle bit back a smile. "Let me finish. All will be explained."

She hoped.

Adam grunted, the sound so much like what her beloved Beast made whenever he was displeased that her heart twisted. For one brief second, he was back with her. Then he glanced at her, questions evident in his beautiful, human eyes.

And the moment was gone.

"As I said, these were the characteristics I was first exposed to, those maddening traits of his, of yours. Then, as time passed, I got to see another side of you. A warm, wonderful, generous, kind, loving side, so eager to please me in every way possible." Belle's voice softened. "That was when I started falling in love with you."

A smile danced across her mouth.

"But, that maddening, impossible side that made me want to tear out my hair and stomp my feet in frustration, and rant and rave back at you, I fell in love with that side, too." She placed both hands on his arm. "Do you see? It was everything.

All of him…you…that I fell in love with. The wild, untamed beast, and the sensitive, civilized man."

Belle saw the confusion in his eyes. Her heart swelled with grief at the hurt she had inflicted. She hurried on, needing to get it over with.

"Since your transformation back to human, you've been a perfect gentleman in every sense of the word. In the month we've been married, you've never once raised your voice to me, even when there have been times you would have been right to do so. In fact," she gave him a soft, wistful smile, "There have been times when I have made absurd suggestions and demands, hoping to get you to disagree with me, to…to put the fire back in your heart, where it belongs. But, alas, every nonsensical thing that poured from my mouth was met with gentle understanding from you. The old Beast, my Beast, was surely dead."

She'd gone too far. What kind of deranged woman berates her husband for being too kind, too sweet, too gentle, too understanding? Maybe she was the problem all along, not Adam. What had she done? If he sent her back to her father and her wretched sisters, it would be no less than she deserved.

She peeked at Adam. As she'd both dreaded and expected, he wore an expression of thunderous incredulity. She gaped as a strangled sound issued forth from him. Fearing that he was choking, Belle jumped up to summon a servant for some water.

She jumped again when Adam's hand shot out, grabbing her wrist.

"Sit," he barked, and the Beast-like tone was so unexpected, that she did as ordered. And waited for him to tell her that she had surely gone too far. That their marriage was over. That she was to leave for her father's home by daybreak. A jumble of emotions warred inside of her. Isn't this what she wanted? Didn't she want to go back home to her father instead of living this life of banal mediocrity?

She closed her eyes, accepting her fate.

"I thought to spare you," Adam said. "You had been through so much torment when I was the creature."

You were never a creature, Belle wanted to burst out. *You were always my Beast.* But she had said enough. It was his turn now. And she would listen, as he had. She opened her eyes and focused on him entirely.

His tone held her hypnotized. "I wanted you to live a charmed life with me. You're a princess now, Belle. My princess. And it is your right. "

"To live happily ever after," she said, turning to gaze out the bay window.

Adam nodded. "I wanted nothing but sweetness and tenderness and love and understanding to surround you." Adam reached over, taking her hand in his. "Can you understand that, Belle?'

She nodded, tears streaming unheeded down her cheeks. "Why didn't you tell me? I would have understood then—"

"I thought you did. It was obvious that you needed to be cherished forever. I assumed you knew it, too."

Belle shook her head. "I know you wanted to give me the best life possible. You've said as much, repeatedly." She sniffed, blinking back the tears. How silly emotions can be after they've been bottled too long. "But in the month we've been married, all you ever do is fuss over me, calling me 'your love,' or 'your flower,' or, my personal favorite, 'your feathered dove.' You do realize, right, that I don't have any feathers to speak of?"

Adam's lips twitched, and for the first time since his transformation, a twinkle appeared in his eyes.

Belle's stomach flipped.

That twinkle.

She knew that twinkle.

It belonged to her beloved Beast.

"I don't claim to know much about the fairer sex. But I am fairly certain that none of you have any feathers. At least not that I'm aware of."

His brows scrunched as he playfully criticized her.

Belle's heart thudded.

First the twinkle. Now teasing.

She cleared her throat. "Umm...what was I saying?"

"Feathers."

"Oh. Yes, feathers. Well...you get the picture, I'm sure."

"Clearly, and in great detail. Thank you for that. "

Belle glanced at him uncertainly. *Sarcasm?* This sudden turn in behavior coming from the human Adam, was so uncharacteristic, she wasn't sure how to react.

"It wasn't easy, you know?" he said, stretching his long legs out before him as he leaned back against the cushions.

"What wasn't?"

"Being the perfect husband. In fact, it was dashedly difficult at times."

"What times?" It took Belle a few moments to realize that she was enjoying this conversation, despite the severity of the situation. They were actually talking. Something that hadn't happened since he was the Beast. And she had not realized just how desperately she'd missed the simple give and take of two people engaged in conversation.

"Well, let me see." A small smile hovered on his lips. Belle's gaze lingered there for a beat too long. It occurred to her that she could lean forward and kiss him. Hard. Right there on his beautiful mouth. The thought jolted her upright, her spine smacking into the back of the settee.

Adam leaned forward immediately, a frown marring his forehead. "Are you all right, dearest?"

She nodded, wondering if he could tell how flustered she was, and after a moment, he sat back, visibly relieved.

"Now let me see. Where was I? Ah, yes. Those times it was so damnably difficult being the perfect husband. Remember when one morning, you decided to fill the castle with peacocks?"

Belle's cheeks flamed. Of course, she remembered. She'd stayed up half the night, conjuring up outrageous demands, in an attempt to get her bland, passive husband to show some signs of life.

Adam's lips twitched. "Your cheeks say it all, My Love. Would you like to know what my first reaction was, when you asked me to buy those wretched birds for the castle?"

Belle leaned toward him with a new and renewed fascination. She shivered, imagining the Beast sitting beside her. Bantering and teasing and laughing. But this was human Adam. Sweet and tender and understanding, to the point of making her want to scream. And yet, he said he'd been behaving that way for her benefit. Goddess, who was this man, willing to make such a supreme sacrifice? For her alone.

Scooting closer to him, she waited, impatient to hear what he had thought of her brilliant plan to introduce an ostentation of peacocks into the castle.

He shot her a grin full of mischief, making her knees weak. "I wanted to tell you that you could certainly have your infernal peacocks, providing you, and you alone, cleaned up after them. And that, my love, you would have quickly found to be a full-time job."

Startled, Belle sat up straight. "That…that's what you really thought?"

Adam inclined his head in assent.

"Instead, you said if it made me happy, you'd order two hundred of them to start."

"I did. But, to be fair, I knew if I suggested a high number you would probably rethink your outrageous demand."

"Which is exactly what happened," Belle muttered, trying not to smile. His eyes were on her, watching her closely. Making her pulse quicken. "Any other times my outrageous demands left you seething on the inside?"

She hoped he couldn't see how flustered she was.

He snorted. "How long do you want to sit here?"

He sat back, clasping his hands behind his head, thinking. "Ah. I have one. Do you remember when you wanted to build a moat around the castle and fill it with crocodiles from the Nile?"

Belle groaned, covering her face, which was most probably going to burst into flames at any second. Had she really been that desperate to see some signs of life in her husband?

"Ah, I see that you do." The cheer in his voice fanned the flames in her cheeks. "And do you recall my reaction?"

"Yes." Belle's voice was muffled through her fingers. "You asked if I wanted the giant maneaters, or the smaller ones that would be happy with the rabbits and other smaller animals around the estate."

Adam chuckled, the delicious sound making her pulse speed up. "Would you care to know my real reaction?"

Belle uncovered her face. "I am all ears."

Adam leaned toward her with a satisfied smile that made Belle's toes curl in a way she'd never experienced before. And she liked it very much. "I wanted to rant and rave and throw a tantrum worse than the cook's two-year-old grandson. I wanted to accuse you of plotting to drive me insane, of the possibility of you actually *being* insane. I wanted to say that even if you swore your undying love for me, even if you gave me ten strong heirs, even if you kissed my feet every day at dawn and dusk for the next fifty years, it still wouldn't be enough for me to get you something that completely and utterly and ridiculously preposterous. Instead, what did I do? Ask you what size you wanted them to be."

Adam reached over, gently tucking a stray curl behind her ear. "How could I possibly have thought that treating you like that, all day, every day, was the right thing to do? I tried to create a fantasy world for you, my Belle, where only good things happen, and it turned into a bad dream. I'm so sorry."

Belle's breath hitched. "You're apologizing for trying to protect me? For loving me enough to change who you are for me?"

Tears blurred her vision as she leaned closer, cupping his face in her palms. "Adam, don't you realize that I love all of you. The sweet, gentle, and considerate you, as well as the stubborn, arrogant, and unreasonable you. That was what made you my Beast. Not the way you looked. The way you *are*."

Adam lowered his head until their foreheads touched. "Would you consider starting over? Giving me another chance to prove to you that I am the same man you fell in love with, despite my rather *unusual* outward appearance back then?"

"Only if you'll give me another chance to show you that I'm not the type of woman to make extravagant, unreasonable demands."

Adam growled, deep in his chest, as he pulled his wife in for a kiss. It took longer than expected, but the Beast finally won his Beauty.

WHILE YOU WERE SLEEPING

Rohit Sawant

"A good morning to you, too."

"Ah, you're going to outlive us all."

The old man chuckled amiably, half waving at the buggy as it rattled away. He was eighty-one. His knees ached. Still, not a day went by when he didn't venture out under the slate-gray sky for a morning ramble. Come rain or cold, he walked down the streets till a blush crept up in the east. He stood at the foot of the castle, the rising sun picked out the high towers. A sense of nostalgia bled in.

Walking homeward, a cloaked figure in the distance gave him pause.

He took his morning walks for years, and, except for a handful of instances, like the time when the baker's boy hurtled past, a spotted mongrel at his heels (he raised his walking stick at the beast and crowed so fiercely that it had the dual effect of forcing the creature to shrink with a yowl and waking half the houses in the area), he saw the same people every day, his surroundings as unchanged as if he ambled through a painting.

The cloaked figure was a first. He couldn't pinpoint it, but something stirred within him. Nothing unpleasant but something...just something.

The only thing he could discern about it, by way of gait, was that it was a woman. Probably one of the scullions sent out on an early errand.

The next morning, the old man slipped on his moccasins, drank a mug of water, and pulled the door open. Stepping forward, he almost bumped into the cloaked figure from the day before, arm half-raised as if about to knock.

Delicate, leathery hands drew back the hood.

"Bless me." He leaned heavily on the walking stick. His mind felt like a busy thoroughfare and a deserted street at the same time.

Crow's feet creased her eyes, grooves bracketed her mouth, the gold of her hair had transmuted to silver, but when she smiled, the sixteen-year-old girl who'd been his dear friend shown through.

He need not head out into the dawn for Dawn had come knocking on his door. As inexplicable as it was, it was true. It was her. It was Aurora.

"Won't you invite me in?"

"Of course." He moved aside to let her pass.

He ushered her to a table and took a seat adjacent, his heart fluttering in his chest in a manner that would've caused him concern for his health under different circumstances.

"How?"

Neither the fact that she should be present in her native kingdom nor the possibility that she might appear on his doorstep surprised him. What did was she *should* have been in her early thirties, having risen from her enchanted slumber, which had lasted some five and a half decades, fifteen years ago.

"I will tell you all, and I pray you shall forgive me for prolonging your anticipation, but before that you *must* tell me how you have been."

"I scarcely know where to start."

"At the beginning."

"At the beginning then. Once upon a time..."

2

A boy named Robert worked in the royal garden alongside his father.

He was nine, tending to the flowers in the courtyard, when a little girl of a similar age walked merrily down the wide stone walkway. A glance sufficed to determine it was the princess. Simply because of the way she dressed and the fact that the queen was at her heel, followed close by a nursemaid.

The trio drew near. The princess, a few paces ahead of the queen, lingered to a halt. Seeing her up close, something fluttered inside him...just something. Part of it was the proximity. The other part a gravid crackle in the air when their eyes met.

They exchanged smiles, and he yanked a luxuriant red rose from a nearby brier and held it out to her. Not because she was a beautiful princess, but because she was a girl he liked.

She thanked him. When Robert only made shapes with his lips, she said, "I'm Aurora," and asked what his name was.

"Robert, princess," said the boy.

"Well, it's nice to meet you, Robert Princess."

They giggled.

Aurora twitched and gave out a small cry for a thorn had pricked her thumb. The queen blanched at the ensuing teardrop of blood and all but swooned and hustled her away.

His father smacked him upside the head and didn't take him to the castle for the next few days.

Resuming work, he successfully evaded the princess until he couldn't and found her in his path. He bowed his head and apologized.

"I know," she said. "No one's ever told me but...I've heard things."

But that's good. You see, now you *know* that you ought to keep away from a spindle. Like any spindle."

"I don't know what one looks like."

"I'll make a drawing of it for you."

"That'd be nice."

For the next seven years, he often brought her smooth-stemmed roses.

"Your name is unusual."

"No, it isn't. It means Dawn."

How fitting.

"What does yours mean?"

"Bright, I think."

Bright. Dawn. A companionable silence fell between them.

"I'm going to call you Dawn."

She asked him with mock-indignation, "What is wrong with my given name?"

"Dawn is just one syllable long, and you don't have to bend your tongue three different ways to say it."

She chased after him, promising she'd lock him up in the dungeon.

A few weeks later, he plucked the last rose he would ever give her. They sat under the lengthening shade of an oak, talking about trivial things.

"Lately, I've been finding myself thinking about...*it* a lot. And it frightens me."

Maybe the curse won't happen, he wanted to say; he wanted to say other things as well. Instead, he held out his palm. She took it.

"It'll be all right, Dawn. I'll save you."

"You are aware that you have to be a prince to pull that off." She half-teased.

He flushed with embarrassment. How ludicrous it sounded now that he voiced it. Like something read in storybooks.

"Why a prince?" Indignation pricked him, the helpless sort only those with rough hands know. Their conversation reached a place where neither of them made eye contact.

"Tradition, I suppose? But don't worry. I doubt any of it shall transpire. I mean, it hasn't until now. Right?"

But it did happen.

It happened the next day.

The kingdom fell into a commotion. A wild tangle of trees and briars grew with nightmarish rapidity around the castle, enclosing it so only the top of the towers showed. Rumors spread about the "Sleeping Sickness."

Robert set out with an axe.

Every time he chopped off a tree limb, it regenerated.

He swung again.

He spent the better part of his youth and early manhood trying to cut through the Thicket. So much so that he was known as the Mad Lumberer.

Eventually, he put down his axe in favor of woodwork.

Decades went by.

He sat in his workshop when a neighbor barged in with the news that a prince had gotten past the Thicket, rather the Thicket had parted to let him through.

The tangle of trees and underbrush withered twice as fast as it had grown and turned to dust. The whole kingdom was covered with this foresty soot for days.

The crowd outside the castle parted to make way for the prince's father. That was the only time Robert got a glimpse of the castle doors before the view was engulfed again. Retreating home he spent a sleepless night.

Their beloved Princess Aurora had risen, as had the king, queen, and councilmen. News followed that she would marry Prince Florimond.

His heart both leapt and broke.

3

Aurora's eyes brimmed with tears.

"You know, I could have you thrown into the dungeon for making me cry."

She told him that it wasn't half as romantic as she'd heard it sung about. As a young girl, she had prepared herself to drop unconscious unceremoniously, awaken to find a strange man hovering over her; one who had kissed her no less—her hand, not otherwise as people are fond of telling.

"My last few waking moments had been delirious. Seeing the spindle up in the turret, being drawn to it—fascinated—as if under a spell because I *was*, clumsily pawing it, the tiny bite on my finger, and after that, it was like slipping into a black pit. I woke disorientated."

Aurora had accidentally elbowed the prince in the face. A few moments later, comprehension seeped in.

After that things fell together, steadily at first then all at once. The prince's father arrived, congratulations were exchanged, and the next thing she knew, she was married.

"I searched for you in the throng of people as I left the kingdom, but later, I realized that I had in my mind your face as I had seen it last and that by then you must've been—"

"Much progressed in age."

She drummed her fingers on the edge of the table. "At any rate, I've finally caught up with you in that area."

"How?" he asked, not believing she'd have an answer; but she did.

Fairy Hippolyta, her fairy godmother, that noble creature who had saved her from entirely falling prey to her wicked sister fairy's curse, was dying and had locked herself up in the hollow bole of an oak.

And with her, the enchantment spell she had cast to preserve Dawn faded.

"In the last few months, I have aged decades, and it has all been rather stressful and confusing...for the prince."

Robert scoffed when she mentioned their awkward exchanges and his weeklong hunting parties from which he'd sometimes return with a whiff of cloying perfume about him.

The kingdom was rife with rumors of her illness. She returned to her native land after visiting her fairy godmother, keeping the journey a secret, which caused commotion at the castle gates. The gatekeeper and driver locked horns.

The latter had announced her as Princess Aurora. Glancing at the old lady in the carriage, the gatekeeper dismissed them and when the driver wouldn't budge, said how they could be tried for impersonating royalty.

"Had we remained there much longer, their squabble would've escalated. In a way, each was doing his duty, and it was partly my mistake. I should have written ahead."

She knew where her old nursemaid lived and alighted there instead.

"I liked it there. I've spent more than enough time behind castle walls anyway. And then I felt something...just something, when I saw you yesterday."

The years fell away from him.

"When I was..."

"Being the most loathsomely inactive person in the world?" He smirked.

"Yes. That." She scrunched her nose, hiking a shoulder. His face lit up; the gesture so familiar that he fancied the companion of his youth peek through at him. But she grew somber as she continued.

"I wasn't completely submerged in darkness. I had dreams."

They held each other's gazes.

He hacked away with his axe, exhausted himself with work so he could fall asleep the moment he rested his back. To dream. Dreams were the only place where he could walk with her. He reckoned her dreams weren't too dissimilar.

"So did I...and I still do."

Dawn and Robert met each other the next day and every day after; and when it was a day like bringing a rose, he would bring her a rose.

FINDING RED

Michael M. Jones

Everyone knows the classic stories. Like the one about a girl and her grandmother, a big bad wolf, and a conveniently-passing woodsman. I'm not sure why this tale, in all of its many formats, has stuck around for so long. Some say that the color red symbolizes blood, or is a metaphor for becoming a woman. They say the wolf represents the fear of the unknown, or the dangers of predatory men. That the death of the grandmother is about growing up or coping with loss. Some people look at the narrative and see werewolves, or sex, or words of warning. "Don't talk to strangers. Don't stray from the path. Beware the forest." There are a thousand different interpretations, some harder to swallow than others. I know the truth: Little Red Riding Hood is about a man and a woman. But not like you'd expect.

It's a love story.

As long as people believe in them and continue to tell and retell them, fairy tales like this tend to persist. They linger; they resonate; they reenact themselves in strange ways. The name's Nick St. Claus. I used to be one of them, until I broke free of the cycle and pursued a new destiny. Now, I play private detective for the Mysteries, putting things right and cleaning up other people's messes. I ply my trade out of Holiday, a strange little town on the outskirts of nowhere, where people like me go to fade away.

As cases go, this one appeared straight-forward. One day, a big bear of a guy, a plaid-wearing lumbersexual, mighty of beard and strong of arm, showed up to spin me a tale of the "girl that got away." We all have those; I've let love slip through my fingers enough times to recognize the yearning in another person's eyes. My client waxed poetic over the redhead who'd stolen his heart before breaking it. His knuckles whitened as he talked about "the other guy" who stole his girl. He growled about the "disapproving grandmother," a bitter anger turning his words into a harsh whine. He wanted me to track down the girl so they could reconnect, so they could rekindle their long-delayed love affair. When he had finished, I shook his hand, took his retainer as an advance against expenses, and went to work. I had my misgivings about my client, but business wasn't so great I could afford to turn it down without giving the job a shot.

Turns out Red hadn't tried too hard to vanish. After a few phone calls, and a substantial donation to Father Aaron, the local priest who tends bar, saves souls, and sells any secret not covered by the sanctity of the confessional, I soon had a lead.

I followed the trail to British Columbia, not too far outside of Vancouver, where, nestled in a suburb, I found a modest two-story house with a well-kept yard and a spotless exterior. It had a warm, homey charm. A minivan was parked in the driveway, and the porch lights were on, even in the late afternoon. I observed from across the street for a while, letting the case's details tumble around in my head. The job required me to confirm Red's presence, then take the information back to my client. I'd be done in time for dinner; with what I'd been paid, I could treat myself to something nice for a change.

Unfortunately, I've never been inclined to take the easy route. Hard experience has taught me to never take the client's word as gospel; people lie. Most of the time, in fact. They bend the truth, hide things, rewrite their own stories. I'm guilty of the same thing. Who isn't?

Determined to hear both sides of the affair, I approached the house. When I rapped at the door, the grandmother answered, a polite smile on her lips but suspicion in her eyes. I gave her my warmest smile in return. She knew me, of course. Everyone who was ever a child knows me, somewhere in their heart. I told her who I'd come to see, and she let me in and offered tea. I accepted, even though I prefer cocoa.

Red joined us in the living room. She'd grown into a lovely young woman, though the bags under her eyes and the baby weight she still maintained spoke volumes, as did the baby toys scattered about the room, and the playpen in the corner. A modest diamond sparkled on her left hand. Like her grandmother, she tensed up at first, sitting on the edge of her chair as though unable to rest for even a second, no matter how much she needed it. The explanation for my visit drew a frown from them both; for a moment, I expected them to toss me out and slam the door in my face.

I reassured them with all the right words, and after a while they settled down and told me their version of what happened. It differed from the tale spun by the hunter. Red told me all about the ex-boyfriend with a sharp axe, a wicked jealous streak, and a quick temper. Throw in a breakup he refused to accept and a mutual friend who helped her escape a bad situation—becoming far more than a friend in the process—and everything made sense. I've always been good at reading truth from lies, naughty from nice, and Red's account felt "right" to me. The grandmother refilled our tea and explained how they'd moved here in search of a fresh start, far from any lingering trouble.

As we were finishing up, the husband came home. I liked him at first sight, but gut instinct told me I'd never want him as an enemy. He still had a feral gleam in his eyes and a sharp, wide grin, and when we shook hands, claws pricked at my skin. He told me, in blunt terms, that he'd do anything to keep his family safe. His pack. He felt a lot more civilized these days, and he returned to the woods on a regular basis to blow off steam, but old habits die hard.

We locked gazes.

I blinked first.

I understood. I couldn't return to my client and report success. The truth is sad: history—and fairy tales—are sometimes written by whoever who has the most to lose. To soothe his wounded pride, my client had revised the story, turning it into one where he killed the wolf, got the girl, and lived happily ever after; that's the one that made it into the books and legends.

The truth just wanted to be left alone.

Before I left, I spent a moment with the baby. He had his father's big, lupine eyes, and his mother's red hair, and he gurgled at me without a care in the world. I didn't want to be around when he started teething. I'd left the toy business behind years ago, so I slipped Red the rest of my retainer and told her to make sure the kid had a good Christmas.

I informed my client that I couldn't find Red. I said his obsession was pointless, a waste of time and money. I urged him to let it go, to leave the past behind before it destroyed him. He yelled for a while. I yelled back. We went out for drinks. Anger turned into weary grief, and we shared maudlin stories about the women we'd loved and lost. After way too much alcohol, and a few rounds of drunken Christmas carols, he spent the night on my couch, snoring like a lonely chainsaw. In the bright light of the next day, he accepted my judgement, and vowed to move on. Thankfully, he didn't press for a refund. The last I heard, he'd met a nice girl who loved hunting and camping as much as he did.

As far as I know, Red, Wolf, Grandma, and the baby are doing just fine and don't care what the tales say about them.

They have their own happy ending.

I'm still looking for mine, but I doubt I'll get that lucky. Like my client, I tend to dwell in the past. One day, it's going to catch up to me.

Told you this was a love story. It's just not *my* happily ever after.

SNOW

Rob Rosen

"That sound." The tiny man gasped. "I recognize it, but surely I must be mistaken. I'm simply an old man hearing what he wishes so dearly to hear."

Still, he followed his ears to the sobs that echoed in the distance. It was a sound he'd not heard in many, many years. A sound that broke his heart so long ago, and yet one he ached to hear again. He often heard it in his dreams, whispering to him from a time long forgotten.

"Perhaps I am dreaming," he said to himself as he traversed the forest, running as fast as his aged, bowed legs could carry him. "Or perhaps it's just a cruel trick of the wind as it courses through these seven hills that surround my home."

But no, for he knew all the sounds of the forest, recognized every noise, both friendly and not; and this one was so very different from any of those. This was something special. Something he had sadly accepted that he'd never hear again, not since that fateful day so many years prior.

Minutes later, he stood a scant few feet from the source, as she cupped her face in her hands and cried her miserable tears. Her once midnight-black hair hung in gray locks around her shoulders. She had clearly aged, as had he, of course. In any case, the woman who knelt sobbing on the forest bed was unmistakable. His soul knew her without seeing the face bent so low that it nearly touched the ground she rested upon.

"Snow? Why is it that you cry so?" His voice cracked, legs barely able to hold him upright now.

She fell back onto her hands and scampered a few feet away. But when her gaze landed upon his grinning face, she smiled timidly in return, her tears drying up.

"My friend," she finally managed. "I cry because I feared that I could not find you. It has been so very long since I've dwelt in this forest, and I have been lost for several days searching for you."

She wiped the salty wetness from her cheeks. "But here you are."

"Yes, Snow, here I am. It seems I have always been able to find you when you've needed me. Is that why you've returned after so long an absence?" His voice came out more stern than he intended, but she had been away for so long, and his heart grew bitter during those years, shrinking to a size better meant for his body.

"Do not be mad, Doc. Had I been able to return sooner, I surely would have."

He hoped she spoke the truth. For of all the creatures he had met in his long life, none had been more honest or sincere than this one. He trusted none more than she. Not before and certainly not since. He softened and crouched on the moss-covered ground beside her.

"I am sorry, Snow. I didn't mean to sound angry. It's just that I was surprised to see you again. And for that, I am quite glad." He gently held her hand in his. She was, he quickly discovered, ice cold. He knew in an instant that something about her was not the same. His years as a doctor had trained him well, after all, though he'd not practiced in a long time. For as long as he'd been alone, as a matter of fact. And that was a long time indeed.

"Come, my friend." He helped her to her feet. "We must get you by a warm fire and feed you. You've been out in this wilderness far too long."

The two walked back through the forest. Doc held Snow's hand tightly for fear that they would forever be separated again. Neither spoke a word. When they finally made it to his tiny cottage in the glade, Snow collapsed on his pint-sized straw bed, clearly exhausted and much worse the wear.

He wiped her perspiring, creased brow and gazed down at the friend he was certain he would never see again. She was still lovely. Age had clearly not diminished her beauty, though something was off. Something was different about her. He couldn't yet put his pudgy, little finger on it, but the Snow White that lay before him had indeed changed.

"What does she need of me now, after all this time?" he whispered as he lay on the floor and tried to sleep, talking to himself out of habit after being alone for so long. "What can an old dwarf like me have that has finally brought her back here?"

When he woke, Snow no longer lay on the cot. Doc bolted up for fear that he had been dreaming, but inhaled deeply at the aroma of eggs and ham, of potatoes roasting on the grill. She had truly returned to him and was, like in the olden days, cooking him breakfast.

He smiled and sighed.

His mind, however, suddenly turned black at the thought that plagued him as he fell asleep: *why have you returned after so long? Why now, my dear Snow?*

But before the thought consumed him, she walked back in and smiled down upon him. That was all he needed to erase his misgivings. It was all he ever needed. Even after working hour after hour in the miserable copper and gold mines that surrounded their home. When his back ached and his joints creaked, the merest hint of her glorious smile made it all right again, made it all tolerable. So he smiled in return and joined her at the table for the glorious meal she had prepared.

"You always were an excellent cook," he said in between hearty bites.

"And you always were an excellent eater." Though she barely touched her own food.

Doc laughed despite the tension that hung thick in the air, but when he'd at last finished his meal, he could no longer keep his peace. "Snow, it's been a very long time since last we faced each other, but not so long that I don't recognize when something is bothering you. Please, tell me what's wrong?"

The smile all at once left her face as she sat rigidly in place.

"Yes, my friend. You are right, as always," she said, haltingly. "But first, pray tell, where are your brethren? When last I saw you, there were six more. Why is there now just one? Did the others move from this valley?"

She actively examined the room as if the others would soon make their appearances, traipsing in one at a time, as they used to do.

And now, it was his turn to sit icily still. He'd been alone for so long that the reasons for their absence nearly escaped his memory.

It now came painfully flooding back to him.

"No, Snow," he managed, his head hung low to his chest in despair. "They're still here. Come, and I will show you."

Tentatively, he arose, and she followed him outside to a clearing behind the cottage.

"Oh no." She cried at seeing the six tiny graves that lay spaced mere inches from each other, at the equally tiny headstones etched with their names. "How did this happen? When did this happen?"

Resigned sadness returned to his heart. "Oh, a very long time ago, I'm afraid. The life of a miner is a hard one, after all. And I suppose their little bodies simply couldn't take it any longer. One by one, they left me until I was as you see me now, old and alone."

Sadness turned into something harder, colder, as their eyes locked. "I tried to send word to you, but never heard back."

"I'm afraid your messages never reached me." Her hand warmed his shoulder. "But that is not surprising. My husband, who when last you saw him was merely a prince, is now king of all the land, as far as the eye can see. And I am his queen. That is to say, *was* his queen. But no longer."

"I'm sorry, Snow. Is he… dead?" The dwarf softened, if only by a hair.

"No. Well, yes. But only to me." Snow slumped in place and turned away from the graves of the once-large clan.

They walked back inside and sat at the table.

"You see, all was not well with our lives."

The dwarf frowned upon hearing about his friend's misfortune. "But I'd often heard that you and the prince lived happily."

"For a time, I suppose. A short time, but not ever after. That is simply what he would have everyone believe." She gazed down at him, a resigned look on her troubled face. "But that is but a fairy tale, my friend. It is what children are told to put them peacefully to bed. It is, sadly, not all as it appeared."

"And that is why you've not returned for so long? You were ashamed of how your life turned out?"

"No, that is not the reason." She hid her face, her agony, from her one true friend, until she could resume her story. "You see, when the prince rescued me from my glass coffin all those years ago, when that accursed apple was dislodged from my throat and I once again found myself among the living, he felt that I was his to do with at his bidding. And I, feeling that I owed him for my very life, tried my very hardest to please him. As I said, for a while, we were happy. Until…"

"Until?" He held her hand and patted her tenderly on the back, hoping to soothe her.

Her gaze drilling down deep into his. "Until I bore him a daughter."

This surprised the little man considerably, his head tingling as he processed the words. For in a kingdom as great as his, the news of a royal child surely would've reached even his remote corner, though it had not.

Not even a whisper of it.

"And why would this cause either of you any unhappiness, my dear?"

"It didn't. At first. But this child was so beautiful, so pure, so perfect, that my husband sent her away. Ah, I see, my friend, that this causes you wonder. But you did not know my husband. What he was most proud of was not his wealth, nor his prestige, nor his vast power. No, what he coveted most in this world was the simple fact that I was the fairest in the land. That his wife, not his daughter, was the fairest of them all. That is how the story went, and that is how he believed it to be. But our daughter was even fairer. This he could not abide by, and so he sent her away. To where, I do not know. This, my friend, is why I could not return to you and the other dwarfs. And this is why I never heard word of them. You see, I have been locked in a room high above the castle, and he has maintained the legend of my beauty all the while. No one has set eyes upon me all this time to question that I was still the fairest in the land. And no one who is still alive to tell about it knows of my child. No one, that is, save for you, now."

"And you've escaped from him?"

His heart beat hummingbird-fast as she nodded in the affirmative.

"And now, you need my help to find your daughter?"

Again, she nodded.

"But how, my dear? I am an old dwarf with no resources and little strength left in my tired body. How can I help find somebody that is meant never to be found?"

At last, she smiled again, lighting up the room as sure as the early morning sun. "But you do have it within your power to help me."

She placed her hand on his.

"Do you not remember what I left in your care after my wedding night, when my evil stepmother perished, and I was, once and for all, free of her?"

Doc raced back to that long-forgotten evening. At once, he seemed to know what she was getting at and why she had returned. After all, he had something she needed.

"The mirror," he finally said.

She gulped, her eyes wide and so blue as to put the sky to shame. "Yes, the mirror. It will know where my daughter is. It and only it. Please, old friend, return it to me so that I may go and seek her out."

"Of course, Snow," said Doc, without hesitation. "It is yours to do with as you please."

He walked to the rear of his cottage and removed a piece of dusty fabric that had been hanging lo those many years. There, as it had been all that time, hung the magical mirror.

A chill ran up his spine when his friend gasped from behind him. "Be not afraid, my dear; it's just a mirror. A mirror that will help you locate your daughter."

"Yes." She almost purred. Her features not show the relief he thought he'd find on her face; it was something else entirely.

Though what, he hadn't a clue.

"Yes, for once and for all, I will find my daughter."

They stood there facing the object on the wall. Doc gazed at his friend's now haughty-looking reflection as she spoke. "Mirror, mirror on the wall, who is the fairest of them all?"

The once inanimate mirror sprang to life. A face suddenly appeared from a swirl of brilliant, sparkling color.

"Ah, that is a question I have not heard in quite some time. But I see that the one that once was the answer to this question is now the questioner," it said.

"No riddles, mirror. Just answer the question," Snow gave the command with a scowl.

"Yes, mistress. But I sense you know the answer already. Still, I will appease you." The mirror's rippling face sneered.

"For many years, it was you who was the fairest, the fairest by far in all the land, but then another was born that even eclipsed your beauty." The mirror grew malicious. "Your very daughter, if I am not mistaken."

"*Yes*. Where is she? Tell me mirror, where is my daughter? I must find her."

"Ah. You truly are your stepmother's daughter, are you not?"

And then, Doc knew what was different about his long-lost friend, knew in a heartbeat why she sought him out. And why she needed to find her daughter so badly.

"Mirror, I have a question," the dwarf suddenly uttered.

"You do?" Snow laced her fingers together in a show of pleading innocence.

"Yes. Mirror, mirror on the wall, does the fairest wish to be found?"

At that, Snow White screeched. "Of course, you little fool, she wishes to be found. She is the princess and my daughter. She needs her mother."

"I think that is not the case." Doc's frown cast long upon his face, which heated up with well-earned anger. "I think that it is you who needs her and not the other way around. That is to say, it is you who *doesn't* need her."

"Little man, may I remind you that you are addressing the queen." Snow's voice dropped low and haughty.

"That you may be, but I see you for who you really are, and I do not need a mirror to show it to me. For it was you who treasured the legend of your beauty above all else. And it was you who has kept the story alive by locking yourself high above the castle so that all would remember what you once looked like and not what you have become. It was you who sent your daughter away, as once your stepmother sent you away. And this, this is the reason you have never come back here, the reason you now seek your daughter, as your stepmother sought you. It is to destroy her, for her beauty must surely grow as yours declines." He once again turned to the object on the wall, and asked, "Is that not correct, mirror?"

"That it is." The mirror had a sinister laugh. "It appears that the apple did not fall too far from the tree. Or should that be *poisoned* apple?"

Snow clenched her fists at her sides. "You both can laugh all you like, but when I find my daughter…"

"You will never find her," came a new voice from the doorway. "For she is in a land far, far away."

The interruption sent a jolt through Doc and spun him around to the majestic shadow of the king.

"Your Highness." Doc bowed as well as his little body allowed him to. Which, suffice it to say, was not very low at all.

"*Husband.*"

"I knew that I would find you here, wife." The king's hatred of her cut through the dusty air. "Though that mirror might be able to tell you where I sent your daughter for her own well being, you will not be able to reach her. And even if you could, and even if your plotting came to its foul conclusion, you still would not be fairest in the land. For as I've sadly come to find out, wife, your beauty has become only skin deep. Like that mirror on the wall, scratch the surface and that is all that you will find: surface."

He promptly frowned, though he stood there regally, ready to cast his sentence.

"For you, my dear, beauty was a means to an end. And now, it will be the end of you." The king raised his royal gilded scepter. "I banish you, my queen, to the place you hold so dear. To the mirror you have come, and to the mirror you shall go. May your soul finally find peace there."

"*No.*" Snow shrieked, but it was too late. For in that land, the king's words were law. And within the swirl that the mirror's face once existed, now emerged his wife's as she had appeared so many years earlier.

Doc bowed to the king, who in turn, nodded and road off to return his daughter to her rightful place.

The dwarf looked into the mirror once again. "Mirror, mirror on the wall, you are once again the fairest of them all. This is what you sought, and this is what you have found. Your beauty will now be eternal. I will be able to gaze upon it until I am no more and be reminded of much happier times. And to those who come across this mirror in the future, I hope they learn the lesson of your folly: to be fair is fine, but to be loved is the true measure of one's beauty."

He grinned as he turned away from her.

SAVING POPPY
Walt Giersbach

Poppy Pachuca crashed back into my life with a bang. Literally. I was nursing a beer and reading *Clinical Medicine* when she drove her car into my garage door. I dropped the journal, saved the beer, and ran to see what'd happened.

"Whoa, shit, Norman, it *is* you." She fell out of the car door and onto the driveway.

The woman I helped to her feet was middle-aged and overweight, her hair was a fright wig and she smelled of brown whiskey.

"Who are you, Ma'am? And what the heck have you done to my garage?"

"Norman," she said. "You don't recognize me? Even you."

"No. Come over to the porch and let me see if you're hurt."

"I'm Poppy. I gave my heart to you. I gave you the best year of my high school career. And my virginity. Well, that was an even trade."

"Ma'am, I knew someone by that name, but she left for California a decade ago. Soon as we graduated. Last I heard she was…oh, something in modeling or the music industry. Movies." No, I couldn't forget that girl. That Poppy was a creature I'd've given my life to hold on to. But the flame flickered out when she left. I remained single, went to college and med school, voted Republican, and locked that part of my past in the closet of my memories.

"All of the above, Norman."

"That's *Doctor*. Hastings. You can use my title since I earned it. Please. And let me look at your knee. You're limping."

"Oh, you're a doctor now. Well, I used to be a damn movie celebrity and a top drawer singer." Her words came out jumbled from the booze, or worse, hysteria. "I sang at the…the baseball field in Wichita. My 'Star Spangled Banner' made the TV news."

"They have a baseball team in Wichita?" Memories crept back, echoes of a girl I'd once known when our world was young and life was a never-ending enchantment.

I flashed to the homecoming parade here in Hawkins, Iowa, during our senior year. She was the first Latina in Hawkins to be elected queen. As the float passed the grandstand filled with dignitaries and spouses on Main Street, she pirouetted, lifted her pink skirt and flashed her moon-shaped ass at Mayor Charlie Gibbons. She wasn't wearing panties. Mrs. Gibbons squealed and seemed to faint. Charlie stood, cursing, and gave Poppy the finger.

She left town within the week, taking her crown with her.

TV reports, in later years, periodically chronicled her skyrocketing to the heights of celebrity. Just as suddenly, she became an untouchable: Poppy grabbing her crotch as she sang the last note of "home of the brave." Her car wrecks in Los Angeles. The police apprehensions she blamed on alien entrapment. Forced rehab. She was a latter-day Grimm fairy tale, a Cinderella in reverse.

"Don't you understand, Norman?" She wailed like a banshee and clawed at my shirt. "I've had a curse put on me. It's aged me thirty years. My youth has been stolen." The lines in her face crinkled like a crushed paper bag.

"That's not scientifically possible, any more than believing in fairy godmothers, Prince Charming or Tinker Bell." This woman grew frightening. It seems often the case that today's celebrities go up like a Roman candle before crashing and burning. The drugs and booze on top of no talent and less education turn them into zombies wandering the green rooms of talk shows and becoming jokes for late night comedians. They're the walking dead. Now I had one of the walking middle-aged standing at my front door.

"It's true," she said. Her face inflated in anger. "I did something to the wrong person and she hexed me out of my youth."

"Wrong person?"

"A movie producer. Don't ever cross a producer, even if she is covered by insurance and studio backing." She laughed in despair. "Mona Gottlieb was producing her first film, and I screwed her husband on the set. A gaffer took pictures and sold them. Boy, that pissed Mona off, enough to put a bullet through his shirt."

Angry at being a mark for these demented ravings, I challenged her. "Prove yourself. Who was the Hawkins homecoming queen in 2004? What happened at the Homecoming Day parade? Answer me that."

"I was queen," she said, "and I mooned that prick Charlie Gibbons. I heard later they sent him up for embezzling the town's tax money."

"Not good enough. The Poppy I remember had a tattoo no one else knew about." I kicked at the falling leaves, wishing this drunk would go away. She wasn't *my* Poppy.

"Everyone knew about it on Homecoming Weekend when I declared my independence." The woman standing on my front walk dropped her cutoffs and bent over, revealing Chinese characters tattooed on her left buttock. "You said it probably meant 'Good taste, cheap dish,' that I copied it from a menu. But you were wrong, Norman. I had it translated, and I know. It says Eternal Love, and eternal means forever in case you didn't know."

"My God, you are Poppy Pachuca."

"Why, thank you very much. Now you're a doctor, and I need help. Change me back. Make me beautiful again."

"Possibly collagen to rejuvenate cell tissue." I examined a face that looked like a chicken pot pie and pondered the therapies. "Hormones, but you need to see a specialist—not a GP in a hick town."

"Norman, I need *you*. We had a thing until I got mad at the morons in this jerk town. I was elected queen, but you were my king."

"Oh, I knew we had a thing, and when you bused out to Hollywood, I realized no one would ever again take me to the heights of passion. The taillights on that bus confirmed your betrayal."

Her face sagged in remorse. "Am I so ugly now? So crammed with mistakes I can never get back on top of the game again?

"Well, not ugly, Poppy. Just a little worn, like a high mileage car."

"I'm the same person you knew, but the crazy life is behind me. Norman, close your eyes and give me a kiss. Please."

Against my better judgment, as a church deacon, medical practitioner and Republican precinct captain, I closed my eyes. I remembered the winsome girl I once gripped in my arms. And I kissed her, deeply, passionately and with regret at all that I'd lost.

The cobwebs of time blew away, and I was shocked to see the Poppy I had known, plus a few years that added maturity and depth. No wrinkles, thirty pounds lighter, dark hair that floated over her face, and a mouth that was made for gobbling up life.

"Poppy." My arms enfolded her. "You really are back."

"Norman, you released me from the curse."

"Poppy, don't go. You have to release me, so I can come back to life."

DRAGONS

Renuka Raghavan

"Don't just stand there, do something. Help her, please. Help her." Tears streamed from Bohdan's eyes as his mother convulsed on the sidewalk, but the fat suit laughed.

"You lowlifes should think twice before shooting shit up your arm," the fat suit said, blowing clouds of smoke into the night, the tip of his cigar glowing a fiery orange.

Desperate, Bodhan tried again.

"Please, sir. You have your cell phone right there." He gestured at the fat suit's waistband. "Call 911."

"What do I get out of it?"

"I don't have money, but I'll do anything."

The man puffed into the air. "Finish what she started."

Bohdan flinched at the suit's open fly and backed away. Men in suits were supposed to be gentlemen and knights, willing to help fair maidens.

Earlier that night, looking at a discarded drawing of a fire-breathing dragon he had found in the dumpster along with their dinner, Bohdan asked, "Mom, are dragons real?"

"No, baby. No such things as dragons. But you, you're my prince, my one and only treasure."

Bohdan smiled. His mother's tender face, half-lit by the moon and half-shadowed by the alley's darkness. The wrinkles of a harsh lifestyle and stress hadn't made his mother any less beautiful.

"Bodie, stay here. I've got someone to meet. When I'm done, I'll come back, okay?"

"Yeah, Mom."

"Hopefully, tonight, I can find my knight in shining armor, yeah? Or better yet, a king."

Bohdan nodded. She'd been looking for her king every night for over a year. He waited alone in the dark alley, but after some time, worry walked him out to the main road. She crumbled on the ground, a needle sticking out of her otherwise clean arm. The fat suit stood over her.

If he submitted to the fat suit's demand, Bohdan wouldn't get any help. But what choice did he have?

"Well, boy? What'll it be? You going to save your Momma, or let her die?"

Bohdan fell to his knees and motioned for the man to stand in front of him.

"And you, you're my prince, my one and only treasure."

In a charged flash, Bohdan snatched the syringe out from the crook of his mother's arm and stabbed it straight through the fat suit's open pant fly, forcing the needle into his flesh. The suit choked and crashed to the ground, firing a large swell of smoke into the air, the fiery embers of his cigar crushed into the sidewalk under his weight. He writhed on the hot ash, holding his groin and cursing Bohdan.

Bohdan reached over him and unclipped the man's mobile phone.

The next morning, Bohdan sat next to his mother's hospital bed and held her hand.

"Thank you, Bodie. You saved my life."

Bodie squeezed her hand, unsure of what to say.

"See, what did I tell you? Princes are real."

"So are dragons, Mom. So are dragons."

ONCE UPON A DIFFERENT TIME

Karen Robiscoe

We're all familiar
with the lore—
of fairy tale people.
The heroes right,
the knights in white,
and princess in the steeple.
But that's not all,
who went to ball,
and found their ever after.
There was, of course,
another force—
of somewhat lesser actors.

The fairies that
stood in for stars,
during dress rehearsal,
close to right,
but just not quite,
for reasons controversial.
Take, for instance,
the history of—
Central Heating-Ella.
Since blood ran cold,
the tale she told,
failed to make novella.

Of course there was,
her hapless cous',
Also known as "Piggy."
Big Toe-lina,

Cut from scene'a,
ate 'til she was Biggy.
A better fate–
than what awaited,
Princess backing soy beans.
the GMO'S—
from Monsanto,
fostered canc'rous breast genes.

Yes, fairy folk
in anecdotes—
must toe writ' lines or go.
Just ask Soul Patch,
Whose shaved blue thatch,
will never be well-known.
Nor will evil—
elven sprites—
Pogo stick to fame.
Since stilts are much—
preferred to Sticks,
If you guess his name.

THREE LITTLE PIGS WALK INTO A BAR, SEE

Marie Lathers

"Three little pigs walk into a bar, see, and…"

"You want that on the rocks, Sammy?"

"Sure, Mickey, rocks. Anyway, three pigs, little, walking…"

"Walking on two feet or four?"

Her voice said she wasn't joking. This was serious, tall-blonde serious. She bent her head to mine, a cigarette dangling out of a delicious mouth. I would have been a fool not to light it.

"Have a seat." I pulled out the barstool next to mine. "Drink?"

She sat and peered down at me—that dame was tall. "Thanks, but not yet. I'm anxious about the pigs." She took a slow drag on her Winston and blew the smoke out through bright pink lips. Her dress matched her lips, except for the black buttons and belt. She looked just like a piece of candy, of the sweetest sort.

"The joke goes down better on ice." I signaled to Mickey. "Another, on the rocks, for my friend here."

"I don't make friends so quickly," she said, putting her hand up like a stop sign. Mickey stood with a glass full of ice, unsure whether or not to add liquid. I lit a cigarette of my own, a Pall Mall, and glanced sideways at her. She eyed my gabardine.

"That's a nice enough suit," she said. "Nice enough."

I blew smoke out over the bar and into Mickey's middle-aged belly. He shrugged, put down the glass, and went off to hose another customer. We were alone, me, my joke, and the dame.

"It's a long one," I said. "A three-drink joke, if you see what I mean. And you aren't even on your first."

She eyed my face now, as if she recognized it from the back page of a newspaper.

"Nice moustache," was all she said.

"It's been good to me." I smiled. I was beginning to get this broad. She was the educated type, someone who probably knew the difference between concave and convex. I peered at her cleavage. Convex.

"You from the neighborhood?" I tested the waters. The only educated dames in the neighborhood were long dead.

"Middle West Side," she said between puffs. "My father was a writer. Of jokes."

I froze. Mickey froze, too. I had never had competition before, not in that neighborhood. Even though this competition was already under six feet of dirt, I was nervous.

"Don't worry." She smirked. "His specialty wasn't farm-animal jokes."

Just when I thought she was warming up to me, she knocked me down, like I was a sad rat in a lobster trap.

"Sammy," Mickey tried helping. "Tell her about the time you made the Mayor laugh. Tell her, Sammy." He was impatient, Mickey. He turned his belly towards the pink dress. "You see, Miss, Sammy was…"

"Sammy, huh?" She planted her gaze on me again. I had to look up to see her. Her black gaze drilled into my nose hairs. "I like that."

Maybe we could get back on a good footing. "Can I ask yours?"

"You can." She swiveled to Mickey. "I'll have that first drink now, but change the ice, it's started to melt." The ice wasn't the only thing melting.

"Mazie. With a 'z.'" The nostril hair drilling recommenced.

"Nice." And it was. The 'z' clinched it. "You should know, Mazie, that my specialty is animal jokes. Farm animals. Cows, donkeys, horses, chickens. I see them in my dreams, those animals."

"Grew up on a farm, huh?" She took the drink Mickey offered her and gulped it down in one shot. "I'll take the second one now. That's two out of three, Sammy."

"I grew up downtown, but a guy I knew in the joint worked on a farm."

"Okay, then, so the pigs—standing on two or four legs?"

"I tell it like I see it. I see them up on two legs. Naked. Walking into a bar."

"Naked, huh? That supposed to light my fire?" She picked up her second drink and took a sip. She held out another cigarette.

I imagined her naked under that pink layer. Curling blond locks falling over breasts capped by inch-long nipples. Bristly hairs starting at her navel and reaching all the way back to her rigid tail. A guy could mess up his face licking those bristles. A guy like me.

"So the bartender says, 'Naked pigs? Now I seen everything.' The pigs sit at the end of the bar, in a row. It's closing time on a Tuesday night, and the regulars have left. It's just the bartender and the row of pigs."

"Naked." Mazie repeated the word like it was the first one she learned as a child. With innocence, and yet underneath that, a hint of original sin. "Why are they naked?"

"That's just what the bartender asked. And pig number one, the one closest to the door, says, 'We lost our clothes in a fire. We lost everything. We're bereft.'"

"An educated pig, huh? I like educated animals." I was right. Mazie was dressed like a high-class hooker and had a high-class vocabulary. Just my type.

"'So, where you staying?' The bartender goes on, 'And the drinks are on the house, since you're down and out…and naked.'" I said the last word slowly. Her tough, bristly arm hairs rubbed against my arm, leaving scratches like bread crumbs showing which way she'd passed. She was close to me and finishing her second drink. I sniffed her perfume—gardenia mixed with dirty sex, the kind that leaves brown stains on the sheets.

"Mickey, another drink for the lady."

She thanked me by moving closer, her convex cleavage up against my shoulder, leaving one of those brown stains I anticipated.

"'We lost our clothes in a fire. We lost it all, house, appliances, yard, clothes, you name it.' The pigs wept. All three in sync. All three sipped from their sherry at the same time. 'You fellas triplets?' The bartender asked, 'You sure do seem to be.' Pig one continued, 'We are, and we've lost it all. No insurance, nowhere to go. Any suggestions on where we can sleep tonight?'"

But Mazie was onto other things that weren't even part of the joke. An educated woman, she wanted a story. The ice melted in her third drink. She took it slowly now.

"Who'd burn down a pig's house, Sammy? Who'd be that nasty?" She said the word "nasty" like she had said the word "naked"—with gusto. Mickey turned away and held his nose at that point, as if he couldn't take the smell. A jealous man, that Mickey. Never lucky with the dames.

"That'd be the wolf," I improvised. It wasn't a joke anymore. This dame was serious, and I had a serious hard-on. Time for some after-hours fun. Time for some rolling in the hay with someone who knew how to roll. I just had to make sure that my ad-libbing didn't ruin the joke. Ruin the joke, and I'd ruin my chances. That's the thing about educated dames who like jokes. One false move, and the fairy tale's over.

"A big, bad wolf?" Mazie stroked my thigh with her hoofed hand.

"Big and bad, yes."

She was nearing the last sip of her drink. "And the punch line, Sammy? The naked pigs and the bartender? Make it good, sugar, make it real good."

Her words came out in fits and starts now, each syllable a grunt. I had to get her out of the bar and into my cheap hotel room. And quick. But if I wasn't going to misfire, I had to change the ending. A lame "No, but I can dress you up with a few more drinks, fellas," wasn't going to cut it. It had to involve a wolf. I searched my memory for a punch line with a wolf. Blank.

"I'm waiting, Sammy," she grunted. She rubbed her suddenly flat nose in my face. Flat and tough, just like I like them.

"So the bartender says, 'Sure, I can help you boys.'"

"I'm waiting, Sammy." Her nose rooted all over me. Mickey's bar smelled like an outhouse. Everyone, including Mickey, had left. We were alone in hog heaven.

"'I got three daughters that look a lot like you boys, but they've got dresses on. If you slip me twenty you're welcome to head on upstairs and take their dresses off. They'll be naked like you and ready to wallow.'"

"You haven't disappointed me, Sammy. Good for you." She could hardly hold the glass up to her mouth to take the last sip, given her hooves. I helped her out, though, and then we went to her place, where she helped me out.

10/25/16 Porcine Problem Drinkers

SWINE

Jaclyn Adomeit

As the clock struck eleven, the three little pigs were cast out from the family farm. Fred understood why Mother Sow wanted them gone, even if he didn't like it. John was lazy, Herbert was a drunk, and Fred, sometimes, bent the truth. Mother Sow forgave the corn-field burning, the swill smuggling, and the bees in her favorite bonnets, but she told the three little pigs that this was the last straw. Fred swore up and down that they had nothing to do with the barn, or the cannon, or the rubber chickens, but the neighbours had taken up their pitchforks and were prepping the tar and feathers. Mother Sow pushed them out the door with a broom handle.

"This isn't the last straw boys. It's an upturned hay-bale." She slammed the door, leaving them to the night.

John, Herbert, and Fred snuck down to the rail yard and hitched an open car. Land soared beneath them, and stars above them, as they sailed away from a small town and small lives.

"We need a plan. If we hitch rail too long, we're gonna get picked up by a chain gang, and I don't wanna lose my figure." John, the oldest, patted his swollen belly.

"What about bank robbin'?" asked Herb, the youngest, "that's what Pop used to do."

"Herb, you chicken-head, that's how pop ended up in the pig pen. You think you're smarter than your own daddy?"

John and Herb quarreled, but Fred sat quietly in the shadow of the crates. John smashed a hoof into Herb's gut. He topped back against wooden boxes. The train car shook.

"Sit down before you knock each other off this polly-waggin' train. I got a plan," said Fred, the middle sibling.

In the dark of the crates, Fred spoke of their Uncle Wilbur who lived this direction on the train line.

The next morning, just before the train landed in the station, they hopped off at Louisville. Brushing off their faces and clothes as best they could, they strolled into the center of town. The general store was nestled in the main square under a small clock tower. Leading the way, Fred entered the shop.

"Good afternoon, boys." The shopkeeper climbed down from a ladder where he had been stocking un-labelled cans on a high, dusty shelf.

"Hello, sir," said Fred, "Would you be able to tell us the way to the Swineson farm?"

"Swineson? 'Bout three miles west of town on Main Street. You boys related?"

"Yes, sir. We're in town to visit our Uncle Wilbur."

"Well, ain't that nice. I hope you boys are 'round to help him with harvest. He could use some strong backs."

"Yes, sir," said Fred. John and Herb nodded along.

"Well, you boys better get gone before the local hens catch wind there is new folks in town to gossip about."

"Of course, sir. Could you answer us one more question? Is there an insurer in town?"

"Mm hmm, the office is just across the street and up a block. What would three little pigs need insurance for? You hidin' diamonds in those grubby pockets?" He laughed at his own joke, then horked up a wad and spat it on the floor.

"Goodness no, sir. I've just heard that all the best towns have insurers these days, and this sure seems like a good little town."

They opened the door, leaving the shop bell tinkling, and hoofed it three miles due west. When they came to the pale yellow farm house, Fred turned to the others. "You two better mind your manners a few days—none of that oinking or hollering. We need old Uncle Willie's help, or we'll have to skip town again."

"Don't you talk to me like that, you little slop-drinker. I know you think you're smart, but I'm the oldest. If you don't listen to me 'n Herb, we're gonna play a little game of Red-Belly Freddy."

Fred dodged John's jab at his stomach, mounted the steps of the porch, and knocked. The unlatched door swung forward with the first thump. "Uncle Wilbur?"

His uncle's head poked around the corner, a coffee cup in his hooves and a startled look on his face.

"Fredrick?" Herb and John craned their heads through the doorway behind Fred. "Herbert? Johnathan? Boys, what in Hog's name are y'all doin' in Louisville?"

Fred stomped on John's hoof to silence his oink in reply. "We had a talk with Mother, and she thought it was time for us to make our way in the world. Since there ain't much room on the Porkter property, she suggested we make our start by coming out here to help you with harvest."

John grabbed Fred's tail hard, and twisted it in return for the stomp. Fred's eyes watered, but he didn't squeal. Herb sniggered.

"Well swine-darn. Thelma, the Porkter boys are here. Get some biscuits in the oven."

After they tucked in for a noon day meal and exchanged necessary pleasantries, Uncle Wilber mentioned that he would love some help with the harvest. "But, you see, fellas, I ain't gonna be able to pay you outright for the work. It's a tough little town. Me and Thelma do all right, but farming ain't no life of luxury."

"We'd love to have and feed you though. The attic rooms are all yours." Thelma gestured to the ceiling with her hooves.

Herb and John's faces fell, but Fred kept a grin fastened on his lips. "Of course we'll help you, Uncle Wilber, and you, too, Auntie Thelma. That's what family is for. And there is no need to keep a roof over our heads. We've got strong backs and quick hands. With a bit of material, we could build up a small place for ourselves in no time."

"Oh, Fred, that's mighty kind."

"That is a mighty fine offer. We've got us some extra bales of straw, and some felled trees that would make good, strong posts. If you boys are up to the challenge and stick around for the harvest, I'll sign you each over an acre in the meadow near the hills. It will be a great place for a little, straw house."

Munching hungrily at biscuits, the three pigs nodded and smiled.

The brothers were not unskilled in manual work. They twisted, and braided, and thatched. Four sturdy trees were chopped and affixed to make four corners and an A-frame roof.

"I'm proud of you boys. Your mother is always making a fuss, but she's had her tail in a twist since she was a piglet. You're good pigs," said Uncle Wilbur.

The day after the straw house was built, Fred walked to the center of town and into the insurer's office. His shirt and face were washed, but both his feet and his tone drawled as he greeted the secretary. She led him in to Mr. W. Ol'Fang's office. The dark, wood-paneled walls contained bookshelves that stretched from floor to ceiling, displaying a barricade of leather bound volumes with golden spines. Ornate oil lamp sconces hung from the wall. Fred's gaze settled on the insurer. He sat straight in his grey tailored suit, with shining cufflinks that matched the yellow glint of his eyes.

"Mr. Swineson, how good of you to come in for a meeting." His razor sharp teeth snapped together as he smiled.

"Actually, it's Mr. Porkter, sir. Mr. Swineson is my mother's brother."

"My apologies, you are new to town, Mr. Porkter. What need do you have of my services?"

"Well, my uncle has been real kind to me and my two brothers and helped set us up with a small piece of land. We've gone and built ourselves a little house out of straw. We wanna make a start in this town. We've been real lucky, but Ma always said that only fools count on their luck to hold out. So I'm here to buy us some insurance."

Winston Ol'Fang's yellow eyes met Fred's. Fred did not blink.

"Your mother sounds very wise, indeed, and you've come to the right place."

Mr. Ol'Fang presented the options, and Fred latched right onto the premium package. Winston ran a long pink tongue over his sharp teeth. Fred felt the hairs on his chin stand up as goosebumps crawled over his skin, but he kept a grin tacked to his cheeks. His hoof met Mr. Ol'Fang's, and they shook. Fred walked slowly out of the office, but as soon as he turned the street corner, he ran all the way home.

The house stood finished for two weeks, then the fire broke out.

Rumors clucked from the beaks of the town chickens that it was the youngest pig's fault. An empty pot left on the fire: coals unattended. A wood burning stove in a straw house was never a good idea. The hens of the town pecked about men being left to fend for themselves.

The mishap did not tarnish three little pigs character. They had already established an agreeable reputation about the town. They assisted neighbours with harvests, attended the weekly church service, and did not frequent the tavern or the town's establishments of ill repute.

Three days after the fire, Fred walked into Winston Ol'Fangs office, papers in his hand and a brother on either side.

"Sir, thank you for meeting with us. I know we should've informed you sooner, but we needed a few days to deal with our loss." Fred passed the paperwork over the mahogany surface of the desk. John and Herb nodded with frowning faces. "It has been quite the shock to get settled and immediately lose all our worldly possessions."

"I see," said the wolf.

"Me and my brothers filled out the paperwork and listed what was destroyed."

Herb let out a snort that turned into a cough.

"We wanted to come in and ensure we could answer any questions." Fred ignored his younger brother.

The wolf tapped his claws on the carved mahogany desk. Fred swallowed the spit that rose in the back of his throat.

"Yes, please sit."

Mr. Ol'Fang turned over the first page of the paperwork and worked through the standard questions. The wolf asked each pig to recite the list of items covered by the insurance claim.

Fred had warned Herb and John that the wolf wouldn't be a fool. The edges of Mr. Ol'Fang's smile slipped and became a snarl as Fred, Herb, and John repeated answers on cue. At the end of the meeting, the wolf assured them that the paperwork was in order, and that his secretary would be in touch soon.

Three curly tails tottered out of the office, and the door closed. As Fred shut the door there was a sound of the tearing of paper and the slamming of paws onto an ornate desk.

A week passed, and the three little pigs returned to Uncle Wilbur's attic. Herb and John behaved meticulously: they were anxious of being thrown out of town. Then, that Monday, a post mule clopped up to the Swineson farm with a letter addressed to Fredrick, Herbert, and Johnathan Porkter. Rushing outside, they opened the letter behind the barn.

"Sooooo-ey," squealed John.

"Hot dog," said Herb.

The two danced a jig with arms intertwined. Fred could nearly see the visions of whiskey, sows, and freedom swirl about their heads.

"Really? All this reaction for a measly one thousand, nine hundred, and sixty-eight dollars? What are we, roosters? Waiting to cock-a-doodle-doo at any and all shiny things that pass our way? This is just the beginning."

"Roosters? What is this hog wash? Not you, not me, or any other Porkter ever had two thousand pig smackers to spend." John chortled and poked Herb in the ribs. "Listen to little red-belly Freddy here. Pulls one con and thinks he's a high horse. Herb and me are taking our share and heading to Tennessee. Freddy can stay here and pretend he's a pony."

"And then what? You two are gonna drink and fondle sows until you have zilch?" Fred took a deep breath and steadied his jaw. "We've got an opportunity here. We could take this and turn it into ten times as much. Then you could drink yourself sick in a pile of sows for the rest of your days."

Herb looked whimsically off into the distance, but John snorted in frustration. "How long?"

Fred smiled. "Only three months."

"So what we gonna do? Have another fire? Ain't anyone going to forget about a fire in three months. Hell, ain't no one in this chicken town gonna forget about a fire for a decade."

"Good thing we are covered for more than fire."

The winter was nearly upon them. With a quarter of the money, the pigs bought logs. They sawed and hammered and nailed. Before the snow flew, they had a log cabin with wood furnishings. It had three bedrooms, a kitchen, a sitting room heated by a cast iron stove, and was nestled into the base of a big hill on the edge of their plot of land.

The day after its completion, Fred walked into the office of Mr. W. Ol'Fang.

When the wolf saw the pig, his jaws clenched and a growl rolled in his furred throat.

"Hello, sir. I am not sure if you have heard the good news, but we've gone and built a new house. A log cabin. It's a lovely home."

"How wonderful, glad to see the insurance coverage served you well."

"Precisely. So you can see why my brothers and I think it is important to insure our new property as well." Fred plopped down in one of the chairs in front of the mahogany desk and leaned back with his hooves on his belly.

The wolf drew a long breath through his furred snout. "You understand, my young pig, that the coverage will be much more expensive. You've already filed a claim, which increases the liability of your coverage. As well, your new residence is worth much more than your straw hut."

"Oh yes, sir, we understand. I want to be sure to employ the premium package as well. It's good to be prepared for anything."

The winter passed for the three little pigs. Their log cabin huffed smoke skyward, and they went about their business. Church was attended and neighbours aided. Often, Fred went for long walks in the hills surrounding the farm and came home with dirt covered hooves. Only once did Herb and John head into town and patronize the most sordid tavern. Fred hustled them out as the brawl began, and before they could be properly identified.

From then on, Fred kept the wooden house well-stocked with whiskey. John and Herb would find that the proximity of drink outweighed the benefits of heading to town. Besotted as they were, they did not remark upon Fred's week-long trips out of town.

One-hundred-and-six days after the fire, a hillside worth of rocks slid down the hill behind the wooden house. A boulder the size of a dairy cow came loose in the spring thaw. It rolled down the slope, blasted through the back of the log cabin, exited the front, and continued on its merry way. The back half of the house crumbled under the weight of the other rocky debris.

The three little pigs and Uncle Wilbur were away, helping raise a barn for the Duckstone family. Fred invited the barn raisers back to the house for a warm up of whiskey beside the fire. When the assembly approached, they saw the roof caved in, a wall blown out, and shattered whiskey bottles covering the front walk. Herb and John sank to the ground, heaving heavy hog sobs.

While comforting his brothers, Fred declined the offered charity and repeatedly voiced his gratefulness for Mr. Winston Ol'Fang. "He has been so good to us. He's a better neighbour than a hen that lays golden eggs."

Fred let Winston Ol'Fang wait for a whole week before Herb, John, and he walked through the insurance office door. The color drained from the wolf's snout as the secretary showed the three little pigs through the office door.

"Thank you for seeing us, sir. It's been quite the ordeal since—"

"Shut your snout. The three of you sit down."

Silent, they sat. Herb and John faces cleaved into grins. Fred's heart beat at his ear drums and he tucked his quaking hooves into his lap.

"Don't you come in here and breathe your hog-wash at me. I know what you did."

Fred raised his hoof, ready to pace off his practiced speech of his whereabouts on the day in question. The wolf snapped his fangs. Fred lowered his hoof.

"Please, don't. I've heard. You were at the barn raising. Everyone saw you there. Your possessions and hard work are covered in rubble."

"Don't forget 'bout the twenty cases of whiskey," said Herb.

"Thirty cases." John sat up straighter in the leather chair.

The wolf took a deep, rattling breath through his clenched teeth, released his claw's grasp from the mahogany desk, and smoothed the fur on his snout. "You may think you've won. But you lard-headed, little squealers listen to me. I will be dogging every one of your footsteps. If I find you have put one hoof out of line, I will huff, and I'll puff, and I'll blow you all down."

Herb and John shuffled in their seats under the wolf's yellow glare, but Fred sat still and returned the wolf's gaze.

"Put the paperwork on the table you miserable swines. Get out."

Two weeks passed. Even Fred was afraid that the wolf found a way to renege on their policy. Then, on a rainy Tuesday, shortly after breakfast, the post mule came bearing a well-timed letter from the office of Ol'Fang.

Fred returned from a trip out of town only the night before, and his brothers bristled with a static charge of fury. More than once in the previous weeks, Fred caught them whispering about how they would be teaching Fred a two-thousand dollar lesson.

Rain tapped at the roof of the farmhouse and the three little pigs gathered in the attic to open their letter. The wooden house had been insured for the high end of its value, and Fred added supplementary policies for every feasible addition with Mr. Ol'Fang's secretary. The policy paid out just over eighteen-thousand dollars.

Herb and John's eyes grew and grew. John laughed. He laughed until he lost his breath and wheezed and snorted for air, then Herb snorted at John. Before long, the two rolled on the floor, barely breathing between oinks and chortles.

Fred walked away from the two rolling pigs and stared out the tiny attic window. It was dotted with raindrops that blurred the grey sky. He gazed down at the check. Pride plucked at his heart, and he felt warm, even in the cold, dull light. "It's just what we needed. Now we can really blow that wolf's coat off."

His two brothers ceased their laughter and sneered at him. They stood up, and pounded their front hooves.

"Don't you even think about it," said Herb.

"We spent a whole winter behavin' and waitin' for this. It's ours."

A tingle of cold fury oozed down Fred's spine. *Their money my snout.* "Think of where we've come from. We had nothing. Now we've got eighteen-thousand dollars."

"And now, we're gonna spend it."

"For only four months that is incredible. But what is six-thousand a pig in the grand scheme of things? A few years of luxury and then back to slogging slop?"

"I'll take luxury."

"Come now, it's the first ten-thousand that's the hardest to make. Why, with this opportunity, we could really make a name for ourselves. The Three Porkter Brothers, look at them go, with wives and mistresses, whole barnyards of servants. Hell, you two could buy yourselves a distillery. I can see it now, 'Herb and John's Hogwash.'"

John lunged at Fred, but Fred jumped down the attic ladder and rolled onto the second floor landing.

John and Herb squealed threats of holding him down and tearing off his tail.

He ran.

Rushing down the stairs, he skirted into the kitchen, then stopped and held the check over the flames of the hearth, just out of the heat of the fire.

John and Herb appeared in the kitchen door.

They froze when they saw Fred.

"You burn that check, Freddy, and we ain't gonna have no brother no more. We're gonna tear off your legs and leave you to bleed like a stuck pig." Malice blazed John's eyes. Herb looked ready to drown from panic.

Fred steeled his gaze. "I'm holding it here so you pork bellies will listen to me. We had nothing. Now we have the chance to be somebody. Not three good-for-nothing pigs whose daddy's in jail, who need to run from town to town till they get hog tied. We could have more than money. We could have power."

The last words silenced even the raindrops on the house windows.

A peel of thunder ripped through the room.

All three little pigs jumped.

"Fine," said John.

Herb humphed. "But this is the last pig-stinkin' time. We ain't going to be able to pull no more insurance schemes with that old wolf though. You heard what he said."

"Don't worry. They say bad things happen in threes."

Fred told Herb and John to go town and order bricks: a whole mansion's worth. They toiled and mortared and laid all spring. On the eve of the summer solstice, the house was complete—the grandest house in town. Along with the brothers' brick laying, Fred hired pipe pigeons to come along and fit the house with indoor plumbing. Three fireplaces warmed the main floor, and more fires illuminated the upper bedrooms. Never had Porkters lived so well.

Fred had the plumbers drill a well for the water that flowed through the house, all sorts of valves and pipes and handles turned this way and that.

Fred paid little attention to a red-furred stranger that lurked in the trees, observing the construction of the brick house.

One night, when all the lights were off, the same red-furred creature, shadowed under a bowler hat, passed into the office of W. Ol'Fang.

"You really think that these swines are going to pull the same scheme again? It's a nice place, perhaps they're starting a real-estate business," he said to the wolf.

"I'm the only one in town with that kind of money."

"Well shucks, maybe they're building it for your furry hide."

"A pig pen is still a pig pen, no matter what the cost. Swine smell would never come out."

"Nonetheless, it looks well-built. No fires or rocks are taking that place down. You know much about this newfangled plumbing they're putting in?"

The wolf lit his pipe, took a deep breath, and blew smoke into the brass lamplight.

"If I was gonna wreck the place, that's how I would do it."

Content with the report, Winston compensated the fox for his cleverness and set to wait. When the brick house was complete, he waited and waited, assuming Fred would come and see him to insure the new property, but as a month elapsed and no pigs passed through the door, he questioned the whole ordeal. He planned to shame the pig and laugh in his face at the prospect of pulling another scheme. Perhaps the fox was correct; maybe they would try and sell it.

On a sunny Thursday, Mr. Ol'Fang sauntered into his office after a lunch meeting and hung his hat. "Any visitors?"

"That old cow stopped in, something about a policy change," his secretary clucked as she took his coat from him. "And the landlord came by, that weasel. He was hissing about a bounced check. I told him there was a mistake, but you should go and see him."

The wolf's snout burned.

"And, yes, a funny note from the Porkter brothers arrived. They mentioned you may want to come and inspect their new property. Something about trouble with plumbing and some water damage."

"Why should that concern me? They have no policy on that pig sty."

"What are you talking about, sir? I put the papers on your desk last week. That handsome Fredrick came in with all the necessary forms. He paid all the fees and went for all the upgrades. They've been such good customers that I ran it all through and put the papers on your desk. You signed the policy along with your daily files last week."

The wolf's breathing caught in his throat.

"You did what?" He could not have done. He would not have done. Those pigs would not take the last of W. Ol'Fang. "You feather covered *chicken-head*."

"Mr. Ol'Fang." She puffed up, spread her wings, and fastened them to her hips.

He lunged at her, but instead of pinning her to the desk, he plowed head-first into the filing drawers. She ran into the street, clucking and shrieking.

Enraged, the wolf rose from the floor. Fire burned beneath his starched collar and he tore at the fabric with his claws, shredding the shirt. He howled up at the brass lamps and bolted out into the street. The wolf ran three miles west to the Swineson farm. Water poured from beneath the front door of the grand brick house. Winston tore the picket fence from its hinges, loped towards the door, and banged on the heavy oak. His claws raked the surface. "You pink little piggies think you are going to pull another scheme on a wolf? I'll huff, and I'll puff, and I'll blow this house down."

They chuckled behind the closed door. "Ooh, the big bad wolf thinks he's gonna blow down a brick house."

Squeals and oinks of laughter sifted through the door, followed by a few sodden hiccups.

"Let the bone-biter try."

"Hey carcass-muncher, come get some bacon."

"Bacon. That old flea head won't be able to afford mutton once we're through with him."

Winston's blood boiled. The oak door flashed red. He ran back through the gate, rushed at the door—*bang*. The oak slab hurled off its hinges, and the wolf burst into the room.

The two little pigs squealed. They tried to run, but their hooves slipped on the soaked-wood floor.

As the wolf tore and munched, the floor of the brick house grew to resemble the red of his vision. Sated, his torn suit steeped in blood, Winston ran out through the empty doorframe into the hills, and disappeared amongst the trees. The trickle of a broken pipe warbled in the hot summer air as a half empty whiskey bottle floated out the front door of the grand, brick house.

Fred was down at the church setting up Fourth of July decorations when Mr. Ol'Fangs secretary came flapping in to make a fuss. "Mr. Porkter. Mr. Porkter. You better come quick. Winston—I mean Mr. Ol'Fang—just tore out of the office in a right rage. He headed up the road to your Uncle's farm."

Fred ran up the street as fast as his hooves could carry him. The hen called after, "If you see Ol'Fang, you tell that fur-face he no longer has a secretary. No one calls me a chicken-head."

Rasping for breath, Fred dashed the three miles west of town. Townsfolk trailed behind. At the brick house, he was met by the torn front gate. Pools of water dotted the front path. They were splotched with red.

Fred knelt and wept outside the gate. When the townsfolk caught up, Fred sobbed that he was unable to cross the threshold. He retreated to the attic. The sheriff was called and kind neighbours cleaned and dried the house as best they could. The wolf was gone, his business collapsed, and no insurance could be claimed for the furniture and rugs damaged by the broken pipe. The neighbours agreed that the loss of a few hundred dollars of insurance money was nothing to Mr. Porkter compared to the loss of his two brothers.

The town hens baked pies and commiserated about how cruel it was for such a nice pig to have suffered so much tragedy. The children around town told each other ghastly tales of the big bad wolf, lurking under beds. If they weren't careful, he would huff and puff and blow their homes down.

After a month in the attic, only opening the door for soup, Fred emerged with two letters to be sent by mail: one to his mother and one to a Mr. F. Roger and Associates.

Again, Fred attended church and received condolences from his neighbours.

Three weeks later, the post mule arrived at the Swineson farm with a letter addressed to Fred Porkter.

Dear Mr. Porkter,

We are terribly sorry for your loss. News of your tragedy reached us in Weedick City. Along with our condolences, we provide our hope that the perpetrator is swiftly brought to justice.

Enclosed is the re-imbursement associated with the life insurance policy held by your brothers and yourself to the amount of $204,922. As per the stipulations, it is paid out to the surviving brother(s) in the case of the loss of any of the aforementioned parties. The valid clause is outlined in supplemental pages attached with this letter.

With greatest sympathy,

Felton Roger and Associates.

THE TWENTY-SEVEN CLUB

Anthony S. Buoni

Psychedelic music and champagne pounded David's head as he drained his fifth flute. Across the bar, a woman in a flowing, tie-dye kimono spilled bourbon over her exposed breasts as a bearded man drank the runoff. Maybe all the drinks had blurred his senses, but David swore that the pulsing tongue lapped the liquor from her nipples in time with the chaotic music pouring from the flashing jukebox in the corner.

Another decadent night in Paris dissolved into a debauched haze.

"Try not to stare." François removed the empty glass and sank it in a small sink behind the bar. "Everyone will think you're strange."

"Do you know how many women you'd pick up in America with that accent?"

François tossed his shaggy hair. "I don't think you realize how many I pick up anyways. Another glass?"

David checked his wristwatch, a present from mother before leaving the states. She'd break out a Bible if she walked into the Rock'N'Roll Circus and saw her youngest son poisoning himself among the European decadence. Rubbing his eyes helped them focus on the watch's numbers. Twelve forty-five a.m.—plenty of time to sleep it off before hitting the studio in the morning.

With wave of his hand, more bubbly appeared.

David's days cycled between piano and booze—blurring the lines between his work scoring a low budget Italian horror film and nights on the town drinking with eccentrics.

Sipping the sweet liquid, his mind drifted to the Lydian scale he recorded earlier.

The mode fit the film's most frightening scene: the Ape Man emerging from the forest, grabbing the scantily-clad blonde bombshell from a polka-dotted picnic blanket and carrying her off into the dense woods as she struggled in its hairy arms. Even though David's music captured the proper mood, the notes lacked something. He needed an extra punch to push the scare over the top and had burnt thirty minutes of studio time trying to figure out the missing element.

Maybe he was trying too hard.

The answer was probably something simple.

Flatten the third?

Play the scale a key higher?

Record the champagne bottles smashing against garbage cans in a seedy alley and then overdub the notes?

Tomorrow, he'd nail the scene. Another drink or two and call it a night…

Four weeks of sessions down. Two remained. Despite the lack of time, he remained ahead of schedule, but he'd never let the filmmakers or the studio heads know. Finishing the project too early meant less pay and less Paris.

Back in the states, he often worked for crumbs, eking out a living by drifting from gig to gig, usually playing a different town every night. The film's producers had vetted him playing improvised jazz in a French Quarter piano bar and offered him the job, all expenses covered by the independent company funding the movie. David jumped at the opportunity, flying to France a week later.

How in the hell could he ever go back to Jonesboro, Arkansas, after tasting the vivid nightlife and counterculture of the City of Lights?

"Mr. Butler. All this merriment, and you're closed in on yourself. With a glass of champagne, no less." Jim Morrison slid in the adjacent barstool and signaled François. "Loosen up, man. Have fun."

"Believe me, I am. Any more fun, and I'd probably get locked up."

"Trust me, that's not fun at all."

Morrison had seen better days.

A few years ago, Jim's cheesecake photos were plastered across countless heartthrob magazines. Providing lead vocals for the Doors had elevated him through the stratosphere where he drank and crooned with Greek gods. People loved him. His sultry baritone delivered dark poetry over the airways, invoking rebellion and sex throughout a generation of seekers. Intense stage performances electrified a restless, changing world alive with youth culture.

His voice changed music and the world forever.

But like everything thrown towards the heavens, the return to earth had been swift.

Tales of his excesses with drugs, alcohol, and women were extreme even in an age of free love. Amazing concerts devolved into fiendish drunken stupors fueled by LSD and insanity. Trouble found Jim in New Haven and Miami; indecent exposure charges still loomed in the western horizon.

David shook his hand as the bartender brought Jim's usual, an American beer and a bottle of cheap vodka.

Jim drained the beer in one mighty gulp.

"Anything interesting happening tonight?" Jim took a swig from the bottle. "Or just the usual Dionysian debauchery?"

David sifted through the evening, trying to remember any particular incident.

With everything and everyone crazy, when flavor and oddity filled each moment inside the club, what qualified something as worthy of retelling to a rock star?

"That sonofabitch dwarf pimp came through earlier, parading around these two young birds I'd never seen before as if they were gold-covered peacocks. He made sure they came by and said hello to every damned person in the bar before they split."

"Anybody leave with them?"

"No. I think it was more like a presale gimmick."

"One thing I will say about this place: lots of characters to fuel my writing."

They had started talking David's third night in town.

Jim heard through God-knows-who about David's work on the soundtrack and approached him wanting to jive about film, music, and books. They hit it off, spending the night talking until they watched the sunrise from the riverbank over a bottle of fine cognac. Since then, whenever Jim sauntered into the Circus, he'd belly up beside David and share war stories, crazy tales of stardom and overindulgence. David loved having an American friend in a foreign culture, especially one so famous.

"Been a hell of a day, brother," Jim said. "I've been writing. Got stoned with Pam and spun some records"

"What are you writing—more music?"

"Nah, poetry."

"Any success?"

"Sure." Sitting up straight, he cleared his throat and closed his eyes. "The hitchhiker wanders through the desert like a snake coiling over a woman's body. The serpent's forked tongue flicks, tasting her mysteries with apprehensive joy. Rain is coming. The floods will wash sin clean so the weary traveler can be born anew."

Jim opened his eyes and cracked a carefree grin that had dropped scores of lustful maidens to their knees.

Damn, how did he make being cool look so easy?

"Not bad, man."

"I want to be remembered for the words. Not all the bullshit, the trouble."

"You have the life, man." David sipped his champagne. "A lot of musicians I know would envy your success."

"Fame is cursed. No one gives a shit about what is really important." Jim swigged from the vodka bottle, chasing the liquor with a sip of a new beer François had deposited. Shoulders slumped, he peeled the edges of the label from the brown bottle. "The sad truth is that music, art, and words are ornamental. Most people don't care. It's all just noise, cacophony rattling in the background as they plod along in their hollow existences."

"That's a tough pill. I'd like to think we're doing something more for people."

"Me, too."

Did he, though? David couldn't tell.

He took another drink of vodka. "How's your score going?"

"Not bad. The movie is schlock, but fun enough to keep me interested."

"Monsters, right?"

David nodded.

"Creature films are really philosophical looks into our fears. It's easy to explore taboo themes when they're portrayed as fictions. Ghosts make excellent vehicles for regret and revenge. Slap some fangs on an actor that's seducing women or cover him in hair and have him howl at the moon, and the audience will sit through a story rife with sexual tensions without their morality or whatever they perceive as their values getting in the way."

"I never thought of it like that."

"Trust me, man. I went to film school. If you're too edgy, viewers tune out. They don't care about real art."

"Hey, now. Your music is art. The Doors released some heady material while pop fluff dominated the mainstream. You called out the end of the sixties with perfect ardor."

"Our sound is a ritual. We call down the moon, shine her light on the darkness that swallowed up the world when our country plunged into Vietnam."

Dave leaned over his champagne, running his index finger over the flute's rim. If the music in the club wasn't so loud, would the glass sing?

"Look, man," Jim said. "I'm not trying to bring ya down. I just think that most people don't get it. Not for real. They stop shaving and don the hippie uniform, but it's just fashion. A mask they wear. They don't really understand the new age bullshit they hide behind. Most of them couldn't think their way out of a dumpster, let alone transform the world into something new and beautiful."

"So, the fairy tale is finally over, eh, Jimmy?" a cigarette-chewed voice interrupted from behind.

Dave, snapped out of the conversation, spun around.

The pimp.

How long had the diminutive man been standing there?

Dick Oswald juggled his cocktail and straightened out his dinner jacket's blue velvet sleeve before shaking their hands. A crucifix hung from a sparkling gold chain dangling around his neck. He reeked of expensive cologne and marijuana smoke, money and seedy class.

Dave knew the rumors and kept his distance from the guy—drug dealers usually brought trouble, and Dick carried pockets full of bad vibes.

"Well, if it isn't the bastard dwarf pimp." Jim raised his beer.

"Jim, baby, I'm hurt. I offer the same thing as you do, cat. Pleasure."

"Pleasure and pain are illusions. People like us treat the symptoms and ignore the cause."

Dick punched David's arm. "Ah, the poet bleeds for us. Let's drink."

They clinked their beverages together and swilled. David wiped away a rivulet of champagne that leaked from the corner of his mouth, a fizzy tear that left stale grapes wafting from the back of his hand.

Jim's lips pulled into his famous, reckless smile. "The buzz around here claims that you got some new meat."

"That's why I'm here. But they're not for just anybody, Jim. The boss instructed me to make sure your needs are taken care of before anyone else."

"I don't need to buy women, Dickie-boy."

"Don't be like that. Everyone has an off night here and there. My girls are beautiful and clean. You could have your pick. What about your friend here?"

Dave held his palms up. The last thing he needed was to return to America with a dripping dick. "Oh, I'm good."

"Look, we can arrange some time at the boss's pool. Get some sun."

"Didn't anyone tell you? I'm a vampire." Jim lifted the vodka bottle. "This is my blood."

Dick huffed. "My boss wants to make it clear that there are no hard feelings about Pam."

Jim shook his head. "We're all adults. Sure, he fucked my girl, but I've got a feeling that his little Marianne hasn't been walking right since I parted her silky legs."

Jim laughed, slapping his hands on the smooth, wooden bar.

David didn't like their new company. Something sinister hung about Dick, and the pimp brought out an unsettling darkness in Jim. "Hey, Morrison, want to hit another watering hole?"

Jim tossed a few wadded bills on the bar and stood. "Yeah, man. I—"

"Wait a second, fellows." Dick placed a hand on Jim's shoulder, pushing him back down on the barstool. "I've got more than whores tonight."

Jim pushed the vodka bottle away. "Tell the Count that I came to Paris to reconnect with my muse, not to be hustled by some two-bit pimp in a flashy jacket."

"Pfft. Screw Jean de Breteuil." Dick leaned closer. "I got the hook up. A little horse to get your junkie girlfriend wet, and something I picked up from the underground for you, a trinket associated with the occult."

"The occult?" Jim asked.

David cringed. Growing up in a religious household and receiving piano lessons for thirteen years from a nun had drilled a deep respect for God into him. He wasn't a perfect Christian by any means, but messing around with voodoo or devil worship was another matter, something more taboo than abusing the body with intoxicants or casual relations.

Consorting with evil meant risking your soul, and David wanted no part in that.

Dick leaned close. "You believe in magic, don't ya, Jim?"

"Well, that depends."

"Don't give me that shit. Everybody knows about you and that New York witch. She's been telling the world that she's your wife, that you two got married in a pagan ritual and drank each other's blood. Did you knock that spooky bitch up, man?"

"Quit jerking me off." Jim yawned. "Let's see what you're packing. Whip it out."

"Isn't that what got you in trouble in Florida?" Dick slapped Jim's back. "Just kidding. Don't give me that look. No, this particular object isn't for any of these people to see. All the normals in here couldn't handle it, ya know what I mean? Let's take this to a proper office where we can do business like gentlemen."

Dick wandered to the back bathrooms, shaking hands with several revelers along the way before vanishing behind the red curtain in the back.

Jim rose. "Let's see what kind of snake oil this rat is selling."

"I should really get back to the Right Bank and crash. I got a lot of work to do tomorrow."

"Aw, don't be like that. Let me at least cop some China for my girl, and we can get out of here. We can share a cab since we're practically neighbors."

"I don't know. That guy gives me the creeps."

"Yeah. Me, too. That's why I need your back. Come on, man. Make sure he doesn't rob me."

"All right," David said, betraying his instincts. Though the situation reeked of trouble, he couldn't turn his back on his friend. It wasn't the proper Christian way.

He followed Jim past couples dancing and friends talking, tapping the blinking jukebox now spinning a Jefferson Airplane 45 before stepping beyond the billowing red curtains separating the main dance floor from the narrow hall leading to the restrooms.

Dick, a cigarette now dangling from his lips, opened the men's room door and extended his arm, ushering in Jim and David with a wan hand.

"Cut the theatrics, Dick." Jim sat against the sink. "You got some H or what?"

"Easy there, cowboy. I got you." Dick pulled a plastic bag from his pocket and passed it to the singer. In one quick motion, Jim swapped folded up American bills for the drugs, the exchange made with fluid effortlessness.

"Thanks, Dick, but we got other shoulders we have to rub tonight." Jim saluted and reached for the door, but the midget grabbed his wrist.

"What about the other thing I got for you? Aren't you the least bit curious what's in my pocket?"

"If it doesn't have jiggling tits or smell like vodka, I'm not interested."

"Oh, but I think you are." Dick reached into his jacket and pulled out something wrapped in a black cloth patterned with intricate designs, handing it to Jim. "No charge. From me to you."

Dave didn't want to see what the pimp had given him. "Throw it away."

"That's no way to treat a gift."

Jim bounced it in his hand. "It's not really heavy."

"It's probably a gun or something that's going that'll involve you in some unnecessary bullshit."

Dick laughed so hard the cigarette flew out of his mouth. "Do I look smart enough to pull that kind of scheme off?"

"Not really." Jim unfolded the layers of cloth, chuckling.

Silver gleamed in the flickering overhead light.

Succumbing to curiosity, David leaned closer. "What is it?"

"A looking glass." Jim turned the antique hand mirror over and the smooth surface flashed. Intricate silver leaves and webs intersected along the circular mirror, crisscrossing into a tightly-woven spiral handle. He admired his reflection. "Narcissus would be proud. Little man, are you calling out my vanity?"

"Of course not."

"And you claim that this is an occult object?"

"Indeed. It's a scrying mirror—well, what remains of a much older magical tool. It'll answer whatever deep, dark questions are lurking in your heart of hearts."

"Where did you happen upon this treasure?"

"Like the other clandestine things I deal in, I'm not obliged to disclose my sources."

"I think it's broken." Jim shook it.

Dick jumped back.

The pimp's sudden movement skipped David's heart.

"Easy with that. It's not some toy. Treat it with respect."

"Looks like any other mirror. It's either broken or you're pulling my cock."

"You know the stories, poet. Sing to it."

"Now I know you're fucking with me."

"I'm telling you, it's no joke. Look into your reflection and sing to the mirror. Offer it a lullaby."

"What do you think, David?"

David shook his head. "He's making a fool out of you. Don't indulge him."

"I can appreciate a joke. Tell the Count this gag is a gas."

Jim held the mirror up into the sky so everyone could see his reflection.

The looking glass's shadow covered his face as he steadied his shaky hand.

Jim's reflected stern gaze and pouty lips looked down on the trio, a moon floating in the bathroom sky.

He cleared his throat before singing to the reflection:

Mirror, Mirror, in my hand;
I sing to thee to understand—
Mirror, Mirror, catch my gaze;
What is left of my days?

The silver designs around the mirror glowed, pulsating with sparkling energy. Ripples danced across the reflection, warping Jim's eyes, nose, and mouth until his features dissolved into a spinning purple vortex pulling into itself.

Jim's grip on the mirror's spiral handle faltered, sending the swirling maelstrom colliding into itself.

"Don't let go," Dick shouted. "Steady, Morrison. Steady."

The color show rearranged itself as Jim steadied his hand. David didn't recognize the translucent faces shifting as if the flickering images in a cartoon flip book. Scores of men and women passed before two he recognized passed.

Jim gasped. "Jimi. Janis."

More faces crossed the mirror's surface. David stopped paying attention around the time a stubble-faced man with unkempt, shoulder-length hair zipped by.

"Look away, Jim," David said, reaching for the door.

Dick held the door shut, shaking his head.

"Huh." Jim lowered the mirror.

"What did you see?" Dick asked.

Jim contemplated the mirror, frowning. "I saw my bathtub and Pere Lachaise Cemetery. Nothing special. Neat trick, but I've eaten a lot of acid before. This display was underwhelming."

"Better luck next time. Keep the mirror. Like I said, a gift."

Dick bowed and exited the bathroom.

David, unsure of what he witnessed or why his knees trembled so, wanted another drink.

"Ready for a shot and a cab?" he asked.

Jim cradled the mirror. "I'll be out in a minute."

"You okay, man?"

"Yeah." Jim dug into his pocket. "Think that vodka isn't agreeing with me."

"I'll get us a couple of bourbons."

Jim nodded.

David pushed out of the bathroom and returned to the main room. A French song he didn't recognize blared from the jukebox. He hadn't realized how quiet the bathroom had been. Everything that he saw in the john seemed like a vague memory, a distant thought or unharmonious piano chord wavering in the air before vanishing forever.

He sat at the bar beside kimono and the bearded man, their lewd display now settled into idle chit-chat, and ordered two bourbon shots from François.

"Where's Dick?" David asked the barman when he returned with his drinks.

"Long gone. He's in and out several times a night, running shit for the Count. Jim's not getting high in my toilet is he?"

"He said he wasn't feeling well."

"Imagine that. The man drinks like a whale and has a headache. Americans."

David sat, putting the pieces of the evening together.

Had Dick played some keen parlor trick on them, or was the mirror actually blessed with magic? If the latter was the case, David hoped his soul hadn't been compromised by being in its ethereal presence.

The amber liquor didn't look the least bit appetizing. He couldn't imagine taking another drink without losing his mind.

Deciding to skip the shot and head home for the evening, he went to the bathroom to offer Jim one last chance at a cab ride home.

He pushed the men's room door open and found François, swearing in French, pulling Jim, from one of the stalls. His eyes rolled back, thick, milky foam spilled from Jim's mouth.

David's world crumbled.

"Is he all right?" David's heart pounded.

"He's fucking dead. Get him home, we don't need this shit here. The pigs will shut the club down for good."

By some ghastly twist of fate, David realized that if he dropped the Lydian mode to A minor and played the recorded scale backwards with a little bit of reverb and fuzz, the music would be perfect for the ape abduction scene.

As François handed Jim's still-warm body to David, glass crunched underneath his feet.

ALICE'S KEEPER

Maren Matthias

My heels click down the hall as I take care with the silver tray in my hands. I had to throw away the slippers I much preferred–she doesn't like to be surprised by my comings and goings. I reach the oak door and tap the gold knocker three times, per her request, before gliding through.

The spacious room is fairly well lit, but the glow of the lanterns bouncing back and forth from the white checks to the black checks on the floors and the walls has a dizzying and dismal effect. A few pieces of furniture, all covered in burgundy velvet, sit around a glass table that is barely a foot off the ground.

I set the tray on the table and circle around myself. Sometimes, she hides in secret wall compartments, but I usually hear her scratching.

Once she managed to remain unseen behind the chaise, but since then, I've learned how the shadows in the room fall.

She must be out in the garden.

On the far side of the room are two French doors, meticulously painted to blend in with the walls. I open them and step into the gray light filtering through lonely clouds.

She's only allowed to take visitors in the garden with an escort.

No one but me is permitted into her sanctuary.

Remember that this is not her rule but mine, yet she seems to agree with it on most occasions.

She is sitting on a bench with her back to me, singing to a patch of daisies:

"A clever flower, bright and quick
When reaching to the sky.
Deceitful in your petals
Much akin to pecan pie.
Respected? Well, I'd wave and nod
To recognize your wit.
But rudeness isn't pardoned,
You're no better than a nit."

"Alice?" I gently touch her shoulder. "You should come inside before the tea gets cold."

She turns and two big, blue eyes stare at me from under the bangs of a short, untidy haircut. I remember the day she cut it. I had walked in on her sawing off small sections at a time with the butter knife.

When I asked her why she didn't prefer to keep her lovely locks, she said, "He loved to braid my hair."

That was the day I lost my slippers.

"Did you know," she said, leaning toward me with a conspiratorial gleam in her eye, "that pebbles and mushrooms share the same secret in their cores? They like to pretend they're indifferent to each other, but I know better."

I nod politely and step off the stone path to let her pass me. She always wears the same dress, and I sigh with dismay every time it needs mending.

I've brought many new dresses for her to try on, but she turns them all away, saying that he liked this color on her. Only once did she grin at the site of a new garment that was various shades of pink and purple. But it hangs, unworn.

On laundry day, she simply lounges around naked.

With great ceremony, she pours two cups of tea and waits. She says it is rude for the server to choose her own teacup. A tattoo of a red heart winks from the triangle of skin between her left thumb and forefinger. I don't know where it came from.

After I've settled in the armchair and lifted my cup and saucer, she places a biscuit in front of each of her guests, puppets, lined up on the chaise. They are strange little creatures: rabbits, mice, queens, and caterpillars. She made them long ago, but I will occasionally see a new feature or new outfit.

Before the hair incident, I also witnessed her sketching a man with a wicked grin and a flourishing arm. Neither her room nor her fingers have borne a trace of him since.

She twirls a black top hat on her finger, winks at me, and tilts it daintily on her head. She points out a new poem she wrote, and I dutifully read.

Did I forget to mention? All over the black and white surfaces of the room are blood red scrawls–at least one new poem a day.

What will she do when she's run out of space?

Her latest beams at me.

Polker Gambling Candy Hearts
The Gardeners play to last.
Boomerangs and Butterscotch
The tar my throat's amassed.

It continues, but I won't trouble you with the direction it takes. While Alice goes on about a time she was once attacked by a hedgehog, I blink at the sight of her skin in the light.

Every so often, the shadows will play tricks on my eyes.

Small white scars stand along her upper arms. For an instant, she wears stripes, as if she were made of them.

But then, I blink again, and they're gone.

I sigh and let her ramble on. She is far beyond the hope of a suitor, and I, now a destined spinster, remain my younger sister's companion.

I try not to be bitter; I do love her so. I only wish I understood how we got to this place.

Have I always been her caretaker?

A dutiful older sister, surely, but has she always needed to be watched so closely?

I can't remember.

I cried in front of her only once. She told me I was as mad as she, and even more so.

I sip my tea.

Will I believe her before the end?

CINDY'S FELLA

Karen Robiscoe

Lucinda gazes at the whimsical sandals she wears; a delicate crisscross of calf-leather straps affixed to cushioned satin soles that feature towering, crystal heels. She pivots and poses in the foot-high mirror, ignoring the bunions and cracked toenails, testimony to a lifetime spent on her feet, and crosses near-sighted eyes to achieve the necessary amount of blur.

There.

Beautiful.

Just like a princess's feet.

"Will you be purchasing those, ma'am?"

Lucinda deflates at the address despite her forty years.

"I guess not. I wouldn't know where to wear them…" No blurring the mask of minimum-wage apathy on the clerk's face as she sits to unfasten the sandal straps. She hands off the heels, pointing to a sensible pair of Keds instead.

"How about those? Do you have those in a size—"

"Eight." The clerk stands to gather her rejects before disappearing behind a shoe-bedecked wall. He's annoyed, pierced lip curved into a hare-lip sneer, and she can't blame him, even if his attitude *is* unprofessional. Why would selling shoes to a haggard, old cleaning woman be anything but annoying to a youth of—oh, she didn't know—twenty or so?

Glancing away, Lucinda watches the lace hand of a tennis shoe clock inch closer to a swoosh symbol standing in for noon. As the glow of fluorescent lighting lulls her into somnolence, she leans heavily into the chair's left armrest to alleviate the chronic pinched disk in her lower back.

She has to get back return to work, soon.

Hard work, too.

Menial.

Lucinda scrubs other people's houses for a living, and every part of her body aches, the stooping, lifting, and brass-polishing parts especially. Twisting gingerly in her seat, she searches out the single display sandal that had initially caught her eye.

God, that Swarovski crystal detail is gorgeous. She licks chapped lips, a visceral hunger growing.

And growing. When the tennis shoe clock barks out the hour—followed by its universally known slogan—the hunger morphs into a sense of déjà vu powerful enough to rewind time. The shoe clock…the too bright, white paint of the wall on which it hangs…the shoe-sized shelves, and splashy brand logos of the store disappear, and her mind whirls to another occasion.

Another shoe.

So many years ago, it's as if it happened to another woman; a woman who'd been waiting for a very different young man to return with a very different shoe.

Shoes, she corrects herself silently, breath so shallow it's almost non-existent. The footwear she'd waited for then had been a good deal more like the sandal she hungers for now.

"Just do it. And do it now. I expected that laundry to be finished a half hour ago. You've plenty more housework upstairs, and I haven't all day to wait for it. My book club ladies will be here any minute. I swear, if I didn't remind you to do your chores, *nothing* would get done around here, Cindy." Her step-mother's directive, barked from the foot of the basement stairs, could be that of a sweat shop boss, or at the very least, a laundromat overlord.

"That isn't my name." Lucinda says to CeeCee's departing back. Futilely, since Lucinda has asked her countless times not to nick her name in that particular fashion—a full six months of countless—but CeeCee just tut-tuts, telling her that she knew how to speak the English language, thank you very much. Lucinda's late mother had called her Cindy—Pop still *did* on occasion—but everyone else was on official notice. The name was synonymous with car crash and no survivors now, in a way that both defied and belonged in Merriam's, but that bitch CeeCee didn't care.

"Don't get lippy with me, young lady." CeeCee pauses mid-climb to glare over her shoulder. "I'll call you whatever I like. I'll tell your father you sassed me, and he'll ground you."

"Pop wouldn't ground me, CeeCee," Lucinda says, with more bravado than she feels. He'd been a loose cannon since Mom died, and CeeCee was pure gun powder.

"There'll be no prom for you tonight." CeeCee resumes her upward trek. "And you're to address me as Mother."

Fucker.

She doesn't dare say it.

"I'm too old to be grounded. I'm a senior in high school," she says to the dryer's hollow drum.

"A senior loser is *still* a loser." Her step-sister underscores observation with an airborne span of ruched satin tossed at Lucinda's head. It cloaks her vision, and her sinking gut tells her just what CeeCee's horrible daughter has thrown. Her prom dress. Wrenching the pale lilac from her head, her jaw drops. There's a disaster-sized, red Gatorade stain on it, now.

"What have you done to my dress?" The hours spent babysitting the very brat in front of her—a pale but plucky clone of her mother—kaleidoscope through her mind. With CeeCee's cheap pay, it took her all year to earn enough money for this dress.

"It's Tiger's fault. His tail wagged my drink right off the nightstand." She turns, grabbing the collar of the Rattweiler on the top step. 'Sides. You can fix it. You're good at cleaning, Lucy."

"I am not."

"Yuh-huh. Super good. Why you think Ma always assigns you all the chores? You're so good you could be a professional cleaning lady, I bet."

"Shut up."

A small whimper escapes the present-day Lucinda still waiting on the MIA shoe clerk.

"You could enter the Cleaning Olympics." The worst thing about the cloddish statement is how true it proved to be. Now *and* then. Hadn't Lucinda considerably lessened the stain with a solution of lemon juice, baking soda, and hairspray? Applied with Q-Tips, an old toothbrush, and surgical precision? Hadn't she carefully ripped, and re-stitched the ruching to disguise what a corsage wouldn't? Add the high polish to which she'd buffed the crystal heels she'd stolen from CeeCee's closet in payback, and it spelled cleaning lady all the way.

The payback was for the stag status her stepmother had "accidentally" relegated her to—telling her prom date she'd "soiled herself" when he'd called to confirm pick-up times—but Lucinda didn't let the lack of escort stop her. Her Vespa was up to the challenge, and her date had only been a plus one, anyway.

The boy twinkling her eyes didn't know she was alive.

"You okay, lady?" The returning clerk asks, breaking Lucinda's reverie with an oddly well-placed inquiry.

"What're those?" The fog of yesteryear clings to her lashes like lenses.

"Easy Striders," the boy says. "We only have the Keds in a seven or a nine, but these are the same."

"They're not." Lucinda says, examining the sneaker's thinner soles, and considerably more narrow instep, ignoring his eye roll. "I suppose I could try the Keds in a nine."

"Look lady, I haven't got all day to—" The incidental appearance of a mid-management type catches his observation short. Lucinda smiles blandly at the beady-eyed, balding fellow pacing quickly by them now, noting a small ink stain below his nametag on his left breast pocket she's pretty sure she could get out as the disgruntled foot jockey makes his escape.

A meandering escape: a gaggle of teenage girls in the store doorway scatter like dandelion fuzz in a wind storm, and throwing back his shoulders the clerk tours the store's parameters—the girls' backsides, too—before swaggering into the back-supply area. When the girls cluster around the coveted, display sandal, cooing and exclaiming, and worst of all, tossing the shoe back and forth, an unbidden sense of possessiveness sparks within Lucinda, and she's suddenly at the fringes of another group of teenage girls; this group in a school gym buried in time.

###

"He *did* come." The cheerleading captain wails. Two, plastic, potted palm trees, and several feet of streamer-draped gym separate Lucinda from where the so-called cool girls gather at the refreshment table, but the voice is too piercing to miss.

"He came *stag*." A collective gasp emits from her cohorts, and Lucinda's lips purse sympathetically for the unknown single. It's hard enough stepping out by yourself...Lucinda peers down at CeeCee's crystal heels, flexing her calf muscles to minimize the trembling the unaccustomed cant causes in her legs. Scrutiny hardly helps.

"I knew Roy wouldn't ask you." A flaxen-haired member of the squad is bold enough to say, tossing her hair as she adds, "He likes blondes. His last girlfriend was blonde."

"He likes redheads," says a carrot-topped girl, tittering and growing more freckled by the minute, and after brunette, black, and quirkier hues add themselves to the mix, the group dissolves into colorful giggles.

"Roy is *so* dreamy."

"The star quarterback."

"The perfect homecoming king. I hope he wins."

"He won't," the cheer captain announces suddenly. "And he won't be perfect for much longer, either."

Fascinated, Lucinda watches as the girl savagely swirls punch in a beveled, plastic bowl, slopping orange slices onto plastic cutlery and paper plates before ladling a dripping, plastic tumbler. After an incongruous pause to wipe the cup's rim, she flounces across the polished wood floor to confront the quarterback under the basketball hoop, where he mingles with his own group of minions.

Lucinda's too far away to hear the nature of their exchange, but even a blind person could read their body language when the cheerleader tosses the cup of red liquid on the boy's ruffled, tuxedo blouse—a stain distinctly reminiscent of the one Lucinda's dress sported not hours ago—and the girl's subsequent charge past her clique.

As the girls hasten to follow their leader to the locker room, the blonde girl bumps Lucinda with enough force to compromise her teetering balance.Tumbling to the floor, Lucinda's cheeks flame. She tries to regain her feet, but the treadless stilettos are no match for the slick parquet, and she lands in a second, Bambi-like heap on the gym floor.

Until the unthinkable happens.

The thoroughly dreamed, but undreamable occurs.

"Let me help you up." A face-saving hand waggles calloused fingers, and as Lucinda's eyes followthe fingers upward, she finds herself looking into the eyes of the boy on whom she'd crushed throughout high school. Whose name, entwined with hers, adorned the interior of every notebook she had. In print *and* cursive, but who could blame her? This was Roy Allman, the junior varsity quarterback.

"I—I." Lucinda stammers. "I'm so clumsy. I don't how that happened."

"I do," Roy says. "Britta ran you down. She toss punch on you, too?"

"I—I...Huh?" Lucinda's confused. Elated, adrenalized, on clouds nine and ten, but confused.

"Your dress." Roy's chin jerks, and looking down, Lucinda sees her careful basting has split its stitches, and the lighter but still noticeable Gatorade stain it had camouflaged adorns her breast like an indelible corsage. Her cheeks burn anew.

"What's your name?"

"Cindy." Lucinda blurts before she can think, clasping her hands to her juicy décolleté, head teeming with so much sensory input that fainting seems a real possibility.

"Cindy." Roy says, and Lucinda's about to correct him, about to explain that was a name for a girl in another life, but she doesn't.

"Such a pretty name. Tell me, Cindy—are you sinful?"

And it's all she can do to shake her head without throwing up.

"I could clean that for you," is what she manages, but he shrugs her off, claiming rental.

"I doubt your date would appreciate that too much." Roy glances around, and Lucinda's head bows as an eternity passes—or maybe just seconds—before that same helping hand cups her downcast chin.

"Hey, now. There's no shame in playing the field. No shame at all.

Roy raises his voice over the band, currently remixing an acoustic David Bowie song.

"Am I right, Bubba?"

"You're always right, Roy." A beefy fellow calls back from where he jigs center court with a plump brunette.

"I'm not about to argue with that big fella. What about you, Cindy? Think you could tackle him?"

"No."

"How 'bout me? Think you could tackle me?"

"No."

"Then let's dance."

And dance they did, right after Lucinda removed her stepmother's gorgeous but impractical shoes, leaving them on the sidelines with a pile of other pumps and purses. She was so thrilled to be on Roy's arm that her knees knocked anyway, and though the dance ended promptly at midnight—to the poignant strains of the Dolly Parton ballad made famous by Whitney Houston—the trembling in her legs never fully abated.

The current day Lucinda's overworked leg muscles spasm in memory, and she massages the cramp, the ache in her heart matching the pain in her leg. Where was that clerk? He clearly wasn't making time with the girls.

A blonde in a skimpy, red mini-skirt struts by in a pair of mismatched heels—one of them *her* sandal, no less, and the other a knee-high boot.

Lucinda flinches when the girl shrieks.

"Oh. I just love this sandal. I *have* to try on the mate."

"But I wanted those," one girl objects.

"Me, too." Another echoes.

"I need a salesperson."

"Shoe boy," a pink-haired girl says.

And in the next instant, a chorus starts, "We need shoes. Bring us shoes."

"And sandals."

"Don't even think about it, girlfriend," the blonde barks, and as she bends to adjust the strap on the too big sandal, she flashes a self-aware smile at Lucinda.

"Those heels are mine." Like a magical incantation, her reply kickstarts Lucinda's interrupted nostalgia trip as subtly as a hog.

"Can I walk you to your car, Cindy?" Roy asks, as the last note of the ballad fades away.

"That's okay." Lucinda says, embarrassed to imagine Roy escorting her to her Vespa. "I have to get my stepmother's shoes—*my* shoes—and…*hey*. Those are my shoes."

The blonde who'd bumped her so rudely earlier looks over, crystal pumps dangling from her fingertips like oversized jewels sparkling in the disco ball reflection, and using her free hand to express a middle-finger sentiment, slips out the fire exit, triggering an alarm that mimics Lucinda's internal panic.

An uncontrollable wail escapes her, and it isn't clear whether it's Roy's athletic abilities that make him react so quickly, or a sense of chivalry, but react he does.

"Did Britta—are those—wait here, Cindy." Roy runs for the emergency door. "I'll get your shoes back for you."

And Lucinda did wait. She waited until she, campus security, and the custodians were the only people remaining in the school gym, but he hadn't come back. And it might have been just as well. She'd been grounded for a full half year after losing CeeCee's shoes, so she wouldn't have been able to see him, anyway.

It wasn't until the obligatory trip home from college that next summer that she'd found out he'd ended up marrying the blonde shoe thief. It seems the girl had fallen in her getaway attempt, breaking a well-deserved ankle, and Roy had fallen, too—but in love. How things might have turned out if she'd stopped him from chasing the girl, she'll never know.

It could very well be they'd have married, and have several—

"Keds. Here's your Keds, lady." The salesman's voice pierces her reverie.

Lucinda starts, disoriented as she regards the young man who *had* returned.

"Your Keds?" He thrusts the box towards her, and when she fails to reach for it, he says, "Didn't you want these in a size nine?"

"Oh, yes." Reality crashes back, settling in with all its bright weight around her, and standing, she walks toward the service counter.

"Those will be fine."

"Aren't you going to try them on?" The boy is already ringing her purchase. "'Cause our return policy is you wear 'em, you own 'em."

"I'd like those crystal heels that blonde girl has on, as well. In every size."

"The mannequin?"

"No, that girl." Lucinda points at the vamping teen wearing *her* shoe. "The one dressed in the red mini-skirt."

"Oh. The one in the stripper heel, and the boot." The boy taps a code into his digital register, the sneer curling right off his face. "Did you say you want them in every size? We got like forty pairs in back. Like…at least. "

"And it still isn't enough." Lucinda breathes, her eyes blurring with an eon of unshed tears as she signs the credit slip. She's so upset she signs Cindy instead of the revised Lucy she's gone by for so many years.

"I'm going to pull my car around front to load them. I'll be right back."

"Hold your horses, lady." The boy says to her retreating back, but Lucinda doesn't turn.

"Cindy Eller." He reads from the charge slip over the PA. "Ms. Cindy Eller. Please return to the counter. Your charge has been denied."

THE HUNTER

William Gilmer

"Jameson on the rocks."

The Hunter watched the young man check the tape in his recorder three times before anxiously setting it on the bar.

"I bet you're getting tired of all these questions by now, huh?" His voice squeaked with nerves and inexperience.

"I never get tired of free drinks, kid. I've told this story to *20/20*, *60 Minutes*, and PETA. As long as people keep picking up the tab, I'm gonna keep telling it."

The Hunter took a generous slug from his glass.

"Well that's not exactly what I'm writing about. Like you said, everybody knows what happened. I'd like to know more about the aftermath, the fallout you've experienced from all of those stories. How has this changed you, as a person?"

A smile walked across The Hunter's face as he tipped his now empty glass toward the waitress.

"I'll tell you what, kid, killing that animal destroyed me. I can't show my face outside this dive without some baby crying. I've broken the hearts of an entire generation of children, and I'm pretty sure they're never going to let me forget it."

The waitress set his new drink on the table, careful not to sully the recording with the loud *clink* of a highball.

"You're still hunting though, right? It is your profession after all."

"*Ha.* I'd be blinded by cameras the minute I slung that rifle over my shoulder. Imagine trying to track an animal with an army of paparazzi behind you. A deaf mule would hear me from a mile away. No, my hunting days are over."

With a quick swig, half of his glass vanished beneath an unkempt mustache.

"What about the documentary? It's a huge hit. Have you seen it?"

"No need, chief. I was there. You seem like a good kid. All you journalists want is some sensational headline. I'm going to give your career a quick jumpstart. I would go hunting again, but only in the hope of seeing that bastard Walt, I'd make damn sure he's dead."

He guzzled down the rest of his drink.

"Make that your article's headline, and you'll sell a couple thousand copies of whatever the hell magazine you write for. Guaranteed."

The reporter, disgusted, hoped to write a story about repentance and moral transformation. The thousands of tears that had fallen during the documentary's infamous death scene were on his hands, and he didn't even care enough to wash them off. Surely, the man sitting before him couldn't be as evil as every other paper reported.

"Don't you even regret it? Given everything that has happened, you wouldn't still take that shot, would you? I have to assume you'd do things differently."

The Hunter's eyes narrowed the same way they did while looking at the crowds, crybabies as he called them, picketing around his house

"You're damn right. I'd still shoot that deer, but I'd make sure to kill that miserable little fawn, too. Let's see Disney make a documentary about a skunk and a rabbit dragging a dead piece of venison through the forest."

Shaking his head, the reporter stopped the recorder, threw a handful of bills on the table, and walked out. He had his answers. A true villain never understands their own.

THE OMEGA WOLFMAN
Jack Haigh

Jim stood on his hind legs and licked at Patrick's mouth, knocking the strawberry flavoured e-cigarette from his lips.

"For fuck's sake, you got mud all over m' Hunters." Patrick pushed Jim to the ground. He spat on a Kleenex and rubbed it over his black wellies. When he was done, he ran his hands across his ruffled quiff, making sure it was still glued in place.

They stood in a small clearing deep inside Fenrir Woods, a rutted dirt track wound its way through the forest. On the track sat a white Golf GTI, its headlights on full-beam, casting crooked shadows across the snow-covered floor. Muffled music seeped through the door, its relentless beat the only thing discernible.

At the edge of the clearing, a small man with the posture and stomach of a pregnant orangutan leant against an old oak tree. A horseshoe of closely cropped hair ran 'round the back of his head. He wore a faded green overcoat and smoked a yellow roll-up that had burnt so far down that he was inhaling skin. His name was Brusco.

"Bloody hell, mate," he said, laughing up a plume of smoke, "you goin' to sniff his bum hole next?"

Jim growled.

"Brusco, shut up." Patrick grabbed Jim by the back of his neck and pulled him upright, "and Jim, stand up."

When Patrick let go, Jim tottered on the spot for a couple of seconds, and then his whole body shook. In one swift moment, his fur was sucked back into his skin, leaving an unkempt tuft on his head, which faded from brown to ginger. With several loud cracks, his muzzle crumpled in on itself and his joints realigned. Useless skin flaked from his ears. His belly swelled. And finally, with a loud cry, his tail retreated, leaving him crouched and naked in the middle of the cold wood.

His mind faded from the streamlined awareness of the wolf to the jumbled fog of contradictions that is human consciousness. His hand shot out to cover his crotch. A trembling smile flickered across his lips before his body folded in half as he brought up the semi-digested remains of a rabbit.

Brusco coughed up a cloud of laughter, whilst Patrick looked away, his lips curled.

"Here." Patrick shook his head and threw a small blue sports bag at Jim. "I've got some mints in the car. Don't want dog breath, not tonight."

Jim nodded, pulling on a pair of white boxers he'd found in the bag, the kind that seemed to be designed to highlight lack of bulge. His slight paunch hung over the big Hugo Boss label. Next came some skinny black jeans and a carefully folded blue shirt that pulled against his stomach.

"Looking good." Patrick threw him the mints. He rubbed his chin. "Something's missing."

Brusco ran his palm over his smooth head. "Do something with his hair Pat. It looks like he nicked it from a LEGO box."

"Yeah, what product do you use?"

"Err…nowt."

Patrick shook his head and pulled a little blue tub of wax out of his bag; the lid emblazoned with phrases like "X-treme" and "to the max." He scraped out a sticky globule with his forefinger and rubbed the lotion out between his hands. It smelt sweet, with the faint tinge of hospitals underneath. After five minutes, Jim had the kind of severe quiff that looks good on pop stars and stupid on anybody else.

"Now, let's have a look at you," said Patrick.

Jim stuck out his arms and gave a hesitant twirl. In the trees above, a blackbird let out a derisive caw.

"Your shirt needs tucking in at back, and you could have had a bloody shave, but overall, I'd say you're fuckable."

"Ta, mate."

"You excited?"

"...Yep," said Jim staring at his shoes.

"Don't say it like that. Lasses like a guy to be confident, they like a guy to be himself. That means you've gotta pretend to like yourself. Okay?"

"Okay."

"Pat's right." Brusco draped his arm across Jim's shoulder. "The ladies don't want a moper, they want a man wi' charm, wi' wit. What you got to do is walk up to her 'n' go, 'a'right luv, they call me Spackle, now how about I fill your crack.'"

Silence.

Patrick grabbed Jim's shoulders.

"Promise me you won't say that."

Jim shook his head when out in the woods, deeper down the path, came the sound they had all been waiting for, the wildly oscillating screech of someone trying to sing whilst wearing headphones.

Patrick clapped his hands together. "Right she's here. You ready, Jim?"

Jim caught himself mumbling his reply and quickly covered it with what he hoped was a forceful and manly grunt of affirmation.

"Good lad. Just remember, women want real men, none of this metro-sexual bollocks."

Jim took in a deep breath. "Okay. I'm a goin' hunting."

He marched off through the woods like a like toddler stumbling across his parents' bed.

Brambles nicked at his jeans as he forged his way through the undergrowth. He stepped out of a thick hawthorn bush and onto a path. In front of him, in her red hoodie, her back turned, the girl.

Jim threw back his shoulders and stuck out his chin. "A'right, luv."

The only reply was the tinny rattle of her headphones.

His shoulders slumped.

"H-hello." He winced at the squeak in his voice. Hand trembling, he reached out and touched her shoulder.

The girl let out a cry and span round, her fists raised.

"Come any closer," she said breathing heavily, "and I'll kick you so hard, your Adam's apple will have two new friends." She nodded down to a pair of Dr. Martens.

Jim stopped on the spot and held up his hands.

"I'm sorry—"

"Shut up. Who the fuck are you, and why are you following me?"

Jim's fear-fuddled mind went blank. He grasped at straws, and pulled out the burning one attached to a red stick labelled TNT.

"Err…I'm Spackle," he said, "Can I…fill your crack?"

A howl, similar to the cry of a wolf, rang out through the trees. Jim crumpled. A dull ache crawled its way up from between his legs to his stomach. Through bleary eyes, he watched as a pair of Dr. Martens turned and marched away, disappearing into the snow-covered forest.

CHARLIE'S CHOCOLATE FACTORY
Nathan Smith

Charlie faced his biggest challenge running the chocolate factory:
the oompa loompas claimed their conditions weren't satisfactory.
They wanted a wage increase. Nay! They wanted a wage
and wanted furnishings for each oompa loompa's cage.
They wanted paid breaks and maximum twelve hour days.
They wanted health insurance and retirement when the last green hair greys.

God, it was awful and, to make matters worse,
they'd taken the steps to unionise first.
They had to be stopped before they discovered H&S laws,
if he had to pay damages, Charlie would go back to being poor.
They'd already discovered protest and adopted it with haste.
Last week, one threw themselves in front of a horse at the fudgesicle race.
They'd walked peacefully to the salted caramel sea.
They'd extracted some salt and celebrated with glee.
One had even refused to give up its seat on the wonkatania.
He'd debated firing them all and hiring from Romania
but EU laws had set in, they were strict and unforgiving.
How could a chocolatier make a reasonable living?
A great idea struck him, a golden ticket of thought,
If they had forgotten their place then they'd have to be taught.
No more complaints about injustice and hurt loompa feelings,
the factory didn't just have glass elevators, it also had glass ceilings.
He took the ring leaders and locked them in chocolate fudge cells
then banned unionization and free assembly as well.
He reduced their rations so they'd have less to eat,
it felt like victory for him, and victory was sweet.

THE EMPEROR'S PIG PRINCESS

Candace Gleave

"Tell me, what do you see?" The emperor asked in a serious tone.

Jonathan focused at the empty plate, perplexed.

"I see nothing," Jonathan said at last.

"You mean to tell me" the emperor raised his voice and pounded his fist on the table. "That you don't see the finest craftsmanship in the entire kingdom?"

Jonathan shook his head.

"Everyone who is anyone can observe this, and they all love it. They told me so."

"I'm sorry, your grace, I see nothing." Jonathan looked closer. Had he missed something?

"Well, skin the ass off my fatted-calf." The emperor's lips curled into a perfect white smile. "You're hired."

Jonathan blinked, confused.

"But I couldn't see it?"

"Precisely." The emperor picked up the empty plate and tossed it at the wall, breaking it. "Because nothing is there... I had the great misfortune of being swindled some years back." He rubbed his head as if the mere thought caused him a sudden headache.

"What happened?"

"Oh, it doesn't matter, a long, cold, walk with shriveled bits does the body good and sharpens the mind. I told myself that day that I will never be swindled again. If I can't see it, then it doesn't exist . . . and I need an adviser whom I can trust will tell me black from white and pink from blue."

"Hence the test." Jonathan grinned, pleased with himself.

"Yes, but you can wipe that shit eating grin off your face." The emperor elevated his voice, hoping to scare his newly appointed assistant.

Jonathan's faced dropped.

"As you are my advisor, and errand boy, you are already behind in your duties." The emperor stood, struck a pose, and shouted orders. "I need a new dress coat by this afternoon. Thursday, by royal decree is now Nude Thursday and sometimes if the town's people are particularly merry, it spills into Nude Friday, but that really only applies to the hired help."

Jonathan had pulled out his tablet and frantically took notes.

"Your most important task, my boy," the emperor, bent low to Jonathan's face. "Is to find me a wife."

"You've been making the emperor's clothes for quite some time," Jonathan picked up a bolt of Chinese silk. "What kind of woman would interest the emperor?"

The tailor peered over his round spectacles. "She doesn't exist."

"What, is he really so picky?"

"The emperor breaks out in a fever and chills at the mere thought of having to wear the same outfit twice, what makes you think that he could be happy with just one woman?"

This impossible task frustrated Jonathan. He bit his bottom lip, anxiety growing.

"She would have to have an impeccable fashion sense," the tailor said.

"That's a start. Anything else?"

"Skinny waistline, long hair, the emperor has a hair fetish, he would grow his own hair out if he could get away with it."

"Not allowed?"

"No, he doesn't have the cheekbones."

"Ah," Jonathan said. "So back to the hair, that's good; does he like blondes or brunettes?"

"Depends on which one of them has back hair."

Jonathan looked up from his tablet. "He's into back hair?"

"He goes crazy for back hair." The tailor suppressed his highbrow snort.

"Okay. That really narrows things a bit. Thanks."

"Happy to help."

"Do you really make him a new dress coat every day?" Jonathan's gaze traced the yards and yards of baroque fabric filling the tailor's room.

"It used to be for every meal." The tailor trimmed a black thread from the burgundy dress coat. "But since the whole ordeal with the swindlers he's made some sacrifices."

"I see." Jonathan examined a golden button.

"Put that back."

"Yes, sir." Jonathan fumbled the button back.

The tailor held up the coat to Jonathan and eyeballed its length. "Yes, a woman with impeccable fashion sense and a good deal of body hair."

"He wants a what?" The plump chef pulled a steamy tray of bacon-wrapped shrimp from the oven.

Jonathan took a deep inhale of the savory aroma, "He wants me to find him a wife. What kind of woman would catch his attention?"

"You see this?" the chef asked.

Jonathan nodded.

"It isn't the shrimp that makes the hors d'oeuvres so delicious, it is the bacon." The chef waved the steam from the pan and took in a deep breath. "I would marry the emperor right now if this was being served at the wedding."

Jonathan shifted his weight, unsure of the chef and his humor.

"A plump woman makes for a good cook," the chef said.

"But you make all his meals?"

"You can never go wrong with a woman who knows how to cook." The chef tapped his nose with his finger. "Bacon-wrapped shrimp."

Jonathan scratched his head, finding this information next to worthless. "So, look for a plump woman?"

"The plumpest."

Jonathan sat in a worrisome state and browsed the emperor's Facebook page. Three hundred pending friend requests sat untouched. Most of the friend requests were from women with names like Candy and Treasure. The pictures they posted on his wall were even worse. Captions and special requests to walk naked were common. Jonathan sent a friend request to a couple of them.

"Working hard to find my wife?" The emperor entered his quarters, wearing his favorite pants and a happy mood.

Jonathan straightened and minimized his browser. "Sir, I am finding it rather difficult to narrow down a suitable maiden for you. Is back hair really that important to you?"

The emperor in the middle of drinking water, choked, and coughed. "Pardon?"

"Back hair, and plumpness, for I know how fond you are of food . . ."

"Back hair and plumpness?" The emperor gave Jonathan a wild look. "What kind of wife are you finding for me?"

"Just teasing you, my lord," Jonathan forced a laugh, hoping that the emperor would forget this mix-up quickly. "Seeing if you are paying attention."

The emperor glared and walked straightway to his full sized mirrors.

"Take note that I am not a man to jest with." The emperor ran his right hand over his black velvet dress coat. "I've been swindled once and won't be swindled again."

Jonathan's dry throat made a loud swallow.

"I do love these pants. Tell me of your progress."

Jonathan turned off his tablet and scrambled for the mail.

"I've sent many inquiries and have received a number of letters." He said, slightly flustered, the truth is the emperor intimidated Jonathan. Since taking the job, Jonathan had developed a chronic case of IBS. Bananas seemed to help.

"And?"

"Um, the most promising is Lady Trinity of Rosedale." Jonathan handed him the letter. "There is no picture, but her father writes of her beauty."

The emperor read the letter and handed it back to Jonathan.

"I would like a meeting." The emperor slapped Jonathan's back, happy that his assistant had done something right.

"Yes, your grace," Jonathan flinched. "And what of the other inquires?"

"Invite them over for tea but arrange an intimate meeting with Lady Trinity."

"I'll get right on it," Jonathan said with a sigh of relief. The assistant was so grateful he responded to Lady Trinity's online dating questionnaire.

"Now, I want you to be absolutely honest with me." The emperor faced Jonathan and looked him with his gaze.

Oh, dear, heavens, what does he want … Jonathan gulped.

"Are these not the finest pants in the entire kingdom?" The emperor's smile doubled as his eyes traced over the exquisite golden sticking. "Just look at my backside."

Jonathan exhaled, troubled. The pants were perfect. If he could only custom tailor a perfect wife for this eccentrically picky emperor. She must have a good backside, he concluded.

The emperor sat amidst three princesses. With a bored look on his polished face, he stared absent mindedly at a rouge hair that needed to be plucked from Sleeping Beauty's eyebrow. Deflated, he poured himself another cup of tea and long for a shot of whiskey.

"I wake up every morning at five – o'clock, and the animals and I start cleaning." Snow White said in a nightingale voice.

All that disgusting, diseased, fur and feet running all over the kingdom, the emperor sipped his tea loudly, demonstrating his distain.

"I would have them clean the bathrooms. I hate cleaning bathrooms." Sleeping Beauty said.

"I've never cleaned anything in my whole life," Jasmine's Persian nose cringed. "It must be dreadful."

"They clean anything I tell them too," Snow White's giggle sounded like a bird, splashing in a bath of water. "Once, I had them scrub Grumpy's personal stains out of his undergarments; the squirrels wouldn't look at me for the rest of the day."

All three princesses broke into airy snickers.

"He really is a horrible dwarf," Snow White said. "Twice now; Doc has tried to kill him."

"I know a guy that is really good with knifes," Jasmine said. "He does all the palace's dirty work, and his prices are reasonable."

"Does he do dragons?" Sleeping Beauty asked.

"Anything," Jasmine said.

"Jonathan," the emperor clenched the arm of his chair. "Jonathan, now, come, now."

Snow White, Sleeping Beauty, and Jasmine silenced their small talk as Jonathan hurriedly approached the handsome emperor.

"Yes, your grace?"

"I have nothing in common with these girls." The emperor couldn't remember the last time he had been subject to such tedious blather. "There is one here that is deathly afraid of spinning wheels? Spinning wheels, for heaven's sake. I will not be forced to have a drab kingdom based on preposterous superstitions."

"It's more of a curse," Jonathan corrected.

"Curse, what? Have you heard a single word I've said?" The emperor felt a sigh coming on and suppressed it. "I can't even begin to rip apart her wardrobe selection. Talk about Wednesday pearls on a Saturday night."

Redness settled on Sleeping Beauty's face, for she overheard the emperor talking about her.

"We were just discussing your outfit," the emperor said.

Sleeping Beauty looked down at her dress and smiled sweetly. "Do you like it? It was made by fairies."

A snarky bully grinned within the emperor's face. "Let me guess, their favorite colors are red, blue, and green?"

"How did you ever know?" Her face lit up.

"Because your dress looks like it mopped-up a bucket of paint vomit," The emperor looked once more at her outfit and confirmed. "Hodge-podge, my dear."

Sleeping Beauty gasped behind her hand. Jasmine and Snow White were equally offened, and Jonathan held back his tactless laughter. Truth be known, Sleeping Beauty's dress really did mirror the emperor's harsh criticism. Perfectly.

"Well at least I can tell what clothes are," Sleeping Beauty poked jest at the emperor's naked lap.

"Please, you wouldn't be sitting here sipping tea if you didn't enjoy the view, honey," the emperor said.

"Well, you aren't charming in the least," Snow White said.

"I'm an emperor honey, not a prince. Jonathan, see to the princesses' needs, I'm afraid my tea has gotten cold."

The emperor stood from the round table and gave a haughty bow. Jasmine returned the gesture and gave him a salty wink.

"If it wasn't for the size of your pussy, my dear, we might have had something." The emperor walked away. Jasmine blushed; everyone pretended not to notice.

Jonathan coughed, hiding his laughter. He made a mental note to remember this forever.

"I can't stand cats." The emperor's voice, broke over the awkward silence.

###

"Jonathan, when I first asked you to find me a wife, I really meant for you to find me a wife." The emperor had been verbally abusing poor Jonathan all afternoon. He fully intended to stop after ten minutes, but the more he lectured the more he enjoyed his rants, and made it a game.

Jonathan was about to have a nervous breakdown.

"I'm so sorry, my lord, I shall do better." Jonathan repeated his earlier apology.

"See that you do." The emperor sat down at his desk, perfectly content.

"Lady Trinity is due to arrive in the kingdom in a few days," Jonathan hoped to cheer up the emperor.

"Is she the one who lives with rodents?"

"No, that's Cinderella."

The emperor shuddered. "When I first heard about that, I gaged and farted at the same time.

"I do find it rather alarming that most of these princesses have father issues and resort to animals for friendship." The emperor had heard of such self-esteem issue. "Best not to take them into my trophy room."

"Indeed," Jonathan said.

"Take note." The emperor stood abruptly from his desk. His vest, trouser combo commanded the very air in the room.

Jonathan pulled out his tablet and waited for instruction.

"Let it be known, I want a woman who is strong, fashionable, beautiful. No wait, scratch that. I want a woman so hot that I covet her and indeed resent her because of her stunning beauty."

Jonathan looked up from his tablet. . . and waited for more vain dialogue.

"Furthermore, I would like a woman who smells of organic fruits and flowers, one who is smart but will still play dumb as to not be as smart as me. I want a woman who will walk around with me on Nude Thursdays and not be ashamed when I am mistaken that it is only Tuesday. Yes, it has happened."

"Do you care about wealth and family relations?" Jonathan asked, getting back to topic.

"I have enough money to buy another kingdom." The emperor's deep and amused laughter wisped through the room. "Though, more money never hurts."

"Okay," Jonathan said. "Who doesn't want a rich, beautiful, woman?"

"The main thing I want is, Jonathan, I want a woman like . . . like me." The emperor sighed as he held up a vanity mirror.

Jonathan erased his notes.

"Sir, may I introduce Lady Trinity of Rosedale and her father, Sir Gawain of Rosedale," the footman announced as the large double oak doors opened to the sitting room.

Jonathan and the emperor stood straight and dignified as they had waited several weeks for this meeting. The nobleman, Sir Gawain was the first through the double doors. The aged man has white long hair that ran neatly down his shoulders. A red scarlet robe hung smartly on his body.

The emperor gasped. Such custom clothes rivaled the tailor's in the emperor's palace, if not surpassed it.

Impossible.

Eyeing the beautiful clothes of Sir Gawain, the emperor straightened his posture and puffed out his chest.

Following Sir Gawain, a, smaller-than-the-average pig, dainty, in fact, walked through the double doors. Her hooves made tiny clicking noises.

"For Pete's sake," the emperor griped, the tiny sound offended his ears. "Clicking."

"I have no idea what's going on," Jonathan blinked, confused at the sight of the pig.

"Let this be a very valuable lesson, Jonathan that you will no doubt reflect on when you are mucking out my stables. Always know what's going on."

"Yes, a lesson I shall never forget," Jonathan agreed.

"An honor to meet you, my lord," Sir Gawain said, with a deep bow as he and the pig finally came to a stop.

The emperor broke into a hysterical laugh. Such a laugh, mockery, and utter silliness, made the room feel stressed and unsure.

"What's this? Sir Gawain, what have you brought me?"

"This, your grace, is my daughter, Lady Trinity."

"I hate to see what the mother looks like," the emperor whispered to Jonathan.

"It is said that she is the most beautiful woman of her generation. All who look upon her, know true beauty and are worthy of her splendor."

The emperor furrowed his brows, like his father always did when cross. "Sir, you've brought me a pig."

"I have brought you nothing of the sort!" Sir Gawain pointed to the pig. "Can't you see her matchless beauty?"

"I see a pig." The emperor pointed at the cloven-hoofed animal and motioned to Jonathan. "My assistant sees a pig as well, correct?"

"It's just a pig, your grace."

Sir Gawain huffed air out of his mouth, in an offended manner. The pig looked up to Sir Gawain.

"They are not worthy of your beauty," he reached his hand out and patted the pig on the head.

The pig snorted.

"Why did this have to take place on a Monday? I have nothing to look forward. Shame on you, Jonathan." The emperor pinched the bridge of his nose.

"My apologies, I can get the guards to escort this man and … pig out."

"Yes. I've had enough of my time wasted." The emperor gestured them away. "Many best wishes to your tailors, Sir Gawain. As to you and your pig my condolences."

Two royal guards passed through the double doors and gazed at the pig. Awe struck, they smiled and then coolly approached the emperor.

"Yes, your grace?" The head guard said.

"Please escort this man and his filthy pig out of my presence," the emperor said.

"Pardon, your grace, but I see no pig. A beautiful maiden stands before you." The guard's gaze traced over the pig like he might want to roll in a sty with her.

The emperor looked at the pig again, and held up his hand. "Did anyone come to work today?"

"At last, someone who is worthy of your beauty," Sir Gawain cheerfully patted the pig.

"This is utter nonsense. Jonathan, call all the guards and remove this man." The emperor took a seat on one of the sofas.

"It will be done." Jonathan exited through the double doors.

"What's her name?" One of the guards asked.

"This is my daughter, Lady Trinity of Rosedale," Sir Gawain said.

"It is a pleasure to meet you." The guard bowed low to the ground. His neatly trimmed beard added grace to his gesture.

The pig squealed happily.

"This is absolutely ridiculous." The emperor huffed, what was taking Jonathan so long.

The double doors opened, and Jonathan led a charge of ten royal guards into the sitting room.

"Remove Sir Gawain and the pig at once. They are swindlers, and they aren't welcome." Jonathan pointed with an angry flair that embodied his emperor's flourish.

The royal guards all scrunched their faces in many different forms of confusion.

"How could such a beautiful maiden be a swindler? She is the most beautiful creature I have ever beheld."

"Enough of this." The emperor pointed to Sir Gawain and the pig. "Get them out of my sight. I shall not be swindled again."

An awkward silence came upon everyone as the emperor marched out of the room. Quick by his side, Jonathan conversed with the emperor in a rushed tongue that indeed, a pig had stood before them.

The next few days, a constant buzz circled the royal palace, excited voices were heard conversing about the beautiful maiden.

"I can't make sense of it." The emperor huffed and poured himself a glass of whiskey. They had been sitting in the emperor's study all afternoon. The wooden desk and brown leather couches were the only things that didn't smell of alcohol.

"I assure you. It was a pig and only a pig," Jonathan said.

"If I were to tell you the number of men who have come and inquired about her. It is staggering."

"Has the whole palace gone mad?" Jonathan ran his hand through his hair.

"If that's the case, I have a lot of firing to do." the emperor finished his glass and poured another.

The two of them sat for a long time in silence. Jonathan troubled in thought about the absurdity of the situation and the emperor second-guessed his ability to rule and behold true beauty.

"I see no other solution." The emperor stood from his desk.

Jonathan jumped in his chair and snapped away from his many, many thoughts.

"Pardon?" Jonathan said.

"By royal default, I would like you to set up another meeting with the pig and only the pig."

"What? Are you sure? Sir, I do believe they are trying to swindle you."

"I know, and I swore that I would never be swindled again, but I have to make certain."

"I will set something up," Jonathan said, disapprovingly, hating to see the emperor made into another royal blunder.

"Good. Now go fetch me a new dress coat, I must look my best." The emperor perked right up with that thought.

The emperor and pig stared at one another in silence for quite some time. Several times, the emperor tried to make small talk, but the pig only squeaked and snorted in reply. His new dress coat was the only cheery thing in the room.

"Are you shitting me?" The emperor said after a long time, sitting in silence.

The pig blinked. It's short, brown, eyelashes held no beauty.

"I know what beauty is. I have an entire palace full of beautiful, stunning, gorgeous things, and you are a pig."

Snort, snort.

"That's all you have to say?"

Snort.

"What makes you so special anyhow?" The emperor stood from his chair and moved very close to the pig, staring at it. "You aren't even very big. You have an unsightly black blob on your hind quarters and you have a slight smell of pee about you. There is nothing beautiful, charming, or fair about you."

Squeal.

"I meant every word."

The emperor sat back in his chair and studied the gold buttons on his dress coat. Rustling and tiny clicks followed as the pig approached the emperor and rested its head on his lap.

"Don't look at me like that." The emperor tried to push her head off his trousers. "These are my favorite pants."

The pig looked up at him with its round eyes.

"Okay, I didn't mean every word." The emperor patted the pig's forehead. "You do smell of pee though."

With the warm touch of the emperor, the pig squealed happily and jumped in his lap.

"By all means, rub your stank on me."

Jonathan entered the sitting room with a puff of stale hallway air.

"Have you made a decision, your grace?"

"Yes, what was the said dowry of this pig?"

Jonathan's jaw dropped, "It is a healthy sum, a plot of land in Rosedale, and their personal tailor will be yours, your grace."

"The very tailor that made Sir Gawain's magnificent scarlet robe?" The emperor's heart leapt.

"Yes, the very one."

"Splendid, arrange the wedding." Delighted the emperor's thoughts bounced frantically around clothes and the many gaudy dress coats that he would parade in.

"Is this another one of your tests?"

"No, no, I am in the right mind." The emperor laughed at the situation. He held up the pig for Jonathan to see. "This little piggy will make my fashion dynasty truly complete. From where I see it, I am the one who gains everything and loses nothing."

"Except for being legally married to a pig."

"Oh nonsense, I'll have the divorce party after the wedding party. Have my worthless, overpaid, lawyer draft the legalities. I get the tailor, in the divorce. Two parties…that means I'll get to wear two suits."

"If this is what you want, I'll make the arrangements."

"See that you do, but in the meantime." The emperor handed Jonathan the pig. "Have one of the maids give this swine a bath. I am starting to lose my sense of smell."

Dressed in an exquisite suit, standing at the altar, with his bride to be, the emperor sheepishly grinned at his pig princess. A tiny pink rose crown rested between her ears. Soon to be married in front of the royal court, his thoughts circled around ordering his new tailor around and see all the many fantastic clothes that would adorn him. He would need a bigger closet; this thought excited the emperor greatly. Standing by his side, Jonathan asked the emperor repeatedly if he was sure and at a moment's notice he would cancel the wedding. With calm reassurance the Emperor signaled the clergy man to begin the marriage ceremony.

"Please take hands," the clergy man said.

The emperor held back a snarky expression as he reached forward and grasped the tiny hoof.

"Marriage is the unity of two beautiful souls."

Jonathan coughed behind him.

"This unity is everlasting and binding. Do you Emperor Tristian take Lady Trinity of Rosedale to be your wife to love and cherish all your days?"

"Yes."

"Lady Trinity of Rosedale, do you take Emperor Tristian to be your husband, protector and provider?"

Squeal.

"Then, by the power of the royal court and his holy majesty, I proclaim you husband and wife. You may now kiss the bride."

Jonathan cringed. "I can't watch this."

The emperor bent low to the ground, very low, and with eyes tightly closed, he thought once more of the tailor, breathed out and kissed his pig princess. A gentle hand grabbed the emperor's. Eyes opened, the most beautiful maiden transfixed him.

"My lady," the emperor said, happily, pulling her close and kissing her again.

Jonathan, rubbed his eyes and inspected Lady Trinity.

"Tell me, dear woman, were you a pig or were tricks placed on mine and the emperor's eyes?"

"A lady never reveals her secrets," Lady Trinity said with a cheeky smile.

"Sure she does," Jonathan quipped.

"Oh, sour puss, we will find you a beautiful swine to marry." The emperor laughed and put his arm around Jonathan. "Rosedale is massive."

With one more kiss, lasting and sweet, the emperor and Lady Trinity waved happily to the royal court who clapped and cheered nonstop.

"Cancel the divorce party," the emperor said through his big toothy grin. "But have them send up the second suit, you'll love it."

Jonathan pulled out his tablet. "Happily ever after, sir."

LOSING THEIR CHARM

M. R. DeLuca

Prince Dapper slipped into the crowded room without a moment to spare. He weaved clumsily around gossiping peasants milling in the aisle, muttering apologies along the way. A fellow prince once told him to never say sorry to inferiors, as a rule, for they not only smelled funny but were prone to ego trips and would savor the role reversal. Dapper wanted further explanation but dared not ask; he simply wanted to learn how to be a good ruler, which he was confident entailed being receptive to his elders' advice. So he absorbed the tidbit into his mental file on proper royal behavior.

He took his seat at one end of the long bench, where the neophytes were relegated. It was a position better suited for viewing than participating. In the middle chair sat a tall, handsome man, the most suave of the otherwise equally suave rulers. He called the meetinghouse to order.

"Greetings and salutations, my esteemed colleagues and constituents. The ladies of the collections of kingdoms composing Happily Ever After have requested this gathering to discuss an urgent matter. Or rather, should I say, a matter they claim is urgent. Gentlemen of the Fairy Tale Council, we are to determine if such claims are legitimate. Gentlewomen, please proceed."

A flaxen-haired woman in the front row of the packed indoor agora stood and curtsied, stumbling before regaining her composure.

"Ma'am, are you okay?" Prince Genteel, another tenderfoot at the other end of the table, leaned forward, ready to rush to her aid.

"Yes, sir. I've simply misplaced my heel."

"Again," came a murmur from the bench.

The blonde bristled. "I ask that my husband keep our personal matters private, or else he be relegated to the couch for a fortnight."

Though Prince Dapper was still in the honeymoon stage with his own lady fair, he sympathized as he saw the older prince slink ashamedly into his chair. In six months' time, he might be sleeping with the dragon in the dungeon, should his tongue betray him.

"Very well." She gestured to the twenty-odd women sitting attentively in the first two rows. "What we have come to accomplish tonight is gaining the right to protect ourselves."

She curtsied again, stiffly, and took her seat.

A king quickly counted. "The twenty-five of you want protection? From what?"

The most learned of them all rose and curtsied, shyly tucking a chestnut tendril that escaped her matronly updo. "Sir, there are more than twenty-five of us, though our small presence here admittedly belies this truth. Some are locked in towers at the moment, or spinning gold, or avoiding the wrath of wicked step-mothers.

"And it is not from what, good sir, but whom. And the whom is you." She steeled her green eyes and sat with a defiantly unladylike plop as the crowd gasped and whispered amongst themselves.

Dapper studied his scarred hands. They had sharpened axes, wielded swords, carried the love of his life to safety.

He couldn't be dangerous. He slayed the beasts; he wasn't one himself.

He hoped.

A younger woman, presumably a girl not even out of the clutches of adolescence, seamlessly rose as her fellow citizen sat. She walked before the long table of distinguished delegates, removed her crimson hood, and curtsied.

A loaf of bread with fang marks in the crust fell out of her basket. She scooped it up and violently shoved it next to the assorted low-lactose cheeses. "This bread will be stale by the time I make it to Boca."

A smirking royal Dapper thought looked too old to be a prince and too young to be a king spoke gave his two cents on the outburst.

"Praytell, miss, how are any of us a threat to any of you? We are in the business of saving you ladies, not hurting you. Frankly, it's more probable than anything else that a little girl like yourself will bludgeon one of us to death with your picnic basket." The contagious guffaws started with the council and rippled until they affected the most insignificant peasants in the far-flung corners of the meetinghouse.

Prince Dapper did not find the remark funny, but he did smile at remembering a rumor that the small girl before him was an excellent marksman singlehandedly responsible for keeping the wolves away.

It wasn't until later that he realized his bemused expression contributed to the notion that the entire council was laughing at her.

The corners of his mouth turned down as the seated leader of their coalition removed her remaining glass slipper and cradled it in her hand before releasing it dramatically. The high-pitched crunch called Prince Dapper, and everyone else, to attention as the painfully beautiful and beautifully painful shoe shattered onto the floor. Nearly everyone's mouth was agape.

"The floor is yours."

The girl startledly nodded. "Thank you."

She faced the council.

"You are all a threat to us. Nay, a realized threat. For years we have lived in squalor, unloved, orphaned, and oppressed. We have switched physical locations but not occupations. We left our childhood homes as passive servants and entered the same roles in our castles, for those as lucky to not live in filthy chambers and among shadows. Our whole lives, we have had our voices taken away, figuratively and literally—" those surrounding the aquatically-inclined woman patted her shoulder consolingly "—and we will no longer stand for these injustices. As consequence, we respectfully demand the council recognize our right to unionize.

"We demand a union that would prevent the members of said council from sadistically and purposely torturing us physically, mentally, and emotionally for the sake of a good story; a venture, in essence, yielding yourselves considerable monetary gain and, not to mention, an exaggerated ego complex."

Prince Dapper's fellow leaders erupted, with a couple dozen men angrily talking over each other in futile attempts to be heard.

The man in the center, in the raised chair, banged his gavel before saying, "If one more husband interrupts his wife, or any other princess, he will be removed from the council permanently. We are here for a dialogue, not merely to hear our own voices."

He turned to the women, his compelling expression a curious blend of intrigue and amusement. "Do continue."

"Actually, I will turn to my colleague, whose expertise exceeds mine in the upcoming matter." She curtsied once again and sat, her cape fluttering around her short legs.

The most learned princess stood and, unlike earlier, now sported her reading glasses.

"Based on my extensive reading of contract law, I have created a legally binding document we request all of you to sign." She handed a copy to each board member. "We want the continual inflicted suffering—borderline beastly, I must say—to cease and desist, and a fifty-percent share of the proceeds corresponding to each princess' respective story of misery. We believe this is more than fair."

Prince Dapper reached for the quill and inkwell before him, but stopped when he noticed no other motioned for a writing instrument.

"Ma'am," said a king after skimming the paper, "you believe us signing this will render the women of Happily Ever After physically safe, ensure their financial autonomy, and grant them broader daily freedoms? Do you honestly believe collective bargaining can do all that?"

"Yes, I do."

The council leader sighed before interjecting himself.

"Ma'am, it is not all of you who should have grievances, but all of us," he said, sweeping his arms before the large, crowded town hall. "Since you were all struggling in the metropolitan areas of our dear kingdoms, those dreadful outskirts, you had practically begged and pleaded to enter our cities upon hills. You asked—no, demanded—that we place our lives in danger, in situations you wouldn't have been in if you all hadn't made deals with the devil on your own accords. And as gentlemen, we were bound by valiance to respond to your maidenly, and suspiciously incredibly helpless cries, by whisking you away to safety. In no case have you demonstrated independence or savvy. Though I believe some of you were genuinely naïve and helpless, I am genuinely convinced more than a few of you used physical attractiveness and knowledge of princely duties of protecting and serving to manipulate your way into the upper echelons.

"Now, you cannot deny you have been treated well for the whole time you've been here, with attending servants and grand palaces and doting though admittedly imperfect husbands. And those women on the outside, whom you wish to protect—if they were worthy of protection, as per the council's judgment, we would have seen to it they'd have received it. That long-haired woman in the tower on the west end? We know she locked herself—she even brought a year's supply of caramel-infused bonbons and back issues of *Princess Weekly*. We also have on good authority that she has a degree in castle mechanics from Folk Tale University, and likely designed her palace of imprisonment. She is no dummy. If she really wanted to escape, she would tie her braid to a notch on the window, rappel herself down, and cut her hair waist-length when she reaches the ground. She simply wants to be a princess, which means attracting a prince, and is doing so by any means necessary."

Prince Dapper knew his wife was accidentally kidnapped by an ogre while strolling through the scariest part of the woods. He repeated this to himself wordlessly, many times.

"This cycle of abuse continues after marriage, too—without naming names, numerous council members have reported their wives forcing them to wear aprons and clean out the cinders in the fireplace, inviting hordes of dwarves and woodland animals to the home at the most inconvenient times and kissing frogs to make them jealous." Prince Dapper knew the accusers in question, and knew these claims were just more than stories. He had once even witnessed Prince Vain's wife give him a distorted mirror and drive him to tears. "If anything, we lost power when you came into our lives, not gained."

Multiple princesses voiced protests, but he banged his gavel ominously once again. Even Prince Dapper was frightened this time.

"Allow me to finish and you will each have your turn." He smoothed his already-perfect hair.

"And you may well know, we protect you in here—the fates you were to have included suicide, murder, and starvation, to name a few. We saved you by deviating your destiny. And this is the price we pay for noble behavior? This cold piece of paper is our thanks? Well," he crumpled the paper in one fist and dropped it on the desk, "this is you're welcome."

The captain of the Princess Swim Team rose without curtsying. She brushed her once perpetually water-logged tresses from her face before launching into her invective. "How dare you. You know none of that is true. You keep us locked away in castles, expecting us to pine for you while you're off gallivanting, doing Neptune-knows-what with Neptune-knows-whom—may my father rest in peace—and keeping us caged like dumb little animals let out only for breeding and publicity purposes. But that pales in comparison to our childhoods under the thumbs of wicked people and no one to look out for us. So yes, maybe not all princesses were perfectly proactive all of the time, but given the circumstances, wouldn't your dreams be crushed? Be silenced?"

She shook from the memory. "You think we couldn't have saved ourselves—but we would have eventually without your help. And then you turn around and sell your personal stories, showcasing yourselves as charmingly brave princes. But you were all just in the right place at the right time. Equipped with a keen marketing spin, you've doing nothing but make yourselves even more rich and powerful and self-absorbed and cruel."

Prince Dapper bowed his head. His own story, a beautifully illustrated tome in an expertly bound hardcover for only $19.95 in local bookstores, fit her words exactly. On the cover he looked wonderfully heroic with his sword and tunic matching his eyes, and his princess had mussed hair and was in an ogre's headlock. And all the royalty checks were in his name, to boot.

"But I'm sick of it." He looked up and saw her cheeks match the enflamed fiery magenta of her hair. "Find someone else to push around. You don't want to sign that paper? Fine. I'm returning to the sea, where I belong."

She stormed out of the building. And one by one, the others followed, openly vowing that that their pasts showed more promise than their futures in Happily Ever After, and that they would return to their old lives with renewed confidence.

The laypeople of the land were now curious as to the council's next step. For that matter, so was Prince Dapper, who had never attended a meeting. Were all such gatherings so eventful?

"Did the princesses just go on strike?" one voice called excitedly from the back.

"Council is dismissed. Everything is fine, go about your day."

The people did as the head council member dictated, dragging their heels as they filed out of the building and into the night, eager to hear of any new, inventive royal rumors come tomorrow's sun rise.

When the place emptied out, Prince Dapper approached the handsome leader. "Sir, why did you let them go? Will they be safe?"

Another thought jarred him. "My wife is still in our castle—she caught multiple warts from the ogre, and is freezing them off as we speak—but what if she eventually joins the others? What will happen to our stories? How will we create heirs to our thrones? How can we be princes and kings without princesses and queens? We need them just as much as they need us."

"My dear lad," the man said as he patted the youngest prince's back, "do not worry your handsome little head. They have never had anything more than delusions of influence and power, and never will. It's just the law of the land. They will be back once they enter the outskirts. They will surely return, pleading for all their old comforts. And to think, the others wanted to handle this matter individually and independently. Never underestimate the power of public humiliation, my boy. It's powerful. We gave the people a show, and now we have them on our side."

"But what if they don't, sir? Return? They looked awfully prepared and angry. And what did you mean by 'law of the land?' What a peculiar expression."

"Come with me."

Prince Dapper followed the king of kings past the others and to a back room, hidden by a bookcase, a square windowless enclosure filled with the rest of the council members. They scribbled, some furiously and some leisurely, but all were poring over books and loose papers. None of the men were fazed by the reveal, and some even smiled.

"He thinks he's finally old enough to know the truth," one murmured.

"Son, do you see these men before you? They—we—are the law of the land. We write our pasts, our presents, and our fates. It is a great responsibility that none of us take lightly. We toil day in and day out concocting the perfect narratives—engaging adventures with valor and despair and triumph, leaving our audiences clamoring for more. We create history. Storytellers like Hans and Jacob and Wilhelm disseminate the finer points of our tales to the greater public—they are masters of their craft, after all—but the core ideas for their writing originate in this very room. It's incredible, the ingenuity these walls have seen. The plots, the conflicts, the trials and tribulations—trust me, no one escapes unscathed. But there is one rule we all agreed upon—all stories end with a Happily Ever After."

He smiled a smile that the neophyte found too natural to be innocent or sincere. Prince Dapper mustered all his strength not to flee.

The senior sat down in his cushioned chair, and pulled its twin beside him, gesturing with a gracious flourish for the junior prince to join the distinguished men of the age-old society.

The nervous young man scanned the elegant tapestries detailing the fairy tales they lived and were in the process of living. The regal chairs before him held eminent royals, princes and kings who ruled longer than he had been alive and had the worry lines to prove it. He had to choose between the open door leading away from these great rulers and the empty chair beckoning him.

He thought of the controlled chaos that unfolded earlier. He thought of the transgressions, the discord, and the manipulation. But he thought the hardest about the fact that he was, in the end, living a fairy tale.

He stepped toward the door and closed it.

Feeling the power surge through his veins, Prince Dapper solemnly took his seat among the giants upon whose shoulders he wished to stand.

ABOUT THE AUTHORS

Adomeit, Jaclyn
Jaclyn lives and writes in Calgary, Canada, where she daylights as an environmental engineer. In her spare time she dances to old records in the kitchen, befriends stray cats, and hops on airplanes with her husband, Rayne, to explore new cultures and new places. You can find out more about her and her work at www.jaclynadomeit.com.

Ashwood, Raven
Raven Ashwood found a passion for reading and writing as well as a love of the dark and creepy at a young age. This drove her to study English Creative Writing and Literature at a small private college in the Midwest. While studying, she found that fractured fairytales was her favorite realm to work in, although she does frequently branch out. Currently, she is a Project Coordinator at a publishing company.

Avery, Shaun
Shaun Avery is a crime and horror fiction fan who has been published in many magazines and anthologies, and also recently co-created a self-published horror comic, more details of which are available at www.comicsy.co.uk. Although a fan of fantasy quest novels as a child, as a jaded adult he has come to the conclusion that anyone who would blow out their friends and family to go on a quest for a person they have never met would probably be a bit of a tool in real life. Hence this story.

Bashe, Kayla
Kayla Bashe is a theater student from the East Coast. Her work has appeared in *Vitality Magazine* and *Solarpunk Press Issue 1*, as well as *The Future Fire, Liminality Magazine*, and the *Outliers of Speculative Fiction* anthology. She tweets about speculative fiction at @KaylaBashe.

Bergloff, Amanda
Amanda Bergloff is a science fiction/fantasy writer who has had stories published by Darkhouse Books (*Stories from the World of Tomorrow*) and World Weaver Press (*Frozen Fairy Tales.)* She is a lover of all things pop-culture and is the editor of the website, "House of Mystery: Comics and More."

Boekstein, Jaap
Jaap Boekestein (1968) is an award winning Dutch writer of science fiction, fantasy, horror, thrillers and whatever takes his fancy. Five novels and almost three hundred of his stories have been published. His has made his living as a bouncer, working for a detective agency and as editor. He currently works for the Dutch Ministry of Security and Justice. Contact him at jaapboekestein.com.

Bond, Charlotte
Charlotte lives in Yorkshire and writes about darkness, whether in the form of horror or dark fantasy. She is due to publish a dark fairy tale novel and a series of horror novelettes for young adults in 2016. She is also a reviewer on the Ginger Nuts of Horror website.

Boyd, Juliet
Juliet Boyd is a British author who writes primarily fantasy and science fiction. Details of her work can be found on her website at www.julietboyd.com.

Brockmeyer, Matthew
Matthew Brockmeyer explores the dark caves and caverns of the human mind using words as his flashlight. His work has appeared in *Cultured Vultures*, *Alephi*, *Timeless Tales Magazine*, *Dark Fire Fiction*, *Pulp Metal Magazine*, and the anthology *100 Voices*, among others. He resides in an off-grid cabin, deep in the hills of Humboldt County, California with his wife and two children. Find more of his work at www.matthewbrockmeyer.com.

Brown, R. Judas
R. Judas Brown has appeared in several anthologies, is working with The Ed Greenwood Group, and serves on the Board of Directors for the Quincy Writers Guild in Quincy, IL. You can follow him on twitter @RJudasBrown, at www.facebook.com/RJudasBrown, or visit his website at www.rjudasbrown.com.

Brown, Tiffany Michelle
Tiffany Michelle Brown is a whisky enthusiast, archer, Aikido practitioner, and writer who lives near the sunny beaches of San Diego, California. She's easily amused by puns, sexual innuendo, and anything otherworldly or magical. Tiffany has published short stories with Liars' League NYC, Popcorn Press, Line by Lion Publications, and Shooter Literary Magazine. To follow her adventures, subscribe to tiffanymichellebrown.wordpress.com.

Buoni, Anthony S.
Living and creating in New Orleans, Louisiana, Anthony S. Buoni haunts swamps and bayous along the Gulf of Mexico, writing, editing, producing, and lecturing about his craft. He's co-edited and co-produced two exciting anthologies: *Distorted* and *Underwater*. Currently writing a New Orleans monster novel, he's also putting the final edits on novels featuring ghosts, zombies, and a café between life and death filled with secrets and philosophy. His next books, a collection of dark short stories and a somber zombie tale, are due for publication sometime in 2017. When not writing, Anthony is a Bourbon Street bartender, underground musician, and DJ, drawing down the moon with new wave, trance, and melancholy tunes. Other interests include film, gardening, comic books, and playing music and video games with his son, Fallon. Visit his blog at nolashadowcat.com and explore working drafts of stories and novels as well as articles and essays about horror culture, music, writing, New Orleans, drinking, and travel.

Burnell, Josh

Josh is the writer of two films, *House By the Lake,* starring James Callis and Anne Dudek, and *Boone: The Bounty Hunter*, starring WWE superstar John Morrison. His passions include horror movies, musicals and Meat Loaf, the singer and the food. He lives in Los Angeles.

Canon, Somer

Somer Canon is a minivan revving suburban mother of two who avoids her neighbors for fear of being found out as a weirdo. When she's not peering out of her windows, she's consuming books, movies and video games that sate her need for blood, gore and things that disturb her mother.

Chelser, Chris

Preferring twisted stories to 'happily ever after' since childhood, Chris Chelser has been writing dark tales about ghosts, monsters, history and human nature for the past twenty years. She lives in the Netherlands, where she shares her life with her family, her book collection, and the demons under the bed. After several digital publications, *The Kalbrandt Institute Archives* is her first book to have been published in print.

Chock, Sati Benes

Sati Benes Chock taught English in Tokyo before getting her MA in Japanese Literature at the University of Hawaii. She currently lives with her family in Honolulu, where she works at an art museum. Her short fiction has been published in a number of online and print publications, including *Amsterdam Scriptum*, *Hiss Quarterly*, *Flash Me Magazine*, *Hawaii Pacific Review*, *Thereby Hangs a Tale*, and *Mouth Full of Bullets.*

Chorney, Saryn

Saryn Chorney is currently a senior editor at People.com. Previously, she was managing editor of MSN's Wonderwall and founding editor in chief of AOL's PawNation. Saryn has been a senior features editor at Us Weekly, dating and weddings columnist for the New York Post, a video correspondent at Conde Nast, and a contributing writer for Paper, iVillage, YourTango and more. Her essay "The Banana Peel" was featured at the L.A. Hustler store's In the Flesh erotica series. A graduate of the University of Pennsylvania, Saryn lives in Brooklyn and enjoys illustration, art house horror movies, playing with cats, and re-imagining myths and fairy tales.

Chu, Ryan

Ryan Chu hails from Southern California but now lives in Seattle. He's a recent UW graduate who likes to read, write and run.

Cooke, Edward
Edward Cooke is a freelance author and technical translator based in York, UK. He has written half-a-dozen stage musicals and one short film. His short stories have been published by Stairwell Books, Runewright, Timeless Tales, Horrified Press and others.

Costanzo, Alisha
Alisha Costanzo is from a Syracuse suburb. She earned her MFA in creative writing from the University of Central Oklahoma, where she currently teaches English. She's the author of *Blood Phoenix: Rebirth*, *Blood Phoenix: Claimed*, and *Loving Red*, and co-editor of *Distorted*, *Underwater*, and *After the Happily Ever After*. Her new novel, *Blood Phoenix Imprinted*, is undergoing serious edits for its 2017 release. In the meantime, she will continue to corrupt young minds, rant about the government, and daydream about her all around nasty creatures.

Csernica, Lillian
Ms. Csernica has published over thirty short stories in such markets as *Weird Tales*, *These Vampires Don't Sparkle*, and *Fantastic Stories*. She has also published a pirate romance novel, *Ship of Dreams, and* two nonfiction ebooks, *The Writer's Spellbook: Creating Magic Systems for Fantasy* and *The Fright Factory: Building Better Horror*. Born in San Diego, Ms. Csernica is a genuine California native. She currently resides in the Santa Cruz mountains with her her husband, two sons, and three cats. Visit her at lillian888.wordpress.com.

Davon, Claire
Claire Davon has written on and off for most of her life, starting with fan fiction when she was very young. She writes across a wide range of genres, and does not consider any of it off limits or out of reach. If a story calls to her, she will write it. She currently lives in Los Angeles and spends her free time writing novels and short stories, as well as doing animal rescue and enjoying the sunshine. Claire's website is www.clairedavon.com.

Dawson, Robert
Robert Dawson teaches mathematics at a Nova Scotian university. When not teaching, doing research, or writing, he enjoys cycling, fencing, and, yes, sailing. His stories have appeared in Nature Futures, AE, and numerous other periodicals and anthologies. He is an alumnus of the Sage Hill and Viable Paradise writing workshops.

DeLuca, M. R.
M. R. DeLuca has short stories published in *Shadows in Salem* and *O Horrid Night*. In addition to the beauty of words, M. R. enjoys numbers, speleothems, and homemade whoopie pies.

DeSantis, M. T.

M. T. DeSantis lives in a small city on the U.S. eastern seaboard and writes full-time. When not working, she can be found practicing yoga, attempting to answer trivia questions at restaurants, and plotting her next adventure.

Dring, Helen

Helen Dring is a writer and teacher from Liverpool, UK. She has always loved Fairy Tales and believes that the oldest stories remain the most pertinent to modern life. She has a MA in Novel Writing from Manchester Metropolitan University and is writing a Young Adult Novel.

Eastick, E. M.

Australian born E. M. Eastick is a retired environmental professional, avid traveler, and writer of no-fixed genre. She currently lives in Colorado.

Fuentes, Megan

Megan Fuentes is eighteen years old and currently attends the University of Central Florida in sunny Orlando. Her passions include writing and education, the latter of which is her intended major. She chose her college for its proximity to Disney World, which should tell you everything you ever need to know about her.

Gibbs, David J.

In the past year, my work has appeared in the following publications; 'The Sirens Call', 'Massacre Magazine', 'Under The Bed', 'Aphelion', 'New Realm', 'Nebula Rift', and 'Sanitarium Magazine'. I have also published two collections of short speculative fiction entitled 'A Taste of the Grave' and 'Once, Twice, Thrice' as well as a novel entitled 'The Walking Man'. My work has also appeared in the following anthologies over the last year; 'Dark Monsters', 'Hidden in Plain Sight', 'Tales From The Grave', and 'Creepy Campfire Quarterly'.

Giersbach, Walt

Walt Giersbach's fiction has appeared in *Bewildering Stories, Big Pulp, CommuterLit, Connotation Press, Corner Club Press, Every Day Fiction, Gumshoe Review, InfectiveINk, Liquid Imagination, OG Short Fiction, Over My Dead Body, Pif Magazine, Pulp Modern, Pure Slush, r.kv.r.y, the Story Shack, Short-Story.Me,* and a dozen other publications. He also writes on military history and social phenomena. Two volumes of short stories, *Cruising the Green of Second Avenue*, are available at Barnes & Noble and other online booksellers. He has directed communications for Fortune 500 companies, publicized the Connecticut Film Festival, managed publicity and programs for Western Connecticut State University's Haas Library, and now moderates a writing group in New Jersey. He blogs at allotropiclucubrations.blogspot.com while also maintaining Web sites devoted to the children's book author Holling Clancy Holling and the Manchester Writers' Circle.

Gilmer, William
William Gilmer is a letter organizer living in Metro Detroit with a girlfriend, teenager, and obligatory cat. When not writing he likes to wonder about the adventures he and Bob Ross could have had together.

Gleave, Candace
Candace Gleave best known for her off-beat sense of humor and snarky dialogue that she packs into every story, makes for an enjoyable read no matter the monster or genre. The two greatest loves in her life are family and writing - chocolate had to go. Candace lives in a little patch of earth called Midvale, Utah. It is there she and her two kids create the world, they love to play in. Want more of her writing, check out her literary delights on Goodreads. goodreads.com/author/show/4841759.Candace_Gleave and follow her on Facebook facebook.com/candace.gleave.

Haigh, Jack
Jack Haigh is a writer of short stories and flash fiction. His works often use his favourite fantasy tropes to satirise modern life. He is currently studying Creative Writing with the Open University. When not reading or writing, Jack works as a gardener, where he spends most of his time thinking about writing.

Hale, Daniel
Daniel Hale writes fantasy and horror in his native Ohio. His short stories have been published in several anthologies, including *The Myriad Carnival*, and *Strangely Funny III*. His first collection, *The Library Beneath the Streets*, is due for release in 2017. He is currently working on his first novel, Faith and Folklore. He can be found at danielhale42.wordpress.com.

Hill, Linda G.
Linda G. Hill is a stay-at-home mom of three boys and the guardian of one beagle and two kitties. Author of the romantic comedy, *All Good Stories*, she concocts tales in her head 24/7 and blogs almost daily at lindaghill.com. She lives in Southern Ontario, Canada.

Hopson, Kevin
Prior to hitting the fiction scene in 2009, Kevin was a freelance writer for several years, covering everything from finance to sports. His debut work, World of Ash, was released by MuseItUp Publishing in the fall of 2010. Kevin has released nearly a dozen books through MuseItUp since then, and he has also been published in various magazines and anthology books. Kevin's writing covers many genres, including dark fiction and horror, science fiction and fantasy, and crime fiction. His blog can be found at www.kmhopson.com.

Iles, Amanda
Amanda Iles lives in New York, where she writes about other worlds. She also copyedits, bakes cupcakes, and drinks lots of coffee.

Johnson, Mary Victoria
Mary Victoria Johnson is the author of two Young Adult novels: *Boundary,* and *The Ashes and the Sparks* (coming summer 2016*).*
Born in the UK, Mary now lives near Vancouver, where she is studying towards her degree in Creative Writing.

Jones, Michael M.
Michael M. Jones lives in Southwest Virginia with too many books, just enough cats, and a wife who always knows what movie he's referring to. His work has appeared in anthologies such as Clockwork Phoenix 3, A Chimerical World, and B is for Broken. He edited the anthology Scheherazade's Facade. Visit him at www.michaelmjones.com

Kibble, Robert
Robert has had pieces published in Every Day Fiction and won the Nottingham Writers Group new writers competition 2015. When not writing, and not suffering the burden of a very much less creative day job, he spends unhealthy amounts of time upset about the lack of a single Russian oligarch with a preference for recreating zeppelins over buying football teams, accidentally collecting whisky, or ranting about the vagaries of modern life at www.philosophicalleopard.com

Kimmel, Daniel M.
Daniel M. Kimmel is a film critic and graduated of Boston University School of Law. He writes on science fiction films for Space and Time Magazine. He was a finalist for the Hugo Award for *Jar Jar Binks Must Die… and other observations about science fiction movies.* His first novel, *Shh! It's a Secret: a novel about Aliens, Hollywood, and the Bartender's Guide* was a finalist for the Compton Crook Award. His new novel, *Time on My Hands: My misadventures in time travel* (Fantastic Books) is scheduled to be released in early 2017.

Landrum, David W.
David W. Landrum teaches Literature at Grand Valley State University in Michigan. His speculative fiction has appeared widely, his fairy tale stories in N*on-Binary Review, Garden of the Goddesses, The Fairy Tale Whisperer, Modern Day Fairy Tales, Black Denim Review*, and many other journals and anthologies. His most recent novellas, *Le Cafe de la Mort, Mother Hulda,* and *The Sorceress of Time*, are available through Amazon.

Lathers, Marie
Marie Lathers writes fiction and creative essays, most involving travel. She has published in Marco Polo Arts Magazine, Slow Trains, Bewildering Stories, and Deep South Magazine.

Lawryniuk, Clara
Clara Lawryniuk is a hopeful romantic who writes poetry and prose. She also writes about intimacy, love, sex and relationships on her blog, Love(r), at theintimacyblog.wordpress.com. Learn more about all her creative endeavors at clarakeepswriting.com.

Little, John
John lives in Western Maryland, where he works as English Tutor and Dairy Goat Farmer. He graduated from the University of Maryland College Park campus with a degree in English Literature and Writing, and is currently pursuing a teaching position overseas.

Matthias, Maren
Maren Matthias is currently living in Chicago, pursuing her fiction writing whilst working at an up-and-coming restaurant in the middle of the theatre district. She jumps from project to project, be it stage combat, musical theatre, housekeeping, or hightailing it overseas to satisfy her restless feet. This is her first publication and she's thrilled to be a part of it!

Michaud, Jenner
Jenner Michaud is a Canadian speculative fiction writer with a leaning towards the dark recesses found at the edge of reality. She enjoys weaving stories that push the boundaries of the possible, even when they go bump in the night and keep her up. Her horror short story *Of Holes and Craters*, as well as anthologies featuring her short fiction, are available on Amazon. Follow her writing adventures on Twitter @JennerMichaud.

Mulhare, R. C.
Born in Lowell, Massachusetts, R. C. Mulhare grew up on a healthy diet of the stories of the Brothers Grimm, Hans Christian Andersen, Charles Perrault and C. S. Lewis, which her mother fed to her in healthy portions, while her Irish storyteller father infused her with a love of narratives and striking characters. She still resides with her family in the Merrimack River Valley, moonlighting in grocery retail when she isn't writing or reading imaginative tales or out looking for hapless princes, princesses or common folk to rescue from harmful spells.

Nelson, Lorraine Sharma
Lorraine grew up in the United Kingdom, the Republic of South Africa, Zambia, Botswana, Canada, and the United States. She has a Bachelor's degree in English Language and Literature, and a Master's in Mass Communications. Lorraine is on the New England Regional Board for the U.S. Fund for UNICEF, and is grateful for the opportunity to do her part in helping children worldwide. She is a wife, a mother, a writer, and a volunteer in the Boston school system. Lorraine is also an avid sci-fi geek, who loves traveling, reading, movies and coconut cupcakes, though not necessarily in that order. She has two horror stories published in anthologies, and two sci-fi stories published in online magazines.

Nikolaidou, Dimitra
Dimitra Nikolaidou is the winner of the 2015 Wyrm's Gauntlet speculative fiction contest. She holds creative writing certificates from the University of Iowa's "How Writers Write Fiction" program as well as from the Open University's "Start Writing Fiction" program. She has written non-fiction for Cracked.com and Atlas Obscura, presented her work at The Fairytale Vanguard (2012) and is currently a PhD candidate researching the cultural values within role-playing games.

Norris, Gregory L.
Gregory L. Norris is a full-time professional writer, with numerous publication credits to my resume, mostly in national magazines and fiction anthologies. A former writer at Sci Fi, the official magazine of the Sci Fi Channel (before all those ridiculous Ys invaded), he once worked as a screenwriter on two episodes of Paramount's modern classic, Star Trek: Voyager and am the author of the handbook to all-things-Sunnydale, The Q Guide to Buffy the Vampire Slayer (Alyson Books, 2008). In late 2009, two of his paranormal romance novels for Ravenous Romance were reprinted as special editions by Home Shopping Network as part of their "Escape with Romance" segment – the first time HSN has offered novels to their customers. In late 2011, his collection of brandy-new terrifying short and long fiction, The Fierce and Unforgiving Muse: A Baker's Dozen From the Terrifying Mind of Gregory L. Norris is being published by Evil Jester Press. He has fiction forthcoming from the fine people at Cleis Press, STARbooks, EJP, The Library of Horror, Simon and Shuster, and Pill Hill Press, to name a few.

Pratt, James
James Pratt lives in southern New Jersey and enjoys writing horror, fantasy, and weird fiction. His influences include H.P. Lovecraft, Jack Vance, Clive Barker, William Hope Hodgson, Clark Ashton Smith, Michael Moorcock, Roger Zelazny, and Stephen King. James's stories have appearing in a number of anthologies including *Canopic Jars: Tales of Mummies and Mummification* from Great Old Ones Press, *Dark Hall Press Cosmic Horror Anthology*, *Alter Egos Vol. 2* from Source Point Press, and *Barbarians of the Red Planet* from Rogue Planet Press.

Quint, Claudia
Claudia Quint writes fantasy, romance, and erotica when she isn't brewing wine, taking care of her society finches, and messing about in her garden.

Raghavan, Renuka
Renuka Raghavan focuses of writing brief dramatic narratives. She lives in Massachusetts with her family and beloved Beagle. Previously her work has appeared in *The Rio Review* and *Boston Literary Magazine.*

Regan, M.
M. Regan has been writing in various capacities for over a decade, with credits ranging from localization work to scholarly reviews, advice columns to short stories. Particularly fascinated by those fears and maladies personified by monsters, she enjoys composing dark fiction and studying supernatural creatures. She currently lives and works in Kyoto, Japan, where she draws inspiration from the country's rich history of *youkai*, as well as the more modern influences of its popular culture.

Robiscoe, Karen
Karen Robiscoe's short stories, essays, creative non-fiction & poetry have appeared in literary journals: Spectrum at UCSB, Postscripts to Darkness, KY Story, Bohemia journal, Steam Ticket Review, Peachfuzz magazine, Dark Light 3, Bibliotheca Alexandrina, Main Street Rag, Meat for Tea, Sand Canyon Review, Midnight Circus, Peachfish magazine, Blue Crow magazine, Lunch Ticket at Antioch, Los Angeles, FTB Press, Poeming Pigeon, Dead Guns Press, and 300 Days of Sun (journal). Online, find my work at Handful of Dust E-Zine, Whistling Fire E-Zine, Art4theHomeless Web-zine, Silver Birch Press, Broken City, and my own dynamic & popular blog: Charron's Chatter. Additionally, my recipes are regularly featured at Hub Pages, and Fowlpox Press released brain-bending, idiom-twisting chapbook: Word Mosaics early in 2014.

Romero, Sita C.
Sita C. Romero is a writer living in the DC metro area. She studied philosophy at Jacksonville University and is currently completing her MFA at Queens University of Charlotte. When she's not writing, she's hiking, knitting or playing boardgames. You can find her at www.sitacromero.com

Rosen, Rob
Rob Rosen (www.therobrosen.com), award-winning author of the novels *Sparkle: The Queerest Book You'll Ever Love, Divas Las Vegas, Hot Lava, Southern Fried, Queerwolf, Vamp, Queens of the Apocalypse, Creature Comfort* and *Fate*, has had short stories featured in more than 200 anthologies.

Rossi, J.
J. Rossi is a Night Shift RN, Connoisseur of Shiny objects and Writer. She enjoys saving lives, kilts, gaining minions, chasing ghosts (or running from them...mostly running) and carrying salt and chalk on her at all times.

Rubin, Randy D.
Randy D. Rubin live alone in a 113 year old haunted house in Virginia. He writes dark fiction and darker poetry. His lunacy knows no limit. His latest horror short story and novelette collection, TOOONG! will be out in late Summer 2016 and his second poetry collection, THE JOINT should hit the streets by November 2016 as part of THE PRISON COMPENDIUM published by EMP publishers. His short story T-BONE is in Happy Little Horrors: ALIENATED anthology and his heartbreaking zombie tale, THE SUSURRUS OF CERULEAN SNOW is out in Volume 1 of Creepy Campfire Quarterly.

Sawant, Rohit
Rohit Sawant's short fiction has been featured in a Lovecraftian anthology titled *Kill Those Damn Cats*. He lives in Mumbai, India. He loves to sketch, and his favorite Batman is Kevin Conroy. You can reach him at rohit-sawant.tumblr.com

Seese, Michael
Michael Seese is an information security professional by day. Or, as his son could say even at age three, "Daddy keeps people's money safe." He has published three books: *Haunting Valley, Scrappy Business Contingency Planning*, and *Scrappy Information Security*, not to mention a lot of flash fiction, short stories, and poems. Other than that, he spends his spare time rasslin' with three young'uns.
Visit www.MichaelSeese.com or follow @MSeeseTweets to laugh with him or at him.

Seitzman, Brian H.
Brian H. Seitzman is a horror author with a background in biology. He shares his home in Worcester, Massachusetts with a hedgehog and an anthropologist. When not writing horrible things, he can often be found looking for mushrooms or exploring old cemeteries – sometimes both at once.

Shipley, Jonathan
Fort Worth author Jonathan Shipley, a SFWA member, writes in the genres of fantasy, science fiction, and horror. He has had over fifty short stories published, and the *After Death* anthology where he was a contributing author won the 2014 Bram Stoker Award. He was also a finalist that same year for the Washington Science Fictions Association's Small Press Award.

Smith, Deanna

Sometime in the late 1980s, Deanna's stepdad and Mom gave Deanna their old Mac Plus computer, and trees all over the world heaved a sigh of relief. Because Deanna writes. About everything. Anywhere. All the time. Writing, drawing, and reading were her passions for years, stumbling cheerfully genre to genre, discovering the fascination of history and music along the way, and then bellyflopped into 3D art. Drama happened, of course, but the upshot is that Deanna now lives in San Bernardino, a home health care worker and caretaker for her younger son and husband, with an older son who consults often with mom on matters of snark. An avid collector of old books – thank goodness for the Internet Archive – always fascinated with history as recorded by people in that time. A lover of fantasy and humor, mystery, science fiction and fact. Steam punk goth. Singer and song writer. Reasonably sane. She also still owns and maintains that Mac Plus.

Smith, Nathan

Nathan Smith is a London-based performance poet. Performing since 2014, his poetry is comedic, dark, and often involves toasters.

Sollazzo, Jody

I am a New Yorker that now lives in Berkeley, CA. I have been previously published. My first story, "Outlier" was published in a David Lynch tribute anthology edited by Cameron Pierce in July 2013. This year I have a story in "Love Hurts: A speculative fiction anthology."

Steiner, Amelia

When one writes to the erratic drum beat of Pileated Woodpeckers and the trill of wild turkeys, one either becomes a poet, or writes essays on self-reliance, or follows Alice into the rabbit hole. Amelia Steiner has chosen the last option. The words which she takes credit for were in fact channeled from creatures flitting by on their way to rendezvous in magical places. But in those hours between Woody's opening overture and the tree frogs' cacophonous calls of raucous courtship, she loves mysteries and sworks on her novel. A few pieces of short fiction are listed in her credits.

Tubrett, Jenn

Jenn Tubrett is a writer from Sydney, Nova Scotia. Her roots are in the Theatre, beginning as an actor she quickly moved to play writing. In 2010, during the Boardmore Theatre's 39th Elizabeth Boardmore One Act Festival of Plays, she took home the award for Best Original Script with her romp comedy *Notte Del Partito*. Tubrett has been published twice previously, both times with local publishing company Third Person Press. First in 2012 with her Sci-Fi/horror short story *Our Last Vacation* as a part of *Unearthed*, volume 3 of the Speculative Elements Series and later, in 2014, with her dsytopian short story *Epilogue* as a part *Flashpoint*, volume 4 of the Speculative Elements Series. *Haunt Us No More* marks her first submission to Transmundane Press.

Turnbull, David
David Turnbull is a member of the Clockhouse London group of genre writers. His short fiction has been published in a number of anthologies, including 'Beware the Little White Rabbit' Leap Books and 'We Can Improve You' Boo Books and more recently 'Creeping Crawlers' Shadow Publishing and 'Frozen Fairy Tales' World Weaver Press. He can be found at www.tumsh.co.uk.

Wagner, KT
KT Wagner loves reading and writing speculative fiction. Occasionally she ventures out of her writers' cave to spend an hour or two in a coffee shop or her garden. Several of her short stories are published. She puts pen to paper in Maple Ridge, B.C., organizes Golden Ears Writers, and attended SFU's Writers' Studio in 2015. KT can be found online at www.northernlightsgothic.com

Williams, Tom
Tom Williams was born in Gower, South Wales, and would have been very happy there if he hadn't gone to London to study at university. He fell in love with London and has stayed there or thereabouts ever since. Tom settled down and began to do all those things grown-ups are supposed to do, with quite a lot of success. But after working in an office for too long he stopped and devoted himself to writing. His first novel is in the hands of an agent, and he is well into a second. Visit him at tomwilliamsauthor.weebly.com.

Wright, Dana
Dana Wright has always had a fascination with things that go bump in the night. She is often found playing at local bookstores, trying not to maim herself with crochet hooks or knitting needles, watching monster movies with her husband and furry kids or blogging about books. More commonly, she is chained to her computers, writing like a woman possessed. She is the author of Asylum, The Invitation and Texas Twister. She is a contributing author to Masked Hearts (upcoming), Ghost Sniffers, Inc.: The Haunting of Zephyr Zoo, Siren's Call E-zine in their "Women in Horror" issue in February 2013 and "Revenge" in October 2013, a contributing author to Potatoes!, Fossil Lake, Of Dragons and Magic: Tales of the Lost Worlds, Undead in Pictures, Potnia, Shadows and Light, Wonderstruck, Shifters: A Charity Anthology, Dead Harvest, Monster Diaries, Holiday Horrors and the Roms, Bombs and Zoms Anthology from Evil Girlfriend Media. Danahas been a contributing writer to Eternal Haunted Summer, Massacre Magazine, Metaphor Magazine and The Were Traveler. She has reviewed music at New Age Music Reviews and Write a Music Review. She is a member of the Horror Writer's Association, Romance Writers of America and has been a presenter at Houston SCBWI. Please follow @danawrite on Twitter.

43756893R00299

Made in the USA
San Bernardino, CA
26 December 2016